The Ojanox

Omnibus Edition

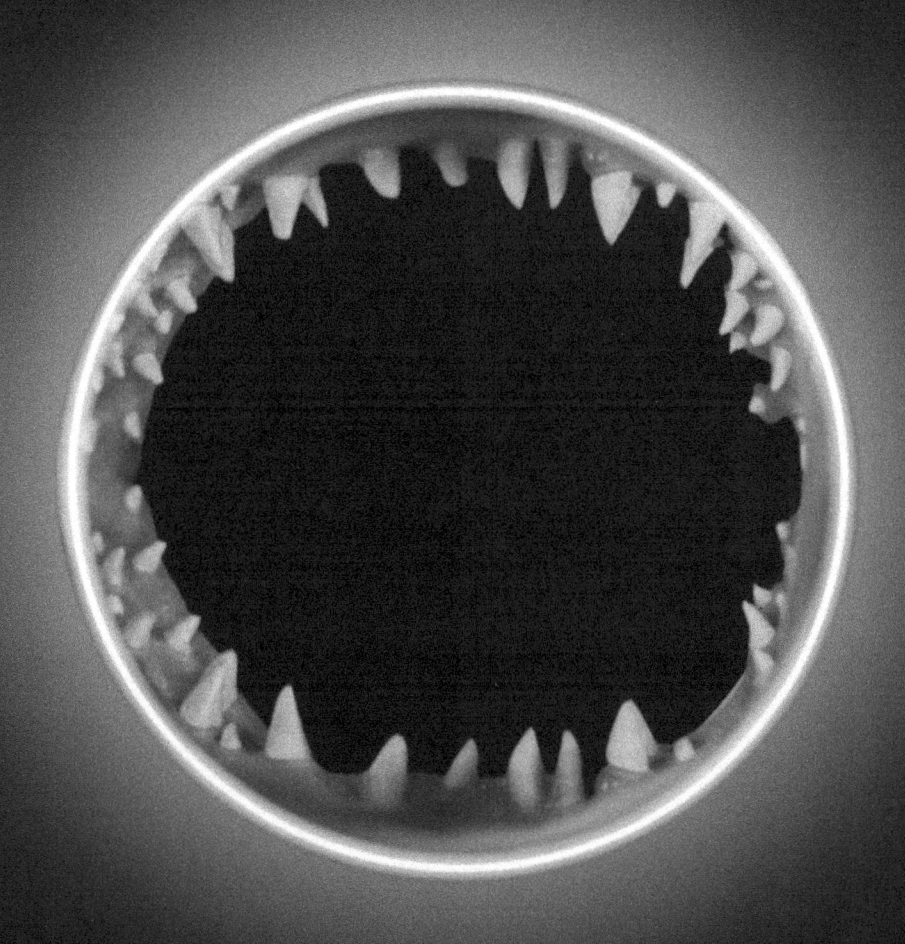

Daemon Manx

Published by Last Waltz Publishing

5 Midland Ave, Pompton Plains, N.J. 07444

All characters in this book are fictitious or used fictitiously with consent. Any resemblance to actual persons living or dead, is purely coincidental.

www.lastwaltzpublishing.com

No part of this publication may be reproduced, distributed, or transmitted in any form or by any means, including photocopying, recording, or other electronic or mechanical methods, without the prior written permission of the publisher, except as permitted by U.S. copyright law.

Edited by Lisa Lee Tone

Original developmental edits by Ben Eads

Library of Congress Cataloging-in-Publication Data

The Ojanox Series / Daemon Manx

TXu 2-417-807 2024

ISBN 979-8-9909628-5-6

Copyright © 2024, 2025 Daemon Manx aka Robert R. Chiossi

Illustrations Copyright © 2024 Christy Aldridge, Don Noble, J.M. DeSantis

Book Cover by Christy Aldridge (Dark Poppy Designs)

Illustrations by Christy Aldridge and Don Noble and J.M. DeSantis

First edition September 2024

All Rights Reserved

Also by Daemon Manx

Abigail
Piece by Piece
Drawn & Quartered with Diana Olney
Hacked in Two with James G. Carlson
These Lingering Shadows
Tales from the Monoverse
Arcranium with Mark Towse
Manx-iety: A Collection of Disturbing Stories
The Ojanox Series: I-IV
Scream in the Dark
Ashes to Ashes
All Fall Down
Lonesome Mountain
Try Not to Die in Arcranium with Mark Towse & Mark Tullius
Deacon: An Assemblage of Nightmares

For Mom
The original storyteller

FOREWORD

GAZING INTO THE ABYSS

The year is 1979. A small New York town prepares to welcome the fall season in all the expected ways: young children bicker and boast over Halloween costumes, secret lovers meet in clandestine corners, and a tortured soul plots wicked deeds. All the while, hidden just out of view, patient and hungry ... an ancient evil lurks.

I know, I know. You've heard all this before. You've read the book, watched the film adaptation, and probably even caught the two-part podcast. If you're a fan of old-school horror, like I am, then you'll swear that you know how the plot will unfold. What the primeval horror is. Who will live, who will die, and even in what specific order said deaths will occur.

Hey, I get it. I thought so too.

But I was wrong, dead wrong. You'll probably be wrong too. And, let me tell you, rarely has it felt SO good to be incorrect. To be legitimately surprised. To revisit a hallowed era of storytelling in such a creative way. Let's be honest: vintage horror is a difficult thing to effectively pull off in today's market. Try too hard and you alienate your target audience, skewing far afield from that elusive "feel". Half-ass it and you're derivative, lazy, or a hefty combination of both.

For anyone who is familiar with his talent, Daemon Manx has, quite unsurprisingly, accomplished something special with *The Ojanox*, making the familiar feel wholly unfamiliar. Pulling us back to the gritty world of late-70s to early-80s horror without stepping on any toes in the process. This is neither an homage nor an emulation. This is a book that could very well have been borne of that halcyon era, resting on some half-askew bookshelf this whole time, just waiting to be discovered. But, as much as *The Ojanox* is a glimpse across decades, it is also a gateway into Manx's mind–one can glean various details about the novelist through the terrors nestled within the typeface.

Much like there are no atheists in foxholes, there are no innocents amongst horror authors. We write from the darkest of depths, from places where light falters and even whispers carry great weight. Yes, the stories we create are ultimately meant to startle, to shiver, and to scare. To invoke those primal sensations of fear and dread. But there is so much more to it than that. We are also, through prose and plot, offering the world a glimpse of our vulnerable sides. Our hopes and fears. The hardships we have endured. Mistakes we've made, and the fallout that followed. From pen to page, our pain is made manifest. Some people suffer for their creations–horror authors put themselves through anguish for their art. And, during this process of composition, this literary baring of souls, we allow ourselves to examine our personal hauntings, be they self-induced or inflicted by others. To exorcise our own demons, keystroke by keystroke. True, we may never completely vanquish the darkness inside us. For many horror authors, those hurts are grafted to our very essence, as much a part of us as blood and bone, woven into the very fabric of who we have become. But, while those shadows may yet linger, we at least get the chance to look our fiends in the eye with an unflinching gaze.

Daemon has never been shy about his personal struggles, of which he has had plenty. I respect both his candor and his fearlessness in facing those dark years. Perhaps that deep well of experience is what gives his writing that extra bit of compelling oomph. Some of us have pint-sized imps on our shoulders, gently reminding us of past indiscretions, tempting us back with honeyed words. Manx has a thousand-pound gorilla clinging to his back, beating its chest and bellowing a mighty roar of misdeeds, yanking at the chains of the past with inhuman strength.

And that, dear reader is what you get with *The Ojanox*. A beast of both the literal and figurative sense. A peek at the demons without ... and those within.

This is a massive story, years in the making, touching on a myriad of topics, many of which are just as pertinent today as they were in '79. From a word count perspective (it shouldn't matter, but we're novelists ... it matters) it is an imposing body of work, rivaling the hefty behemoths of the era, as is only fitting. From my first involvement with *The Ojanox*, I have always maintained that Daemon writes like Laymon, but with a more literary bent. This isn't a knock at all: Laymon penned some classics. He was great at concepts, with a knack for the perverse and deft skill at setting a scene. The only place I was occasionally left wanting was with the narrative voice itself. Daemon rectifies that shortcoming with the ease of raw ability, wrangling words in the best of ways. In all honesty, it wouldn't shock me in the slightest to see Manx and Laymon sharing space on bookstore shelves in the not-so-distant future. I am hard pressed to think of an indie author who deserves it more.

But don't take my word for it. See for yourself. Curl up in your favorite space, dim the lights, crack open *The Ojanox*, and step into the town of Garrett Grove. What you find just might surprise you.

Jack Wells
Author of *Jack of All Trades* and the *Monochrome Noir* series.

Trick or Treat

I hope you will indulge me just a little before diving into the book, as the origination of *The Ojanox* is almost as interesting as the story itself. I began the writing process during the spring of 2020 while I was serving my final year of incarceration in a halfway house in Newark, New Jersey. Yes, you read that right. I spent nearly a decade in state prison prior to that. The short story: I made some terrible mistakes because of addiction (rarely are addicts known for making good ones), and that landed me in a very dark place.

But that was only the beginning of my journey because prison is where I finally got clean (Eleven years and four months as I write this today) and it's where I turned my life around. But something else happened while I was serving my days behind the wall. I started writing again. Addiction had stolen everything I loved, and my creative muse was only one of the casualties. But as the fog lifted, my desire to create returned, and it was in a cold, lonely cell where I started to live once again.

By the time I reached the halfway house, years later, I had written dozens of short stories and novellas but had never tackled any larger projects. It was January of 2020, and I had just received permission to leave the halfway house for a few hours a day to attend college in person. I even got a couple months under my belt, and then Covid hit. The house was put under quarantine lockdown, and no one was allowed to leave. Unfortunately, the virus had already found its way into the building.

And that was life for the next seven months. We started out with almost three hundred men in the facility, and that number quickly diminished to less than a hundred. We all got sick during that time, some more than others, and many of the men were taken back to the prison system's medical facilities ... never to return.

To pass the time, I started writing what I thought would be a short story, one that encapsulated the feeling and the mystery of Halloween the way I remembered it as a child. I sat down and wrote the first lines of what is now chapter one, and *The Ojanox* was born. Within a few days, I realized this was not going to be a short story. I had no idea just how massive it would be, but I was about to find out.

I owned a portable word processor called the Alpha Smart 3000, originally intended for my college classes. If you're not familiar, The AS3K is a battery-operated unit with a small screen that allows the user to see three lines of script at a time. There are eight files you can fill with text, but once they are filled, you must transfer the data to a Word doc and zip drive. I would fill the files every night, writing from 6p.m.–11p.m. non-stop. The next day I would use the house's library computer to transfer my work and ultimately free up space for another night of writing.

I should mention that I shared the room with ten other men who were anything but quiet. Who can blame them? We were all stir-crazy. While they were listening to music, playing poker, and screaming to one another in the confines of our 12 x 12 room, I would don my headphones, crank up the tunes, and write, write, write.

And yes, it was like that. I wrote in a fever; the words flowed as if they were coming from somewhere other than me. It was very stream of consciousness, but it was also methodical. During the day, I would map out the next ten scenes in outline, and that night, I would write. Oddly enough, not once did I experience even an ounce of writer's block.

On October 30, 2020, I typed the words *The End* and looked down at a massive file containing 520K words. I had finished the first draft in six months. Seven days later, I was released.

THE OJANOX

Now would come the hard part. The rewrite. Little did I know, I would be rewriting this beast for the next four years and editing out over 160K words, all for the betterment of the story, I assure you.

Now it's true that this story was created under some very adverse conditions. You could even say it is a byproduct of that suffering. But that's not why *The Ojanox* was written in such a short period of time. To be honest, I have been working on this story since I was ten years old myself. Like Troy Fischer, when I was in fourth grade, I had a Halloween party and built a haunted house in the garage. Yep, you guessed it, it was called Scream in the Dark. In *The Ojanox*, many of the settings, themes, and circumstances are inspired by my memories of Halloweens gone by and my own life experiences as well. However, this story isn't just a tribute to my own childhood but to childhood itself. If I have done this correctly, it is to pay respect to that initial sense of mystery we all felt when we heard our first ghost story, to that chilling fright when we saw our first horror movie.

Although the coming-of-age factor is just a small portion of this story, as *The Ojanox* is pure horror with its fair share of violence, I mention it because that's where it started for me ... when I was a child. My love for horror, that is.

If I got any of this right, I hope you are taken back, if only for a moment, to that innocent time in your life when you set out to grab a pillowcase full of candy on Halloween and returned home with all the peanut butter cups you were hoping for ... and more.

Daemon Manx

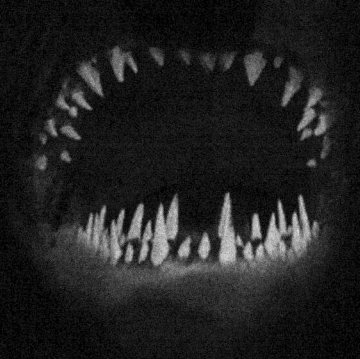

Part One

"There is a presence, delivered on the breeze, that only shows itself on Halloween. You feel it in the shiver crawling up your spine and hear it in the rustle of fallen leaves." ~ Lois Fischer

PROLOGUE

Saturday, October 24, 1979

7:30 p.m.

Felix Castillo eased his foot off the gas pedal, bringing the Con Edison utility truck to a stop at the quiet intersection. He proceeded left onto Mountain Avenue, entering the wooded residential development, and made his way towards the dead-end cul-de-sac of Foothills Drive. Sycamores and maples lined the quiet street, most of their leaves already turned deep shades of orange and rust from the seasonably crisp autumn temperatures. Lumbering along at a snail's pace, the electrician checked himself in the rearview and did a double take. The grinning face staring back at him was almost unrecognizable. It'd been a long time since Felix had anything to smile about, and its presence felt out of place. It wasn't like he was depressed or any sadder than the next guy, he just wasn't happy, and his awareness of the malady had grown more acute over the past few months.

Most of the men who worked for Con Edison were already married or had steady girlfriends, of which Felix had neither. A good number of them had children, something Felix was sure he did not want ... until recently, maybe. Having bounced around the foster care system as a child, Felix had always longed to be a part of a family, a real family, one he could call his own. But he'd never been able to connect with a woman on a deep enough level, emotionally or physically. And Felix Castillo had come to accept the idea that that ship had sailed. Up until a few weeks ago, that is. A recent development in his life had changed the way Felix thought about a lot of things ... a development named Mandy Griggs. Felix laughed as he scanned the rearview a second time, ran a hand through his thick, black hair, and allowed his smile to widen until it filled his entire face.

Glowing eyes burned orange against a darkened backdrop of night; carved-out jack-o'-lanterns sat on almost every porch, staring back at Felix as he passed. Plastic skeletons and stuffed bedsheet ghosts hung from tree limbs, swaying like pendulums in the cool October breeze. Felix slowed the truck even further with his face pressed to the window, admiring the yard decorations. The town of Garrett Grove sure did Halloween right. Nearly every front lawn was done up, with each house trying to outdo the next. And with the big night only a week away, it looked like every kid in the Grove would be coming home with a pillowcase full of candy.

Felix turned the truck around at the end of the cul-de-sac and backed in beneath a canopy of overhanging pines. Foothills Drive was his favorite place to park, with only four houses on the entire block, all set far back from the road. The perfect spot to catch an hour or two of uninterrupted shut-eye. As a lineman for the electric company, he preferred the night shift and took all the overtime he could get. Most nights were quiet, with the occasional fried squirrel on a transformer or a fallen tree limb over a power line. Storm season was a different story; from late November through early March, Felix could count on no less than thirty extra hours a week. But tonight, there wasn't much going on in his corner of the world, which consisted of Warren, Parker Plains, and Garrett Grove. And from where he sat beneath the shadow of Garrett Mountain, all was quiet, as if the world had gone to sleep.

Turning off the engine, he listened to the low hum of static from the dispatch radio. The volume was set just loud enough to wake him if he were called. He fumbled for his pack of smokes, rolled down the window, and lit a Marlboro Red.

The blazing glow of the Ford's cigarette lighter illuminated the entire cab of the truck.

Felix drew on his smoke and scanned the sports section of the paper. Oct. 24, 1979, **Billy Martin Punches Marshmallow Salesmen, Puts Job in Jeopardy**.

"At it again, huh, Billy?" he said, putting the paper to the side. He yawned and leaned against the seat, allowing thoughts of Mandy to fill his head once again. A vision of the girl in her waitress uniform caused his smile to return, although it was a bit more wicked than the previous one he had worn.

Mandy Griggs worked the morning shift at Wilson's Diner on Route 3. She'd been flirting with Felix for the past month now, but he'd been afraid to make a move. Still, he loved the way her skirt hitched up when she stood on her tiptoes to grab the peach cobbler from the top shelf of the display case.

"You sure do like this peach cobbler," she had teased.

In truth, the cobbler tasted like shit, but it was the only pie on the top shelf. And Felix enjoyed watching Mandy reach for it—so much so, he had packed on a few pounds as a result.

He had a good idea Mandy had moved the pie up there on purpose. She'd been extra flirtatious lately, had started to wear just a little more makeup, and the top button of her blouse seemed to drop one each day——which had been unbuttoned dangerously low to begin with for a family restaurant. As if it had been delivered with a sledgehammer, Felix finally got the message and asked Mandy out. He took her to the Warren Drive-in to see the movie about the haunted house on Long Island and was thrilled to learn that Mandy's blouse could be unbuttoned a hell of a lot more in private.

He couldn't wait to see her again. Strawberry blonde hair and blue eyes, the girl had everything, including a great rack. Felix shifted in his seat, getting excited just thinking about her. *I wonder if she's free tomorrow night—I could go for a double feature.*

He took one last drag from his smoke and pitched the butt out the window. A light garble of static from the radio broke the silence but only for a moment. All was quiet. With the cool air waltzing in against his skin, Felix stretched out and shut his eyes. He thought more about Mandy, happy he had finally asked her out, even happier he could stop eating all that God-awful peach cobbler. Now he didn't need an excuse to get her to hike up her skirt.

The breeze picked up, sending a cold chill racing through the cab of the Ford. It was followed by a scraping sound, as if someone had skidded across the pavement just outside the truck. Felix straightened in his seat and turned toward the street. He reached to roll up the window and hesitated, listening for the furtive sound to return. His heart rate escalated as possible scenarios played out in his head, each one more outrageous than the previous. *What the fuck was that?*

The scuffing could have been caused by an animal, but Felix doubted it had been made by a small one. There were mountain lions and deer living in the woods behind the small development, more than a few bears as well. It was also the week before Halloween, and the idea that someone was hiding in the dark, intent on messing with him, presented itself as a valid possibility. He waited for what felt like an hour, listening, his senses agitated to high alert. He started again as a rattling of dried leaves skirted across the cul-de-sac, carried along by the sudden breeze. Felix watched them tumble over the asphalt and shook his head in relief. "Get a grip, man," he said, realizing he was jumping at shadows.

He smiled once again, but the feature twisted as a frigid rush of air blasted him in the face, silencing his breath like a noose. Felix tried to focus on the wave of distortion before him. He blinked and opened his eyes in time to see it reach for him. It latched onto either side of his skull and yanked him forward. Titanic pressure flooded his brain and bore into him with a vice-like urgency. Every muscle in his body spasmed as if he'd been hit with a cattle prod. He struggled to free himself, but the force was gargantuan. Before he could scream, Felix was ripped out of the driver's side window, breaking four fingers as he fought to hold on to the steering wheel.

Felix didn't know he was airborne until he landed. He came down in the middle of the street with his shoulder shattering on impact. The scream rising in his throat stagnated and never left. The unseen force was on top of him in a heartbeat, biting with the velocity of a chainsaw. He attempted to focus on his assailant, but his vision was obscured by a swirling cloud of darkness. The stench of cold copper invaded his sinuses and filled his lungs. Fighting to speak, Felix lay on his back staring up at a desperate October sky. A vision of Mandy found its way back as the beast forced itself inside and violated him. It was cold at first but quickly escalated with the intensity of frostbite, then his blood boiled over like hellfire. The night crept in, fading to a toxic grey as Felix was drained. His last thoughts were of Mandy leaning over the counter, her blouse unbuttoned dangerously low.

THE OJANOX

Felix smiled and slipped away with the God-awful taste of peach cobbler lingering on his tongue.

Chapter 1

Meanwhile

Less than a mile away

Lois Fischer sat cross-legged at the large coffee table with the focused attention of ten fourth graders hanging on her every word. She slid the candle towards her and leaned forward, allowing the delicate flame to cast dancing shadows across her face. Meeting the stare of each child for a brief second, Lois paused for dramatic effect. Then she dropped her voice an octave and began to speak.

"There is a presence, delivered on the breeze, that only shows itself on Halloween. You feel it in the shiver crawling up your spine and hear it in the rustle of fallen leaves. A menacing darkness has entered the town, and it knows where you live. It lurks in the shadows, it hides in the woods, waiting for you to take the shortcut through the graveyard. It holds no physical form but watches through the eyes of the jack-o'-lanterns as you make your way home from school. It circles from above, waiting for you to trip and lose your footing. Then it strikes!" Lois raised her voice and slapped her hand against the coffee table, causing a chorus of gasps to erupt from the entranced group of children. She paused once again, then continued.

"Like a raven seizing a shrew. You fight to breathe as you struggle to escape its grip. But it's too late. You succumb to its gravity, paralyzed with fear, and may never know the beast by name ... for it has many names. And it's older than time itself. Only then will you understand what has been delivered on the breeze. Only then will you know the beast by name. You say it with your dying breath ... Ojanox."

"Ow-jo-knocks?!" Troy Fischer cried, zeroing in on his mother's sapphire-blue eyes, his own nearly the identical shade.

"No, honey," Lois said, leaning over and ruffling her son's overgrown mop of hair. "It's pronounced, Oh-Ja-Nox."

"Well, that's not scary. Whoever heard of an Ojanox?"

Lois shrugged and returned the candle to the center of the table, illuminating the faces of the ten boys and girls dressed in their Halloween costumes. Beyond the swath of candlelight, the Fischers' living room looked like a scene ripped from the pages of a Bram Stoker novel. Fake cobwebs covered every surface, from the olive-colored love seat to the Pioneer stereo. Half-concealed plastic spiders lurked from their perches, ready to pounce. Glow-in-the-dark skeletons stood in the far corners of the room, and rubber bats hung suction cupped to the windows and the front of the RCA color television set.

Halloween was Troy Fischer's favorite holiday, and it showed. Of course, he loved the candy, but there was more to it than that. It had something to do with what his mother described in her ghost story, although he thought the name of the monster was somewhat silly. There was a strange sense of ominous wonder in the air this time of year, a feeling of tension and mystery that Troy associated with Halloween. This year had brought an added element of excitement with the coming of Troy's second annual Halloween party. This was the first time that Wendy Sirocka was able to attend. The girl had moved to town just last month. Troy also had a special surprise waiting in the garage for his guests ... one that was guaranteed to make them scream.

"I thought it was scary," said Kelly Rainey, who wore a Raggedy Ann costume and sat so close to her friend Caroline Smith, she was almost on top of her. "What about you?" she asked her friend.

THE OJANOX

"Really scary." Caroline nodded in agreement, the baggy fabric of her Raggedy Andy costume flopping in time.

"Yeah, that was a good one, Mrs. F." Mike Barnes wore a cowboy costume and sat next to his neighbor, Jeff Campbell, who came dressed as Captain Kirk.

"I don't know, Mrs. Fischer," Tommy Negal said. "I don't scare too easy, but it was pretty good."

Troy examined the boy's thrown together hobo outfit and concluded that Tommy had put zero thought into his costume and come up with it at the last minute. Fixing his Dracula fangs for possibly the tenth time in the past five minutes, Troy bared his teeth and checked out the rest of his friends' costumes. Beth Dorn and Terry Wallen both dressed like babies in footy pajamas. And Scott Cole had come as Frankenstein, complete with neck bolts and head piece, and was looking like the clear winner for best costume.

Although *Star Wars* had been out for just over two years and was still all the rage, none of the boys had dressed as Luke Skywalker, Han Solo, or even Darth Vader. The only guest to arrive as a character from the movie was Wendy, who wore a Princess Leia costume. With her long black hair set into tight buns against the sides of her head, the young Italian girl looked exactly like the *Star Wars* heroine. Troy turned to her, feeling the strange fluttering inside his chest once again, and wished he had dressed as Luke Skywalker and not a stupid vampire.

"What did you think?" Troy asked with a tremble in his voice. "Um, about the ghost story, I mean."

"I liked it." Wendy looked back at him, her big chestnut-colored eyes catching him like a deer in the headlights.

Troy coughed, almost swallowed his Dracula fangs, and quickly turned away.

"Who's ready for some cupcakes?" Lois asked, rising to her feet.

"Aw, Mom," Troy said. "It's time for Scream in the Dark."

"I think your friends would like some cupcakes first," she said, making her way to the kitchen and turning on the lights. "Then you can have your haunted house."

Shouts in favor of cupcakes told Troy he was outnumbered. He let out a theatrical sigh, then thought it might be better to scare his friends once they had full stomachs. *Tommy will probably puke.* Troy laughed, but his smile faded as thoughts of Robert Boyle came to mind. Rob was his best friend, had been since their first day of kindergarten. The two boys had worked most of the past week constructing Scream in the Dark, using cardboard they had liberated from the dumpster behind Marcos Playmart to fabricate the labyrinth walls. The boys had originally intended to operate the entire show themselves with the help of Troy's older cousins, Eric and Billy Tobin, who were secretly waiting for the festivities to commence.

Troy and Rob had worked out all the scares and gimmicks on their own, and each had a vital role to play in the night's production. Then Rob had gotten sick at the last minute and been unable to come to the party. To make matters worse, there were others who couldn't be there as well. Both Ben and Erin Richards, the only twins in Troy's class, had also missed school on Friday due to an illness. Whatever Rob had appeared to be going around. But the absence that Troy felt the most, even more than that of his best friend, was his father. Don Fischer had missed a lot of family dinners lately and not been home to help the boys with their construction. And even though he had said, "I wouldn't miss it for the world, kiddo," when Troy asked if he would be home in time for the party, he still hadn't come home from work.

Troy looked up to the wall clock, noticing it was almost eight, then turned his stare to the family portrait hanging next to it. A picture of his mom, dad, and himself, taken a little more than a year ago, smiled back at him and caused him to smile himself. As his friends gravitated to the kitchen to retrieve their cupcakes and juices, Troy's mind wandered to just a few days before when Scream in the Dark was still in its early design stages.

Troy and Rob had begun constructing the haunted house Wednesday after school. They continued their work on Thursday, but there was still much to be done, and they knew they'd be lucky if they finished in time for the party. It had started to get late, and Rob said he had to be home by five-thirty for dinner. So, the boys made plans to finish the following day, and Rob set out for home on his bicycle. His house wasn't far, just under a mile if you stuck to the town's paved roads. Which was something the boys rarely did; the paths through the foothills were the perfect shortcut and their preferred route of transit. A network of trails snaked through the undeveloped woods of King County, separating

Mountain Avenue from Foothills Drive, then continued up the north side of Garrett Mountain.

Miss Davis, the third-grade teacher, had taken Troy's class there on a field trip last year. She told them how the Lenni Lenape tribe had lived in the area for centuries and that the paths through the foothills were old game trails used for hunting. Scott Cole had even found an arrowhead, which sparked a treasure hunting frenzy in the entire class. After that, Rob and Troy returned to the foothills every chance they could; arrowhead fever was at an all-time high.

After Rob had left, Troy continued to plug away in the garage until he was called into the house. He was handed the phone to find Rob's mother on the line. "Troy, this is Mrs. Boyle. Robert isn't home yet," she said. "Is he still there?"

"Um, n-no," Troy said. "He left, like, an hour ago. But I wouldn't worry; he must've stopped to look for arrowheads on the trail." He cleared his throat, then told her how Rob would probably be home any minute. Which is exactly what happened, and Rob walked through the front door while Troy was still on the line.

"Thank you, Troy," Mrs. Boyle said. "Rob will call you later, if he can still walk after the beating he's about to get. But it's not looking good."

When Rob didn't show up for school the next day, Troy figured Mrs. Boyle had kept good on her word and given him a good licking. He called his friend as soon as he got home, only Mrs. Boyle answered.

"I'm sorry, Troy. Robert's sick and can't come to the phone." She said it was probably the flu and doubted if Rob would be able to make it to the Halloween party.

Troy had felt his chest deflate as if all his ten-year-old dreams had been crushed with one fell swoop. It was devastating that Rob might not make it to the party; even worse, they had planned to go trick-or-treating together, and Halloween was only a week away.

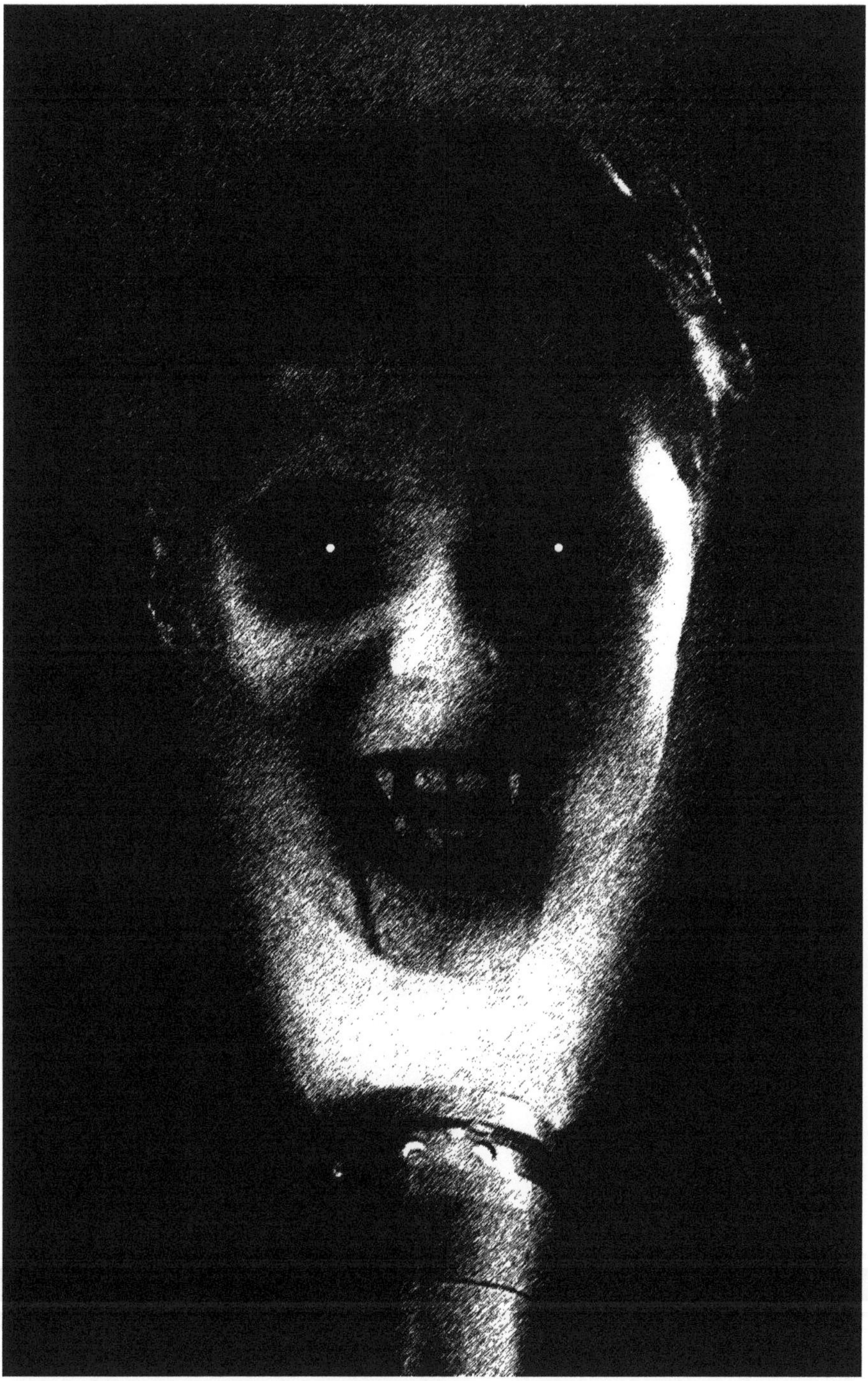

Chapter 2

After the cupcakes were devoured, the children walked single file out the front door, into the cool, crisp night. Candles had been set along the walkway leading from the porch to the Fischers' garage. Troy guided his friends with a flashlight held beneath his chin; Wendy followed a close step behind, bumping into him every time he stopped to speak.

"I warn you, what you are about to see may give you nightmares," Troy said, trying to sound like Bella Lugosi. "There are things inside that want to eat you!" He shouted the last two words, causing Wendy and several of the other girls to scream.

"Come on, let's go, Count Dorkula," Mike said, inciting a fresh fit of laughter.

"Follow me then ... if you dare."

The front of the garage had been blocked off with thick sheets of cardboard painted black. Troy led the children to the right, through a makeshift door, and ushered them into the darkness. Once the last child was inside, the door slammed shut behind them and Troy stopped short to block their path. The walls of the narrow hallway were tight on either side, with no room for the children to turn around. Suffocating night closed in around them, making it impossible to see. Cries of discomfort and confusion started much sooner than Troy had anticipated. He continued to hold his ground and remained silent, allowing their disorientation to escalate. But the total darkness and claustrophobia proved too much for his friends, and they started to panic.

"What's going on?" Beth cried out. The sound of hands slapping against the cardboard walls of the hallways echoed throughout.

"I can't see anything. Stop touching me!" Terry yelled. There was a folly of grunts and groans as the tangle of children pressed against one another.

"Hey!" someone else screamed.

Troy stifled his laughter and pictured what was about to happen.

"This is stu—" Mike's voice was silenced as the tiny hallway exploded with a flurry of sound and vision. The blinding pulse of a strobe light and the ear-piercing blare of tortured screams assaulted the children like mortar fire. Arms reached for them, clawing and grabbing, materializing from the very walls themselves. Unknown to the children, they had been standing inches away from the window of a cage. The Tobin brothers howled like wild animals from behind the bars that covered the opening. Both wore werewolf masks and clawed at Troy's friends, who were now screaming and desperate to get away from their attackers.

Troy held his ground, refusing to budge; there was nowhere for the trapped children to go as his cousins played their part to the fullest. One of the kids had started to cry, and Troy was pretty sure it was Tommy. *Oh boy, here comes the puke.*

The strobe had disorientated everyone as planned, and the screams played through the giant boom box had come on at the perfect moment. Troy jumped as something brushed up against him and took his hand. It had been Wendy. The strange fluttering returned, causing his heart to pound so hard he felt it in his throat. Sweat started to slick his brow, and for a moment, Troy forgot where he was. The sight of his cousins in their wolf masks snapped him back to the moment. He returned the flashlight to his chin and shouted to be heard over the noise.

"Quick, follow me ... this way." He pulled Wendy by the hand and led everyone through the door behind him.

The next hallway was covered in webs. Two black lights mounted to the ceiling illuminated the glow-in-the-dark spiders that began to descend upon them.

"Don't let them touch you. They are highly venomous! One bite, and you are a goner!"

The children followed him out of the room as the arachnids continued to drop on them. Troy was pretty sure he had scared the daylights out of everyone and figured he'd move them along to the next big scare.

He stopped at the next door. "I don't know what's in here, but it doesn't sound good." The squealing sounds of rodents filled their ears. "I hope you're not afraid of rats!" he shouted over the din.

They entered a room even darker than the first, making it impossible for the children to see the rubber hoses lining the floor. Billy, Troy's oldest cousin, operated the mechanism controlling the rat hoses from the safety of his hiding place on the other side of the wall. The shrieking cries of vermin pumped through the hidden stereo speakers was deafening.

"Oh my God! I stepped on something!" Caroline screamed.

"They're everywhere!" someone shouted.

The further they walked into the room, the deeper the carpet of hoses grew, making it feel as if rats were being crushed under their feet. Troy felt his smile threaten to take his entire face as he noticed how lifelike the sensation of the rats really felt.

"One's in my hair! Get it out!"

Troy squeezed Wendy's hand and pressed forward, leading his friends out of the rat menagerie and through another doorway. They entered a room longer and wider than the others, which took up nearly one third of the entire garage. A deep crimson glow bathed the room in a blood-like wash as organ music, piped in from some unseen source, provided the demonic soundtrack.

"This can't be good," Troy said, leading them further inside.

The room before them revealed itself to be a graveyard. Headstones were set with names written on them: I.P. Daily on one and Bob Frapples on another. A small fence separated the children from the far side of the room, where a large coffin sat propped against the wall.

"I better check this out." Wendy tried to hold onto his hand as Troy pulled away. "Don't worry, I'll be right back." He popped the small capsule into his mouth without anyone noticing and stepped over the fence.

The other children held their breath and watched Troy approach the coffin. His cape hung inches from the floor as he walked through the graveyard and knelt beside the casket. "That's what I thought," he gasped.

Eric Tobin lay inside the coffin waiting for his cue, and that was it. He bolted upright and seized Troy by the shoulders, pulling him toward the sarcophagus. Troy screamed and bit down on the capsule.

The boys struggled for a moment as Eric pretended to sink his fangs into Troy's neck before releasing him. Troy fell backwards toward the fence. Blood dripped from his mouth as he looked up at his friends and screamed. "Get out! While you still can!" He collapsed on the floor. A second later, Eric started to rise from the coffin.

The children jumped back into the wall behind them and clamored about to find an exit. They pounded against the cardboard, which appeared as sturdy as brick and refused to budge. They tried every surface but couldn't find a way out. Kelly and Caroline screamed as several of the kids knocked into them. The sound of one boy crying was distinct above the insanity of noises.

"I think I found it!" Wendy shouted and pressed up against what she thought was the exit. The others followed, jamming the little girl against the wall. Together, they clawed at the slit that had to be the doorway.

Eric emerged from the coffin and stepped over the fence. He raised his arms towards the frightened children and moaned.

"Why isn't it opening?" Kelly whined.

"Push harder," Tommy cried, ready to puke.

"Stop it. You're crushing me," Wendy shouted.

With a sudden rush, the door flew open, and the mass of boys and girls tumbled out onto the Fischers' driveway, safe and unharmed. The cool October air vaporized their breath, revealing it in exaggerated plumes of condensation.

"Oh my God! That was so scary," Caroline gasped.

"Cool," Jeff agreed.

Troy and his cousins scrambled out the back entrance of the garage and listened to the conversations from their hiding place.

"That wasn't scary. It was pretty dumb, if you ask me," Mike said, leaning against the side of the house.

It was the exact cue Troy had been hoping to hear. He gave his cousins the okay signal and the boys broke cover, jumping out of the darkness from the side of the garage, screaming and grabbing at the other children. Eric and Billy had donned their masks and tore after Mike and Tommy, who ran from the driveway with the werewolves in hot pursuit. The rest of the group scattered for a moment, then regrouped and started to laugh. Troy joined them, with his smile growing wider by the second. Every trick and gimmick had worked like a charm, just as he and Rob had planned.

"You scared me half to death." Wendy approached Troy and punched him in the arm.

The other kids chimed in, voicing their approval as well. Jeff patted him on the back, Scott and Caroline told him what rooms they liked best, while Terry and Beth continued to hug each other, attempting to steady their nerves. The sound of Mike and Tommy screaming in the distance helped everyone shake off the fright Troy had given them. A few moments later, they were all giggling and laughing it up.

"How did everything go?" Lois asked as she entered the driveway.

"Great," Troy said with a ribbon of fake blood clinging to his chin.

"Was it a graveyard smash?"

"Mom!" Troy rolled his eyes and shook his head.

"Well, I thought it was funny," she said. "There's some pizza left if anyone's still hungry." Lois turned and headed back into the house, and the other children followed, leaving Wendy and Troy alone in the driveway.

"You really liked it?" Troy asked. "Scream in the Dark?"

"It was awesome. Could you show me again?"

"Well, it won't be the same without Eric and Billy working the lights and stuff." Troy couldn't think of a reason why she might want to see it again. *It won't even be scary now that you know what happens.* But Wendy insisted.

"That's okay. I just want you to show me."

"Well okay. Follow me then." He opened the first door, revealing the hallway with the cage set in the center of the wall. The strobe light still flashed at a tantric pace, making Troy feel lightheaded as he led Wendy by the hand. Then she stopped, tugged on his arm, and pulled him back. Troy turned around, but before he could react, Wendy kissed him. It was quick and awkward as her lips pecked him half on his bottom lip and half on his chin. Troy felt the blood rush to his face and the sensation of pins and needles dancing over every inch of his skin. A lump the size of a softball formed in his throat as the narrow hallway tilted to the left and threatened to knock him off his feet. He had been blindsided by her forwardness, having never kissed or been kissed by a girl before. Wendy stepped back, bit her lip, and smiled.

"Umm," Troy managed.

"I like you, Troy," she said.

"Umm, you do?"

"Yes ... do you like me?"

"Umm ... yes." The ability to speak slipped further from his grasp.

Wendy took a step forward and kissed him again. He was a bit more prepared this time and managed to pucker his lips and offer a feeble kiss back. It was a gallant effort for the ten-year-old boy.

But the moment was brought to an abrupt halt when Billy and Eric chased Mike and Tommy back into the driveway. The four boys huddled outside the door as Troy and Wendy nervously exited the garage. The guilty-as-sin look they both wore was unseen by the other children. But when they entered the house, it was noticed immediately.

Call it mother's intuition. Lois Fischer watched her son and his new friend as they took their pizza and retreated to the living room, away from the other kids. The forty-five of the Monster Mash spun on the turntable for the umpteenth time in a row, and the hyper banter of the ten fourth graders made Lois's head swim. From what she could make out of the conversations, Scream in the Dark had been a total success. A satisfied grin lit her face as she entered the living room to offer Troy and Wendy a refill of juice, and to conduct a little snooping as well.

"More Kool Aid?" She approached with a pitcher.

"No thanks, Mom." Troy fidgeted in his seat, shifting his gaze to the floor.

"No, thank you, Mrs. Fischer," the little Italian girl said with a blush.

"Did you have a nice time, Wendy?" Lois asked, her smirk growing wider by the second.

"Yes."

Troy continued to squirm as if his underwear was too tight.

Lois tried her best to stifle her laughter at the sight of her son. The kid was a mess compared to Wendy, who played it as cool as a snow cone. *This one is going to be a handful.* Allowing a devious smile to slip, she started to head toward the kitchen, then turned back. "Oh, Wendy," she said.

"Yes, Mrs. Fischer?"

"You've got something on your chin." Lois dropped the bomb, then waited at the entrance to the kitchen to witness the reaction.

Wendy rubbed her hand against her face and came away with a red smear on her palm. Lois watched as the child's face flushed crimson like the fake blood on her chin, a near identical match to the color and location of the stain that Troy wore. Wendy's jaw dropped as she stared down at the stain. She quickly looked up at Lois, then back at her hand, and finally turned to Troy, who still had no idea his mom had figured everything out in less than two minutes. But Lois could see the realization in Wendy eyes; the girl knew she'd been caught and darted from her chair and ran toward the bathroom. *Girls really do mature quicker than boys.*

Wendy left Troy in a huff, racing past Billy and Eric Tobin just as they entered the room.

"That was radical," Billy said to his younger cousin, shoving the last bite of pizza into his mouth. "To be honest, I thought it was gonna be dumb, but you really pulled it off. Can't wait till next year."

"Did you see their faces when we jumped 'em?" Eric asked, still wearing his werewolf mask. "I thought the one kid was gonna piss himself ... he might have."

"You guys were great," Troy said, looking up at his cousins. Billy and Eric could have almost passed for twins if Billy wasn't six inches taller than his younger brother. With their sandy-brown hair and sapphire-blue eyes, they looked like nearly grown versions of Troy, and resembled Lois as well. "The graveyard was awesome. They were stuck, just like we planned."

"Piece of cake," Billy said. "No way I was letting them out."

Billy had barricaded the door from the other side, using a board of sheet rock and his own teenage strength.

"Right on!" Troy said, trying to sound cool to the older boys.

"Whatever, dork!" Billy laughed and punched his younger cousin in the arm. Although it had been a friendly blow, it stung just the same. Troy did his best not to show it. The three boys looked up as Wendy returned to the living room with no sign of the incriminating smear on her chin. Troy's entire body went rigid as she walked across the shag carpet towards him. Billy examined his actions and threw him a wink. "Well, kiddo," he said, clapping Troy on the back. "We gotta scram. Big night, if you know what I mean."

"Um ... not really." Troy shrugged his shoulders, clueless to Billy's suggestion.

"Well," Billy said, raising his eyebrows as Wendy passed him. "Give it a couple years and you will. Oh, and I get to be the vampire next Halloween."

"I got something even scarier planned for next year."

"I don't know about that, kiddo. You really outdid yourself. Well, see ya later, squirt."

"Where are you boys off to?" Lois popped her head out of the kitchen.

"You know, big date, Aunt Lois." Billy offered an exaggerated wink. "Can't keep the ladies waiting."

"Hmm-mmm." She smirked. "Well, be careful driving. I know there won't be any drinking involved, right?"

"We're not old enough to drink, Aunt Lois," Eric said, lifting his mask to kiss her on the cheek.

"See you soon." Billy kissed her as well, and the Tobin brothers exited out the front door. Eric replaced his mask and howled all the way to the car.

"Is your mother picking you up, Wendy?" Lois asked.

"Yes, Mrs. Fischer. She should be here any minute now," Wendy said politely. "Thank you for having me." Wendy's mother and father were divorced, and her dad lived in Warren. And although her mom had tried to fill Wendy's head with cautionary tales of how horrible men were, Wendy had a willful mind of her own. Sometimes a bit too willful for her own good.

Troy thanked his friends, who agreed it had been a radical haunted house and a groovy party. Then, one by one, the children's parents arrived in their Pintos and Toyotas, honking their horns to announce their arrival.

When Wendy's mother showed up, Troy walked her to the door and opened it.

"That was a cool haunted house, Troy." She bit her lip again.

"I'm glad you liked it. I hope it wasn't too scary," he said, feeling the confidence swell within him.

Lois listened from the kitchen while Troy exercised his newfound bravado.

"I was okay." Wendy stepped onto the front porch, hesitated, then doubled back. "Because you were there." She stuck her head in the doorway and pecked him on the cheek. "See you Monday at school." She darted off the steps, raced across the lawn, and jumped into the backseat of her mother's station wagon.

Troy watched her leave, then shut the door. He turned to find his mother, Scott, Kelly, and Caroline staring at him with giant grins plastered to their faces.

"Troy's got a girlfriend," Caroline snickered.

"Troy and Wendy, sitting in a tree," Kelly ribbed.

Before Scott could add a clever comment of his own, the fortunate sound of a car horn broke the tension. Kelly's mom had arrived to drive the three of them home. They ran down the stairs as if on cue, shouting, "Thanks, Mrs. Fischer, great party. See ya Monday."

Troy had been spared ... almost.

His mom continued to grin at him from her perch at the top of the stairs.

"What?!" he blurted.

"I didn't say anything." She walked back to the kitchen and added, "Think you can help your mother clean up, Romeo?"

"Aw, Mom!" Troy let out an exasperated sigh, shook his head, and followed her into the kitchen.

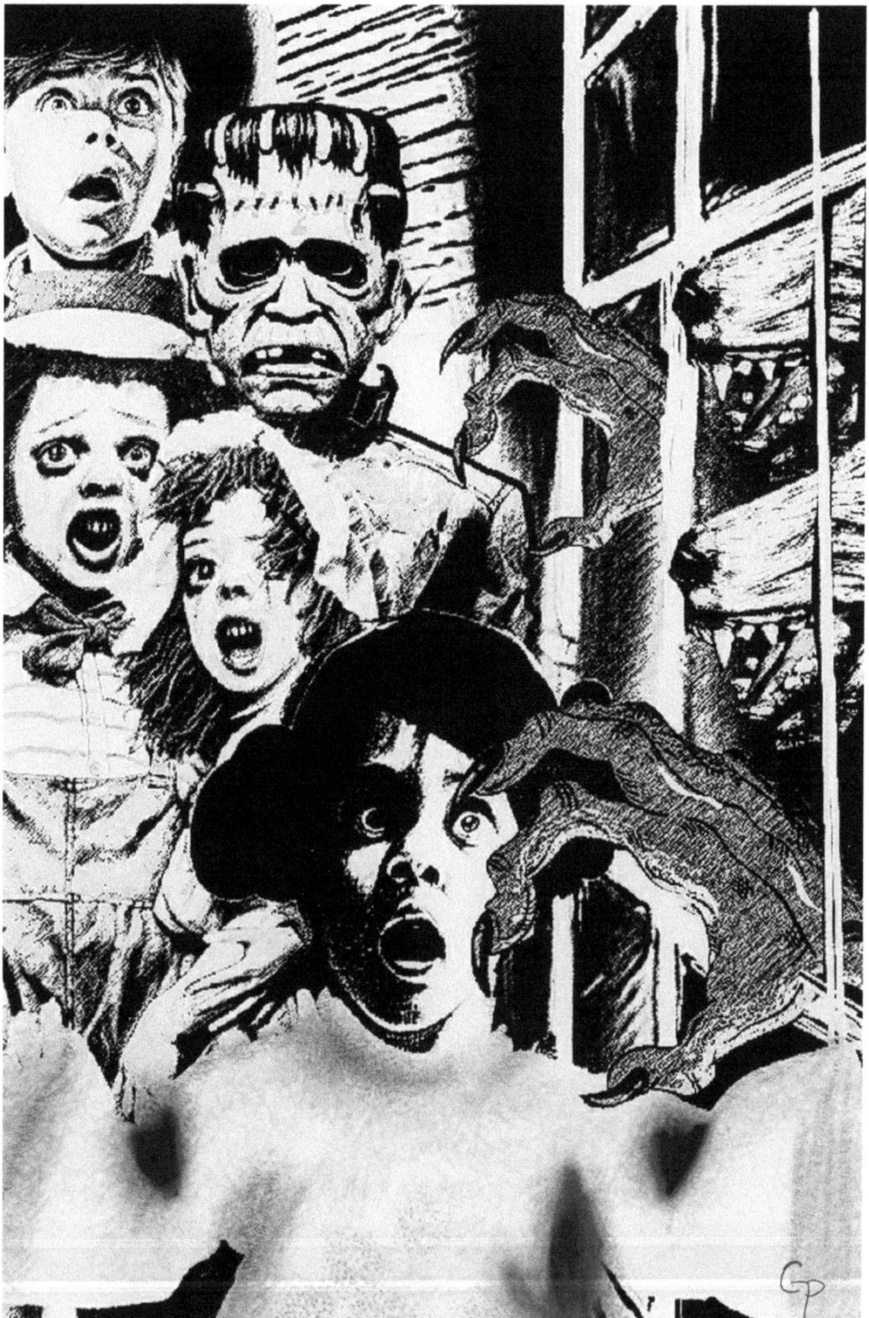

Chapter 3

Mountainside Park sat at the top of Mountain Avenue and wasn't much more than a glorified dirt parking lot at the end of a dead-end road—but the view was spectacular. Here, one could see the entire town of Garrett Grove, from the steeple of the Lutheran church, all the way to the banks of the Lenape River, and everything in between. Mountain Avenue—known to the locals as Mountain Ave—sat on the north side of town, originating at the base of the foothills. Then it took a steep climb up the side of Garrett Mountain, where it dead-ended at the park. It was a favorite spot for family picnics on Sunday afternoons and teenage make-out sessions on Friday and Saturday nights.

But to call Mountain Ave a dead-end wasn't entirely accurate. Although the road was closed where the park had been established, the old extension continued well past the barricade and snaked up the mountain a good mile and a half further.

The weed-strewn, pothole-filled old extension, which had been closed for decades, corkscrewed and twisted up the mountain like a crooked politician. This treacherous piece of blacktop led to the Mountainside Sanatorium, which sat vacant at the summit in a state of rot and decay. The sanatorium had been built in 1890 to house consumption patients. As tuberculosis spread like wildfire during the 19th century, sanatoriums in isolated locations began to pop up across the country, the idea being that contagious patients would greatly benefit from the open setting and spacious properties. These facilities promised a certain level of accommodation to those who could afford them. However, Mountainside was anything but a place of comfort and grace.

As the disease had reached pandemic proportions, the sanatoriums were forced to open their doors to the public. This led to an indigestible level of suffering. Patients were left to waste in overcrowded sick rooms as TB stole their breath. There was no cure, and there was no relief. There was only pain and desolation. Finally, the first consumption patient was cured in 1949 with a drug called Streptomycin. Mountainside Sanatorium closed its doors in 1952, but not before the stain of despair saturated the ground. The building had been left standing there ever since.

The copper wiring and light fixtures had been stripped by scrappers looking to make a few extra bucks. Most of the windows were shattered, and nature crept in through every possible crevice. Graffiti covered most of the walls, and beer cans and cigarette butts littered the floors. But other than that, the place was intact.

The sanatorium looked as if it had been abandoned in a hurry. Gurneys and beds still occupied the rooms and halls, files were left in cabinets, and furniture still sat in the doctors' offices. It was like the place closed overnight, as if the staff had made a run for it.

Now there were more rumors about the sanatorium than facts. It had become such a sour piece of the town's history that most people pretended it never existed at all. So it sat at the top of Garrett Mountain in a state of disrepair, growing more mysterious with each passing year. The only visitors were the occasional vagrants, and teenagers looking for a place to drink and make out. Since Garrett Grove didn't have much of a vagrant problem, and the old road was lined with potholes large enough to swallow a small child, the place didn't get many visitors. However, there was nothing more determined than horny teenagers looking for a place to screw.

The six high school students stood in the abandoned parking lot beneath a blanket of stars, staring at the ominous structure. The place was enormous and loomed before them in the darkness like a monolith. Several buildings jutted out from the main structure, and smaller houses called "the cottages" peppered the outskirts of the property. That was where the hospital staff had lived.

"There's no way I'm going in there," Debbie Horne said. Her straight, dark hair hung to the small of her back, resembling the pop singer Crystal Gayle, or so she liked to think. Unfortunately, thinking she looked like Crystal Gayle didn't make Debbie's brown eyes any bluer and it didn't make her look anything like Crystal Gayle, but she was still pretty enough for Billy Tobin. "You couldn't pay me to step one foot in that place."

"What?" Billy cried. "After we walked up the whole damn mountain, you're gonna chicken out on me?" He wrapped his arms around her and groped just a little. "I'm not gonna let anybody get you, baby. I promise."

"Stop it, you pig," she said, halfheartedly fending him off.

Eric Tobin let out a howl, still wearing the werewolf mask from the party. "Oww." He panted and pretended to bite Susan Smith on the neck. She pulled his mask off and kissed him on the lips.

"Easy, boy," she said. "You don't have to beg."

Susan was Caroline Smith's older sister, which was obvious. Both girls wore the same blonde curls and revealed identical dimples when they smiled. Susan and Eric had been dating since their freshman year, and this wasn't her first visit to the sanatorium, but she could remember how freaked out she had been. She knew exactly what Debbie was feeling, being her first time and all. Also, Debbie and Billy had been dating for less than a month.

"Anybody want a beer?" Mick Petrie asked. He had known Billy and Eric for years and gotten into nearly as much trouble as the two brothers. Mick was the jock of the group, and even though he was stronger and faster than his friends, he still followed Billy Tobin around like a faithful servant. He and his girlfriend, Allison Aigans, had been to the old sanatorium more than a few times before.

"Oh yeah." Billy grabbed a can for him and one for Debbie. "So, what do you want to do, stand here in the dark all night?"

"No," Debbie said, opening her beer. "I guess not."

A crescent moon shined down and blanketed the massive complex in a silvery-blue light. Shadows jumped from the overgrown scrub grass that wove its way between the cracks in the pavement. The structure, a sour face at the top of a haggard body, kept a silent watch, an imposing silhouette against a backdrop of night. Billy cast the beam of his flashlight across the front façade of the old hospital, revealing paint that had peeled away to nothing and loose brickwork that had broken free. Not even the vines creeping up the front of the building were able to hold it together. Eventually, the entire place would crumble to the ground. The light caught a family of raccoons as they scurried across the front steps.

"What the hell is that?" Allison ran behind Mick and latched onto him, her skin-tight corduroy slacks swooshing as her thighs rubbed against one other.

"Maybe it's the knob goblins," Mick answered. "I hear they feast on virgins—oh wait, you have nothing to worry about."

She slapped him. "Very funny, asshole."

"Well"—Billy pulled Debbie closer—"you don't want the knob goblins to get you. I can make sure they leave you alone and fix that whole virginity thing tonight."

Debbie opened her mouth to reply but stopped when something else darted across the front steps of the building. It was dark and low to the ground, much larger than a raccoon, but there was nothing recognizable about the form. It shot from the left to right like a bullet and was too fast to follow. Billy jumped as it passed through the beam of the light. The others had seen it too and reacted the same.

"What the hell was that?" Mick started.

Debbie screamed and hid behind Billy.

It registered as a blur, moving too quick to even cast a shadow. Billy tried to follow its path with his flashlight but was unsuccessful. He swept the beam to either side of the hospital's main entrance, surveying the grounds, but couldn't find anything.

There was movement behind them, furtive and threatening. It was more like a sensation than an actual sound. Intuition screamed. Something was rapidly approaching from the darkness; the entire group turned as if on cue. Billy cast the light into the murk only to reveal a parking lot of overgrown weeds, empty and deserted.

"I don't like this, man." Eric's voice was little more than a whisper. "We should get out of here."

For a moment, they stood there, breathing heavily into the cool night. Silence fell like a blanket; even the crickets were hushed, as if they had been erased from existence. Something just beyond the reach of the light waited. They all felt it. A predator lurking in the shadows. The only sound Billy heard was his heart thrumming in his chest. He nearly screamed when Debbie pulled herself behind him and whispered in his ear. "We need to leave ... Now!"

The others remained still, waiting for Billy to tell them what to do. Instead, he stood there, focusing on the patch of earth just beyond the reach of the light. He could almost see the hazy image—wavering—black against black; it made his eyes hurt to look at it. Whatever was out there had stopped moving.

It was watching them.

The night grew deathly still, and a low-lying ground fog crept in at the edge of their periphery. Billy turned to Debbie and took her hand. "Let's go," he mouthed to the group, just loud enough for them to hear. He started to walk back toward the road but found it impossible to restrain himself from running and tore off in the direction of the old extension as if his head were on fire.

"Come on, let's go!" he screamed to the others.

They didn't need to be told a third time and followed close enough to be on his heels. No one said a word. Fear and panic took root and nearly paralyzed them. If it hadn't been for Billy, they would still be standing in the darkness, exposed and vulnerable.

They descended the steep slope of the extension, being as careful as possible not to break an ankle on the loose asphalt or in any of the numerous potholes. Billy had an overpowering urge to look over his shoulder but didn't dare. He was sure whatever was out there was hunting them. He sensed its pursuit as they made their way further from the old building.

Susan cried out as her feet tangled on a branch in the road. She fell hard to the pavement on her hands and knees. Eric rushed to her side to help as Billy paused to cast the light in their direction. The air above them parted in a flurry of disruption as something passed just inches from their heads. Billy felt his ears pop as the presence descended upon him. It had shot down from the top of the mountain and nearly scalped them. The attack was followed by the scraping sound of loose gravel disturbed in the gloom further down the hill.

Now it was in front of them.

"It's fucking hunting us, Billy!" Eric shouted.

The girls cried as the group huddled close together in the middle of the deserted road. Casting his flashlight in frantic, searching sweeps, Billy prayed nothing would be illuminated; he knew whatever was out there would be unbearable to see.

"What the fuck are we going to do, Billy?" Debbie clung to him, terrified and trembling.

Billy felt close to tears himself and didn't have any answers. He continued to sweep the perimeter with the light, the beam jumping from the tremble of his grip. A strangled cry escaped from his lips when Mick took hold of his shoulder.

"What the hell is that?" Billy's voice shook.

"I don't know, but I have an idea." Mick spoke low and deliberately. "We're gonna count to three. Then I need you to shine the light up the hill, and I'm gonna make a run for it."

"No way, you're not leaving me," Allison protested.

"Don't worry; I'm the fastest one here." Mick had been on the track team since sixth grade and was the fastest kid in school. "I'll head into the woods and then double back. I'll probably get to the car before you do."

"I can't let you do it, man," Billy said.

"You don't have a choice," Mick reassured him, gripping his shoulder. "Three. Two. One." Mick sped off like a bat out of hell, and Billy trained the light up the hill to help guide him.

The sound of scraping gravel echoed below their position. Then the air above them rippled once again, as if a flurry of wings had taken flight. It felt oppressive as it passed overhead and pursued into the night after Mick.

"Come on, quick!" Billy ran, and the others followed.

Their feet skidded and slipped on the loose gravel, but somehow, none of them fell as they barreled down the side of the mountain. Billy yanked at Debbie's arm, pulling her behind him. Eric and Allison flanked Susan to help her along. With every frantic step, they prepared for something to swoop down and carry one of them off into the night.

They crashed into the gate at the bottom of the hill and skirted around it toward the park. Billy let go of Debbie's hand and pulled out his car keys. He unlocked the driver's side, and everyone poured into his Charger through the one open door. Then he jumped in and slammed it shut behind him. Sweat ran down the back of his shirt as he tried to catch his breath. The others stared back at him, wide-eyed and panting. No one spoke.

Billy didn't know what to do. He wanted to go after Mick but was too scared to propose the idea. He put the key into the ignition and sat behind the wheel, waiting for something brilliant to come to him. He was out of ideas.

"We can't just leave him out there." Allison broke the silence. "We have to do something."

"Okay, okay," Billy replied.

"We have to do something, Billy," she cried.

"What the hell do you want me to do?!" he shouted. "If you got any ideas, I'm all ears."

"Easy, bro," Eric said. "Let's just sit here a second and figure this out."

"We can't just sit here. Mick's out there ... he needs our help!" Allison insisted.

Billy felt like jumping into the backseat and strangling the girl but managed to control himself. Before he could reply, the car shook as something heavy landed on the hood. The girls screamed, and Billy turned on the headlights. Perched in front of them, illuminated in the glow, stood Mick, grinning like a clown. He was flushed and out of breath, but he was smiling. He walked around to the passenger side, and Eric let him in.

"You scared the crap out of me," Allison said, pulling him into the backseat. She threw her arms around him and kissed him.

"Ouch." Mick flinched. "That hurts."

"What is it?" Susan asked. "Turn on the lights, Billy."

Billy hit the interior lights and turned to find Mick bleeding from a small wound just below his jaw.

"What happened?" Allison had gotten some blood on her when she grabbed him.

Mick put his hand to his neck to stop the bleeding, which didn't appear too bad. "I ran into a branch or something. It was hard to see, but I think I lost it in the woods. I don't know what the hell's out there, but it sure is fast. Damn thing was right on me too."

Billy started the car, put it in drive, and skidded out of the dirt parking lot. He looked back at Mick in the rearview mirror. "Are you okay, man?"

"Never better." Mick smiled. "Except for one thing."

"What's that?" Eric asked, concerned.

"I dropped the beer." Mick started to laugh, but no one joined him.

The tires chirped as they met the blacktop, with Billy's foot pressed firmly to the floor. He didn't like how pale Mick looked but was happy to put some distance between them and the mountain. He turned on the radio to help lighten the mood, and Buck Dharma's voice filled the cab of the Charger. Billy didn't appreciate the way the singer insisted that he shouldn't fear the reaper, so he turned off the radio and drove in silence.

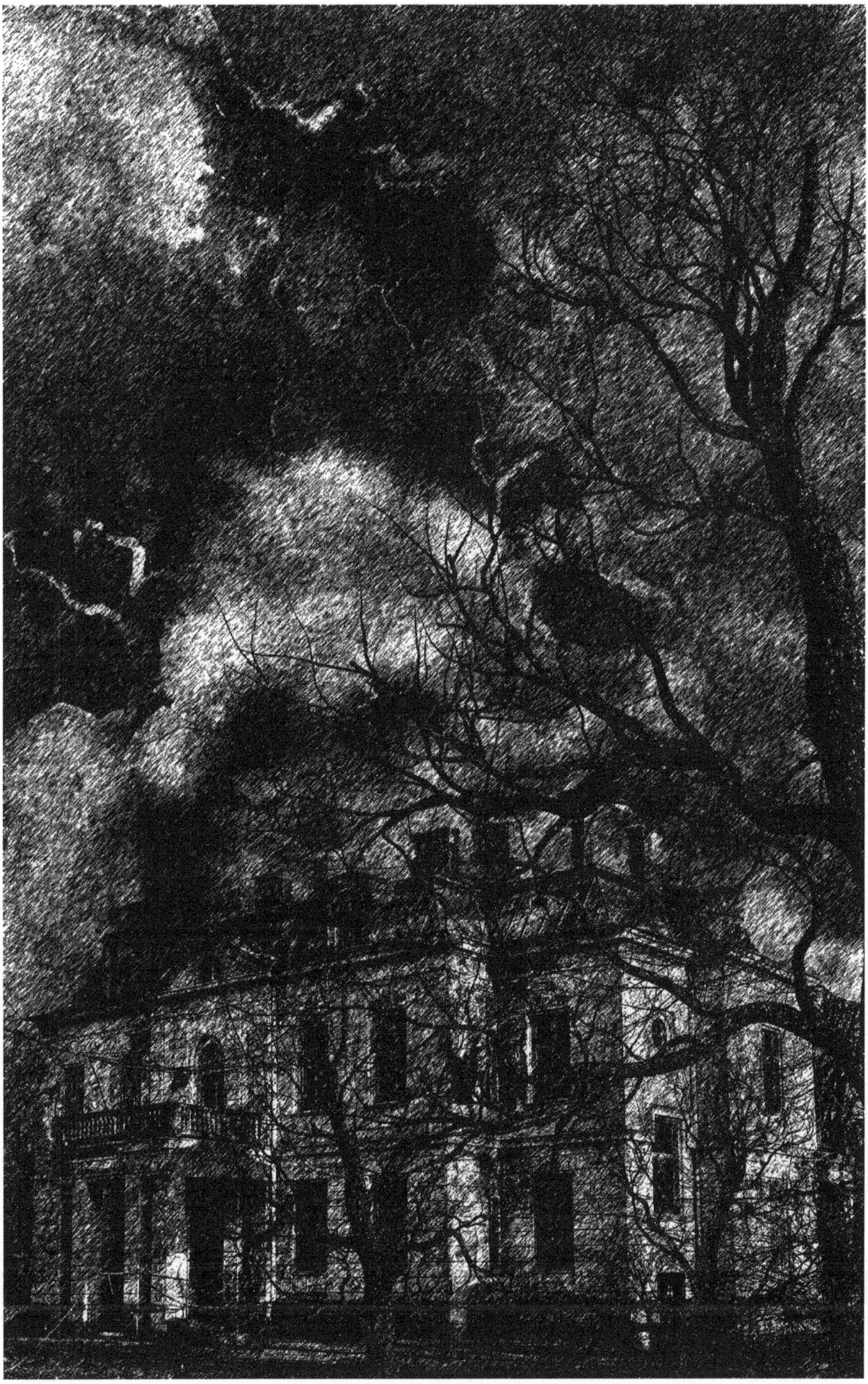

Chapter 4

After all the guests had gone home from the party, Lois watched her son as he absentmindedly tossed paper cups and plates into the trash with a giant grin plastered to his face. "I've never seen anyone so happy to throw out trash," she snickered.

"Huh?" Troy hadn't heard a word.

"Your friends looked like they had a nice time."

"Oh yeah," he said. "It was awesome. You should have seen it, Mom. We scared the heck out of them."

"Umm-hmm, and Wendy looked like she had a nice time."

"Yeah. I mean, I think she did." His face darkened a shade.

"She's pretty. Don't you think?"

"Mom," he pleaded. "Stop it."

"Okay, kiddo. Just don't grow up too fast?" Lois kissed the top of his head.

"Sure, no problem." Troy scanned the kitchen for a diversion to escape from the conversation. "I'm gonna take out the garbage," he said, lifting the bag from the can and heading for the door.

"Thanks, sweetie," she called to him. "Make sure you blow out all the candles."

"Okay, Mom."

"And close up the garage too."

"Got it," he said and walked outside.

Troy threw the garbage into one of the metal cans his father kept on the side of the driveway. Donald Fischer had wanted to be there to help with his son's haunted house but had been unable because of work. Don was a geological engineer for DuCain Industries. The company had been cutting into the mountain on the far side of town for the past decade. Troy had no idea what needed to be done at a quarry on a Saturday night, but his father had said something big happened earlier in the week, that he and a few of the other men would have to burn the midnight oil. Troy had no idea what that meant since DuCain wasn't in the oil business. As far as he knew, they mined minerals and supplied crushed stone for construction. Although, he wasn't exactly sure about that either.

Troy followed the path to the garage, pausing to blow out the candles along the way. He stopped in front of the large overhead door and reached up to grab it. Gripping the handle, he began to pull down. A loud thud, as if something significant had fallen inside, caused Troy to jump. He stood there listening.

All was quiet. He thought maybe the piece of sheet rock Billy had used as a barricade might have fallen over. Then he noticed the strobe light was still flashing and realized he had left the other lights on as well.

Troy entered the strobe-lit hallway and walked past the cage into the spider chamber. He proceeded into the rat menagerie and was gripped by an unshakable sense that he was no longer alone. An icy chill caused the wispy hairs on his arms to prickle; it crept in between his ribs and wrapped around his heart. Despite the rising tension fluttering inside his chest, Troy's legs continued to propel him forward. Step by step, he maneuvered through the darkness and navigated his way across the carpet of rubber hoses. Carefully, he opened the door to the graveyard room and scanned the area, waiting for his eyes to adjust to the dull glow cast from the crimson lightbulbs.

The dimly lit room revealed itself in a wash of scarlet shadows as Troy took another step inside. The fence and the headstones, even the coffin, all appeared as he had last seen them; nothing looked out of place. Troy exhaled and began to turn when a splash of motion caught his attention. A gasp rose in the back of his throat but was silenced, the saliva in his mouth drying up like it had been hit with a blow torch. Behind the coffin against the far wall, the scarlet shadow shifted once again.

Arctic fingers gripped him on either side of his head, then spread downward until the ice water settled in his arms and legs. Unable to move, Troy stood frozen in place with his eyes focused on the dark figure in the corner of the room. The intruder stood facing the far wall with their back to him. Even in the dull amber glow, Troy thought it must be a child, as the figure appeared roughly the same height as he. Not sure if he should call out or turn and run, he stood there trying to grasp a rational explanation. *Is that Tommy ... or Mike?* It was possible his friends had returned to pay him back for scaring them. Troy examined the room to see if anyone else was hiding in the shadows. But he had watched his friends leave when their parents picked them up. He dismissed the notion as he suddenly realized the identity of the figure in the darkness.

"H-Hello," the word cracked from his parched mouth.

The young boy slowly turned toward him. Scarlet shadows danced across his face and revealed his features—it was Rob.

"Rob, what are you doing?" Troy asked.

The child was barefoot and dressed only in his pajamas. Troy noticed his friend's feet right away; they were scraped and cut and covered in dirt. Rob's mouth hung open; his eyes stared back blankly at Troy. Even in the crimson light, his face was visibly ashen and grey, with deep purple streaks on his cheeks and lips.

"Are you okay? What are you doing here?" Troy asked again.

Rob took a step toward him and then another. The boy raised his arms and closed in on Troy.

"Stop playing. You're scaring me."

Rob opened his mouth, allowing a low, guttural hiss to escape. He took another step forward and backed Troy up against the wall. Then Rob lunged at him but suddenly stopped like he had changed his mind at the last second. He looked up at Troy, blinking and confused, as if he were in shock.

"Troy," Rob said in a voice as weak as dust. He scanned the room and then looked down at his bare feet. "Troy, what am I doing here?"

Before Troy could answer, Rob collapsed into his arms. He struggled to hold him, but the boy was as heavy as a sack of wet flour. Troy could feel the heat pouring off his friend's body as he attempted to ease him to the floor. Then Rob's eyes rolled back in their sockets, and he started to convulse.

"Mom!" Troy screamed. "Mom, help! Something's wrong with Rob!"

Donald Fischer and Mark Gold sat at their desks in the large trailer that served as the site supervisor's office. Mark's desk was covered with topographic prints of alternate blast sites. He shifted through the seemingly endless rolls of blue paper with a cigarette suspended from his lips. Smoke lifted into his squinted eyes and rolled over a set of brows so thick, they resembled a pair of Gypsy Moth caterpillars. Donald was on the phone attempting to quell the shitstorm that had blown up in their faces. Early Tuesday morning, routine blasting had revealed a large cavity in a cliff wall on the north face. It was initially thought to be part of an old, abandoned mine, although there were no records indicating the presence of one. Still, it was possible; they came across them from time to time. Which was dangerous as hell due to the pockets of methane they often contained.

It was Don's job to verify safe blast sites. And everything had looked green across the board. Seismic tests hadn't revealed any cavities or abnormalities in the topography. No one was more surprised than he when the smoke cleared and the cave's small opening was revealed.

The markings on the rock near the entrance determined they hadn't uncovered any mine. The ancient symbols resembled hieroglyphs. From what Don could tell, the blast had opened either a burial site or a tribal habitat. Whatever it was, it was old as hell and would prove to be one giant pain in the ass. Not only would he have to determine an alternate blast site, but he was required to report the findings to the historical foundation. They would no doubt send in a group of artifact geeks who would descend on the quarry like a plague of locusts and infect it in a similar way.

The presence of methane had not been detected, but that didn't mean the cave was safe. A small group of engineers and miners were sent into the cavity to determine if the place was structurally sound enough for the scientists to mess around.

Walt Taylor was the first man in; he had served as a tunnel rat in Vietnam and was the best surveyor the company had. The man was as skinny as a birch tree and looked like you could knock him over with a harsh word, but Walt was full of grit and one tough bastard. He inspected the cave and then reported back to Don. "You're not gonna fuckin' like it, boss."

Don braced himself for the bad news.

"There's a ton of stuff in that cave," Walt continued, "artifacts ... all that kinda crap, ya know? It was an important place to someone, tell you what. There's also bones in there, and I mean a fuck load. It could be a burial site. I'm willing to bet those museum guys'll be crawling around in there for months."

Don's stomach did a cartwheel and then turned sour. It was official; the north face had just become a shitshow, and he was the master of ceremonies. He envisioned the ass reaming he would get from old man DuCain and nearly puked. His life was about to become extremely difficult.

"I can do that," Don announced into the phone.

Mark looked up at him through a veil of cigarette smoke.

"Absolutely, I will be sure of that. Okay, I'll be expecting him." He hung up and buried his head in his palms.

"Do I want to know?" Mark put the cigarette out.

"We got a guy coming in on Monday." He checked his scribbled notes. "Dr. Stephen Thompson, curator for the Museum of Natural History, he's supposed to be some type of artifact specialist. We're to give him whatever help he needs."

"What kind of help does he need?" Mark asked. "You go in the cave, you take out the stuff, and you leave."

"Yeah, it isn't as easy as that, apparently. No one is to disturb anything until he gets here."

"What are we supposed to do until then, babysit a hole in the rock?" Mark leaned back in his chair and laced his hands behind his head.

"Well, the guy gets here Monday. It should be easy enough to keep it tight till then. We'll park a dozer in front of the entrance and put up a couple of signs."

The phone rang on Don's desk; both men stared at it for a moment.

"You going to answer that?" Mark asked.

Finally, Don picked up. "Hello, Fischer." A wash of grey drained his face. "Slow down, Lois. What happened?"

Mark furrowed his tangle of brows and looked at his partner.

"Is Troy, okay? Good. He did what? In his pajamas?" Don felt every muscle in his face tighten. "Look, I'm leaving now. I can be there in a half-hour. Is Troy with you? Okay, okay, just try to calm down. I'm on my way." He hung up the phone and bolted from his desk.

"What happened?" Mark asked.

"It's one of Troy's friends; Lois had to bring the kid to Chilton. Found him in the garage in his pajamas."

"What the hell ... pajamas?" Mark winced.

"Look, I'll call you when I know more. Lois is freaking out. I got to go." Don jetted out the door, leaving Mark alone in the trailer.

● ● ●

Lois heard Troy scream from inside the house and knew it was a matter of life or death. She dropped the plate she had been washing and hit the front door at full sprint. She found Troy kneeling over Rob, with the boy convulsing on the garage floor. He was dressed in his pajamas and had started to turn blue. Lois rolled him onto his side and felt the heat radiating from him. His fever had to be close to 105.

"How did he get here?" she asked. "Did he walk all the way in just his pajamas?" Lois looked at Troy, who appeared on the verge of tears and unable to answer.

Nothing made sense, and there was no time; Rob was fading fast. She cradled the boy's head to prevent him from smacking it against the floor as he shook. Then she instructed Troy to retrieve her purse and car keys from inside the house. By the time he returned, Rob had stopped convulsing, and Lois had begun to carry him to the car. Troy helped get him in the back seat, and they sped off. Lois clutched the wheel and prayed; she wasn't sure if Rob would last the two-mile trip to the medical center. *Christ, this kid is on fire.* Now that he was out of the red glow of the garage, Lois could see just how grave he looked. The boy could have already passed for dead; she hoped it wasn't too late. His lips were dark blue, and deep scarlet circles spread out beneath his eyes. The rest of his skin was the dusty white of a corpse. She pushed the Impala's accelerator to the floor, running every traffic light along the way.

She skidded to a halt in the Chilton Medical Center's parking lot in front of the emergency room entrance. Two orderlies rushed to their aid.

Rob was ushered into the emergency room through two batwing doors situated behind an oval reception desk that sat like an island in the center of the large waiting area.

Lois called Rob's parents from the reception desk and tried to explain everything she knew, which wasn't much. Mrs. Boyle had no idea her son had even left the house, and Lois couldn't answer any of her questions. She wasn't sure what had happened herself. The boy had shown up out of nowhere. Minutes later, Karin and Bob Boyle burst through the side entrance and blew past Lois and Troy. They stormed the front desk, where a middle-aged woman sat behind the counter, and were ushered into the emergency room to join their son. Lois and Troy hadn't been allowed in because they weren't family, also because Rob's condition was critical.

They returned to their seats in the waiting area, frantic and in shock, with Troy still wearing his vampire costume and Lois wringing her hands as if they were wet. Minutes later, a young nurse jiggled towards them, her two-sizes-too-small uniform looking more like a coat of white paint.

"Mrs. Fischer, I'm Nurse Gilmartin."

"Yes, how is he?" Lois stood up. "Is he going to be all right?"

"The doctors are with him now. They're trying to bring his fever down. You did good by driving him here. He might not have survived if you waited any longer."

Lois listened and continued to wring her hands.

"His temperature is over 106, but the doctors are doing everything they can. I was hoping you could tell us what happened. Can I get you a cup of coffee or maybe something cold?"

Donald rushed into the building and ran to them. He took Lois in his arms and hugged Troy. "What happened?" he asked, out of breath.

Lois picked up her purse and began to rummage through it. She pulled out a pack of Parliaments. "Mind if I smoke?" After several drags, which appeared to steady her nerves, she did her best to explain what happened, from the moment she heard Troy scream to finding Rob on the cold garage floor. Troy managed to fill in the rest. He told them how Rob had been standing there in a trance and how strange his friend had acted.

"It was like he was coming after me, like he wanted to hurt me. Then when I called to him, it was like he woke up from a dream. He didn't know where he was."

"He's delirious from the fever. I'm surprised he was able to stand at all," the young nurse said.

"I'm sorry." Donald checked the girl's name tag. "Nurse Gilmartin, I'm confused. If Rob is that sick, how the hell did he walk all the way in bare feet and pajamas?"

"I can't answer that, Mr. Fischer." She turned to Troy. "Could I get you a cup of cocoa?"

Troy looked to his father, who nodded his approval.

"I think I'll take you up on that coffee, if that's okay?" Lois added.

Nurse Gilmartin nodded to Donald, who shook his head yes. "I'll be right back," she excused herself and disappeared down the hall.

"What the heck happened, Troy?" Donald asked. "I thought you said he had the flu. How do you think he walked out of the house without his parents even knowing he left?"

"I got no idea, Dad ... really. He didn't come to school, and you should have seen the way he looked at me. I thought he was gonna strangle me or something. He scared the crap out of me."

"Language, Troy," Lois snapped.

"I'm sorry, Mom," he apologized and turned back to his father. "I have no idea how he got there or how long he was even in the garage. He must have been really upset that he missed the party. Maybe he felt good enough to come over."

"In his pajamas? I don't know, kiddo, but I'm proud of you." Donald hugged his son. "That was brave of you tonight. I hope he's going to be okay. His poor parents." He trailed off as Nurse Gilmartin arrived, juggling the coffee and cocoa.

The doctors continued to work on Rob for what felt like half the night. Finally, Karin and Bob exited the emergency room looking haggard and drawn out. They joined the Fischers in the waiting area and filled them in on what they knew so far. Rob's temperature had dropped a few degrees, and he was being given fluids. No one could explain how he had left the house, let alone how he walked nearly a mile in his condition. The doctors were cautiously optimistic at this point and said it was a good sign they were able to bring his temperature down.

The Boyles thanked Lois and Troy for helping Rob and told them there was no reason to stay any longer. They said they would call in the morning with an update. The Fischer family reluctantly left the medical center.

Later, as Troy lay in his bed praying for God to watch over his friend, he replayed the night in his head. It felt like weeks had passed since Wendy kissed him in the garage, though it had only been a few hours. And even though he knew his friend was very sick, something about what happened didn't sit right. It was the way Rob looked at him in the garage and how he had come after him. It felt like Rob had wanted to hurt him. Troy could have sworn Rob had acted as if he was ... hungry. That was it; he had been searching for a way to describe it. Rob had sized him up like a late-night snack.

    He lay awake, reliving the scene over and over. It wasn't until much later that Troy was able to fall asleep. He felt like he had just closed his eyes when he woke to the sound of police sirens racing up his street.

Chapter 5

Sunday, October 25

At 6:15 a.m., Ted Lutchen found himself at the scene of the first murder in his eighteen-month career as a deputy for the Garrett Grove Sheriff's Department. The clean-cut patrolman, who looked like he had just stepped off the football field after throwing the game-winning touchdown, had responded to several traffic fatalities and even a suicide during his brief time on the force. Garrett Grove was in no way a booming metropolis, and murder had never been a problem before. However, it was 1979 and times were changing. Ted figured if an actor could run for president, then anything was possible, even a murder in Garrett Grove. He proceeded to block off the cul-de-sac at the end of Foothills Drive and put on his most authoritative face. With trembling hands and his heart jackhammering like a greyhound with a case of pre-race jitters, he did his job and prayed the other officers couldn't tell that he was jumpier than a cat in a bathtub.

The victim lay in the street approximately twenty feet from a Con Edison company Ford. Sheriff Carl Primrose and Deputy Gary Forsyth continued to examine the body and the vehicle's contents while they waited for the county coroner to arrive.

Burt Lively had been shaken from his sleep by a phone call from Sheriff Primrose at six twenty. At first, he thought it was a joke … it had to be. No one got murdered in Garrett Grove. He struggled to shed the sleep from his old, foggy brain and focus on the news coming through the phone line. Then he noticed the alarm in the sheriff's voice and digested the magnitude of the situation. His friend wasn't joking; there had actually been a murder in Garrett Grove. He needed to haul his ass out of bed and get down there right away.

Burt pulled up to the barrier at the end of the block. He jumped out of the black sedan carrying a medical bag. His hair was closer to salt than it was to pepper these days, and it looked as if he hadn't bothered to run a comb through it before leaving the house. The suit jacket he had thrown on was wrinkled and full of lint as if Burt had slept in it. He approached Deputy Lutchen, who moved one side of the wooden police barricade and allowed him to pass through.

"Morning, Mr. Lively." The deputy nodded as the short man passed him in a huff.

Burt joined Sheriff Primrose, who knelt over a large white sheet that covered the body. The sheriff removed his black Stetson cowboy hat, looked up at his old friend, and squinted. Fine lines etched a face that had been weathered more from experience rather than age itself; getting sent to Vietnam had done that to a lot of men his age. "I'd say good morning, Burt, but we both know that's not likely." He pulled the sheet back far enough for the coroner to see. "His name's Felix Castillo, from Warren. He was a lineman for Con Ed."

The dead man lay on his back with his head turned slightly to the right. His eyes were closed, and he almost looked as if he were sleeping. A circular mark on his neck was the only visible wound; several deep punctures dotted the outer edge of the bruise, with one larger incision in the center.

"What do you make of this, Burt?" he asked.

Burt bent down to get a closer look. He took a pair of surgical gloves from his pocket and pulled them on. Then he turned the man's head to examine the other side of his neck and returned it to its original position. The coroner pressed his fingers against the wound and lifted the sheet to examine the rest of the body.

"As far as I can tell, that's the only wound. But I've never seen anything like that before," the sheriff said. "What do you suppose did that?"

Burt lifted the head again, pressed his fingers into the soft flesh of the man's cheek, and released. He examined the pavement near the body and stood up with a confused look. Burt circled the area, then walked to the truck where Deputy Forsyth was busy collecting evidence.

"Howdy, Burt." The deputy removed his yellow-tinted Aviator glasses and offered the coroner a Donny Osmond smile.

The old man ignored him and proceeded to investigate the cab of the truck; Burt mumbled something under his breath and continued to huff. Gary Forsyth watched as the coroner rooted through the cab, searched underneath the seat, and then looked around the passenger's side of the vehicle. Burt paced back to the body and lifted the sheet again. He looked even more confused than he had a moment ago.

"What's going on, Burt? I can see those wheels turning." The sheriff waited patiently.

"I'm confused, Carl," Burt said. They had known each other far longer than either would care to admit and worked together countless times. The old coroner was one of the few individuals in town who called the sheriff by his first name.

"Look at this." Burt put his hands on the man's throat and spread the wound. The large puncture in the center of the circular mark opened, revealing a one-inch slit in the man's neck. "That's his carotid artery." He pointed. "Right there. I can't tell you what the hell made this mark, but I can tell you a couple things right away."

Carl winced. "Well, spit it out. You waiting for me to buy you a goddamn drink, or what?"

The old man took his time examining the victim's head and torso once again. "Well, Carl, you tell me. Where the hell's all the blood? Wound like that, this guy would have bled out like a spigot. There should be one hell of a mess, but I don't see much blood."

A dried smear of dark crimson had crusted at the corner of the man's mouth, and a few drops speckled the area around the wound. Other than that, the only sign of blood was a small spot the size of a silver dollar on the man's shirt, just below the neckline.

"So, what are you telling me, Burt?" Carl squinted his eyes even tighter.

"Well, I see a few possibilities. But none of them make all that much sense. Of course, murders rarely do, but what do I know? I suppose that's your job."

"Oh, for Christ's sake! Would you spill it already!"

"Okay. This guy should have bled like a stuck pig. And unless I'm missing something ... there isn't any blood anywhere. So, the way I see it, either this guy was murdered somewhere else, which is possible—I suppose." Burt paused to wipe his glasses with a handkerchief he pulled from his jacket pocket and continued. "But ... there's not enough blood on his clothes for that either. So, whoever killed him must've changed his clothes after they whacked him. Oh yeah, they must have washed him up pretty good too 'cause this guy should be covered in blood."

Carl shook his head and grimaced. "I'm not buying any of that. And neither are you."

"Doesn't sound likely," Burt agreed. "By the way the guy's laying, I'd say he didn't put up much of a fight. If I had to guess, he was thrown from over there somewhere." Burt pointed toward the truck. "Just a guess," he continued. "But what I do know? From his skin color and lack of rigor mortis, I can tell you there's very little blood left in his body. Little of anything, for that matter."

Carl looked up and down the street and studied the area of pavement close to the body. "You said there were a few possibilities."

"Well, they all lead to the same result. Someone removed the blood from the body."

Carl shook his head and cringed. "Don't you dare say like a vampire."

"Of course not like a vampire—more like a vacuum cleaner, by the looks of it, big old heavy-duty sucker, at that. Whatever did this was very efficient. You know how messy it can be to drain a body?" He didn't wait for a reply. "Well, I do. Whatever did that was very efficient indeed."

"So, what happened to the blood, Burt?"

"That sounds like police work to me. You'd be looking for about ten or so pints, give or take. I'm guessin' you'll know it when you find it."

"If that's your idea of a joke, I'm not laughing. People don't get murdered in Garrett Grove—not in my town."

"Well, Carl," Burt said, "I hate to tell you, but this guy didn't kill himself, and he didn't die of natural causes. If you ask me, he was murdered. And as far as I know, Foothills Drive is a part of *your* town. So, I guess people do get murdered in

Garrett Grove—at least they do now." Burt checked his watch and looked down the street. "The meat wagon will be here soon. I'll let you know what I find out after I perform the autopsy."

Carl took his hat off and ran his fingers through his hair. "You know, Burt, you really got a way of pissing me off." He picked a piece of lint from the black Stetson, then placed it back on his head. "I suppose I don't have to tell you to keep a lid on this."

"I suppose you don't," Burt replied. "But I doubt you'll be able to keep this news from spreading." He nodded toward the barricade, where a group of neighbors were in the process of interrogating Deputy Lutchen.

"Oh Christ." Carl scowled.

"Yeah, you better go take care of that before the kid folds under pressure."

Burt watched as Carl approached the gathering crowd with his hands raised. "Okay, folks, please step back and let us do our jobs." The neighbors retreated to their homes but continued to watch from the safety of their closed windows and drawn curtains. Minutes later, the county coroner's "meat wagon" turned the corner and pulled up to the barricade.

Carl locked eyes with his old friend and shook his head. "What the hell is going on here?" he whispered under his breath as he scanned the neighborhood. "What the hell?"

● ● ●

Ben and Erin Richards had been unable to attend Troy Fischer's Halloween party because they were sick. Their mother, Sally Ann, had stayed up half the night setting cold compresses and monitoring the twins' fevers. The kids had the flu. Erin was running at a steady 102, which had her concerned, but at one point in the night, Ben's temperature had shot to nearly 104. She had put him in a cool bath and given him an adult aspirin, which managed to bring the fever down slightly. But the poor things were miserable. It took Sally Ann everything in her power to get them to eat even a few tablespoons of Lipton Soup. Erin usually loved the Ring-o-Noodles, but tonight, they hadn't eaten a half bowl between them.

The twins continued to toss and turn throughout the night. They sweated through their pajamas and soaked their bedsheets. Sally Ann changed their clothes and watched over them till they both finally fell asleep around 3:30 a.m. Then she retreated to the living room, worrying as only a mother could, and began to nod off herself. Her husband, Dennis, was in their bedroom and managed to sleep through the night undisturbed. Sally Ann had let him; he was currently working nights at the plant, and by the time he dragged himself home every morning, he was exhausted. Saturday into Sunday was his only night off, and she knew if she woke him, he would have been fit to be tied and taken it out on her.

She did everything she could to not aggravate Dennis these days. He never actually hit her, but there were times he had come close and given her a firm shove. Once, he grabbed her arm so hard, the bruises had lasted for two weeks. *It wasn't his fault,* Sally told herself. Dennis was trying so hard to keep the bills paid and food on the table, plus he had a lot of responsibilities at the plant since the layoff. They were lucky he still had a job; nearly half the men at Faber Manufacturing were standing on the unemployment line. Dennis had a right to get a little angry every now and then. Times were tough, and the gas shortage had everyone on edge. Also, Dennis was livid at the idea of an actor running for president.

"I'd vote for Walter Matthau before I voted for Ronald Reagan. Whoever heard of an actor as president? What's next, Sammy Davis Jr. as Secretary of State?!" he screamed one day over the breakfast table.

Sally Ann had listened and agreed with Dennis's rants. What did she know about politics, anyway? She didn't care much about that stuff. She'd liked Kennedy, but that was because she thought he was handsome. These days, she was happy Dennis was still working and she had time to take care of the twins and the house. Besides, Dennis liked things a certain way, and she liked it when he was happy. It was a whole lot better than when he was not.

Last night had been rough, and Sally Ann hoped she could catch a few winks before Dennis woke up. She had an hour or so before he would be looking for his coffee and bacon, just enough time for a little catnap.

Seconds after she closed her eyes, Sally Ann woke to the faint sound of Erin calling for her. The child's voice was whisper-thin. At first, she thought she was dreaming and her daughter was speaking to her from far away. She opened her eyes to find the girl standing nearly on top of her. Erin held out something in her hand to show her mother.

"Mommy." Her voice was barely a breath; she sounded as if she had something in her mouth. "My tooth fell out."

She had to be dreaming; both kids had lost the last of their baby teeth over a year ago. The girl spoke again, finally commanding her mother's full attention.

"Let me see." Sally felt the heat billowing from her. "Oh my God!"

One of Erin's top incisors lay in her hand. The root was red, and there was blood on her palm. Sally opened Erin's mouth to examine her. There was a large gap where her tooth had been.

"Erin, what on Earth happened?" Sally cried.

"I don't know, Mommy; I felt it in my mouth." Erin swayed on her feet, and Sally steadied her.

"Dear God, baby, you're on fire."

"I don't feel good, Mommy." Erin shook for a short second and then bent over and vomited onto the floor.

Sally watched in horror as Erin retched. What came out of the child smelled like death. The little bit of soup she had eaten was expelled in a deluge of dark red blood. She coughed, and a second tooth flew from her mouth and landed in the mess. Sally screamed for Dennis with little concern as to what kind of mood he would wake up in. She scooped up Erin, who immediately began to shake in her arms. "Dennis, wake up!" she screamed again.

Erin began heaving and violently flailing in her arms as Dennis rushed from the bedroom in his boxer shorts.

"What the hell's going on out here? I'm trying to—" He stopped when he saw the state of the living room and his daughter convulsing. He grabbed Erin from Sally and nearly slipped in the vomit. "What happened?"

Before Sally had time to answer, Ben started screaming as if his fingernails were being ripped out with needle-nose pliers.

Dennis stared at his wife with disbelief and panic in his eyes. "Sally," he pleaded. "What the hell is going on?"

Sheriff Primrose was busy instructing his deputies on the steps he wanted taken to secure the crime scene and exactly how he wished the paperwork to be handled when a voice broke over the police band.

"Dispatch to Sheriff Primrose, you out there, Sheriff?" Tara Jefferies called from the station.

"What now?" He reached into the cruiser and grabbed the handset.

"Yeah, I'm here. What's up, Tara?"

"Sheriff, there's a problem at the Richards' place on Mountain Ave. Both kids are really sick. Sally Ann called half out of her mind. Pretty serious, by the sound of it, Sheriff. I think the little girl is having a seizure or something … over."

Carl looked to the end of the cul-de-sac; the Richards' place was only a stone's throw through the woods. "Okay, Tara. I'm right around the corner. I'll meet the ambulance there." Carl jumped into his car.

"10-4, Sheriff, over and out."

"Ted," he shouted to his deputy. "Hop in; you're with me. Gary, secure the scene and get started on the paperwork. Send what you can over to Burt."

"Will do, Sheriff," Deputy Forsyth yelled back.

Sheriff Primrose and Deputy Lutchen sped off down Foothills Drive with the cherries flashing. A minute later, the guys in the meat wagon followed with the body of Felix Castillo bagged and tagged.

Deputy Forsyth approached Burt with the man's credentials in a plastic bag. "I'll log all of this in and get it over to you right away."

"I don't think there's any rush on that, Gary." Burt took off his glasses and wiped them with his hanky. "It's not like he's going anywhere."

"If you say so, Burt." The deputy laughed. "All the same, it won't take long either way."

"You sure about that, Gary? By the looks of it, I'd say you're about to have a pretty busy day." The men could hear the siren from the ambulance as it raced down the Boulevard towards the Richards' house on Mountain Ave.

"Yeah," Gary agreed. "You might be right."

Chapter 6

At 4:47 a.m. on Sunday morning, Robert Boyle stopped breathing for nearly three minutes. Dr. Ethan Ziegler, the attending on-call physician, immediately proceeded to administer CPR with the assistance of Head Nurse Doris TenHove. She attempted to breathe life back into the boy as the doctor pumped his chest repeatedly. They had just managed to bring Rob's temperature down a couple degrees when the boy flatlined. His parents were ushered out of the emergency room to allow the staff space to work.

Dr. Ziegler fought to revive Rob until he himself was sweating and out of breath. He was prepared to call the time of death, then pounded on the boy's chest several times with a clenched fist. The child inhaled deeply but struggled to breathe on his own. He was rushed into the ICU, put on a ventilator, and had not regained consciousness.

Rob's face was sallow, and his cheeks had sunken in. Dark circles surrounded his eyes, and his lips were blue. Ziegler ordered a run of full blood work and was waiting for one of the nurses to meet him in the ICU when he was paged over the medical center's intercom system.

"Dr. Ziegler, report to emergency. Dr. Ziegler, report to emergency, code blue."

Ziegler ran toward the double emergency room doors. Blue was the center's code for critical emergency. The soles of his shoes squeaked on the polished tile as he tore through the hallway.

The place was frantic with orderlies, nurses, sheriff's officers, and two patients who had just arrived. Dr. John Malcolm, the chief of medicine, focused his attention on a young girl, while Nurse TenHove attempted to stabilize a boy about the same age. Both children were in the throes of grand mal seizures. The girl dripped blood from her mouth and had more than likely bitten her tongue. Ziegler rushed to the nurse's aid and rolled the boy onto his side to prevent him from hurting himself.

Ziegler recognized the identical symptoms he had witnessed in the Boyle kid. His mind raced to worst-case scenarios and attempted to draw a correlation between the cases. The paramedics ran down a laundry list of symptoms they'd recorded since first entering the home. Ziegler listened but was distracted by the hysterical cries of the children's parents in the waiting room. *What the hell kind of flu is this?* None like he had ever seen. The Boyle kid had been dead for almost three minutes, and these two weren't far off. The boy felt as if he were on fire, and the girl looked as bad as Robert Boyle had. Whatever this bug was, it was nasty as hell.

Ben Richards finally stopped seizing, and Ziegler was able to take his vitals and start an IV. His temperature was 105, and his sister's was over 106. They needed to ice the children and stabilize them as fast as possible. In the adjacent room, he could hear Nurse Gilmartin attempting to calm the frightened parents. But the situation had escalated, and she was losing control by the second. Finally, a booming male voice shouted, "Nobody's gonna stop me from seeing my kids!"

Dr. Malcolm looked up at the sheriff. "Could you help her out there? We can take this from here."

The sheriff and his deputy rushed into the waiting room to diffuse the situation. Badges had a way of grabbing people's attention, especially during times of emergency.

Dr. Malcom lifted the girl's eyelids to find her scleras bloodshot and pupils dilated. He examined her mouth and gasped; the child had lost nearly all her front teeth. Ziegler watched as the chief of medicine examined the girl and checked his own patient. The boy had also lost several teeth, not baby teeth either; the children were losing their permanent bicuspids and incisors.

"Do you see what I'm seeing, Ethan?" Malcolm called to him.

"I see it, Doctor," Ziegler replied. "I have no idea what I'm looking at, but I see it. This isn't any flu. Is it, Dr. Malcolm?"

"None that I've ever seen." Dr. John Malcolm's face drew tighter. "Three children in one night. We need to figure out where the hell these kids have been and who they've been in contact with."

"Wait a second, Doctor. I know where you're about to go with this, and we don't know anything about it yet."

"Exactly!" Malcolm shouted. "We have to act now while there's still a chance to stop it. If it's that contagious, it may already be too late. We need to get everyone who's been in contact with these kids under quarantine. ASAP!"

The staff in the emergency room stared at the chief of medicine as his words echoed like a thunderclap off the stark-sterile walls.

● ● ●

Once the Richards children were stabilized and admitted into the ICU, Dr. Malcolm ordered the wing to be cordoned off. He was headed toward his office when Dr. Ziegler approached him. "Dr. Malcolm, do you think I could have a word with you ... in private?"

Malcolm cast a cautious stare over his bifocals at the young doctor. He liked Ziegler and believed he had a bright future. He still had a way to go, but he was attentive and an excellent diagnostician. What he didn't like about Ethan Ziegler was his cavalier attitude. There was something about the way Ziegler carried himself that rubbed John Malcolm like a sandpaper washcloth. Especially the way he handled himself around the nurses, not to mention, the guy was a bit of a hippie, always looked like he needed a haircut and had to be close to thirty-five.

They walked down the hall together and entered the chief's office. The place smelled like pipe tobacco, and not the cheap kind. Two ornate bookcases stood in the back corners, flanking a wall covered in diplomas, certificates, and awards. A massive dark wooden desk sat at the room's epicenter, serving as John Malcolm's command post.

The old doctor sat behind the desk and held up his hands. "I know what you're about to do; you're going to try to talk me out of calling in the quarantine. But I'm standing my ground on this one."

"No way, Dr. Malcolm. This is your call. You've been in this town a lot longer than I have, and I know you believe this is the best course of action." Ziegler delivered his words with the sincerity of a used car salesman.

Malcolm paused, expecting at least a little resistance. "You're damn right. I'm glad you see it my way."

"Of course. You're the chief of medicine, and I trust your opinion." Ziegler had the same persuasive way with the nurses. "I was just going to suggest a couple scenarios I'm sure you've considered."

Malcolm gave him a puzzled look. "Such as?"

"Well, I was going to mention, since you've decided to initiate quarantine, Sheriff Primrose and his deputy are officially off duty. That's nearly a quarter of this town's police force. Which I imagine could complicate matters?"

John shook his head and leaned back in his chair. "Hmmm." He motioned for Ziegler to continue.

"I imagine it won't be a problem for whoever is at the center already. But you're going to need police officers to find everyone who's been in contact with those kids over the past three days ... possibly longer."

"I know, Doctor. It's one giant mess, but I don't think we have a choice." Malcolm tilted his head and looked down over his bifocals once again. "I take it you have a suggestion, Dr. Ziegler?"

"Well, sir, the Boyle kid has been sick since Thursday. I'm guessing the Richards kids, about the same. None of the parents have taken ill in that time, and the Fischer boy spent the whole week with all three children; he isn't sick either. Surely one of them would have shown symptoms by now."

"We don't know that," Malcolm said.

"I'm just saying this could be something else entirely. We're not going to know until the blood work comes back. And if we cripple the police force, we'll have to call in the state authorities."

Malcolm's furrowed brow softened a bit. "I don't want to see anyone else get sick."

"Chances are it already would have happened." Ziegler blew a piece of hair out of his eyes. "The kids are in the ICU, and no one gets in or out without the proper protection. We'll monitor them around the clock. That gives us time to run the blood work and rule out everything else before you call it in. In the meantime, tell the sheriff your plans just in case, so he can prepare. We'll instruct everyone to limit their interactions for the next twenty-four hours, just until we know."

Ziegler presented his case with the confidence of a defense attorney. He cleared his throat, adjusted his tie, and continued. "Twenty-four hours of monitoring and tests, full disclosure with the authorities, and if you still feel the same tomorrow, make the call. This way, we'll have a chance to figure things out, and the sheriff will have time to set up whatever preparations he may need as well."

Dr. Malcolm pulled a pipe from his breast pocket and held it for a moment. Then he struck a wooden match and took several puffs of the tobacco. It smelled like cherry and oak. "I hope to God I don't regret this, Ziegler. Twenty-four hours—that's it! If we don't get this thing figured out by then, I'm pulling the plug."

Ziegler smiled. "Great."

"Not so fast." The old doctor took a couple quick pulls from his pipe. "I'm putting you in charge of all the tests. First, I want you to oversee the blood work and go over everything with a fine-tooth comb. Then you'll need to coordinate with radiology, get some chest x-rays, find the kids' dental records, and that's just for starters."

Ziegler appeared to shrink two inches as his chest deflated and shoulders folded inward. "I've been on for almost twelve hours, and I'm scheduled to be off tonight."

"That's not going to be a problem, is it?" Dr. Malcolm didn't wait for an answer. He stood up and headed for the door. "Glad to hear it. I'll check in later to see what you've got," he said and left the office.

Ziegler stood there feeling like he had been kicked in the teeth; somehow, it had blown up in his face. While he honestly believed it was much too soon to initiate a quarantine, his intentions to sway Dr. Malcolm hadn't been selfless. He had plans with Jackie Gilmartin this evening and was pretty sure the young nurse was as eager to see him as he was her. He'd been performing routine examinations on Jackie for a good month now, and tonight, she had promised to leave her nurse's uniform on.

He checked his watch; it was already past eight a.m., and he hadn't eaten anything since well before midnight. He decided to grab a quick cup of coffee and a snack from the cafeteria before seeing Peter in pathology. It was going to be one bitch of a day.

Dr. John Malcolm pulled Sheriff Primrose to the side and spoke to him privately. He told him what he knew so far, what he didn't, and what his plans were if they couldn't come up with anything solid in the next twenty-four hours. Carl thanked him for his discretion and for giving him a fair heads-up before calling in the quarantine. He promised the chief he would make sure the Fischer family were aware of the situation and would talk to them himself to see if anything had been missed. The twins' and Robert Boyle's parents were still at the medical center and agreed to cooperate. It was unlikely any of them would have left the building anyway, not with their children in critical condition and still in the ICU.

The emergency room staff and paramedics who dealt with the twins agreed to limit their contact with the public to a bare minimum for the next twenty-four hours as well. That took care of everyone involved except for Nurse Gilmartin, who had snuck out as soon as her shift ended. Head Nurse TenHove tried to reach the girl repeatedly at her apartment but had been unsuccessful so far. Possibly, she had stopped to get something to eat or pick up a few things at the store before going home. TenHove assured Dr. Malcolm she would continue to try until she contacted the young nurse.

Carl dropped Deputy Lutchen off at the station with strict orders for him to take the rest of the day off and not leave the house. Hopefully, this would all be over soon. If not, they would have a whole lot more to worry about than a lost day of work. Then he contacted Deputy Forsyth to see how the paperwork was coming on the Castillo case. Minutes later, Carl arrived at the home of his former high school sweetheart, Lois Fischer.

Chapter 7

Sheriff Carl Primrose pulled into the driveway and sat for a moment listening to the steady hum of the police cruiser. He had spent a long time trying to forget the past and was completely unprepared when it snuck up and sucker punched him. It all came back in a vivid wash as if it were yesterday.

Lois met Donald Fischer during her sophomore year at Penn State while she and Carl had been attempting to prove that a long-distance relationship could actually work. The truth was they seldom did, and by the time Lois returned to Garrett Grove, she and Carl were history. Not that he had wanted it that way; for Carl, Lois was the love of his life, and he never fully got over it.

"It will be good for us to spend some time apart," she had told Carl the week before she left for college. "By the time we see each other again, you won't be able to resist me."

Carl had parked the Mustang at the top of Mountain Ave. It was a favorite spot for teens even in '67. "I can't resist you now," he had said. "I don't see how being apart could possibly help."

Lois had her heart set on going to Penn State and been on cloud nine when she got accepted; it was all she could talk about. "We'll see each other on holidays and over the summer. Oh yeah, don't forget spring break. You'll see; things won't be all that different." And she had believed every word of it.

From the top of Mountain Ave, they could see the floodlights over the high school football field and damn near all of Garrett Grove. The moonlight glinted off the steeple of the Lutheran church and lit up the Lenape River as if it were the Ganges. But it all struck Carl as out of focus and not nearly as bright as it had in the past.

"Maybe I should apply to Penn State? Who knows, I might get accepted." But Carl knew that was a pipe dream; he didn't have the grades for it.

"You'd hate it, and you know it." She leaned over and kissed him while the Beatles played through the Mustang's A.M. radio, a sappy ballad about how far away all of Paul McCartney's troubles seemed. It was surreal. "I could never forgive myself for making you miserable."

"I wouldn't be miserable. I'd be with you," he assured her but knew he was lying.

"What about the sheriff's department? It's all you've talked about for the last two years. You're just gonna throw that away?"

Carl had known she was right; he'd wanted to be a deputy for a lot longer than two years. His father had been the sheriff of Garrett Grove, and Carl planned to follow in his footsteps. It had been his dream since he was old enough to see out the windshield of his father's police cruiser from the safety of the old man's lap. Allan Primrose had let his son hit the siren and flash the lights every time they drove past Bell's Hardware. It made Carl feel special, and he wanted to be just like his dad. Sheriff Primrose, the first, was a well-respected man in town and for good reason. He went out of his way to help people simply because he liked to do it. And Carl was a chip off the old block. He couldn't imagine a better job than helping and protecting the people in his own town.

"You're going to be Sheriff of Garrett Grove one day, and you're going to be damn good at it," Lois told him. "I can't let you give that up for me. I just couldn't live with that."

"I can't live without you, Lois. I love you."

"I love you too."

That night, they made love in the Mustang at the top of Mountain Ave. It hadn't been their first time, and probably not even the last. But looking back, Carl thought it was the last time that counted.

Lois went to Penn State, and they called each other every day, at first. She came home for the holidays, and he'd even driven there a few times to see her. Then she decided to take a few summer courses. After that, they began to talk less and less. A minute here, five minutes there. The calls became more infrequent. Carl tried to reach out every chance he could but found her either heading off to class or busy with homework.

When she called him out of the blue one day, he could tell right away by the sound of her voice and knew what she was about to say. Lois said she was sorry, that she still loved him and didn't want to hurt him.

"Well, don't do it then!" he yelled over the phone. "I knew this was going to happen, and what did you say? You said it would be good for us. You said it would make us closer." He could hear her crying on the other end.

"I'm so sorry. I still love you, Carl."

"So, what's the problem then, Lois?" She didn't answer him.

She had started to cry, then finally blurted it out: "I'm pregnant, Carl."

He had to think about it for a moment, and then it hit him. Carl hadn't seen her in over four months. Lois had been seeing someone else, and the prick had knocked her up.

"What's his name?" The phone had grown heavy in his hand as arctic waves leached through the earpiece into his head. *How can you do this to me? You—you're my life. I—I can't.*

"D ... Donald," she said between sobs.

"Do you love him?" he asked again, and again, he waited for a reply.

"You're not saying. So, either you don't, or you don't want to tell me that you do." He had wanted to scream but knew it would only make things worse.

"I guess that's it then?" He waited for her to say something otherwise, but she never did. He had lost her, the only girl he had ever loved and ever would.

"I'm sorry, Carl. You deserved better." Her words, nearly impossible to make out through her tears. "I love you," she said and hung up the phone.

He had stood there frozen with his heart bleeding inside his chest. All the years, every dream they had shared, was over. Carl had been certain his world would never be the same ... and he had been correct. Three weeks later, he was drafted and sent to fight in Vietnam.

It was strange that he could remember it all so vividly. The sting was still bitter, although it had mellowed with age. *Time heals all ... almost.* Carl did his best to shake it off and focus on the matter at hand. This was no time to be floating around in the clouds. There had been a murder with an unexplainable cause of death. Now, three kids were clinging to life in the ICU with something possibly a whole lot worse than the flu.

He turned off the cruiser's ignition and pushed all thoughts of his high school sweetheart to the back of his mind. That was until he saw Lois standing in her kitchen, and the memories flooded back like the Lenape River during storm season.

● ● ●

Butchie Post watched Jackie Gilmartin from the front seat of his Chevy Monza as she entered Wilson's Diner at nine a.m. Sunday morning. Her nurse's uniform clung to her hips, but Butchie focused on the way it showed off her giant tits. He thought they looked like cantaloupes wrapped in white cotton. Jackie hadn't looked half as good back in high school; she hadn't blossomed yet. She sure as hell hadn't had tits like that, or Butchie would have noticed.

In truth, Jackie had started to bloom her senior year, but Butchie had been kicked out by then. He got expelled during the middle of his sophomore year, which was fine by him. School was for pussies anyway. And it had been that douchebag Jimmy Reilly's fault; he was the one who had gotten Butchie kicked out in the first place.

Butchie entered the world as Marion Arthur Post but adopted the moniker Butchie for obvious reasons. His mother named him Marion; she said that his father resembled the Duke. Butchie never met his dad, at least not that he could remember. The guy skipped out when Butchie was still shitting his diapers. He'd seen a couple pictures of Mark Post but didn't think the guy looked anything like John Wayne. What the hell was his mom thinking when she married him, anyway? Butchie figured she must have been drunk that year. Why would that year be any different than the rest?

He chose the name Butchie after watching *Butch Cassidy and the Sundance Kid*. Now that was one cool-ass cowboy, not no pussy like John Wayne. He had taken a lot of shit as a kid with the name Marion, not to mention he was the only boy in the class without a dad.

"Mary, Mary, look at the fairy." One of the many brilliant limericks the children had created to tease him. Another incredibly original one was "Marion the Fairion, where's your daddy, little girl?". It didn't rhyme, but it had the same effect.

The taunts and constant name-calling had hurt. And when he told the other children his name wasn't Marion, it was Butchie, it only made the teasing worse. That had gone on well into the third grade, but by then, Butchie experienced an early growth spurt. Also, getting left back in the second grade gave him the advantage of brute strength over his younger classmates. Then one day, he discovered he had the power to shut their twisted pussy pie holes. And he liked the way it felt.

Joey Turner and Gilbert Duncan had been ripping Butchie for a good week. The two boys followed him home from school one day, taunting him as he walked up the Boulevard towards Foothills Drive.

"Mary, Mary, quite contrary. Why you such a fucking fairy?"

Butchie pretended not to hear them as he walked toward his house on Mountain Ave. But the boys keep calling to him, over and over.

"Hey, Mary. I heard your momma's a drunk; that's why your daddy left her."

Butchie had started crying. They had no right to talk about his mother, and he could feel the pressure building up inside him like a teapot just before it started to whistle. He walked faster, but the children continued to follow.

"Mary, Mary." The boys matched his pace.

"Hey, where are you going, Mary?"

Butchie took off running, and Joey and Gilbert chased after him. He pumped his legs as fast as he could but knew they were closing in. He approached the shortcut through the foothills and decided to take it. He turned left onto the dirt path and into the woods. Joey followed him with Gilbert right behind.

"Hey, sissy, where are you going?" Joey called.

"Yeah, don't run, mommy's boy," Gilbert yelled.

Butchie's lungs burned, and his heart threatened to explode. His fear escalated to the tipping point. Then, a thunderous crack erupted inside his head, loud and concussive. He howled, sounding more like a wild animal caught in a trap than a frightened little boy. Joey and Gilbert realized a second too late they were in deep shit, as Butchie turned and went ballistic.

First, Butchie slammed his clenched fist into Joey's jaw as the child tried to stop short. The force of the blow and the pursuing child's own momentum resulted in one bad-ass wallop. Joey's feet flew out from under him, and he landed hard on his back. Gilbert didn't have time to stop either and nearly ran over his friend. Which gave Butchie enough time to seize him by the hair on the back of his head. He dragged Gilbert off the path and ran him face-first into the nearest tree. Gilbert fell to his knees, screaming, with his nose shifted almost two inches to the left and spouting like a geyser.

Butchie turned back towards Joey, who was struggling to get to his feet.

"Okay, okay. I'm sorry; stop it! I'm sorry!" the boy cried.

Butchie bent down and picked up a branch about two inches thick and three feet long. He checked how it felt in his hand and took a couple practice swings as he walked back to where Joey scrambled.

He raised the log above his head and brought it down on Joey's shoulder. The boy's collarbone snapped like a toothpick. Butchie smiled when the child screamed. He raised it again and brought it down harder the second time.

"My name is BUTCHIE!" he yelled as he slammed the stick down on the child's ribs.

"My name is BUTCHIE!" Into his stomach.

"BUTCHIE!" His knees.

After that day, there wasn't a soul in Garrett Grove who would so much as look at him sideways, let alone call him anything other than Butchie. Marion Arthur Post was dead. Long live Butchie the Destroyer.

Joey and Gilbert eventually healed, but their experience was a lesson for all. Butchie had stuck up for himself that afternoon, and everything changed after that. Soon, he began to look for fights, just to add a little excitement to his day. He had taken crap for so long, and now that the shoe was on the other foot, he liked just how comfortable it felt. He was good at beating the snot out of pussies, enjoyed it too. And why shouldn't he? They had it coming. It wasn't long before Butchie started getting suspended for fighting.

How Butchie had gotten as far as high school without getting kicked out sooner was an accomplishment in itself. And to have made it into his sophomore year was nothing short of a miracle. The teachers and principal felt somewhat sorry for the boy. His father had abandoned him, and his mother had a bit of a problem with the bottle. Who wouldn't be a little angry? However, Butchie Post wasn't just a little angry; Butchie was disturbed, and not just a little. The boy was a raging psychopath. He was constantly in trouble for one thing or another. On one occasion, he smashed the windows of his English teacher's car and spray-painted the words *Die Pussy* on the hood. There was the constant fighting, of course, but the final straw was the day he waited in the boy's bathroom for Jimmy Reilly.

He targeted Jimmy earlier that year and made the kid's life a living nightmare. Just before Jimmy entered the bathroom, Butchie lit a cherry bomb and threw it into the toilet. Unfortunately for Jimmy, the firecracker went off just as he opened the stall. Butchie couldn't have timed it better. The ceramic shattered as the cherry bomb exploded, sending lacerating pieces of the broken toilet flying in every direction. Jimmy's face looked like he'd been run through a blender. And that was the end of Butchie Post's academic career; he was expelled, and Jimmy's parents pressed charges. Butchie spent eighteen months in the Barre Oaks Youth Correctional Facility. And almost lasted a whole day without getting into trouble. But Butchie learned fast that no matter how tough you thought you were, there was always someone tougher.

Butchie had been beating on smaller kids from the backwoods-sticks of Garrett Grove. He hadn't faced any real resistance yet and thought he was hot shit. But Barre Oaks housed boys as old as eighteen from all over the state. Cities like Millville and Burlington were home to some pretty rough neighborhoods. Nothing like the small town Butchie had grown up in.

The biggest problem that followed Butchie into the correctional system was his government name, Marion. The guards as well as the inmates seized the opportunity and ran with it. He arrived on a bus full of young men ranging in age from fifteen to eighteen. Butchie was at the younger end of the spectrum but by no means the smaller. And he probably would have been fine if it hadn't been for the name and the giant chip on his shoulder.

The new recruits were stripped, thrown into a cold shower, and processed. Butchie was approached by a guard that towered over him by a good two feet, with a forehead the size of a cinderblock that protruded nearly as far as his chin. The Neanderthal looked down at his clipboard and burst out laughing.

"Marion Post," he yelled loud enough for the other cops, as well as the busload of new inmates, to hear. "Marion?"

"It's Butchie," he said.

"Did you say something? I didn't tell you to speak, Marion," the cop barked in Butchie's face. Three of the goon's cronies closed in around Butchie like sharks circling a wounded seal.

"You want to repeat that, Marion?" the cop screamed. Spit flew from his mouth onto Butchie's face.

Butchie may have been hard-headed, but he wasn't a complete idiot. He knew there was nothing to be gained from an encounter with Mighty Joe Young and his band of merry dicks. He shook his head and looked at the floor.

"That's what I thought, Marion." The cop flipped through his paperwork. "Dorm three, bunk seven. Next!"

That's how it started, and it only got worse from there. The boys had to walk naked and barefoot to their dorms through the entire complex. The inmate population screamed and whistled as they passed. Some threw toilet paper and food at the new fish, and by the time Butchie arrived at dorm three, he was covered in ketchup and pop and in need of another shower.

He quickly learned of a strange phenomenon in the prison system: gossip traveled faster here than it did at the beauty salon. By the time he reached the dorm, there wasn't a soul in the facility who didn't know his name was Marion.

The first fight happened in the shower. Two guys, who didn't look like much of a threat, began ribbing him about the name. Butchie stuck up for himself and taught them a pretty good lesson, leaving one with a shiner and the other with a busted lip.

"My name's, Butchie," he spat and figured it was over.

But it was far from over. The two guys he fought were low-ranking members of the Bristol Boys, and the rest of the gang didn't appreciate that some guy named Marion had bested two of their own. Later that night, they followed Butchie from the mess hall and jumped him when he passed the woodshop, dragging him inside. Butchie squared off and stood his ground. "I'm not afraid. I'll fight all of you," he had said.

One of them seized him from behind as two others grabbed each of his arms.

"Let me go," he screamed. "I'll take all of you."

A large Italian-looking kid with greasy black hair and an even greasier face stepped up. Butchie figured the kid had to be the leader as he struggled to free himself.

"You're right about that," the kid said. "You will *take* all of us."

Butchie didn't follow what the guido meant until the other three pushed him to the floor face first. He tried to free himself, but there were too many of them. One of the boys grabbed the back of his jumper and yanked at it. The material ripped easily, exposing him. Then they were tearing at his boxer shorts. *What the hell are they trying to do?* Then it hit him. They were trying to do him. The guido knelt over Butchie while the others held him down, then he took him.

He had never been with a woman in his life and had never known his father. His first sexual experience was on the cold concrete floor of the woodshop in Barre Oaks. After the first boy finished, the next one jumped on him, and then the next.

They laughed and called him Marion as they raped him, then left when they were done. He lay there for nearly an hour, seething with rage and humiliation. A bitter morass like no other clawed its way inside him. It gripped Butchie's black heart and twisted. And had there been an ounce of humanity left in Butchie Post prior to that moment, it had been silenced once and for all that night on the woodshop floor.

The Bristol Boys were by no means the only predators who stalked the halls of Barre Oaks. And although they were deviant in their idea of hierarchy, they followed a specific code, and they took care of their own. Butchie's service to the gang had turned out to be some insane form of initiation. He continued to fight back and got his knuckles bloody when the opportunity presented itself. But he also took his beatings and nights on the woodshop floor and kept his mouth shut. He never said a word, primarily out of humiliation but also out of pride. It was evident the Bristol Boys had found a new recruit, and everyone in the facility knew what that involved. All the while, Butchie stayed to himself and took it like a man ... so to speak.

Vinnie, the leader of the group who had introduced himself most intimately that first night, had taken a liking to Butchie. And not in the obvious sense. Vincenzo "Vinnie" Rozgoni from Millville respected how Butchie stood up to him and always tried to get a few licks in first. Most of all, he respected how the guy kept his mouth shut. Other fish usually sang after the first time. Of course, they were dealt with accordingly. But Butchie was different, and Vinnie liked that. The kid had passed his initiation.

Butchie had been picking up cigarette butts outside the administration building when Vinnie and another boy, who was built like a brick shithouse and looked about as bright as one, approached him. Butchie prepared to defend himself; he dropped the bag of butts and clenched his fists.

"Relax, Post. I want to talk." Vinnie stopped in front of him.

Butchie expected the other guy to grab him or hit him from behind. He watched the kid, ready to knock out a few of his teeth.

"I got something going on tonight. Some prick over on A Unit needs to learn who runs this place. Want a chance to be on top?" Vinnie asked.

After all that Butchie had been through in the past three months, it was hard to believe that Vinnie was being straight with him. *Is he asking me to join the Boys?* It sure sounded like it, but did it mean what he thought? Judging from what the group had done to him, Butchie figured as much.

"This is a one-time offer. I ain't gonna ask twice." The boys stood there waiting for Butchie to reply.

There was a good chance they were just messing with him and decided to add a whole new element of foreplay to the game. But there was also a chance that Vinnie was on the up and up. Either way, Butchie figured he had nothing to lose. Not like his situation could get much worse.

"I'm in," he said.

An evil grin spread across Vinnie's greasy face like a germ. He held his hand out to Butchie, who reluctantly shook it.

After chow, he met up with the gang in the bathroom on A Unit. Butchie half expected them to jump him and laugh at what a sucker he had been, but that's not what happened. An older red-headed boy entered the bathroom with his chest puffed out and arms held a distance from his body, as if his biceps were too big to walk right. A real cocky douchebag, by the looks of it, and Butchie disliked the guy the second he saw him.

"Get 'em, boys!" Vinnie shouted, then waited as the rest of the gang swarmed their new target like a colony of fire ants.

"Not so tough now, are you, Cunningham?" Vinnie approached the cocky ginger before the kid could say a word and shoved a rolled-up sock in his mouth. A dirty one, by the looks of it. The Bristol Boys wrestled him to the floor, tore at his jumper, and stripped him. Finally, Vinnie turned to Butchie, who, up until that point, had only been watching. "Let's see what you got, Post," he said.

Butchie didn't need to be told twice and had gotten worked up seeing someone else face down on the floor for a change. Turned out, it wasn't any different than what he had learned that day in the woods. The day he finally stood up to Joey and Gilbert. It felt a whole lot better to give it than it did to take. And Butchie gave it like a champ; he passed his initiation with flying colors and enjoyed himself in the process ... very much, in fact.

That had been almost ten years ago. Now, as Butchie watched Jackie Gilmartin enter Wilson's Diner, he visualized the look in her eyes when he finally got the chance to shove a rolled-up sock into her mouth. He pictured himself forcing her to the floor of his shed and ripping the back of her nurse's uniform at the seams. A quick glance at his watch told him the supermarket had been open for fifteen minutes. Butchie had lost track of time, awash in the sourness of his thoughts. The girl would have to wait. The shed behind his house wasn't going anywhere, neither was the roll of duct tape in his glove compartment. He'd been following Jackie for the past two weeks, waiting for just the right moment. But this wasn't it. He needed to pick up a few things for his mother and something special for himself. He hoped Jackie was patient and swore he would make it up to her. She was going to love what he had done with the shed. He just knew it.

Butchie exited the car and walked into the A&P supermarket. He caught a glimpse of his reflection in the sliding door and liked how he looked, his big barrel chest and squared-off jaw. If he hadn't grown his hair into a mullet, he could have passed for that cowboy in the movies, the one with the eye patch in *True Grit*. Butchie couldn't remember the actor's name and imagined he was probably just another Hollywood pussy.

He grabbed what he needed and left the store, immediately noticing Jackie's car was no longer in front of Wilson's. He stepped onto the sidewalk and stopped short. Two kids had parked their bicycles right next to his Monza. Butchie's blood sizzled when he saw the little homos walking into the candy store. They had left their bikes propped up on the kickstands, right there on the sidewalk—as if they owned the damn place.

Butchie stormed over to where the first bike was set up, his bags of goodies clutched tightly in his arms. He raised his foot and kicked the bike over with a firm boot to the seat. The two boys looked back in horror as the bicycle crashed to the sidewalk. Tommy Negal saw the man had kicked over Jeff Campbell's bike and couldn't help but laugh. But he was immediately sorry he did.

Butchie turned to him and screamed, "Don't you fucking laugh. I'll knock yours down too." He kicked Tommy's bike with every ounce of tainted fury in his black heart. It crashed to the pavement like a lead balloon. Then Butchie spit on the bikes, got into his car, and peeled away from the curb.

Chapter 8

Troy sat at the breakfast table, pushing scrambled eggs from one side of his plate to the other. He wasn't hungry but pretended to enjoy it for the benefit of his parents. The past twelve hours had been difficult to process, and Troy wasn't sure he had even fallen asleep. But he figured he must have because he remembered dreaming about sirens.

The party had been a hit, and all his friends loved Scream in the Dark. Mike and Tommy cried like little girls when Billy and Eric chased them down the street. Troy snickered just thinking about it, then recovered and shoved a forkful of eggs into his mouth. And Wendy had kissed him! *Did that really happen?* The entire night felt like a dream. *It sure did!* She asked to see the haunted house, just the two of them, and then ... *Wham!* It was weird at first; she'd caught him by surprise, and he didn't know what he was supposed to do. Then it happened again. Troy thought he might have done a better job the second time. He knew the older kids did something with their tongues called French kissing. But didn't think he would like that very much; it sounded gross. He grimaced at the runny eggs on his plate.

For weeks, he'd imagined what the night of the party would be like. Ever since Rob had come up with the name for the haunted house, Scream in the Dark. He thought it would turn out awesome, and it had, but not in a million years did he think that Wendy would actually kiss him. He couldn't wait to tell Rob.

Troy's stomach soured at the thought of his friend, and he lost what little was left of his appetite. It must have killed Rob to miss the party. He was probably so upset, he got out of bed and walked over in his pajamas just to join them. Too bad everyone had already left. But Rob had been really sick and looked terrible, even scarier than Troy did with his vampire makeup on.

And there was something else about the way Rob looked at him. *It was like he didn't even see me.* Then Rob had lifted his arms and come after him. It was as if—

"Troy, eat your breakfast," Lois said.

"I'm not very hungry," he replied.

"Eat up, sport," Don added. "There are children in Africa who are starving."

"They can have the rest of my eggs," he pouted.

Don and Lois exchanged a stifled laugh. That had been a good one; they both nodded. Lois pushed Troy's hair out of his eyes. It was getting long, and he needed it cut. "Just one more bite. Do it for me?" she asked.

Troy scooped a forkful into his mouth and bounded from the table as if he had been released from the electric chair. He took his plate to the garbage and scraped the rest of his breakfast into the can. A loud knock at the front door caused all of them to jump.

"I'll get it," Troy shouted, running out of the kitchen.

Sheriff Primrose stood on the front porch with his cowboy hat in his hands. "Good morning, Troy." He smiled. "How are you feeling today, partner?"

"Hi, Sheriff Primrose. I'm good, thanks; we were just finishing breakfast."

"I hope I didn't come at a bad time."

"Not at all, Sheriff," Don called from the kitchen. "You're just in time for coffee. Come on in."

Troy opened the screen door and let him in as Lois looked around the corner. "Milk and sugar, Carl?" she offered. They had worked past much of the awkwardness years ago, for the most part.

"Just black," Carl said, ascending the steps leading to the bi-level's second floor, two at a time.

"How are things at Chilton?" Lois asked. "I haven't heard from Karin or Bob and didn't want to call just yet. You know, if—"

"That's why I'm here, actually." He rolled his eyes in Troy's direction, and Lois understood what he was implying.

"Troy, do you think you could see if the paper is here yet?"

Troy headed out the front door as Don poured the coffee. "So, what's going on, Sheriff? We heard the sirens earlier, and I'm guessing you didn't stop by for Lois's coffee."

Carl took a seat at the table and set his hat on an empty chair.

"No, that's not why I'm here." He paused, taking a sip from his mug. "What I'm about to say doesn't leave this room. Not a word."

Lois raised a hand to her lips. "Oh my God, Robert didn't—"

"The boy is in ICU at the moment." Carl stopped her. "The doctors are running tests on the other kids as well."

"Kids?" Don raised his voice. "What do you mean, other kids?"

"The Richards twins were rushed into the emergency room early this morning. They're showing similar symptoms. Doctor Malcolm believes we might have a situation here. How are you both feeling? How about Troy?"

Lois and Don looked at each other as if the oven had exploded. "We're fine," Don said. "Everyone's fine. We're still talking about the flu, aren't we, Sheriff?"

"The truth is they don't know yet. And if we can't get it figured out quick, we might be looking at a quarantine. That means the three of you and everyone else who was there last night."

"Dear God!" Lois gasped and covered her heart.

"I need you folks to stick around the house today, at least until Malcolm gets a handle on this." He decided not to say how the Boyle kid had nearly died last night and wasn't about to tell them how the Richards twins were losing teeth faster than a couple of hockey players. "I'm sure he'll have this straightened out by the end of the day. Just here to cover all the bases. If you guys could avoid going out or seeing anyone, I'd really appreciate it."

"We were going to go to church at ten, but I'm sure Troy won't mind if we miss one Sunday." Carl could see Don was trying to sound calm but was on the verge of freaking out. Lois, however, was having a harder time of it.

"They must have some idea what it is. Rob had the flu. He was delirious and had a fever, but it was just the flu, right?" she said, her voice rising slightly.

Carl looked across the table at her. She was scared, and she had every right to be. "More than likely." He tried to reassure her. "You know how Dr. Malcolm can be. This is just a precautionary measure, probably all for nothing."

"You're probably right." Lois relaxed a little. "Doc can be a little much at times."

Carl turned to Don. "Would you mind if I asked Troy a couple questions about last night? I'd like to see if he saw something we might have missed, if it's okay with you."

"I guess." Don hesitated. "Sure, no problem."

"Paper's not here yet," Troy shouted as he entered the house.

"Hey, Troy," Don called. "Why don't you show the sheriff all the work you did on the haunted house?"

Troy ran into the kitchen; his mood suddenly lifted an inch or two. "It's called Scream in the Dark. Rob came up with the name. We did all the work ourselves, and I thought up the rat room."

"Rat room?" Carl stood up from the table. "I have to see this."

Troy's eyes lit up as he led the sheriff out the front door.

Billy and Eric Tobin were told by their father that neither of them would be leaving the house until the backyard was raked and the leaves were bagged. Billy had been up all night trying to understand what happened at the sanatorium but had no luck so far. He woke to find a note from his father, reminding him about the yardwork, and decided to get an early jump on the leaves. Eric was still dragging his ass inside.

They'd been there countless times before, and nothing like that had ever happened. Sure, the place was spooky, but that was the whole idea. It was easier to comfort a girl out of her panties after she had a good scare and a couple beers. And since Halloween was only a week away, it seemed like the perfect place to bring their dates.

But something was up there, and it had chased them down the mountain. Billy didn't have a clue what it might have been, but it was fast as fuck. And it flew over their heads like a goddamn screaming eagle or something. It was big, whatever it was.

He spent more than half the night trying to piece it all together and still had no idea what it could have been.

When the thing initially passed through the beam of the flashlight, it didn't look real. Billy tried to remember what he had seen as he raked the same pile of leaves for a second time. It hadn't been solid; it was more like ... He tried to remember. Then it hit him. *Smoke!* It had looked like smoke when it passed through the light, not solid enough to make a shadow and not entirely there.

"Do you hear yourself?" he said out loud. "Smoke?"

He tried to shake off the idea, but it held firm. Whatever was up there had waited for them, just beyond the reach of the light, as if it were intelligent.

"It freaking chased us," he whispered. *What's smart and fast and can fly like that?* It had to be an owl or some big-ass bird of prey. That was probably it, one big-ass bird of prey.

Eric finally stepped outside with sleep in his eyes and his hair a mess. "You're up early," he said.

"Butt-munch, it's almost ten o' clock. We should be halfway done by now," Billy told his younger brother.

"I couldn't sleep. That shit scared the living crap out of me last night." Eric grabbed a roll of hefty bags and tore one open.

"You and me both. I still can't figure out what the hell was out there. Some kind of bird, I guess." Billy dropped the rake and walked over to Eric. "It freaking flew over us, right? Then it waited for us like it was smart."

"I don't give a crap what it was. I should have never let you talk me into going up there in the first place." Eric rubbed a sleep crumb from his eyes.

Billy punched him hard enough in the bicep to cause Eric to drop the bags.

"Asshole, whatcha do that for?"

Billy shouted at him. "You wanted to go up there just as much as I did, dickweed. Don't say you didn't!"

"You didn't have to hit me, for Christ's sake," Eric whined.

"Stop being such a baby. I'm trying to make some sense out of this shit, and you're not helping."

"Okay, I don't know, yeah, maybe it was a bird, a smart bird. Is that better?"

Billy wanted to hit him again but managed to hold back. There was barely a two-year age difference between them, but sometimes it felt like a thousand. Eric had always been the baby of the family, and it still showed. He never took anything seriously, and Billy didn't think he stood much of a chance with Susan Smith. It wouldn't be long before she got tired of Eric's idiotic behavior.

On the other hand, Billy figured he might be giving Susan a little too much credit. She had been unfazed by Eric's antics. In fact, she appeared enamored with his crap. Maybe the girl was just as much of a dipshit as Eric.

"I just want to figure out what the hell it was," Billy explained.

"I get what you're saying, Bill. I'm just saying that I don't really give a fuck. It chased us, and it scared the shit out of me. I'm never going up there again, and that's what I think." Eric had a point, but it still pissed Billy off.

"Mick could have been killed last night. Don't you feel like we should go back and look around, try to figure out what the hell is up there?" Billy tried to guilt his brother a little.

"NO! No, I don't feel that way at all. I feel like we should forget about that fucking place, go back to school tomorrow, and never talk about it again. That's how I feel about it."

"I'm going up there, and you're coming with me." Billy pulled the older brother card, the trump card. "We're gonna finish raking these leaves, grab Mick, and we're going back to the sanatorium, and that's final."

Eric didn't continue to fight. There was no use; Billy had played his hand, and there was no way to win after that. "As long as we're back before it gets dark, and we bring one of the shotguns." Those were his demands.

"Oh yeah," Billy agreed. "We're gonna bring a couple of 'em."

●●●

Carl followed Troy into the garage. He didn't know what to expect and was taken aback by the amount of detail he saw. It was hard to imagine that a couple of ten-year-olds had built it themselves. The place had definitely taken a great deal of hard work. They entered into a tight hallway with a cage window set into one of the walls.

THE OJANOX

"I stopped here." Troy showed the sheriff. "It was really dark, and no one could get past me. Then Billy turned on the strobe light and the tape recorder. Billy and Eric were in the cage, and they tried to grab everyone."

"I bet that scared the pants off your friends." Carl had to admit the kid had done a hell of a job. "Did you think of that yourself?"

"Yeah, that was my idea," Troy boasted. "Me and Rob built the whole place in just a couple days."

"I'm impressed. You've got quite a talent. Might want to get into the movie business someday."

"What do you mean?" Troy raised his eyebrows.

"Well, they have guys in the movie business called set designers who build everything you see on film. They make the haunted houses, the laboratories, sometimes they even build entire towns. Sounds like something you'd be darn good at."

"You really think so?" An epic smile filled his entire face. "You think I could do that?"

"I think you could do anything if you put your mind to it," Carl said, patting Troy on the back.

"Gee, thanks, Sheriff." Troy showed him into the spider room and explained how the plastic arachnids were suspended from the ceiling by lengths of fishing line that ran into a secret hallway on the other side of the room. Eric operated a wheel from inside the hidden space and had lowered the spiders onto the children's heads. The hallway was a small tunnel where all the secrets to Scream in the Dark were hidden. It was where the rats and spiders were operated, and it allowed access to the cage. It also served as a command center where the Tobin brothers could work the strobe light and boom box.

The next room was even more involved than the first two and showed off the level of creativity the boys possessed.

"Where did you get these ideas, Troy?" Carl asked as he tried to navigate the rubber hoses. It was easy to imagine he was walking over rats. With the added effects of darkness and tape-recorded rodents, the kids must have been terrified.

"Once, I was walking in the backyard and stepped on the garden hose. I got scared because it felt like I squished a mouse or a snake. I thought it would be even scarier in the dark; pretty cool, huh?"

"Pretty cool indeed."

They stepped into the graveyard room, and Carl took it all in. "Is this where you found Rob?"

"Yeah, I was taking out the garbage, and I heard something. I thought maybe it was a raccoon. So, I walked in, and he was standing right there." Troy pointed toward the corner of the room beyond the headstones. "He was just kinda staring at the wall."

"What happened then?" Carl asked.

"Well, I wasn't sure it was him. I think I said hello."

Carl listened as he stepped over the small fence into the graveyard. He scanned the room, from the red bulbs on the wall to the materials used to construct the fence and coffin. He noticed the cardboard headstones that read I.P. Daily and Bob Frapples. *Genius.* He laughed and looked back at Troy. "Then what happened?"

"He turned around, and I saw it was him. He looked terrible. Rob was supposed to dress as the vampire. He was gonna jump out of the coffin."

"In there?" Carl pointed at the coffin.

"Yeah, that's when I saw how bad he looked. He had big circles under his eyes, and his face was like a ghost."

"I bet it was pretty scary to see him like that," Carl said, bending down to take a closer look inside the coffin.

"Not until he tried to grab me," Troy stated.

"What do you mean, tried to grab you?" Carl raised his head.

"He didn't recognize me at first; it was like he was in a trance. Then, he started walking towards me and put his arms up like this." Troy held his hands out like Frankenstein's monster. "Then he hissed and tried to grab me."

Carl furrowed his brow in disbelief.

"Then ... it was like he woke up and didn't know where he was."

"You think he was sleepwalking?"

Troy thought about it for a second. "I guess so. I mean ... yeah. He was probably sleepwalking. Um, Sheriff, do you think Rob is gonna be okay?"

Carl nodded and offered a thin smile. "I'm sure your friend is going to be just fine." A small object on the floor caught his attention; he leaned forward to pick it up. He held it between his fingertips, studying it for a moment. "You don't think Rob was sleepwalking, do you, Troy?" He placed the object into his shirt pocket.

"No, sir. I guess not."

THE OJANOX

"Why not?" Carl asked.

"Well, you should have seen how he looked at me." Carl sensed Troy getting worked up and didn't want to push the boy any further. Still, he needed answers.

"How did he look at you, son?"

Troy searched for the exact words to say and shifted his eyes to the floor.

"Just between you and me, Troy. It might help your friend," Carl assured him.

Troy finally spit it out. "He looked at me like ... like he was hungry."

●●●

Carl thanked Donald and Lois for the coffee and then shook Troy's hand. "Thank you for showing me around the Scream in the Dark. I wish I'd been here to see it in action." He placed his hat on his head and straightened it out.

"I would appreciate it if you could do what I asked," he told Lois and Don. "I'll call you tonight and let you know what's up."

"Sure, Sheriff," Don said, then shook his hand. "If there's anything else ... you know. And if you see Karin and Bob, tell them not to hesitate, whatever it is."

"Will do," he replied. "Thanks again; sorry to bother you on a Sunday." He nodded to Lois.

"Good to see you, Carl." She smiled.

Sheriff Primrose climbed into his cruiser and turned the engine over. He waved to the Fischer family where they stood on the front porch. Then he reached into his front pocket and pulled out the small object he had found on the garage floor. He turned it over in his hand. A giant knot grew deep inside him as he studied it.

It was a human molar with dried blood covering the root. Carl had a good idea the tooth belonged to Robert Boyle. The child had likely lost it while convulsing.

He hadn't shared the discovery with Don or Lois, and he sure as hell wasn't about to tell Troy. Carl felt sick to his stomach. This wasn't good at all, and it sure didn't sound like the flu. He prayed Dr. Malcolm would figure this out soon. Carl had enough on his own plate. There was an ongoing murder investigation with no defined cause of death, and he needed to get in touch with Burt as soon as possible.

Static from the police band broke the silence. "Base to Sheriff Primrose. Are you there, Sheriff? Over."

The knot in Carl's stomach tightened like a noose around his neck. The tone in Tara's voice told him she wasn't calling with good news. He picked up the handset and paused. For the fortieth time today, he asked himself, *"What the hell is going on around here?"*

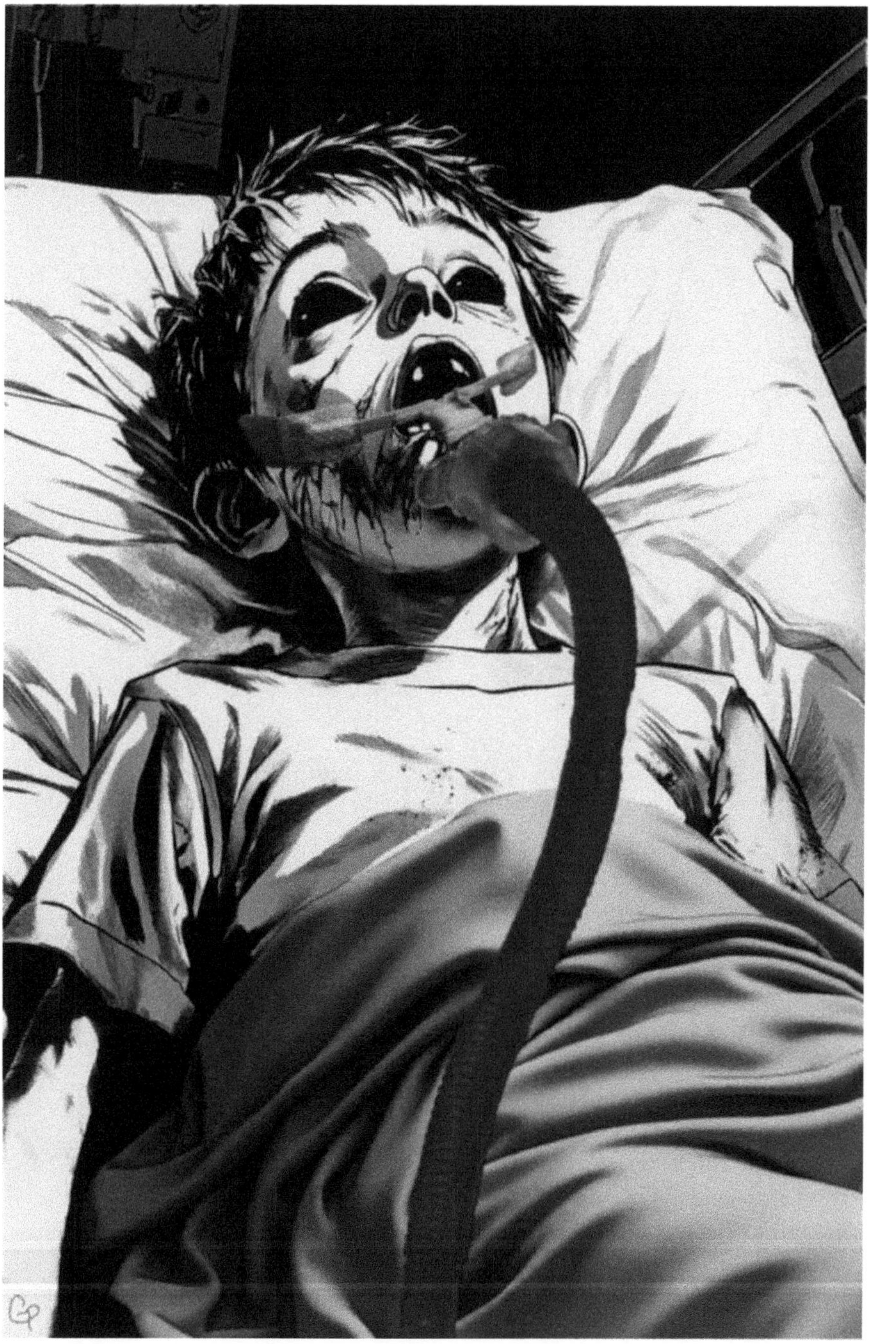

Chapter 9

The medical examiner's office was located on the Boulevard near the Chilton Medical Center. The front part of the brick-faced building housed a small reception area and an even smaller office where Burt kept his files, a desk, and a hidden bottle of booze. The rear of the building held the morgue, the laboratory, and "Old Smokey" the incinerator. This was where all the heavy lifting was done. Burt opened the back door, stepping out of the harsh stainless steel coldness of the morgue, just as the meat wagon pulled into the secluded parking area behind the building.

Burt Lively had served as the King County medical examiner for longer than even he could remember. During those years, he had witnessed far too many senseless deaths. The morgue was usually filled with a mix of natural causes, automobile fatalities, and the occasional hunting accident. There had only been a few instances of the latter, but they had stuck out in Burt's mind. Once, a forty-five-year-old man had ventured out at the start of buck season but neglected to clean his 12 gauge before leaving the house that morning. A field mouse had found its way into the barrel of the man's Mossberg and built a nest over the winter. With several hours to go before sunrise, the guy parked himself in his tree stand and waited for a hefty 8-pointer to pass. Whatever did walk by had had a lot more luck than that poor bastard did. The guy grabbed his shotgun and fired at what he thought would be the talk of the lodge. Instead of discharging a slug into the heart of the animal, the barrel exploded in the man's hands and blew half of his face off. What a mess.

Another hunting-related death that stuck out in Burt's mind happened in '73 when a massive blizzard crippled the entire state for a week and a half. A second hunter, with an equal amount of luck, had gone out just before the snow started falling. He must have gotten disoriented in the whiteout and been unable to navigate his way through the forest. Park rangers found him weeks later after the bulk of the snow melted. By then, damn near every creature on the mountain had taken a bite out of the guy. But King County usually wasn't that exciting, and they'd never seen anything close to what the sheriff's department found on Foothills Drive early this morning.

Burt walked back into the morgue, opened the icebox, and pulled out the long retractable shelf. He went to his office to check his answering machine and waited for his guys to transfer the body to the freezer slab. There were no messages, not that he expected there to be. He told Deputy Forsyth there was no rush and imagined he wouldn't hear anything until later in the day. He returned to the morgue to meet Abe and Tony as they wheeled the gurney through the back entrance. The men positioned it next to the slab and unzipped the black body bag. Then, they transferred Felix Castillo onto the cold steel of the freezer shelf. Abe started to push it back in when Burt stopped him.

"Don't worry about that, Abe," Burt told his driver. "I want to check on a couple things first."

"No problem," Abe answered. "Is there anything else we can do before we head out?"

"No, I've got it from here. Sorry to call you guys in on a Sunday morning. Thanks for your help." Burt had already begun to examine the corpse and barely noticed when Abe and Tony walked out the back door and closed it behind them.

The old coroner pulled on a fresh set of gloves, then positioned a sizeable fluorescent light with a retractable arm directly over the body to help his tired eyes. Stark white light illuminated the corpse, arresting every shadow in the room. The light revealed the victim's face, and Burt did a double take. Felix Castillo's cheeks appeared flush with color, which seemed more than a little off.

This morning they had been a pale shade of blue, the hue you would expect to find on a dead body that had been left outside in the cold or one devoid of body fluids. Now his cheeks were almost pink, and he looked as if he couldn't have been dead for longer than an hour, two at the most.

Burt checked the wound and recoiled with a start, quickly removing his hands as if he had touched a flame. "What on Earth?" he gasped, then slowly returned his fingertips to the man's neck. Felix Castillo had been ice cold less than three hours ago when Burt examined him on the street. Now the man's skin felt closer to seventy-five or eighty degrees, maybe even higher.

"What the hell is going on?" he whispered to the empty room.

The phone rang, causing Burt to jump. "Oh, Jesus Christ, Burt. Get a grip, will ya?" He moved to turn off the light, then thought better of it and left the morgue to answer the phone.

"This is Burt," he said.

"Hi, Burt, it's Gary. I've got some info, but there isn't a whole heck of a lot I could find out." Deputy Forsyth paused.

Burt sat at his desk and took out a notepad and pen. "Okay, what have you got?"

"Well, as we already knew from his ID, his name's Felix Castillo, age twenty-nine, from Warren. He worked for Con Ed for the past nine years, no next of kin."

"None?" Burt asked.

"Zero; no parents, no wife, and no kids."

"Jeez, poor bastard. That's even sadder than dying in the middle of the street."

"If you say so, Burt." Gary cleared his throat. "No medical conditions, no arrest records. His boss said he was a model employee. Worked as much overtime as you could throw at him."

"I guess that would explain why he had no wife," Burt added.

"If you say so, Burt," the deputy repeated.

The back door of the morgue suddenly slammed. Burt looked up from his notes. "Is that you, Abe?" he called. There was no response.

"Are you there, Burt?" Gary asked.

"Huh, yeah, hold on one second, will ya?" Burt covered the receiver with his palm and called out, "Hey, Abe. What's going on back there?"

Burt waited for Abe to answer but only heard the motor of the freezer. "Hey, Gary, let me call you back in a minute."

"You got it, Burt." The deputy hung up.

Burt put the receiver back on the cradle and entered the hallway. "Abe," he called as he walked towards the examination area. "I told you I was good here. No need to hang around any longer."

He rounded the corner. "Abe, what are you de—" Burt stopped short in the entranceway. "Jumping Jesus Christ!" He stared in disbelief. The room was silent; Abe had not entered through the back door and neither had Tony. The area was completely empty. The freezer shelf was exactly where Burt had left it, except Felix Castillo's body was no longer on it.

Burt ran to the back door and burst into the parking lot. It was empty as well; no Abe, no Tony, and no Felix Castillo. His mind raced to draw a logical conclusion but was unable to. Every possible scenario ran back to an impossible dead end. He had never lost a corpse before and had no idea what the protocol was for such an occurrence. Someone had to have come in the back door and stolen it. He thought about the call he needed to make. Carl was going to blow a gasket. This was bad. *Jesus Christ, this is so very, very bad.*

"What in the name of all things holy?" Burt asked the empty parking lot. The sound of the wind was his only reply.

● ● ●

Dr. Ethan Ziegler had been running on fumes for the past six hours and been at the center going on eighteen. He checked his watch to confirm. His back ached, his head throbbed, and the coffee from the cafeteria sat in his gut like a rock. Dr. Malcolm had been ready to quarantine Chilton's east wing and the emergency room staff, as well as Sheriff Primrose and one of his deputies. But Ziegler managed to convince him otherwise, mostly because he didn't want to get stuck there himself, which is exactly what happened. And Malcolm left him in charge of the whole shooting match. A grocery list of tests needed to be executed and evaluated, from x-rays to blood work with a full tox screen, even urinalysis. Sadly, he wasn't any closer to diagnosing the children than he had been when they were first admitted. He needed answers by six tomorrow morning, or Dr. Malcolm was going to pull the plug and call in the quarantine. *If it comes to that, I'll have much bigger problems to deal with.*

He swallowed the last gulp of his coffee, got up from his desk, and made his way to the lab.

"Good morning, Dr. Ziegler." A young candy striper with shoulder-length blonde hair passed him, pushing a cart of books and stuffed animals. She wore a pink and white uniform that hugged her figure, making her look like an hourglass-shaped peppermint stick.

He nodded to the girl, and on any other day, he would have stopped and chatted her up, but there was no time for that. Ziegler opened the door to the lab and barged in on a heavy-set man with a thick black mustache who looked up when he entered the cluttered lab.

Peter Gillick, the lab tech, worked for the center long before Dr. Ziegler had been hired. He was a big man, and not just tall either. Peter stood well over six-four and looked like he hadn't missed a meal during his entire career. His massive figure engulfed the microscope in front of him like a water buffalo sipping from a shot glass.

"Hey, Doc." Peter nodded.

"Peter. Got anything?"

The big man winced and tightened his enormous lips. "You realize blood work takes time? Not to mention it's Sunday, and I'm the only one here." Peter shifted on a stool that creaked in protest under the strain. "By the way, I'm good. Thanks for asking."

"I'm sorry, Peter," Ziegler offered. "It's been a hell of a day. I was hoping you had something. I guess not."

"Well, I didn't say that. It'll still be a few hours before the rest of the results are in, but I did find something interesting."

Ziegler raised his head and took a lunging step forward. "So, you got something?"

"Take a look at this, Doc." Peter backed away from the table, allowing Ziegler to look into the microscope.

"This is a sample from Erin Richards," Peter explained as the doctor examined the slide. "As you can see, there isn't any sign of a viral agent present. However, there is an elevated concentration of white cells, indicating an infection. But—"

"Am I seeing this right?" Ziegler asked and raised his head.

"I was asking myself the same thing when you walked into the room."

"Poison?" Dr. Ziegler looked back into the microscope. "I mean, is that what I'm seeing? It looks like these kids have been poisoned."

"Yeah, I think so. Except this isn't like any poison I've ever seen. And I'm still not entirely convinced that's the only thing going on here. There is a bacterial signature you can see that has attacked the red blood cells. It behaves much like a parasite, attaching itself and feeding, almost like a tick."

"Is it the same in all three children?"

"Identical," Peter answered.

"Then they all came in contact with the same toxin. If that's even what it is," Ziegler said more to himself. "A bacterial parasite of some variety."

The sample taken from Erin Richards clearly revealed a foreign agent. The infection had compromised the integrity of the plasma, causing her blood proteins to denature. In an attempt to fight off the infection, the girl's immune system kicked her white blood cells into overdrive. They had begun to destroy the red cells where the toxin was centralized. Her body was eating itself.

"They're not going to last much longer unless we figure out exactly what the hell this thing is." Ziegler felt the icy fingers of time tightening around his throat. "I've never seen anything like this. What do you make of it?"

"At this point, Doc, I don't even want to guess. Toxicology will take another hour or so. We'll have a little more to go on when that's finished. I called in a couple of the other techs, and they should be here any minute." Peter checked his watch: eleven thirty.

"I don't know how much longer those poor kids can last."

"I know, Doc." Peter grabbed a pipette and a box of slides from the counter. "As soon as I have something, I'll call you. I'm doing everything I can."

"Thank you. Page me when you've got something." Ziegler walked out of the lab and sped off as fast as he had come.

The blood work confirmed the evidence of an infection, which was obvious from the high-grade fever. The agent attacking the children's red blood cells possessed the qualities of a poison. It also contained a biological signature, like that of a single-celled bacterium. It was unlike anything Ethan Ziegler had ever seen. Erin's body was feeding on itself in an attempt to fight off the foreign invader, one nasty bacteria or poison or whatever the hell it was. By the look of it, Ziegler believed it might be a hybrid of the two, if that was even possible. Up until a few minutes ago, he hadn't thought it was. But now, he wasn't so sure. He tore down the hall toward radiology and passed the same blonde candy striper from before. She smiled at him and probably batted her eyes, but Ziegler didn't even notice.

Robert Boyle lay in room 3 of the ICU wing. He had been placed on a ventilator early that morning after becoming unable to maintain his respiration. Sweat ran from every pore of the child's body, and he had lost nearly ten pounds since Thursday. His color was near that of a corpse—pallid, pale, and almost blue. Two of his teeth had popped out when the doctors inserted the breathing tube, and the rest had fallen out shortly after, as if his body was too weak to hold on to them. Nurse TenHove entered the room in a full-protective body gown with head gear.

His parents hadn't left the building since they arrived and had only been permitted to visit from no closer than the doorway. As a courtesy, the staff provided rooms for both families to wash up and rest. Dr. Ziegler prescribed the mothers a light sedative to help them relax ... if only slightly.

Nurse TenHove recorded Rob's vitals and checked his IV. She registered the stats in the boy's chart, then hung it back at the foot of the bed. Taking one last look at the child, she turned and left the room.

Robert Boyle opened his eyes and stared up at the ceiling. His dark pupils had consumed the irises, making his eyes as black as tar. A transparent film shuttered across them from side to side; a secondary eyelid much like an amphibian's had developed. It shielded out much of the bright fluorescent light, which was too painful to look at directly. Then Rob closed both sets of lids and lay there listening to the steady pump of the ventilator.

Carl stood in the morgue with his hands on his hips and a look on his face that a mother might give a child who repeatedly stuck pennies into the wall outlet. He'd gotten the call from Tara and known right away by the tone of her voice it was bad news. But he never could have imagined.

Burt stared back at him, even more puzzled and confused.

"Let me get this straight. You're telling me you *lost* the body?" Carl asked again.

"It was right here." Burt motioned to the freezer shelf with both hands. "I just started examining the guy when the phone rang. It was your deputy. Couldn't have been more than five minutes. Then I heard the door slam and figured Abe came back for some reason. But it locks from the inside. So, I thought maybe some kids were trying to break in or something."

"And what about Abe and your other guy?" Carl searched for the man's name.

"Tony," Burt answered. "It wasn't them. I called on the radio. Abe was parking the wagon in the lot at the medical center."

"So, where's the body, Burt?" Carl took off his hat and scratched his head. "Correct me if I'm wrong, but the guy didn't walk out of here on his own. Please tell me that's not what you're suggesting."

"Of course not!" Burt shouted. "What do you take me for, a goddamn fool? I know the guy didn't walk out of here on his own, Carl. Somebody came in here and stole the body!"

Carl pursed his lips and replaced his hat on his head. "Okay," he said. "We have a body snatcher in Garrett Grove. I'm sure you checked the rest of the drawers. Not to insult you, but I'm having a hard time swallowing any of this."

"Goddamn it, Carl!" Burt stormed to the freezer in a huff and began to throw open the doors to prove he wasn't entirely out of his mind. "Look, nothing here." He opened one after the other, then slammed them shut. "Nothing in here either. I'm not crazy, Carl. Someone had to come in here and take the body." He opened the last door revealing it, too, was empty. "Satisfied?"

"Not even a little. First, you tell me I should be on the lookout for a missing ten pints of blood, and now I need to issue an APB for the body that goes with it. I'm not very satisfied at all." Carl examined the empty freezer shelf where the body had lain. The retractable fluorescent light still shone down onto the cold stainless steel.

"I know how this looks," Burt said.

Carl stared at his friend. "Do you? How does it look, Burt?" He continued to inspect the shelf and the door to the freezer.

"It looks like I've lost my damn mind!"

"Yep, that's what it looks like." Carl was about to move the fluorescent light out of his way when he noticed something. He leaned in closer and then fished a plastic bag out of his pocket. "Hey, Burt, take a look at this."

The coroner walked over to the shelf to see what the sheriff was looking at. Caught in the retractable arm of the fluorescent light was a swatch of black hair. "Son of a bitch!" he exclaimed.

"Does that look like the color of the victim's to you?"

"Son of a bitch," Burt repeated.

Carl turned to him. "Dammit, Burt!" he snapped.

"Absolutely, dark black and coarse. The only guy in here with hair that dark in the past six months."

"Would I be correct in assuming that this light is cleaned regularly?" Carl waited for a reply.

"You would."

"And by the looks of it"—Carl mockingly gestured toward the large amount of grey on his friend's head——"this hair doesn't belong to you."

"Obviously." Burt rolled his eyes.

"Let me ask you something else, Burt." Carl studied the position of the light and the patch of hair caught in the hinge of the arm. "Has this light moved since you left the body and went in the office to answer the phone?"

The coroner thought about it for a second. "Nope, that's exactly where I left it. Yeah, right where I left it."

"Are you sure you didn't move this light?"

"I didn't move the damn light, Carl. It's in the same exact place I left it," Burt insisted.

Carl took a step back to view the examination shelf from a different angle, then approached it again and intently studied the patch of hair in the hinge. "You'd say the guy was about a buck-eighty, give or take?" Carl asked.

"Yeah, give or take, sounds about right," Burt replied.

"Took two guys to lift him onto the table; I imagine it would take two guys to carry him out as well. Would you agree?"

"Yeah, two guys, sure. He's dead weight. You know how hard it is to move a body."

"Burt, do you think two guys could lift Castillo off the table and carry him out the door without moving the light? I mean, they would have had to move the light, right?"

Burt studied how close the light was to the shelf and scratched his head. "Son of a bitch! You're right. I don't get it."

"What do you make of that?" Carl took a penlight out of his holster and illuminated the patch of hair. "Is that a piece of the guy's scalp?"

Burt looked closely. There was a decent-sized piece of scalp attached to the hair. Carl pulled it free with a pair of tweezers and dropped the evidence into the plastic bag. He handed the bag to Burt and took his hat off. "Could you hold these for a second?"

Before the old man could ask him what he was doing, Carl climbed onto the shelf and lay down in the position the body had been. He took extra caution not to disturb the position of the light. "Is this the way the body was laying?" he asked.

"Are you nuts, Carl?" Burt studied his friend with concern. "Yeah, that's how he was laying, but you're out of your damn mind."

Carl slowly sat up from his prone position; he lifted the top part of his torso until the tip of his head was an inch away from the light. If he allowed himself to sit completely upright, he would hit his scalp on the hinge, exactly where the patch of hair had been.

"You got to be shitting me." Burt's jaw dropped as he watched Carl's head graze the hinge exactly where Castillo's would, if he had ...

Carl and Burt stared at each other. Neither said a word.

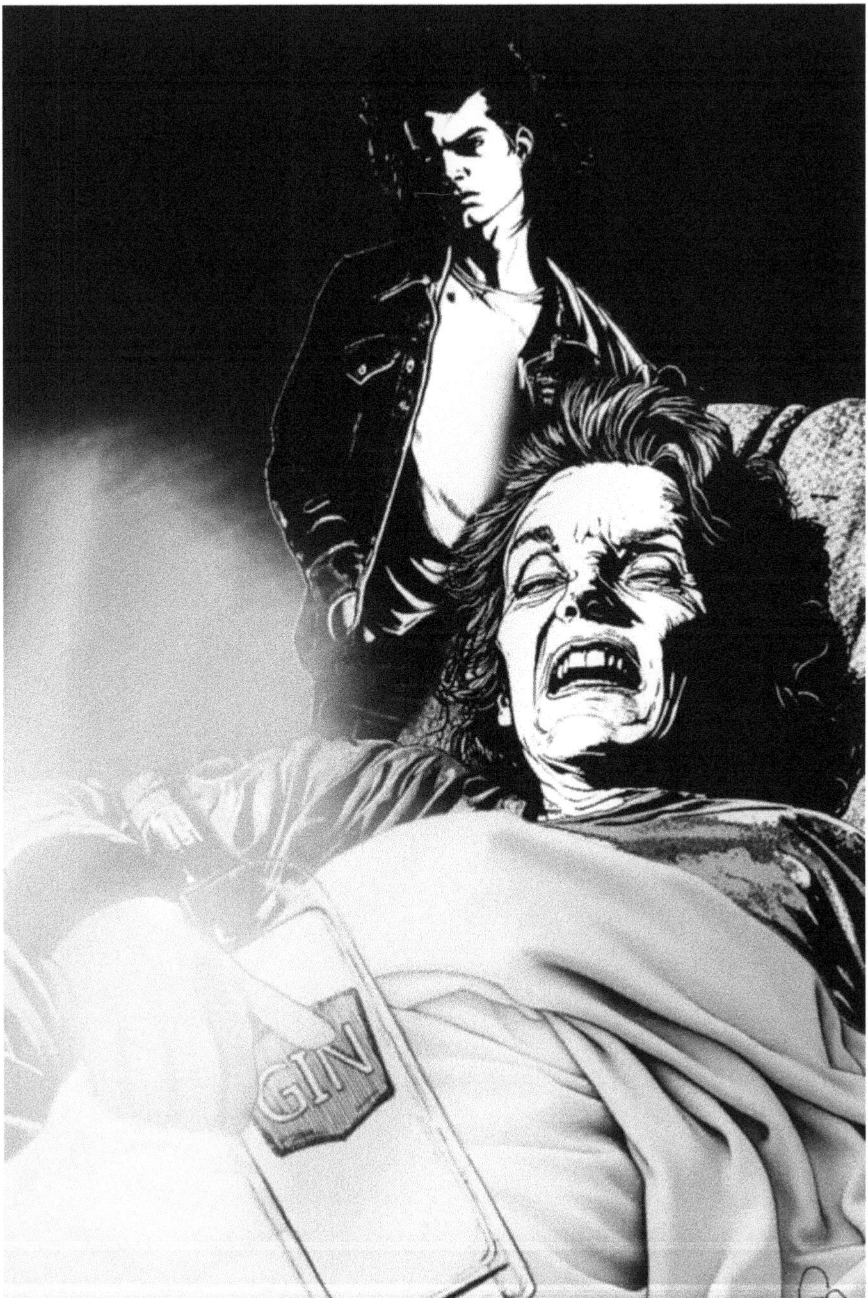
GIN

Chapter 10

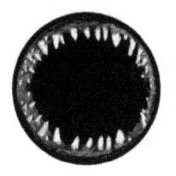

Butchie Post flipped the Spam over in the cast iron skillet and was greeted by a waft of sizzling goodness. The kitchen was poorly lit in the house he shared with his mother, Margaret, the same house he had grown up in, and the one he had come back to when his time at Barre Oaks had been paid in full. The old ranch wasn't much to look at. It needed a paint job, the gutters were overflowing with pine needles, and the yard was in serious need of attention. The place was structurally sound, but the interior was dank with the reek of stale cigarettes, as if the windows hadn't been opened since Kennedy was in office. The wallpaper was a musty shade of sour, the carpet smelled like a wet sock, and it wouldn't hurt if someone had taken the time to throw out the stacks of old newspapers and magazines that had taken over like an infestation.

Margaret had never been the happy homemaker type, and Butchie was ... well ... Butchie. After her husband left, Margaret did her best to raise her son, but it had been an uphill battle. The boy was a handful. She'd been in and out of the principal's office regularly in a futile attempt to keep the kid in school. And Butchie hadn't made it easy. When he was finally kicked out and sent to Barre Oaks, her two gins a night turned into three and then four. It wasn't long before she needed a couple shots in the morning just to steady the old nerves. Not like it was a problem or anything. Who didn't need a drink or two every now and then? Besides, the house was paid for, and she had her disability. Butchie had come home and gotten a decent job at the quarry. So, it wasn't like she was taking food out of their mouths to buy booze.

Margaret loved her son, and Butchie loved his momma. He flipped the Spam over in the pan one last time. Nice and crispy, just how she liked it. He buttered a piece of toast and fixed her a plate, then brought the food to her in the living room, where she sat watching Abbott and Costello. The comedians were dressed in baseball uniforms and performing their "Who's on First" bit. Margaret laughed and took a long sip from her Gilby's and tonic. A Pall Mall sat perched between her fingers with a two-inch ash defiantly clinging to the end.

"Here you go, Momma." Butchie placed her meal on a folding tray that sat next to her recliner.

"You're such a good boy, Butchie. Give your momma a kiss." She raised a cheek to her son, who kissed it and smiled. Margaret laughed again at the men on the television while Butchie went back into the kitchen and grabbed the items he had picked up at the A&P.

Margaret had needed Spam, bread, and two packs of smokes. Butchie's requirements were equally as simple. He headed out the back door, stepping onto the porch, and looked out into the woods behind his house. This time of year, one could expect to see an occasional buck or doe eating acorns on any of the numerous paths that cut through the foothills. Once, Butchie even spotted a mountain lion that must have gotten brave and ventured from its den on Garrett Mountain. Today, the trails behind the Post house were empty, and that was just the way Butchie liked it. He didn't need anybody disturbing him this afternoon. Butchie had a few things he needed to take care of before Halloween. He gazed at the old shed, set at the far edge of his property, and his mind went right to thoughts of Jackie Gilmartin in her white nurse's outfit. It was going to look good torn to shreds on the floor of the shed. Butchie felt himself getting excited just thinking about it. He shook it off; he had a job to do.

He set the two shopping bags on the picnic table and sat down on a moldy patio chair. From the first bag, he removed the two dozen Red Delicious apples he had bought for the trick-or-treaters. He'd taken great care to make sure each one was shiny and crimson, with not a blemish or a wormhole in the bunch. *The kids are gonna love these.* Based on Butchie's own awful eating habits, he should have known that no kid in his right mind wanted to get an apple for Halloween.

Still, somehow, he thought it was a good idea. Butchie's vision was obscured by his dark intentions.

He removed a sewing kit from the second bag, an extra box of needles, a roll of paper towels, and a bottle of Ipecac. He remembered playing in the garage when he was either five or six, back when his mom still called him Marion. There had been a shelf full of cans and bottles with automotive solvents and household chemicals on it. He couldn't be sure if he had drunk from the bottle, but Margaret told him she had walked into the garage and found young Marion downing a bottle of brake fluid. She called the family doctor, who recommended she give the boy a shot of Ipecac. Fortunately, she had a bottle of the vile liquid in the house and forced fed several spoonfuls down her son's throat. At which point he vomited up the entire contents of his stomach and then some. He remembered that part, and even though he thought that he probably didn't drink the brake fluid, he never wanted to experience the Ipecac again. So, he learned his lesson about playing with bottles and stayed out of the garage.

Butchie sat in the early afternoon sun and got to work on his project. He set a large Tupperware bowl in the center of the table, removed the paper towels from the wrapper, and uncapped the Ipecac. The liquid smelled repulsive and brought back the traumatic childhood memory. Yet somehow, he managed to keep his breakfast down and continue.

He poured the medicine generously onto a handful of paper towels, then proceeded to rub the liquid over the skin of the apples. When he was finished with the first coat, he poured more of the medicine onto the fruit directly and let them sit in the Tupperware bowl to soak.

After he was satisfied that the apples had been sufficiently bathed in the Ipecac, he opened the sewing kit and the box of needles. Using the thimble, he began to push the tiny daggers into the apples. *Three needles per apple should do the trick.* Any dickweed kid who bit into one of these bad boys was sure to come away with a treat. If the little shits happened to miss the needles for some reason, the Ipecac would surely do the trick. Butchie thought better about his work and decided to insert a fourth needle into the pieces of fruit, pushing them in with the thimble far enough so they were undetectable.

He filled the bowl with the dangerous treats and, for good measure, poured the remainder of the liquid over them. He couldn't wait to hand these fuckers out to the neighborhood kids. *Trick-or-Treat my fat dick.*

The voice of a young boy broke the silence as well as Butchie's concentration. "Oh yeah, you and what army?" the kid shouted.

It was the two fartbags who had parked their bicycles next to Butchie's Monza earlier that morning. That had really pissed him off, but now the little dick lickers were riding on the paths just behind his house. He watched as they crested a small hill and disappeared into the woods.

"Oh no you don't, you little fuckwads. Not in my yard." Butchie jumped from his chair and bounded down the steps of the porch. He ran into the woods after the boys with blind rage coursing through his veins. They had a lot of nerve riding their bikes on his property.

The land between Mountain Ave and Foothills Drive was state property and open to the public, but Butchie didn't see it that way. Most of the time, kids were smart enough to avoid the section of the paths bordering the Post property, unless, of course, they were looking to get the ever-living shit kicked out of them. Tommy Negal and Jeff Campbell weren't the brightest kids in the fourth grade and hadn't realized they'd driven their bikes within earshot of the town lunatic. It was a mistake neither of them would regret for long.

Ziegler stood before the back-lit panel, staring at the impossible images in front of him. It had to be some type of mistake; surely there was something wrong with the equipment. It happened. That was the problem with technology; it wasn't foolproof. Even the most advanced systems showed faulty readings from time to time. But there had been no mistake, and what he was looking at wasn't the result of faulty equipment or inaccurate readings.

He'd ordered chest x-rays to be taken of the children in the ICU, and all the images had come back the same. The techs in radiology had been so startled by the initial results, they'd taken a second set of photos. Which hadn't been easy with the Boyle kid on a ventilator. Now, looking at the results, Ziegler imagined it wouldn't be long before the Richards kids were on ventilators as well.

Both the first and second sets of x-rays revealed the same thing. The children's internal physiology had been altered. The lung capacity of the children had decreased by nearly thirty percent. Not just their ability to take in and process air, but the actual size of their lungs had been reduced. It was as if their bodies were being subjected to the effects of extreme pressure. And that wasn't even the most startling abnormality the photos revealed. The children's hearts had increased in size and were nearly twice as big as a ten-year-old's should be. It was impossible, but the x-rays didn't lie. The proof was sitting in front of him.

There wasn't a germ on the planet capable of that. Ziegler was in way over his head and knew he had made a horrible mistake by convincing Dr. Malcolm to change his mind about the quarantine. It was a race against time to find an answer that might save these children. And Ethan Ziegler was losing confidence in his ability to do that. Not to mention the growing probability that through his hubris, he had released an unidentified contagion back into the populace of Garrett Grove.

Fuck ... Malcolm was right ... this is all my fucking fault!

It waited ... watching ... listening ... ready to feed. It heard the echoes and felt the ground move from behind the walls of its prison. Then the rock shifted, and light swarmed the darkness. Free at last. It had been tricked by the simple creatures it once controlled and fed on. They had lured it into the shadows and trapped it with their magic. But they would pay. It rushed from the cave, thirsting and famished, ready to exact revenge upon the ones. But the creatures were different. The worshipers of the Great Spirit, the ones who prayed to Ketanëtuwit, were no more. A new race had emerged, evolved over time. The new creatures had built machines to bend the will of the environment. They were fascinating. It sensed the heightened consciousness and intellect immediately; their thoughts were deafening, and the capacity of their emotions was limitless.

But it was vulnerable in its present state and needed to find a den. It didn't dare risk exposing itself, even though it was famished. It had been too long since it last fed.

Still, it understood restraint, which it had exercised with the younglings, draining its reserve even more. When it finally consumed, it had been ravenous. The emotions of this new race were like nothing it had ever ingested. Their desires had evolved, their emotions were refined, and their fear was glorious. Their nourishment was deliciously intoxicating. It had been driven to a frenzy by the salacious thoughts of the one called Felix and drained the vessel dry, an unavoidable mistake. Now, there was great work to be done once again. Vessels to be drained, consciousness to be absorbed, and innocence to be devoured. Nothing satiated its hunger like the innocence of the younglings. Their fear was exquisite.

Tommy and Jeff pretended their bicycles were X-wing fighters as they navigated the asteroid belt behind Butchie's house. They were presently mounting an attack on the Death Star.

"Red One to Gold Leader, he's on your tail, defensive maneuvers," Jeff yelled, with dust spitting from his back tire.

"Roger, Red One. I'm on it." Tommy hit the brakes and pretended to fire laser cannons at an enemy TIE fighter.

"Gold Leader, I have a shot. Cover me," Jeff shouted and pedaled faster towards his imaginary target.

"Copy that, Red One. Take your shot when you're ready." Tommy followed close behind. Loose sand took to the air as they tore through the trails that had been carved into the woods so long ago.

It watched the young ones from where it hid. The creatures passed within feet of where it waited and never noticed it. They had evolved in many ways but had lost their primordial instincts; they could no longer sense the threat of a predator. It followed unseen, like a vapor.

"I'm taking the shot, Gold Leader." Jeff fired his cannons at the Death Star. "Direct hit, let's get out of here before she blows."

Closer...

The boys followed the path to the right, around a large oak tree, and headed in the direction of the creek. The trail took a slow downgrade, their tires bouncing over ruts in the dirt formed by heavy rains. The woods grew darker around them as they drew closer to the small stream.

Closer...

Tommy and Jeff were feeling pretty psyched about blowing up the Death Star. Jeff imagined being kissed by Princess Leia as she hung the medal of bravery around his neck. He turned back to yell at Tommy but was suddenly lifted from the seat of his bicycle. For a full second, he was aware of the feeling of weightlessness ... then, there was nothing but *Darkness*.

Tommy had about a half a second longer than Jeff to register what was happening. He watched as his friend was lifted from the seat of the bicycle in front of him. It seized Tommy and held him by the throat, making it impossible for the boy to breathe. Tommy opened his mouth to scream as his eyes rolled back into his head. But by then, it was over.

● ● ●

Butchie saw the two little rump rangers riding their bikes on his property and had run after them. The pricks were yelling and screaming like they owned the place. But this was his yard, and he was about to teach them a lesson they weren't soon to forget. He heard them calling each other things like red and gold and imagined it was some type of code for sissies. Butchie knew these trails better than anybody. He ought to; they were his. The queer baits were headed toward the creek, and the trail was a dead end. Butchie cut into the woods; willows slapped at his face and stung like tiny wasps. It was familiar ground, not far from where he had finally stood up for himself all those years ago. And he was about to stand up again. He could feel his excitement growing at the thought of confronting the little pussies. He thought he might even show them a little trick he had learned in Barre Oaks.

The boys had stopped yelling. Butchie listened as he approached the creek. Taking a running leap, he cleared the little brook and landed on the opposite bank. He continued to run, never missing a step. Butchie exited the woods and emerged onto the path. The little humps would be just around the next corner. The air in his lungs began to burn; he had worked up a sweat, not to mention he could feel the heat in his balls growing hotter by the second. He bounded up the trail and turned the corner.

Butchie stopped short in his tracks.

The kids' bicycles lay in a tangle where they had come to rest half on and half off the path. The back tire of one still spun mindlessly. Butchie thought he must be seeing things; some type of trick or illusion of light played with his vision. He attempted to register what he saw but was unable.

The two kids hung in the air about three feet above the ground; their arms and legs dangled from their motionless bodies. Butchie struggled to see if anything was tied around their necks; they looked as if they had been lynched. But there was nothing. The children simply floated before him, suspended by some invisible force. "What the f—"

He sensed the presence at once. It was easy for evil to recognize itself. Butchie was overcome with the urgency to run but found it impossible to move. He knew if he didn't react, he would never get another chance. He finally tried to turn, but it was too late. It rushed him like a gust of wind. Suddenly, it was in his mouth, entering through his eyes, and forcing itself into his ears. It violated every part of him. He was invaded like never before, nothing like the way he'd been taken in Barre Oaks. For a moment, Butchie felt it inside his head. Then it spoke, and he knew he had been chosen. He had only been chosen once before, by Vinnie and the Bristol Boys. It was good to be selected; it meant you were important. It meant you were a giver, not a taker.

Butchie was lifted off the ground as it entered him and revealed in detail the great work that was before him. His feet hung several feet above the dirt as it consumed him, and Marion "Butchie" Post ceased to exist.

Chapter 11

Wilson's Diner maintained a steady flow of customers throughout the week, then picked up considerably on Saturday and Sunday. Dick Wilson owned the place and could usually be found slinging burgers and deep-frying potatoes behind the grill. On the rare occasions when Dick wasn't there, his nephew Josh piloted the ship.

It was nothing more than your typical greasy spoon, but it was the only diner within a twenty-mile radius. Which was great for business but bad for the town's cholesterol. Today's lunch had been busy like most Sundays. Amanda Griggs, who everyone called Mandy, like the girl in the song, had worked the floor. Mandy was twenty-five and quite the looker, which kept the truckers and quarrymen coming back. Who didn't love a pretty face? She was good with the kids, friendly, courteous, and she knew how to flirt a fat tip out of every guy that walked into the joint. One of her favorite moves was to unbutton her blouse as far as gravity would allow, then lean over the counter to offer the truckers and quarrymen an eyeful. The girl sold more peach cobbler than any other waitress who worked there, and Dick had seen how she did it. In fact, Dick was thinking about moving the chicken liver to the top shelf just to see how much of the disgusting paste Mandy could peddle by standing on her tiptoes and showing off her ass cheeks. Dick was willing to bet he'd have a hard time keeping it in stock.

When lunch was over, only a few customers remained. A family of three sat at a table near the window finishing their meal, two men from the quarry had just paid their bill, and Dr. Malcolm sat in the far booth, keeping to himself. The chief of medicine had started to visit the place a bit more frequently since his wife, Rosie, passed away two years prior. They were married nearly forty years. She had always been a big woman and had struggled with diabetes for a long time. But she lost the battle in the end.

Rose Malcolm doted over her husband for as long as she could. Right up until she became unable to make breakfast for him in the morning. Most people believed John would pass shortly after Rose. Married men usually didn't fare well after the death of their spouse.

So far, Dr. John Malcolm proved to be an exception to the rule. Most likely, it was the job that kept him vital. However, as the song goes, to everything there is a season. John knew he was getting a little long in the tooth and it was time to let the young bucks do some of the heavy lifting. So he hired Ethan Ziegler, a talented young surgeon and a damn good diagnostician. But John wasn't ready to be sent to the glue factory just yet. Although the hours were getting to him, he was concerned if he acquiesced to Mother Nature's call to leisure, it wouldn't be long before the girls at the beauty parlor were saying, "Poor old Dr. Malcolm, he just wasn't the same after his Rosie passed. He died of a broken heart".

Besides, plenty of patients in Garrett Grove preferred seeing the chief of medicine rather than young Dr. Ziegler. Some felt Ziegler was a bit too casual. Also, there was talk about his relationships with a few of the nurses. That didn't necessarily make him a bad doctor, but it made some of the older population uncomfortable.

Jackie Gilmartin had been running the bases with Dr. Ziegler regularly and had shared their recent exploits with her roommate, Mandy Griggs. Jackie liked to stop by Wilson's after work for a bite to eat and a little conversation. The girls shared every detail about their sex lives, and Mandy loved hearing about the randy Dr. Ziegler, who had an excellent bedside manner.

That morning after work, Jackie told Mandy about her and Ziegler's plans for this evening. The girls had made a bit of a spectacle of themselves during the breakfast rush. Which was pretty much the case whenever they were together. It was impossible not to notice them, with Mandy hanging half out of her skirt and blouse, and Jackie in her skintight nurse's uniform.

In turn, Mandy shared all the spicy details about her date at the drive-in with Felix and told Jackie how she had used the old cobbler trick on him. Her attempts to get the electrician's attention were successful, and they had gone to see *The Amityville Horror* up in Warren.

"How was the movie?" Jackie had asked.

"So good," Mandy answered. "We watched it three times."

That's when the girls started to cackle like two mother hens, which raised the eyes of everyone in the place.

"Mandy, don't you have tables to serve?" Dick scolded from behind the grill.

She poured Jackie a fresh cup of coffee, then leaned over the counter and whispered, "I'll be right back. Dick's a little grouchy today."

"Maybe you should offer him a slice of cobbler." Jackie smirked, which resulted in another bout of uncontrollable giggles. After breakfast, Jackie went home to the apartment to rest up for her big date with Ziegler.

Mandy approached the far booth where Dr. Malcolm sat alone.

"Can I get you anything else, Doc?" she asked as he sipped at his coffee, reading the Sunday paper.

"Thank you, hon. I'm good for now." He covered his mouth as he spoke, as if he was concerned that he might have food in his teeth. Although Mandy didn't realize it, Dr. Malcolm had chosen the far booth to avoid contact with the public.

Mandy set a stack of plates at the sink where Roger was busy scraping and washing. He was still in high school and worked as the busboy/dishwasher on weekends and after school. He was a cute kid, and Mandy liked to tease him a bit. Nothing serious, just enough to get him flustered and make him blush. She messed up his hair as she walked towards the back door, making sure to brush her hip against him as she did.

"Hey, Dick. I'm gonna take five out back," she called to her boss.

"Take the garbage with you," he barked.

Mandy rolled her eyes and grabbed the garbage can near the sink where Roger worked. She bent over far enough to give him a good look down the front of her blouse. She met his eyes as he scanned her rack. "See anything you like?"

He blushed as Mandy took the garbage and left out the back door. She stepped outside into the bright afternoon sunshine. It had been a warm October, but Mandy could tell the temperature was about to start dropping. Leaves had already begun to change colors on the oaks and the maples in town. And Garrett

Mountain was starting to show large swatches of orange and burgundy on the north side.

The area behind Wilson's was a small lot the restaurant shared with Goldie's Beauty Parlor. Both businesses used it for deliveries, and it was where the garbage dumpsters were kept. A breeze whipped across the short stretch of blacktop, churning leaves into a mini cyclone in the center of the pavement. Mandy shivered as the cool air hit her bare legs and arms; it was going to be an early winter. There would be snow on the ground this time next month.

Mandy carried the garbage to the bin.

"Meow." A ginger-striped alley cat milled around the dumpster, looking for a free meal.

"Hey, Scraps," Mandy called to it. She had been feeding table scraps to the cat for several weeks and had aptly named it. She bent down to pet it. "How are you today, cutie?"

Scraps raised its head to be scratched more efficiently.

"Are you hungry?" she asked, removing a half of a turkey sandwich wrapped in tin foil from her apron. She set it down in front of Scraps, who tore into the offering like it was filet mignon.

The wind blew through the back lot again, kicking up an old newspaper and sending it wafting on the breeze. The rattle it made as it cartwheeled across the pavement spooked the cat, and Scraps retreated under the dumpster.

Mandy looked over her shoulder at the back door of the diner and the small alley separating the two businesses. A man stood in the shadows of the buildings; she had not noticed him until now. She drew in a sharp breath at the sudden sight and then relaxed when she recognized the familiar Con Ed uniform.

"Felix, what are you doing here?" she called to him.

He stood near the far wall, then stepped back and disappeared into the alley.

Scraps inched his head from beneath the dumpster and hissed. Mandy stood up and straightened her skirt. She and Felix had had a wild night at the drive-in, and she'd been looking forward to the next time they could see each other. They did it in the backseat of his car as the Lutz family battled the forces of evil on the big screen. It was obvious Felix had enjoyed it just as much, and even joked about meeting her behind the diner one day for a little afternoon delight. She had no idea he was serious.

THE OJANOX

Mandy had laughed it off but had secretly been aroused by the proposal. When Felix didn't come in this morning at his usual time, she thought he had used her. But he was here now. She couldn't believe he had actually picked today to surprise her. She found it incredibly exciting.

"I don't have enough time, baby," she called to him. "Dick only gave me a few minutes to take out the trash."

Mandy went to where Felix had been and peered down the alley. He had walked to the end and was standing with his back to her. *Cat and mouse, hmmm. This guy knows just how I like it.* She followed him down the alley.

"Baby, I don't have time today. Dick is expecting me back any minute," she explained. Still, she knew if he tried, she would let him have her. But that didn't mean she had to make it easy on him; she had to play a little hard to get. Mandy cursed herself for having worn her granny panties to work today but hoped Felix wouldn't mind too much.

Felix stared at the wall with his shoulders slumped and his back to her. There was something stimulating about the game he had initiated. Mandy could feel herself getting worked up as she approached him.

"Felix, baby, what are you doing here?" she asked coyly. "I didn't think you were going to show up today." She walked up to where he stood and watched him sway to the left and right as if he were listening to music.

"Baby," she said and touched his shoulder.

Felix spun around like an uncoiled spring and grabbed her, his hand clamping around her throat. He held her tight and stopped the air from entering her lungs. At first, she thought it was part of the game and found it thrilling, then she saw his face.

Felix stared back at her through a pool of onyx; his eyes were completely black, like they'd been filled with Indian ink. The veins in his face had bulged and ruptured. They spread out beneath his eyes like scarlet spider webs, making him look like he had aged a hundred years overnight. His neck was black and bruised, and there was blood on his shirt collar. Mandy tried to scream as he lifted her off the ground by the throat. Then he pulled her closer and opened his mouth impossibly wide.

Dear God!

His breath smelled like rotting meat. Mandy gagged as his grip tightened even more.

She didn't have to think about it for long. Felix opened his mouth wider still, his lower jaw descended with a sickening clack as the bones unhinged and dislocated. With the speed of a serpent, he drew her in and smothered Mandy's face with his gaping maw. The world was blocked out when Felix's putrid lips slurped against her skin. As she began to lose consciousness, she felt it rush into her. It forced itself into her mouth and down her throat. She thought it was his tongue for a second, except it was cold and horrible and tasted like death. She gagged and convulsed as her feet dangled above the ground. Her skirt rode up above her thighs as it took her. When Felix was finished, he tossed her to the pavement. Mandy's last clear thought before the lights went out was, *Oh no, my granny panties are showing.*

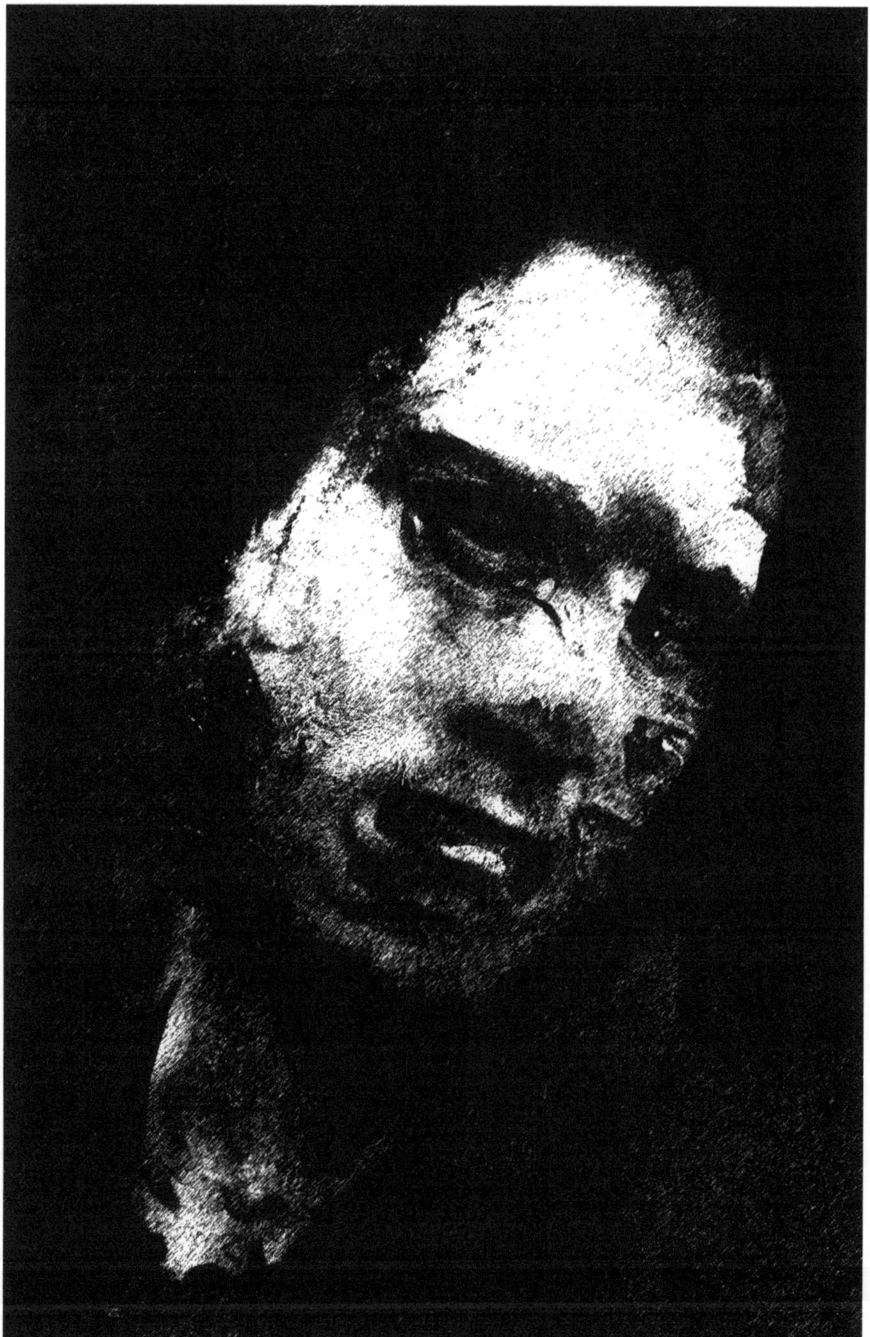

Chapter 12

Billy and Eric had been unable to focus their attention on raking the yard for different reasons. Billy was determined to get back to the top of Mountain Ave to discover what had stalked them last night. And if they happened to run into it, he intended to put a full load of buckshot into the fucker. Eric, on the other hand, just wanted to get Billy off his back. He wasn't interested in returning to the sanatorium, and he damn sure didn't want to run into that thing again. He was only going because Billy was making him. And whether they found it or not, he planned to never go back there again. He prayed they wouldn't find anything.

The Tobin brothers beat on Mick Petrie's front door for nearly five minutes before their friend finally answered, looking like something that had been pulled out of a litter box.

"What's up?" Mick opened the door with dark circles etched beneath his eyes, as if he had just rolled out of bed.

"Whoa, you look like shit," Billy said. "Allison kept you up late, huh?"

"No, man, she left right after you dropped us off." He rubbed his eyes and yawned. "What time is it anyway?"

"Past noon. You just getting up now?" Eric asked.

Mick didn't answer. He squinted at the midday sun and winced.

"Get dressed," Billy said. "We're going back, and you're coming with us."

Mick looked at him the same way that Eric had. He held no desire to go back up the mountain and was about to stand his ground. But he knew it was pointless to argue with Billy. His friend had a severe big brother complex and was used to getting what he wanted. It didn't matter what anyone else said. It was Billy's way or the highway. He was a master at debating and could outlast anyone in an argument. Billy was relentless.

"Man, I just got out of bed, and besides, I feel like shit." Despite his complaining, however, Mick knew he wasn't getting out of it.

"Get dressed and stop acting like a little bitch." Billy pushed his way inside, and Eric followed. A long staircase led to the main floor of the house; wallpaper depicting Revolutionary War battle scenes stretched upward toward the high ceiling. "We have to go back up there to find that thing. I brought the 12 gauge and the twenty-two. We're going to put it down." Billy passed his friend and then stopped; his attention focused on a large red splotch on Mick's neck.

"What the hell is that?" Billy pointed.

Mick reached to touch his neck, but Billy prevented him before he could. "Don't touch it, man. That doesn't look good at all. You got poison oak or something."

"Oh shit," Mick said as he raced up the stairs and headed to the bathroom. "That's all I need right now."

"Where are your folks?" Eric called after him.

"They went to my aunt's house for the week. They won't be back till Friday." The light came on in the bathroom. "Oh, shit! I got fucking poison oak!"

"I told you," Billy shouted from the living room. "Use some calamine lotion and get dressed, for Christ's sake."

A minute later, Mick came out of the bathroom with calamine lotion drying on his neck. Eric walked up to him and checked out the rash, which had already begun to blister.

"Jeez, dude, shit looks nasty. That's a pretty bad case of poison oak, might even be sumac." Eric winced. "Bet it itches like a bear."

"Not really. I didn't even notice until dickhead said something."

"Good," Billy pressed. "Throw some clothes on, and let's get going. We'll wait for you in the car." Billy smacked Eric in the bicep as he headed to the front door. It was Eric's cue to follow and Mick's to get his ass in gear. Once again, Billy Tobin had gotten his way.

THE OJANOX

They filed out of Billy's Charger and stood in the dirt lot of Mountainside Park. Eric studied the sun, which was still high enough in the sky to relieve his apprehension, if only just a little.

"Okay, just to be clear," Eric said. "If we don't find anything, we're outta here. We ain't hanging around, we ain't getting sidetracked, and we ain't staying after dark ... right?"

Billy opened the trunk and removed the shotgun and the rifle. "Stop being such a little bitch and take this." He handed the .22 to Eric.

"I want the twelve." Eric held out his hand.

"I don't think so. This thing will knock you on your ass. Here you go."

Eric reluctantly accepted the rifle and grabbed an extra box of bullets from the trunk.

Mick, who was distracted by the rash on his neck, carried the bottle of calamine with him and obsessively continued to reapply it.

"Okay, let's go," Billy said, shoving extra shells into the pockets of his jacket, and slammed the trunk. A minute later, they set off up the old road.

Autumn had begun to take root on Garrett Mountain. The grass that wove its way through the cracks in the old pavement had turned brown and withered since the summer. Overgrown trees, once trimmed back to the side embankments of the extension, crept in and overhung the road. A good fifty percent of their leaves had turned gold or changed over to a dark burnt umber. Scores of them now littered the broken asphalt. They rattled across the road, swept along on the breeze, sounding like maracas as they danced over the crumbled pavement.

The road leading to the sanatorium looked even worse during the day than it had at night. Giant ruts eroded by the heavy rains and ankle-breaking chunks of loose asphalt littered the entire way. Cracks as big as fists zigzagged like lightning bolts in every direction. In some areas, full trees pushed their way through the blacktop, forcing broken pieces of the road up around their trunks.

Billy, Eric, and Mick carefully navigated the dangerous obstacle course as they made their way up the steep side of Garrett Mountain. They neared the halfway point when Mick started freaking out. He began scratching at the rash on his neck like a mangy dog. "Son of a bitch!" he yelled. "This shit is driving me nuts." He pulled off his jacket, which must have been rubbing up against the poison oak rash, and dug into his neck with his fingernails.

"Easy, dude," Eric said. "You're gonna make it worse. You're scratching it raw."

"Relax, man," Billy tried to calm him. "Let me see that stuff." He took the bottle of lotion from Mick and examined his friend's neck.

"Man, you've really scratched the shit out of yourself." Mick's neck had turned deep red and swelled. The blisters were so pronounced around the perimeter of the rash, Billy thought they almost looked like scales, like something you might see on a fish.

"It's bad, isn't it?" Mick continued to squirm.

"Well, it isn't good, but I never heard of anyone dying of poison oak. Might be sumac. But I think you'll live."

"Gimme that stuff." Mick grabbed the lotion out of Billy's hand and poured it directly onto his neck. Which seemed to help, and he relaxed a bit. After a few more dabs of the liquid, he was ready to continue.

They passed the spot where they had been ambushed the night before. There wasn't any evidence from the encounter other than some freshly kicked up asphalt and the branch Susan had tripped over. Nothing seemed out of the ordinary, although there was hardly anything ordinary about the old deserted road to begin with.

They could see the crest of the hill from where they stood with the sun in front of them, big and bright and shining directly in their faces. Suddenly, a figure appeared at the top of the mountain. Large and intrusive, clearly a masculine presence.

The boys shielded their eyes to get a better look. But the man was completely bathed in the shadow of his silhouette as his figure eclipsed the sun.

"Who the fuck is that?" Eric's voice grew shrill.

"I got no fuckin' idea," Billy answered.

A gust of wind kicked up, rattling a throng of freshly fallen leaves across the boy's path.

"I don't like this, Bill. Let's get the hell out of here." Eric turned to him.

"What the fuck? It looks like that lunatic Butchie Post," Mick said. "Don't ya think?"

"Shit, I hope not," Eric said. "I'd rather run into the demon bird from Hell than that psychopath. Let's go."

But it was too late for that; Billy had already decided to instigate. "Hey, asshole!" Billy screamed at the man. "What the fuck are you doing?" Billy didn't give a shit who it was; he was holding a 12 gauge Mossberg with two in the barrel.

The man didn't reply. He stood there in silence, staring down at them from his vantage point. The figure lifted his arms to the sky with intention, making him look like a cross between Moses parting the Red Sea and an Old West revival showman summoning the rain.

"You got to be shitting me," Mick spat under his breath. "I'm sure that's him. Look at the hair."

Everyone in town knew Butchie Post and avoided the guy like the plague. He was more than dangerous; he was psychotic. Billy squinted to get a better look. The guy sure looked like he had a mullet just like that jerk-off Post did, but it was hard to tell with the sun in his eyes.

The man stood there with his arms raised above his head like a Broadway dancer, and then something happened. The area around his feet started to move. It looked like heat waves rising off the pavement. Only it wasn't nearly hot enough for that, and it felt as if the temperature had even dropped some in the past few minutes.

The asphalt continued to weave in strange hypnotic waves, making it difficult to focus on. Then the illusion spread outward and moved toward them down the mountain.

"Are you seeing this, guys?" Mick asked. "What the hell is going on?"

"I think we better get out of here." Eric held the .22 at the ready.

The road appeared to melt in front of them, twisting and buckling before their eyes. Then, whatever it was started to spread faster, and suddenly, they could hear it. At first, they thought it was the wind. But it grew louder, and the boys realized the sound was coming from the mountain itself. By the time the moving waves descended a third of the way toward their position, the boys could see what it was, and suddenly, the peculiar noise made sense. It wasn't the wind at all. It was a hiss. The road was hissing.

"Jesus Christ!" Billy screamed.

"Are you fucking kidding me?" Eric shouted.

Thousands of snakes covered the road, making their way towards them. The coiling and winding of their bodies had caused the pavement to appear as if it were moving. It had looked exactly like waves. But now the boys could see them clearly enough to make out the individual bodies. Eastern diamondbacks and timber rattlers slithered toward them, mixed with corals, kings, copperheads, cottonmouths, and a horde of other serpents.

The snakes gathered at the maniac's feet at the top of the road, where they entwined around his legs. Their hissing grew louder and more intense as they made their descent; the sound of their rattles and the scraping of their bodies against the blacktop was so loud it drowned out the wind.

Billy turned to the others. "I'm not seeing this, am I?"

"Let's get the fuck out of here!" Eric screamed, and finally, Billy agreed.

It looked like every snake in King County had been dispatched to intercept them. And as impossible as it was to accept, it looked like the lunatic at the top of the hill was controlling them, like he had summoned them with his arms stretched out to the heavens. But that was just too insane to be real.

Billy realized it had been a horrible idea to come back. There was something terribly wrong with Garrett Mountain. "Yeah," Billy cried. "Let's get the fuck out of here!"

Both he and Eric turned to run, then realized Mick still hadn't moved. Eric went back for his friend and grabbed him by the arm, but Mick stood frozen in place, staring up at the man on the hill. Then he pivoted his head and focused on Eric with eyes that had turned solid black. The irises, the pupils, and the sclera looked like coal, as if they had fossilized.

"What the f-fuck, Mick? Are you okay?" Eric stammered, but his friend just stood there gawking at him with eyes as dark as the far side of the moon.

Mick's arms hung slack at his sides, and his bottom jaw hung open as if he were in a catatonic state. A thin line of saliva slipped off his lip and fell onto his shirt. From somewhere deep within his throat, it originated, a low, guttural growl like that of a bear or wolf. It happened so fast, Eric didn't see it coming. Mick lashed out and clamped onto his wrist with the speed and accuracy of a cat. Eric attempted to pull his hand free, but Mick held on with vice-like strength. An ear-splitting shriek echoed off the mountain like an air horn as Mick opened his mouth wider and threw his head back.

Despite how terrified he was and how every nerve in his body screamed at him to run, Eric was unable to move. He could only stand there, transfixed by the beckoning dark of the boy's eyes. It was impossible not to stare at them; they looked as if they were ... moving. The ink wells of Mick's eyes swelled and then pushed outward like they were about to pop from his head. They doubled in size to the point of bursting, and something inside them emerged. Eric watched in horror as a soot-like mist poured forth from Mick's black sockets.

The same strange substance lifted from his friend's open mouth and nostrils. It was dark and dense like the smoke from burning rubber. The cloud spiraled and churned in front of Mick's face as it flowed out of his orifices in a flood.

In a dizzying flash, the dark cloud propelled itself at Eric like a bullet. The boy's head was thrown backward as the toxic mass forced itself down his throat and into his nostrils. At first, he felt his insides freeze. Then his lungs began to burn as if they were on fire. A second later, Eric's shoulders slumped, and the cloud enveloped both of the boys.

Billy watched it happen, unable to say a word. He felt the piercing dagger of guilt slip between his ribs and penetrate his heart. *Eric, no! Don't let it touch you.* He wanted to run to his brother and pull him away from Mick but was too terrified to go near either one of them. *I'm sorry.* The cloud that swirled about their heads darted in furtive circles, making clear its ill intentions. And the first of the snakes had closed in on their position. A large cottonmouth wrapped itself around Eric's boot and coiled at his feet. It was joined by the approaching throng of serpents, which quickly gathered around the boys, attracted by the strange transfer.

Billy found himself drawn in by the swirling smoke, hypnotized by the tendrils that darted around Eric and Mick in a frenzy. Then he remembered he was holding a shotgun. He raised the Mossberg in the direction of the lunatic on the hill. *It has to be that fucking Post asshole.* And the army of serpents reacted in unison; the hoard of vipers raised their heads and struck out at him.

Billy prepared to fire, then felt the first snake dart across his sneaker. He looked down as a large copperhead slid across his foot and turned to strike. He jumped back, but they were everywhere; they covered the road, they wrapped around the other boys' feet, and they were on top of Billy as well. He backed away as even more emerged from the tree line behind Mick and his brother.

"Eric, wake up!" Billy pleaded. But Eric didn't move or was unable to hear him. The snakes pursued. He didn't realize he was crying as he stepped away from the army of reptiles that threatened to cut off his escape. Billy searched for an exit route down the mountain and found none. The serpents blocked the way; they had cornered him from nearly every direction.

Billy jumped when the large rattler struck. He was sure he had been hit, then realized it had only grazed his jeans. He retreated further from where Eric and Mick still stood with the strange smoke swirling about their heads like some demonic halo. Billy was forced back toward the tree line and further up the mountain. He jumped over the reptiles, but they continued to pursue him, separating him from his brother and friend.

The lunatic at the top of the mountain hadn't moved and was now covered in snakes. They hung from his arms and around his neck; they climbed his legs and blanketed the entire road. Again, Billy raised the 12 gauge, and the agitated throng of snakes shot toward him as if they knew his intentions. He turned and fired into the writhing mass of serpents. The buckshot scattered the snakes, but they were immediately replaced by hundreds more.

Eric and Mick turned toward him. The onyx cyclone increased in speed and changed direction. It focused on Billy with intention and purpose as another snake struck and nearly connected. He turned and fled into the woods, where it was considerably darker. Somehow the sun had already begun to set. *How long have I been here?* He ran blindly into the thick, and then he felt it. It bit down hard into his ankle, and Billy screamed. Then another one hit him on the leg; the pain was incredible. Billy fell to the forest floor screaming as dozens of sharp teeth ripped into his flesh.

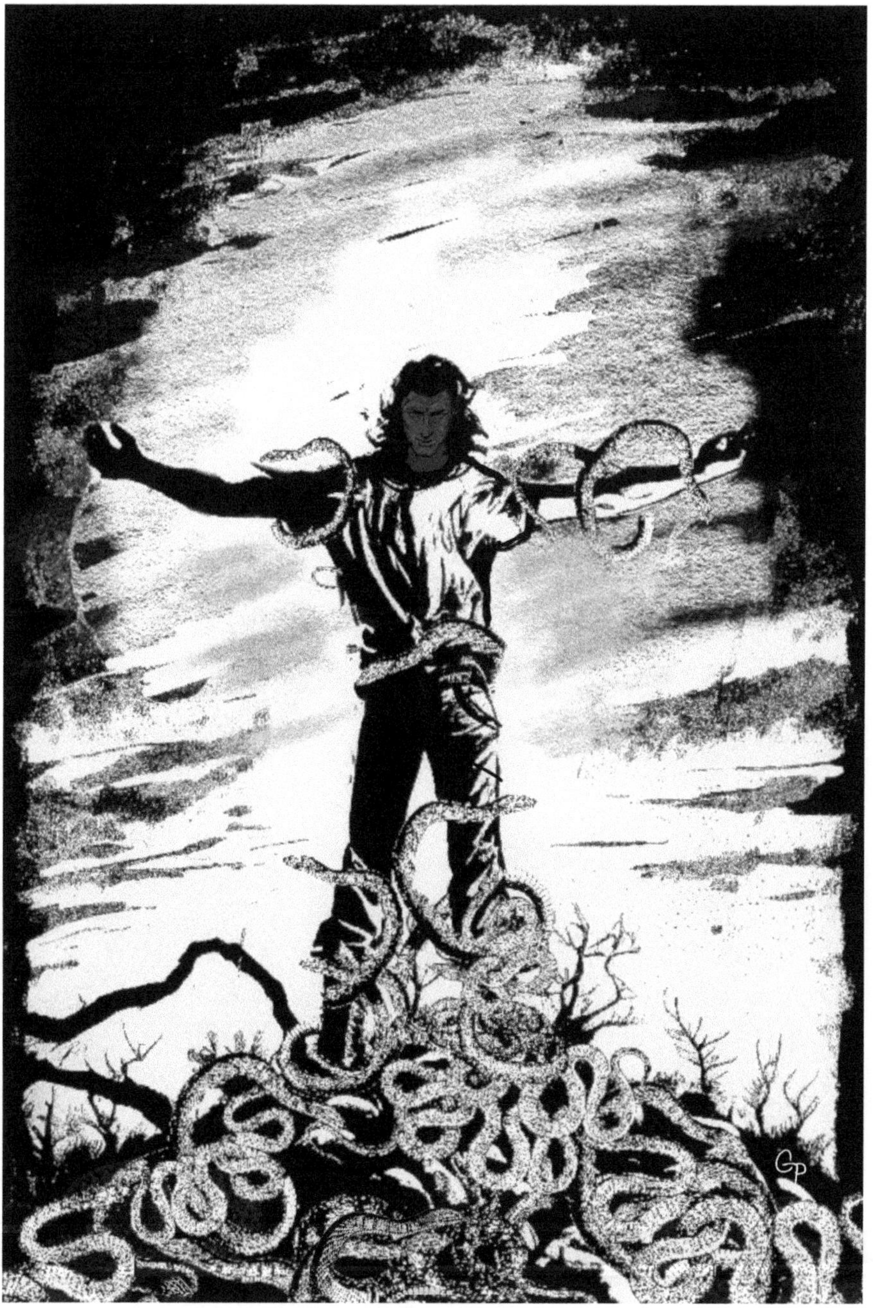

Chapter 13

Father Kieran McCabe blessed himself before the altar in the Our Lady of the Mountain church. Walking below the vaulted ceiling, past rows of solid oak pews, he looked to his right at one of twelve stained glass windows that elaborately decorated the building's exterior walls. Refracted glints of crimson, blue, and gold were cast inward through images of Christ and his Passion on the cross, filling the entire church with a warm, welcoming glow.

Kieran had come to serve the parish exactly ten years ago in August. It was easy to recall because it had been the year of the massive traffic jam on the New York State Thruway. As he was making his way south to Garrett Grove, thousands of young adults were making their way north to a music festival intended to last all weekend long. And the traffic had been at a standstill. If that wasn't enough to make it memorable, the half-naked occupants of the minibuses and convertibles who had taken to flashing their whatnots at him as he passed certainly did. He recalled feeling embarrassed by their lack of modesty.

But that was ten years ago, and he'd been a different priest back then. Of course younger, just twenty-five at the time, but he'd been different in other ways as well. It was a strange time in the world. The war had been at full speed, and men he had grown up with were losing their lives in a country that no one had ever heard of until then. Kieran was only a few years out of seminary school at the time and been serving under Father Michael at Saint Benedict's.

Kieran had answered the call to the priesthood and never questioned the decision, nor had he ever felt that he missed out on anything by doing so. However, during the early years of his service, he lacked the confidence that only came with age and wisdom. He thought a great deal about the men who were risking their lives in Vietnam. The idea of so much death and suffering affected him on a spiritual level, and he came to believe his services might be better met as a chaplain in the armed forces.

Father Michael had listened to the young priest explain the sense of guilt he was experiencing. It didn't seem appropriate for there to be so much suffering while he lived contently, not when he was the one who had taken a vow to do the Lord's work.

"War is not the Lord's work, my son," Father Michael had told him.

"I realize that, Father. But I feel as though my services may be better utilized elsewhere."

Father Michael had been spiritually transitioning young priests for many years and seen nearly every crisis of faith imaginable. There had been similar pleas over a decade ago when men were sent into Korea. "Do you believe the Lord is calling you to the war in Vietnam?"

Kieran allowed the question to resonate. He didn't know for sure but thought it was possible. "I don't know, Father, but I think so."

"Father Kieran, you do realize you would be putting your own life in danger if you were to volunteer your services?"

"I understand, Father."

"I see." The old priest scratched his head and took a sip of wine. "You know you're not on this earth to end suffering? You're here to spread the word of our Lord, Jesus Christ." They both blessed themselves, making the sign of the cross on their foreheads and chests. "There are army chaplains who are trained to deal with what those men are going through. I think it is admirable you feel compelled to answer the call, but I don't see the logic in that path."

"Yes, Father." Kieran was disappointed, but he was not about to overstep his ground and risk angering Father Michael. "I appreciate your consideration in the matter, Father. It has weighed heavy on my heart for some time now."

"Yes, I can see that it has. But perhaps the answers you seek may be found elsewhere." Father Michael finished his glass of wine.

"I don't follow you, Father." Kieran said.

"I spoke with the archbishop earlier this week. There is a small parish in need of spiritual direction. Father Joseph Scott has suffered a heart attack and is not faring well. I believe you know Father Joe?"

"I do. I am so sorry to hear that, Father. Is he going to be all right?" Father Kieran asked.

"He is expected to recover, but it is unlikely that he will be fit to serve the parish in the same capacity."

"That's terrible. Father Joseph has done so much for the diocese. His presence will be sadly missed."

"I should think so." Father Michael poured himself another glass of the sacristy wine. He offered some to Kieran, who passed. The young priest had not yet acquired a taste for it.

"The archbishop is looking for someone to fill Father Joseph's shoes in Garrett Grove, and I believe this may be your calling. I couldn't think of anyone better suited for the job. Of course, I told His Excellence I would discuss it with you. He was concerned you may not be ready for the position, but I assured him you were."

Father Kieran was both embarrassed and flattered by his mentor's confidence in him. "Do you really believe I'm ready for my own parish, Father?"

"Well, my son, I think the real question is: do *you* believe you are ready for your own parish, or do you think you would be more useful in Vietnam?"

Father Kieran didn't have to think about it for long, and that had been the end of his spiritual crisis. He believed he wasn't doing enough, that he might be of better service as a chaplain in Vietnam. But Father Michael presented an alternative and thought Kieran might better service the Lord by leading his own parish. So, he accepted the position.

Father Kieran had made the trip from Utica to Garrett Grove the Thursday before Woodstock. Bumper-to-bumper traffic had shut down the northbound lanes on the thruway, and Kieran was practically the only one on the road traveling the opposite way. Girls with flowers in their hair hung out of the windows of their parked vehicles and waved to him. Some held up signs that read, *Make Love Not War*, and more than a few of the young ladies flashed him as he passed.

It embarrassed him to see the boldness of youth in all its glory exposed on the thruway. But it also filled him with a sense of affirmation. He had made the right decision. There was still work to be done here in America, just as there was work in Vietnam. Father Michael had chosen him for the position in Garrett Grove. A message was delivered in his time of crisis; it had been the work of the Lord.

Kieran watched the young souls stranded on the interstate and became convinced he had been chosen to help and pray for them. He was uplifted during that trip and offered a clearer image of the priest he was truly meant to be. A sense of direction swelled within him, and he felt his confidence grow. He experienced a spiritual awakening.

He wasn't the only one who had been given something that day. Many of those who made the trip to watch Janis Joplin, Crosby, Stills, Nash, and Young, and Jimi Hendrix took away a memory that had nothing to do with sex, or drugs, or rock-n-roll. The children of Woodstock returned home to tell their friends the story of the priest in the Chevy sedan who had honked his horn and given the peace sign to every girl that flashed him.

● ● ●

Sunday morning Mass had gone well, and Father Kieran shared the parable of the Good Samaritan. Our Lady of the Mountain held three services on Sunday: seven, ten, and noon. The ten o'clock service was typically the busiest of the three, with the seven a.m. being the warmup. Noon Mass was usually thin, but today had been slower than expected.

Still, Father Kieran did a fine job and faithfully delivered the message he had been called to do. He blew out the candles on either side of the entrance and exited the modest church through the stained glass front doors. He held his bible in his left hand, dipped the fingers of his right into the holy water, and made the sign of the cross. Allowing the door to swing closed behind him, he walked outside.

A strong breeze gusted, rattling the leaves of the maples in front of Our Lady of the Mountain. The church sat far back on a large piece of acreage situated between

THE OJANOX

Sunset Road and Mountain Ave and had been aptly named for its position in the heart of the foothills of Garrett Mountain. Pines and cedars lined the parking lot, except for a few areas where trails had been cut into the terrain centuries ago. The church was built in the fifties, and the land had been cleared by contractors hired by the diocese. Father Kieran heard that the original builders found a small fortune worth of arrowheads and artifacts during the construction. And to this day, treasure fever still ran high. It was common to see children scouring the woods behind the church, hunting for a trophy they could show off to their friends.

He walked across the parking lot and headed to the rectory, thinking he might enjoy a nice glass of wine. Father Michael would have enjoyed one himself if he were still alive. But sadly, his old mentor passed away last year, peacefully in his sleep. Father Kieran had spoken at the funeral and delivered the eulogy.

As he ascended the steps of the rectory, he paused for a moment. Out of the corner of his eye, a movement in the woods captured his attention. Father Kieran turned in time to see what looked like a hulking shadow darting in and about the trees at the edge of the parking lot. It traveled quick and was hard to follow. It was too fast to be a man and far too big as well.

He stood on the steps of the rectory, waiting. Then it moved again. This time he saw it more clearly. It looked like smoke; it was dark, almost brownish black in color. It was hard to tell exactly how big it was, but judging by how high it stood against the trees, it appeared to be no less than fifteen feet tall. The strange shape darted behind the great pines, passing quickly through some of them. Kieran inhaled deeply and scoured the woods for any signs of fire. He didn't smell anything ... not that he thought he would. By the way it moved, Kieran didn't believe it was smoke at all.

His heart quickened at the sight, and a chill gripped the back of his head just behind the ears. Again, he watched the shadow as it paused for a moment, concealed behind a thatch of fir branches, and then shot into the open, only to disappear behind the next swatch of trees. There was something very wrong about it. There was purpose in the way the form traveled, an intelligence; nothing moved that way by accident. It appeared as if it were ... hunting.

It started out as nothing more than a tremble, just the faintest shake in the very tips of his fingers. But it quickly progressed. Kieran's hands began to move uncontrollably, and then the tremors spread up his arms and settled into his chest.

Fear seized him like a glacier, as if he had been plunged into a bath of ice water. It wrapped around his heart and threatened to stop it where he stood. It was evil, and it was only a stone's throw from his doorstep.

He struggled to pull himself away from the incapacitating fear that gripped him. He made the sign of the cross with sweat-slicked fingers and began to pray. *"Yea, though I walk through the valley of the shadow of death, I will fear no evil."*

Father Kieran preached of such; he warned his parishioners about Satan and the fires of Hell. And although he knew every word of it to be true, he had never witnessed anything malevolent or supernatural. As a Catholic priest, he'd heard of numerous accounts and read even more documentations of possessions and manifestations, but he had never witnessed anything firsthand. Now, gazing upon the presence in the woods before him, he knew he finally had. *"By the power of God, cast into hell Satan and all the evil spirits who wander through the world seeking the ruin of souls. Amen."*

The shadowy figure passed through the forest with furtive intention, then disappeared. Father Kieran prayed as he watched it vanish. "Hail Mary, full of grace," he said as he opened the door to the rectory and rushed inside. He locked it behind him, then proceeded directly to the table with the decanter of sacristy wine and poured himself a full glass. He swallowed it in two gulps and quickly poured himself a second one.

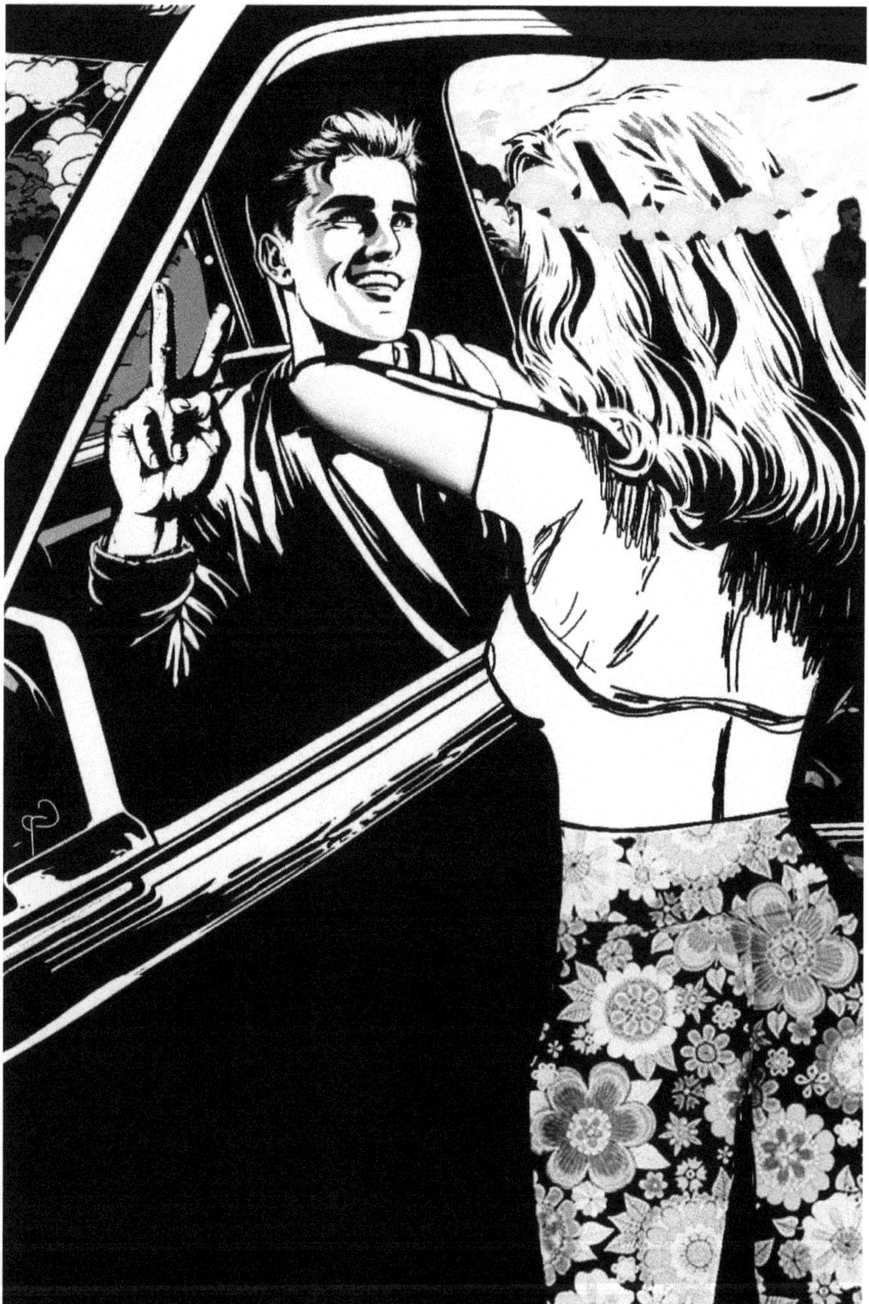

Chapter 14

Deputy Gary Forsyth drove north on Route 3. In another mile, he would reach the Gables Bridge, which spanned the Lenape River, one of only two routes in and out of Garrett Grove. He slowed the cruiser and turned into the front parking lot shared by Wilson's Diner and Goldie's Beauty Parlor. Only a few vehicles were in the lot. He recognized Dick's green Maverick and Dr. Malcolm's Caddy. The old doc had been hitting the diner regularly since his wife had passed away.

Gary was about to make the trek into Warren to look through Felix Castillo's locker at the Con Edison plant. He'd spoken to the man's supervisor and gotten the green light to interview a few of Castillo's coworkers and check his belongings. Warren was the Grove's closest metropolis, but it would still take over an hour to get there.

He entered the diner and saw the old doctor sitting in the corner. "Afternoon, Dr. Malcolm. How are you today?" The aroma of deep-fried potatoes and heart disease hung in the air like a lard-filled piñata.

The doc looked up from his paper and smiled. "Hello there, Deputy. Nice to see you."

Dick noticed the deputy and met him at the counter.

"Deputy Forsyth, what's the good word?" Dick smiled and greeted him.

"Hey, Dick." He nodded. "I was looking for a cup of that jet fuel you been peddling."

"Sounds good. Is that for here or to go?" Dick looked over his shoulder into the back and then lowered his voice. "Mandy's around here somewhere." He winked at the officer.

Gary returned the smile. "That's to go, but I'm tempted to stick around for a couple hours."

"Milk, no sugar, right?"

"You got it."

Dick made the coffee and checked the back again. "Hey, Roger, you want to see what's taking that girl so long? She took the garbage out over fifteen minutes ago."

Roger took his apron off, hung it up, and walked towards the back door, which opened before he got there. Mandy stumbled in, cradling her head in her hand. Her skirt had ridden up her thighs, and her hair was messed.

"What the hell happened to you?" Dick barked.

Mandy lowered her hand to reveal a bruise on her forehead and her lipstick smeared across her cheek.

"Jesus, Mandy." Roger hurried to her side as she nearly toppled off her high heels. He scooped her up and helped her out of the kitchen, into one of the booths. Deputy Forsyth and Dr. Malcolm witnessed the state of the young girl and rushed to her aid.

Dr. Malcolm pushed his way through the group, forgetting he had been trying to distance himself, and knelt beside her. He lifted Mandy's chin and looked into her eyes. She had a nasty scrape on her forehead, and judging by her lipstick, she looked like she had been smooching in the back lot. He held up three fingers in front of her.

"How many fingers am I holding up, dear?"

"Three. I'm fine, Doc. I must have slipped outside by the dumpster." She blinked a couple times. "Really, I'm fine."

Malcolm was unconvinced and continued to examine her eyes as if he wasn't exactly happy with what he saw.

"What the hell happened?" Dick leaned in. "You were out there for over fifteen minutes. You said you were coming right back. And look at you, your lipstick's all smeared."

Mandy blushed. "Oh, excuse me a second, just let me clean up a bit."

"I think you should sit down for a little while," Malcolm told her.

"I'm fine." She pushed her way through the crowd of men and headed to the ladies' room.

Deputy Forsyth remained quiet and took mental notes. Mandy looked like she had been roughed up a bit. He had questions but thought it might be better to ask them in private rather than in front of her boss and the doc. He sipped his coffee and then pulled out his wallet.

"What do I owe you for the coffee?" he asked.

"It's on me, Deputy," Dick replied.

"No chance." He took out a dollar and left it on the bar.

Dick leaned over and whispered to him. "I'll bet she was out there with that lineman guy."

"What guy would that be?"

"The guy that works for the power company," he answered.

Gary raised his eyebrows. "Really?"

"I don't know his name. Freddy or something. Comes in after his shift every morning to flirt with Mandy and eat cobbler. They've been hitting it off pretty good, if you ask me." Dick confided in the deputy.

Mandy exited the ladies' room a bit more put together. She had fixed her makeup, straightened her skirt, and was using a piece of toilet paper to blot the scrape on her forehead.

"So, what the hell happened out there, missy?" Dick asked.

Mandy sat at the counter next to the deputy as Dr. Malcolm studied her.

"It was that guy, wasn't it?" Dick asked. "He was back there, wasn't he?"

Mandy blushed. "Yeah, Felix stopped by, and we talked for a second, that's all."

Deputy Forsyth choked on his coffee and almost spit it across the counter.

"What the hell did he do to ya?" Dick raised his voice. "Did the bastard hit you?"

"No," Mandy answered. "Felix isn't like that. He stopped by to say hi. I kissed him, and then he left. I was petting Scraps, and I think the little kitty must have gotten under my feet and tripped me."

"I told you to stop feeding that fleabag!" Dick shouted.

"Scraps is a good kitty. He's just hungry."

"Does your boyfriend work for the power company, Mandy?" Gary spoke up.

"Yeah, do you know him, Felix Castillo? He's worked for them for like ten years now."

Forsyth stared at the girl with his mouth open. Had he heard right? "Your boyfriend is Felix Castillo, black hair, Italian, works for Con Ed?"

"I just said that. I guess you *do* know him?"

Forsyth got up from the stool. "You said he was just here. Felix Castillo was just here?" Gary Forsyth had been the first officer at the scene to find the body of Felix Castillo face up on the cold pavement at five thirty this morning. So, either Mandy was hallucinating or the entire Sheriff's department had made a colossal mistake. At this point, he wasn't sure which it was.

He walked through the kitchen toward the back door. "Out here?" he asked and stepped outside. It was a small lot with two garbage dumpsters and a small alley separating the diner from the beauty parlor. First, he checked the dumpsters and walked around them. A skittish, orange-colored cat mewed as he passed. Then Gary crossed the lot and entered the alley to find it empty as well. Convinced there was nothing to be found, he returned through the diner's back entrance.

Dr. Malcolm remained at Mandy's side and continued to examine her eyes. "I don't think you have a concussion, but it wouldn't hurt for you to stop by the center and let us take an x-ray of that pretty little head of yours."

"Thanks, Doc. I'll probably come by with Jackie a little later." Mandy smiled. "I think I just want to go back to the apartment and take a hot bath." Mandy and Jackie's place wasn't far, just about a mile back into town.

"I'm not so sure you should be driving, the way you stumbled in here like that," Dr. Malcolm asserted.

Deputy Forsyth was unsure how to proceed. Mandy had to be lying about Felix, and her story about tripping over the cat didn't sound right either. There was something strange going on, and Mandy Griggs was hiding something. That much he was sure of. Still, it was hard to believe she had anything to do with the death of Felix Castillo. The girl just didn't have it in her. But Gary liked the idea of solving the murder on his own. No doubt there would be a promotion in it for him if he pulled that off.

"I'll drive you home, Mandy," the deputy said. "I was just headed up—" he stopped. "You can pick your car up later if you're up to it."

She smiled at him. "Thank you, that's sweet. I guess you're right. I probably shouldn't drive."

"How long ago did Felix leave?" he asked.

"I'm not sure really, my head's still kinda fuzzy. We were only out there for a few minutes, then he left."

"If that creep laid one finger on you, I'll break his legs!" Dick barked again.

"Don't be silly, Dick. Felix is one of the nice ones. He just showed up to say hi, and I gave him a little kiss, that's all."

The deputy studied her as she spoke. There was nothing about her body language or anything he could see in her eyes to indicate she was lying. But the facts were the facts; Felix Castillo was dead, despite the yarn Mandy was spinning. If she was lying, she was damn good at it. Hopefully, he would learn more on the drive. If there was any way to get to the bottom of this, it was by going along with whatever game Mandy Griggs was playing. She would slip up and say something eventually. Gary was counting on it.

"Make sure you have Nurse Gilmartin keep an eye on you until we get that x-ray." Dr. Malcolm smiled. "Doctor's orders, okay?"

"Thank you, Dr. Malcolm. I'm sure I'll be fine." She stood up and wobbled a bit on her high heels. Deputy Forsyth grabbed her and helped her to the door.

"My hero," she said. "Thanks for the help, guys. Thanks, Dick; thanks, Doc; see ya later, Roger." The young dishwasher hadn't said a word. He simply watched as the older men swept in and took care of everything.

"I hope you feel better, Mandy," Roger finally said, but she had already walked out the front door.

"Real smooth, Romeo." Dick snarled at the boy. "Don't you have some pots to wash or something?"

"Yeah, boss." Roger slumped his head and went back to work.

●●●

Dr. Malcolm had been on duty for twelve hours before placing Dr. Ziegler in charge. He didn't want to leave but was running out of steam long before the Richards twins had arrived. At sixty-five, John Malcolm couldn't work the marathon shifts that he used to. He considered retirement a little more this year than he had the year before. But in the end, it had only been a consideration and not a thought he acted on. He wasn't ready to be put out to pasture quite yet; maybe he would feel differently next year.

As much as he hated to leave the medical center, he needed to refuel. A quick bite to eat at Wilson's and a couple hours of rest in his own bed, then he would rush right back and be good to go. That was the plan.

He pulled his Caddy into the driveway. He and Rosie had raised three boys in the house on Midland Ave; now they all had children of their own. John had eight grandchildren, and the two oldest were enrolled at Dartmouth, studying medicine.

Rosie, the love of John's life, had needed her insulin three times a day, and it became more complex as she got older. She'd never been the healthiest of eaters, which drove John nuts. He tried everything he could think of to get his wife to take her health seriously. He didn't keep junk food in the house and had filled the refrigerator with vegetables and healthy snacks. But he couldn't watch over her all day. He knew she was cheating on her diet by her glucose level; the strips didn't lie. He was a doctor, after all. Rosie had a sweet tooth, and eating made her happy. It killed John to feel he needed to deprive her the enjoyment. But if it was going to save her life, he was willing to be the bad guy.

Rosie didn't understand how serious her condition was and refused to listen to John's constant pleading. That was until her right foot had gone gangrene and needed to be amputated. She ended up losing all the toes and several inches of the foot. After that, her disease progressed rapidly, partially due to the challenges of the missing foot but also because Rosie had fallen into a horrible depression.

John divided his time between Rosie and work and even hired a nurse to care for his wife when he couldn't be there. But no matter what he did, it never felt like enough. It tore him apart to think that he wasn't doing everything he could for her. He often thought he might have saved her if he'd left the job and dedicated every waking hour to watching over her. But it was unlikely to have made a difference, and it wouldn't have been good for either of them. There was no saving Rose Malcolm by that point, and John needed the job at the medical center as much as he needed her.

After Rosie died, John immersed himself into work even more. It became his only way of dealing with the loss. He just wouldn't be John Malcolm if he didn't have Chilton. He was the chief of medicine, after all. It was as much a part of him as his white hair. And now he had a new protégée to groom and mold. Ethan Ziegler was talented, but without John's guidance, he was likely to get himself jammed up, one way or another. If the guy was lucky, he would only knock up one of the nurses. But there was always the potential he could mess up on a far grander scale. So, John decided to stick around, at least until he was confident Ziegler could handle things on his own.

Now, he was pretty sure that day had come. John admired the way Ziegler stood up to him about the quarantine. It'd been a good idea to wait twenty-four hours, which allowed John the time to think. There was a lot more involved than he initially considered. He would have crippled the sheriff's department, knocked out the ER staff, and very likely started a panic in Garrett Grove. He was still concerned about the children in the ICU and would be back at their bedsides as soon as he got a few hours' sleep himself. But Ziegler had been right: they needed more information to go on before they did anything, and he was confident the young doctor had things well in hand.

John entered his spacious home and immediately felt the emptiness; it had been like that since Rosie had passed. She possessed a personality that had filled the place. Now it was more than just empty; it was barren. His footfalls echoed off every harsh surface as he made his way up the stairs. John inhaled, certain he could still detect the fading scent of Rosie's perfume. Estee by Estee Lauder; it had been her favorite.

For months after her passing, the fragrance permeated the house. It helped him feel as if she was still there, like he wasn't alone. There had been just a dapple left at the bottom of the bottle, which John continued to spray on her pillow once a week. The flowery intoxication warmed the bedroom with memories of Rosie that waltzed throughout the entire house. It greeted him when he returned home from work, kept him company when he ate his dinners by himself, and filled his dreams with visions of his beautiful wife and the aroma of her sweet perfume, each pump lasting long enough to keep her memory lucid. Then, slowly, it would fade, little by little, till it was barely detectable in the air. At which point, John would remove the bottle from Rosie's nightstand, inspect how dangerously low the contents had become, and repeat the process. Another flowery spray onto the pillowcase where she once laid her head.

It had been over a year since John used up the very last of the perfume, and although he was certain he could still detect the fragrance in the air, it was more of a memory than actually there. Sadly, nothing in this world ever lasted forever, except for maybe memories themselves. John walked down the hall and placed his keys on the dresser. There was enough time for a few hours of sleep. He took off his shoes, laid on the bed, and stared at the ceiling. He hated coming home now that Rosie and the perfume were gone and couldn't bring himself to purchase another bottle. Something about that didn't feel right, almost like cheating. He let out a deep sigh and stretched his hand to the side of the bed where Rosie had slept and placed it on her pillow.

"I miss you, Rosie," he said to the empty room.

Chapter 15

Deputy Gary Forsyth drove Mandy Griggs back to the apartment she shared with Jackie Gilmartin. She sat in the passenger's seat of the cruiser as he made his way down Route 3, obeying the speed limit. It was against departmental protocol to allow occupants to sit up front, but Gary wanted Mandy to feel as comfortable as possible. After all, she'd been dating the guy they found dead this morning and had implicated herself at the diner. Mandy claimed to have been with Felix only moments before the deputy's arrival. Which made her either a witness, an accessory, or completely full of shit. Forsyth was still trying to figure out which one it was. He hoped she might slip up and reveal something but knew there was little chance if she believed he suspected her.

Could it be she's that good and she is completely playing me? He studied Mandy as she checked her makeup in the mirror.

There's no way. No one is that good of an actor.

Still, there was something off about the girl. If she was involved with the death of Felix Castillo, then she had to realize Gary was on to her by now. But she didn't appear nervous, not even a little bit. She was more than convincing.

What the hell are you hiding? Gary wanted to get on the horn with Sheriff Primrose and tell him what he had discovered but didn't dare. He had a better chance of uncovering the truth if he used a bit more discretion.

Mandy shifted in the seat, her skirt riding up her thighs, revealing an eyeful that Gary had a hard time not checking out.

"You say you tripped over the cat in the alley and that's when you bumped your head?" He tried to keep his eyes on the road and study her reactions at the same time.

She pressed her lips and reapplied some lipstick. "Yeah, I think so." She returned the passenger mirror to the up position. "I guess I hit my head pretty good because the whole thing is a little fuzzy right now. But I remember Scraps. I think I fed him today."

"Well, by the looks of it, you hit the pavement pretty hard. You're gonna have a bit of a knot, I'm afraid," he told her.

She looked at him. "Does it make me look ugly, Deputy?" She batted her eyes.

"Not at all. I don't think anything could do that."

Mandy smiled and batted her eyes some more. Gary knew girls like Mandy needed to be complimented a lot and figured it was the best way to proceed with his line of questioning.

"Do you really think so?" she asked.

"Are you kidding? You're probably the prettiest girl in town. Everyone knows that. You must see the way all the guys look at you."

"You're embarrassing me, Deputy Forsyth."

"Well, I didn't mean to do that. I just meant you shouldn't worry about that bump on your head too much. It will go away in a couple days, and no one will ever notice."

She slid closer to him across the cruiser's large front seat. Gary took his eyes off the road for a moment and looked at her; she smiled back at him. His plan was backfiring. Now she thought he was trying to hit on her. *Quick, jackass, change the subject.*

"So, you've been dating this guy from the power company?" he asked.

The question didn't seem to faze Mandy all that much; she continued to smile at him as if he was a late-night snack. Gary's heart raced as his palms went slick against the wheel. He had steered the conversation in the wrong direction and struggled to get it back on track.

"Felix, you said his name was, right?"

"Yeah, Felix, Felix Castillo. He's a nice guy. We went to see *The Amityville Horror* last Saturday at the movies."

"That sounds nice. Did you go to the Warren Drive-in?"

She slid closer.

"Uh-huh." Mandy bit her lip as she answered. "The Warren Drive-in." Her voice had gone raspy, sounding as if she'd just woken up or she was deliberately trying to sound sexier.

Gary was glad the entrance to her apartment was just up on the right. He used the turn signal and pulled into the parking lot.

"You were talking to Felix before you fell by the dumpster?"

"I think we were in the alley," she answered, her voice dreamy and far away.

Forsyth began to feel a bit lightheaded himself. He blinked a few times as he guided the cruiser through the lot and pulled into a parking place.

"You and Felix were in the alley; what were you doing in the alley?" Gary's eyes felt heavy; it suddenly became difficult for him to keep them open. He tried to shake it but was unable. He felt like he had been drugged. *God, did she drug me?* He tried to remember if Mandy had been near his coffee. He thought it was possible. He tried to move his hands, but they were just too heavy.

Mandy slid her body up against him and whispered in his ear. "Well, we were in the alley so Felix could fuck me." She grabbed the deputy's crotch and began to rub him.

Gary couldn't move. A wave of heat washed over him like a shot of morphine. He tried to resist but couldn't; she must have drugged him. He waited for her to remove the pistol from his holster. *How could I have been so stupid?* He had completely underestimated this clever, clever girl.

Mandy pressed her mouth to his ear and slipped her tongue into it. He shivered from the chill that entered him. It felt as if she were penetrating his brain. Bright white light flashed in his eyes as her tongue buried deeper into his ear canal.

Then Mandy unbuttoned his pants and unzipped his fly. Forsyth couldn't tell if he was still breathing. Her hand burned like a cinder as she grabbed him. She took it out and stroked it violently. It was painful yet wonderful at the same time. He was helpless to stop her, not that he entirely wanted to. She leaned forward and put him into her mouth. Her head moved up and down as every muscle in the deputy's body seized. She continued the motion until he began to convulse. She brought him to the edge and then sent him over. Gary experienced the most powerful orgasm he had ever had in his life.

Gary stiffened in excruciating pain as something entered him. It slid into his guts and exploded; it had come from the girl's mouth. His eyes rolled back into his skull as the sensation ripped into him like a blade. Deputy Forsyth passed out as Mandy shared her gift with him, just as Felix had shared it with her.

The girl finished what she had been instructed to do. Then she checked her makeup in the mirror as the deputy sat behind the wheel convulsing with drool spilling from his bottom lip.

Mandy straightened her skirt and exited the cruiser. She let herself into the apartment and walked up the steps.

"Hello, Jackie," she called to her roommate. "I've got something I want to show you." The black onyx of her eyes reflected the hallway light as she made her way to the bedroom where Jackie lay sleeping.

The top of Carl's head lined up perfectly with the hinge of the light above the autopsy shelf. Several strands of what appeared to be Felix Castillo's hair, along with a piece of his scalp, had been caught in the mechanism's retractable arm. Which made no sense. If someone had come into the morgue and removed the body, they certainly would have had to move the light. There was no other way. Burt and Carl remained silent for a moment longer, trying to register the implied impossibility. Carl's analytical mind reached for a tangible rationalization, while Burt's less grounded imagination was off to the races.

"I don't get it," Burt said, finally breaking the silence. "I just don't get it."

Carl swung his legs over the side and hopped off the shelf. Burt handed him his hat. "I've heard you say that sometimes during an autopsy, a cadaver can move on its own. Tell me about that."

A wash of relief softened Burt's face. "Of course. That has to be it. You know, I thought for a second there that old Felix here just kind of—" Burt held his arms and walked a few steps like Frankenstein's monster.

The sheriff held up his hands to stop his friend. "Could we please focus here, Burt? I'm starting to get a headache, and I got a lot on my plate right now."

"You're right. I'm sorry." The coroner lowered his arms. "Well, as a cadaver goes into a state of rigor mortis, the body does a whole bunch of crazy shit."

"Crazy shit, that's the clinical definition?" Carl asked.

"Cadaveric spasms, or postmortem spasms," Burt clarified. "The muscles and ligaments start to contract and tighten. The gasses in the body escape, and, well, it's pretty disgusting. Sometimes, an arm will twitch, and it could even shoot up into the air."

The sheriff nodded his head. "Could a body sit up from a prone position?" he asked.

"It's not impossible." Burt seemed pleased. "That must be what happened."

"That's what happened, huh? Well, during the rigor mortis process, is it common for a body to also climb off the damn table and let itself out the back door?"

"No." Burt knew it was no time to be clever. "Someone had to come in and remove the body."

"That doesn't make a whole lot of sense." Carl squinted. "Who the hell goes around stealing bodies from the morgue?"

Burt figured it was best not to say anything and shrugged his shoulders.

"You know, Burt, I'm gonna have to question your men and get their stories. I don't even know how I am supposed to report this. You have any idea how this will look when I tell the State Police there's been a murder and we seem to have lost the body?" Carl took a deep breath. "Do you have any idea how that looks, Burt?"

"It looks pretty bad."

"It looks terrible." Carl took his cowboy hat off and scratched his head. "On top of this, I got Dr. Malcolm about to quarantine the dang medical center."

"Hold on, what quarantine? You didn't say anything about a quarantine."

"It's not like you gave me a chance. I'm trying to conduct a murder investigation, and I get a call that my medical examiner has lost the body."

"All right," Burt said. "I deserve that. I do. So, what's this about quarantine? What's going on?"

"Well, it's possible I may have exposed you to a virus."

"What?!" Burt shouted. "A virus?"

"Dr. Malcolm isn't sure. He needs to run more tests before he knows anything. But last night, three kids were admitted into the emergency room with similar symptoms."

"What the hell's wrong with them?" Burt asked.

"Thought it was the flu, at first, started a couple days ago. High fever, chills, body aches and pains," Carl explained.

"That sounds like the flu to me."

"There's more. The Boyle kid stopped breathing for nearly three minutes. The doctors were able to bring him back, but he's on a ventilator now. Also, the Richards twins were having seizures, and the little girl started losing her teeth."

"Jesus Christ, Carl. It sounds like those kids have been poisoned." Burt sprinted out the door toward his office.

"Where the hell are you going?" Carl called to him.

"I've come across something like that before."

Carl followed Burt into the office; his friend had removed several books from the shelf next to his desk and began flipping through the pages.

"You really think it sounds like poisoning?" the sheriff asked.

Burt continued to rifle through the pages, not hearing his friend's question.

"You might be able to help out at the center. I'm sure Dr. Malcolm could use all hands on deck. It's not like you have an autopsy to perform at the moment."

"Is there any way the children could have come in contact with the same substance?" Burt asked.

Carl nodded. "I suppose; they don't live all that far apart … Damn! The kids practically live next door to each other."

Burt looked up from the manual with concern on his face. "Where do they live?"

"Oh shit," Carl said under his breath. "The Richards twins live on Mountain Ave, and the Boyle kid lives on Foothills Drive. Their houses are only separated by a small stretch of woods."

"You're shitting me, right?"

The sheriff continued. "I'm not shitting you. We were right in front of the Boyle kid's house this morning. That's where the body was found."

Chapter 16

Before dinner, Troy gave his mother and father a tour of Scream in the Dark. Neither of them had seen the finished project. Lois had been around while the boys were building it but given them their privacy. Don had promised Troy he would assist with the construction, but when the cave was discovered and the shit had hit the fan, he had to go back on his word. He'd been put in charge of the whole cave fiasco, which meant long days and even some night shifts. He swore he would make it up to his son and said he would be there the night of the party. Which was another promise Donald Fischer was unable to keep.

Don's responsibilities at the quarry were already demanding without the added aggravation the recent find presented. He was the geological engineer for DuCain and one of only a handful of men in the state certified in demolitions. The weekly blasting that occurred on-site was executed under Don Fischer's direct guidance and supervision. It was the crux of the process that earned the men of DuCain their bread and butter. Now he had additional responsibilities to contend with. He was in charge of maintaining the integrity of the cavern until the proper authorities arrived tomorrow, and then he was supposed to act as some type of spokesperson-slash-liaison once they did. Don was to give them whatever they needed to make their work easier so they could get the hell off his job site as fast as possible. Which meant more time away from home.

The long hours were only part of what kept Don from his fatherly and husbandly duties. He'd been consumed with work long before the cavern was discovered. Even when he was home, he was never entirely there. Troy had noticed it a little, and Lois quite a bit more.

"You did this all by yourself?" Don asked as the three of them stepped into a room filled with spiders. Standing well over six feet tall, he needed to duck to avoid brushing against the glow-in-the-dark arachnids. Even in his thirties, Don had a baby face and been told more than a few times that he resembled a certain member of the Fab Four.

"Well, Rob helped too," Troy answered.

Don hadn't meant to remind him. "I'm impressed, kiddo."

"Sheriff Primrose thinks I could work in the movie business one day." Troy brightened a bit.

"The movie business." Don lifted his brow. "Is that something you're interested in?"

"I don't know, never thought about it before. Sounds kinda cool, though."

They walked over the rubber hoses on the floor and stepped into the graveyard room.

"Wow," Don exclaimed. "This is something else. I feel like I'm in a vampire movie."

Troy stepped over the small fence and walked up to the coffin lying on the floor.

"I brought them inside and then came over here to investigate. Eric was in the coffin. He grabbed me and pretended to bite my neck. Everyone got so scared, but they couldn't get out because Billy was holding the door shut. It was awesome!" Troy beamed with pride.

"You've got quite an imagination, kiddo," Don said. "You would be a great movie director or producer."

"Director ... producer, what do they do?" Troy looked at his mother.

"I'm not really sure, honey."

"Well, they're the guys in charge of everything. They're the ones who come up with all the ideas," Don told him.

"Oh," Troy looked as if he were concentrating intensely. "Sheriff Primrose said something about being a set designer."

"Sure," Don agreed. "Those are the guys who build the stuff. But I see you as a creator, a thinker. The producers are the real thinkers. You liked *Star Wars*, right? Well, George Lucas produced and directed it. Who do you think thought of R2D2?"

"Steven Spielberg too," Lois added. "He made *Jaws* and *Close Encounters of the Third Kind*."

"Then that's what I wanna be when I grow up. A producer or director like George Lucas and Steven Spielberg. I'll make a vampire movie, but not in black and white. Something super scary with a crazy haunted house in it." A massive grin spread across Troy's face as he explained.

"I'd pay to see that," Don said.

"So would I," Lois agreed. "Say, who's ready for dinner?"

"I am." Troy was always ready to eat and had been growing out of his clothes a little too quick for Lois's liking. She wished he could stay young for just a bit longer.

"Why don't you go get washed up, and your father and I will follow you in a second," she said.

Troy ran out of the garage and left Lois and Don in the graveyard. She folded her arms and looked at him.

"This is where I found them. It was horrible. Rob was having a seizure. I thought for sure he was going to die." She paused, then added: "You really should have been here."

Don shook his head and exhaled deeply. "You know I can't help it, Lois. Old man DuCain put me in charge of the whole site. This damn cave fiasco has my hands tied. They need me up there a little more these days."

"What about us? We need you too. Troy needed his father's help; this was so important to him."

"He did a pretty good job on his own. I'm sure Troy understands." Don raised his hands and shrugged. "He's fine."

"Don't be so sure about that. Rob nearly died last night, and he isn't out of the woods yet. Trust me, Don, Troy isn't fine."

"I didn't mean it like that," he tried to explain. "Believe me, I wish I could have been here. But things are crazy right now. What do you want from me?"

There it was. They were the exact words he used years ago back in college. Lois had been infuriated then and wanted to tear his eyes out. *"What do you want from me?"* he had asked her. The memory made her want to slap him still today.

Lois Middleton met Donald Fischer at Penn State during the spring of 1969. He had been working towards his master's, studying geosciences, and tutoring math to make a little extra cash. Lois was an English major working towards a degree in literature. When it came to prose and composition, she was a wiz, but she had taken statistics as one of her electives and was lost in the class. Her professor had recommended she either find a tutor or accept the statistical probability she might fail the course.

She saw a bulletin board in the student lounge with a list of tutors and took down a few numbers. Donald Fischer had agreed to help her with her math. The first thing she noticed about the boy was how much he looked like Paul McCartney, with his shaggy Beatles haircut and pretty boy complexion. She felt guilty for thinking he was cute since Carl was still her boyfriend, even though he was miles away in Garrett Grove.

They met three times a week to study statistics and probabilities. Donald was funny and made her laugh, and Lois had begun to receive passing grades, thanks to his tutelage.

The war in Vietnam was in full swing, and it was common to see organized rallies on campus. Also, there was a large population of kids being referred to as hippies. Lois and Don didn't exactly fit that category despite Don's long hair. But they did enjoy the music played at the bars on campus and some of the local bands.

He asked her out one Friday night; his friend's band was playing in Altoona. At first, she declined, but Don wouldn't take no for an answer.

"Just a friendly date," he said. "I swear, I'll be a perfect gentleman."

He was very charming, and Lois had to admit she really did want to go. So, she agreed to join him.

They made the drive to Altoona and enjoyed the show. The band played songs from Jefferson Airplane, Grateful Dead, and Jimi Hendrix. They drank Yuengling beer, which was brewed right there in Pennsy, and they had a great time.

Lois felt guilty being infatuated with the cute senior. But she couldn't help it. And somewhere between the beer and the music, she stopped thinking about Carl. She told herself it was because she'd been drunk; that's why she had slept with Don. At least that's what she told herself the first time. The second time she couldn't use that excuse. Then she said it was because she was lonely. After that, she stopped making excuses. By that point, she was just having fun.

She enjoyed her Friday nights with Don and had started to avoid Carl's calls. But Lois felt horrible and completely torn. She loved Carl; he had been her first, and they had planned a future together. But Don was intelligent, had dreamy eyes, and was a respected senior on campus; when she was with him, she felt respected too.

They had sat in the front seat of his car one night, smoking cigarettes and drinking Yuengling. "What are your plans after college?" she asked him.

"Well, after graduation, I think I'll take a couple months off to travel a little, you know, see the country a bit."

She rested her head on his shoulder and listened to his heartbeat. "I mean after that, what are your plans for the future?"

"Oh, that's easy. I'm applying to the Yosemite Geological Society in California to study the fault line and tectonic shift."

"I have no idea what you're talking about," she said and kissed him.

"I don't expect you to," he said. "It's just more boring geology stuff. Not very exciting at all, at least not to most people. Guess I'm a nerd."

"Maybe a little, but that's okay." She rubbed his chest hair. "What else? Do you see yourself getting married or having kids? I bet you'd make a good father."

"Na, not me," he said. "I need to focus on my career and get on my feet before getting married. I feel like I need to do things in the right order. First, make money, have the career and the house. At least, that's the plan."

"That makes sense," she said. It was then Lois realized their relationship had been nothing more than a college fling. Don hadn't been all that serious about her, and although she'd been infatuated with him, that was probably all there was to it. She enjoyed the time they'd spent together but suddenly felt guilty for dating him behind Carl's back. That's when she decided she would stop seeing Don.

Two weeks later, Lois found out she was pregnant. She cried for nearly a week straight before she built up the nerve to talk to Don about it. She didn't know how he would react; actually, she had a good idea and was regretting it. She didn't expect anything from him and was pretty sure that's how he would want it as well. Still, he was the father, and he deserved to know.

They met at the student center; it was where he first agreed to tutor her.

"Lois, how have you been?" he greeted her as he sat down.

She faked a smile and gave him a peck on the cheek. "I've been better, to tell you the truth."

"What's wrong?" He looked concerned and took her hand.

Lois sat there trying to find the words and braced herself for his reaction. She had cried so much over the past week and could feel she was about to start again. She held it in for as long as she could, then burst into tears.

"What's wrong, honey? Tell me." His voice almost comforting.

"I'm sorry, don't hate me," she said. "I—I'm pregnant, Don." She hadn't felt any better.

He sat there with his mouth open as if he were waiting for a fly to come along and land on his tongue. His face had gone white as he stared at her.

"Please say something."

"Um, you're sure?" he asked awkwardly.

"I'm sure."

"It's mine?" Lois glared at him. "I mean, of course it's mine, I just ... well. How did this happen?"

She gave him the same look. "I think you remember how it happened. You were there."

"I-I know how it happened, but I thought we were careful. We made sure, you know."

"These things aren't a hundred percent. There's always a chance. I guess this is one of those times." She watched him fidgeting in his chair. *This is horrible.*

"So, what's next?" He looked at her as if she should have it all figured out by now.

Lois hated him for that. She didn't expect anything from him. She just thought the right thing to do was tell him she was going to have his baby. She immediately regretted the decision. "I don't know what's next," she snapped. "I go back to Garrett Grove, and I raise my baby. That's what you usually do with them." She continued to cry.

"What about ... um, you know," he said under his breath.

THE OJANOX

"An abortion?!" she shouted, attracting the attention of over half the students in the center.

Donald's face turned beet red, and he motioned for her to keep it down.

Lois lowered her voice. "I'm not getting an abortion from some backstreet butcher. I would never. I am going back home, and I am going to have my baby. I just thought I should tell you, that's all."

"What do you want from me?" he asked, and she had hated him even more. *How dare you put that on me, you bastard!*

"I don't want anything from you, Donald," she hissed, then stood up and walked out the door.

"Lois, wait." He ran after her. "Wait!" He caught up and stopped her. "That came out all wrong; you caught me off guard, that's all." Lois turned on him, ready to strike. "Look, I'm not going to let you run off, and I'm not going to leave this all on your shoulders. This isn't just your responsibility."

"Stop, Don. You don't want this." She offered him the out; all he had to do was walk away.

"Don't tell me what I want, Lois. I can't let you do this on your own. That's my baby too." Donald took her hand and pulled her close.

"Don't do this." She allowed him to comfort her. And then she allowed him to make an even bigger mistake.

Lois agreed to marry Donald Fischer even though she knew he didn't love her and doubted she had ever loved him. It seemed like the right thing to do for the baby. She would finish the semester and then return to Garrett Grove. Donald would stay and finish out the year and graduate with his degree. Then they would get married and find a house somewhere close to her parents. It wasn't the way she had planned for her life to end up, but it was still a plan. It had all been so difficult up until that point, but the hardest thing she would ever have to do was still ahead of her; she had to tell Carl. She owed him the truth.

She called him and had been straight with him, for the most part. She told him about the baby and about Donald in not so many words. But Carl had asked her questions she simply couldn't answer. He asked if she loved Donald, and she had remained silent. She couldn't say yes; it would have been a lie. But she couldn't tell him no either. She knew Carl would have tried to talk her into coming home and letting him support both her and the baby. And she couldn't let him do that. She had already hurt him enough. In the end, she never said a word, and allowed

Carl to think what he would. She wasn't sure if it was the cruelest thing she'd ever done or the kindest.

Lois made the trip home the same weekend a certain young priest was making his way down the New York State Thruway. Neither of them ended up where they thought they would. Lois Middleton Fischer and Father Kieran McCabe had discovered the same thing in very different ways, that no matter what your plans might be for the future, God's plans would always come as a surprise. There was nothing a little girl from Garrett Grove or a priest from Utica could do to change that.

Don graduated with his master's degree, moved to Garrett Grove, and married Lois. He got a job as a geological engineer for DuCain Industries and never made it to Yosemite. Troy was born later that year and quickly became the apple of his mother's eye. He had been a breech baby and nearly killed Lois on the way out. She'd been unable to have any more children afterward, which may have had a little to do with the incredible bond between the two of them. Troy had her blue eyes and sensitive heart, and he inherited Donald's intellect, which was a good thing, but other than that, he was a momma's boy.

Don loved Troy just as much as his wife did, but he wasn't the most affectionate of fathers. It just wasn't how he'd been raised. And since Don spent his days at work while Lois stayed home with Troy, it was only natural the boy would have a stronger bond with his mother.

Now, standing amidst the cardboard graveyard of Scream in the Dark, Lois stared at Don with her arms folded and her face turning redder by the second. "What do I want from you?" she repeated. "I want you to act like you give a shit about your son and spend some time with him. That's what I want from you."

"I am doing everything I can to keep a roof over our heads and food on the table." Don counted his sacrifices using his fingers to accentuate his point. "I go to work every day so you can be here when Troy comes home from school. I can't help that it keeps me from being around the house. I got responsibilities." His voice rose to a shout.

THE OJANOX

"Rob could die. Do you have any idea what our son is going through right now?" Lois threw her arms up in the air. "I guarantee, Troy is not fine. He might act like he is okay, but he doesn't know what to think. Rob is his best friend, has been since his first day of kindergarten. Could you at least act like you care?"

Don took a defensive step backward and attempted to make peace. "I don't want to fight here. I'll talk to him, all right?"

But Lois wasn't hearing it. It was always the same story. "Just talk to your son and spare me the bullshit!" she shouted.

●●●

Troy heard his parents from where he stood outside the garage. They were fighting about him again; it seemed like every time they fought, his name was brought up. He knew it was his fault that they were having such a hard time getting along but had no idea what he had done. *Maybe it's my grades. I swear I'll clean my room when you ask. Please stop fighting.* A hundred different reasons presented themselves; not one of them even came close to identifying the root cause of his parents' problems. Troy wiped the wetness from his cheeks and listened as they continued to yell at one other.

"Rob is his best friend, has been since the first day of kindergarten." The voice of his mother carried to where he stood in the driveway.

No!

He knew Rob was sick, but not for a minute had he thought his friend could actually die. The tears came faster and harder. *Rob can't die.* They had known each other for as long as Troy could remember; he was his best friend, his only friend, and had been since …

Troy remembered that very first day of kindergarten. It was so long ago, and he had been so little. It was hard to recall all the details. The conversation about school was something his mother had kept bringing up, and he remembered feeling excited about the idea of it, at first. Then the day finally arrived and all the fear along with it. He had never been away from his parents without at least the comfort of his grandparents to fill the void. The idea of it suddenly became a very scary reality.

Lois had dressed him in what she called his school clothes and fussed over his hair till she finally said it was perfect. She let him sit in the front seat of the car like a grownup, which made him feel important. Then they pulled up to a big yellow building that Troy had never seen before, and panic started to set in. She held his hand as they walked through the front doors into an enormous hallway; the ceiling was so high it made Troy feel tiny, like an insect on the sidewalk. The place smelled funny too, like the stuff his mom used to clean the bathroom, which made him even more uneasy.

There were other people there as well, looking at him, watching what he and his mother were doing. A woman and a little girl walked ahead of them, then disappeared behind a large door. A moment later, the woman exited alone, holding a tissue to her eyes, trying to hide the fact that she was crying.

His mom had looked down at him, smiled, and squeezed his hand, but it didn't give him the confidence it was intended to.

He recalled the door opening onto what appeared to be an army of people. There were long tables set with small chairs lining either side. Little boys and girls packed into the room accompanied by their mothers, and everyone was talking at once.

"You must be Troy," a pretty woman said to him.

He nodded yes but was too overwhelmed to speak.

She bent down closer to eye level. "I'm Miss Boriello, and I am going to be your kindergarten teacher. It's very nice to meet you, Troy." She had long brown hair and wore a kind smile, and Troy liked her already, which put him somewhat at ease, but he was far from comfortable.

Miss Boriello and his mother exchanged a few words, and his mom nodded. Then she led Troy to an empty seat next to where a young Robert Boyle sat talking to his mother.

"Hi, my name's Rob. What's yours?" the little boy asked.

"T ... Troy," he replied.

"Don't be scared, Troy," Rob said. The boy seemed awfully grown up, and Troy liked that. "My mom said we're going to get cookies and juice later."

Troy wondered why his mother hadn't told him about the cookies. That was probably why everyone in the room was so excited. Overstimulation made his head spin; the scene was a cross between a parade and a circus, with children talking over one another and mothers struggling to be heard above the commotion.

THE OJANOX

That was when Miss Boriello walked to the front of the room and spoke. "Mothers, it's time." And the moms reacted as if it had been rehearsed. Lois bent down and wiped her cheeks.

"I love you, honey. Have a great first day of school. I'll be back in a couple hours." She kissed him and slowly walked to the door along with all the other mothers.

What's happening? Alarms went off in his head. *What?* She was leaving him here with all these strangers? She couldn't do that. "Mommy, no!" he cried as she walked out the door wiping her eyes.

The last of the mothers left, and the place erupted like a volcano. Children jumped up and chased after them. They pounded on the giant door as Troy sat in his seat, frightened and confused. Most of the kids began to scream and cry, but he was still unable to move. He looked to his right and noticed the boy named Rob had remained in his chair as well. The vivid memory became a snapshot image seared in his mind. It would never leave and was probably the cornerstone of what would make Troy Fischer and Robert Boyle inseparable best friends.

Miss Boriello stood silent at the front of the room and allowed the pandemonium to ensue for several moments. Then, she began to rummage through a brown grocery bag sitting on her desk.

Troy couldn't remember if he had cried but was pretty sure he had. He was overwhelmed by the panic going on around him but was comforted by how Rob handled it. That was probably the only reason Troy didn't freak out.

Rob sat with his hands folded, a perfectly behaved little boy, while the other kids in the room went ballistic. He appeared unfazed by the insanity that threatened to rip Troy from his chair at any moment. Then, something happened that Troy would never forget. A single tear rolled down Rob's cheek and clung to his chin for a moment. It wasn't followed by a second or a third, and Rob made no attempt to wipe it away. Even to Troy's five-year-old perception, the moment struck him as significant. And from that day on, Troy Fischer and Robert Boyle were as thick as thieves; neither hell nor high water could keep them apart.

Miss Boriello had set up paper plates and called out over the cacophony, "Who wants chocolate chip cookies?"

The screaming ebbed to a dull roar. The children had something else to focus on. And that was Troy's memory of his first day of school. Chocolate chip cookies,

Rob Boyle, and a single tear. It was a memory that would last him the rest of his life.

Chapter 17

Ethan Ziegler sat in his office staring at the toxicology results. All three cases yielded identical conclusions: bloodborne pathogen. The children had ingested the same contaminant, a poison that infected the blood. However, this poison was unlike any he had seen before. It possessed the qualities of a parasitic bacterium, along with some other anomalous attributes as well.

The only good news: it wasn't an airborne contagion. The contaminant had to enter the body through either an exchange of fluids, transfusion, or ingestion. As far as he could tell from the blood work and the lab results, there was no need to worry about an outbreak. Which didn't make him feel much better. He still had no idea what the children had gotten into and no clue how to help them. Antibiotics were doing little if anything to fight the bacteria. But their fevers had gone down somewhat, and none of the patients had experienced any more seizures throughout the day, which was a good sign. Perhaps they simply had to let their own metabolism do the job. That was if their immune systems didn't kill them first. At the rate their white blood cells were attacking the red, it was amazing they were alive at all. Ziegler still had no answer as to how their organs had mutated at such a rapid rate. And although the threat of quarantine was over, the children's struggle to survive had just begun.

Dr. Malcolm woke precisely two hours after he had fallen asleep. He showered, had a cup of coffee, and was back at Chilton before the sun set. He passed through the emergency room, greeted his staff, and checked on the new arrivals. There had been only one; Denny Birch arrived with a Hula Popper fishing lure firmly attached to the side of his head. The man had spent Sunday afternoon fishing the banks of the Lenape River under the Gables Bridge when he hooked a decent-sized brook trout. He attempted to set the hook and jerked the line a bit too hard, yanking the lure completely out of the fish's mouth. The Hula Popper rocketed like a guided missile, out of the water and right back at him. Four out of six hooks now pierced the man's cheek and forehead. Denny claimed he wasn't in any pain. The Jack Daniels he'd been drinking since eleven a.m. may have had something to do with that. It also might have played a part in his momentary loss of muscular coordination as well.

Dr. Freedman, a gangly man with coke-bottle glasses, was busy removing the lure when Malcolm passed through the ER. He stopped and looked while Freedman snipped one of the hooks with a set of pliers. "Catch anything today, Denny?" Malcolm asked.

"A couple. You should have seen the one that did this to me, had to be close to five pounds, Doc," the man slurred.

"Ahh, the one that got away. Well, there's always next week." Dr. Malcolm continued his rounds. "Carry on, gentlemen."

The place was quiet, which was typical for a Sunday evening. Dr. Malcolm nodded to the nurse at the front desk, who was relatively new and filled in for Nurse Gilmartin on her nights off. He entered the hallway and headed directly towards Dr. Ziegler's office. A young candy striper turned the corner as he passed the lab. The sound of the girl's shoes squeaking on the freshly buffed floor echoed off the walls. He finally arrived at his destination and walked into the office. The young doctor sat at a desk with several reports in front of him.

"Dr. Malcolm, I'm glad you're here." Ziegler stood up and shook the chief's hand.

"So, what have we got, son?" Dr. Malcolm asked. He took a seat in front of the desk, and Dr. Ziegler returned to his own.

"Well, take a look at this, sir." He handed a clipboard to the old doctor. "I've run the blood and toxicology, and I think we've narrowed it down a bit."

Dr. Malcolm removed a pair of bifocals from his coat pocket and looked at the front page of the clipboard. He studied it for a long moment in silence. Then he flipped to the next page and examined that as well. "Any idea what type of toxin they ingested?" he asked.

"That's where things get a bit strange, I'm afraid." Dr. Ziegler handed him another report. Malcolm studied it.

"Parasite?" He turned back to the blood work. "I don't feel very relieved. I'm glad to hear it isn't a virus, but this is rather inconclusive. A bacterial parasite doesn't mean the community is safe from infection. Granted, they would have to come in contact with the same substance or source as the children. Which means we need to figure out where these kids have been in the past week."

Dr. Ziegler rubbed his eyes. He'd been on the floor for over twenty-four hours and only gotten a few minutes sleep here and there. "I've been working on that and was about to go talk to the parents. But I wanted to have some answers before I did, and I wanted to talk to you first. I thought about asking Burt Lively to check out the school tomorrow, and then get permission to check out the kids' bedrooms. They could have picked up something in the classroom or on the playground."

"If that were the case, I think we would have a lot more than three sick kids. But it couldn't hurt." He looked at his young protégée. "You look like hell. When was the last time you slept, Doctor?"

Ziegler leaned back in his chair and attempted to stifle a yawn. "I had a few winks here and there, but I've been on the floor for over twenty-four hours now."

"I appreciate your dedication, Dr. Ziegler, but I think you better go home for the night. I'm sorry I left so much on your plate; I couldn't have trusted anyone else to get the job done. I knew I could count on you."

Ziegler did a double take. "Thank you, Doctor. But we're still far from knowing what's going on here. I could stay a bit longer and help out."

"Absolutely not! You're no good to anybody half asleep. Now go home and get some rest. That's an order. Dr. Freedman and the rest of the staff are here. I'll check in on the kids and talk to the parents. Then I'll call Burt first thing in the morning and see what his schedule looks like." Dr. Malcolm stood up and opened the door.

"Are you sure, sir?" Ziegler asked.

"Absolutely; see you tomorrow, son." He exited and turned down the hall toward the ICU.

●●●

Carl steered the cruiser north toward the Richards house on Mountain Ave with Burt sitting next to him in the passenger seat. The body of Felix Castillo had disappeared from the medical examiner's office in broad daylight, and there was no explanation other than the possibility it had been stolen. It was a slim possibility at that, but Carl didn't rule it out since it was almost Halloween. He'd seen teenagers do some pretty stupid things this time of year, although nothing quite as bizarre as messing with the dead. At the moment, it was the only working theory.

Carl picked up the radio handset and spoke. "Sheriff Primrose to base. Come in, Tara." He let go of the button.

"This is Andrea, Sheriff. Tara went home an hour ago. I've been trying to reach you for a while. I guess you were away from your radio." Andrea Geary was the night dispatcher and relieved Tara Jefferies at five o'clock on Sundays. *Jeez, is it that late already?* He had been running around like a one-legged man in an ass-kicking contest all day and barely had time to eat the sandwich Burt shared with him at the lab.

"I didn't realize it was so late. What's up, Andrea?"

"We've had two separate calls in the last hour. One from Sarah Negal and the other from Beth Campbell. Their sons went out earlier today on their bicycles and were supposed to be home hours ago."

"Well, it's not like the kids even missed dinner yet. I wouldn't be surprised if they lost track of time and are out playing somewhere. They'll find their way home as soon as they get hungry."

"I suppose you're right, Sheriff. I said the same thing." Andrea's voice broke up. "I told them I would contact you and let you know about the missing boys."

"They're not missing, Andrea," he corrected her. "It hasn't even been a full afternoon yet. Trust me, boys have a way of losing track of time, especially at that age. What grade are they in?"

"I believe Jeff and Tommy are in the fourth grade." Burt looked at Carl. The Richards kids and Robert Boyle were in the fourth grade as well.

"Well, like I said, I'm sure the boys will be walking through their front doors any minute. Who's on duty tonight?"

"That's the other reason I was trying to get a hold of you, Sheriff," Andrea said, her voice breaking up again. She had a habit of putting her mouth too close to the microphone. Every time she did, her voice cracked and distorted. At least she didn't say "over" after every sentence like Tara did. She continued. "Deputy Rainey and Deputy Kovach are on tonight, but that's not why I was calling. Deputy Forsyth was en route to the Con Ed plant in Warren to check out a lead on the Castillo case."

The Sheriff waited for her to continue. *Maybe it would be better if she did say over.* "Is there anything else, Andrea?"

"I haven't been able to get in contact with him for a few hours now. He doesn't answer his radio, and I even tried him at home. No luck there either."

"Did you try reaching him at the power plant?" He figured the answer was yes but still had to ask.

"That's the thing, Sheriff. He never showed up at the plant. He told one of the supervisors he was on his way. But I called up there an hour ago, and he never made it." The static stopped when she released the button on the mic.

Carl looked at Burt; neither man said a word. He wondered if he'd gotten the dates mixed up and it was April Fool's and not the week before Halloween. Burt looked out the passenger window and pretended not to listen.

"I'm sure Gary will show up at the station or the plant any minute now. Keep trying to reach him. I'm with Burt Lively, and we're on our way to the Richards residence on Mountain Ave to check out a lead."

"A lead? On the Castillo case, Sheriff?" she asked.

He thought about the coincidence of the murder victim being found outside the home of Robert Boyle and the strange illness that had afflicted the children. "I'm not sure yet, Andrea. I'll let you know if I find something," he paused, "over," then replaced the handset.

The sun was low in the west, and the sky had just begun to turn purple. It would be dark soon, which would make it next to impossible to find anything.

Carl looked across the cab of the cruiser at his friend sitting in the passenger seat. "I'm not sure what we're looking for here, Burt. Do you think we're just going to stumble across whatever made those kids sick?"

"I don't know. But I'll bet all three of them play in those woods. I've always found in forensics to look for commonalities. If you ask me, the foothills that separated the Boyle and Richards houses are a pretty big commonality."

Carl smiled at his friend. "You wait till now to start making sense." He pulled the cruiser over to the side and parked near the Richards' driveway. He decided to enter the woods from the Mountain Ave side rather than Foothills Drive, due to what had taken place earlier that morning. He didn't want to raise any eyebrows and wanted to avoid answering any unnecessary questions from the neighbors. They exited the cruiser and cut through the yard, then took one of the paths into the foothills.

Dr. Ethan Ziegler felt guilty about leaving the center but was grateful Dr. Malcolm let him go; he was exhausted and had nearly fallen asleep at the wheel on his way home. But despite how tired he was, he had every intention of taking a quick shower and calling Jackie Gilmartin as soon as he freshened up.

The hot water hit him like a deep tissue massage, peeling away the past twenty-four hours like the skin of an onion. He sat on his bed in his bathrobe with plans of seeing the young nurse. But Ethan Ziegler never made it to the phone. He stretched out on the bed and was asleep before his head hit the pillow.

As Ethan Ziegler was closing his eyes, Erin Richards was opening hers. What had once been a normal ten-year-old girl barely looked human at all. Most of Erin's hair had fallen out; her long blonde locks lay beside her head on the pillow. Her skin hung loose on her face in flaps that resembled gills, sagging beneath her eyes and cheeks and the sides of her neck. It had lost its elasticity and no longer fit the child's face.

The eyes that stared up at the ceiling were as black as obsidian, with a secondary set of lids that blocked out much of the UV light from the overhead fluorescents.

The girl's lips had pulled back and grown thin, and her jaw had dislocated and dropped, allowing her mouth to hang open in an oval. It had only been an hour since the nurse checked on her, but most of the changes had occurred within the past fifteen minutes. Erin was mutating into something, and the process wasn't quite finished yet.

Sharp teeth erupted from her mouth like tiny arrowheads. A thick, black fluid coated them at the gum line as if she had begun to bleed oil.

The presence scanned the room, assessing every detail, taking in its surroundings. With every soul it devoured, it gained more knowledge. It consumed the essence of Erin Richards and assimilated her consciousness. Everything she had ever been was as much a part of it as the shaman of the creatures who had called themselves Lenape. All the beings it had consumed throughout the course of its lifespan were absorbed with one sole focus: evolution. Every thought and every memory of their fleeting existence added to its potency. It fed, it controlled them, and then it assimilated.

The creatures of the past had referred to it by many names. It had been called Nue and Vetala. Names like Penanggalan, Almesty, Ah Puch, and Ahk-Mah had been used, and more recently, the ones called Lenape had referred to it as Mantantu. It searched the minds of its new acquisitions; did they have a name? The one called Tommy had been thinking of one before it was consumed. The Jeff-creature had been thinking the same. They thought of the name as it ravaged them; they had called it ... Ojanox.

Every race had given it a name when their own existence was near an end. This civilization would call it Ojanox. It was pleased with this identity.

It searched the thoughts of Erin Richards and instructed her. The strange creature sat up and pulled the IV needle out of its arm. It studied the machines that monitored the child's vitals and focused its power at them. The heart monitor stopped working, and the other devices turned off as well. The Erin-creature threw her bare feet over the side of the bed. She had work to do.

Chapter 18

The sky had just begun to darken as Carl and Burt entered the woods behind the Richards house. They followed one of the dirt paths that had been cut into the foliage centuries ago by the Lenni Lenape Indians. The entire state had been home to the Lenape tribe, who believed Garrett Mountain possessed a divine connection to the spirit world. Burial sites were constantly being discovered in the Grove, and the kids in town were always turning up arrowheads.

Carl Primrose grew up in Garrett Grove and had scoured these very woods as a child. He played Davey Crockett and pretended he was Roy Rogers on the same path he and Burt now walked on.

The sun sank lower in the western sky, and long shadows stretched out before them. Carl removed a flashlight from his belt and focused the beam on either side of the path.

"What do you suppose we're looking for, Burt?" Carl turned to his old friend, who was only inches behind him. "Jeez, give me a little room, would ya."

"You got the only flashlight, and I don't want to fall and twist an ankle. I'm having a hard enough time keeping up with those long legs of yours." Burt stayed right behind the sheriff.

"Well, try not to trip me in the process," Carl told him. "Any idea what we're looking for?" he asked again.

"No, not really," Burt replied. "But I got an idea we'll know it if we find it."

"That doesn't help much. What do you think, like mushrooms or a poison frog, or something like that?" Carl pointed the light onto the path in front of them. Daylight was fading fast; soon, it would be full dark and impossible to find anything.

"Hold on a second." Carl bent down and directed the light onto the soft ground in front of him. He studied the dirt, then checked the woods on either side of the trail.

"What do you see, Carl?" Burt asked.

"Probably nothing," he answered. "Couple sets of bicycle tires, pretty fresh by the looks of them too."

"Those kids your dispatcher told you about, they were out on their bikes when they went missing, weren't they?"

"They were." Carl studied the two distinct sets of tracks. One of the bikes had a thin tread that was worn out more on the left side than the right, and the other set had knobby treads. Carl thought they were possibly made by a three-speed and one of those small motocross bikes. He got up and started to follow them. "Try not to step directly on the tracks. Put your feet where I do." Carl showed him by walking on the side of the trail, not completely in the woods and not on the dirt.

"Okay," Burt told him. "Just go slow. It's getting dark as hell out here."

The tracks followed the path, and it became clear to Carl that the motocross bike had been trailing the three-speed, by the way the knobby treads overlapped the thinner ones. He also believed the marks had been made some time today. If they had been older, there would have been animal prints on top of them. There was a hell of a lot of critters in these woods.

"I can't see shit, Carl. We should come back in the morning." Burt tugged at the sheriff's arm.

Carl ignored him. Instead, he bent down and focused the light onto the dirt again. A large bootprint revealed itself in the soil. The grass and weeds on the right side of the path had been trampled; someone had cut through. The owner of the print had taken a few steps along the trail and then disappeared into the woods on the opposite side. The grass was disturbed in that direction as well. Then Carl measured the mark by placing his foot next to it and noticed the print was a good three sizes larger than his own size eleven. The guy who had left it was one big son of a bitch.

"I don't like this," Burt whined.

"Easy, old man. I'm not thrilled about it either, but I think we're on to something. Don't worry, I won't let anything happen to you."

A loud noise cut through the night; it came from the tree line on the side of the trail. The men stopped in their tracks as something large thrashed through the grass and fallen leaves. Something big stepped out of the woods in front of them and grunted. Carl jumped back, and Burt screamed.

● ● ●

Dr. Malcolm passed the young candy striper on his way to the ICU. He nodded, and she returned the smile. The girl's name tag said Cyndi, not Cindy with a y at the end, but Cyndi with an i. "She looks like a Cyndi with an I," Malcolm muttered under his breath. The girl was young and blonde, somewhere around eighteen to twenty years old. He wondered if she had a crush on Dr. Ziegler. Now that was a contagion most of the young ladies at Chilton had contracted.

Before entering the ICU, Malcolm stopped in the changing room. He donned a protective paper gown, face mask, and eyewear. He also grabbed a fresh pair of surgical gloves. Now that they knew they were dealing with a parasitic bacterium, he didn't want to take any chances, since the method of transfer was still unknown. The protective garb reminded him of his time as the head of surgery back when Rosie was still alive. It had been a happy time for them. They'd been younger, and Rosie had still been relatively healthy; at least she hadn't been extremely unhealthy. His hair had been dark and thick, and Rosie, who had always been a full-size woman, was still a bit curvy. For some reason, John had done a lot more reflecting today than expected. He took a long, deep breath, hoping to catch a scent he knew he wouldn't find, and left the changing area.

The intensive care unit consisted of six individual rooms, occupying an independent wing of the medical center. Here, all the critical cases were referred as well as any patients who required solitary confinement. Since the Boyle child was the first to be admitted, Dr. Malcolm walked down the hall and opened the door to check on him first.

The room was bathed in a brilliant white light, so intense Malcolm's eyes were unable to adjust. Without warning, a sharp pain centered in the middle of his forehead. He grabbed his temples and nearly collapsed. Then his ears started to ring—loud and intense, like a whistle being blown inside his head. He rocked back and forth, swaying to a melody that only he could hear.

For a brief moment, John possessed the clarity to realize something was wrong, that he was in mortal danger. But the thought was silenced as if a blanket had been thrown over it. The ringing in his ears faded and was replaced by words he couldn't quite understand. And then he smelled it.

Faint, like the first flowers of spring, their fragrance caught on the breeze and carried through an open window. It lifted from the room and caressed his senses, gently but growing stronger by the second. *Estee ... Rosie's perfume.* But it was impossible; he had used the last of the bottle over a year ago. Still, it was as real as the memories that flooded his head and the voice that spoke to him. He heard it clearer now and could almost make out the words.

"Come sit with me, John," the voice said. "It's been so long since you sat with me."

John Malcolm knew that voice. How long had it been since the last time he heard it?

But John was so tired and found it almost impossible to keep his eyes open. He had no idea they were already closed.

The voice spoke again. "John, come sit with me."

It can't be; I have to be dreaming. John Malcolm forced himself to open his eyes and focused on the figure sitting on the bed in front of him.

The room wavered like a mirage, and the image faded into view. She sat before him, smiled, and patted the bed beside her. "Come sit with me, John."

He continued to sway in place as the vision grew clearer. "Rosie, what are you doing here?" he asked, an uneven smile infecting his face.

Rosie Malcolm sat on the bed, wearing a dress John had bought her over twenty years ago. He couldn't remember the last time he had seen it on her, but it had always been his favorite.

Her hair was exactly the way she had worn it back when he was the head of surgery. She would set it in curlers for hours just to get it right; John remembered she called it a bouffant. He thought it had made her look like Annette Funicello. Rosie looked good, exactly like she did in his dreams.

"What a silly question. I'm here to see you, of course," she said. "Now come over here and sit next to me, handsome."

John was propelled across the room, no longer in control of his own body. His arms hung limp at his sides, the clipboard fell from his grip and landed on the floor, the papers it held scattered. But John didn't notice. He stared into Rosie's deep, dark eyes. They were so dark they were almost black. *Rosie had green eyes*—the thought was silenced. He was drawn toward her as if a rope were fastened around his chest. There was no sense in resisting, not that he could if he wanted to. John's mind and body were no longer his own.

"Rosie," he said. A thin line of saliva fell from the side of his open mouth. "My Rosie."

His feet slid against the floor.

Rosie's smile grew wider. Her big, dark eyes focused intently on John as he approached the bed. Somehow, they grew darker and wider.

A strange thought echoed from somewhere within, something John had seen once in a cartoon. *Hey, Rosie, what big eyes you got... to have.* A noise escaped from deep in his throat. It was intended to be a laugh but was closer to a whimper.

Rosie's smile broadened as if she knew what he was thinking and found it funny herself. Then, she opened her mouth and smiled, exposing at least three rows of razor-sharp teeth the size of broken Chiclets.

Hey, Rosie, what sharp teeth you got ... to have.

● ● ●

Carl and Burt collided, nearly sending each other sprawling into the woods as the beast emerged from the shadows and onto the path in front of them. Carl instinctively dropped his hand to the gun on his hip. With his other hand, he raised the flashlight in the direction of the creature. It grunted and then squealed as the light fell upon it. A large black sow had burst out of the darkness and stood in the middle of the path. It snorted a warning, then several piglets filed out of the woods. The little ones gathered around their momma, who stared down the path in the men's direction. They remained still while the sow sized them up. Once she was satisfied there was no threat and all her babies were accounted for, she darted into the woods on the opposite side of the trail, with her piglets close behind.

Carl, who had been holding his breath, released it. Wild pigs could be nasty and were known to attack, especially when it came to protecting their young. *That was too damn close.*

"I think I pissed myself," Burt said, sounding relieved.

Carl looked back at him and smiled. "Your secret's safe with me." He let out another deep breath and chuckled. "Because I think I might have pissed a little myself."

They laughed, thankful for the tension to have dissipated. Burt slapped Carl on his back. "Let's get out of here. We're not doing any good stumbling around in the dark."

"Yeah, I'm with you there." The sheriff directed the light across the path where the sow had stood with her babies. A glint of reflection flashed back at him from further down the trail; the beam bounced off something shiny and metallic.

"What the hell is that?" Burt asked.

But Carl was already walking toward the object.

The night grew silent and closed in around them. "Do you hear that?" Burt held his breath.

"Hear what? I don't hear anything," Carl replied.

"Exactly. What happened to all the crickets? They should be hollering up a storm." Burt followed Carl as the path took a gentle turn to the right. Finally, the light came to rest on the object that had caused the reflection.

Two bicycles lay overturned on the side of the trail. Carl approached and examined the tires. He motioned for Burt to be careful not to step on any of the tracks. One of the bikes had a thin tread and was in fact a three-speed. The other one had the name *Mongoose* written on the frame; it was a motocross bike with knobby treads. The bicycles lay half on the path and half off. Judging by the zigzag and skid marks, it looked to Carl as if the bikes had crashed into each other.

"I bet these belong to your two missing boys," Burt said.

"I'd have to agree. It looks like they were discarded in a hurry." The sheriff cast the light in the direction the bicycles had been heading. Then he lit up the woods on either side of the trail. "That's strange," he said, confused.

"This whole damn day has been strange," Burt said, looking over his shoulder into the darkness. "What part are you talking about?"

Carl cast the light on the area where the bikes lay. "Well, usually when you get off a bike, you step on the ground, but I don't see any footprints anywhere. It doesn't look like anyone even walked through the woods on either side."

The coroner followed the light to see what his friend was talking about and, sure enough, couldn't find any footprints near the bikes or on the trail. "That is strange," he said. "What do you make of it?"

"I haven't got a clue." Carl pulled his walkie-talkie from his hip. "Sheriff Primrose to base, come in, base."

Andrea's voice broke the silence with a garble of static. "Go ahead, Sheriff."

"I think I might have a lead on our two boys. You said they were out riding their bikes this morning?"

"It was a false alarm, Sheriff. Both of their mothers called; the kids came home for dinner just like you said."

Carl looked at Burt and shrugged. "They didn't happen to mention leaving their bikes out in the foothills, did they?"

"Neither of them mentioned anything. Why do you ask, Sheriff?"

"Well, I found two bicycles out here in the woods. Think it's odd someone would just leave them here."

"I can call back and check."

Carl pointed the light down the path and then back onto the trail. "Yeah, could you look into that for me? Has Deputy Forsyth checked in yet?"

"Still no word, Sheriff. He never made it to Con Ed either." Her voice broke up from being too close to the mic.

"Damn," he said under his breath. "Well, we're gonna head out and have another go at it in the morning. Have you heard anything from Dr. Malcolm?"

"Negative, Sheriff. Were you expecting him?"

"Probably not yet," he said. "Let me know what you find out about the bikes."

"Will do, Sheriff." Andrea terminated the transmission.

Burt Lively crept close enough to Carl that he was practically standing on top of him. He listened intently to the conversation and was more than ready to leave. "I got a bottle of scotch back at the lab. Thirsty?" he asked.

"If you're buying, I'm thirsty. Let's get the hell out of these damn woods, Burt," Carl replied.

It was the best thing Burt had heard all night.

The thing sitting on the bed next to Dr. John Malcolm looked nothing like his dead wife. It bore no resemblance to Robert Boyle, the child who had worn the skin that now covered the grotesquely mutated creature. And the stench that suffocated the room smelled nothing like Estee Lauder. It parted its lips, exposing the saw blade that had erupted from its gums. An oil-like saliva slipped out the side of its mouth as it manipulated the old doctor. Insatiable hunger radiated inside the small beast; euphoric intoxication consumed it as it prepared to strike. John Malcolm's eyes rolled back in his skull as the creature rushed forward. The presence poured into him and began to devour, gorging itself on consciousness and lifeblood. It nibbled away at the useful parts like a rat tearing through the trash. Munch ... munch ... munch!

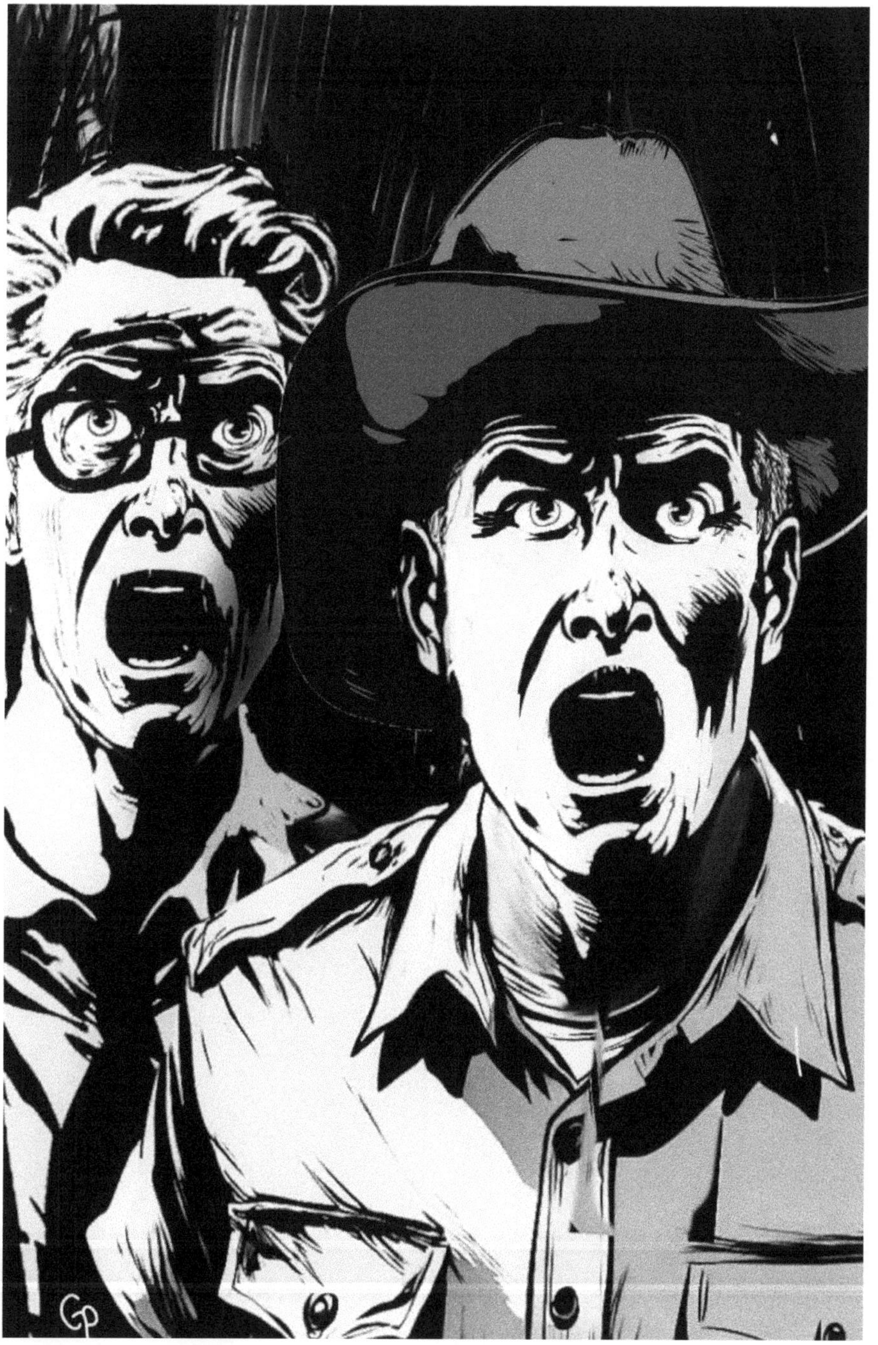

Chapter 19

Dennis Richards sat in the cafeteria drinking a Tab and growing more impatient by the minute. Both of his kids were in the intensive care unit, and he wasn't even allowed to see them. On top of that, not a single nurse or doctor had shown their face in over an hour to let him know just what the hell was going on. They had to have some information by now. He got up from his chair, stormed out of the cafeteria, and headed to the desk outside the ICU wing. Dennis's temper hit critical mass when he arrived at the nurses' station to find it empty and not a soul in the hallway either.

"Where the hell is everyone?" he called out.

The hall was silent. He walked down the wing into the ICU and called out again. "Hello, is anybody there?" He listened. "Where the hell is everybody, for Christ's sake?" Earlier, the door to his son's room had been open, but now it was closed. The cold fluorescent light crept from under the door. A shadow passed through it, causing Dennis to start. Someone was in the room. "Hello, nurse, doctor. What's going on? I want to see my damn kids."

Dennis felt his blood boil as heat flushed his face with rage. He threw open the door and stormed into the room. The bed was empty, and his son was gone. In fact, there was no one in the room at all. It didn't make any sense; he was sure he had seen someone moving about. He was positive.

He checked to the left and right of the door, but the room was so small there was really no need. A discolored stain saturated the center of the empty bed, soiled and wet from the boy's sweat. Dennis noticed the clumps of hair covering the pillow where his son had laid his head.

"What have you done to my boy?" he screamed. Then it hit him; the foul odor was consuming, hard, noxious, and oppressive. Dennis gagged and took a step backward.

"Where is my son?!" he howled into the empty room.

There was a shuffling sound, and then there was movement. He had enough time to realize something was above him just before it grabbed him by the throat.

Ben had gotten out of the bed as instructed. Had crawled across the floor on all fours, scurried up the wall, and clung to the ceiling, where he had waited. It dropped onto the man and dug into him with its newly grown teeth. Then it drained the vessel and added Dennis Richards to the collective.

Karin Boyle had been unable to sleep, even with the help of the valium. Bob sat in a chair beside the bed, attempting to comfort her. "I'm sure Dr. Ziegler will be along any second with some good news," he told her.

"I'm scared, Bob. He looked terrible. You saw him. What's wrong with our boy?" She had been crying nonstop since they arrived last night.

"I don't know, baby," he said, stroking her hair. "I don't know."

"I thought it was the flu; he only had a fever. He said he didn't feel good when he came home on Thursday, and I was so mad because he was late. I yelled at him and told him I was gonna give him the beating of his life." She tried to control her sobs but was unable. "Oh, Bob, what if—" She couldn't finish.

"Stop," he said. "Don't do that to yourself. You're a great mother, don't ever doubt that. You didn't do anything wrong. Rob loves you."

She felt guilty for being mad at her son. What if she never got the chance to say she was sorry? He had worked so hard, and the Halloween party was all he had talked about. Then he had gotten sick. Karin blamed herself for the whole thing. She wished she could go back to Thursday night when Rob had come home late. She would have done everything differently.

There was a knock at the door that startled them. Then Dr. Malcolm entered the room and smiled. "What's all this?" he said. "I think you should follow me. There's a young man who wants to see his parents."

Karin jumped out of bed, and Bob got up from the chair. "Is Rob okay? How is he?" Bob asked.

"Oh, God. Thank you," Karin cried. "Is it true, Dr. Malcolm? Is he going to be all right?"

Dr. Malcolm smiled and rubbed the back of his neck. "Well, why don't you come see for yourself," he said and exited the room.

Bob and Karin followed the chief of medicine down the hall toward the ICU. He opened the door and let them inside. They rushed in, and Dr. Malcolm slammed it behind them. Robert wasn't in the bed.

"What's going on here, Doctor?" Bob screamed and tried to turn the doorknob. It wouldn't move; someone was holding it shut from the other side. Whoever it was had to be as strong as a bull. It couldn't be Dr. Malcolm.

"Open this door, dammit." Bob pounded against it.

"Bob!" Karin cried. "Dear God!"

Bob turned around and was hit by a stench that scrambled his guts. The hot tang of rotted meat filled the room like vapor. Then he heard it, the furtive sound of malicious intent, like an angry hornet trapped in a Dr. Pepper can. Gooseflesh pricked his skin as the strange sound grew in intensity and the overpowering stink punched him in the face. He covered his mouth just as two figures jumped from the floor onto the bed. Bob knew immediately that one of them was his son. "No."

Robert's body had changed, morphed into something deformed, insectile. The second creature had gone through a similar disfigurement. It focused on Bob with dark, bulbous eyes and began to preen itself.

"Oh my God!" Karin screamed as the small creatures propelled themselves toward them. The couple tried to back out of the way, but their attackers were lightning-quick and had them before they could move.

Rob seized his mother by the throat with hands that had grown talons. His claws dug into Karin's flesh as he drove her to the floor. She heard Bob struggle for a moment and then only a terrible gurgling sound.

Rob landed on his mother's chest and fed on her consciousness. Karin felt the icy presence enter her brain and projected a final thought. *I'm sorry, Rob, please don't be mad at me. I love you.*

The Boyles were added to the brood.

Carl and Burt drove back to the coroner's office, where a bottle of scotch waited for them. It wasn't going to make their problems go away, but it would make them a bit more bearable. Carl picked up the handset and spoke. "Leaving the foothills now. Did you find out anything yet, Andrea? Any word from Deputy Forsyth?" He prayed for at least a little good news.

"Affirmative, Sheriff," she replied. He let out a sigh of relief and waited for her to continue. "Deputy Forsyth dropped the squad car off about fifteen minutes ago. He got held up at Wilson's Diner. Apparently, Mandy Griggs had a little car trouble, and he gave her a ride home."

The men exchanged a smile. Everyone in town knew Mandy, and Carl had an idea there was a bit more to the story than Deputy Forsyth had told the dispatcher. He figured Gary would have a different tale to tell when it was just the guys.

"He never made it to the power plant," she continued, "said he'd head up there tomorrow."

"I'll bet," Burt said. Both men laughed.

"What about the kids? Did they leave their bikes in the woods today?"

"Kids said their bikes were stolen outside the A&P this morning. They came home late 'cause they were walking around town trying to find them and lost track of time." Andrea was full of good news.

"So, the case of the missing boys is solved." Carl smiled at Burt. "Someone left the bikes in the foothills. Tell the parents we found them behind the Richards house near the creek."

"Will do." She paused. "Sheriff, Dr. Malcolm called."

"He did?" Carl crossed his fingers, waiting for the other shoe to drop. This was where she would hit him with the bad news. "What did he say?"

"He said there's no need to worry, the children are showing signs of improvement, and there's no need to be concerned about contagion."

Carl eased against his seat and smiled. "That's great news." All Andrea had to do was tell him someone had found Felix Castillo's body, and most of his problems would be fixed. "Well, it certainly has been a long day."

"You can say that again, Sheriff. You need anything else?" she asked.

"Just a glass with some ice in it, dear." He laughed.

"Well, have one for me, Sheriff. Have a good night."

"I'll have two for you, Andrea. Good night." He returned the handset to the dashboard.

Burt tilted his head in question. "Guess the kids weren't as sick as he thought. Sounds promising."

"I'm surprised too. If you saw them last night, you would have said, no way. No way they would be doing better so soon. I guess Dr. Malcolm figured it out."

"Yeah, I guess so." Burt creased his brow.

"That only leaves us with one problem, Burt." Carl took a dig at his friend. "You realize how much trouble the two of us are looking at, don't you?"

"You think I don't know?" Burt shook his head. "I still can't explain it any other way than someone playing a sick joke. It's almost Halloween, you know?"

"Well, don't think different of me for bringing this up." Carl paused and thought carefully about what he was about to say. "If I report this like I should, you're bound to lose your job. I'll get my ass reamed, but the state will surely see you swing, buddy."

"Yeah, I was wondering how long it would take you to mention that."

Carl let out an exaggerated exhale. "I can't believe I'm about to say this, and if any of it leaves this car, I'll deny every word."

"What are you trying to say, Carl?"

"This guy Castillo didn't have any family, no next of kin. Maybe I don't have to make that call just yet. Let's see if the body turns up. It's not like anyone's coming in to identify him."

"I can't let you put your ass on the line like that," Burt told him.

"I really don't see how you have much of a choice. If I call it in now, you'll lose your job and probably your pension along with it." Carl paused for dramatic effect and to let his friend realize the magnitude of the situation. "Now, if we wait and the body never shows up … God forbid, you fill out the autopsy report and burn it."

"Huh … burn what?" Burt asked.

The Sheriff continued. "You turn on the incinerator, and I don't care what you burn. Burn that damn suit you wear every day. I will report that we have no leads, and it becomes a cold case, and that's that. Now, if by some miracle the body does show up, then I will call you and let you know that we found the body you reported stolen. I can't believe I am saying this, but I don't feel like I have much of a choice."

"Carl, I—"

"Listen, old man, you worked for my father when he was sheriff, and you've always been a good friend. I wouldn't do this for anyone else in the world. But I can't stand by and watch you lose your job and retirement just for being, I don't know ... a really irresponsible coroner."

"That's fair," he said. "I deserve it."

"Right now, we're going to go back to that lab, you're gonna break out that bottle, and we're gonna get drunk. Who knows, maybe Felix Castillo will be there waiting for us, and you can buy him a drink too."

"I don't know what to say, Carl." Burt rubbed his eyes.

"Well, don't say anything yet because I could still change my mind."

"You're a good friend, Carl. Thank you."

"Like I said, Burt," he looked at his friend, "I could still change my mind."

Sally Ann Richards finally managed to fall asleep, thanks to the valium Dr. Ziegler prescribed. The staff had allowed her and Dennis to rest in one of the unoccupied rooms on the same floor as the ICU ward. Unfortunately, they were still not allowed into the room with their kids and were only able to see them from as close as the doorway, since Dr. Malcolm was still concerned about contagion.

But Sally Ann couldn't understand why she was being prevented from seeing her children. If she was going to get sick, surely, she would have already. She'd been with them round-the-clock since they first came down with fevers. Poor little Erin was losing her teeth. It was horrible. Sally Ann was helpless to do anything, and on top of that, she was thoroughly exhausted. She hadn't slept at all, except for the few minutes before Erin came to her in the living room and vomited.

Now, thanks to the tiny blue pill Dr. Ziegler had given her, she slept restlessly, tossing and turning, falling in and out of consciousness. Dennis had turned the lights out before heading to the cafeteria, leaving the room dark and quiet. The only light was from the streetlamps in the parking lot. It filtered through the blinds, casting long shadows against the far wall.

Sally had been plagued by repeated visions from the previous night. In her dream, she was asleep in her bedroom on Mountain Ave. But then she was suddenly expelled into wakefulness by an urgent need to tend to her children, who were sick and in pain. Although she would try to be quiet as she left the bed where Dennis lay sleeping, every step she made on the hallway floor felt as loud as hammers on concrete. No matter how careful she tried to be, she would either trip over something in the hall or knock over a table. At which point, Dennis would charge from the bedroom, screaming, and start to shake her. That's when Sally would wake up, confused and unsure of where she was. Until she recognized the shadows on the far wall and remembered she was still in the center and her babies were so sick. Then, laying her head back down against the pillow, the valium would kick in, and the dream would start all over again. Repeatedly, she would find herself back in her own bed, lost in the spin cycle.

Sally had just awoken from the nightmare and looked around the unfamiliar dark room. *Where am I?* Confusion dominated for a moment, but soon she realized where she was: still at Chilton, exhausted and completely drained. Then … she heard it, faint and gentle like the movement of fabric on flesh. There was a soft rustle near the door of the room, and Sally thought Dennis must be sitting in the dark and had fallen asleep himself.

"Den, what time is it?" she called to him.

There was another soft rustle that almost sounded like paper being dragged across the floor. The sound drew closer to where Sally Ann lay.

Rustle … Scrape … Rustle.

"Dennis, is that you?" Sally's eyes focused on a small shadow as it approached the side of her bed. Then the shadow spoke.

"Mommy … I don't feel so good," Erin whispered in a garbled voice that was no longer human.

Part Two

CHAPTER 20

Monday

Jared Neibolt turned right onto Sunset Road, making his way into Garrett Grove. He pushed the truck a bit faster than usual and checked his watch to find it was almost five a.m. Right on time. It wasn't the early morning hours he minded; Lord knew there were worse jobs than delivering bread for a living. Still, having to make the arduous trek over Garrett Mountain for only two stops was a royal pain in the ass. The Grove was the most remote destination on his route, and he wished he didn't have to come here at all. But since he didn't make the schedules, there was no point bitching about it. With any luck, he would get promoted to manager in June and his truck driving days would be over. *No more trips into bum-fuck Garrett Grove, and no more hemorrhoids.*

It was still dark at five a.m., with an early morning ground fog making visibility even more difficult. Jared squinted to focus on the stretch of pavement before him, then turned on the high beams, which did little to help. But with barely another vehicle on the road, he relaxed some, pressed the gas pedal a bit harder, and turned up the radio. The sound of the Ramones filled the cab of the truck, making him feel like he wasn't completely alone.

He bobbed his head and sang to the music, unaware he was now doing over forty-five in a twenty-five mile per hour zone. He sailed past the high school and entered a rural stretch with fields and drainage ditches on either side of the street. Then, for one disastrous moment, Jared took his eyes off the road a second time.

It smashed into the bread truck with the velocity of a cannonball, causing the entire vehicle to shudder. Jared jumped in his seat and attempted to slam on the brakes, but it was already too late. He white knuckled the wheel with his heart beating triple time in his chest and his mind racing to figure out what happened. He thought he had hit a deer or a bird had flown into the grill. Then he saw the man's face as it smacked against the front windshield.

It sounded like he had driven into a wet tree. The guy's head bounced off the glass, and for a fleeting moment, time stood still. Jared stared into the man's eyes and watched as life exited his body. There was nothing but darkness left inside him ... cold, blank darkness. Jared fixated on the dead man's stare and wanted to die himself. A second later, the guy was airborne and thrown over thirty feet into a drainage ditch on the far side of the road.

Jared continued to jam on the brakes, bringing the truck to a screeching halt, then exited the vehicle, shaking and ready to vomit. "I killed him. Oh my God, I killed him!" he cried.

He made his way to where the body had landed and looked over the embankment. It was horrible. The man lay face down, half submerged in the muddy water and a tangle of weeds. His body was now twisted in a most unnatural way, and the sight of it made Jared's stomach lurch. He doubled over and spilled his breakfast onto the side of the road.

It's all my fault. What do I do, what do I do? There was no radio in his truck, and Jared had no idea where the nearest phone might be. He had never even been issued a parking ticket, and now he had killed someone.

Jared nearly died a second time when Deputy Kovach turned on the cherries and hit the siren behind him. The officer pulled the cruiser to the side of the road and exited the vehicle. "What seems to be the problem, sir?"

"Thank God! He stepped out of nowhere. I didn't even see him. One minute I was driving, the next he's right in front of me. Oh my God ... I didn't even see him!" Tears streamed down Jared's cheeks, and his hands had begun to tremble.

Deputy Kovach walked to the embankment and looked over to find the body embedded deep in the mud as if it had come down like a meteor. He then led

Jared to his cruiser and instructed him to have a seat in the back while he moved the truck off the road. "I need to secure the scene before someone comes along and hits one of us," he told Jared, who nodded but didn't hear much of what he had said.

The fog was beginning to thin, and the sun had just started to rise as Deputy Kovach went to the embankment and looked down into the ditch a second time.

"Poor bastard," he hissed. "And I thought *I* was having a bad day."

Chapter 21

Donald Fischer arrived at the quarry long before sunrise and several hours ahead of any of the other employees. He typically enjoyed the early morning solitude but doubted if today would be all that enjoyable. The Museum of Natural History was sending a representative to inspect the artifacts in the cave. The guy's title was Curator of Tribal Antiquities ... or something like that, but to Don, that was just a fancy little label for giant pain in the ass. He didn't give a hill of beans what some crusty old geezer from the museum did with the cave or the crap inside it. He needed the old fart to make it quick and leave so he and the rest of the men could get back to work. Production had come to a grinding halt since the recent discovery, and with winter just around the corner, layoffs wouldn't be far behind.

As a geological engineer, it was Don's job to determine and prepare safe blasting formations in the topography of the DuCain quarry. Granted, it wasn't as prestigious as mapping the shift of tectonic plates at Yosemite, but it paid the bills. In truth, he had given up aspirations of getting to California long ago. *That's life: man plans, and God laughs.* Donald Fischer believed God had been getting a good laugh at his expense for some time now.

He opened the office trailer, walked across the scuffed linoleum floor, and put on a pot of coffee. Mark Gold and the other foremen would arrive later, but not before Don had enjoyed the peace and quiet of his first cup of morning Joe. It was all about the small victories, which was exactly what happened last night.

Sheriff Primrose had called the house around nine o'clock with the good news. Robert Boyle and the Richards twins were all doing better, and there was no need to worry about contagion. Don had been cleared to go to work, and Troy was allowed to attend school. Don had been more than relieved. Although he loved his family dearly, he felt another day in the house was more than he could stand. Lois had been on his case more than usual. Everything he did lately seemed to piss her off. He couldn't help that he was needed at work, and she should be able to understand that. *It's this crummy-ass job that puts the food on the table.*

Lois had urged him to have a heart-to-heart with Troy, which had gone well. *Kids are resilient as hell, especially at that age.* Troy had been somewhat pensive, but he wasn't in the sad state that his mother made him out to be. Thankfully, Rob was on the mend, and with any luck, the events of last Saturday night would soon be forgotten. Besides, Don had enough on his own plate to worry about.

The pressing matters at hand had everything to do with the cave and the shutdown of production that sent old man DuCain into a tailspin. It crossed Donald's mind more than once that all their problems could be solved if a pocket of methane actually did explode, taking out the cave and everything in it as well.

Don had even gone inside the cavern himself and taken a look around. It certainly appeared different from the typical cache of bones or occasional tomahawk they usually found. The cavern was huge. Much too big to have gone undetected by his equipment. There was no explanation as to why it didn't show up on his initial readings. It just didn't make sense.

The opening revealed by the blast was large enough for a man to fit into, but it was impossible to determine just how far the cavern extended into the mountain. There were bones in there, a lot of them, not all of which looked entirely human. And the place was loaded with artifacts, including weapons. All appeared to be in excellent condition.

Just thinking about it twisted Don's stomach into a sour knot. He grimaced as he poured a cup of coffee and walked across the narrow trailer, with its scattering of blueprints covering every inch of wall space, and took a seat behind his small but organized desk. He had just taken his first sip and was startled by a knock on the trailer door. His stomach twisted a notch tighter. The other supervisors and quarrymen never arrived before seven, and the guy from the museum wasn't due till even later. The knock came again, soft but deliberate. Don got up and opened the door.

"Good morning." An attractive woman stood in the doorway.

"Good morning," he said, taken aback by her presence. The woman had dirty blonde hair and bright blue eyes. She looked somewhere in her early thirties and wore a toothy smile. Don figured she was either lost and had somehow stumbled across his trailer or she worked for the newspaper and had heard about the recent discovery.

"Can I help you?"

"I hope so. I'm looking for Donald Fischer. Do you know where I could find him?"

"I'm sorry. I'm not allowed to speak to the press about anything yet," he said, trying to be polite but curt at the same time. "You'll have to talk to the people from MNH."

"I'm not with the papers." She held out her business card. "I'm *with* the museum, and I'm supposed to meet with Mr. Fischer this morning. Do you know when he'll be in?"

"I'm sorry." He took the card and examined it. His lips pinched together in a scowl of confusion. "I was expecting—"

"You were expecting a man, probably an old man at that." She smiled and held out her hand. "I take it you're Mr. Fischer."

"Um-Donald Fischer, nice to meet you." He shook it and read the card a second time, **Dr. Stephanie Thompson, Curator DDAH.**

"Likewise, Mr. Fischer." She nodded and offered a look of understanding. "Don't be embarrassed. I get it all the time. No one expects a woman to do my job."

"Um-a, no, it's not that. My boss told me to expect a Dr. Stephen Thompson, so I naturally expected a man. An old one at that."

They both laughed, which seemed to ease the tension. "Is that coffee?" she asked and pushed her way past him through the tight doorway. "I could sure use a cup."

"Do come in." Don's eyes widened as she made her way to the coffee pot, helped herself to one of his mugs, and poured a cup. "Please, make yourself at home."

Had she turned out to be an old geezer, Don would have been put off by the straightforwardness, but Stephanie Thompson had caught him off guard and momentarily disarmed his defenses. She stood no taller than five-two, maybe three, at the absolute most, with a whole lot of spunk packed into a small package.

"My dad had his hopes set on a boy. Wanted to name me after my grandfather. Then I came along. Ta-da!" She held up her hands and took a bow. "So, he changed the Stephen to Stephanie, and well, there ya go." She took a sip of coffee. "This is good, full strength. Well, Dad was the curator for the museum and passed the ambition onto me, his oldest child—not a boy." She finished with a huge smile.

Donald watched as she took her coffee, walked over to his desk, and sat in his chair.

"So, when the museum says Dr. Thompson will be showing up, everyone naturally expects an old man. Then I walk in. And they all react exactly like you are right now, Mr. Fischer."

"Don is fine."

"Great, Don," she continued without taking a breath, "so, what have you got up here? I hear it's quite a find. I'm dying to get a look. When can we go up there?" She had only had a couple sips of coffee and was already bouncing off the walls. Don couldn't imagine what she would be like if she snorted a line.

"As soon as the sun comes up and my engineers arrive. There are strict regulations about working in confined spaces. I realize the relics and contents of the cave belong to the museum, but the cavern is on DuCain property. God forbid there is a cave-in or something. Everyone's safety is my responsibility."

She smiled and nodded her head in agreement. "Of course. I was just seeing how far I could push you." She flashed a smile that made her eyes look even brighter.

"I'll bet that works most of the time."

"You have no idea." She winked and leaned back in his chair.

"Actually, I think I do." Don had been regretting this morning's meeting, but there was something about Dr. Thomson that he liked quite a bit.

"Have you been inside? I hear there are intact skeletal remains. Is that true? Are they intact?"

Don didn't know if they were intact or not, but there were an awful lot of bones in there. He told her as much as he could but still had some questions of his own. How long did she expect the excavation to take? How long would his job site be shut down, and just how many more visitors he could expect to show up?

She told him it was too early to tell. The museum had flown her in from DC and rented a house in town for her and her family to stay. But she expected to be in Garrett Grove for no less than two months.

"Two months! How could it take so long?" His jaw nearly hit the floor.

"If there are as many artifacts in that cave as you claim, I think I could be here much longer."

Donald's shoulders slumped and his chest deflated.

"You should be happy," she said.

"Why on Earth would I be happy? If the quarry doesn't produce, there will be a lot of hungry families this winter."

"Well, Mr. Fischer, as the curator for the museum, I'm authorized to reimburse you and your company for the time and inconvenience this excavation may incur. So, when I say you should be happy, trust me—you should be. Because I have a ledger full of blank checks to help ensure your cooperation." She raised her coffee mug and offered a smile that Don was sure had broken a thousand hearts.

"We've never been offered anything like that before, and artifacts have been turning up for a long time at this quarry."

"Well, let's just say the museum is very interested in that cave and wants to make sure that you and everyone else involved is compensated."

"I've got to say, Dr. Thompson." Don raised his own mug. "I think I like you a whole lot more than some crusty old man."

● ● ●

Sheriff Carl Primrose woke up at six a.m. with a dry mouth and a splitting headache. Thanks to one too many scotch on the rocks, he had a good old-fashioned hangover. After the day he had had ... he deserved it. And Burt had deserved to pay for the drinks. He replayed yesterday's events in his head as he made coffee, then drank two large glasses of water and waited for it to brew.

He and Burt had gone back to the coroner's office and hashed out a plan to solve both of their problems. Carl wasn't thrilled with the idea, but their options were limited. He had become a cop to help people but never imagined that might involve covering up the missing body of a murder victim. Burt had screwed up—big-time—and the old man was his friend. *If you can't help your friends, then what good is the damn badge?* Still, the more he thought about it, the more it gnawed at him.

He sat at his kitchen table, listening to the inner debate rage on. Other than that, the house was silent. The large kitchen with its dark walnut cabinets, the three bedrooms, and two full baths ... all quiet. Carl had never married, and there had been no little Carls running around. At this late point in the game, he highly doubted that either would ever happen.

His breakup with Lois had been difficult, and Carl fully expected to spend the rest of his life pining over her. But life had other plans. And in 1969, he was drafted by the United States Army and sent to Vietnam.

Having grown up in Garrett Grove, Carl had been no stranger to the wilderness. But the jungles of South Vietnam weren't like any of the woods he'd seen growing up. Carl was drafted and shot through basic training like a human cannonball. By the time he found himself in the heart of it, he had a lot more to worry about than Lois Middleton.

He met Ralph Pinkerton at West Point during an eight-week blur that passed quicker than a summer afternoon. The men bonded instantly and were assigned to the same platoon. The training had been difficult, and it wore them ragged. It felt like they were always running, from the time they woke up until they passed out ... mile after miserable mile. But the training had leaned them, hardening the softness that growing up in places like Garrett Grove had afforded.

On one of the rare occasions when they weren't completely exhausted and had managed to stay up late, they'd gotten to talking about girls. What else was there to talk about? Ralph told Carl about his fiancé back in Tempe. He had shown Carl a picture of Kerrie Ann; the guy had done pretty well for himself. "What in the hell does she see in you?" Carl had teased his friend—kind of. Ralph wasn't a pretty boy by any means. He had a large forehead, which made him look slow, and a big nose, which had been broken at least once. The guy sure wasn't going to win any beauty contest, but somehow, he had scored himself a knockout with Kerri Ann. He probably pulled it off because Ralph was one funny son of a bitch. Even with all the shit going on around them, Ralph could always make Carl laugh. Apparently, it had worked on Kerri Ann; the guy must have laughed the panties right off her. Kerri Ann was back in Tempe, Arizona, with a bun in the oven, waiting for the big guy to come home so they could get hitched.

In turn, Ralph asked Carl if he had a girlfriend back in Garrett Grove, and Carl had answered the question with just one word. "No." He didn't elaborate, and he never mentioned Lois's name. Not once during his entire deployment did he ever talk about her. He had managed to push Lois out of his mind as if she never existed—almost. However, there were moments in the darkest hush of night, just before he fell asleep, when he would think about her, sitting in the passenger seat of his Mustang with the moon shining, illuminating the Lenape River like it was the Ganges.

Carl and Ralph's platoon sergeant gave them two pieces of advice when they arrived. The first was to keep their heads down, which was relatively easy to do. The second little tidbit was to keep their socks dry, which was next to impossible. The country was wet. Even when the sun was out. It rained nearly every day, and, supposedly, they were there during the dry season. They had been told it was a jungle. But from what Carl had initially seen, it looked more like a swamp.

That first week, they had been spared from seeing any real action. But their reprieve was short-lived, just enough time to get used to the sound of mortars in the distance. And then it was on top of them.

The concussion of artillery fire was something you never got used to; it rattled your brain and shook the fillings out of your teeth. Survival instinct sent a direct order to the legs: Run! And that's what got most kids killed in Vietnam. The second a greenhorn took off running, the snipers drew a bead and took him out. It was damn near impossible for most to override the flight mechanism. The ability to hunker down and keep a level head was an acquired skill that didn't come easy; it went against every natural urge. But once you learned how to control it, it stuck.

There was one thing that had stayed with Carl more than anything else. It wasn't the molar-rattling concussion of artillery fire. It wasn't the constant battle to keep his socks dry in a place that was wetter than the Great Swamp. And it wasn't the Volkswagen-sized mosquitoes that wanted to carry him away in the night. The thing that stuck in Carl's brain and never left was the nauseating smell of rotting fish.

During one unforgettable day of their deployment, Carl and Ralph's platoon had crossed over the Mekong Delta to find thousands and thousands of dead fish rotting on the surface of the water. The weather had been sweltering, and the fish lay putrefying in the Asian sun. The stench was all-consuming. It filled the men's sinuses, crept into their mouths; it saturated their clothes and permeated the air. It was everywhere, and it wouldn't go away.

That was the scar that stayed with Carl and never left. It had hit him like a fifty-caliber round to the chest. Now, even the faintest scent of fish, cat food, or anything that remotely resembled seafood would render him incapacitated. For most of the men who came back from Vietnam, loud noises or the sound of fireworks brought on that thousand-yard stare. But for Carl, it was the smell of fish that brought him back to the Delta and the memory of all that blood. It had been everywhere.

There were ten men in their platoon, and Carl had taken point. Guys that went by the names of Hacksaw and Tank had been his brothers-in-arms. There was Tennessee and Tucson, who were both from Florida. Then Sergeant Wilkins, followed by Little Joe and Big Joe, which left Goober and Ralph, who were bringing up the rear. The choppers had dropped them in the middle of that mess of fish. It never crossed Carl's mind how it had gotten there in the first place.

They were waist-high in the brackish soup of the Delta with the sun beating down on them like a clenched fist and the stink coming off the water making them gag. The flies were everywhere, and the bastards bit too. The problem was you needed to walk with your M-16 raised above your head when navigating the fish guts, and that left you wide open for the little fuckers to land on your neck and face and gnaw the shit out of you.

The floating carcasses parted like the Red Sea as the men passed through them. Carl had navigated a safe path through the ocean of fish and brought the platoon to land. Nearly every man arrived at the water's edge; they had all stepped in practically the same exact spot that Carl had.

Somehow, they all missed the land mine submerged twenty feet from the bank. All of them except for Ralph. The big guy knew he had triggered the damn thing too. There was just enough time for him to yell, "Loo—"

THE OJANOX

The water erupted like a marinara geyser where Carl's friend had been standing. A thick mixture of pulverized fish and what remained of Ralph Pinkerton rained down on them, painting the world a nauseating shade of crimson. Ralph never made it out of Vietnam, and he never made it back home to Kerri Ann. She and Ralph's parents had likely received a standard letter from the president, stating how deeply sorry he was to inform them and how Ralph had fought bravely to defend his country. But he hadn't fought bravely; he had stepped on a goddamn land mine. Kerri Ann would be raising the child by herself. No doubt, the kid would come out with a large forehead and a big nose just like his father, a father he would never know. Now, even the thought of fish turned Carl's stomach and filled him with the memory of how it tasted to have Ralph's blood in his mouth. That was Carl's thousand-yard stare. And he never told a soul about what happened that day on the Delta, not even Burt.

* * *

Carl found himself sitting at his kitchen table staring at a coffee pot that had stopped percolating ten minutes ago. He grimaced as the taste of dead fish faded to a whisper. Finally, he went to the pot and poured a mug. The magic brew began to work instantly, pushing the hangover to the side and the memory of the Delta back into the shadows.

The house was silent. No wife and no kids for Carl. And that was the way he wanted it, which allowed him to focus on the job—or so he told himself. It was easy to maintain your defenses when you didn't let anyone get too close, and since the death of his father, Burt had been his only real friend. The marriage bug had never bitten him. *You can't miss something you never had.* Carl had even managed to convince himself that he believed it.

* * *

It recognized the darkness in the one called Butchie. There was work to be done, and this one would make the perfect soldier. Before the sun had risen, Butchie was dispatched. He smashed the window of Billy Tobin's Charger, then put the vehicle in neutral and pushed it. It had been easy for Butchie, who was much bigger and stronger than he had been less than a day ago.

The dirt lot at Mountainside Park, where the car had been left, sat above a steep slope that ended in a valley of thick woods owned by the state. The car hopped the embankment and was gone. It picked up momentum as it careened down the slope. It bounced over rocks and sailed between trees, then finally smashed into a large boulder at the bottom of the ravine.

There was still more work to be done, but it would be difficult to operate in the light. That had never been its domain; its home was the darkness, and its soldiers were sensitive as well. It could tolerate the great heated orb when it absolutely had to, if it needed to feed or defend. But it was far too dangerous to do so now. First it needed to grow its ranks, to build its army. It dispatched the one called Butchie, and Butchie was happy to be of service.

● ● ●

Margaret Post had drained the last of her gin and fell asleep in front of the TV watching Johnny Carson. She sprawled out in her favorite recliner with the cadence of her snores harmonizing to the static of the television. She was used to Butchie staying out late, and last night had been nothing out of the ordinary. He was usually home in time to make breakfast and to see if she needed anything. Margaret didn't hear the back door creak open or the sound of boots on the kitchen floor.

It stood over the woman, watching her sleep. A lingering sense of affection stirred in the one called Butchie. The presence within appreciated the raw emotion this vessel was capable of. So many flavors and textures. It had tasted Butchie's rage and the hunger incited by the one called Jackie. It knew what Butchie craved to do to her and now possessed the memories of what he had done to others in the past. But the Butchie-vessel was capable of other emotions as well. These creatures referred to it as love, and it was delicious.

Butchie stepped closer to the woman as static buzzed on the television.

She opened her eyes and looked up, still half asleep. "Butchie, is that you?"

"It's me, Mamma," Butchie replied, his voice deep and garbled like it was being delivered through a mouthful of dirt.

THE OJANOX

He parted his lips and allowed the presence to spill forward. The Ether forced its way inside her, and Margaret Post surrendered to the consciousness.

Chapter 22

Father Kieran McCabe had kept a vigilant watch over the Foothill's woods from his bedroom window at the rectory. The dark presence that had revealed itself after yesterday's Mass initially looked like an enormous waft of black smoke, but Father Kieran recognized it for what it was ... true evil.

He had always been a practical and non-superstitious man; however, he was a man of God above all else, and with that came acceptance for the unexplainable. The Catholic Church trained priests who specialized in exorcism and demonic possession. It was kept relatively quiet, with most of the public thinking it was only in the movies. But Father Kieran knew the truth behind the Hollywood scenario. His mentor, Father Michael, believed it necessary for his young apprentice to learn everything there was to know about demonic possession and the forces of evil that preyed on the weak of faith. He revealed in detail the countless cases of men and women who had received the sacrament of exorcism and been healed by the church. There was a vast library of sacred literature available to the clergy on the subject, and Kieran had made use of the knowledge.

It was easy for him to accept the presence in the woods for what he believed it to be, a demonic aberration. After witnessing the strange smoke-like miasma that darted furtively through the trees yesterday, Kieran had taken up post in his bedroom and watched the woods from behind the safety of his blinds.

There had been more shadows in the trees last night, different than what he had seen yesterday. People were walking through the foothills in the dark, heading somewhere with a particular destination in mind. It wasn't only men and women; there were children as well. Not all of which traveled upright like humans. Some walked on all fours, others hopping like frogs or some type of reptile. Father Kieran had watched the figures as they made their way through the dark woods, and prayed.

"Through my fault, through my fault, through my most grievous fault, I have sinned ... in my thoughts, in my words, in what I have done and in what I have failed to do; Father, forgive me."

He had kept his post by the window with his bible in one hand and a wine glass in the other. And by the time the sun started to rise, Father Kieran had been good and drunk. Now he lay in his bed sleeping, turning restlessly from side to side. Strange images filled his dreams and tormented his soul. Godless creatures pursued him through the woods. In his nightmares, he ran from them but kept getting lost in the endless forest. They hunted him, feeding on his fear with an unquenchable thirst and a tireless resolve, and had been dispatched by Satan himself.

Kieran fled until the path before him dead-ended at the base of a great cliff. With nowhere left to turn, he began to ascend the steep incline, his legs growing ever more sluggish by the second. He clawed his way up the rock face as his fingernails bent back and broke against the unforgiving stone. All the while, the creatures continued to close in on him. He struggled to breathe ... fought to breathe. His muscles screamed in pain, and his soul cried out as he desperately struggled to save himself.

Inch by inch, he scaled the sheer cliff wall, blood oozing from his fingertips and terror ripping through his heart. He could hear the grunts and growls of the beasts as he took a lumbering final step and missed his footing. Then ... he was falling. Kieran watched the world rush up at him with the sensation of terminal velocity overwhelming his overtaxed brain. He awoke a second before his body hit the bedroom floor. In the survival flight of the nightmare, he had rolled out of bed in a desperate attempt to save himself. For some time afterward, he lay there crying and shaking, trying to discern what of the previous day had been real and what had been a nightmare. It took him over an hour to convince himself that any of it had happened at all.

Tara Jefferies looked up from her position at the dispatch desk as Carl walked into the station with the brim of his Stetson pulled down to the top of his sunglasses. "Good morning, Sheriff," she said. "Rough night?"

He removed his hat but left the glasses on. "Why are you yelling?" he whispered. "Is the coffee ready?"

"Yep, I'll bring you a cup."

"You're the best," he said, then proceeded to his office. Not bothering to turn on the lights, Carl hung his hat on the rack by the door and sat at his desk. The office, the hat rack, and the desk all belonged to his father before becoming his. He rubbed his temples and wondered how many hangovers the old man had nursed sitting exactly where he was now. Allen Primrose had been a bourbon man, good old No.7. It wasn't to Carl's liking, but on those occasions when he needed a little spiritual guidance, he would sit at his father's desk and pour a glass of Captain Jack. Usually, it helped. Whether it was due to the channeling of the old man's spirit or just the quiet time, he couldn't say. Either way, it was here where he did his best thinking. Probably his best listening as well. Listening to his intuition, his thoughts, but, more importantly, listening to his gut. Carl Primrose had come to respect that cautionary voice he referred to as "his gut". Lord knew it had saved his bacon more times than he could even count. It had gotten him out of Vietnam in one piece, and it had saved his neck as a sheriff's deputy as well.

Carl had drawn his weapon three times during his career. The first time, as a rookie, he'd been called in to help search for a hunter who had gotten lost in a blizzard.

A combined effort of sheriff's officers and volunteer firemen combed the mountain looking for the lost hunter but had no luck finding the man. Carl and his partner, Tim Colbert, continued searching in the knee-deep snow and had ventured out past the abandoned sanatorium.

There were old cottages on the hospital property, connected by an elaborate maze of underground tunnels. The hospital staff had lived in these cottages and used the tunnels to travel back and forth to work. Carl and Tim thought if the lost hunter had made it this far, then maybe he had found his way into one of the buildings.

The place had been deserted for a long time, even back then. The windows had been shattered, and there wasn't a visible surface that hadn't been marked with graffiti. The officers approached the first building, and alarms went off in Carl's head like an air raid siren. His gut screamed, *Something's wrong*, and he listened. He pulled his service revolver and held it in the ready position. A fetid odor, impossible for either man to ignore, saturated the air like a summer storm. There was something inside the building. Judging by the stench, Carl doubted if that something was still alive.

Carl entered the narrow hallway with Tim several steps behind him. Immediately, they noticed the carnage on the floor. Dried blood and animal hide coated the old linoleum. They had discovered the source of the stink, but that didn't set Carl's nerves at ease. He tensed up, walked into the next room, and froze in his tracks. From somewhere in the shadows, a deep growl echoed off every surface, making it impossible to tell which direction it had come from. Then ... in one heart-stopping second, a sizable mountain lion leaped from the furthest corner of the room and propelled itself at the two officers. Carl reacted and fired his revolver three times, putting the great cat down. He had been ready because he listened to his gut, and it had saved both his and his partner's lives.

There had been the other incidents when he had drawn his weapon and even more occasions when his gut had saved his hide. Now whenever it spoke, Carl paid close attention.

Tara entered the room with his coffee. "Here you go, Sheriff." She set the mug on his desk.

"Thank you," he said, taking a sip. "Have you heard from Deputy Forsyth this morning?"

"Not yet. Gary's on the graveyard shift tonight. You want me to get him on the line?"

"No, that's okay. He was following a lead yesterday. I suppose it can wait till he comes in later." Carl considered asking one of the other deputies to handle it, then thought better. Gary Forsyth was one of his senior men, and since Burt had screwed the pooch, it was best to let Gary get to it when he did. Besides, Carl had a better relationship with Gary than with some of his other officers. Deputy Kovach was strictly by the book. And Deputies Rainey and Lutchen were still new on the job. Carl was considering some rather unprofessional measures, which made this a job for Deputy Forsyth's capable hands.

"Who's on patrol this morning?" He took another long sip from the mug.

"Kovach and Lutchen."

"Good, anything on the burner?"

"A call came in from Alice Tobin. She and Will were out of town yesterday. When they got back, they found a note from Billy and Eric. The boys said they'd be home late but never showed up. Alice is worried."

Carl knew Lois's nephews Billy and Eric Tobin all too well. The boys had been giving him a hard time since he and Lois started dating. *Hard to believe it was that long ago.* Carl had been a kid himself when he first met Lois's sister and brother-in-law, Alice and Will Tobin, and their two little terrors, Billy and Eric. Billy couldn't have been any older than six at the time, and Eric had been younger than that. But even at that age, the boys were always getting into something. Eric, the younger of the two, probably would have been okay on his own. But Billy was the alpha big brother and the mastermind responsible for nearly every premature grey hair on Carl's head.

He and Lois had been invited to their house for dinner one Sunday afternoon. It was early December, with a good layer of snow already on the ground, which was easy for Carl to remember. He would never forget the damn snow. He picked Lois up at her house, and they had driven over in his Mustang. The car wasn't great in the slush, but he sure as hell wasn't about to put chains or snow tires on his pride and joy.

Alice and Will welcomed him into their home and introduced Carl to their two little ones, Billy and Eric. They were nice enough kids, not snotty or spoiled, as many were, and appeared relatively behaved for the most part. If anything, Carl thought maybe the boys were a bit too well-behaved but didn't think too much of it.

Will took their jackets, hung them up somewhere in the house, and returned a moment later to talk baseball with Carl. Both men were diehard Yankee fans, that much they could agree on; however, when it came to the topic of who was the greatest player of all time, they were at an impasse. Will sided that it was Mickey Mantle and could not be swayed despite Carl's every attempt to prove it was Roger Maris. And there was no changing either man's mind, but there was one other thing that they did agree on. They both despised the Boston Red Sox with an equal passion. Alice and Lois had gotten into a conversation of their own that had nothing to do with baseball but had everything to do with getting around the bases. Alice wanted to know if Lois and Carl had started doing it yet. They had, so the women had an awful lot to talk about as well.

That was about the time that Billy and Eric went outside to play in the snow. A fresh layer had recently fallen on the existing six inches already covering the ground, and altogether, there was about nine inches of snow and ice. By the sound of it, the boys were having the time of their lives.

When it was time to eat, Alice called the kids into the house. They came in like a pack of wild dogs, hooting and hollering, dragging clumps of snow up the stairs. They continued to laugh about some inside joke that was clearly the funniest thing either of them had ever heard.

After dinner, Carl thanked Alice and Will for having him and prepared to drive Lois home. Will retrieved their jackets and saw them to the door. Carl kissed Alice on the cheek and extended his hand to all the men in the family. But Billy and Eric were still giddy by whatever had entertained them before dinner. So, Lois and Carl left out the front door, and that's when he realized that the keys to the Mustang were no longer in his jacket. He rechecked each individual pocket, hoping he had just missed them the first time. Then he checked the ignition and under the seats as well. But they were nowhere to be found. Which didn't make any sense since he was a fanatic about that car and never careless with the keys.

Lois went back into the house to see if they had fallen out where Will had put the coats. He had laid them on the bed, but the keys weren't there either. By that point, it was rather obvious what Billy and Eric had been laughing about. Will threatened the boys with a beating that neither of them would forget, and they folded like patio furniture.

Apparently, Billy had gone into Carl's jacket while the men were busy talking baseball. Then he and Eric had gone outside and buried the keys in the snow. However, neither of the boys could remember exactly where they were. The closest that Billy could narrow it down to was somewhere in the backyard.

The property wasn't huge, but it was big enough. And it was useless to retrace the boys' footprints since they had traipsed through nearly every square foot of the backyard. To make matters worse, it had already started to get dark.

So, the search for the Mustang keys began. The four adults started to dig in every possible place the boys might have buried them. The children themselves appeared to feel bad about what they had done, but that did nothing to improve the situation. Carl dug through the snow with his bare hands until his knuckles were raw, imagining how good it might feel to bury both of the little rugrats neck deep and then forget where they were. It had taken over two hours for the four adults to scour the backyard before Will triumphantly stood up with the keys in his hand. By then, Carl had been praying that Will would keep good on his word and beat the tar out of the little brats. That had been his first encounter with the Tobin brothers.

The second time was in '72. Carl had been back from the war for a little less than a year and working for the Sheriff's Department. Billy Tobin must have been around eleven or twelve at the time. Carl had just parked his cruiser in front of the municipal building to monitor the flow of traffic on the turnpike, when from out of nowhere, Will Tobin's station wagon screeched past with two tires on the curb and two in the street. The car jerked hard to the left and bolted into the opposite lane of traffic, then lumbered back into the correct lane—for the most part. Carl recognized the vehicle and thought Will must be drunk. Which would have been a shock because he had never known the man to be a drinker.

"Jumpin' Jesus Christ!" At first, it didn't look as if anyone was sitting in the driver's seat, then it all made perfect sense. He saw the very top of Billy Tobin's blond head, just barely high enough to look over the steering wheel, as the car passed. The little shit had no doubt lifted his dad's keys. *Figures. The kid can't be any older than eleven, and he's already a goddamn car thief.* Billy had decided to take the wagon out for a little joyride and was about to kill himself or someone else in the process.

Carl hit the lights and sirens and took off after him. Billy must have seen the cruiser pursuing him and panicked. Fortunately, he wasn't a skilled enough driver to put much effort into his evasion, and as soon as Carl pulled behind the wagon, Billy jerked the wheel far too hard to the right. The car lurched onto the front lawn of the Lutheran church. It mowed down a large hedgerow of lilacs and rolled to a stop a few feet before crashing into the front steps of the church. It was a wonder the car hadn't been totaled.

Carl opened the driver's door to find Billy Tobin sitting behind the wheel with a shit-eating grin on his face and Eric in the back seat crying his eyes out. No doubt his older brother had forced him into tagging along. Carl wanted more than anything to put Billy in handcuffs just to show the kid what it felt like. And had almost done it too. The only reason he hadn't was because he didn't have cuffs small enough. Will and Alice arrived minutes later to pick up the boys and their car. It had been a close call, and Carl hadn't been amused; it could have easily turned tragic.

As far as kids went, Billy wasn't even all that bad. Lord knew he wasn't anything like Butchie Post, who was just a menace to society. That guy was really going to kill someone one day. If they were lucky, they would get him back behind bars before that happened. Butchie had done an eighteen-month stint in Barre Oaks and come back even worse. Billy Tobin was just too active for his own good. He was into everything and great at getting other kids to follow him. The boy was a master manipulator and a persuasive character ... He was also one giant pain in Carl's ass.

Alice Tobin was forever calling the station. "Billy didn't come home last night. Billy disappeared for the entire weekend." And by the time Carl took the job as sheriff, he was tired of hearing, "Alice Tobin is on the line".

When Billy got older, it became a whole new set of problems. The boy had discovered girls and had damn near lost his mind chasing pussy. He was constantly staying out hours past his curfew—if he made it home at all. Carl had caught him in the act no less than a dozen times. One night he pulled up behind him at the top of Mountain Ave and approached the car to see Billy Tobin's ass pumping away like a jackhammer. Carl had turned his flashlight on the couple. The girl's face turned bright red, but Billy just smiled and gave him a look that said, *Yeah, you caught me again.* So Carl took full advantage of the moment.

"Mr. Tobin," he said. "I just caught you up here last night. When are you going to learn your lesson?" Carl had made it up, but Billy's date didn't know that. The color of her face had gone from embarrassed red to crimson fury. Carl walked away laughing, knowing that Billy wasn't going to finish what he had started unless he took matters into his own hands—literally.

On another occasion, Carl caught him back in the same exact parking spot. He turned the flashlight on the kids to find the young lady with her head in Billy's lap, working extremely hard to please the boy. She almost bit it off when Carl knocked on the window. Billy jumped up as the girl clamped down on his pecker and drew blood. Carl had a difficult time keeping a straight face when Billy rolled down the window. "Mr. Tobin. I'm glad to see that the doctor was able to help you out with those crabs."

The girl looked as if she were about to vomit. But by Carl's count, Billy Tobin was still up on him. It would be some time before the kid was paid in full for the whole car key incident.

● ● ●

"Sheriff," Tara repeated. "I said Alice Tobin called. Billy and Eric never came home last night."

"I heard you, and if I know Billy Tobin, he's out there with his kid brother having a hell of a lot more fun than either of us." *Probably shacked up with a couple of girls and a case of beer.* "Did you tell her not to worry and the boys'll be home as soon as they're done screwing or they run out of beer?"

"Not those exact words, but I told her they would probably be home any minute now."

"Thank you." Carl lowered his head and rubbed his temples.

"Kovach to base! Come in, base."

Tara left the office and headed to the dispatch desk at the sound of the deputy's call. "Go ahead, over."

"Additional units required on Sunset Road, just north of the high school. Over."

Carl jumped up from behind his desk, grabbed his hat, and was out the front door without waiting to hear the rest of the transmission, the voice in his gut screaming at him the entire way.

● ● ●

Donald Fischer sat at his desk listening to Dr. Thompson relive her life's story. The woman had the energy of a three-month-old Labrador pup and hadn't stopped talking since she entered the trailer and helped herself to his coffee. But Donald didn't find it rude and thought it refreshing to see a woman so inspired. She was passionate about her work and had earned the degree, not to mention the endless hours of research. She'd published countless papers, and there had even been an article about her in *National Geographic*.

"I think I remember that article. It was in the rain forest issue."

"So you're the *one* who read it. I'm impressed," she said, working on her second mug. "So, Donald Fischer ..."

"Call me Don."

"One condition. Drop the whole doctor thing. I'm Stephanie or Steph. Deal?"

"Deal."

"So, you're in charge up here. Geosciences?"

"Yep, geological engineering. I was hoping to study tectonic shift and fault lines, but here I am." He shrugged. "You know what they say, all the best-laid plans."

"I don't buy that. Never stop planning and never stop chasing your dreams. If that's your passion, that's what you need to follow. I got to admit, I'm glad to have you here. It's going to be helpful having a geologist on board, especially if the site turns out to be what we hope."

"What are you hoping for?" he asked, a bit more curious than he had been a moment ago.

"I'm afraid I can't tell you that."

"Hmmm, secrets, huh? I got to tell you, Stephanie ... Steph. I'm not a big fan of secrets. Not on my job site. Not when I have to answer for what goes on."

"No secrets." She crossed her heart with her index finger. "I'm just a bit superstitious, and I don't want to say anything to jinx myself. Once we get in there and start looking around, I will tell you everything I can, but until we—"

"You keep saying we. You mean *you* and *your* team, right?"

"Actually, you're on the team as well. Mr. DuCain said he would be happy to lend us his best engineer. I think his exact words were, 'he's at your disposal.'" She fished out a set of papers from her back pocket and leaned across the desk.

Don walked over, took them, and started to read. They were signed by Charles DuCain and stated that he was to assist Dr. Thompson in whatever way necessary to help expedite the excavation. Mark Gold would be covering his position. Everything appeared to be in order, but Don intended to call his boss the first chance he could. However, it did make sense that old-man DuCain would want one of his own men on the inside, acting as a supervisor while the museum folks poked around.

He studied the woman who had stormed into his Monday morning and turned it upside down. He knew he should be pissed off but wasn't. And for some reason, the idea of poking around inside the cave with Dr. Thompson sounded like it might just be the diversion he needed. At least for a little while. Since he was getting paid to do it, who was he to argue? Stephanie Thompson looked at him from across the desk and offered a contagious smile. *Well, I didn't see this coming.*

Chapter 23

Carl arrived at the scene of the accident only a few minutes before Burt. Although the fog had burned off and the sun had risen, it was still chilly. Their breath hung in long plumes as they exchanged pleasantries.

"You look how I feel," Burt said, still wearing the same wrinkled brown suit he'd had on yesterday.

"Oh yeah? Well, you're about to feel a whole lot worse when you see this." Carl walked with him to the side of the road and pointed over the embankment.

"Oh Christ. Poor bastard." Burt winced at the sight of the body in the ditch. The guy had been thrown and landed face first in the mud with his head and shoulders entirely submerged. His legs and arms were bent at impossible angles, and it looked like Burt's men, Abe and Tony, were going to have a hell of a time getting the body out.

"I hope we aren't going to make this a habit. I don't think I could do this again tomorrow," Burt joked, then realized it probably wasn't a good idea. "I'll check for an ID. Has anyone gone down to see if he's carrying any?"

"Not yet." Carl looked back at the bread truck and cruisers parked on the shoulder. "Kovach had to stay with the vehicles, and the driver is all freaked out."

"I can imagine," Burt said, removing a pair of surgical gloves from his pocket and pulling them on. "Okay. I'll take care of it."

Carl questioned the truck driver and instructed Deputy Kovach to assist Burt and his men with the body. They definitely had their hands full. The driver, Jared Neibolt from Warren, admitted that he had been speeding—a little—but swore he had been wide awake and he didn't drink. "Never touched the stuff." He told Carl the guy had just walked in front of him. "Like he was in a trance or something."

Carl listened to the man's story, took notes, and was fairly convinced it had been just an unfortunate accident. And although he didn't see any reason to arrest the guy, he still instructed Mr. Neibolt not to leave the state in case he needed to get in touch with him for further questioning.

Burt and the other men manage to wrestle the body from the ditch and placed the mud-caked remains on the side of the road. Deputy Kovach checked the guy's pockets and didn't find a wallet or any form of identification. In fact, the man didn't have anything on him at all.

"All right, Abe," Burt said. "Let's get him bagged up and back to the lab. We'll get him cleaned up there."

"Any idea who our John Doe might be?" Carl approached the men.

Burt shrugged, and Kovach replied, "Not yet, Sheriff. He didn't have any ID on him, and there isn't much to go on. I could follow the coroner back to the lab and get some prints once they hose him down."

"That's okay. You stay on patrol. I'll follow them over and grab the prints." Carl bent down closer to examine the body and nearly gagged. "Jeez, Burt. Should he smell that bad already?"

"It's all that shit he's covered in. It gets pretty nasty in those drainage ditches." Burt made a sour face and stepped back while Abe and Tony transferred the body into the large bag and zipped it shut. Once it was placed into the meat wagon, they could all breathe a lot better; the foul stench had lifted some.

●●●

Troy sat behind his desk at ten minutes to eight, waiting for class to begin. He fidgeted in his seat, staring at the fourth-grade mascot positioned at the front of the room in the corner next to the blackboard. Henrietta, the full-size human skeleton, wore a long black wig with curls that hung past her clavicle and a yellow button-down cardigan sweater. He smiled, leaned back, and reflected for perhaps the tenth time this morning, not sure what it was about today that reminded him of his first day of kindergarten. Maybe it had something to do with the weather, which was cool and crisp, nearly a snapshot image of that unforgettable moment. It had all stuck in Troy's memory like a wad of bubble gum in the carpet: walking into the strange school for the first time, sitting next to the boy named Robert Boyle, and that solitary tear that defined their friendship for years to come. He had overheard his parents talking yesterday in the garage, and it sounded like Rob was a lot sicker than anyone thought. Then later, his mom told him the good news: Rob was feeling better. With any luck, they would still be able to go trick-or-treating on Halloween, which was now less than a week away.

Before class, the students had gathered at the back closet, as they usually did, hanging up their jackets and putting their lunches away. Today, the hot topics of discussion were the awesome Halloween party and ... Troy and Wendy. The teasing had already begun, which didn't bother Troy as much as it would have only a week ago. He felt like he had changed in some way over the weekend; he felt cooler, wiser, maybe even older. And when Wendy pulled him inside the closet and pecked him on the cheek, he felt even better. Now, leaning back at his desk, with his fingers laced behind his head, Troy couldn't wipe the smile off his face if he tried. He was definitely feeling older.

Scanning the room, Troy noticed that even more of his friends were out sick today. Of course, Rob wasn't there, or Ben and Erin Richards, who hadn't been able to make it to the party either. But now, both Jeff Campbell and Tommy Negal's desks were empty, and they had been fine on Saturday night. He looked back at Wendy, who sat a few seats behind him. She offered a huge smile, making Troy feel self-conscious and nervous. He quickly turned toward the front of the class. *Maybe I'm not that cool after all.*

Then Miss Walsh, the fourth-grade teacher, entered the classroom accompanied by a young girl that Troy had never seen before. She was cute and blonde and hid behind the woman when they walked through the door.

"Hello, class," Miss Walsh said. "I'd like to introduce you to a new student who will be joining us. This is Janis Thompson. She's from Washington, D.C., our nation's capital, and her mother is a friend of mine. So, I want you all to make her feel welcome."

The class knew what was expected of them and responded in unison. "Nice to meet you, Janis."

The whispering started within seconds, mainly from the girls in the class. The boys, however, didn't say a word. They were too busy staring, most of them with their mouths hung wide open.

Janis was pretty, with long hair styled like Farrah Fawcett Majors from the TV show *Charlie's Angels*. She had bright blue eyes, also like the actress, but that wasn't what had all the boys spellbound. They had never seen anything like it before in their entire lives; even Troy found it impossible not to stare. The girl pulled them in with a magnetic power, and the boys were helpless to resist. How could they? Janis was the first fourth-grade girl who had started to grow boobs ... and they were hypnotizing.

●●●

Carl finished up at the scene of the accident and headed over to the coroner's office. By the time he entered the building, Burt and his men had disrobed the body, placed it into a large basin, and were in the process of washing off the thick layer of filth. The horrible stench hit Carl like a sledgehammer the second he walked into the morgue, causing the coffee in his stomach to do the Hustle.

"Christ, Burt, that isn't drainage runoff."

The coroner didn't respond; a look of grave concentration etched his face as he focused the spray of the shower nozzle onto the body The pressurized water blasted the muck from the corpse and sent it spiraling down the drain. Burt washed off the man's broken legs and arms and then began the task of rinsing off his torso. The dark filth had seeped through the guy's clothing, soiling nearly every inch of him, but his head and upper body were by far the dirtiest.

Burt grimaced as the silt and slime were jetted away. He aimed the water onto the guy's chest and then onto his neck, dissolving the mud quickly and revealing what lay beneath. He jumped back and nearly dropped the nozzle as the water exposed the area of skin just above the man's shoulders. Burt leaned in to get a better look. "Jesus Christ almighty!" he shouted.

Carl, who had stood back avoiding the overspray, approached the basin to see what startled his friend. The water had revealed a mark on the man's neck: a dark round bruise with several deep perforations along the perimeter and one incision in the center. It was identical to the wound they had seen yesterday morning on Foothills Drive.

"Let me see that." Carl took the nozzle and directed the force of the water onto the man's face, making quick work of the muck concealing his features. First, the jaw was revealed, then the cheeks, and, a second later, the rest of the corpse's face, including his dark black hair.

Burt jumped back another two feet and screamed once again. "That's not possible!"

Carl stared with the world cartwheeling in his periphery. Burt was right; it wasn't possible. There was no way in hell he was looking at what he thought was in the basin. Holding his breath, Carl blinked hard to refocus, then took a step forward. An icy chill raced through his nervous system and settled in the base of his spine. He slowly exhaled and stood over the body. There was no denying its identity. Felix Castillo lay before them, in far worse shape than the first time he had been brought into the morgue.

His face was still recognizable, but it had changed considerably, and not just from the results of getting creamed by a truck. The skin beneath his eyes sagged in loose folds, overlapping his cheeks, and were covered in an almost reptilian texture of lamella-like scales that also peppered the man's forehead and the bridge of his nose. His mouth had grown disproportionately as well and was much wider and longer than it had been only yesterday.

Carl grabbed a pair of surgical gloves from the table and pulled them on. He bent down and lifted the man's upper lip, exposing the most significant change to have occurred. A chorus of gasps filled the morgue. Several rows of small, jagged barbs crowded Castillo's gumline, giving his mouth a threatening resemblance to that of a piranha or a shark.

"Dear God," Carl whispered.

"God's got nothing to do with that." Burt watched from a safe distance. "What the hell happened to him?"

Carl pulled the corpse's lip back even further and jumped when a loud pop escaped from deep within its throat. It happened without warning; Castillo's lower jaw flew open, dropping as if it had dislocated, and an oversized serpent-like tongue slid out of his mouth. It lolled to the side, nearly nine inches long, slender, and black, and tapered to a sharp point that looked an awful lot like a weapon.

The men recoiled in unison. Burt hid behind Carl, whose gut was now screaming. Abe and Tony both retreated from either side of the basin like a pair of synchronized swimmers, and no one said a word. The only sound that Carl heard was the thundering of his heart inside his chest, pumping like a freight train. His palms grew slick inside the rubber gloves, and the muscles in his neck tightened. Listening to the voice in his gut, he instinctively backed away and lowered his hand to the butt of his revolver.

After several tense seconds with nothing further happening, Abe leaned forward to get a better look. He didn't even have time to react. Felix's eyes flew open, and his serpentine tongue rocketed toward Abe like a guided missile. It wrapped around the man's throat and lifted him off his feet. Abe beat at the oil-slicked tongue with his clenched fists and opened his mouth to scream. The only sound to leave his lips was a strangled gurgle. A dark splash danced between them, if only for a second. It looked as if a shadow had been thrown in Abe's direction, but it happened so fast that no one was sure what they had seen. Abe gagged as the tongue tightened around his neck and pulled him closer toward the basin.

Burt made a desperate run towards the office, crashing into one of the lab tables, and Tony tripped over his own feet as he headed for the back door. Carl, who had been listening to the voice in his gut, was the only one who kept his head. He drew his revolver without thinking, instinct guiding his arm. Body on autopilot. Aim, exhale, squeeze.

The first bullet hit Felix in the chest, resulting in an ear-splitting shriek that echoed off every smooth surface in the morgue. The thing in the basin tried to sit up, but the broken bones in its arms and legs made the effort impossible. There was an audible crunch followed by a sickening snap as Felix attempted to right himself. It twisted and writhed when Carl put a second slug into its chest, and then it threw Abe across the room like a wet beanbag. The medical assistant crashed against the wall on the far side of the morgue with a tremendous thud and fell to the floor in a lifeless heap.

The snake-like appendage redirected its attack onto Carl, lashing out at him, snapping like the bands of a slingshot. Ducking to the right, he avoided it by inches and fired a third round into the thing's chest. The tongue retracted, and the body started to convulse in a violent fit. It flipped and slapped against the porcelain of the tub like a fish on hot pavement. Carl pulled the trigger a fourth time, burying the .38 caliber slug into the center of Felix's forehead. The odor of

THE OJANOX

burnt gunpowder filled the air; it combined with the stench of the creature laying in the basin, and the thing that had once gone by the name Felix Castillo finally stopped moving.

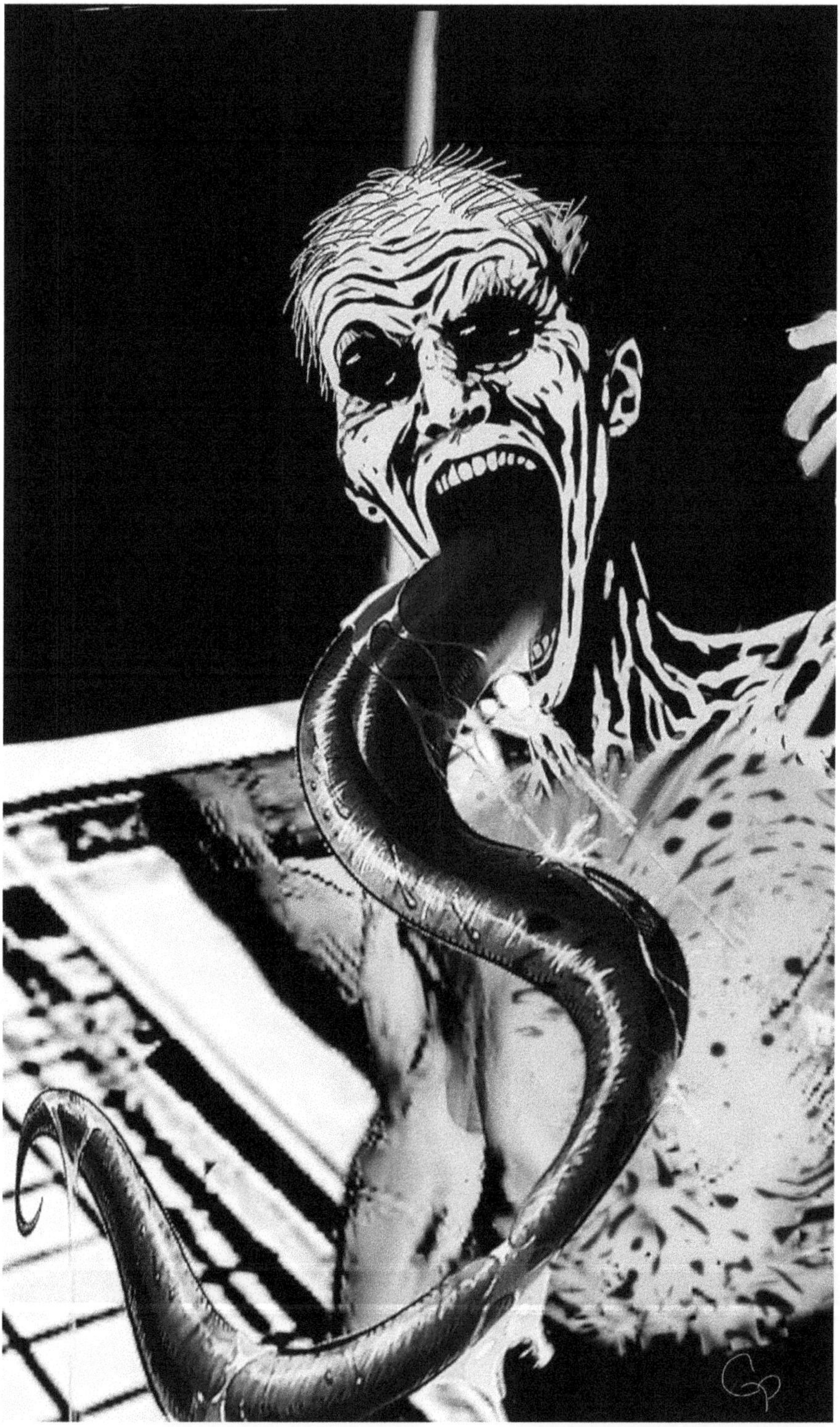

Chapter 24

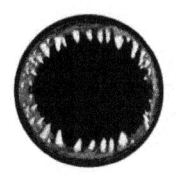

In just a few short hours, Janis became the most popular kid in class. Such a feat had never been accomplished by any other child in the history of Garrett Elementary. At least, the boys were impressed. The girls, on the other hand, felt differently about Janis Thompson. She had disrupted the hierarchy of the pride with one fell swoop of her magical powers. Even Troy wasn't immune. Fortunately, he had the recent enchantment of Wendy's own persuasive influence as a protective shield; however, that didn't make him invulnerable to the occasional peek at the goods.

Mike Barnes and Eric Helmsworth were drawn like iron filings to her strong magnetic presence. The boys gravitated towards Janis during lunch, introduced themselves, and made some valiant—yet awkward—attempts to impress the young lady. But she didn't appear interested and kept looking over at Troy and Wendy, who had gone off to the far side of the playground to eat lunch together. Until only a few hours ago, Wendy had been the new girl in class. She had moved to town just last month, but the overall reaction to her arrival had been far less grandiose.

"What's the big deal? I don't understand why they're all acting that way," she told Troy. "Nobody acts that stupid when a new *boy* starts school."

"Yeah," Troy said through a mouthful of Oscar Mayer bologna. Although he was no fan of the deli meat, he obliged when Wendy asked to trade for his peanut butter and jelly sandwich.

"Boys are so stupid," she said, eyeing Janis's flock of admirers. "Except you; you're different."

Troy didn't think he was all that different but maybe just smart enough to not make a total fool out of himself. He had *definitely* noticed the new girl, but even at ten years old, Troy knew you weren't supposed to stare when your girlfriend was watching.

Is Wendy my girlfriend? They had never actually talked about it, but he figured you didn't get kissed by a girl unless she wanted to be your girlfriend.

As if on cue, Wendy blurted, "So, aren't you going to ask me to be your girlfriend?"

Troy choked on the bologna and swallowed. "I um, thought um—" The truth was he didn't have any idea what he thought. However, Wendy was more than capable to do the thinking for both of them.

"What did you think, silly? Don't you know that you have to ask me? That's how it works. You ask me if I'll be your girlfriend, and then I say, I'll think about it. Jeez, everybody knows that."

Troy felt the heat rush to his face and was sure he had turned a deep shade of red. "Um ... will you be my girlfriend?"

"I'll think about it." Wendy smiled and took a bite of her sandwich with a look of satisfaction smeared across her face.

"I heard there's another *Star Wars* movie coming out next year." Troy changed the subject and hoped he didn't look like a total goof. "Maybe we could go see it."

"*The Weekly Reader* said George Lucas has nine movies he wants to make. That's why the first one was called *Part IV, A New Hope*."

Troy was more than a little impressed that a girl knew so much about his favorite movie. "Really? I always wondered about that. That's so cool. What else did it say?"

"Well, they said it's gonna take a really long time for all the movies to come out. We'll be grownups before they're finished making them."

"Oh man, I don't know if I can wait that long." A shadow cast over the area where they sat, interrupting the moment.

"Hi," a voice said.

Troy and Wendy looked up to find the new girl had left her gaggle of admirers and now stood before them.

"Hi," Wendy replied.

"Hi," Troy managed through a mouthful of bologna.

"Can I sit with you guys?" Janis asked. "Those boys are acting silly."

Troy looked over his shoulder and noticed Mike and the other boys staring in their direction as if something important was about to take place.

"Sure," he said.

Wendy straightened her back and stared at him.

"I'm Janis. What're your names?"

"I'm Wendy, and this is my boyfriend, Troy."

Troy squinted and turned, unsure if he had heard her right. *That was fast. I guess you're done thinking about it.*

"You're from Washington?" Wendy asked as Janis sat down between them.

"Yeah, well, I was born in Florida, then we moved to Washington later, when my mom got a job at the museum."

"Your mom works at a museum?" Troy asked, his interest piqued.

"She's an archeologist and studies artifacts." Janis wore a huge smile that almost seemed to sparkle when she spoke, and Troy understood why all the boys wanted to be around her. It was a smile that made you feel good inside, one that made him want to smile as well.

"No way, that's so cool!"

"We were just talking about *Star Wars*," Wendy said. "Did you see it yet?"

"Are you kidding?" Janis's smile lit up her entire face. "I saw it three times. It's, like, my favorite movie ever."

Troy didn't know why Wendy acted so weird when Janis first approached but noticed a change in the girl when the conversation switched subjects.

"Who's your favorite character?" Wendy asked.

"Princess Leia, of course!" Troy had a feeling Janis would say that.

"Mine too," Wendy agreed. "I liked her because they never make girls the heroes in movies. She was more of a leader than Luke and Han."

"Yeah, that's why I like her too."

"But they had to rescue her from Darth Vader," Troy said.

The girls both turned and gave him a set of looks that made Troy feel like he had said something stupid.

"She was a lot braver than both of them. Han only wanted the money. And Luke was just a kid." Janis turned to Wendy and smiled.

"I guess so." *I should stop talking.* But Troy was unable to control himself. "Wendy said there's gonna be more movies."

"I *said* there were going to be *nine* movies." Wendy's face tightened as if she had eaten a lemon. "At least that's what George Lucas wants to do."

"I read that too in the *Weekly Reader* at my old school." Janis smiled but still appeared distracted by the group of boys who continued to stare at them. "Why are those boys acting so weird?"

"Ignore them. Boys are immature," Wendy said. "My mom says boys mature two years slower than girls."

"The boys in my old school acted like that too. They were fine last year. But when we came back in September, they were different. Like they changed over the summer."

Troy pretended not to pay attention as the conversation shifted. *I know why they're acting funny.* He continued chewing his sandwich and praying at the same time. *Please don't ask me why they're acting funny, please don't.*

"You're a boy, Troy," Janis said, causing the bologna to ferment in his throat. "Why are they acting so funny?"

A cold sweat broke on his brow. *What the heck am I supposed to say now?* He looked at Wendy for support, but there was none to be found. With nowhere else to turn, he looked back at Janis, who only sat there staring at him with her great big trouble-making eyes.

"Um-um, I don't know." He cleared his throat; a piece of half-chewed bologna flew from his open mouth and landed in the grass.

"Well, you sure sound like you know." Wendy narrowed her eyes and stared him down. "Spill it, Troy."

"Come on. You know," he said, nodding at his chest and then looking back at the two girls. He repeated the movement a second time, motioning downward and then up at the girls with his eyebrows raised.

"What's he doing?" Janis asked. "I don't get it."

"Come on, Troy," Wendy said. "Just say it."

He felt it in his face, hot pins and needles spreading across his cheeks like a rash. Certain he was about to faint, Troy scanned the playground, looking for an escape route. The two lionesses had lured him into a false sense of security with talk of

THE OJANOX

Star Wars and trapped him. Troy cleared his throat a second time and struggled to think on his feet. Unfortunately, that wasn't one of his strong suits, and he folded under the pressure.

"It's because you have boobs! There, I said it! Are you happy? They never saw a girl in class with boobs before, and they can't handle it!" Troy felt like he had caught on fire and was sure he would pass out any second. *Jeeze, I can't believe they made me say it.* He wiped his brow and braced himself for the backlash.

Wendy and Janis stared at him for what felt like a lifetime without either of them saying a word. Then they turned to each other, smiled, and burst out laughing. Troy didn't understand. He expected Wendy to go ballistic and was sure Janis would have gotten embarrassed or offended.

"What? Why is that so funny?"

"Cause we're messing with you," Wendy said.

"W-what do you mean?"

"Do you really think I don't know about my boobs? Come on, Troy. They're kinda hard to miss, don't you think?" Janis continued to laugh until tears appeared in the corners of her eyes.

"You were so nervous," Wendy blurted. "Every girl in school knows why the boys are acting like a bunch of second graders. Anyway, I'm proud of you. I didn't think you would say anything. Maybe not all boys are as immature as my mom says." She leaned over and punched him in the arm, apparently giving her seal of approval.

Janis stopped laughing long enough to punch him in the other arm. "You're all right, Troy. That was very cool. You're the only guy who was ever honest about my boobs."

Troy felt like he would die if she didn't stop saying boobs. He needed to change the conversation, but once again, that came to thinking on his feet, which just wasn't going to happen. He cracked a smile and let a weak laugh fall out the side of his mouth.

"My mom's working late today," Janis said. "Would you guys like to come over after school for a snack?"

"Sure, but I have to ask my mom," Wendy told her.

Janis gave Troy a look that made him even more nervous than the whole boob conversation.

"I got to ask my mom too-um—probably."

"Great," Janis had taken their answers for yes, and a minute later, the bell rang, calling the children back into the building. Lunch was over. "You can meet my dog, Peanuts. She looks like Snoopy a little."

The three children grabbed their lunch boxes and headed back inside with the eyes of the entire fourth-grade class watching their every move.

Chapter 25

Garrett Grove had been home to the Lenape tribe long before any white man stepped foot on the continent. They lived harmoniously with nature, the spiritual world, and prized peace above all other attributes. Nestled in the foothills of Garrett Mountain, the land had been called Kittatinny by the Lenape, which loosely translated to Endless Mountain; however, Lonesome Mountain was a more accurate interpretation. Their tribal civilization was situated in the valley, flanked by the Lenape River on one side and King Lake on the other.

Still today, there were only two access routes in and out of Garrett Grove. The first was County Road 202 via Route 3, a long stretch of wooded highway spanning the Lenape River by way of the Gables Bridge. The bridge was old and in desperate need of repair; however, a simple patch job wasn't going to cut it. The unfortunate truth of the matter was that the Gables Bridge didn't have many winters left in it.

The other route was even more treacherous. Sunset Road was a twisting, turning, nerve-wrenching stretch of pavement that traversed the south face of Garrett Mountain. With a sheer rock wall towering above the road on one side and a steep drop on the other, it wasn't for the faint of heart. Before the road had been built, the isolated area was even more inaccessible, making the Grove the ideal location for the peaceful civilization.

The Lenape tribe worshiped the Great Spirit and believed in a mystical healing power generated within the land itself. From the mountain, they received their greatest gifts: food, protection, and life. Their tools and pottery were made with natural materials that came directly from the mountain as well.

The Lenape tribe occupied the area longer than anyone could be certain and had vanished before the first colonists arrived. And although archeologists knew the truth about what happened to most of the indigenous people (genocide perpetrated by the European settlers), that hadn't been the case on Lonesome Mountain. By the time the Grove was settled, the Lenape had already disappeared.

There were countless stories of lost civilizations from all over the world. *National Geographic* had published a piece about the subject and included the story of the Lenape in the article. Dr. Thompson, being the chief expert on the subject, was interviewed. She'd been studying the tribe since grad school and was fascinated with the mystery of their disappearance. Although she wasn't inclined to say anything just yet, she hoped that the DuCain expedition would reveal some of the answers to that mystery.

The cavern was declared structurally safe and appeared to extend well past the forty to fifty feet recorded during the initial inspection. Work lights, powered by a generator set up just outside the cave entrance, were installed and now illuminated all but the furthest reaches of the chamber. Stephanie and her team would have to limit their research to the main area until a secondary set of lights were added.

The entire party wore hard hats bearing the DuCain logo, as well as glow-in-the-dark safety vests. Stephanie's team consisted of herself and three coworkers: Joe Hillman, a fellow archeologist; Gail Herd, Stephanie's assistant and photographer; and Barry Knolls, a historian. Don completed the party of five and was the only DuCain representative.

Long shadows stretched out across the cavern floor and danced upon the walls as the men and women passed in front of the work lights. Upon entering, the first details to catch Don's eye were the elaborate cave drawings. Colorful murals covered nearly every inch of the stone surfaces. The vibrant depictions had held up exceptionally well over the centuries. Not only was the vividness of the murals striking but their complexity and size were daunting, with some taking up entire walls. Images of men, women, and children engaged in some type of ritual were illustrated in one of the scenes. Another was decorated with reproductions of various animals, many of which were recognizable; however, some appeared to have been made up.

Skeletal remains littered the floor; many that were intact, while others, nothing more than a random scattering of bones. What could have been some breed of large cat lay next to the skeleton of a child. The proximity of the two suggested to Don that they perished together.

Stephanie, who had finally stopped talking for the first time all morning, focused intently on the murals, pointing out the various details to her assistant. The young girl dressed as if she were going on safari, in tan shirt and fatigues with nearly a dozen pockets in each, all jammed with extra rolls of film and various camera equipment. Gail followed Stephanie's lead, taking pictures at a feverish pace. The sudden flash momentarily blinded Don, who was looking in the wrong direction. A large white dot filled his vision for almost a full minute before it faded.

"Gail, take a couple shots of this." Stephanie pointed to a figure in the foreground of the first painting. "I want to get these developed as soon as possible." The girl continued to click away, exhausting roll after roll of film.

Don's eyesight slowly returned as he stood behind the women, trying to see what they were interested in. The wall that held their attention extended about ten feet into the cave from the entrance. The mural portrayed the Lenape gathered around one of their own, who was either being buried or honored, it was difficult to tell. It looked like a ritual, possibly a funeral for a chief or a holy man. The man on the ground was dressed in an elaborate gown and headdress.

The following scene showed the same man being buried as his fellow tribesmen cast handfuls of dirt onto him, confirming that the previous scene had been a funeral. Finally, the third painting, which Stephanie and Gail appeared most interested in, showed the same holy man chasing three children. He was dressed in the same gown and headdress from the other scenes, only now it was stained darker—the same color as the dirt he'd been buried in.

The man's eyes were painted black, a stark contrast to their white color in the previous scenes. Something else was strange about him as well: his jaw hung open, disproportionately larger than it should have been. It was hard to make out the details in the dim light of the cave, but to Don, it looked as if the strange mouth was filled with tiny, pointed teeth. Also, a dark cloud of smoke, resembling a wreath, had been painted around the holy man's head, obscuring many of the finer details of the image.

Gail exhausted an entire roll of film on this mural alone before she and Stephanie moved on to the other areas of the cave. They made their way to where Joe and Barry worked, recording information about the bone formations. Joe was the older of the two men, with a horseshoe of unruly grey hair nestled around a perfectly smooth bald head. Barry, on the other hand, didn't have a bald patch on his body. He wore his thick hair on the long side, his beard was unkempt and tangled, and even the hair on his arms looked as if it had erupted from his skin in bristly patches. Don overheard a little of what was being said by the group. *Would you look at that … What do you make of this … See I told you,* was some of it before he moved on to his own investigation. Then something caught his eye.

"Don, just be careful not to disturb anything. We have to inventory every item before any of it can be moved. Thank you." Stephanie didn't wait for a reply, nor did she ask for one.

Don was too focused on the cave itself to take it personally. The flash of the camera had revealed something he hadn't noticed before. He leaned in close to the cavern wall and examined the composition of the rock. *What the hell?* The entire cave was comprised of a massive deposit of lodestone, an iron ore also known as magnetite. It suddenly all made perfect sense, the reason why his equipment hadn't detected the cave before blasting. Lodestone was a natural magnetic ore, known to throw off compasses and interfere with electronic equipment. Don hadn't even considered the existence of the mineral because of how uncommon it was in the area. He felt foolish for having missed such an obvious answer, but it still came as a relief. *Thank God. It wasn't my fault after all.*

Gail took more pictures of the skeletal remains, and as the flash went off, Don turned his head away from the glare. The strobe lit up the area of the cave in front of him, revealing several random shadows. He crouched down to inspect the marble-like objects littering the floor, being careful not to disturb anything.

There were more pieces of the lodestone, only these had been formed into perfectly rounded spheres that resembled musket balls. Don knew the Lenape had manufactured tools, which was evident from all the arrowheads that had been found in the area, but this seemed awfully sophisticated. He wasn't a historian or an archeologist, but he was familiar with minerals, and he knew it took a great deal of patience and talent to wear a piece of iron ore into a perfect musket-sized ball. The flash went off again as Don got up and walked to where the rest of the party was gathered.

Stephanie and Joe were crouched over two of the skeletons that appeared to be relatively intact, neither of which could have measured any longer than four feet in length. Don figured they were the remains of children. Next to them were several animal skeletons. One looked like it belonged to a large cat and the other from some type of reptile. The jawbones on both skulls were massive and filled with incredibly sharp-looking teeth. What surprised Don the most was how the bones and everything else in the cave had been so well-preserved.

"Are dig sites always in such pristine condition?" he asked.

"Almost never," Stephanie said. "This is an amazing find. I wish my father was here to see it."

"He would be very proud," Barry told her.

"You know, Don, this is *your* discovery. Of course, Mr. DuCain owns the site, but you're the one who told the men to blast here. You're about to become famous."

Not knowing how to reply, Don smirked and shrugged his shoulders. He turned back and watched Barry focus the beam of his flashlight onto the rib area of the cat skeleton. There were several dark objects embedded into the bones and some others scattered on the floor close to the remains.

"What do you suppose these are?" Barry asked, leaning in closer.

"I have no idea," Joe answered.

"Lodestone," Don said.

They all looked up at him. A smile slowly spread across Stephanie's face. "What?" she asked.

"That's lodestone ... magnetite. The whole cave is made up of it. Those little guys right there have been shaped into marbles or some kind of musket ball. And I can tell you one thing, that wasn't easy to do."

"Are you sure?" Barry asked.

"Well, I'm sure it's magnetite. And judging by the way they're embedded into the bone, I'd say, yeah ... I'm pretty sure they were used as weapons."

"I'd have to agree," Stephanie said. "I told you, Joe. This is the proof we were looking for. Come on, Gail, get a few shots of this."

Gail took more pictures in rapid succession. The constant flashing made Don dizzy, but now that his eyes had adjusted and he could see a bit more clearly, he noticed there were other weapons in the cave as well, all of which appeared to be comprised of lodestone.

"I thought you said that the Lenape were a peaceful people?" he asked.

"That's right; they were," Joe said.

Don surveyed the cave, inspecting the skeletal remains and the random piles of bones that were everywhere. Then he focused on the hoard of weapons stacked against the walls and the tiny musket balls littering the floor, some of which were embedded into the ribs of the one creature. "Well." He rubbed his eyes and took it all in. "You could have fooled me."

Chapter 26

Dr. Ziegler arrived at the Chilton Medical Center at twelve thirty-five p.m. He entered through the emergency room doors and passed the reception desk where Head Nurse TenHove was stationed. The grey-haired woman held a clipboard in one hand and the house phone pressed against her ear with the other. She looked up at Ziegler, pursed her lips, and shook her head as if in disapproval. *Looks like someone needs to get laid.* The next thought to enter Ziegler's head was an image of Jackie Gilmartin, who he expected to find at the front desk instead of sour-faced Doris TenHove. He and Jackie had special plans last night, but after working a triple shift, he passed out without even looking at the phone. Then after sleeping late through the alarm, he hadn't had time to call her before leaving for work. Besides, he was anxious to check on the condition of his three young patients. He nodded to the head nurse, making his way through the reception area, and proceeded towards the ICU wing.

"Hello, Dr. Ziegler," a female voice said. He turned to find the young blonde candy striper and quickly checked her name tag. Cyndi, with an i.

"Hello, Cyndi," he said, noticing her full, pouty lips and the inviting blush of her cheeks. "How are you today?"

"Fine, thank you." She smiled, batted a pair of big doe eyes, and that was all it took. Ziegler forgot what he was doing, stopped in his tracks, and looked her up and down. He immediately started doing the math in his head. *She looks too young, but I've seen her here in the afternoon, so she's not in high school. At least eighteen ... right?*

"You've been working quite a lot lately." He leaned against the wall and brushed the hair out of his eyes.

"Oh, I took the fall semester off from college, so I have a lot of spare time on my hands."

College girl. Ding-Ding-Ding!

"Oh really." He squared his jaw and tilted his head toward her. "So, what do you like to do for fun? Don't tell me it's all work and no play."

Cyndi fed him a devilish grin and leaned forward to whisper in his ear. "Meet me later, and I'll show you."

The young candy striper turned without saying another word and left him leaning against the wall. She walked off, jiggling in all the right places, and Ziegler was helpless to look away. *That was too easy. Like taking candy from a candy striper.* He watched as she disappeared around the corner, and intended to take her up on her proposal as soon as his schedule allowed.

He remained there for a moment, basking in his glory, then remembered his current objective and headed towards the intensive care unit. He entered the dressing room, washed up, and donned the necessary protective gear.

Dr. Ziegler walked down the hall dressed in a full body gown, surgical gloves, and face shield. He stood before the closed door of Robert Boyle's room, rechecking for any breaches in his clothing. After a thorough inspection and satisfied that he had taken every necessary precaution, he placed his hand on the cold steel of the doorknob and entered. Ziegler stopped as the sound of his footsteps echoed off the back wall of the vacant room. Robert Boyle was gone, along with any sign that he had ever been there at all. The bed was now made, the machines were missing, and the entire place had been scrubbed top to bottom. The lingering smell of industrial-strength disinfectant was the room's only occupant.

Dear God! Ziegler's mind attempted to latch on to any logical explanation but could only come up with one. The child had died. *This is my fault*, repeated in his head, *this is my fault.* He exited and ran down the hall to Erin Richards's room. His heart clenched in his chest as he grabbed the doorknob and pulled. A strangled gasp left his lips. The room was as empty as the first, with no sign of the little girl. *This can't be.* Ziegler couldn't even imagine a scenario as to why he hadn't been notified. Dr. Malcolm would have called him right away if something happened to both children.

Spinning one-eighty on his heels, he bolted toward the room where Ben Richards had been admitted. He crashed through the door and froze. Silence greeted him from the shadows of the empty room. *What the hell is going on here?* Feeling like he had been kicked in the chest, Ziegler returned to the hallway and dialed Dr. Malcom's office on the house phone. He stood there with his mind jumping to dangerous conclusions as he waited for the man to answer for well over a minute.

"Come on!" he shouted, slamming the receiver down. A second later, Ziegler was sprinting down the hall at top speed. He turned the corner and nearly collided with two nurses blocking his path. He swerved just in time, tripping over his own feet but somehow remaining upright, and continued on his way. He barged into the chief's office and stopped short. The lights had been left on, reports were scattered on the desk, but Dr. Malcolm was not there.

"What the hell?" He struggled to catch his breath. The children had been in terrible shape; there was no denying that. Still, Ziegler knew that if even one of them had passed, Dr. Malcolm would have called him right away. And the man would have sent the goddamn National Guard to rip his ass out of bed if something had happened to all three.

He peeled his facemask off and picked up his boss's phone.

"Yes, Nurse TenHove; this is Dr. Ziegler. Could you page Dr. Malcolm for me?"

"I'm afraid Dr. Malcolm isn't here."

"What?! What do you mean he's not here?"

"I'm sorry. I was under the impression you kn—"

"I don't know anything. Where are the children that were in the ICU, and where is Dr. Malcolm?"

"Dr. Malcolm is with them. He called a colleague in Oswego, and they were transported to the toxicology center late last night."

"When did this happen? Why wasn't I notified?" Ziegler shifted on his feet.

"I believe sometime between three and four a.m. I was under the impression that Dr. Malcolm had notified you. Apparently, he made the decision after examining the children last night. Let's see ..." There was a rustling of papers as she paused to look. "Here it is; at three thirty-seven, Dr. Malcolm signed all three of the patients to be transported to the care of the Oswego Toxicology Center for further testing. Dr. Freedman was here as well. I imagine one of them left the paperwork either in your mailbox or in your office."

"Nurse TenHove, don't you find it a bit strange to transport patients at that time of the night?"

"It's really not my place to say. I'm sure Dr. Malcolm had a good reason for doing so."

"Is Dr. Freedman on the floor?" he asked.

"I haven't seen him. But that doesn't mean he isn't here somewhere."

"Thank you." Ziegler hung up and made a beeline toward his own office. He pulled off the rest of his protective clothing on his way, then walked in and found the reports on his desk. There was a cover sheet that had been signed by Dr. Malcolm.

Dr. Ziegler,

Sorry not to have called you, but it was late, and you had already put in a triple shift. Your test results proved tremendously helpful and allowed us to narrow down the toxins, potentially a viper; however, the bacterium is unknown. There is a toxicology specialist that has agreed to help. I have accompanied the children and their families and will be in Oswego. I will be in touch periodically. Until then, I trust that Chilton is in safe hands under the care of Dr. Freedman and yourself. He is a seasoned vet and won't steer you wrong. Again, thank you for your dedication to the welfare of the patients; this is a commendable attribute that will no doubt look excellent on your review.

Regards,
Dr. John Malcolm

Ziegler felt somewhat relieved but still had a lot of questions. He flipped through the pages of reports to find several pictures of what appeared to be puncture wounds. *That can't be.* He had checked the kids thoroughly and hadn't found any marks at all. However, the first image showed the signature bite mark of a viper with bruising around the infected areas. The name on the report said Robert Boyle. It was a close-up of the bottom of the boy's foot. *How could I have missed such an obvious wound?* Ziegler doubted that whatever was making these children sick was any type of snake venom, at least none that he had ever seen. The following photo was the back of Erin Richards's ankle, depicting the same type of wound, a snake bite. The third was of Ben Richards's big toe.

Ziegler didn't consider himself a snake venom specialist by any means, but he had treated plenty of hunters who'd been bitten by timber rattlers and cottonmouths in the past. The children's blood definitely had a toxin in it, but the rest of their symptoms didn't fit the classic mold of hemotoxic envenomation. Surely Peter Gillick or the guys in toxicology would have picked up on that right away. He was desperate for answers and needed to see what Dr. Freedman knew about the late-night transportation.

He called the man's office and got no answer, then he checked the emergency room and didn't find him there either. None of the attending staff had seen Dr. Freedman since earlier this morning; Ziegler figured he was probably catching a few winks in one of the empty rooms.

However, finding Dr. Freedman wasn't the only thing on Ethan Ziegler's plate; he had rounds to make and other patients to attend to. For now, he needed to trust that Dr. Malcolm had made the right call concerning the children. He set off on his rounds and was quickly consumed with the workload.

Felix Castillo's body had finally stopped moving—for the second time, possibly the third—and neither Carl nor Burt were about to give it the opportunity to get up again. With Tony's help, they moved the corpse to a lab table and secured it with a roll of duct tape. Carl tightly wrapped the tape around the arms, legs, and chest, taking extra precaution to cover the mouth and fasten the head to the table. It was the business end for most animals and reptiles and had proven to be the case with Castillo as well. The thing's tongue was long and powerful and had tossed Abe across the room like a dishrag. Carl had unloaded three bullets into Felix's chest, which hadn't done anything but piss it off. The final bullet had hit him in the head, and that one did the trick.

None of the men said much after that. There were no answers anyone could offer, and they were all thinking the same thing: Felix Castillo had been dead Sunday morning. Dead as Dillinger, no question about it. When the body disappeared yesterday afternoon, Carl had been willing to put his badge on the line to cover Burt's ass. Even he hoped it was a prank and that a few kids had stolen the body. Except that's not what happened. Felix had walked in front of a bread truck early this morning, presumably rendering himself dead for the second time. That was until he got up again and killed Abe Gorman, who hadn't even seen it coming.

They moved Abe's body to one of the tables and checked his vitals, but the man was gone. Carl had just finished securing Felix with the duct tape when Burt tapped him on the shoulder. "Um, we all just saw that. Castillo was dead. He was dead yesterday when we found him, and he was dead when he got hit by the truck this morning."

"I know." There was little else he could say. "I know."

"But that's not possible." Burt's voice rose a full octave. "Dead guys can't do that. What the hell was that, anyway? That's like a goddamn frog or snake's tongue. What the hell happened to this guy?"

Carl took a long, deep breath and released it slowly. "I have no idea."

"That thing isn't human. I don't know what happened to him, but he didn't look like that yesterday." Burt's hands shook as he motioned toward the man taped to the table. "It's like he's mutating or something."

"Is there any of that scotch left?" Carl asked.

"Yeah, I think so."

"I need you to go get the bottle, and I want you to take a good shot. You're hysterical."

The old man didn't need to be told twice. He sprinted to his office, retrieved the bottle, and unscrewed the cap. He took a long swig, then returned to the morgue a moment later. He offered it to Carl, who accepted the drink and passed it to Tony. It helped, at least for the time being.

"Look, I'll agree this is something we've never seen before, but there has to be a logical explanation." Although Carl couldn't think of one.

"That's a vampire," Tony blurted out.

"That's not helpful." Carl shook his head. "There's no such thing."

"Then what the hell do you call that?"

"I don't call it a vampire!" Carl shouted. "I'd call it unexplainable. I'd call it a mutation. But I sure as hell wouldn't call it a goddamn vampire."

Burt took another pull from the bottle. "He's right, Tony. That's not helping. We've all seen the movies, and whatever that is, it sure isn't a vampire."

Carl removed his hat and rubbed his temples, thankful that the scotch had relaxed Burt some. "The truth is we don't know anything about Felix Castillo or his background. For all we know, he could have been born with some rare mutation. And that's why you're gonna cut this son of a bitch open, and were gonna get to the bottom of this, right here and now."

Carl watched as Burt's face drained to an impossible shade of white. "Who? Me?"

"You're the coroner."

Tony took the bottle and tilted it back. "Look, this guy started walking around after he died, like a vampire ... I'm just saying, if it walks like a duck."

Carl felt the heat rise in his chest but held back while Tony finished.

"And it just killed Abe. I mean, shouldn't we tape him down too? Just to be sure."

Carl and Burt looked at each other for a brief, tense moment. Burt shrugged his shoulders, and Carl raised his eyebrows. "That's not a bad idea," Carl said, grabbing the duct tape. Together, the three men proceeded to bind Abe's body to the gurney, taking extra care to secure his mouth.

Chapter 27

Troy, Wendy, and Janis set out after school with the eyes of the entire class on them. Boys who had been enchanted by the new girl found it unacceptable how she had bonded with Troy so quickly. And the girls in the class watched and whispered as well. Janis and Wendy noticed them gossiping and found it exciting, although Troy was oblivious to what was going on. He was also unaware that his innocence and ability to remain unaffected had somehow proved him worthy in the eyes of his two new friends.

As they made their way across the parking lot, Wendy handed Troy her *Brady Bunch* lunch box. "The man is supposed to carry our things," she said, taking Janis's *Starsky and Hutch* container and handing it to him as well.

Troy struggled to find a comfortable position, now juggling three lunch boxes—including his own with a picture of the Fonz on the front—and nearly dropped them all in the process. Then Wendy took both her and Janis's notebooks and dumped them into the pocket of his knapsack. The extra weight set him off balance, but Troy straightened his back, stood tall, and managed to exude a little extra bravado. *Jeez, I had no idea being someone's boyfriend was such hard work.* With the straps already digging into his shoulders, he gritted his teeth and prayed that the walk to Janis's house wasn't all that long.

They made their way past the municipal building where the sheriff's department and courthouse were located, then cut behind the first aid squad/firehouse. A baseball diamond sat perpendicular to the buildings, with a path etched into the grass just beyond centerfield. The route then cut across the railroad tracks and led the children to the small community called the Village. From there, it was just a few side streets to Janis's house.

When they arrived, they found Janis's aunt in the driveway and two moving men carrying a sofa. She saw the children approaching and abandoned what she was doing. "Well, what do we have here?" she said with a smile. Troy thought the woman looked like an older version of Janis, with dark blonde curls and a contagious toothy grin.

"Aunt Lynn, these are my new friends, Wendy and Troy. They're in my class. Can I show them my room?"

"Nice to meet you, Wendy, Troy." She shook both their hands. "Sure. Are you guys hungry? I think we have some chocolate chips and milk?"

"Yes, please." It was unanimous.

"Your mom won't be home for a while, hon. Try not to get in the movers' way, and I'll bring up some snacks in a few minutes."

"Thanks, Aunt Lynn," Janis replied and headed toward the house with her blonde curls bouncing as she went.

"Thank you," Troy and Wendy added as a small white beagle with black spots bounded out of the house and intercepted them, its tail wagging so hard it looked like it might throw out a hip.

"Hi, Peanuts." Janis bent down to let the pooch lick her face. "How's my good girl?"

"She really does look like Snoopy," Troy said.

The dog greeted him and Wendy with equal enthusiasm. They took turns petting and scratching her ears till she rolled over on her back in the grass, exposing her belly, clearly in heaven. A second later, Janis entered the house, and the rest of them followed.

The place was filled with cardboard boxes and stacks of furniture wrapped in blankets. There weren't any pictures on the walls or plants hanging in the windows, and the children had to zigzag around the maze of clutter just to get to the staircase. They carefully stepped over the piles of books on the steps and made their way up to Janis's bedroom. Troy gasped at the immaculate state of it.

Janis's bed had already been set up, and the room looked as if she had lived there for years instead of just a few days.

"My aunt got here last week, but my mom and I didn't come till Saturday. So, this is my new room." Janis threw her hands out as if she were revealing a magic trick.

Troy's attention shot to the *Star Wars* movie poster hanging on the wall above her bed. It was the big one that had been used in the theaters.

"Wow, that's so cool!" He gawked at the size of it.

"Thanks." She walked over to a bookcase. "Check this out." The shelves contained all the *Star Wars* action figures. The princess stood front and center, flanked by the rest of the characters on either side.

"Oh my gosh," Wendy said. "You have every figure. I only have the princess. You're so lucky."

"Na." Janis shrugged. "My dad buys me lots of stuff since my parents got divorced. I don't really see him much, so he sends them to me." She took one of the figures from the shelf and handed it to Wendy. "Here, you can have this one. I got a couple."

Troy had almost dropped the lunch boxes several times along the way, and then again coming up the stairs. His arms trembled from the strain as he released his hold and set them to the floor. Then he wiggled out of his knapsack and placed it down as well. Peanuts didn't miss a beat and inspected each item thoroughly, making sure to sniff every square inch of the lunch boxes.

"This is super cool for a girl's room," he said, trying to work the cramps out of his hands and shoulders. "I mean, it's not all girly and stuff."

"Thanks ... I guess." Janis took a case off her shelf and placed it on the bed. She unfastened the snaps and lifted the lid. Troy let out an exaggerated gasp when Janis revealed the treasures inside. Within the case were over a dozen separate compartments lined with cotton. Inside each chamber sat individual arrowheads, spearheads, and smaller objects that looked like sharks' teeth.

"No way!" He leaned in closer. "Where did you get all of those?"

"My mom gave them to me. She works for the museum and finds this stuff all the time." The children focused on the box of artifacts, noticing the perfect condition of the arrowheads. Labels were inserted into the compartments as well, depicting where each item had been found along with a date and name of tribe.

"Your mom found all of these?" Wendy held on to her action figure as she studied the arrowheads.

"The woods in town are called the foothills, and you can find arrowheads there too. Scott Cole found one on a class trip. I go there with Rob all the time, but we still haven't found any yet." Troy told the girls about his adventures, trying to sound impressive but doubting there was much of a chance. Not with all the cool trophies Janis already had. Her reaction caught him by surprise.

"Really? Maybe we could all go together. As long as you don't mind looking for arrowheads with a couple of girls." Janis flashed an exaggerated smile.

"I don't mind; that would be cool." Troy had no idea that at just ten years old, Janis had already figured out how to get exactly what she wanted from the men in her life and been practicing on her dad since her parents got divorced. "I'll show you guys anytime. Maybe Rob will feel better and can come with us." Which gave him a great idea. "What are you both dressing as for Halloween?"

"Princess Leia, of course," Wendy said, rolling her eyes. "You already saw my costume, silly."

"I bet you look exactly like her," Janis said.

"You should have seen her. She looked awesome," Troy agreed, causing Wendy to blush and shove him.

"You missed Troy's party. He made a haunted house in his garage that was so scary. Oh my God, even the boys were scared. Tommy Negal was crying," Wendy said. "There was one room that was full of rats. You could feel them crawling on your feet. But my favorite room was the one with the strobe light." She winked at Troy.

"That sounds like a lot of fun. I wish I saw it."

Troy stood a little taller with his newfound confidence swelling within. "Well, I was supposed to start taking everything down, but I wanted to wait for Rob to get better. You know, so he could walk through it one last time since he helped build it. I bet my parents would let me show it off again if you wanted to see it. I call it Scream in the Dark."

"Scream in the Dark," Janis repeated. "That's so cool. I want to see it."

"I'll ask my mom and dad tonight and see what they say. Oh no!" Troy blurted. "I forgot to call my mom. Can I use your phone?"

"Who wants a snack?" Janis's aunt entered the room with a tray of chocolate chip cookies and a pitcher of milk, causing Peanuts to jump up with her tail beating like a windshield wiper.

"Yes, please," Janis answered for all of them. "Can Troy use the phone to call his mom?"

"Sure." Lynn set the tray down on the nightstand. "Right this way, Troy." She led him out of the room and left the girls with the cookies and milk. They dug in.

"How long have you and Troy been boyfriend and girlfriend?" Janis asked with half a cookie in her mouth.

"Well, we kinda liked each other since I moved here last month, but—" Wendy leaned in and whispered. "I kissed him at the party, and today he asked me to be his girlfriend."

"You did?" Janis bounced where she stood. "He seems nice, not stupid like the other boys."

"Yeah, that's what I like about him too. I mean, he still gets a little stupid every now and then but not as much as the other boys. He's different, probably because he spends more time with his mom than his dad. You're gonna like Mrs. Fischer; she's cool. Too bad you weren't at the party. She told us a scary story; it was far-out."

It was Janis's turn to lean in and whisper. "Did you guys really kiss?" Wendy nodded yes. "What was it like? Were you scared?"

Wendy giggled, then looked over her shoulder to make sure they were still alone. "I was at first. I didn't really know what to do. So I did it again."

"Oh my God!" Janis's voice jumped an octave, and she covered her mouth. "You did it twice?" She started to giggle as well.

Wendy smiled and nodded her head. They were both laughing when Troy walked back into the room but stopped as soon as they saw him.

"What's so funny?" he asked.

The girls exchanged a quick glance. "Nothing, just girl talk," Wendy told him and shoved a cookie in her mouth.

"Have some chocolate chips," Janis offered, and Troy didn't need to be told a second time. They were Chips Ahoy, his favorite. Apparently, they were Peanuts's favorite too, who waited patiently underfoot for any crumbs to fall. "We should all go trick-or-treating and dress as the characters from *Star Wars*. Troy, you can be Luke, and Wendy is already Princess Leia."

"Don't forget Rob. He can be Han Solo if he feels better," Troy added.

"Who will you be?" Wendy asked.

"That's easy." Janis opened her closet door and poked her head inside. She rummaged around for a few seconds, rearranging and searching within until she appeared to have found what she was looking for. She struggled for a moment and then popped her head out and jumped toward Wendy and Troy. She growled at them with a full-size Chewbacca mask covering her head.

"Oh my God, that's the best!" Wendy shrieked.

Troy couldn't control the excitement brimming within him and felt as if his smile were too big for his face. "We're going to look so cool! Don't forget the costume contest at school on Friday. We'll definitely win."

He turned his attention to the collection of arrowheads and finished his last cookie. "Janis, what are those little things on the bottom row?" He pointed to the perfectly pointed triangles that looked like tiny arrowheads.

"Those are teeth." She picked one up and handed it to him. "My mother said no one really knows what they belong to. There was a Native American colony that disappeared in the 1400s."

"Back in the time of Columbus?" Wendy asked.

"I think even before that. It was named Cokia, or something like that. It's called America's forgotten city, and it was a huge civilization in Illinois. Then, one day, they disappeared, just like that ... vanished."

"What happened to them?" Troy asked.

"No one knows for sure. But my grandfather was one of the archeologists on the excavation, and he told my mom everything about it."

"Really, what does she think?" Wendy studied the tooth in Troy's palm.

"She never really said. But the museum she works for found a whole bunch of these weird teeth and some strange animal bones."

"Maybe they got eaten," Troy said.

"That's what I think too."

"What kind of animal is it?" He flipped the item over in his palm, noticing how it resembled a piranha or a shark's tooth.

"An Ojanox," Wendy said. "That's definitely an Ojanox tooth, if you ask me."

Troy looked at her and shook his head. "Come on, my mom made up that story." He turned to Janis. "She's a great storyteller ... usually. She was trying to scare us at the party, so she made up a Halloween story. It was pretty good too, until she made up a dumb name for the monster. She called it an Ojanox."

"Sounds pretty scary to me," Janis said, taking a closer look at the tooth herself. "Looks like it could be an Ojanox tooth, if you ask me."

"I told you, Troy. Don't disagree with the girls," Wendy said. "Everyone knows girls are smarter than boys."

Troy was smart enough not to disagree. He kept his mouth shut and smiled. *Man, it's hard being a boyfriend.* It took a lot more practice and patience than he'd imagined. Now he knew why the other boys in school didn't have girlfriends. It was a full-time job.

Although he wasn't consciously aware of the occasion, it had been a pivotal day in Troy Fischer's life. He learned just how different boys were from girls and how hard it was to look cool in front of them. He struggled to say the right things and not act immature because if there was one thing his new friends were focused on, it was how fast girls matured compared to boys. It wasn't like he could forget since Wendy had made it a point to remind them, more than just a few times. It made Troy feel like a traitor to have to agree with them, but given the audience, he didn't think he had a choice.

Troy couldn't wait to tell Rob everything that had happened. In one action-packed Monday, he had become Wendy's boyfriend and met the new girl in class. He had already decided that Janis and Rob would become instant friends when they all went trick-or-treating on Halloween. He couldn't believe how cool Janis was. *Whoever heard of a girl collecting arrowheads and teeth and even having a Chewbacca mask?* Troy wouldn't have been surprised if his new friend had the entire costume hidden somewhere in her closet.

When it was time to go, he told the girls goodbye and set off with plenty of time to spare. He didn't want to get home late after being allowed over to his new friend's house for the first time and hoped to go back to see what other cool things she collected. Janis thanked him for coming, told him she would see him tomorrow, and Wendy decided it was time to leave as well. Together, they walked to the end of the block, where Wendy needed to turn left and Troy to the right. He knew it was customary to kiss your girlfriend goodbye but still wasn't comfortable with the practice. Again, Wendy proved that girls really did mature faster than boys and kissed him on the side of the mouth. Then she spun on her heels and quickly walked away.

"See you tomorrow," she said, and skipped off in the other direction.

Troy headed home with his chest inflated and a new spring in his step. He swung his lunch box in long arcs, feeling like the first man to climb Mt. Everest. Taking in his surroundings, he checked out the Jack-o'-lanterns on the front porches, the fake cobwebs in the windows, and the spooky decorations set on nearly every lawn. Freshly fallen leaves of every color danced across the grass, adding a soundtrack to the seasonal displays. Troy had always loved autumn, with the sense of mystery and wonder that it brought. But today, it felt as if a whole new element had been added to the mix. He figured that had something to do with his new friends ... the girls, who had somehow enhanced the mystery of the season. There was something taboo about the way Wendy made him feel. Troy had no idea he wasn't the first boy to become enchanted by the fairer sex. He couldn't describe the way he felt, and had it been 1679 instead of 1979, he might have called it witchcraft, which wasn't that far from the truth. Still, for Troy, it was a wonderful surprise accentuated by the coming of fall. The wind appeared to sense his mood and tossed his hair just as he crossed over the railroad tracks and cut across center field.

He passed the municipal building and backtracked his way to the school. From there, he needed to zigzag through a couple side streets to get from the Turnpike to the Boulevard. Instead, Troy opted for a more direct route and cut through the graveyard behind the Lutheran Church. He usually walked this way with Rob, the two boys noticing the dates and names on the headstones along the way. One of the oldest ones they had seen dated back to 1806, although many were too worn to read and could have been much older.

Troy and Rob had been walking through the graveyard when they first decided to use the names I.P. Daily and Bob Frapples on the headstones in their haunted house. He remembered that day well and laughed under his breath, then quickly stopped, remembering where he was. As if sensing his thoughts, the wind picked up and the temperature felt like it had suddenly dropped several degrees. Troy continued on his way past the old burial markers; David Swift, Beloved Husband and Father 1824-1878. Another one read, In Loving Memory Abigail Rosewood 1912-1965. He zipped up his coat to block the wind and stopped in front of a grave he hadn't noticed before. The inscription read Sheriff Allen Primrose Loving Father 1922-1976. *That must be Sheriff Primrose's dad.* Troy wasn't sure if he remembered him.

Another gust of wind raced between the headstones, causing a branch to snap somewhere in the distance. Troy jumped and turned in the direction the noise had originated. The tree limbs now bent back against the strong breeze, and the leaves had started to turn themselves inside out. He scanned the area behind him, checking the gravestones, and caught the slightest flicker of motion, as if someone had ducked behind one of the large mausoleums. A cold wind raced a shiver across his scalp, and Troy was overcome with a sense of vulnerability and an unshakable notion that he was being watched. The sky above him grew darker, looking as if it might rain any second. He started to walk again, faster now, with the feeling growing stronger with every stride. He'd heard the stories of what happened to kids who walked through graveyards alone but always thought it was something grownups made up to keep them from trespassing. Troy quickened his pace, using all his willpower to not look back over his shoulder once again. He could see the fence that bordered the main road and double-stepped his way toward it.

He heard another noise behind him, as if someone had coughed or shouted, only this time it was much closer. Now Troy was certain there was something behind him and it had started chasing him. Fear sizzled in his blood like boiling oil, making his face tingle with pins and needles. His legs threatened to cramp and glue him in his tracks, but survival kicked in, and Troy broke into a full sprint. The second he took off, it screamed—an agonizing bellow that sounded like a howl mixed with a shriek. There was a flash of movement he saw in the corner of his eye, of something running parallel on his right. It darted out from behind the tombstones and disappeared behind another. Then he noticed something else moving on his left. *Oh God, there's two of them.* They were trying to pin him in the graveyard and cut him off before he could reach the gate. He couldn't tell who or what was trying to ambush him, thinking maybe they were dogs or even a couple of men, but he wasn't about to stop to get a better look.

Troy had never been the most athletic kid in school, but he was a ten-year-old in good health, and he had a plan. He knew if he ran straight for the gate, the men, or whatever it was, would edge him out and catch him. Instead, he dodged left and headed toward the part of the fence closest to him. Troy prayed he could get there before the assailant on that side could reach it; he also figured this would throw off the one on the right, who was even closer. He pulled the straps on his knapsack tight so the contents wouldn't shift and throw off his balance. Then he tossed his lunch box into the air and over the fence, which prompted another horrifying shriek. That sound hadn't been made by any person, and now Troy was positive there were wild animals after him. Which made it that much worse. *Who knows how fast these things can run?* Lightning flashed, and a second later, the sky turned dark black as the first drops of rain started to fall.

Troy could almost make out the figure on his left, cutting through the graveyard and heading straight toward him. He also sensed the presence of another one close behind. Focusing only on his escape route, Troy zeroed in on the large oak tree closest to the fence and sprinted as fast as his legs would allow. The shrieks were much closer now, howling and growling from multiple directions, and Troy wondered if there were even more than two pursuers on his tail. Taking a running leap, he grabbed on to the lower limb of the oak and pulled himself up to the next branch. He scrambled from limb to limb, then swung his legs out over the wrought iron spikes and dropped to the grass on the other side. Without thinking, he ran into the street, across the Boulevard with his heart screaming and tears in his eyes. Troy was suddenly halted by the sound of screeching tires and looked up just in time to see the grill of the vehicle barreling down on him.

Deputy Ted Lutchen slammed the brakes of the cruiser, stopping less than a foot in front of Troy Fischer. He hopped out of the car and ran to him. "Are you crazy, kid? I almost killed you."

"They're chasing me!" Troy cried and fought to catch his breath. His heart thundered in his temples like a marching band.

"Who's chasing you?" Deputy Lutchen looked toward the graveyard where the boy had just come from.

"I-I-I dunno. They're fast, howled ... screamed." Troy bent down and put his hands on his knees.

"I don't see anybody. It was probably just some kids messing with you. Are you sure you didn't just get freaked out?" Another flash of lightning lit up the sky and was followed by a low rumble of thunder. Then the heavens opened.

"Hop in, kid. I'll give you a ride home. You live around here?"

"Pine Street," he told the deputy and jumped into the backseat.

The cruiser sped down the Boulevard with several sets of dark eyes watching from the shadows of the graveyard. The owner of one of those sets had seen the boy clearly. It dug its newly formed talons into the granite headstone and let out a strangled cry that could have passed for human ... almost. The mournful noise the creature made sounded as if it had screamed a single word. "*Troooyyyeee!*"

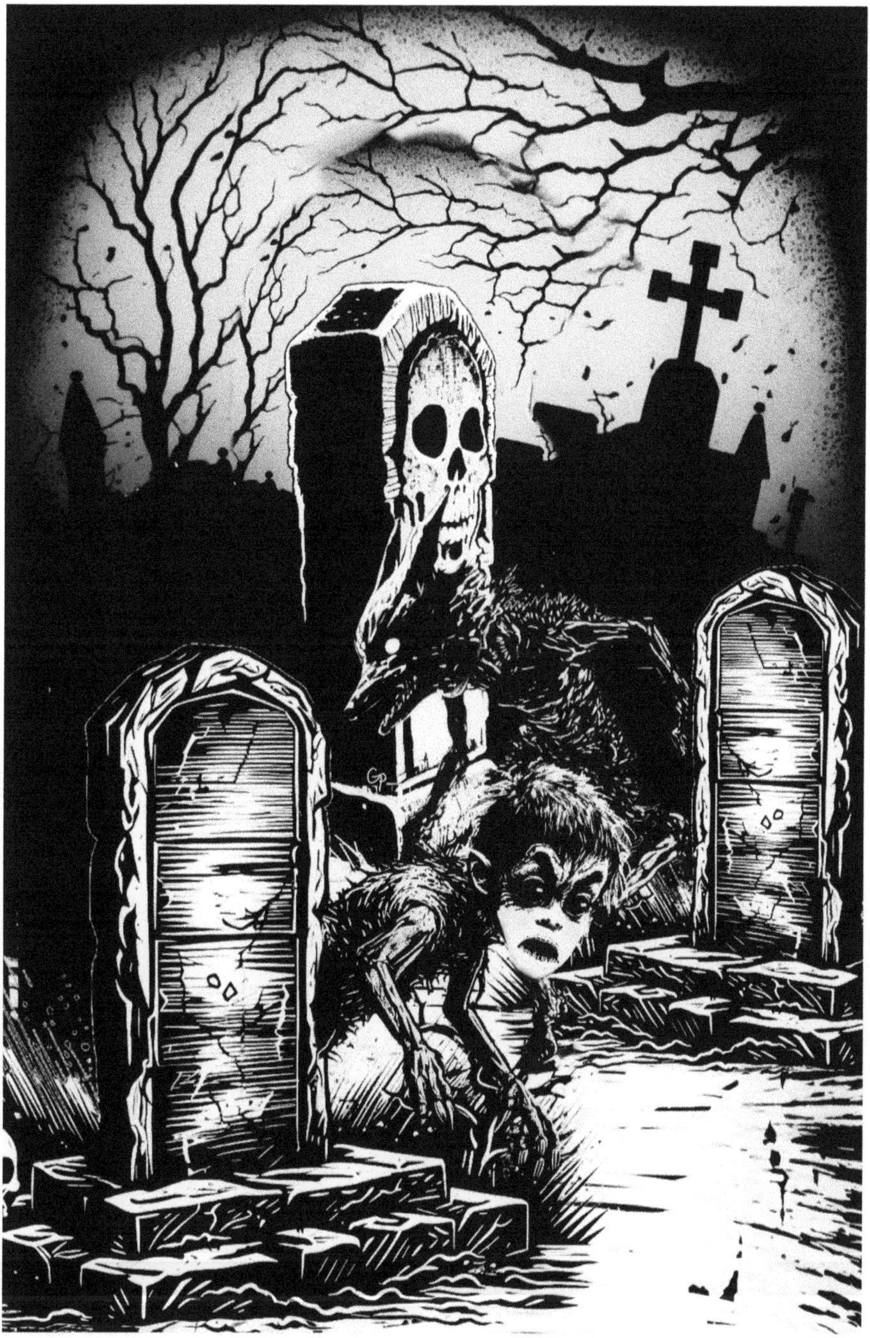

Chapter 28

The rain came down heavy and sudden, and it was already dark by the time Burt started the autopsy. There was no such thing as vampires, on that they were all in agreement. Everyone except for Tony, who stood at the back door, chain-smoking one Pall Mall after another. However, they were also in agreement that Felix Castillo had exhibited some very vampire-like qualities. He had mysteriously defied death more than once. First, from a neck wound that resulted in a total depletion of his blood. And although it couldn't be determined, Felix appeared to have turned into something similar to what killed him. Which only supported Tony's vampire theory and pissed Carl off even more.

Still, it was a regular bullet to the head that put Felix down for good. Not holy water, a crucifix, or a wooden stake through the heart. The fact that the first three shots hadn't even slowed him down was more than troubling. It was possible that the bullets had missed the man's vital organs; unlikely, but it was possible. However, the one to the head had sealed the deal, the same as it would to any normal human being.

For no other reason than to cover his ass and ease his mind, Burt had taken the crucifix from around his neck and pressed it to Felix's forehead. Everyone, including Carl, held their breath, half expecting the thing to start thrashing about and smoking. But nothing happened; there was no smoke and no reanimation either.

"Try Abe," Tony said from the safety of the back doorway. "Go ahead, try it on Abe. You'll see."

Burt shrugged and took the cross to where Abe was secured to the gurney. He held his breath again, then placed the cross on the man's forehead. Nothing happened.

"Thank you, Dr. Van Helsing." Carl exhaled. "Do you think we could get on with cutting this guy open already?"

The thing on the table that entered the world as Felix Castillo had left as something entirely different. Burt first checked the man's eyes. His pupils had tripled in size, blacking out the irises and corneas. It appeared that, for whatever reason, they'd developed to adjust quicker and more efficiently to darkness. At least that was Burt's immediate theory. Transparent flaps resembling a second set of lids were visible as well, which also supported that postulation. The man's skin was waxy and grey and hung loose as if he had lost a great deal of weight or there was just too much of it. And Burt wasn't about to examine the mouth or the tongue, at least not yet.

The smell that saturated the room when he cracked open Felix's thoracic cavity was so putrid that Carl and Tony had to step outside while Burt removed the organs. "Dear God! Carl," Burt called from the lab. "You have to see this."

Carl returned to find his friend removing a muscle as big as a horse's heart from the man's chest. "That can't be his heart!" He stared at the massive organ.

"It can't," Burt said, "but it is. Also, his lungs have shriveled away to nothing. I can't explain that either, but it looks as if he no longer needed oxygen to survive. Judging by the size of this heart, I'd say he still needed blood—and a lot of it. I see where you shot him, missed the lungs completely. Not that I think it would have mattered if you hit them. They're desiccated, all dried up and useless." Burt removed a tissue sample and placed it in a stainless steel basin next to the one containing the heart.

"Have you ever seen any of these conditions before? Is there a disease that can do this?" Carl asked.

Burt looked at his friend as if he had asked him to set his lips on fire. Then he stepped away from the body and began preparing slides. "I've never even heard of *anything* that can do this. As crazy as it sounds, this guy looks like he's turning into some type of lizard or reptile."

Carl leaned over the body and squinted. "I hate to agree, but that's exactly what it looks like."

Burt cut a small section from the tissue, set it on the slide, then he placed it on the microscope and turned on the light. He stared into the lens for a long time, focusing and refocusing. Finally, he stood up, rubbed his eyes, and swayed on his feet as if he might pass out. "What the hell is it, Burt?" Carl asked.

"We better call Dr. Malcolm—right away."

Lois Fischer answered the door to find Troy and Garrett Grove's youngest deputy, Ted Lutchen, standing on her front steps looking like a couple of drowned kittens. Even in the heavy rain, she could see the tears streaming down her son's face and the stern look in the deputy's eyes. She threw open the door, and Troy rushed into the house and wrapped his arms around her without saying a word. Lois started to speak, then stopped and turned her head to Deputy Lutchen. Ted looked back at her and raised his eyebrows. Lois braced herself for what she was about to hear.

She let the deputy inside while doing her best to comfort Troy, who appeared to have relaxed some, now that he was back home. When the tears finally subsided, Lois lifted his head by the chin and looked him in the eyes. She smiled and kissed his cheek.

"Why don't you go dry off, honey. We can talk when you're ready."

Troy nodded, then headed upstairs and made his way to the bathroom. When he was out of earshot, Lois turned to the deputy and lowered her voice. "Wha—?"

"Your son is fine, Mrs. Fischer," Ted said. "But ... he was running across the Boulevard, and I almost hit him with my cruiser." Lois's hand reached to cover her mouth. "He said something had been chasing him ... in the graveyard. It's possible maybe some older kids were messing with him, but I didn't see anyone else."

Lois felt the color drain out of her face as the deputy explained. "Thank you for bringing him home. Can I get you a towel to dry off, or a cup of coffee? You must be freezing."

"No, thank you. I have to get back to work; we're a bit understaffed today." Ted turned to exit the house, then lowered his voice as well. "Just one thing, Mrs. Fischer. Your son said *something* was chasing him, not *someone*. I thought I should mention that."

Lois thanked him again as he left out the front door and ran across the lawn into the downpour. She rushed up the stairs and joined Troy where he stood before the bathroom mirror drying himself off. He looked terrified, which was more than worrisome. Troy didn't scare easily; he was a horror fanatic and had spent much of his time building the haunted house with all its frights and surprises. *Maybe all this scary stuff is getting to him after all.*

"What's going on, kiddo?" She smiled and mussed his hair.

"They chased me, Mom. I was walking through the graveyard, and there were at least two of them. God, they were so fast." His voice grew shrill, and he looked as if he might start crying again.

"You know I don't want you in there."

"I know, but me and Rob walked through there before and nothing ever happened." Lois had a good idea what was really going on. Troy wasn't fine, despite what his father insisted. Her son had recently found his best friend close to death, and that was a lot for anyone to deal with, especially a ten-year-old boy.

"Promise me you won't do anything like that again."

"I promise. I'm sorry." Tears welled up in the corners of his eyes and spilled out onto his cheeks. Lois hugged him and drew him as close as she possibly could.

"Th-they were so f-fast, Mom. They almost got me. I-I had to climb over the fence."

"Who was chasing you, baby?" She lifted his chin again and looked in his eyes.

"Animals. I only saw them f-for a second. They ran kinda like dogs, but they h-hopped too."

"Do you think they were coyotes? They've been coming down off the mountain a bit more lately, or maybe someone's dogs that got loose."

"It wasn't coyotes or dogs. They screamed, and I think they were hunting me."

"That sounds scary." Lois didn't know what to think but knew that Troy believed every word of it. "I would have been scared too, honey. Would you like some hot cocoa? You're freezing."

He nodded and buried his head into her bosom again. "Mom?" His voice sounded impossibly small.

"What is it, baby?"

"You know that story you told us at the party?"

Lois had to think. Although it had only been two days, Saturday night felt like a lifetime ago. Then she remembered the ghost story she had told the kids. It was something she had written back in college, some of it at least, the rest she had made up on the spot. "Why do you ask?"

Troy pulled his head away and looked up at her. "I think that's what it was, the things that chased me. It was just like you said; it watches when you walk through the graveyard, waiting for you to fall. I think that's what it was. I think it was the Ojanox."

Carl rubbed his eyes and looked into the lens of the microscope a second time. No matter how hard he tried, he couldn't get it to focus and finally quit in frustration. "Christ! Will you just tell me what I'm supposed to be looking at?"

"That's a bacterial infection!" Burt said. "If I had to guess, I'd say it's parasitic."

"Like in the children?" Carl's eyes focused on the old man.

"I don't believe in coincidence. This guy died in front of the Boyle kid's house. And all three of those kids live less than a block from each other. Dr. Malcolm needs to confirm if this is the same infection. But I'd bet my prick on it." Burt removed a hypodermic from a drawer and approached the gurney where Abe's body was secured. He watched the man as he took the blood sample.

"What are you doing?" Carl asked.

"Following a hunch. With Abe's help, I think we'll find out how this infection is transmitted." Burt prepared a slide with Abe's blood and transferred it to the microscope. He stared through the aperture and jumped back a second later. "Bingo!"

Tony pitched his cigarette out the back door, where he stood a safe distance away from the bodies. "Is it the same?"

"Identical," Burt said. "Same cellular pattern exactly, except ... What the hell?" He refocused the scope, then changed the magnification level.

"What is it, Burt?" Carl asked.

"These cells are still active. His white blood cells are attacking the red. That shouldn't happen, not in a body that's been dead for over an hour. This blood is alive." All three men turned to the body duct taped to the gurney. Burt's cross still sat on Abe's head where he had left it.

"That's not possible; we checked his pulse," Carl said, making his way toward the body. He leaned over and touched the man's wrist. There was no pulse, but the body was warm ... too warm. "Christ, Burt! He's still hot."

Tony shrank further back until he was almost standing in the parking lot. They all focused intently on the man secured to the gurney, watching for the slightest twitch or warning sign. Half a second later, Abe's eyes shot open as if they had been spring loaded. Large black pupils zeroed in on the men, then Abe began to buck and twist, struggling to free himself from his bindings. The tape held fast—for the moment—but the man continued to flail about on the gurney, nearly tipping it over in the process.

Carl pulled his revolver and pointed it at Abe's head; dark, toxic eyes fixed on his every move. Satisfied that the duct tape was indeed holding, Carl lowered the weapon. Then an awful noise erupted from Abe's mouth, filling the morgue with a repulsive shriek that bounced off every metal surface in the place. Carl pictured a dozen razor-sharp teeth exploding through the man's gums.

Grabbing one of the stainless steel basins, Carl threw it over Abe's face. Then he took the duct tape and fastened it to his head and to the gurney as well. *Better safe than sorry.*

"Get me the phone, Burt."

The coroner ran to his office and came back a second later pulling the phone along with a mile of cord.

Carl picked up the receiver, dialed, and looked to the back door. It stood open, but Tony was gone; he had run out into the storm.

"Yes, this is Sheriff Primrose. Could I speak with Dr. Malcolm, please?" He paused. "He what? Oswego? I thought he said the children were doing better ... uh-huh ... uh-huh, yeah, I'll hold."

"What's going on?" Burt asked.

"Malcolm's in Oswego. Left last night and took the kids with him. Some toxicology center or something."

"Just like that? What did he find out?"

Carl shrugged and motioned for Burt to hang on one second. Then a familiar voice came on the line.

"Hello, this is Dr. Ziegler."

"Hi, Doc. This is Sheriff Primrose. I didn't know Dr. Malcolm transferred the children."

"I just found out myself. Happened around three thirty this morning, which struck me as odd."

"That doesn't sound right, not without alerting you or myself first. You were working on the lab results. Dr. Malcolm said you suspected a possible toxin or a bacterial infection."

"To be honest, it's nothing I've ever seen before," Ziegler continued. "Dr. Malcolm left a report on my desk indicating the possibility of snake venom, which seems unlikely, if you ask me."

"Snake venom?" Carl and Burt turned toward the mutated body of Felix Castillo.

"It didn't sound right to me either. But Dr. Malcolm is the chief of medicine. Besides, there wasn't anything I could do."

"I think we may have a related case, Doctor. Would you mind looking at something for me?"

"Are you sick, Sheriff? You aren't showing symptoms, are you?" Ziegler's voice wavered.

"No, I'm fine. I think it would be better if we just show you."

"We?"

"I'm with Burt Lively at the coroner's office. Is there any chance you could swing by here?"

"I suppose I could sneak away and be there in about half an hour. What's at the lab that's so important it can't wait?"

"Like I said, Doctor, I think it would be better if you looked for yourself."

"Is everything all right, Sheriff?"

"I'll see you in a half-hour." Carl hung up the phone and turned to Burt. "Is there any of that scotch left? I think we're going to need it."

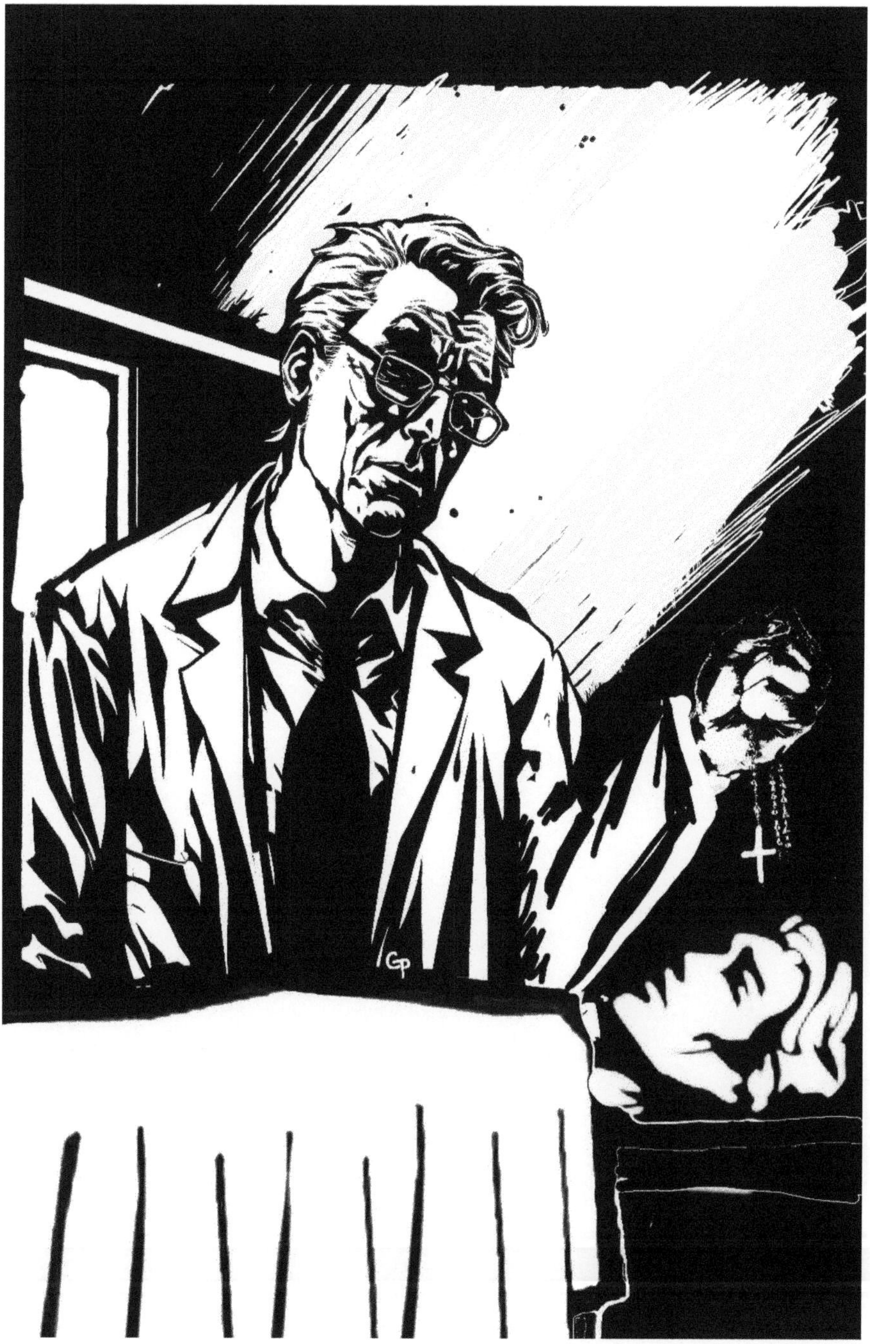

Chapter 29

Carl and Burt congregated under the awning at the rear entrance of the morgue. It had started to rain even harder, and the dull glow of the yellow lamp hanging from the building did little to illuminate the parking area. Occasional flashes of electricity etched the sky, casting long shadows across the slick blacktop and the men's faces. They exchanged a tentative look when Dr. Ziegler pulled into the lot. Moments later, the young doctor opened the car door and stepped out into the deluge. Ziegler spotted the men and ran to where they stood; he was soaked by the time he reached the back entrance.

"Hello, Sheriff, Mr. Lively. I must say you have my curiosity piqued. What's this all about?" He shook their hands.

"Thanks for coming, Dr. Ziegler." Carl said. "Before we begin, you need to promise you won't tell anyone what you see here. No one but Dr. Malcolm."

"If this is a medical concern, I am sworn to secrecy."

"It is," Burt said. "But you better hold on to your stethoscope."

Ziegler turned to the coroner and furrowed his brow. "Gentlemen, if this is some kind of a joke, *now* is not a good time. I have patients that requi—"

"It's no joke, Dr. Ziegler," Carl said as they entered the morgue.

The first thing Ziegler noticed was the overpowering stench of decay that hung in the air like a wet blanket. He covered his mouth and nose to try to block it out.

"Dear God! How many bodies do you have in here?" he asked. "Are they supposed to smell that bad when you work on them?"

"No, Doc," Burt said. "Definitely not after only thirty-six hours."

They approached the lab tables, and Ziegler immediately spotted the body of Felix Castillo where it lay putrefying beneath the bright fluorescent light. Then he focused on the duct tape that had been used to fasten him down. Sudden movement on the other side of the room drew his attention to the man on the gurney. A stainless steel basin had been secured to his head, and he was bound as well. The man struggled to free himself from his bindings.

Jesus Christ! Ziegler's heart raced into overdrive, and his flight instinct kicked in. He ran for the door, but Carl slammed it shut before he could reach it. "Not so fast, Doc." Ziegler spun on his heels and tried to take off in the other direction, but before he could, the coroner jumped in front of him and blocked his path.

"What the hell is going on here?!" Ziegler turned again and came face-to-face with Carl, who seized him by the biceps and held him fast.

"I need you to calm down, Doctor. We're not going to hurt you."

Ziegler motioned to the man on the gurney. "Who the hell is that, and what have you done to him?"

Burt approached the frightened doctor and placed his hand on his shoulder. "Doc, if you would just take a look at the slide on the microscope, I'm sure this will make much more sense."

Carl loosened his grip and walked Ziegler to the counter.

Seeing that his options were limited, Ziegler bent over the instrument and peered into the lens. He studied the sample for a moment, then let out a long gasp. "Where did you get this? It's identical to the infection we found in the children."

"That's what I figured," Burt said. "Dr. Malcolm mentioned you believed the infection was a toxin with a bacterial signature?"

"Yes, and that's what you have here as well. If I didn't know better, I would say they were taken from the same subject."

"I found this infection in both of these men," Burt said.

"Dr. Ziegler." Carl addressed him in a calm, deliberate tone. "I need you to keep an open mind for what I am about to show you." He led the doctor to the dissected body of Felix Castillo.

Ziegler noticed the abnormalities immediately; a Y-incision revealed the open chest cavity. *Dear God. That's not possible.* The man's lungs were shriveled and had wasted away to nothing. Then he saw the enormous heart in the basin. *That couldn't have come out of this guy.* Ziegler leaned in closer to focus; the skin on the man's face sagged and hung loose, almost as if he had at one time been obese and then lost a tremendous amount of weight.

Burt pried open the man's eyelids. "Look at this, Doc."

The subject's eyes were entirely black.

Ziegler gasped but remained silent.

Then Burt used a pair of tweezers to reveal the translucent folds that had grown over the man's eyes. They looked like a secondary set of lids.

"Dear God, what happened to this man?"

"He died, Doctor," Carl said flatly.

"Obviously."

"No, this man was found dead in the middle of Foothills Drive yesterday morning." Carl looked to Burt to fill in the blanks.

"I inspected the body, and the only wound I found was this." Burt lifted the tape, revealing the strange punctures on Castillo's neck. Ziegler creased his brow and examined it as Burt continued. "The man's blood and body fluids were depleted when we found him, and there wasn't a drop at the scene."

"His name is Felix Castillo," Carl said. "He was transported here around nine o'clock yesterday morning. At eleven o'clock, the body went missing. This morning, a delivery driver hit Mr. Castillo on Sunset Road."

"How did the body get there?" Ziegler shook his head, not sure if he was following.

"It walked." Carl held up his palms. "Just stay with me a little longer. The guy was covered in mud, so we didn't know it was Castillo. But we sure noticed the stink. We brought him back here and washed him off. That's when he woke up. He opened those giant black eyes and stared at us like we were a couple of late-night snacks. Then this ... thing shot out of his mouth and killed Abe."

"That's Abe Gorman? The medical assistant?!" Ziegler suddenly noticed the scrubs the man was wearing. "What happened to him? Let him go!"

"That's not a good idea," Burt said as the body on the gurney jumped and twisted against the tape.

"Would you both take a few steps back?" Carl produced a pocketknife and approached the body of Felix Castillo.

"I don't think you should do that," Burt said. "You saw what that thing did to Abe. What if it wakes up again?" He took several steps away, pulling Ziegler along with him.

Carl positioned himself at the back of the table behind the man's head. He held on to Castillo's chin with one hand to keep the mouth from opening and then sliced the duct tape with the knife. Ziegler gasped when the face was revealed. The dead man's mouth had transformed into something straight out of a horror movie; it had grown longer and more circular, with flaps of extra skin that now hung loose like silly putty.

Carl nodded to Burt, and the old man pushed Ziegler back several more steps. Then the sheriff pried open the man's mouth and plunged the knife inside. He fished around for a moment, then began to pull his blade upward. *Dear God.*

The sheriff lifted his knife and revealed the hideous appendage attached to the business end. It looked like an eel, slimy and black and pointed at the end. It stretched out as if it was made of rubber, unraveling from some unlimited source like clowns exiting a tiny car. Carl continued to remove it from the man's mouth as Ziegler watched with his heart doing the Hustle and his sanity threatening to jump off the rails. When he was finished, Carl had revealed a tongue that measured over three feet long.

Ziegler swayed, feeling like he might pass out. The next thing he saw was the bottle of scotch that Burt shoved into his hand. *Oh, thank God.* Ziegler unscrewed the cap and took a long slug of the liquor.

"What the hell is that thing?" Ziegler said, wiping his eyes.

Carl let the tongue retract into Felix's mouth and went to work with the duct tape. "I was hoping you could help us figure that out."

"Are you telling me this all happened after he died?" Ziegler took another healthy swig.

"It used that ... tongue thing to grab Abe," Burt said. "Tossed him around the room like a goddamn puppet and killed him. Then Abe woke up, and he was just like it."

Carl approached the gurney where Abe was bound. He cut the tape securing the basin to the man's head and slowly lifted the pan covering his face. Abe immediately reacted and started bucking and twisting to break free. He stared up at them and focused on Ziegler with a pair of coal-black, lifeless eyes. Carl replaced the basin a second later, which appeared to relax the thing on the gurney.

"This is impossible, all of it!" Ziegler shouted.

"I think whatever killed Felix Castillo infected him with your parasite or bacterium." Carl folded the knife and slipped it in his pocket. "And when he attacked Abe, he passed it on to him."

Ziegler held on to the bottle and listened as Carl continued.

"This toxin, or whatever the hell it is, got these men up and walking after they died, like some kind of freaking zombies or something. If those kids have been infected by the same thing, we need to get to them right away."

"But they've been transported to Oswego. The toxicology center."

"You said Dr. Malcolm suspected some type of snake venom?" Burt asked. "This doesn't look like that to me."

"I didn't think so either. But I had no way to question him about it. When I arrived this morning, he was gone."

"Vanished in the night, huh?" Burt nodded.

Ziegler pointed to Felix's forehead. "That looks like a bullet wound."

"It was the only way to get him to let go of Abe. I shot him three times in the chest first; didn't do much. But that one did the trick."

"I should take a look at Abe," Ziegler said. "If there's any way to save him, maybe I can help."

"What exactly do you have in mind, Doc?" Burt asked. "Whatever you do, you do *not* want to get too close."

"Dr. Malcolm blew this year's budget on some new equipment that's supposed to change the way we look at the human body. It's called MRI, short for magnetic resonance imaging. Cutting-edge stuff, really. We have a technician specially trained to operate it, but I've watched him a few times. I'd like to get Abe into the chamber and take some pictures, see what's going on in his brain—but we'll need to secure him to a wooden plank. There can't be any metal at all. It'll interfere with the imaging and probably destroy a million-dollar machine in the process."

The thing on the gurney thrashed about as if in response to what he had said. The stainless steel basin covering its head wobbled like a capsized ship, and the men were helpless not to stare at it.

"Is there any other way?" Burt asked. "Like an x-ray or something."

"I'm afraid not. The metal from the gurney and the basin would also interfere with an x-ray. To see what's really going on in the soft tissue, it's got to be the MRI machine."

"Well, if we're really going to do this, I have an idea." Carl removed the radio from his hip and depressed the button. "This is Sheriff Primrose to any available officer. Come in."

A squelch of static flooded the tiny speaker. "This is Deputy Rainey, Sheriff."

"What's your twenty, Rainey?"

"I'm behind the station. I was just about to start my patrol."

"I need you to grab the riot gear from storage. The body armor, the helmets, and some of those large cable ties? I want you to bring them to the morgue."

"Could you repeat that, Sheriff? It sounded like you said bring the riot gear and cable ties to the morgue?"

"Roger that. Come to the back entrance. I'll meet you there." Carl waited for a reply.

"Ten-four, Sheriff."

The body on the gurney twisted and arched its back against the restraints. The duct tape did its job and continued to hold it securely in place ... for the moment at least.

Chapter 30

Although the worst of the storm had passed, it continued to pour well into the evening. Occasional whips of lightning sliced the ozone like a machete through silkweed, followed by the rolling growl of thunderheads clashing in the distance. Deputy David Rainey exited the cruiser and stepped out onto the rain-slicked blacktop behind the morgue. Petrichor emanated from the earth and fused with the dark odor seeping out the back door of the building—damp and crisp tainted with a dash of pestilence. He spotted the three men standing at the rear entrance, looking like they were about to blow the charge on a bank vault. The suspicious movements of the men made him even more apprehensive than he already was. *What the hell is this all about?* Rainey was still a rookie, just a few months longer on the job than his younger coworker, Ted Lutchen, and had never travelled further than fifty miles from his hometown of Garrett Grove. In fact, he still lived with his parents and kid sister, Kelly, in the three-bedroom Cape Cod he had grown up in. He took another apprehensive look in the men's direction and made his way to the back of the cruiser. For the life of him, he couldn't imagine why the sheriff needed riot gear at the morgue.

Sheriff Primrose approached the cruiser with Burt Lively and Dr. Ziegler from the medical center behind him. He went straight for the riot gear and started to distribute it. "I need you to put these on," he said, passing out the helmets and body armor.

"Am I missing something, Sheriff?" the young deputy asked.

"We don't have time for questions right now," Carl said. "I need you to gear up and help restrain a suspect. Follow your orders to the letter, and I'll brief you later."

Rainey did as instructed and donned the riot gear while the other men did the same. After they had strapped up, the sheriff inspected each man's vest, helmet, and face shield, then gave them the go-ahead. Carl ran into the building, Burt and Dr. Ziegler followed close behind, and Rainey brought up the rear.

The overwhelming stench of death smacked Rainey in the face the second he entered the morgue. He gagged as the contents of his stomach shifted and felt his heart cramp inside his chest. Then he saw the man bound to the gurney. The figure writhed in a most unnatural fashion and struggled to break free from the duct tape securing him. *What the fuck?* A shiver sliced through Rainey's groin like an arctic blast at the sight of the stainless steel basin taped to the man's head.

On a table adjacent to the gurney sat a wooden stretcher with leather straps wrapped throughout its handles. Rainey knew right away that the sheriff intended to transfer the body from the gurney to the stretcher, then bind it in place. Sheriff Primrose quickly positioned himself over the man's head while the doctor and coroner ran to either side and grabbed his arms.

"I need you to hold his feet, Deputy. And for God's sake, don't let go, no matter what happens." The sheriff held a pocketknife in one hand and used the other to remove the basin.

What in the name of—? Rainey stared down at the thing laying before him. Its giant dark eyes darted around the room and focused directly on him. Rainey was helpless to look away. The man strapped to the gurney was Abe Gorman, the meat wagon driver. Except it wasn't exactly Abe ... not anymore. Something terrible had happened to him; his face had distorted and grown grotesquely disproportionate. Rainey felt the bile rise in the back of his throat and swallowed hard to force it down.

He grabbed Abe's legs as instructed and froze, unable to do anything but stare into the endless sea of black. His pounding heart echoed in his temples as he struggled to digest what he was seeing. Abe's face contorted and twisted in an aggressive fit of rage. And his eyes—*dear God*—were huge and dark and all-consuming. They stared back at David Rainey and penetrated him. He shifted his gaze to avoid looking directly at the awful obsidian eyes until it started to hiss, breathy and slow like a serpent. A second later, the most God-awful sound spilled out of the creature. The unbearable shriek filled the room and gnawed into the deputy like nails on a chalkboard. His head began to swim, then he started to feel queasy. Rainey bit down on his bottom lip and fought to regain his composure.

David ... the voice echoed from inside his head.

"You got him?" The sheriff gripped Abe underneath his chin, and the coroner produced a wide leather muzzle from his pocket.

"Here we go. You ready, Rainey?" Carl shouted. "Are you okay, David?"

"Fine, Sheriff. Ready," he said, and the voice spoke again.

David ... relax.

Carl cut the tape securing Abe's head to the gurney, then ripped it free, exposing his mouth. Burt passed one end of the leather strap under the man's neck and looped the other across his jaw. Together, they worked to secure the muzzle while Abe heaved and bucked as if he'd been thrown into a fiery pit. Ziegler grabbed the stainless steel basin a second before it was knocked off the gurney onto the floor.

Abe continued to writhe, with every muscle in his body screaming to break free. The men struggled to subdue him but were halted by a sudden tearing sound as Abe ripped through the restraints securing his legs. He kicked wildly and bucked against the table, then the tape securing his torso began to loosen as well. Rainey gazed into the creature's bottomless pits of black and was lost.

"Dammit, Rainey!" Carl shouted. "Hold him down!"

The deputy released his grip and stepped away from the gurney. Carl looked up to find himself facing the barrel of a service revolver. He froze as Deputy Rainey leveled it with his head.

The creature continued to thrash while Burt and Ziegler fought to control it. But their hold on it was waning, and it was getting loose.

"Deputy Rainey, lower your weapon!" Carl screamed. "That's an order!"

David ... shoot himmmm.

The voice was cold and intrusive and bore into him like a drill. Rainey pulled back the hammer of his revolver, sensing the pressure of the trigger against his index finger. It was heavy ... so heavy, and the urge to squeeze was impossible to resist. Moreso, he wanted to do it; he wanted to pull the trigger.

David ... Now!

David closed his eyes, stopped fighting, and squeezed.

Ziegler raised the stainless steel basin like a broad sword and brought it down with a sickening *thwack!* It connected with the deputy's hand a second before the gun went off. The slug passed less than two inches to the right of Carl's ear, breaking the air like the crack of a whip. The deputy's weapon was knocked from his hand and sent flying across the room. Ziegler raised the basin a second time and slammed it against the deputy's helmet, cracking the faceplate and knocking the man out.

Carl didn't wait; he cut the remaining tape binding Abe to the gurney as the doctor and coroner clamped down. Together, the three men lifted and transferred him to the stretcher. They fastened the straps around the body, restraining his arms, legs, chest, and head. The leather proved far superior to the duct tape and prevented the man from moving almost entirely. Finally, Ziegler replaced the basin over the thing's head and stepped away.

Panting and out of breath, Carl walked across the room, picked the deputy's gun off the floor, and stuck it into his waistband. He took the cable ties from his back pocket and handed some to the other men. He secured Deputy Rainey's hands together while Burt and Ziegler went to work on Abe, fastening the man directly to the oval openings in the plank.

"What the hell was that?" Burt's voice cracked.

"He was going to kill you." Ziegler fought to control his breathing. "That wasn't your deputy. Did you see him?"

Carl had seen it and knew Ziegler was right. Somehow, the thing on the table had taken control of Deputy Rainey and had almost killed him. *What in the hell are we dealing with here?*

Chapter 31

Night fell an hour after the storm started. The sound of thunder and the drone of the constant downpour helped suppress most of the screams that would have otherwise alerted the citizens of Garrett Grove. Tommy Negal had returned home late Sunday afternoon after spending most of the day in the foothills' woods with his friend Jeff Campbell. Both boys had gone to bed early, feeling feverish and achy; neither had made it to school. Tommy had stayed in bed ... listening. A gnawing voice spoke from within him; he was unaware as it ransacked his consciousness. It took what it needed, and then ... it left a little something in return. Everything that Tommy knew, every thought he possessed was sorted and filed away.

It was a gatherer, a consumer, a collector. A reaper of emotions and flesh. Ojanox was the last word on the boy-creature's lips. It was as good as any name it had been called in the past. It didn't matter what they called it. It was power, it was thought, and it was eternal. It had dominated this rock since the dawn of time. Now, there was so much more to feed on, knowledge to consume, fear to devour, and desire to satiate its hunger. There was so much food!

Tommy lifted his head in the darkness of his bedroom with a mind full of thoughts no longer his own. He got to his feet, leaving most of his hair on his pillow, and entered the hallway. The visitor watched through his eyes as he descended the stairs and walked into the room where his parents sat with their backs to him.

The boy lifted his head and opened his mouth, allowing the ear-cracking shriek to escape from his throat. Sarah and Otto Negal turned to find their son's black eyes fixated on them ... then they noticed his teeth.

Sarah tried to scream but was silenced when Tommy sprang like a panther onto her. He buried his face into the woman's neck and bit down. Sarah's eyes rolled back in her head as the child ripped a mouthful of flesh from her throat. Her arms flailed for a second, then fell limp at her side.

Otto was helpless to react and stared for far too long. Finally, he lunged at the boy and attempted to pry him off his wife. Tommy jumped up, landed on all fours, and snarled at his father with Sarah's blood covering his lips. Then he threw his head back and howled through a mouthful of tiny razor-sharp teeth. Otto managed only a feeble moan before Tommy hushed him for good. The child tore into his father like a chainsaw while the voice in his head screamed with pleasure. None of the neighbors on the block heard a sound; what little noise there was had been masked by the storm.

● ● ●

The area behind Wilson's Diner tended to flood when it rained. Roger, the dishwasher, ran into the heavy downpour with a bag of garbage in each hand. He splashed through a large puddle, soaking his foot all the way to the ankle. The entire lot was several inches deep, and by the time he made it to the dumpster, he was soaked from head to toe. He tossed the trash and allowed the metal lid to crash back into place. A sudden blur leapt from the shadows and onto the dumpster, causing Roger to jump backward. At first, he thought it was Scraps, the alley cat that always hung around, but he knew cats hated water and he dismissed the idea. Then he noticed the size of the figure before him, which wasn't any cat. This thing was huge.

Stumbling backward, he tripped as the shadow launched itself into the air and landed in front of him. It was dark and impossible to make out any of the its features, but it was obvious that it was a person. A strangled cry escaped his lips as the figure crawled towards him. Crouching like a gargoyle, it hobbled closer on its spindly arms and legs, then Roger noticed the bra and panties. It took another step forward, and Roger could see that it was a woman and she was practically naked. *Dear God.* He recognized her. *It's Mandy!* Only she had changed.

The waitress had lost almost all her hair, and her body looked as if it had withered away. Her bones were visible beneath her tight skin, which looked almost grey in the darkness of the storm. Mandy crab-walked across the blacktop at full speed and charged toward Roger. He turned and sprinted through the puddles toward the door but was stopped in his tracks when a tidal wave of rainwater erupted in front of him. A second figure splashed down, lowered its head, and sized him up. This one looked like Mandy's roommate, the nurse at the medical center, but not exactly. Something awful had happened to her as well.

Roger backed away, and the creature closed in on him, propelling itself forward like a spider. *What in the name of God?* He blinked against the driving rain and struggled to focus on the impossible vision. An extra set of arms protruded from the woman's ribcage. Only they didn't look much like arms. The appendages were black and hairy, as if she really was turning into some type of spider.

The air was knocked out of him as Mandy landed on his back and drove him to the pavement. Her taloned fingers sank into his skin as Roger landed face first in the dirty water. Struggling to breathe, he fought to shake the girl off him, but the other one was on him before he could do a thing. He choked on a mouthful of dirty water while the girls held him down and ripped into him. They consumed pieces of his flesh and then dug into his head to feast on the good parts. Before he surrendered, Mandy lowered her awful mouth to his ear and spoke in a gravelly voice, just loud enough to be heard above the pounding rain. *"See anything you like?"*

● ● ●

Jeff Campbell discovered his mother and father preparing dinner in the kitchen and decided to share something with them. It was the very same something that Tommy Negal had shared with his own mom and dad. One thing was certain, neither of the boys or their parents would ever have to worry about such menial diversions as cooking, going to school, or watching TV ever again. When Jeff was finished, he left the house and scurried across the street to where his classmate

Mike Barnes lived. The light was on in the boy's second-floor bedroom. Jeff crouched in the driveway, then using the newly developed muscles in his lower legs, he propelled himself ten feet into the air and landed on the garage roof. He clawed his way up the ridgeline to the boy's window and peered inside to find Mike seated at his desk doing his homework; a Batman comic sat on his opened textbook.

Mike jumped at the sudden noise. It wasn't much more than a tap against the window, but he had been engrossed in his comic and not expecting it. He looked up from his desk and was met only by his reflection against the darkened pane. *Just the storm.* He leaned back in his chair and turned the page. The second time it happened, Mike was a bit more prepared for the faint clicking at the glass, as if the wind had kicked some debris and tossed it against the house.

Click ... Click ... Click

It happened again, sounding like someone throwing pebbles.

Click ... Click ... Click

Mike set the comic book aside and got up from his desk. He walked to the window and strained to look through the darkness and pouring rain. He pressed his face against the glass.

Click ... Click ... Click

Mike unlatched the lock and lifted the lower pane. He squinted and drew in closer to the screen to get a better look. Then he saw it. Just the outline at first. There was something outside on the roof. *Oh, my Go—*

The thought was silenced in a heartbeat. Jeff tore through the screen and seized Mike by the head, his hands clamped around his friend's neck, and ripped into his skin. He yanked the boy out of his room and pulled him into the night as if he weighed no more than a throw pillow. Mike landed on the wet shingles and began to slide down the slick incline of the roof. Before he could think, Jeff was on top of him, and they were both falling. By the time they hit the driveway, every thought the child ever had was consumed and added to the collective. Now it knew everything about the one called Mike. It knew his sister's name was Melissa. It knew that Melissa was downstairs. It also knew that the back door unlocked.

THE OJANOX

The creature that had once gone by the name of Robert Boyle waited outside, watching the house. It crept on all fours like a massive beetle, making its way to the side of the garage. This place ... Scream in the Dark. It drew upon the catalogue of memories and came to a vision of the two children working together, building. Troy ... It had come close to taking the boy earlier in the graveyard and had tasted the child's thoughts. Now, it craved to possess him, to add the one called Troy to its collection. It yearned to savor his fear. Nothing satisfied its hunger like fear.

A blinding light illuminated the creature where it hid; it quickly retreated behind the building. The vehicle stopped, and a man exited. It was the one called Fischer, the boy's father. As the man approached, the creature inched slowly from the shadows to the edge of the house. It made its way closer, ready to pounce, ready to feed. Lightning flashed, casting a brilliant aura, momentarily freezing it in its tracks. It no longer looked anything like Robert Boyle, the boy it had once been. Its features now far more primal, hunched and reptilian; its dark eyes seeing everything in the darkness as the man entered the house. It waited ... it watched ... it hungered ... Troyeeee.

Father Kieran sat in the kitchen of the rectory with a glass of wine in front of him and the good book opened to the Revelations of John. He read from the Scripture every day and typically favored the Gospels for his after-dinner meditation. However, tonight he believed that one of John's other books was a bit more fitting.

The shadows in the woods had stopped moving shortly before daybreak, just as Kieran knew they would. *For the light is the Lord's domain; there is no evil that can prevail in the light.* But now that the storm had arrived and the sun had set, the creatures were traveling once again. Some of their numbers walked much like humans, upright and on two legs. But there were many that didn't resemble anything even remotely human. They leaped from shadow to shadow, traveling swiftly on all fours like beasts. *They are Satan's Imps*; he knew it to be true. *The children of the Dark One have come to Garrett Grove to test the flock.* He prayed for guidance and waited for a reply. His only answer was to immerse himself in the word of the Lord.

"And I saw, coming out of the mouth of the dragon and out of the mouth of the beast and out of the mouth of the false prophet, three unclean spirits like frogs."

Father Kieran blessed himself. He had witnessed these very creatures last night as he watched from behind the curtains of his bedroom window. *Dear Lord, tell me what you would have of me.* He made the sign of the cross and continued reading.

"And they assembled them at the place that in Hebrew is called Armageddon."

There was a sudden noise at the back door, causing Kieran to jump. His breath stopped, causing his lungs to tighten and clench within his chest. It sounded like something significant had fallen outside, just beyond the threshold. Father Kieran waited and stared at the doorknob, expecting it to turn at any moment and the beasts to burst through. He listened with an icy sweat breaking on his brow and the book trembling within his grasp. Again, just over the sound of the wind, he heard a rustle. And then the voice of someone outside.

"Help."

It was too soft and weak to be real, but Kieran was certain he had heard it.

"Thy will be done, Lord," he said as he got up from the table and approached the door. He held his breath, reached out, and took the handle in his hand. Kieran pulled it inward and froze. He gasped at the sight of what lay before him.

"Help me, Father."

He rushed into the night without concern for his own safety. "Dear Lord, what happened, my child?" he asked.

● ● ●

Dr. Stephanie Thompson arrived home late from work, thanks to an exciting first day at the DuCain excavation. Her daughter and sister had dinner ready and waiting. Together, they sat on the floor eating tuna sandwiches and drinking Kool-Aid, with a houseful of unpacked boxes and plastic-wrapped furniture towering around them. Peanuts performed her doggy-duty to the letter, scarfing up even the tiniest of crumbs that happened to fall to the floor, while Janis told her mom everything about her first day at the new school and the cool friends she had made.

"You already have new friends?" Stephanie set her sandwich down and leaned forward. "That was quick. Tell me about them. What are their names?"

"Troy and Wendy. They came over after school. They want me to see the haunted house that Troy made in his garage. It's called Scream in the Dark, and it's supposed to be really scary. Wendy and Troy are boyfriend and girlfriend, and they have another friend named Rob, but he wasn't in school today. We're all gonna go out trick-or-treating ... if that's okay."

Stephanie felt her smile grow wider by the second as Janis relived her entire day without taking a single breath. *Is that what I sound like*? She knew that she did but imagined most people didn't find it quite as adorable on her as when it came out of a ten-year-old. Janis was the spitting image of her mother, just a miniature-sized version. In fact, all three women who sat together looked incredibly similar, with the same wavy blonde hair hanging in long ringlets past their shoulders and the same exact shade of pale blue eyes. "You had a big day. Did you have any time for school, or was it just one big party?"

"Oh no, we got to hear about the guy Tolkien, who wrote a book called *The Hobbit*. Miss Walsh said she was going to start reading it to us." Janis took a large gulp of the red Kool-Aid and continued. "Oh! I showed Troy and Wendy the arrowheads you gave me and the little teeth from Cokia."

"Cahokia, sweetie," she said.

"Cahokia, and Wendy said that they were from an Ojanox."

"Where did she come up with a name like that?" Lynn asked.

"Troy's mom told them a story at the party about a monster that only comes out at Halloween. It hides all year long and only comes out in the fall; it's called the Ojanox."

"Well, honey, no one really knows what those teeth belong to, but I'm pretty sure there's no such thing as an Ojanox. I bet it was a good story, though." Stephanie brushed a long curl of Janis's hair and tucked it behind the girl's ear.

"Yeah, I know." Janis took a bite of her sandwich.

"I was telling the movers where to put the couch," Lynn said. "Then here comes little Miss Social Butterfly walking up the street with her two friends. I gave them milk and cookies and let Janis show off her toys."

Stephanie smiled and tossed a piece of crust to the dog. "You said Troy and Wendy are boyfriend and girlfriend? I hope you aren't thinking about things like boyfriends yet. You're only in fourth grade, and you know how I feel about that."

"I know, Mom. Don't worry. The boys at school are dorks. They were all staring and acting dumb because I have boobs."

Stephanie nearly choked on her sandwich, and Lynn just escaped spitting Kool-Aid through her nose. The girls shared a very open dialog in the household, and Janis's early development had been a topic of many conversations.

"Yes, baby. Boys can be very immature. They are two years behind you when it comes to maturity. They can't help it, though; they don't know any better."

"Except Troy. He's different than the other boys." Stephanie gave Lynn an apprehensive look as Janis continued. "We were talking, and I asked him why all the boys were acting so weird."

"You did? Well, what did he say?"

"At first, he got really embarrassed, but me and Wendy kept asking him, and finally, he said, 'They're all acting stupid because of your boobs. They've never seen a girl in class with boobs, and they don't know how to act.'"

Stephanie felt like her eyes might pop out. She worked to control her expression for several seconds before she started speaking again. "He did? It sounds like Troy is different, all right. I'd like to meet Troy and Wendy next time you guys get together."

"Okay. Troy's going to ask his parents if me and Wendy could come over and see Scream in the Dark before he takes it down. Maybe you could meet him them?"

"Wendy and I." Stephanie said. "And what can you tell me about your friends' parents, anything?"

"I'm not sure about Wendy's parents, but I know Troy's mom tells scary Halloween stories and his dad works at the quarry."

Stephanie paused again; she hadn't told her daughter that her current assignment had taken her to the quarry. "What are your friends' last names?"

"Wendy Sirocka and Troy Fischer."

Stephanie's cheeks hurt from smiling so much. It had truly been a day for surprises. Troy was Don Fisher's son. *I bet Troy is different than most boys. Like father, like son, I guess.*

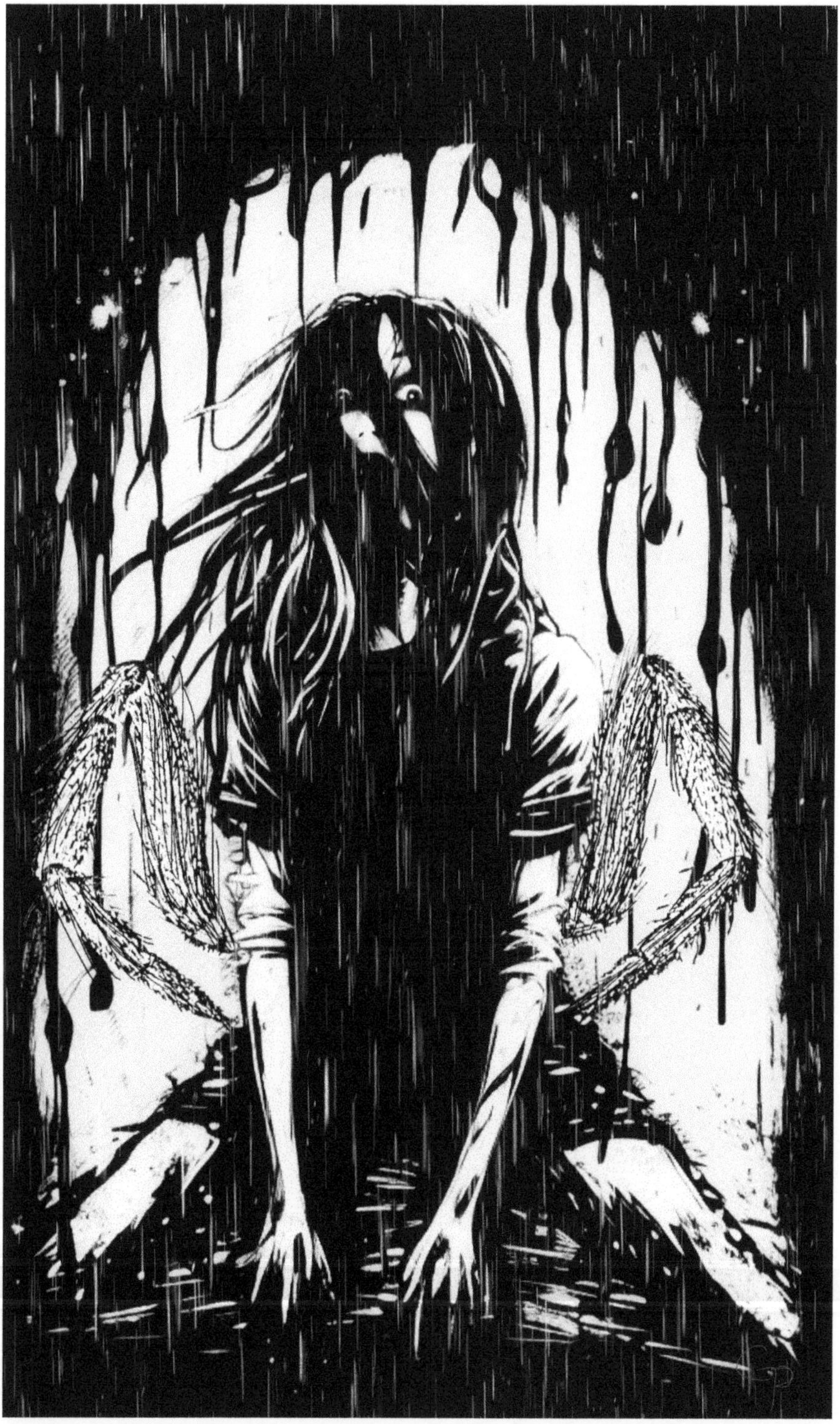

CHAPTER 32

The meat wagon pulled up to the rear entrance of the medical center with Sheriff Primrose, Dr. Ziegler, and Burt Lively crowded together in the front seat. In the back was something that could no longer be described as Abe Gorman, tethered to the wooden stretcher, and Deputy David Rainey, who lay bound and unconscious on the floor.

Carl backed the van up to the loading dock. He turned off the engine and scanned the area for activity. "Looks like the coast is clear."

"Okay," Ziegler said, grabbing the door handle. "I'll check inside. If I'm not back right away, just hold tight."

"Hey, Doc." Carl grabbed his arm. "You might want to take off the body armor first."

Ziegler looked down at the vest and the rest of the armor he still wore and shook his head. He removed the protective gear and discarded it onto the floor. Then he exited the van and let himself in through the back service entrance of the medical center.

Carl and Burt watched the man enter the building and offered each other a tentative look. The parking lot was quiet ... too quiet for Carl's liking. And sitting there in the dark made him feel more like a criminal than the town's sheriff, even though it wasn't unusual for the meat wagon to be parked in the loading area, where it was used to transport bodies.

"How do you suppose we're going to get this thing in there without drawing attention?" Burt asked, removing his vest. Carl shrugged and continued to scan their surroundings. They stripped off the rest of the riot gear and waited till the back door swung open and Dr. Ziegler stepped outside. The man gave them the *all clear* sign and waved to them.

"Here we go," Carl said, tapping his fingers against the steering wheel. "Showtime."

They exited the vehicle and met the doctor at the rear of the van. Burt opened the back door, and together, he and Carl removed the stretcher, leaving the unconscious deputy lying on the floor. Then Dr. Ziegler led them inside to a gurney he had placed near the entrance. They set the stretcher down, and Dr. Ziegler covered Abe with a large sheet that almost made him look like just another patient—almost.

The men wheeled the gurney down the hall with Ziegler leading the way, first taking a right down an adjacent corridor and then following the doctor to the left. They arrived at a large steel door without running into a single staff member. Ziegler ushered them in and turned the lights on in a small reception area. They quickly maneuvered the gurney into the room, and the doctor closed the door behind them.

"That went well." Sweat beaded on the doctor's forehead. "Follow me."

Ziegler led them through the only other door in the reception area. They entered a room that looked to Carl like something straight out of a *Star Trek* episode. He had never seen an MRI machine before or even heard of one. It was ominous and threatening, a beast of a mechanism that took up the entire room. A massive cylinder that resembled a giant torpedo tube fixed with keypads and dials surrounded a flat table where the patient was intended to lay.

"Is he secured enough for this thing, Doc?" Carl asked.

"It will have to do." Ziegler check the straps and bindings that secured Abe to the wooden plank. "Doesn't look like he's able to move much, to me. Hopefully, this will give us some answers."

"If you say so, Doc." Burt stared at the thing on the stretcher. "But I got a feeling it's too late for that."

THE OJANOX

They transferred the wooden plank onto the table of the machine. Carl rechecked the cable ties and nodded to Ziegler, satisfied that the man was bound securely. The leather strap around Abe's face, the bindings, and ties all appeared to be doing the job. Carl felt reasonably confident they would hold and were almost safe enough to remove the basin that still covered the face—almost.

Ziegler told them it would take about twenty minutes for the imaging to register. Shortly after that, they would see the results. Hopefully, the MRI machine would reveal much about the changes that had occurred in the man's organs and soft tissue.

"If you'll both follow me." Ziegler pointed to an adjacent room with a large glass window that resembled a recording studio.

He led them through a thick, padded door into the next room. Carl was the last man to leave the chamber; he grabbed the basin covering Abe's face and wheeled the metal gurney into the room. The overhead light came on automatically, revealing a tight space that looked even more like the inside of a spaceship than the chamber itself. A large instrument panel took up the area in front of a window overlooking the machine. A sea of dials and buttons covered the entire back wall of the room. Carl examined the staggering amount of equipment packed into the cramped quarters and gasped. *This shit probably costs more than every house on my block combined.*

"Would ya look at all this stuff. Do you know how to operate this thing, Doc?" Burt asked.

"I've got a pretty good idea. I guess we're about to find out. Besides, once it's on, it does all the work itself." Dr. Ziegler flipped a large switch on a circuit panel and proceeded to turn on the smaller sub-circuits. Lights began to flash across the board and on the instruments covering the back wall. The entire room began to buzz with electricity as Ziegler turned a large dial on the board and depressed a button beneath it. The MRI machine in the adjacent room came to life; small yellow lights flashed on a panel near the top of the cylinder. The sound of a churning motor could be heard above the noise of the other instruments.

Ziegler turned another dial, and the table retracted into the heart of the cylinder. Abe's body was swallowed by the circumference of the imaging system. The only parts of the man that remained visible were his shoes.

The intensity of the motor grew louder as the instrument cycled to operate. Carl and Burt exchanged an uneasy look and waited for the process to begin. The noise the machine made was unnerving. From inside the room, a loud, sporadic thudding began. There was a jarring buzz, followed by more of the thunderous thudding.

"Is it supposed to do that?" Carl asked, watching for any movement from within the chamber.

"It's fine. We just have to wait. About twenty or so minutes." Dr. Ziegler exhaled and wiped his brow.

A horrifying shriek erupted from the chamber, loud enough to drown out the thudding of the instruments and cause each man to jump. The thing inside the machine screamed in anguish.

"What the hell is going on?" Burt shouted.

Ziegler pressed his face to the window to get a better look. Abe began to buck and twist violently inside the cylinder. The man shook with such great force that the stretcher itself began to shudder against the table. The next sound that erupted from the man sliced through the air like a lance and threatened to pop the soft membranes of their eardrums. Dr. Ziegler lunged for the instrument panel and proceeded to power down the machine. Carl saw what was happening inside the chamber and stopped the doctor before he could.

"Don't do that. You need to see this!"

Ziegler looked up through the glass to see what the sheriff was talking about and immediately stopped what he was doing. A dark cloud had begun to permeate the inside of the chamber. It rose from Abe's body and appeared as if it was seeping out of his pores. The man continued to struggle against his restraints, shrieking and howling, as the cloud grew thicker and took on more density.

"For fuck's sake!" Burt cried, but no one could hear him over the tormented wail of the thing inside the MRI machine.

The stretcher crashed against the table. The dark mass that had formed above the body darted forward and was halted as if it had hit a barrier. Half a second later, it was pulled backward into the heart of the machine. Carl focused on the strange cloud; it looked like it was attempting to escape from the chamber. But the smoke was unable to breach the outer edge of the cylinder. Abe howled with such insane intensity, Carl was certain the man had shredded his vocal cords. Then the cloud folded in on itself, collapsed, and vanished. The body of the man inside the chamber stopped moving.

THE OJANOX

Carl, Burt, and Dr. Ziegler stared through the glass, trying to see where the strange substance had gone. There was no sign of it anywhere. "I think it's dead," Burt said.

Ziegler cycled down the machine and retracted the table from the chamber. He turned off the main power at the control board, which resulted in a most unnerving silence. The body on the stretcher lay motionless. A dark black fluid ran from its eyes and ears.

"Any idea what that was, Dr. Ziegler?" Carl could still hear the sound of the man's screams echoing in his ears.

"Whatever it was, it's also in the children." Burt's voice cracked. "That's your poison right there. That machine just sucked the infection out of Abe and killed him in the process."

Ziegler opened the door to the imaging chamber and walked in to inspect the body. Carl followed. They approached the side of the table with Burt bringing up the rear. Abe was dead ... for good this time. A tar-like fluid ran from his open orifices and pooled on the table beneath his head. Ziegler examined the man's eyes to find their original shade had returned. He checked for a pulse, looked at his watch, and recorded the time of death. "Eight fifteen."

"I suggest we get this body out of here and go check on my deputy. Then we can discuss just what we think we saw here tonight." Carl looked at Burt and then at Ziegler to see if they had anything to add. No one did. "Okay then, let's get out of here." They transferred the body to the gurney and let themselves out the way they had come in. Carl didn't feel like they needed to operate in secrecy anymore. Now they really were just transporting a dead body.

●●●

Deputy Rainey regained consciousness sometime later. He held an ice pack to the side of his head but could recall little of what happened. Tilting his head back, he took a slow pull from the bottle of scotch. "I don't remember any of that," he said.

The four men gathered in the lab, recounting the night's events. The dissected corpse of Felix Castillo lay just a few feet away; next to it rested a black body bag containing Abe Gorman, the man who had once driven the very vehicle he had been transported in.

"You pointed your gun at the sheriff," Burt said. "You were going to kill him."

"Try to remember, son." Carl sat across from him, holding his hat in his hands. "We were getting ready to move Abe, then something happened. What can you tell me?"

"I'm not sure." Rainey squinted. "I remember an itch. You know, like the kind you get in the back of the throat. Except, it was in my head. I know it sounds crazy."

Carl leaned back. "Like a headache or something like that?"

"Not exactly." The deputy paused and took another sip. He stared at the floor in front of him as if the answers might be lying there. "I remember someone calling my name. Next thing I know, I woke up in the van."

"You discharged your weapon." Carl pointed to the bullet hole in the freezer door.

"I-I would never try to hurt you." The deputy's voice wavered, and he appeared on the verge of tears. "I'm sorry, Sheriff."

"I forgive you, son," Carl told him. "In fact, I don't believe it was you who tried to kill me tonight. I think that thing got in your head and made you do it."

"Why would it only affect him?" Burt started to pace the floor.

"Well," Ziegler said, "I could think of several possible explanations. Now, it didn't happen until the sheriff took the basin off its head. And when he did, the deputy was looking right at it. That's when he started acting crazy."

"That's right!" Rainey shouted. "I looked up, and it was staring right at me. That's when I heard someone call my name."

Ziegler nodded. "Also, the deputy was the only man who was armed, other than you, Sheriff. It saw you as a threat. You're the one who killed Castillo, after all."

"Well, Doc." Carl stood up. "Why wouldn't it just jump into my head, make me shoot myself or something?"

"Not sure; it's just a theory, really. But I'm guessing you're not easily influenced. No offense, Deputy."

"Yeah, he's right about that, Carl," Burt said. "That thing probably got a taste of your sour ass and spit you back out."

Carl cracked a half smile and met the doctor's stare. "You need to get in contact with Dr. Malcolm immediately. If he's with the children, he is in way over his head. We've seen how it spreads, and if even one of those things got out ... Christ, if that truck hadn't come along and flattened Felix Castillo, there's no telling how many we'd be dealing with right now."

"That's what worries me, Sheriff," Ziegler said. "Castillo disappeared a full day before that truck hit him. What if he got to someone already?"

The sudden hush that fell over the men was broken by a blast of static from the radio on Carl's hip. Andrea's voice crackled through the tiny speaker: "Dispatch to Sheriff Primrose. Come in, Sheriff Primrose."

Carl's gut clenched as he reached for the radio. The other men stared at him with the same look of apprehension on their faces.

"Go ahead, Andrea."

"Sheriff, we have a few situations. There's a house fire at Sixteen Poplar, the Barnes residence. Also, Deputy Forsyth never made it in. I called Deputy Kovach to cover for him, but there's no answer at Forsyth's house, and I can't seem to get in touch with him."

"I'm on my way. You said Sixteen Poplar?"

"10-4 Sheriff. Sixteen Poplar. Oh, one other thing." Carl braced himself. "The Tobin boys still haven't come home. Alice is really starting to worry."

"Roger that, Andrea. Deputy Rainey is with me, and we're on our way. Over and out." Carl replaced the radio to his hip and started to move. "Doc, I need you to get in touch with Dr. Malcolm as fast as possible." He turned to Burt. "I want you to burn these bodies, pronto."

"Abe too? Wouldn't his family—" Burt stopped in mid-sentence as if he thought better of what he was about to say. "Yeah ... it would probably be best if no one saw them. I'll take care of it right away. Oh ... Carl?"

"Yeah?"

"Be careful out there, for Christ's sake."

Carl put his hat on and nodded to his friend. He bent down to adjust his sock and came up with a small-caliber pistol in his hand. He handed it to the coroner. "You too, old man." He left the office with Deputy Rainey at his heels.

Donald Fischer walked through the front door to find Lois and Troy sitting at the kitchen table. He could tell right away that something was wrong, something far more serious than him being two hours late for dinner ... again. Tear stains were visible on Troy's cheeks, and his eyes were bloodshot. However, Lois's eyes told a completely different story, one that Donald was certain he didn't want to hear.

"What happened?" He rushed up the stairs and into the kitchen.

Troy lifted his head to his mother but didn't say a word. Lois kissed him on the cheek and then turned to Don. "We had a little scare this afternoon. Troy was almost hit by a car."

"What?" Don raised his voice. "Didn't you look both ways?"

"I-I guess not." Troy took a ragged breath and wiped his face. "I cut through the graveyard on my way home."

"You did what!? We talked about this. You know I don't want you guys walking through there, even if it is a shortcut." Donald felt Lois's laser-bolt stare sear into him from across the room and decided on a different approach. "Why were you guys walking through the graveyard?"

"It was just me." Troy's voice shook as he spoke. "I went to a friend's house after school and cut through the graveyard on the way home. There was something in there ... following me, like an animal or something. Th-then ... I heard them, and they started chasing me. I ran, Dad, but they were so fast, and-and-I don't know. I was so scared; I ran into the street, and I guess I didn't look." By the time Troy finished telling the story, a stream of fresh tears coursed down his face.

Don got down on one knee and hugged his son. He looked up at Lois and lifted his brows. She shrugged her shoulders in reply; apparently, she didn't know what to make of Troy's story either.

"Hey, kiddo." Don released him. "What do you think it was?"

"I don't know, Dad. I-I didn't get a good look." His tears ebbed to a trickle.

"Okay, kiddo." Don knew it wouldn't help any to interrogate his son. "Just promise me you'll stay out of the graveyard from now on. Okay?"

"I swear. I'll never go in there again."

"Say, I got some news you might think is cool." Don figured he'd try changing the subject. "We were blasting on the north face last week, and we discovered an old cave."

Troy's eyes widened. "Really, was there anything inside it?"

Lois went to the oven, removed a plate of left-over roast beef and potatoes, and set it on the table for Don.

"That's why I didn't say anything before." Don nodded to Lois. "In fact, there are *a lot* of artifacts in there. I couldn't tell you because we were waiting for the archeologists from the Museum of Natural History to arrive."

"That's Janis's mom! I was at her house today." Troy's face brightened a full shade.

"You mean Dr. Thompson?" Don asked.

"Yeah! Wow, Dad, you should see all the arrowheads and teeth she gave Janis. They're so cool."

Lois cut in. "Dr. Thompson from the museum is *Janis's* mother, and she is working at your job?"

"Well, it isn't *exactly* my job. It's a DuCain job, and the museum is working in the cave. It's my responsibility to make sure they don't get in the way so everyone else can get back to work."

"What's in the cave, Dad? Come on." Troy fidgeted in his chair; he appeared to be feeling much better.

"You wouldn't even believe it. Everything looks as if it could have been left there only a few years ago, except for the bones, of course."

"There's bones?"

"Oh yeah, lots of them, human and animal. There are murals on the walls too. So colorful and vivid. But you know what's really amazing? The entire cave is comprised of lodestone, which is another name for magnetite. It's a magnetic iron ore used to make magnets. The Lenape tribe made weapons out of it. They sanded the stone into these little balls, like the kind you'd use in a slingshot or a musket."

"That's radical. You don't think they would let you take us up there, do you?"

"I doubt they'd let anyone in who doesn't work for the museum, not until they finish what they need to do first. They're still taking pictures and making a list of everything in there."

"And you were in the cave while they were doing all of this?" Lois asked.

"Well, yeah. Mr. DuCain wants me to represent the company and make sure his interests are considered. I am the go-to guy for the museum personnel," he boasted and messed Troy's hair.

Lois folded her arms as Don began to eat his dinner. "You're working with Dr. Thompson then, in the cave?"

He took a bite of the roast beef. "Uh-huh, but I tell you what I'll do. I'll tell the doctor that you're interested in artifacts and see what she says. Who knows, maybe she'll let you and your friends see the pictures. I don't think it hurts that you're friends with her daughter." He shoved another forkful into his mouth and grinned at Lois.

She turned her back and walked to the fridge.

"Want some pudding, kiddo?" she asked.

"Yes, please." Troy smiled. "Do you think I could wait a couple days before I tear down Scream in the Dark? I know you need the garage back, but Janis wants to see it, and I was hoping she and Wendy could come over so I could show it off one last time."

Lois and Don exchanged a look and nodded to one another. They had always been good at reading each other, even though they weren't all that good at talking.

"Your mom and I will discuss it. Okay?" Don leaned over his plate, a bit more curious than a moment ago. "*Both* of your friends are girls, Wendy and Janis?" *When the hell did this happen?* Troy hadn't expressed an interest in girls yet, not that he knew of.

"Yeah," Troy squirmed a little more, "but it's cool. As soon as Rob gets better, I won't be so outnumbered. It's really tough hanging out with two of them."

"You don't say?" Don coughed and almost spit his dinner onto the table. He looked up at Lois again. "How do you mean?"

"I dunno. You really got to think about what you say. It's easy to look stupid. It's like they're testing you all the time ... ya know?"

Lois rubbed her son's head and placed a can of pudding in front of him. Donald swallowed and leaned in closer. "Get used to it," he whispered. "It's gonna be like that for the rest of your life."

Troy picked up his spoon and dug in. "Oh man! That sounds exhausting."

"It is, kiddo, it is."

Lois turned toward the sink and ran the tap. She lifted the window an inch and started to wash the dishes. It had finally stopped raining, but occasional sizzles of lightning continued to light up the sky. She smiled and listened to the Fischer men talk about the great plague that had suffered the male species for centuries, the great scourge of women.

Chapter 33

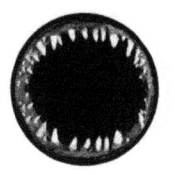

Garrett Grove's volunteer fire department responded to the house fire at Sixteen Poplar. Both the ladder truck and the pump were at the scene when Carl and Deputy Rainey arrived to see the billows of thick grey smoke still lifting into the air. The entire block was a beehive of activity. Firefighters continued to fight the blaze from every angle, and it looked like they had it under control. The sheriff exited the cruiser and spotted Deputy Kovach, who had taken point on crowd control by securing the perimeter and keeping the on-lookers at bay. Carl made his way across the street and approached him.

"We couldn't get inside. The entire place was lit up by the time we got here. Neighbors called it in." Deputy Kovach had soot marks on his cheeks and hands. "No sign of the family. Christ, I hope they weren't inside."

"Andrea said this is the Barnes residence." Carl scanned the gathering crowd. "Any of the neighbors see or know anything?"

"There isn't anyone home across the street," Deputy Kovach checked his notepad, "the Campbell residence. The other neighbors seem to think the Barnes family was probably home at the time."

"All right. Well, see what you can find out from the other neighbors. Deputy Rainey!" Carl shouted. "Give Kovach a hand questioning the crowd." Carl walked toward the house and entered the driveway of Sixteen Poplar. Firemen were in the process of soaking what remained of the smoldering structure, and the last of the flames appeared to have died out. However, radiating heat still poured off the burnt timbers, and the smell of charred, waterlogged wood filled the air. Carl surveyed the damage from where he stood and prayed that no one had been home at the time. He walked up the drive, stopping at the two cars parked near the garage, and knew there was little chance of that. His stomach somersaulted with the realization that the Barnes family had more than likely been home when the fire started. He feared there would be some grizzly discoveries once the smoke cleared.

He was alerted by the commotion as two firemen kicked in the front door and entered the house. They dragged a hose from the pump truck and sprayed the interior as they walked inside.

Carl checked the vehicles to find nothing out of the ordinary. He then followed the driveway to the garage, where a litter of broken glass peppered the asphalt. He inspected the windows and noticed that all the panes on the garage door were still intact. Wondering where it had come from, he backed up and looked on the roof. The reflection of the streetlight glinted as if it were caught in a thousand tiny mirrors. Slivers of broken glass spread out across the wet shingles in a wide pattern. Carl strained to see the single window on the gable side of the house. It had been smashed; the torn screen hung from the frame along with a portion of the window itself. It looked like it had blown outward or something had jumped through it. *Maybe someone got out after all.* But there was no sign of survivors, at least not in front of the house. *Better check out back.*

"Hey," he called to the group of firemen gathered on the lawn. "Did you guys knock that window out?"

An extra-large fireman in full protective gear removed his helmet and face mask, revealing a boyish face and thick handlebar moustache. It was Bob Jones, the chief; Carl knew him well and genuinely liked the giant man. "Howdy, Carl. We haven't been up there yet."

"Your men didn't break that window, Bob?"

"Wasn't us. Maybe someone got out."

"Okay, thanks." Carl left Bob and the rest of the crew to finish their work and made his way to the back of the house. He pulled a small flashlight from his belt and inspected the lawn as he proceeded. The grass hadn't been disturbed, and there was no broken glass as far as he could tell. He continued around the house until he came to the back screen door.

It hung open with the top hinge ripped off. Carl approached the entrance and stopped. It was still too hot to enter without proper protection; he would have to wait for the place to cool down before he could go in tomorrow with the fire inspector and look around. He backed away from the door and bumped into a stone statue set on the top steps. Turning around, he cast his light onto the small figure and froze. Carl leaned in closer. Something on the stone surface shimmered in the beam. He touched the circular stain and noticed it was still sticky. He examined his fingers in the light. *Blood* ... A small drop had come to rest on the statue. Someone had either come out of the house bleeding or they had gone in that way. Carl's gut told him what he already suspected. They weren't going to find the Barnes family inside the house after all. In fact, no one was going to find them, and if they did, they were going to wish they hadn't. Felix had infected at least one person before getting hit by that truck. If he had walked out of that morgue at three on Sunday afternoon and hadn't been found until five the following morning, he had been out there for fourteen hours. *Fourteen hours ... Jesus Christ!* If they were lucky, Felix had only infected one or two and not dozens. At the moment, Carl Primrose wasn't feeling very lucky at all.

The Thompson family continued to share their day's experiences with one another. Stephanie was more than thrilled that Janis had gotten on so well and prayed they would be able to stick around long enough for her daughter to finish out the school year in Garrett Grove. Lord knew they'd been bouncing around a lot lately. She hated uprooting the family repeatedly, but that was the job and she had to go where the museum sent her.

They talked and they laughed until it had gotten late. Stephanie knew tomorrow would be a busy day for all of them and told Janis it was time to wash up. The girl was still excited but tired from an eventful day; she kissed both her mother and aunt goodnight and went off to bed. Stephanie said she was exhausted as well and went to her room once she and Lynn finished cleaning up the remnants from the meal.

However, she hadn't been as tired as she let on; there was something she had been curious about since the afternoon. Her bedroom was still littered with unpacked boxes, and after raking through a few of them, she found the one she was looking for. Cracking the packing tape and digging through the contents, Stephanie came across the large binder. She opened it and flipped to the picture on the first page. It showed a cave painting, far more primitive than the murals at the DuCain site. The hands that created the art belonged to a race that had vanished long before the Lenape had crafted their own designs. Still, the subject matter was oddly familiar.

The picture revealed a dark-skinned woman being tended to by the members of her clan; she appeared to be suffering or sick as the healers of her tribe treated her. The photograph on the opposite side of the page showed a secondary scene. The same dark-skinned woman had undergone some type of trauma. Her features had transformed into something grotesque and inhuman. She looked as if she had de-evolved into something primitive. This was evident by how she chased after her healers on all fours. And although it wasn't an exact replica of the murals they had seen today, the likeness was uncanny. Tiny pointed teeth lined the woman's mouth, similar to the ones depicted in the murals at the DuCain site. The skulls that Stephanie's team had found today also contained mouthfuls of those same awful teeth. She focused closer on the picture. As the mutated woman pursued her healers, a strange shadow appeared to follow her. It looked as if it originated from her body, as if she was expelling it.

Stephanie flipped to another set of pages titled "Cahokia." There were photos and newspaper clippings that dated back to the 1920s. They showed a massive excavation that had taken place. The Cahokia civilization was one of the countless unexplained mysteries that archeologists loved to speculate on. Stephanie's father had been fascinated with America's forgotten city and devoted much of his life's work to finding an answer to the strange disappearance. Stephanie followed in his footsteps and wrote the thesis for her doctorate about the archaeological evidence found at the colony's site.

There were several working theories as to what led to the disappearance of nearly 40,000 people. Cahokia was a thriving centralized hub of religion and politics by the year 1000. It also went by the name The City of the Sun and, by all rights, could be considered a kingdom. It had been the largest North American civilization, spanning from the Great Lakes and covering much of the southeastern region of North America. Some historians believed environmental impact played a major role in the disappearance of the tribe. Evidence of previous floods and periods of drought could possibly explain a mass exodus, but that evidence was inconclusive. Still, something had occurred near the year 1200 that started a catastrophic chain of events. Lack of resources, including food and wildlife, led the nation into war and an increase in ritualistic sacrifices, which ultimately resulted in the extinction of the people. By 1250, Cahokia had fallen, and by the 14th century, the great nation was nothing but a memory.

But Stephanie didn't subscribe to any of those theories and neither had her father. They both believed that the correlation of the die-off in the area's wildlife revealed more about the period than anything else. The evidence indicated that nearly all biological life had disappeared in the area somewhere between the years 1200 and 1300. And there had been some valuable clues left behind, clues that only senior members of the dig team had been privy to. Dr. Edgar Donavan, the lead archeologist of the expedition, had shared that information with his oldest daughter, Stephanie.

The next page in the binder displayed two photographs. The first had been the source for much hypothetical speculation and controversial disagreement from Stephanie's peers. The photo depicted what appeared to be the jawbone of an animal. The same small, razor-sharp teeth lined the bones of the animal's jaw, much like the teeth depicted in the cave paintings. The jawbone was found during the Cahokia excavation and appeared to be somewhat canine in nature. Only not exactly canine; there were qualities of the bone that looked prehistoric reptilian. And there were other anomalies as well. In fact, there were at least three distinct biological features found within the singular bone. But that wasn't what had perplexed the original scientists the most. The back molars of the jaw appeared to be human; not only did they resemble human molars but it was almost certain that they were. Two of the rear molars contained gold fillings. A rudimentary dentist had drilled out cavities in the teeth and packed the malleable alloy into the holes. There was no reason to suspect that a dentist would perform this type of procedure on an animal, certainly not one as strange as this. Stephanie believed that the jawbone had belonged to a human, one that had undergone a drastic mutation and changed its physiology.

Other excavations had led to similar finds, revealing hybrid fossils of human and animal remains combined. In most cases, it looked as if the bones were in the process of mutating into a creature that had never existed. At least no creature ever documented by paleontologists. Stephanie believed the reason they had never been documented was because they were a combination of species from different periods. It was evident in the jawbone that human, canine, and Jurassic qualities had been somehow fused together. These weren't anomalous findings either. Fossils exactly like the jawbone had turned up all over the world from myriad cultures. The Lenape cave was the most recent of these findings, and Stephanie hoped it would prove to be her Rosetta Stone. *This could be the discovery that ties it all together.* The secret was in the murals. They were in far better condition than any of the other cave paintings they had inspected in the past.

If only you were here to see this. Her father had inspired her to continue the search, and he had been right. All those years ago, he had been onto it and been so close to the truth. Stephanie touched the book that had once belonged to Edgar Donovan. "Oh, Dad, you should be here," she said.

The last picture in the book finally made sense. She hadn't been able to understand the significance of it before. But after today, thanks to Donald Fischer, she understood much more. The picture was taken of several weapons discovered during the excavation. There were a few arrowheads, a dagger, and several spear tips. All the weapons had been fabricated from the same material ... magnetite, an iron ore also known as lodestone.

● ● ●

Lois picked up the telephone and dialed Karin Boyle's number. She'd been reluctant to bother her at home after everything she and her family had been through in the past few days. But Carl had called last night and said that Rob and the other children were on the mend; however, Lois hadn't heard a thing since.

She let the phone ring, waiting for Karin or Bob to pick up, but no one answered. She waited a bit longer, hung up, and then dialed the center.

"Chilton Medical, how may I direct your call?" a woman's voice greeted her.

"Hello, this is Lois Fischer. I brought a young boy into the emergency room on Saturday night."

"Yes, Mrs. Fischer. I was here Saturday as well. What can I do for you?"

"Well, I was wondering how Robert is doing. I was concerned, and I haven't heard anything since yesterday."

"Well, Mrs. Fischer, I am really not supposed to give out that information to anyone who isn't family."

"Oh, I see." Lois waited for the woman to continue.

"But I know how worried you were about the boy." The woman lowered her voice. "So ... don't tell anyone I told you, okay?"

"Of course," Lois said.

"Well, late last night, Dr. Malcolm transferred all three of the children to a toxicology center in Oswego."

"Oswego. Why on Earth did he do that?"

"Apparently, he believes that the children may have come in contact with the same toxin. He mentioned something about snake venom."

"Snake venom? I thought Robert was being treated for a bacterial infection."

"I'm not sure, Mrs. Fischer. In fact, that's all I really know."

Lois thought for a moment, then continued. "I suppose both Karin and Bob made the trip with Robert. I tried to reach them at home, but they weren't there."

"Yes, I would imagine they did."

"Is there any chance I could talk to Dr. Malcolm? If he isn't too busy."

"Oh, I'm sorry, but Dr. Malcolm accompanied the families and is in Oswego assisting with the patients." The woman paused to clear her throat. "I think Dr. Ziegler is in his office. He may be able to answer some of your questions. Would you like to talk to him?"

"If I may. Thank you."

"Remember, Mrs. Fischer. I didn't tell you anything."

"Of course. Thank you for all your help." Lois waited to be connected, and after several rings, the doctor picked up.

"Dr. Ziegler," he answered.

"Hello, Dr. Ziegler. This is Lois Fischer; I hope I am not calling you at a bad time."

There was a pause before the man replied. "Not at all, Mrs. Fischer. What can I do for you?"

Dr. Ziegler was Troy's physician and had known the family since he started working at Chilton. Lois trusted him and thought he was a good doctor. "I was concerned about Robert Boyle. He and my son are good friends, and well ... we brought him in the other night to the emergency room."

"Is Troy feeling all right? I know he was in close contact with Robert."

Lois's pulse quickened at the man's reaction. "I was under the impression this wasn't contagious like Dr. Malcolm originally believed. Sheriff Primrose told us there was a possibility of quarantine and that we should stay home yesterday. But then he called later and said that Robert was somewhat better and there was no need to worry."

Ziegler cleared his throat on the other end. "Yes ... that's exactly right."

"Oh, because the way you asked about Troy, it sounded like you might be worried about something serious." Lois thought carefully about what she would say next. "Dr. Ziegler, are Robert and the other children all right? Should I be concerned for my child's safety?"

"Dr. Malcolm transferred the children to a toxicology center up state. I was just about to call and check on their progress."

The man's voice had changed. *What are you hiding, Dr. Ziegler?* "You didn't answer my question, Doctor. Should I be concerned for my child's safety? Is there a chance that Troy could catch what Robert has?"

"Mrs. Fischer." He cleared his throat and paused again. There was a rustling of papers on the other end of the line, and Lois could tell he was more than just uncomfortable. "I can tell you with one hundred percent certainty that if Troy had what Robert has, he would already be showing symptoms. There would be no hiding it; you would know."

"So, you believe it *is* contagious and *not* a snake venom or some type of poison?" She had no choice; she had started down this line of questioning and couldn't stop until she got an answer that satisfied her. Ziegler was hiding something.

"Um, who told you that?" he asked. "Where are you getting your information from, Mrs. Fischer?"

Lois cursed herself for overplaying her hand; she thought about her next move and hesitated for a moment. But if there was even a chance that Troy was in danger, she was prepared to do whatever it took. "Well, Dr. Ziegler, I've known Carl since before he had to shave. I spoke with him earlier, and he recommended I call you. And as Troy's doctor, I trust you have my son's best interests in mind."

She knew she had crossed the line by using Carl's name and there would be repercussions, but she had no choice.

"I assure you, Mrs. Fischer, there's nothing more important to me than the welfare of *all* my patients. And since Robert and the other children have been transported to Oswego, you have nothing to worry about."

"Hmmm-mmm, let me ask you this. What if Robert and the other children weren't in Oswego? What would you tell me then?" Troy didn't know how right he had been when he told his father that men had to think fast around women, and Lois Fischer knew Dr. Ziegler was no exception to the rule.

The doctor paused for a long moment; there was another sound of papers moving and the rattle of a door, as if the man had checked outside his office. He returned a moment later and lowered his voice even more. "Mrs. Fischer, if that were the case, I would suggest that you and your family strongly consider going on vacation. I hear Florida is lovely this time of year."

Lois felt a massive lump well up in her throat and almost dropped the phone. Had she heard him correctly? *Did he just tell me to get the hell out of town as fast as possible?* Lois Fischer had pushed it as far as she dared with the good doctor and knew there would be backlash from Carl for her manipulation of the man. But she had all the information she needed, at least for the moment. "Thank you very much, Dr. Ziegler," she said, her voice trembling and on the verge of tears.

"Mrs. Fischer," Ziegler said more directly. "This conversation never happened." He hung up.

Lois's heart throbbed as she remained clutching the phone like a baseball bat. She struggled to wrap her head around the words he had said. *Florida is lovely this time of year.* But Carl had told her the children were improving. *Just what the hell was wrong with them, anyway?* Surely, she and Troy had been exposed to whatever Rob had. Ziegler said he would have already started showing symptoms. Lois tried to think if Troy had appeared sick in any way. He seemed fine, but there had been the incident in the graveyard. That was odd behavior, but he had only been scared. He didn't seem sick. The phone started to beep in her hand; she hadn't realized she was still holding it long after the doctor had hung up. She laid the receiver on the cradle.

Lois walked down the hall to her son's room and peeked in on him. He was in bed reading a comic book, nothing strange. Then she passed the den where Donald was busy looking over some paperwork he had brought home. She didn't want to tell him what Dr. Ziegler had said; it would only lead to a conflict. Lois knew exactly what she had to do, but she would have to wait until tomorrow. *I need to talk to Carl and get to the bottom of this.*

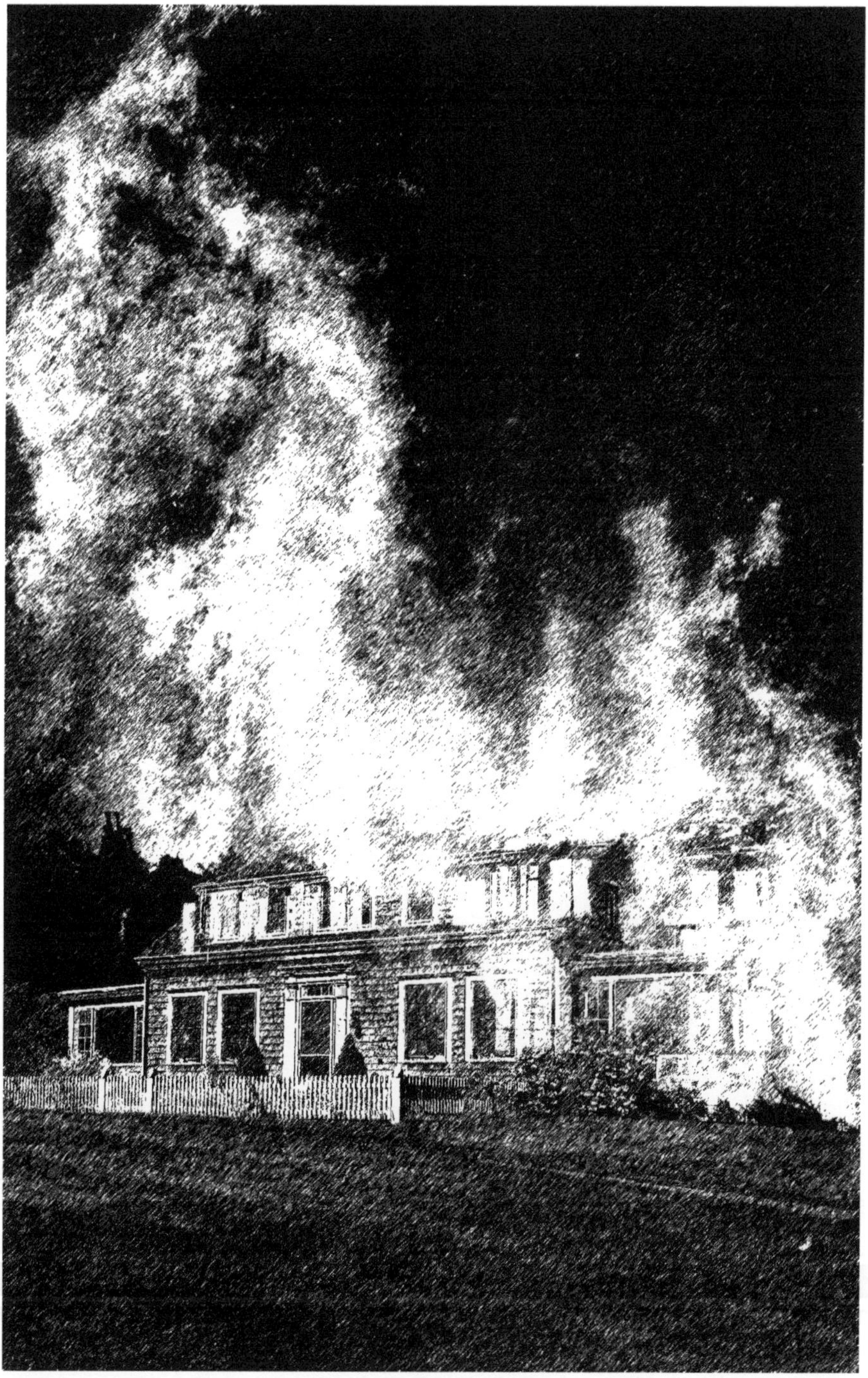

Chapter 34

Father Kieran had carried the boy into the downstairs bedroom of the rectory, where he remained unconscious, looking as if he had lost a fight with a mountain lion. The priest did everything he possibly could for him, but the child was dehydrated and in shock. Kieran offered him a few drops of water at a time but didn't want to overdo it at first. Surely the boy needed the liquid, but too much too soon would cause him to choke. Kieran slowly offered him a bit more.

The boy moaned and shivered while some violent nightmare plagued his dreams. There was no telling how long he had been wandering the woods or what evil he might have encountered out there. Kieran could only imagine that he'd been lost in the woods for a couple days, judging by the state he was in. Large punctures tore into the material of the boy's jeans, leaving dark crimson stains that traveled from his hips to his ankles.

He had lost a lot of blood. Most of it had already dried; however, some of the deeper wounds appeared fresh. Kieran took a large pair of shears and slit the leg of the boy's jeans.

"Dear God." The priest let out a gasp as the wounds were revealed. He exposed the boy's other leg. On the table beside the bed, he gathered what medical supplies he could find in the rectory. A large pair of tweezers and some disinfectant, along with bandages and rolls of gauze, were assembled neatly within reach.

The kid was in bad shape; his legs had sustained massive puncture wounds and deep lacerations. Father Kieran immediately discovered what had caused the injuries. He used the tweezers, grasped at the object, and pulled. It came out easily, though it had been lodged a good three-quarters of an inch into the boy's flesh. Kieran examined the massive thorn; the tip was covered in blood. It was much bigger than the thorns that grew at the base of Garrett Mountain, and Kieran suspected that this one had come from somewhere deep in the woods, where it had been growing wild for ages. He dropped it into a bowl, making a sound like a penny being tossed into a dish at a carnival, then went to work on the other intruders that impaled the child.

The boy moaned while the priest removed the massive splinters from his legs. Fresh blood oozed from his open wounds and stained the sheets he lay on. Once Kieran had removed all the thorns he could find, he cleaned the wounds with disinfectant and bandaged the worst of them, wrapping the child's legs with the gauze.

He offered the boy more water, allowing him only a few sips at a time. *Thank you, Lord.* Kieran believed it was a good sign that he was taking in fluids. Still, he knew that infection would be the real threat. The boy was going to need antibiotics and proper medical attention, but ...

Father Kieran rechecked the window. *Dear God, there's so many of them.* Now the creatures were traveling in two directions, some toward the mountain and some headed into town. He knew it best not to call an ambulance or the authorities for the risk it might put them in, not with the beasts so close to the rectory property. He opted to tend to the child himself rather than put anyone else in harm's way. *We will wait it out together, my son.* The boy stirred and moaned in his sleep.

"Help me," he said, his voice sounding cracked and dry.

Father Kieran rushed to his side and leaned in close. "Tell me, son, what is your name?"

The boy opened his eyes for a moment and allowed the weakest gasp to slip through his lips. *"Billy,"* he said.

Evading the truth didn't sit well with Dr. Ziegler. In the past, he had exercised discretion and avoided certain particulars to maintain an air of professionalism. But he had never outright lied before—or, in this case, withheld the truth from a patient or their family. Having to dance around Mrs. Fischer's questions left his stomach feeling sour, like he had swallowed a peach pit. He told himself he had given the woman enough information to use her own discretion. After all, he did warn her of the potential danger without exactly spelling it out. But telling himself that didn't make him feel any better about it.

Ziegler finally found the number to the toxicology center in Oswego and dialed the phone. A man picked up on the second ring.

"ECHO Toxicology, this is Adrian. How may I direct your call?"

"Hello, Adrian, my name is Dr. Ziegler. I'm calling you from Chilton Medical in Garrett Grove."

"Hello, Doctor. What can I do for you?"

"Well, my chief of medicine, Dr. John Malcolm, is there, and I was wondering if you could find him for me?"

There was a long pause, and for a moment, Ziegler thought he had been disconnected. "Hello, Adrian. Are you still there?"

"I'm sorry, did you say Dr. Malcolm?"

"Yes, that's correct. He would have arrived sometime yesterday with the children we transferred."

"Could you hold for one moment, please?"

Ziegler was put on hold before he could answer, and after about a minute of waiting, another voice came on the line.

"Hello, this is Dr. Klein, the chief administrator. You are Dr. Ziegler. Am I pronouncing that right, Doctor?"

"That's right. I'm calling from Chilton Medical in Garrett Grove."

"I'm sorry, but my assistant was a bit confused; he said you were looking for a—" There was a rustling of papers, then the doctor replied, "Dr. Malcolm, is that correct?"

"Yes. Dr. Malcolm, he transferred three children to the care of your facility. They would have arrived early this morning sometime."

"Dr. Ziegler." The man paused. "There's no Dr. Malcolm here, nor have we had any patients transferred from your facility."

Ziegler's heart jumped into his throat and stagnated. His mouth went dry as he attempted to speak. "A-are you quite certain?" He nearly choked on the words. "The children's names are Robert Boyle, Erin Richards, and Ben Richards. All are ten years old and have been exhibiting cellular degeneration caused by a potentially unknown bacterium."

"I'm quite sure I would have remembered any patients exhibiting symptoms as extreme as that. ECHO Toxicology is more of a research facility, and we have very few patients on the premises at any given time. Perhaps your chief of medicine transferred the children to another facility."

Ziegler had a pretty good idea that Dr. Malcolm and the children weren't going to be found in any other facility. He didn't need to inquire any further.

"I'm sure that's what happened," Ziegler said. "I'm sorry to have bothered you, Doctor. Thank you for your help."

"You're quite welcome, Dr. Ziegler. Sorry I couldn't be more helpful. Goodnight."

"Goodnight." Ziegler hung up and stared at the phone. *Oh God, this is my fault.* He had no idea what they were dealing with when the children were brought in. *I should have listened to you.* Dr. Malcolm had been right all along. Quarantine would have been the correct course of action, and he had talked the old man out of it. And for what? So he could get laid.

Things may have turned out the same regardless, but at least it wouldn't have been on his shoulders. Ziegler believed the worst thing he could do was allow a contagious variant of the flu loose in Garrett Grove, but he had ended up releasing something much worse.

There was no doubt; the infection that attacked the children was the very same bacteria that had mutated Felix Castillo and Abe Gorman. The result would also be the same for the children as it was for those men. But for some strange reason, the transformation had taken much longer to manifest in the three ten-year-olds. Now, it was only logical to assume that Dr. Malcolm and the children's parents had been infected as well.

This is bad; this is so bad. Only a few hours ago, the laws of medicine and physiology applied. He had been trained that everything could be explained with scientific method, that through research and observation, a logical conclusion could always be concluded. But Ethan Ziegler had seen things tonight that changed all that. He could no longer trust what he believed to be the truth. Dead bodies didn't get up off the table ... or did they? He raked his hands through his hair, clenched his fists, and racked his brain for an answer. *Come on, man ... think.* But no matter how hard he tried, there was no logical answer to be found.

He had been staring at the phone for almost twenty minutes before he finally tore his eyes away and looked up at the bulletin board. Several notices were held in place with large red ladybug magnets. He studied the colorful design on the back of the bug, bright red with black dots. The circular patterns of black reminded him of Abe's eyes just before they had put him into the MRI machine ... just before it had killed him. Ziegler wondered if Dr. John Malcolm now had eyes that resembled the dots on the backs of the ladybugs. Big, black, lifeless eyes.

Chapter 35

Tuesday

Donald Fischer arrived at the quarry at five-thirty a.m. to find Dr. Thompson sitting on the steps of his trailer with two Styrofoam cups in her hands.

"Good morning, cowboy," she said, handing him a cup. "I brought the coffee today."

"Bright and early, I see. Kind of figured you would be." He skirted past her up the wooden steps and unlocked the trailer door.

"Big day," she said and followed him inside. "It's hard to sleep in when you've got the discovery of your career just sitting there."

"I can imagine." Don turned on the lights, approached his desk, and took a seat. He motioned for Stephanie to join him. She pulled out a nearby chair and sat directly across from him. "My son said he met your daughter yesterday. She made quite the impression."

Stephanie laughed. "I heard nice things about Troy as well. Janis said he made a haunted house in your garage."

"Yep. He calls it Scream in the Dark. He did one hell of a job too."

"He did that all by himself? Quite the motivated little man. Must run in the family."

"He had some help from his friend ... Rob. Known each other since kindergarten. Unfortunately, Rob caught the flu, so Troy had to finish it up. And to be fair, he's a lot more motivated than his old man. Doesn't take much to run a quarry. I know it looks glamorous, but I assure you, once you get past all the dirt, dust, and guys named Rusty, it really isn't."

Stephanie laughed and threw her head back. "You're modest ... That's a good quality. But don't be so hard on yourself. Nobody's life turns out exactly as planned. Unless, of course, your last name's Rockefeller or Kennedy." She tilted her head and made a face. "Even then, it's not guaranteed."

Don laughed and nodded. "True, although it looks like it worked out pretty well for you—pursuing your dream and all."

She took a sip of coffee and leaned back in the chair. "It did, but this wasn't *my* dream. It was my father's. I only picked up where he left off and ended up finding a passion for it."

"Really?" He placed his elbows on the desk and folded his hands under his chin. "Well, don't keep me in suspense. What was it? I'm guessing you wanted to be an astronaut, no wait, an Air Force pilot?" He laughed.

"Not even close, funny man. If you must know, it was ballet. And I was damned good at it!" She twirled her arms at her sides and mimicked taking a bow.

Don had been doing his best keeping his eyes off her legs as she sat across from him but could no longer help himself. She had worn shorts to work again, despite the chill in the air. "I could see that," he said, trying not to stare. "You're strong and petite and look like you'd be easy to pick up." He realized what he had said and felt the heat rush to his face. "I-I didn't mean it like that. I meant ... you know, as a dancer. I'm sure it helps to be small so the guy can throw you around." *For Christ's sake, just stop talking.*

She smiled and watched him squirm. "You're not very good at talking to women, are you?"

"No," he said, taking a quick sip from his cup. "Not at all."

"Actually, it's kinda cute." She leaned in and lowered her voice. "The truth is, I *am* easy to throw around." She winked at him and smiled.

Don choked on his coffee and almost dumped the Styrofoam cup in his lap. He made a valiant effort to recover, sitting up straight and wiping his chin, but Stephanie was already busting a gut.

"Relax, cowboy. I'm just messing with you. My God, you should have seen your face. I wish I had Gail's camera. Talk about a Kodak moment. Speaking of, I told the team to be here by seven. I was hoping to get started right away. Is someone else taking over the daily glamour of the quarry while you babysit me and my guys?"

Don still hadn't fully recovered, but he felt a bit better. The woman was a pistol, and he appreciated her energy. "Yes, Mark Gold will cover me while I play in the dirt with your team."

"So, aren't you going to ask me what happened?"

"Why did you never become a dancer?"

Stephanie leaned back in the chair and kicked her foot up onto his desk. Don's eyes followed the slope of her calf all the way to the curve of her thigh. Then she twisted her leg, exposing the inner side of her knee and a great deal of the rest of her as well. An angry scar lined with a severe number of stitch marks formed a circular pattern around her kneecap. "Torn ACL," she said. "I had the lead in *Swan Lake*. It was a big deal. And when you're small like me, it's easy for the anchor to, I believe you said, 'throw you around.' Well, I landed wrong and tore my ACL, and that was the end of my dancing career. It healed fine, but it was never strong enough to dance again. Besides, who wants a dancer with a big, ugly scar on her leg?"

Don felt hypnotized and found it impossible to pull his stare away from her perfectly toned thigh muscle. "It's not ugly at all." He finally looked up to find her staring at him.

"Why, Mr. Fischer, you *do* know how to talk to women after all." She slowly removed her leg from his desk, taking her time and never breaking eye contact.

Donald felt the heat flushing his face again but managed to handle it better this time. "So," he said. "Now that you've seen what's in the cave, is it everything you were hoping you would find?"

"Everything and more." She looked down at the floor and folded her hands in her lap. "These murals are in pristine condition, and the artifacts—the preservation of the site is impeccable. I've never seen anything quite like it before."

"Really? What makes this site different from others?"

"Well, there are many factors that could explain the unique preservation. It doesn't appear as if the elements were able to penetrate the cave; that's a big one. Also, geographic location, the summers aren't too bad in this part of the country. And who knows, maybe it has something to do with the rock itself. You said the cave was made of magnetite. That's got to be rare."

"It's usually found in smaller deposits in Asia and on the west coast. You'll hit a vein here and there, but never an entire cliff face. Not like this, not in the northeast. It makes me wonder why the Lenape chose this location in the first place."

"It makes sense when you think about the lifestyle of the tribe. They were a spiritual and mystic civilization. They used crystals and stones to stimulate the chakras. I'm sure you've heard what people are saying about the healing powers of magnets. Maybe the Lenape knew something we don't."

Don didn't know about that. He was a man of science and had never been into all that cosmic idealism. Still, as a geologist, he had to admit there was something about the makeup of many geological formations that defied logical answers. There was Stonehenge, for one, and the crystal skulls left by the Toltecs in Lucasio, Mexico. Also, numerous civilizations had discovered the magnetic quality of lodestone and utilized it. But he had never heard of anyone using an entire cave of the ore as a burial site, if that's even what it was.

"Is the cave a burial site? I mean, it looks like it, but I thought they typically used mounds."

Stephanie raised her eyebrows. "That's the million-dollar question. Obviously, some type of ritual took place in that cavern, but I'd be lying if I told you I knew for certain. I'm hoping to find out an answer by getting in there and digging around."

"I've been thinking about the pieces of lodestone found in the ribs of the skeletons," Don said. "What do you think that's all about?"

The smile on Stephanie's face dropped for a fraction of a second, as if she were searching for a quick answer. "I'm not sure of that either."

Don studied her face, looking for a chink in her armor. *Did she just lie to me?* He checked his watch. Stephanie's team would be arriving soon.

"Well, I guess I should put on some more coffee. I think we're gonna need the energy." He left his desk and walked across the trailer.

"Sounds like a plan, cowboy," she said.

THE OJANOX

Miss Walsh entered the classroom and stopped in the doorway with her mouth hung open while she studied the room. More than one-quarter of the seats were empty. She checked the clock above the blackboard just to make sure she had the correct time. Eight o'clock on the nose. She'd heard there was a flu bug going around, and it wasn't only her class that had been affected. The fifth-grade class was missing six students yesterday, and the third-grade class had just as many absentees. It was too soon for flu season to be hitting so hard. It was still only October.

Miss Walsh took a seat at her desk and asked Scott to lead the class in the Pledge of Allegiance, followed by "America the Beautiful." Afterward, it was time for show-n-tell. "Who would like to go first?"

Troy had completely forgotten that Tuesdays were show-n-tell day. He looked around the class and noticed that Rob was still out. *Aw, man.* Erin and Ben hadn't made it back to school either, along with Tommy and Jeff. And now there were even more kids out sick. Mike Barnes wasn't in his seat and neither was Beth Doran or Terry Wallen. *Jeez, I better not catch the flu. I don't want to miss Halloween.*

Troy had woken up a little later this morning than usual and rushed out the door after breakfast. His mom seemed a bit preoccupied as well and burnt his Eggos on the first try and had to make him a second batch.

The other children hadn't forgotten that today was show-n-tell. Even Janis had brought something to show the class, and it was only her second day. Troy turned around to Janis, who had been given the seat behind him, and whispered, "I forgot to bring in something for show-n-tell. I'm so stupid."

The little blonde girl shrugged her shoulders and smiled in reply. Troy turned back as Caroline Smith made her way to the front of the class and revealed an x-ray of her father's arm. While cleaning the gutters, Mr. Smith had fallen off the roof and broken the bone between his wrist and his elbow.

Troy felt a tap on his back and turned around to find Janis holding a Luke Skywalker action figure. "Here," she said. "I was gonna give this to you at lunch to help you make your costume, but I guess you can have it now." She handed the small figure to him.

"Oh my gosh, thank you. That's so cool!" He looked back to where Wendy sat, held up the action figure, and smiled. Wendy's face pinched tighter than Troy thought was possible. Her lips pressed together, and she shot him a look he had seen countless times in the past. *That's the look that Mom gives Dad.* He had an idea he had done something wrong but hadn't a clue what that might be. He turned around quickly, scared he might do something else to earn another one of those looks. It was getting harder to be a boyfriend by the minute. *I'm not ready for this.*

When it was his turn for show-n-tell, Troy proceeded to the front of the class and displayed the action figure. He looked at Janis and then looked at Wendy, then back at Janis, and then at Wendy again, and then ... he started to panic. The little blonde girl brimmed with pleasure when he told the class how his new friend had given him the figure to help him make his costume for Halloween. But this brought out an entirely different reaction from Wendy. She looked pissed. *Jeez, what the heck did I say?* He cleared his throat and told the class about their plans to dress up as the characters from the movie and how he hoped Rob would be better by Saturday so he could be Han Solo. His eyes darted from Janis to Wendy, with his heart racing like a soap box car. Troy's palms started to sweat, and even his fingers felt slick, and for a second, he was sure the small action figure would slip from his grasp. He held on to it tighter and finished up by saying they were going to win the costume contest on Friday because he had seen Wendy's Princess Leia outfit and she looked exactly like her. Wendy's face softened, and a bright smile quickly spread like a case of the flu. Troy exhaled, feeling like he had been granted a stay of execution. *Man, I'm so confused.*

At recess, the trio retreated to a corner of the room for a little pow-wow. Wendy walked up and punched Troy in the arm, which he took as a good sign. Apparently, what he had said made Wendy forget about giving him dirty looks.

Janis had worn a baggy sweatshirt to school, and the boys appeared to settle down a few notches. In fact, the whole class seemed a bit more subdued than they had been the day before, maybe because so many kids were out sick.

"I asked my parents about showing you guys the haunted house, and they said they were gonna talk it over," Troy said. "That's usually a good sign. I'll ask them if tomorrow night is okay."

"Great." Janis smiled. "Did you get started on your costume yet?"

"Um, no, I had a little situation on the way home yesterday. Oh, I almost forgot, my dad knows your mom. The cave they found at the quarry is the one she's working at."

"Really, that's weird. She didn't say anything about it. And we were talking about you last night."

Troy wondered why Janis and her mother would have been talking about him. He didn't know, but for some reason, it made him feel good. He smiled and turned to Wendy, who was definitely *not* smiling—not even a little. Troy felt his own smile falter, then fall to the floor.

Wendy's face had pinched up again like she'd just eaten something sour. "What do you *mean* you had a little situation yesterday?"

Troy's hands started sweating again. "I um … I was walking home and cut through the graveyard. It was getting dark and started to rain. Well, it felt like someone was following me. Then I heard this scream and these things started to chase me." Janis's big eyes focused on him as he retold the story, and Wendy's mouth hung open. She didn't look mad anymore. "I started running, but they tried to cut me off. They weren't dogs, and they weren't kids either. So, I ran for the big tree by the fence. I climbed it and threw myself over. I was so scared, I ran into the middle of the street, and Deputy Lutchen almost hit me with his car. He had to drive me home because it was raining so bad."

The girls stared at him for a tense moment. "Are you kidding around and trying to scare us?" Wendy asked. "'Cause it sounds a lot like your mom's ghost story. You know, the Ojanox?"

"That's what I thought too. I asked my mom about it, and she said she made the name up. But I don't know if I believe her. It felt like she wasn't telling me the whole truth."

"Was it one Ojanox, or maybe a couple of them? Do you think that's what was after you?" Janis asked.

Troy didn't want to admit that he thought the stupid made-up monster from his mom's story really had chased him through the graveyard. He knew that wasn't the way you impressed girls.

"I don't know what to call it. Ojanox sounds about right, though. All I know is they were after me, and they weren't friendly."

"Do you think they're still there, in the graveyard?" Wendy asked.

"I don't know, but remember what my mom said? It comes around this time of year. So, it might be here for a while. I was so excited about Halloween and dressing up as *Star Wars* that I didn't even think what could happen if those things are still here on Halloween. We could be in big trouble."

"Not just us but all the kids in town," Wendy said. "Troy, swear that you're not lying to us. If you're lying, I'll tell the whole class that you let us put makeup and a dress on you."

"Whoa," he yelled. "I'm not lying. It really happened, just like I said."

Janis leaned closer and lowered her voice. "I think you should both come over after school. I have to show you something."

Troy wondered what other surprises the new girl had to show them. Janis had certainly turned out to be an interesting individual with her arrowheads and *Star Wars* toys and Chewbacca mask.

"I don't know if my mom will let me after what happened yesterday. I'll see if I can call her at lunch to ask, but I doubt it," Troy said.

"What do you think?" Janis asked Wendy.

"Yeah, I can go."

Troy already felt left out and decided he would do whatever it took to get to Janis's house after school. Exactly how he would pull it off was another problem altogether. When Miss Walsh called the children back to their seats, the three agreed to talk later.

"Not a word to anybody," Wendy instructed them.

It was exhilarating, and Troy felt as if he had been accepted into a secret club. He especially loved the attention.

●●●

Lois hadn't slept well and woke up with too much on her mind. She burnt Troy's breakfast on the first try and forgot to put the coffee in the percolator. She didn't even realize it until she poured herself a cup of hot water and ended up having to drink tea instead.

Dr. Ziegler's words continued to resonate in her head. *Since Robert and the other children have been transported to Oswego, you have nothing to worry about.* She had used Carl's name to manipulate the doctor. And it worked like a charm.

But Dr. Ziegler said something else that had kept her awake most of the night. He said if Rob and the other children were in town, it would be a good idea to consider taking a family vacation. *I hear Florida is lovely this time of year.* In other words, Ziegler had told her to get the *hell* out of Dodge.

She couldn't talk to Donald about it. It was hard enough to talk to him as it was. There was only one person she could talk to, and that was Carl Primrose ... her ex. If anyone knew what was going on, it was Carl. She didn't want to jump to conclusions but found it impossible not to. There was something in Ziegler's voice. He had been hiding something; that much was obvious. But there was more than just that ... The man had sounded scared.

Lois had finally managed to feed Troy breakfast and get him to school. Unable to control herself any longer, she drove straight to Carl's house, only to find his driveway empty. He was already at work. Lois tried the front door, just to be sure. She mustered her nerve, walked up the steps, and knocked.

There was no answer. Lois knocked louder and waited. "Damn," she said under her breath and considered heading to the station to talk to him. She checked her watch, saw it was eight thirty-five, and thought better about bothering him at work. She decided to come back later and drove home, running through every possible scenario of what might be wrong with Robert and the other children. *What the hell do you know, Dr. Ziegler?* She needed to find out.

Chapter 36

Shortly after eight-thirty a.m., Sheriff Primrose met Bill Hamilton, the King County fire inspector, and Bob Jones, the fire chief, to inspect the house fire at Sixteen Poplar. Bob's men had battled the blaze and brought the fire under control late last night. The pump crew remained on the scene to continuously douse the ashes and watch for any flare-ups. Now, just a few hours after sunrise, the embers had cooled, and it was safe for the men to walk the ruins of the house. Bob Jones had already canvassed the scene last night, but this was the first time the inspector and sheriff were able to see the place themselves.

After finding the blood near the back door, Carl was concerned about what discoveries they might find inside the house. But he was more worried they'd find nothing at all. And it was beginning to look like the Barnes family had not been in the home when the fire broke out.

Chief Jones led the men through the front door and brought them down a hallway to the kitchen. "This is where it started." Bob showed them to the stove. "It looks like the burners were left on. Apparently, they were cooking dinner. But you'll be able to tell us if that is correct or not."

"It looks that way from what I'm seeing." Bill Hamilton pulled a pair of Clark Kent-framed glasses from his coat pocket and examined the dark flash points near the back of the stove. "But we'll get it all straightened out."

"I take it you didn't find any bodies?" Carl asked.

"None at all, Sheriff. Not even a family pet," the large fire chief said. "My men turned the place upside down, and there isn't anyone here. Good news. Strange they would start supper and then leave the house."

More than strange. Carl knew how unlikely that was and wondered if either man thought the same. Sure, the family could have escaped once the fire started, but wouldn't they have run to a neighbor's house or been outside when the fire department arrived? Nothing about that scenario sounded plausible.

Carl followed Bill and Bob through the rest of the house, assessing the damage. The place was totaled, the furniture, the contents, and the structure. It had been a family's home just yesterday. One of the many families that Carl had taken an oath to protect. The children had done their homework at the kitchen table, they had played Candy Land on the living room floor, and they watched Bob Hope on the family television set. Carl's heart ached as if it had been skewered with an ice pick. He knew in his gut that the Barnes family would never know they had lost their home and everything in it. Which was hardly a consolation. They had met a far worse fate.

Carl removed his hat and rubbed his forehead, feeling the lump growing in his throat. He needed to talk to Ziegler and see what the man had found out. Hopefully, he had gotten in touch with Dr. Malcolm and had an idea of what they were dealing with.

Dick Wilson stood at the grill with a scowl on his face. He flipped an omelet and slapped it down hard, as if the egg and cheese concoction owed him money. Mandy hadn't shown up for work and wasn't answering her phone. He had called his only other waitress, Amy Sterling, but the girl was unable to cover Mandy's shift. Typically, Mandy's absence would have been nothing short of a catastrophic event, and even though it had set Dick into a tailspin, it could have been far worse. Of all days for the girl to go AWOL, she had picked the slowest day the diner had seen in years. With only one table occupied and a few seats taken at the counter, Wilson's Diner looked as if its usual patrons hadn't bothered to get out of bed.

Dick's nephew Josh finally agreed to come in and lend a hand. He busied himself while Dick sneered and barked out orders from his position behind the grill. Josh approached the counter and refilled the mugs for a few men who worked for Con Edison, the power company. "Can I get you guys anything else?" he asked.

"Yeah," joked one of the men. "You can get Mandy. I sure as hell didn't come in for the coffee."

"You and me both." Josh nodded and smiled. "She didn't show up, and we haven't sold one slice of peach cobbler all morning."

"And you're not gonna if *you're* serving it," another man chimed in, spurring a fresh fit of laughter from his coworkers.

"The garbage isn't going to empty itself!" Dick shouted. "Do something about that, will ya?"

Josh set the check on the counter in front of the men. "Whenever you're ready," he said, then grabbed the garbage bag and let himself out the back door into the lot. He was met by a breeze that smacked him in the face and sent gooseflesh rippling down his arms. The area near the dumpsters tended to act like a wind tunnel, catching the breeze and swirling it around between the buildings and the back fence.

Josh checked the lot and looked down the alley, trying to locate the stray cat Mandy had more or less adopted. She'd fallen in love with the poor thing and been feeding it for months now. The little guy was never going to leave and had no reason to, not with the constant supply of leftover greasy food that the diner's employees provided.

He pulled out a plastic bag containing a few pieces of ham. He threw the garbage into the dumpster and checked the area again, not seeing Scraps anywhere. Josh emptied the meat onto the ground near the wheel of the dumpster, then headed back to work. *Where are you today, kitty?* He thought maybe the cat was like the men in the diner who would only eat peach cobbler if Mandy was there to serve it. Scraps was really *her* cat after all.

Josh crossed the lot and was about to open the back door when he heard a rustling behind him. He turned back to see Scraps had poked his head out from underneath the dumpster and was munching away. The cat paid no attention to him and continued to devour its meal. "I guess you were hungry after all," he said and went back into the diner. Dick was already barking a new set of orders the second Josh walked in the door.

● ● ●

Doris TenHove attempted to juggle not only her job as head nurse but the duties of three other staff members who had not shown up for work that morning. To make matters worse, not one of them had bothered to call in. Nurse Gilmartin was perhaps the most surprising out of all the no-shows. The girl was always punctual and dedicated to the job, even though lately she appeared a bit preoccupied. And Doris had an idea why. She suspected that Jackie and Chilton's resident ladies' man, Dr. Ethan Ziegler, had started playing doctor together. Not that Doris could blame the young nurse. *Damn, if I was twenty years younger, I'd teach you a thing or two about anatomy myself, Dr. Ziegler.*

Doris called Jackie's apartment repeatedly but was unable to contact her. In addition to Nurse Gilmartin, Kate Wallen was scheduled to be in at seven, and there had been no answer at the girl's home either. Kate still lived with her parents and her kid sister, Terry. Surely someone should have been at home to answer the phone. The other missing girl was Angela Shupp. Doris heard there had been a fire last night on Poplar Ave. That was practically next door to where the Shupp family lived. She prayed that the fire hadn't affected Angela's house. It was more than peculiar that she should get no answer from all three girls' homes.

Angela had been scheduled to work pediatrics, and Kate was slotted to cover the reception desk, where Doris busied herself answering phones and pulling her hair out. She continued trying to find someone to cover the girls' shifts but had no luck. Many of the nurses were unable to come in, and a large percent of the ones she did call hadn't answered either. To make matters worse, Jackie was one of her top ER nurses, and her presence was urgently needed.

There had been a bad car accident this morning on Route 3, and the occupants of the vehicles were currently being treated in the emergency room.

Doris looked up in time to see Michelle Marks and Joseph Santos preparing to exit the building. Both Joe and Michelle worked the paramedics unit for the center and had responded to the car accident. Doris waved them over to the reception desk. "Are you both still on call?"

"Yeah. What's up?" Joe asked.

"I have three nurses who never showed up, and I need help. Is there any chance you could lend a hand for a little while?"

Michelle nodded. "Of course, just tell me where you need me."

"No problem," Joe said.

"Great!" Doris felt as if she had been thrown a life preserver. "Michelle, could you report to Pediatrics? And Joe, you're needed in the ER. Thank you so much." As if on cue, the phone at the reception desk started to ring on three separate lines. Doris suddenly wondered if her life preserver had been made of lead.

Baxter ran from one side of the kennel to his empty water dish and stared at the bowl, panting. He had been barking for the past two hours, but no one showed up to feed him or to fill his water. He looked toward the house, then jumped against the fence and let out several loud barks.

Baxter belonged to Tommy Negal. He had become a member of the family when he was just a ten-week-old German Shepherd puppy and been a loyal companion ever since.

He sensed there was something wrong last night and whined and howled with concern. He struggled to escape from his pen and even tore one of his pads on the fence in the process. But Baxter had been unable to free himself and been upset all night.

Now he was hungry and thirsty and knew that something terrible had happened to his family. He continued to pace across the pen and flipped his water dish, hoping to find a drink. When he finally got tired of running in circles, he laid his head down on the cold concrete and let out a mournful whine. He missed Tommy.

Chapter 37

Donna and Angelo Franco lived just a few doors down from the Barnes residence at Ten Poplar Ave. The newlywed Italian couple were younger than most people on the block and had moved in last year. Donna was the first one to call the fire department last night. She had looked out her front door to see flames wicking out of the Barnes's kitchen window. Hoping to help, she and Angelo ran to their neighbor's house before the fire trucks arrived and pounded on the front door. Angelo even tried to get inside, but the blaze was already out of control and made it impossible. The young couple watched in horror along with the rest of the neighborhood as the home was consumed by the inferno.

It hadn't occurred to Donna last night amidst all the confusion, but this morning, she realized she hadn't seen Beth or Jerry Campbell among the crowd of concerned neighbors. Beth and Jerry lived directly across the street from the Barnes house. Donna knew the two families were close, and their boys were good friends. It was odd they hadn't ventured out of the house.

After Angelo left for work, Donna got to thinking. She was worried sick about what had happened to one family on the block and now wondered if she had reason to be concerned for another. She looked out her front window and noticed the Campbells' Buick was still in the driveway and had been there all night.

She tried to mind her own business, but the more she thought about it, the more it bothered her. Unable to contain her concern any longer, she threw on one of Angelo's sweatshirts and walked out the front door. The air smelled like burnt wood and wet smoke, thick and overwhelming. Donna crossed the street, walked up the driveway, and knocked on the Campbells' front door. There was no answer; she knocked again, harder this time, and waited, but there was still no answer.

"Oh well. In for a penny, in for a pound," she said, walking around the side of the house and into the backyard. Donna froze in her tracks as if gripped by a sudden frost. Her heart stopped, then fluttered, and a cold sweat slicked her palms. The screen door had been left open; it caught the autumn breeze and swung back and forth in lazy arcs. "Hello," she called out, loud enough to be heard.

She took a step forward and approached the house with caution, as if she were walking up on a sleeping hornets' nest. The interior door was open as well, and from where Donna stood, there appeared to be no one inside.

"Hello," she called again, rapping her knuckles against the doorjamb. She poked her head in and yelled out, "Hello, it's Donna from across the street. Is anybody home?"

There was still no answer. She looked through the open door into a dark, quiet living room and took a step inside. There was a smell in the air, one she couldn't quite place. It was deep and thick like metal, but there was something else to it as well. It reminded her a little of burnt toast but not exactly. Donna took several more steps and was overpowered as the odor knocked her over the head. *God, what is that?* She covered her nose and mouth with her hand.

The living room opened into a hallway that led up a small staircase. Donna tiptoed up the stairs, and the odor grew stronger with every step. She could see the kitchen just over the rise of the stairs. The lights were on, and it had suddenly started to feel much warmer in the small stairwell. By the time Donna reached the second to last step, she could feel the heat pouring out of the kitchen in waves.

"Hello," she called as she topped the staircase and entered the kitchen. *Dear God!* She gasped at the state of the room. A frying pan lay face-up on the floor along with whatever had been cooking in it. A bowl of salad had been discarded and scattered across the floor as well. The food rested atop a dizzying pattern of long, dark smears that had dried to a dark crimson brown. *My God, that's blood!*

The stains looked as if someone had been butchered and then dragged across the tile. Dozens of footprints had tracked through the blood while it was still wet and led into the living area of the house. Donna's head swam; she could feel the heat rising inside her and was certain she would either pass out or vomit. The burnt toast smell was now all consuming, and the heat was unbearable. Then she saw it. Flames flickered on the front burners of the stove. The oven had been left on as well; the dinner within it had burnt away hours ago. Her heart pounded in her temples, and she started to hyperventilate. She knew she should turn off the oven and the burners, and running out of the house as fast as possible felt like a solid plan as well. But the fear crippled her, and no matter how desperately she tried to take that first step, Donna found it impossible to move a muscle.

Please, God, help me.

Donna couldn't think straight and knew if she didn't react soon, she never would. She held her breath and forced herself to count down from five in her head. When she got to one, she skirted around the blood on the kitchen floor and turned off the gas. Then she ran through the kitchen, tore down the stairs, and burst into the living room. She flew out the back door like a cannonball exploding from the deck of the Jolly Roger. Donna ran home before the first tears hit her cheeks. But by the time she reached her house, she was hysterical. She smashed through the front door and fell to the carpet, unable to call the police or even her husband. It was forty-five minutes before Donna was able to pick up the phone.

● ● ●

Deputy David Rainey arrived at the home of Gary Forsyth to check on the whereabouts of his fellow officer. He immediately noticed Gary's pride and joy sitting in the driveway, a black Camaro Z28. Rainey exited his cruiser, walked up the drive, and laid his hand on the hood of the car. *Cold.* He proceeded to the front door and rang the bell. The chime sounded from inside the small hallway, and Rainey waited nearly a full minute before he rang it again. There was no reply.

"Hey, Gary. Are you in there, buddy?" he called up to the second-floor window. Again, there was no answer. Rainey tried the knob, which clicked open, allowing the door to swing inward. "You home, Gary?" He stepped inside and stood there for a moment listening. The place was silent.

Rainey had seen some crazy shit in the past twenty-four hours and wasn't about to go off half-cocked. He pulled his service revolver out of his holster and held it pointed toward the ceiling. "Gary," he called again.

He took several slow steps across the burgundy-tiled foyer and poked his head around the corner with his gun leading the way. He headed to the staircase and ascended them two at a time. A muffled noise echoed from somewhere on the second floor. There was a soft thud and then a rustle, like something had moved in one of the back bedrooms. Rainey swallowed and stood motionless. He heard it again, the sound of someone walking across a wood floor.

He eased back the hammer on his revolver and crept down the hallway, one step at a time. The noise was coming from the bedroom at the end of the hall. He reached the door and paused outside, listening to the furtive movements within.

Another thud, louder this time, almost caused him to discharge his weapon on the spot. There was definitely someone inside. Rainey took a long breath to steady his nerves, raised his foot, and kicked as hard as he could. The flimsy door flew inward, and Rainey rushed into the room, pointing his gun at the intruder. "Don't fucking move!" he shouted.

The woman screamed and dropped the lamp she had been holding, along with the dust rag she had been using to clean it. She raised her arms to shield herself as splinters of wood from the shattered jamb were thrown her way.

"Who are you? What the hell are you doing in here?" Rainey shouted at the now hysterical woman, who continued to shield her face and cry. Then he noticed the headphones on her head and the radio clipped to her waist.

He lowered the weapon and raised his arms to show he wouldn't hurt her, then pointed to his own ears. The frightened woman got the gist of what he meant and removed the headphones; loud music blasted from the tiny speakers.

"Who are you? What are you doing here?"

"You scared the shit out of me," the girl cried. "I'm Claire ... Claire Rizvi. I clean the place for Gary. You can call him. He'll tell you." The girl looked about nineteen or twenty years old, with long, dark hair pulled back tight into a single braid. She dressed almost completely in faded blue denim, with the exception of her Pink Floyd concert T-shirt.

"Gary didn't show up for work today. Have you seen him?"

"No. I saw his car out front and thought he was home; my boyfriend dropped me off. There was no answer, so I let myself in. I have a key, see." She held up a house key to show him.

"So, he wasn't here when you got here? Did you notice anything strange, anything out of the ordinary?" he asked, holstering his weapon.

"Everything looked the same as usual."

"Okay, I'm sorry I frightened you, Miss Rizvi. Let me help you clean that up." He motioned to the broken lamp on the floor.

"It's okay, I got it. That's what I get paid for anyway; next time just yell or knock or something."

"Actually, I did. You didn't hear me with the headphones on. You might want to turn them down a little bit."

"Cool, isn't it?" She unclipped the radio and held it out to him. "It's a Walkman, they just came out. Now I can listen to Floyd everywhere I go."

Rainey had seen the commercials for the Walkman and planned on picking one up for himself at the Radio Shack in town or the Crazy Eddie's up in Warren. And even though he wanted to show his interest, he was on the job and fought the urge. "If you don't mind, I'm going to take a look around. I'll let myself out when I'm finished. Sorry again for startling you, Miss Rizvi."

"It's cool," she said. "See you around, Deputy"—she looked at his name tag—"Rainey."

He searched Gary's house and found nothing out of the ordinary or peculiar in any way, then let himself out and called base. "Deputy Rainey to dispatch."

"Go, Deputy, over," Tara answered.

"It was a no-go at Deputy Forsyth's place. The maid is here, and she hasn't seen him either. His car is in the driveway, but there's no sign of him."

"That's strange. I hope he's okay. I'll relay the message to the sheriff. Thank you, Deputy Rainey, over."

"Roger that, Tara, over and out." He started the cruiser and backed out of the driveway. Rainey had a feeling that something bad had happened to Gary Forsyth, and no one had been there with a stainless steel basin to save his ass either. Of course, it was just a feeling, but it was a strong one. *Christ, I hope I'm wrong.*

Tara Jeffries terminated the communication with Deputy Rainey and prepared to radio Sheriff Primrose just as the phone rang. "Sheriff's Department, how can I help you?"

"P-p-pllee." The words were impossible to understand, but the voice was female.

"Ma'am, please calm down," Tara said. "Take a deep breath and tell me what's wrong."

"M-m-my n-name is Donna." The woman continued to cry and stutter.

"Yes, Donna. What seems to be the problem?"

Tara could hear the woman forcibly drawing in a long-exaggerated breath and then expelling it on the other end of the line. Finally, the woman sighed and sounded like she had regained an ounce of her composure. "I think someone's been killed. Th-there was so much blood; it was e-everywhere."

"Okay, Donna. Where are you? Who do you think was killed, hon?"

"My neighbors, Jerry and Beth Campbell." Donna's breaths hitched on the other end of the line. "Th-They live at Fifteen Poplar. There's blood all over the kitchen. I-it was everywhere."

"Okay, Donna. Where do *you* live? You said they're your neighbors?" Tara wrote the information on the blotter in front of her.

"I live at Ten Poplar."

Dear God. Right next door to the house that caught fire. "I'm sending an officer right now." Tara was about to radio in the report when a second line started ringing. "I have to put you on hold for just one second, Donna." But the woman on the other end had already hung up. Tara answered the second call. "Sheriff's Department, how can I help you?"

"Yes, this is Alice Tobin." The woman was also crying but controlled herself a little better than Donna had. "Billy and Eric still haven't come home. I know something's happened. Please help us?" She sounded defeated.

"Yes, of course, Mrs. Tobin," Tara said. "I will send a deputy over right away. Just hang in there, ma'am. I'm sure we'll be able to locate them."

"Thank you, the address is Seventeen Garden Drive."

Tara was about to disengage the call when a third line started flashing. *What the hell is going on here?* "A deputy will be right over, Mrs. Tobin."

"Thank you," the woman said and hung up.

"Sheriff's Department. How can I help you?"

"Yes, this is Brian Miller. I live on Stanhope Road. My neighbor's dog has been going nuts since late last night. Ordinarily, I wouldn't call, but the poor thing sounds like it's in distress, like something's wrong. I knocked on the door, but no one is home. The dog is in a pen in the backyard. He's one big German Shepherd, and there's no way I'm going near it without the family around. I thought you might want to check the place out. They love that dog. There's no way they would leave it alone all night."

"Sure, Mr. Miller. What's the address?"

"One Thirty-Three Stanhope Road. It's Otto Negal's house, and I live at One Thirty-Two."

"I'll send a car over as soon as I can."

Tara turned to the radio and waited for the phone to ring again. When it didn't, she spoke into the mic. "This is base to any available unit. Come in, over." As soon as she finished the transmission, the phone started to ring once again.

●●●

Dr. Ziegler had spent hours trying to locate his chief of medicine and the missing children by calling every toxicology center in the state. He struck out with every attempt; none of them had ever heard of Dr. Malcolm. Ziegler knew he was in over his head and needed to contact Sheriff Primrose as soon as possible. But by the time he finished with his phone calls, it had been well past three a.m. and he was beyond tired. He didn't bother to drive home. Instead, he found an empty room on the second floor, sat in one of the chairs, and racked his brain trying to figure out just what the hell was going on.

Ziegler had been on a rollercoaster since the Boyle kid arrived Saturday night, and it felt like every move he made since was the wrong one. He had been sure that using the MRI machine was the only way to see what was going on inside Abe and how the infection had affected the soft tissue. But the man had died during the procedure. *Just what the hell happened in there?* None of them could explain the strange dark cloud that had permeated the interior of the chamber. Whatever they were dealing with was powerful and able to control Deputy Rainey without even touching him. It almost killed the sheriff and would have killed the rest of them if it had been successful. Something had been inside of Abe. *Was that cloud the infection? Can an infection be visible outside the host's body?*

Ziegler asked himself a thousand questions and fell asleep in the dimly lit quiet of the room on the second floor without finding a single answer. He ran his brain in circles till it finally turned itself off. He didn't open his eyes until an orderly woke him Tuesday morning.

"Dr. Ziegler, I'm sorry. I was hoping I might find you," the orderly said.

"What time is it?"

"Just after nine. Nurse TenHove and Dr. Freedman have been looking for you. They're a bit understaffed this morning."

Ziegler jumped up, shaking off the sleep. "Thank you," he said and headed to the bathroom to freshen up.

He had intended to contact the sheriff immediately upon awakening but stepped into a beehive instead. Many of the staff had not shown up for work, and those who did were overwhelmed. He located Nurse TenHove, and she immediately sent him to help Dr. Freedman in the emergency room with the victims from the car accident. Several of the patients were in critical condition. Ziegler dove in and focused on the job at hand. His call to the sheriff would have to wait till later.

● ● ●

Burt arrived at the morgue early Tuesday morning to dispose of the ashes of Felix Castillo and Abe Gorman. He had left the office shortly after the incinerator finished running its cycle, with the interior of the giant oven still too hot to open. He started his day with a strong cup of coffee and the glamorous job of removing the remains, using a large steel dustpan to scoop the ashes into the trash. Despite what most people liked to believe, there was nothing sacred or dignified about death. It was messy and oftentimes humiliating. Burt knew that better than anyone. It had been his bread and butter longer than most marriages lasted these days.

THE OJANOX

Old Smokey, the morgue's incinerator, was an amazing piece of equipment, capable of reducing the human body to a pile of ash. Often, there were some bones and teeth left behind on the first go-round, but nothing fully intact. Most of the time, they, too, were rendered dust in the wind. Burt scooped up an undignified panful of cinders and paused as something hard rattled against the steel. *What the hell?* He sifted the ashes into the trash, waiting for the harder items to surface. Burt gasped as the lighter dust fell away and he found himself looking at what remained in the bottom of the pan. The small triangular-shaped teeth that filled Felix Castillo's mouth had withstood the incredible heat of the incinerator and remained unfazed.

"That's impossible," he said, examining the small objects. Burt had run the incinerator two full cycles to make sure nothing was left behind. He transferred several of the specimens to a container and examined them as yesterday's events replayed in his head like a crappy disco tune. Burt tried to wrestle with logic and reason, but after seeing what happened to Castillo and what Castillo had done to Abe, he was having a hard time of it. Something inside those men had changed them, and it sure as hell wasn't the flu. It was a lot more contagious than influenza and made the Black Plague look like a case of the sniffles.

The thing inside Abe had controlled the deputy and used the man like a tool. Burt hated to keep thinking it, but the damn thing had some very real vampire traits about it. *Look into my eyes.* He let out a nervous laugh. Being a Catholic, Burt had always imagined that Satan probably looked a lot like Nosferatu.

The big question that kept getting snagged in his head was *What the hell happened in the MRI?* It looked as if the machine had somehow extracted the infection from Abe and killed him in the process. If that was the case, then the answer lay in the inner workings of the machine itself. Unfortunately, Burt didn't know Jack-squat about an MRI machine, other than it extracted pictures of the body's soft tissue using magnetic resonance. And anyone who went to medical school could tell you that much.

It continued to eat at Burt how Dr. Malcolm could suspect snake venom. There was no way the bacterium that infected Felix and Abe was any type of reptile toxin or anything that even resembled one. Burt's next thought sent an icy shiver up his back. *What if it got Dr. Malcolm like it did the deputy?* If this thing was powerful enough to manipulate a deputy and make him try to kill the sheriff, then couldn't it control an old doctor and make him do just about anything? It could make him pick up the phone and lie about his patients, and it could feed the staff and the sheriff any false information it wanted to. It could also allow the children to simply walk out the back door. *Dear God.* Burt realized he had just given this thing a consciousness, and dammit if it didn't make sense. He needed to get in touch with Dr. Ziegler immediately.

Burt picked up the phone and dialed. A frantic woman on the other end answered. "Chilton Medical, please hold."

"Wha—" Chilton was never so busy you got put on hold. Burt could remember it happening maybe twice in the past. And those rare occasions had been under the most extreme circumstances. One time involved a four-car pileup on Route 3, and another happened the year the Lenape River overflowed the King Dam and flooded the south end of town. The early thaw combined with heavy rains swelled the watershed, and the county hadn't released the flood gates in time. Those who were caught in the frigid water succumbed to hypothermia within minutes. It had been a nightmare.

Finally, the woman came back on the line. "Thank you for holding. How can I help you?"

"Good morning, Doris. This is Burt, could I please s—"

"Oh, thank God," she said. "Burt, I am in a real pickle here. I have three nurses out sick, my lab tech never showed up, and about a half dozen other staff members decided to take off from work as well."

Burt listened with an impending sense of dread swelling within him. That many employees being sick on the same day, he doubted it was a coincidence and was almost certain his concerns for Dr. Malcolm had just been validated.

"If you aren't too busy this morning, I could really use an extra set of hands." Burt could hear it in Doris's voice; she was in over her head.

He told her he would be right over since there was little left to do at the morgue. Besides, he had known Doris for years and still held a man-sized crush for the woman. He also needed to talk with Ziegler as soon as possible. He hung up the phone and started to run out his office door, then grabbed the small jar of teeth he had collected earlier and stuffed them in his coat pocket.

THE OJANOX

Father Kieran struggled to keep the boy's fever down throughout the night. The child had started to shiver, and the heat continued to radiate from his body. He needed medical attention, but with the creatures still roaming the woods, it had been too dangerous to risk it. Kieran had placed two ice packs under the young man's armpits, checked his dressings, and wrapped him in a blanket, but he wasn't sure any of what he was doing was the correct way to treat the boy.

He had said his name was Billy. The boy was clearly in shock and suffering from exposure, and there was little that Kieran could do. However, there was always one thing that helped more than anything else. Father Kieran made the sign of the cross on the boy's forehead and on his own as well, then he opened the bible to the Gospel of James, rested the gold-bound book on the young man's chest, and prayed.

"And the prayer of faith will save the one who is sick, and the Lord will raise him up. And if he has committed sins, he will be forgiven."

Father Kieran kept a vigil over the boy until the cloak of night was pulled back like a shroud. The sky grew increasingly brighter with the morning's first light, and Kieran knew he was in the presence of the Lord. The darkness had passed, and the child stopped shivering. It felt as if his temperature may have dropped a little as well.

Kieran ran to the window to find that most of the creatures had vanished into the woods. In another hour, the last of them would be gone as well. The priest knew he couldn't risk putting another soul in danger and would have to take the boy himself. The child had already been spared once from the creatures, and Kieran had the Lord to protect him. He started to turn from the window when a sudden movement from the opposite direction caught his eye. The beasts had been traveling north towards the mountain, but what Kieran now saw was headed south. He watched as a family of raccoons darted from the woods and crossed the church parking lot. They were followed by no less than two dozen squirrels. "What on Earth?" he whispered. A large black bear stumbled out of the woods accompanied by a pair of mountain lions. Kieran gasped as possums and badgers joined in the parade and ran across the rectory parking lot. There were chipmunks, and groundhogs, and even a few wild boars. The animals were running as if they were being chased, fleeing from whatever it was that had invaded their home. They were trying to get as far from Garrett Mountain as possible. Father Kieran again made the sign of the cross on his forehead and prepared himself for the work at hand.

Carl entered the station just as Tara hung up the phone. She shot him a look of wide-eyed panic, then picked up the second line that had been ringing. She gave him the universal sign for stop as he prepared to enter his office; the affirmative palm of her hand told him something was wrong. He watched as she wrote something down and told the person on the phone that a deputy would be along shortly. He took his hat off and walked around the counter to the dispatch station to find a shopping list of calls she had fielded.

"Thank God you're here. The whole town has gone insane." Carl braced himself, knowing it was bad. "Possible homicide at Fifteen Poplar. A neighbor called and found blood on the kitchen floor but didn't stick around to see if there were any bodies. She was too freaked out."

"Jesus Christ, I was just over there." *That's right across the street from the Barnes place.* Carl's gut twisted. "I'm on my way. Call Deputy Rainey and have him meet me there."

"10-4, Sheriff. Also, the Tobin boys never made it home. It's officially a case of missing persons now. Mrs. Tobin is frantic."

Goddammit, Billy, what are you up to now?

"Okay, send Kovach; he'll know what to do." Carl threw his hat on and attempted to exit the building a second time.

"There've been a few other calls as well, Sheriff."

"Anything life-threatening?" He was halfway out the door.

"Not exactly."

"Call Ted in and send him to the most important one first, have him work his way down the list." As Carl descended the front steps, the phone started ringing again. "Call me on the radio if you need me," he yelled and jumped into his cruiser.

THE OJANOX

Carl hit the cherries and siren and sped out of the municipal parking lot just as Lois Fischer was pulling in. He didn't see her as he sped down the Garrett Turnpike towards the south end of town. And by the time Lois had turned the Impala around, he was already gone.

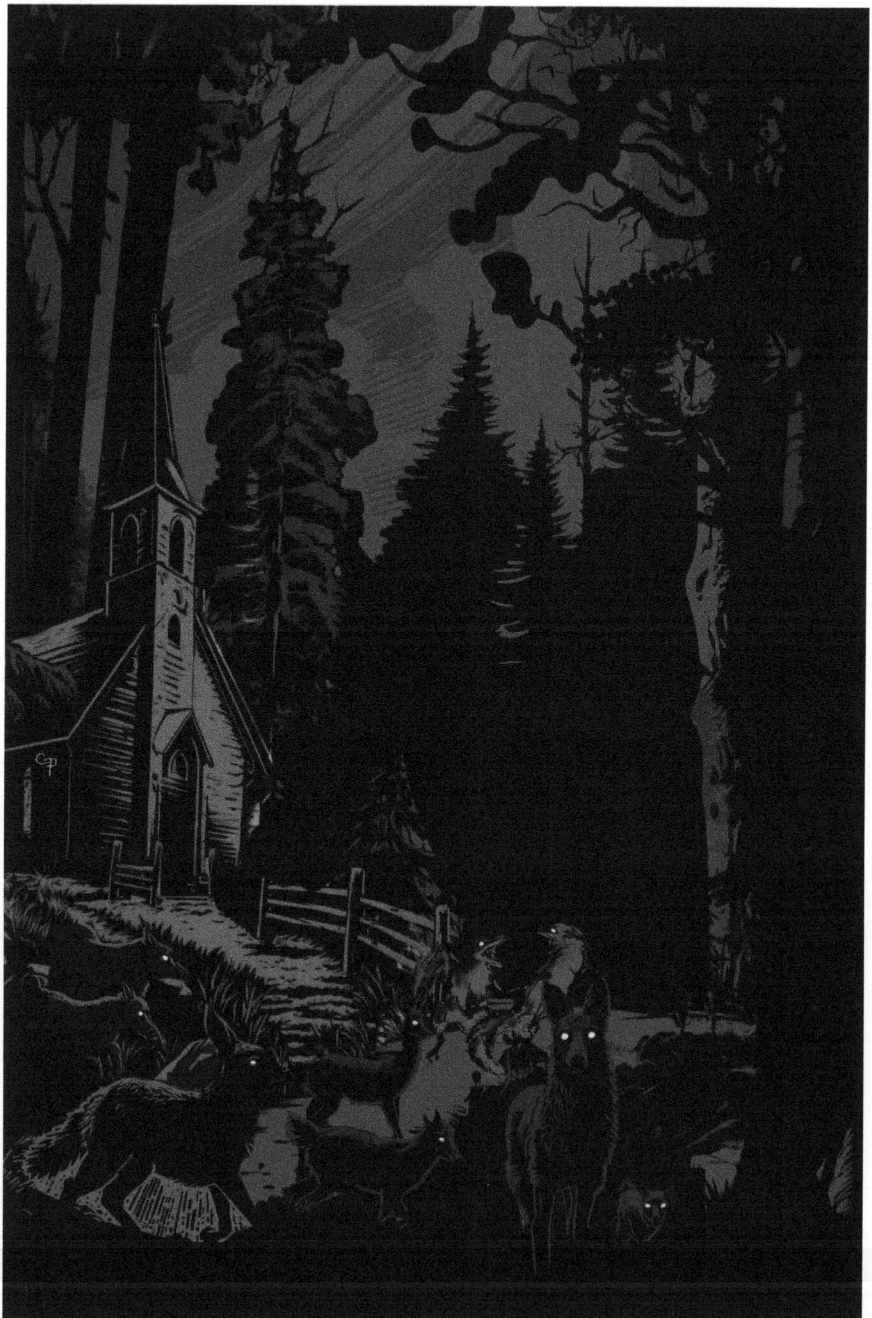

Chapter 38

Sheriff Primrose and Deputy Rainey arrived at the Campbell residence within seconds of one another. They exited their vehicles and noticed the man and woman approaching from the opposite side of the street.

"Hello, Sheriff." The man wore a black silk shirt, unbuttoned enough to reveal the chain and gold crucifix that hung to the center of his chest. "I'm Angelo Franco. My wife made the call." He held on to the woman, who appeared visibly distraught, with fresh tears in her eyes and her hair knotted in curly black tangles.

"What happened?" Carl asked.

"Donna was worried about the neighbors and went over to check on them. The back door was open ... Said there's a lot of blood. She called me at work, and I came right home."

"Okay, I need you to go back inside and don't open your door for anyone other than me or my deputy. We'll be over soon," Carl instructed them.

"Of course, Sheriff." The man led his wife across the street and back into their house.

Carl nodded to Rainey with a look of understood risk, then turned toward the house and drew his weapon. Rainey followed his lead and did the same. "I'll take the front, and you take the back. And for God's sake, David, don't shoot me."

The deputy feigned a halfhearted smile. "Don't worry, Sheriff, that was a one-time thing." Deputy Rainey crept around the side of the house and proceeded to the back door while the sheriff checked the front, only to find it locked. Carl tested the door, rocking it slightly in its jamb. It didn't feel all that solid, and he figured it would only take one forceful push in the correct spot.

He pressed his shoulder against the door and backed up. Then Carl threw himself against the oak with the full force of his body, and the jamb splintered at the latch. The door swung inward as he rushed into the house.

Carl smelled the blood right away; it was strong, acrid, and overpowering. He heard Rainey ascending the back staircase like a Muskox in heat. "Front hallway clear," Carl yelled.

"Back room clear," Rainey answered.

Carl made his way up the front steps and met Rainey in the kitchen. Mrs. Franco hadn't exaggerated. The blood was everywhere. Judging by the look of it, there had been a struggle; the family had most likely been ambushed while they were preparing dinner. Food, cooking utensils, and gore littered the floor. There were tracks from several different prints, one of which was barefoot and led out of the kitchen down another hallway. Carl motioned for Rainey to follow him. They entered the living room, where the struggle had continued, judging from the mess. Someone had been dragged into this part of the house and bled onto the carpet before moving on.

More tracks led down the main hallway to a closed door. Carl followed the trail towards the room with the deputy on his heels. Silence consumed the house. All was still except for the intrusion of their footfalls on the carpet and the sound of the officers breathing. Standing at the bedroom door, Carl counted down from three. When he got to one, they burst into the room, with Carl sweeping left and Rainey covering the right. The bedroom was empty.

A large king-sized bed sat in the center of the room, where a massive pool of blood had soaked into the mattress. It looked as if someone had been laid out, bled to death, and then been removed sometime later. The paisley-printed curtains covering the windows suddenly ruffled inward from the force of a breeze entering the room. One of the windows had been left open. Carl pulled the curtain to the side and looked down at the windowsill, where several bloody handprints remained. "Jesus Christ!"

"They left through the window?" Rainey asked.

"That would be my guess."

They continued to check the rest of the house but were unable to find anything, including a body or a weapon. Then Carl radioed Tara and sent Rainey across the street to interview the couple who reported the incident.

"Sheriff Primrose to base."

"Come in, Sheriff, over."

"Tara, could you get in touch with Burt and see if he could meet me out here on Poplar?"

"Sure, Sheriff. I'll do that right now, over." Tara picked up the phone and dialed the medical examiner's office. She let the phone ring until the answering machine finally picked up.

"I didn't get an answer, so I left a message."

"Okay. Did you send Kovach to talk to the Tobin family?"

"I did, and Deputy Lutchen is taking care of the other calls. I think we got everything pretty much under control. How are things out there on Poplar?"

"Well, it's just as Mrs. Franco reported; there's a lot of blood, but there aren't any bodies." He didn't want to say anything else to his dispatcher, not just yet.

"Oh my, Sheriff. It sure has been one crazy week."

You have no idea.

Deputy Kovach had just finished interviewing Alice and Will Tobin when Deputy Ted Lutchen arrived at the Negal residence to investigate the neighbor's noise complaint. There was no answer when he rang the front doorbell, but he could hear the dog howling in the backyard. He rapped hard against the wood frame with his knuckles and waited. "Hello, Sheriff's Department. Is anybody home?"

The dog continued to carry on as if its ass was on fire. After waiting several minutes without an answer, Ted proceeded around the side of the house and let himself into the backyard through a large wooden gate. He first came to an oblong-shaped above-ground pool that had been covered for the fall. Then he noticed the pen and the giant German Shepherd pacing back and forth within. The massive dog locked eyes with him, stopped barking, and began to wag its tail.

Ted approached the pen as slow and non-threatening as he possibly could. "What's all the fuss about, buddy?" The Shepherd stood up against the pen on his hind legs to greet the deputy, his long, pink tongue hanging from the side of his mouth.

Ted noticed the two overturned water bowls and that the concrete beneath them was bone dry. "How long has it been since you had a drink?"

The dog reacted, wagging his tail even harder. *Poor thing, you're thirsty as hell.* He scanned the yard and located a garden hose attached to the house. He walked over, turned the water on, and dragged the hose to the pen. The Shepherd jumped against the fence as Ted squirted the water directly into its mouth; it lapped and slurped it up as if it hadn't had a drink in years.

"Damn, I guess you were thirsty. Where's your family?" Ted read the tag on the dog's collar. "Baxter," he said as the dog gulped down the cool water. "Where's your family, Baxter?"

Once Baxter had drunk his fill, Ted threw the hose to the grass and approached the back door. The Shepherd let out a few disapproving barks and returned to pacing in his pen.

"Easy, boy, I'll be right back." Ted knew he was a bit of a softy when it came to animals and already liked this dog, a lot.

He ascended the steps and looked through the back kitchen window. At first glance, the place appeared to be in order ... Then he saw it. Pressing his face against the glass, Ted scanned the first-floor living room and noticed the television had been left on. His internal warning system red-lined. Less than two feet from the television, a recliner had been upended. The cushions lay next to it on the floor. He couldn't be sure, but it looked as if the cushions from the sofa had been thrown about as well. "This is Deputy Lutchen requesting backup," he called into his radio. "I'm located at One Thirty-Three Stanhope Road."

"Roger that, this is Deputy Kovach responding."

"10-4, Deputy Kovach." Tara's voice came over the radio. "Deputy Lutchen, Deputy Kovach is en route to your position. Copy that? Over."

"10-4, Lutchen out." Ted backed away from the door and prepared to kick it in. He hesitated and then tried the knob. It turned easily in his hands, allowing the door to swing inward. "Sheriff's Department! Is anyone home?" he shouted into the solitude of the empty kitchen.

THE OJANOX

The house remained as silent as a corpse while Baxter continued to raise holy hell in the backyard. As Ted prepared to enter, the distant echo of a siren reassured him that Deputy Kovach's approaching cruiser was only minutes away. Feeling it was safe to enter with backup en route, Ted proceeded into the house.

The kitchen was empty, and nothing appeared out of place. The counter was clean, and the small Formica table surrounded by its cushioned vinyl chairs all seemed in order. He walked into the living room, where the recliner lay tipped over on its side. The cushions were tossed, and a bowl of popcorn lay scattered on the floor like New Year's confetti in Times Square.

Something happened here. Deputy Lutchen took extra care not to disturb anything as he tiptoed around the popcorn and fallen furniture.

The sound of the cruiser's siren grew louder and then cut off. Ted looked out the front picture window to see Deputy Kovach getting out of the vehicle. He opened the front door for his partner and let the man into the house.

"What do you have?" Kovach asked.

Lutchen pointed to the state of the living room as Kovach entered. "A neighbor called and reported the family dog had been barking up a storm since last night. I checked, and the poor thing hadn't had any water in a long time. I gave him some from the hose."

Kovach nodded and pointed to one of the cushions on the floor. From what Ted could see, it looked like the underside was either wet or stained.

Kovach removed a ballpoint pen from his pocket, leaned down, and carefully used it to tip the cushion over. The opposite side revealed a dark scarlet stain in the shape of a handprint, smeared at the fingertips. The edges of the stain had dried and turned brown.

The men looked at one another, their hands dropping to their guns simultaneously. Not only had something gone terribly wrong in the house, but there was a chance that the perpetrator was still inside. They scanned the room and surveyed the exits. A hallway ran past the kitchen to a staircase leading to the second floor.

They remained still for a moment, listening for anything out of the ordinary. Ted stared intently at Kovach as one of the floorboards above their heads creaked ever so lightly. Frozen in place, they continued to listen. It came again, the faintest creak; something was moving upstairs. Whatever it was couldn't be big, either that or it was being cautious. *Creak!* A third time. Ted felt his heart rise into his throat and prayed that Kovach, his senior officer, wasn't half as freaked out as he was.

Deputy Kovach moved towards the staircase, and Ted pushed himself to follow. Slowly, they ascended each riser, trying not to alert whoever was hiding upstairs. The top landing opened onto a bathroom with bedrooms on either side. The door to the left was open, and upon quick inspection, there appeared to be nothing out of the ordinary inside. However, the door on the right was closed, and that was where the noise had originated from.

The officers took position on either side of the door with their weapons drawn. Kovach put his hand on the knob and waited. He gave Ted a nod of acknowledgment and, in one motion, turned the handle and pushed the door forward. The men swung their weapons in on the empty room. Ted prepared to yell "freeze!" but held back at the last second.

There could be no doubt that the owner of the bedroom was a little girl. The entire place was pink, from the paint to the bedspread and even the curtains. It reminded Ted of cotton candy.

They stood in the doorway for a moment with their weapons at the ready. *Creak.* It was soft and barely audible, but one of the floorboards on the far side of the room had shifted as if under stress. There was something underneath the bed. Ted felt his throat tighten and go dry with the realization. He waited for Kovach to take the lead.

"Cover me," Kovach said with his weapon trained on the floor. The senior officer took a step forward and approached the small, twin-size bed that could only belong to a child. Then, holding his weapon in one hand, he used his other to take hold of the bed. He nodded to Ted and flung the mattress and box spring with ease. It overturned quickly and fell against the wall, exposing the small figure that had been hiding beneath.

The child screamed and backed away, clutching what looked like a board game to her chest. A scatter of dolls and toys littered the floor where she hid.

"Whoa, easy, easy," Kovach said. "We're not going to hurt you. We're sheriff's deputies."

The girl screamed and buried her face behind the board. She trembled and screeched like a feral cat as she clawed herself further away from the men. Her hair was tangled and matted, and her clothes were stained. Ted could see the poor girl had urinated on herself. There was no telling how long she had been hiding underneath the bed.

Kovach reached out and tried to grab the child, but she lashed out at him. Ted shook his head and holstered his weapon, then slowly entered the room. Scanning the area, he took notice of a picture frame on the child's dresser, a family portrait of the girl with her brother and parents; the name engraved on the frame read, Dawn.

"Hi, Dawn," Ted said, lowering himself onto one knee in front of her. The girl's eyes widened in response to the sound of her name. "My name's Ted, Dawn. That's your name, right? Dawn? That's a pretty name."

Kovach watched as the rookie stepped in and took control of the situation.

"You know how I found you?" Ted smiled as she shook her head. "Baxter told me. He was worried about you. So, he called me over to find you."

"Baxter can't talk," the little girl said in a voice as small as a tear.

"Well, he was barking, so I went into the backyard. Then he started looking at the house. That was his way of telling me to go find you. Baxter's a good dog, isn't he?"

"Y-yes."

"Do you want to go thank him and bring him something to eat?"

She slowly nodded, her head barely moving at all.

Ted extended his hands and offered his kindest eyes. Dawn reacted and allowed him to take her in his arms. He carried her out of the bedroom past Deputy Kovach.

Cradling Dawn against his shoulder, he hid her face from the mess in the living room and headed straight to the kitchen. He filled a glass of water from the tap and offered it; she eagerly sucked down half the contents. "Are you hungry?" Ted grabbed a box of donuts from the counter and handed her one. Dawn accepted and shoved it into her mouth. Then Ted opened the door to a large pantry and found a jumbo-sized bag of dried dog food, which he scooped up with one hand as he transported Dawn with the other and exited the kitchen.

The girl's demeanor brightened at the sight of her dog, and Baxter lit up like a Roman candle when he saw her. He started whining and running in circles around his pen.

"Baxter won't bite me, will he?" Ted asked.

"No." She smiled. "He's a good boy."

Ted put Dawn down and let her stand on her own as she opened the pen. The enthusiastic dog bound from the kennel and proceeded to lick the girl's entire face. After slobbering on nearly every inch of her, he sniffed her up and down and whined, apparently concerned about the smells coming off her. But it appeared the dog was most interested in the bag of dog food. Ted watched Dawn upright the bowls and begin filling them herself, managing to spill only half of the bag as she overflowed Baxter's dish. The dog didn't seem to mind. Baxter tore into the kibbles like a Hoover attacking an army of stray dust bunnies.

"Wow, he sure was hungry. You must have been hiding for a long time?" Ted knelt to meet the child at eye level.

Dawn looked at him and nodded. Her big eyes welled with tears.

"Can you tell me what happened, Dawn?" He didn't want to push but needed answers.

"It was Tommy."

"Tommy, is that your brother?"

She stroked the back of the dog as he polished off the rest of the food.

"What happened to Tommy?"

"He killed them. He killed Mommy and Daddy." Dawn latched onto Ted and buried her face into his neck. Baxter whined and looked up for a minute, concerned but not enough to tear himself away from his food. He hadn't eaten in a very long time.

●●●

Don Fischer instructed four of his men to set up a second generator outside the cave and snake an extra fifteen hundred feet of electrical cord through the six-foot opening. An additional arsenal of high-powered floodlights was carried in along with the rest of Stephanie Thompson's own personal gear. Once the last of the lights were set in place and the generator was fired up, searing illumination penetrated the furthest reaches of the endless chamber, dispelling every shadow.

The original area where the team worked yesterday extended deep into the earth, far beneath the bedrock of Garrett Mountain. This initial chamber was the widest portion of the cave, although now it appeared to be more like a tunnel. The expansive cavern narrowed as it stretched back and sloped gradually downward into the earth; there was no telling just how far it went.

Don also set the team up with an array of portable lanterns and flashlights. The cave, now free from shadows, was as bright inside as it was out, allowing Stephanie to point out the nuances that had gone unnoticed in the darkness. Gail followed her lead and began taking pictures of the elaborate murals.

Joe and Barry once again gravitated to the skeletal remains and dove right into the process of cataloging and recording. But for Don, the big mystery was the cavern itself and the presence of the lodestone. Now that he was aware of the magnetite surrounding him, he felt more in tune with the subtle pull it influenced upon his metallic equipment. Holding his flashlight close to the rock surface, he noticed the way it was tugged toward the wall. He could feel it in everything from the buckle of his belt to his steel-toed boots.

Yesterday, they had only been able to see so far into the darkness. But now, with the unlimited visibility, Don was able to safely navigate his way toward the back of the cavern. The walls were decorated with even more murals. Scene after scene, there appeared to be a chronology to them, a progression that was noticeable. It was apparent the Lenape had been telling a story through their art. All of it struck Don as familiar in some way. *Where have I seen this before?*

He resumed his trek into the endless tunnel within the rock. The ceiling dropped, and the walls drew in closer, but the cavern continued to stretch on and on. Nearly a half dozen more murals covered the walls on either side as he made his way inward. It was impossible to say how far he had traveled or just how deep below the surface the cavern extended. Feeling his ears pop, Don knew he had descended at least a full atmosphere's worth in pressure. He ventured a bit further until he found himself in front of an opening in the rock wall, slightly smaller than the one at the entrance to the cave. A blanket of endless night stared back at him. Don cast the beam of his flashlight into the darkness and leaned forward. On the other side was another great chamber; this one was massive, far bigger than the one he just walked through. The weak beam of light was all but absorbed by the suffocating black of this new chamber. From what Don could tell, the void was endless. Somewhere in the murky distance, the faint sound of water dripping off the rock surface echoed back at him. He cast the light onto the floor and didn't find one. It was impossible to know if there was a safe passage through the chamber or a bottomless drop. This was one of those places that killed both the skilled and the foolish alike.

Donald turned to leave and bumped into Stephanie. He jumped back, finding himself face-to-face with her. "Christ, you scared the crap out of me."

"What are you looking at?" she asked, not bothering to back up.

"I was surveying the cavern to see how far it extends and noticed all these murals." He cast his light against the walls, but Stephanie didn't bother to look.

"I think you know how dangerous it is to go off on your own in a place like this?" she said with a smirk on her face.

"I do. There's a chamber on the other side of this opening, and I don't see a floor. It could be a very far drop."

"Really?" She attempted to poke her head inside to get a better look, but Don stopped her.

"Nobody goes in there without my guys checking it out first, even then, not without the proper gear. The last thing we need is for this to turn into a rescue situation or, God forbid, something worse."

Stephanie stood there for a moment longer before turning back toward the entrance. "Fair enough, Mr. Fischer. Maybe you could bring your flashlight over here and show me the rest of the murals you found?"

They left the entrance to the great chamber and proceeded to the relative safety of the main chamber. Don noticed the flashlight as it trembled in his hand; he had been shaking. He was certain it had more to do with his proximity to the dangerous drop-off and nothing to do with how close he had been standing near the young doctor.

● ● ●

The second Burt Lively entered through the emergency room doors, he was flagged down by Doris TenHove and put to work. Joey DeStefano, who worked in phlebotomy, had been one of the many employees who hadn't shown up, along with Dean Childers, one of the lab technicians. Doris let Burt decide which position he felt comfortable filling. Naturally, he opted for the lab.

"Thank you for coming over so quickly." Several lengths of Doris's grey curls had come undone and hung loose from her nurse's cap. But to Burt, the woman looked as lovely as ever.

"Well, maybe you could make it up to me and let me take you out for dinner on Friday." He leaned over the counter and raised a pair of bushy eyebrows. They had been playing the flirting game for years without it ever developing into anything. Both were married to their jobs, but Burt was more than just a little interested. Doris was close to his age and carried a few extra pounds in the back, an attribute Burt was defenseless against.

Doris fixed her hair and pretended to blush. "Why, Mr. Lively. I'm afraid you couldn't handle me if you got me. I might give you a heart attack."

"I couldn't think of a better way to go. Come on, give an old man a break, or do you want me to beg?"

"I tell you what, old fool. If you hustle your buns down to the lab and get to work, you might not have to buy me dinner. I might just give it to you right here on the counter."

Burt choked and almost swallowed his tongue. He felt the heat rush throughout his body and turn to steam. Doris TenHove dangled the goods under his nose, leaning over the counter while he stared with his jaw hung slack. Then she gave him the shoo sign by waving her hands, indicating he was dismissed. Burt left the reception desk grinning like a fool. At sixty-two, he had no more resistance to the powers of the feminine sex than a fourth-grade boy.

Burt passed through the ER on his way to the lab with his mind somewhere in the clouds and not on where he was going; he nearly ran right into Dr. Ziegler.

"Burt, what are you doing here?" Ziegler asked.

"Looks like you're a little understaffed today. I told the pretty nurse I would pitch in and lend a hand."

Ziegler looked at the reception desk and spotted Doris TenHove. He raised his brows, and his eyes widened as he opened his mouth to speak.

"I-um-a, I'm glad you're here. We really must talk." The doctor checked his watch. "Unfortunately, it will have to wait. Meet me in the cafeteria at one o'clock."

Burt looked around the emergency room. There were at least four occupied beds, which was unusual. Not only was there an absence of staff, but there appeared to be an influx of patients. Burt tried to push what he was thinking to the back of his mind, but it was impossible. *So, this is how it starts.*

CHAPTER 39

Sheriff Primrose instructed Deputy Kovach to tag and log all the physical evidence he could collect at the Negal residence. Similar instructions had been given to Deputy Rainey regarding the home of Beth and Jerry Campbell, but without the assistance of the medical examiner, there was only so much that could be done. The absence of victims at either scene prevented the events from being filed as murder investigations; however, there had been a witness at the Negal place. Dawn Negal had seen something, but the girl was in shock and only five years old. Ted Lutchen was able to bring her around somewhat, but her condition was delicate, and there was no way she could be subjected to rigorous questioning. The sheriff was hoping they might coax a little information out of the girl, but first she needed to see Dr. Ziegler to make sure she wasn't suffering from something a bit more serious.

Carl pulled into Chilton's parking lot just as Ted opened the back door of his cruiser and lifted the child out. He cradled her in his arms and approached the sheriff.

"Sheriff, this is Dawn Negal." Her tiny fingers dug into the collar of his uniform. "Want to say hi, honey?" She shook her head and clung for dear life. Ted shrugged his shoulders and nodded.

"Looks like you found a friend. Hi, Dawn. I'm Sheriff Primrose. The doctor is going to take a look at you."

The girl began to squirm and cry.

"Do you want Deputy Lutchen to stay with you?"

The answer appeared to be yes and seemed to calm her down.

"Okay, then."

They entered the medical center to find the place a flurry, with nurses and orderlies running every which way. Carl made eye contact with Dr. Ziegler as he emerged from behind a drawn curtain. He rushed over to where they stood.

"You must be Dawn. I heard how cute you are. I guess they weren't kidding." Ziegler produced out a lollypop from his lab coat pocket. "You look like a cherry girl. Am I right?"

Dawn nodded as Ziegler pulled the wrapper from the candy and handed it to her.

"Do you think you could do this in a quiet room? She's been through a lot," Carl said to Ziegler, lowering his voice.

"Sure, if you'll just follow me." Dr. Ziegler led them down the hall away from the bright lights and commotion of the ER. He opened the door to an examination room and showed them inside. Dawn continued to suck on the lollipop but latched on to Ted's collar when he attempted to place her on the exam table. However, she did allow the deputy to sit down with her on his lap, and even remained still as Ziegler checked her heartbeat and looked in her eyes. Carl waited and held his breath.

⬤ ⬤ ⬤

Father Kieran loaded the boy into the backseat of his Buick and transported him to the medical center. It had been difficult, but he prayed for strength, and the Lord had provided. *Praise God.* The child continued to moan and stir in his unconscious state as Kieran pulled up to the emergency room entrance and laid on the horn. Having been alerted to the commotion, two orderlies rushed to the car, pushing a gurney. Kieran directed them to the boy in the backseat, then stood back as the men lifted and transported him inside.

The child was whisked away to an open bed in the ER, and the priest was directed to the desk, where an older nurse worked. He gave her all the information he could about the boy, omitting how long he had waited before bringing him in and not mentioning a word about demonic apparitions.

The only thing Father Kieran knew about the boy was that his name was Billy. He wasn't a member of the parish, at least not recently. Maybe when he was younger. But it was difficult to remember every child that walked through the doors of the church, even in a town as small and isolated as Garrett Grove.

Doris told him that the young man looked familiar but couldn't place his name. More than half the teenage boys in Garrett Grove saw the inside of the emergency room at one point or another, whether it was for a broken arm, a couple dozen stitches, or something a bit more life-threatening. And without proper identification, there was only so much they could do, so the young man was admitted under the name William Doe.

Lois drove down every side street in a vain attempt to locate the sheriff. She'd heard police sirens multiple times throughout the morning but had always been too far away to follow them. Finally, she returned home just before noon to use the restroom and refuel. She was heating a bowl of clam chowder when the phone rang, and she picked it up immediately. "Hello." She half-believed it might be Carl calling.

"Hi, Mom," Troy greeted her.

"Honey." Lois's heart fluttered, and she clutched the phone in a death grip. Her thoughts went straight to worst-case scenarios, assuming something was wrong. "Is everything okay? Why are you calling in the middle of the day?"

"I'm okay. The principal let me use her phone. I wanted to see if I could go over Janis's house after school."

"Oh, I don't know if that's such a good idea." After Troy had nearly been killed from running into the street, Lois felt she had every right to be a bit frugal with her son's extracurricular activities.

"Aw, please, Mom. I promise I won't walk through the graveyard. Janis lives right by the school in the Village. I don't even have to go that way, really."

Lois considered his request, which wasn't all that unreasonable. He would be with two other children, and the Village was only a few blocks from the school. "I guess so, but I'll come pick you up at five. I don't want you walking home alone, and I want to meet Janis's parents."

"I think her mom will still be working with Dad. But her aunt will be there. You can meet her."

Lois felt the muscles in her back tighten at the mention of Janis's mother and Don working together. If she didn't know any better, she might have mistaken what she was feeling for jealousy. *That's ridiculous.* She and Donald didn't have that type of relationship. It was hard to say what type they actually did have. They had only stayed together for Troy. Everything she had ever done had been for Troy. He was her entire world, and she hated to deprive him of anything that brought him happiness. So, Lois acquiesced to her son's request, as she knew she would, just like she always did.

"You said she lives in the Village. What's the address, kiddo?"

"Twenty-Two Village Road, right around the corner from Wendy."

"I'll be there at five on the dot."

"Thanks, Mom. I love you."

"I love you too, kiddo." She was about to hang up and added, "Be careful, honey."

"I will, bye."

Lois sat in the kitchen alone. She had gotten used to being alone throughout the day. Ever since she had taken Troy to his very first day of school. The house had felt so empty without him there. But as time passed, she learned to deal with the unnerving silence and even managed to block it out.

Troy had been such an animated child, as most children were. But Troy was hers, and he was her only one. Every first experience for him was a new one for Lois as well. His first taste of ice cream made her feel as if she had never savored the decadent treat before. His first step, his first words, she had seen it all as if through his eyes. Donald missed out on most of those firsts, and it hadn't even fazed him. It didn't even occur to him that Troy had mastered enough of the English language to put a sentence together until one unforgettable night. It was late, and Lois had spent most of the day chasing Troy around the house. She was exhausted and didn't even stir when the boy started crying. Donald walked into Troy's room to find his son toddling in his crib, waving a bottle that had been drained dry. "Fill 'er up, Pop," a one-year-old Troy had said, and Donald nearly pissed his pants.

He later returned to bed and woke up Lois. "I think if he's old enough to say, 'Fill 'er up, Pop,' then he's old enough for us to take away the goddamn bottle."

That had been a funny one; Lois could always count on Troy for a good laugh. And Donald had been furious, which made it even funnier. Maybe if he had been around more or paid closer attention when he was home, Donald would have known that his son had been talking for nearly two weeks by that point. But even when Donald was around, he was never exactly present, and that had always been the biggest problem in their marriage. He had almost choked on his roast beef last night when Troy said he had spent the day with two girls.

Lois felt as if her little man was growing up way too fast. Just four days ago, she figured out that Troy and Wendy had been kissing, and now he was spending his afternoons at another girl's house—with them both. At this rate, she couldn't imagine what his high school years would be like. Lois thought about the day she told her parents she was pregnant and envisioned a similar situation involving her son. *Don't you dare do that to me, Troy.*

The sudden sound of police sirens cut through the silence like the slamming of a door. Lois tried to discern their location but realized they were somewhere on the other side of town. There had been an awful lot of police activity this morning; this had to be the third time she heard sirens. *Carl's really got his hands full.* As if on cue, her mind started to wander into the land of *what if*, as it frequently did. It was always the same questions she asked herself. *What if I hadn't gone away to college? What if I stayed in Garrett Grove and married Carl? What if I never broke his heart ... What if?* They were questions she would never know the answers to, but still, she continued to ask them almost constantly. The ultimate answer to all of them was always the same. If she had done any of it differently, she might never have had Troy, and that was a blessing she wouldn't trade for anything, not even for Carl.

Her concentration was shattered by the sound of the phone ringing on the counter. Lois jumped and answered it. "Hello."

The voice on the other end was hysterical but clearly recognizable. "What is it, Alice? What's wrong?"

"Oh God, Lois. Billy and Eric are missing. The police just left. Th—" Alice broke down, unable to finish what she had been saying.

"What?" Lois thought back to Saturday night, the last time she had seen her nephews. They had helped Troy with the haunted house. It seemed impossible what her sister was saying. Surely there had to be some type of mistake. "Slow down, Alice. I don't understand. What happened to Eric and Billy?"

Her crying continued, but Alice managed to control herself enough to form a coherent sentence. "The boys. Will and I went to visit his brother, and when we got back, they left a note. They said they would be home late." She nearly lost what little composure she had but was able to continue. "They never came home Sunday night, and then we never heard from them yesterday. Oh God, Lois, the police just left."

Lois attempted to get her mind around what her sister was saying. Her nephews had been missing since Sunday, and she was just finding out about it now.

"Why didn't you call me sooner, Alice? Why did you wait so long?"

"You know the boys. I kept thinking they would be home any minute. And the police said they couldn't do anything until they were missing for forty-eight hours."

"You've got to be kidding me! You should have called me. Carl would have come right over, I'm sure of it."

"Oh, Lois, I don't know what to do." Alice broke down and sobbed into the other end of the phone. Finally, Will came on the line.

"Hello, Lois?" he said.

"I'll be right over." Lois slammed the phone down, grabbed her purse, and was doing twenty miles over the speed limit before leaving her block.

⬤⬤⬤

Wendy and Janis waited for Troy near the tire swings while he called his mom. The girls passed the time talking, mostly about boys, and of course, Troy's name had been mentioned more than once. The story he told them about his walk home yesterday was a major topic of discussion.

"Do you think Troy really saw something in the graveyard?" Janis asked.

Wendy had come to school with her hair styled similarly to how Janis wore hers. Now the girls could easily pass for a miniature version of two-thirds of Charlie's Angels. "If Troy said something chased him, you can bet it did. He doesn't lie, not like other boys. He's just not good at it." The girls looked up as Troy exited the back doors of the school. "I don't know what he saw, but if it scared Troy, it had to be really scary."

Janis listened while her new friend applied reason and rationale to help understand their problem.

Troy jogged over to the girls with his lunch box in hand. "My mom said yes, but she wants to pick me up at five. So, whatever we do, we gotta be done by then." He sat down next to them and dug in. "I got peanut butter 'n jelly. Mmm, grape too."

Wendy opened her lunch box and removed an egg salad sandwich, which Troy spotted out of the corner of his eye. He hated egg salad more than getting a haircut and prayed that Wendy wouldn't want to trade again.

"Here you go." She handed him the egg salad and ripped the PB&J from his tightly clenched fist.

The look of defeat must have been written on his face, as Janis smiled and held out a sandwich in her small hands. "I have salami and cheese, Troy. Do you want to trade?"

He didn't know what to say. Had she really just offered him salami and cheese, the holy grail of the deli sandwiches? It was too good to be true.

"Sure." He accepted the trade-up, fully expecting a negative reaction from Wendy. However, the PB&J had had a calming effect on the girl, and she didn't seem to mind.

It was nearly a full minute before any of them spoke. Troy imagined they were all probably thinking the same thing but no one wanted to be the first to bring it up. He was just happy he didn't have to eat egg salad.

A few mouthfuls later, Wendy broke the silence. "If you had to guess what they looked like, how would you describe them?"

Troy had given it a lot of thought since yesterday. And although he hadn't gotten a good look at either of the creatures, he had caught a glimpse of the one on the left. "It was really weird. They were fast but not too big. Maybe a little smaller than a kid, or about the same size. It kinda ran like those African dogs with the big shoulders."

"Hyenas," Janis said.

"Yeah, like hyenas. Only, they ran a little, and then they kinda hopped too, almost like a frog. I never saw anything like that." He took a bite of the salami and chewed as fast as he could.

"Hmmm," Wendy said. "Why do you think they were in the graveyard? Do you think they live there?"

Troy thought about it as he chewed the delicious meat and swallowed. "I don't know … maybe. But I doubt it. I think something like that needs a lot more room. I think they would get bored in the little graveyard."

"That makes sense," Janis said. "Predators need a large hunting ground. Something like that would probably need a lot of land, like a park or the woods."

"The foothills!" Wendy slapped Troy in the shoulder, almost knocking the sandwich from his hands in mid-bite. "There's no bigger woods in town than the foothills. If they live anywhere, I bet that's it." The look of satisfaction that crossed her face suggested she was pleased with her deduction. Troy thought it made her look smart and admired how Wendy was able to figure things out so fast. It had only taken her a few seconds. He was glad she was on his team.

"That makes sense." Janis took a small bite of her egg salad and set it to the side. "Do you think they live on the mountain and came down because they were hungry?"

"I guess," Troy said. "But there's a lot to eat on the mountain, and the mountain lions hardly ever come into town. These things were brave." Troy noticed Janis wasn't eating the sandwich and started to feel bad. He wondered why she had traded in the first place if she didn't like egg salad. It didn't make sense.

"Maybe they don't eat animals," Wendy stated. "I mean, they chased you. If they ate animals, they could have gone after a squirrel or a cat or something. Maybe they preferred boys and girls. You know like the … Ojanox."

"I need to show you something in one of my mom's books. It has to do with those little teeth, you know, the ones I have in my case?"

Troy had been thinking about those dangerous-looking teeth ever since yesterday, and if he had to guess, he would have said that Wendy was right. Those things that chased him probably had teeth just like that.

And it was as simple as that. It wasn't even a consideration that the teeth in Janis's case might belong to an animal that had gone extinct eons ago. The children had their own mystery to solve and had each concluded a correlation. Something had chased Troy through the graveyard, Janis's mother had given her teeth from some mysterious creature, and Mrs. Fischer had recently told them the story of the Ojanox. The connection was elementary. The teeth obviously belonged to an Ojanox, and that was what had chased him. Garrett Grove had an Ojanox problem.

The big question was: what do you do when you have an Ojanox problem? Janis was the one to make the suggestion. "In her book, there are a bunch of pictures of those teeth, and then there are other pictures too. Pictures of weapons. I think that's what you need to use to kill them. I don't think you can use just anything."

"You mean like a werewolf?" Wendy said.

"Or a vampire?" Troy added.

"Yeah, that's what I think. I want you guys to look and see for yourselves."

The bell rang to call the children back into the building. Troy watched Janis wrap up the rest of the sandwich and place it into her lunch box. He figured if he got the chance, he would ask her why she had traded in the first place. The second bell rang as they beelined back into the building. The other children had been watching their pow-wow. However, there were now fewer eyes to watch than there had been yesterday.

● ● ●

Perhaps the quietest place in the medical center was the lab where Burt Lively sat working alone. How could he say no to Doris TenHove? He'd been playing cat and mouse with the woman for the better part of a decade now, and she'd always dismissed his advances and acted uninterested. But today he just might have melted the old girl's icy heart, even if it was only just a little. She'd been pleased with his eagerness to lend a helping hand and promised him a good time in return. Either she was finally coming around or just sick and tired of turning him down. Whichever it was, Burt would take it; there was nothing wrong with accepting a little pity sex.

There was a saying that guys Burt's age came to respect as gospel: *Never trust a fart, and never waste a boner.* If Doris TenHove was willing, he damn sure wasn't going to waste that boner.

The lab was quiet except for the occasional doctor checking on the status of their tests. Burt pushed through a mountain of work that had piled up since yesterday, which was nothing more than a stack of files. The results of several biopsies, an array of blood samples, and an abundance of reports. Nothing all that taxing, but it felt good to get out of the morgue and be around the living. The only human being Burt had a semi-healthy relationship with was Carl, and that was often debatable. Before that, it had been Carl's father. He had been friends with Allen Primrose for years, but Burt had been a different man in those days. He and Allen grew up together in Garrett Grove. They went to school together, played cowboys and Indians on the trails of the foothills, and when the world went to war for the second time that century, they joined the army to go kill Krauts together.

However, they were soon split apart. Allen was a born soldier and found himself an infantryman; he was sent into France and then on to Berlin to aid in the liberation of the city from the Nazi regime. Burt, on the other hand, already had a few years of medical school under his belt and became a corpsman for the Army. He ended up in Poland. Burt's division swept through Auschwitz as the last of the Nazi generals were choking on their cyanide pills. The ones that remained were rounded up by Burt's platoon and executed on-site ... the lucky ones, that is. Those that weren't lucky enough to have eaten their own bullet or one issued by Uncle Sam found themselves corralled and set loose into the same cages they had used on their captives. The platoon released the Jewish prisoners and let them do with the German soldiers as they pleased. It was a bloodbath, and the prisoners showed no more mercy than they had been shown themselves.

It affected Burt horribly. Though he had initially joined the Army for that very reason, to kill Nazis, he didn't have the heart for it. Burt was a healer and wanted to help the German, Austrian, and Polish Jews they had found emaciated and at death's door in Auschwitz. Sadly, Burt's division were unable to help those poor people and had ultimately been responsible for killing a great deal of them as well. The prisoners were starving. Burt had never seen how bad the human body could look when it was deprived of nourishment for such an extended time. He instinctively did what the rest of the American medics were doing and gave the prisoners food. They gave them whatever they had available. The rich, filling food that had fed the Nazi generals was there for the taking, and these people were close to death. Burt's platoon liberated the stockpiles and distributed it amongst the emaciated faces with their outstretched hands. They needed his help, and he had given it to them, and it had killed them by the truckload.

The men, women, and children had been starving for longer than any American soldier could even imagine, and their bodies had undergone tremendous physiological changes. Their stomachs and digestive tracts had grown used to being empty. Their organs had shrunk and been in a state of shock. The rich food that the Germans had eaten, as well as the American's own rations, acted no less effectively than the gas chambers. Some of the prisoner's stomachs burst and ruptured due to the strain of over ingestion. Others grew violently sick and developed acute colitis and gastritis. The results were the same, and they died just as horribly, if not worse, than at the hands of the Nazis. Burt had joined the army to kill people, and he'd gotten his wish.

Allen returned home to tell stories of the people he freed in Berlin and tales of German women who had shown their appreciation to the American soldiers. Burt returned with a darker view of humanity and a terminal disinterest in life. He no longer felt fit to pursue the field of medicine. How could he trust himself to diagnose a patient and treat them properly after the devastating mistakes he and the other men had made in Poland? It had been a dark time for Burt. While the world was celebrating the victory and America was patting itself on the back for saving the day, Burt was receding into himself. He damn sure didn't feel like a hero. Shit, even the Russians had done a better job, since they were used to starvation. Stalin had prepared them. They saw the people in the concentration camps and had tossed them a single potato—"Here you go, make soup."

Allen helped his friend through it and forced Burt to get out of bed on days he would have simply hidden away. He drove Burt to class and forced him to finish med school. Burt still didn't believe he had what it took to become a doctor, but he was willing to pursue what he started. Allen forced him to go on double dates, and when Allen met Carl's mother, it was Burt Lively who made the toast at the wedding. Allen had brought Burt back from a darkness that easily could have consumed him, and Burt owed the man a lot more than a few kind words on his wedding day. He owed him his life.

It was Allen who suggested that Burt become a medical examiner. He was at the top of his class when it came to lab work and discerning abnormalities of the various systems. If he didn't want to be a diagnostician, at the very least, he should consider forensics. He would make one hell of a specialist. It was settled, and the position of medical examiner proved to be a place where Burt found himself comfortable. At least he didn't have to worry about killing anyone. That was an off-color joke he told only Allen ... every now and then.

Burt watched Carl grow up and took to the boy as if he were his own. Allen let young Carl tag along quite a bit, and it was obvious the kid would one day follow in the old man's footsteps. Then Carl himself was sent to war ... a very different war. One that was on the television and wasn't pretty. Not that war ever was. Still, there were some things the public didn't need to see and never needed to know. The media had filled a lot of people's heads with images that changed the way America looked at the young men who went to Vietnam. And the soldiers got nothing like the hero's welcome that Burt's generation had received.

Carl returned in one piece, making it home just in time to say goodbye to his old man. Allen died the following year, and Burt delivered the eulogy at his funeral. Suddenly, he and Carl were the only family either one had left. Carl's mom had passed away young, and Burt never found the right gal to settle down with. He looked at Carl as a son, and that son grew to be a friend—a damn good one, at that.

Burt arched his back and listened to his joints crack. He opened another file and went to work transferring data to the blood catalog. Checking the clock, he noticed he still had some time before his meeting with Dr. Ziegler. Lord knew they sure had a lot to talk about.

Chapter 40

Dawn Negal had spoken briefly to Ted Lutchen at the crime scene but withdrawn into herself and grown silent once again. Carl didn't want to push the child but was desperate for answers. She was the closest thing to a witness they had. It was apparent that something horrific had taken place in the house, yet somehow, the girl had managed to survive.

Dr. Ziegler checked her vitals and gave her something he called apple juice to drink, although what he had given her contained far more vitamins and nutrients than regular apple juice. He asked routine questions as he examined her, but she still wasn't talking. It was possible there were too many men in the room. Carl whispered in Ziegler's ear, then said something to Ted. A moment later, he spoke up. "Dr. Ziegler, do you mind if I have a word with you outside for a moment?"

"Sure," the doctor answered. They stepped out of the room and waited by the door. Ziegler lowered his voice. "If I sense this is going the wrong way, I will end it."

"Of course," Carl said.

They listened outside the door as Deputy Lutchen began to speak.

"Don't be scared, Dawn. I won't let anything happen to you." She wrapped her arms around his neck like a cat about to be thrown into a bathtub. "Whoa, that sure is a tight grip. I didn't know you were so strong. You must eat a lot of spinach. Is that it? Do you like spinach?"

She shook her head and shoved her thumb in her mouth. Ted didn't have children of his own, but he knew it couldn't be a good sign. It had probably been years since she last sucked her thumb, and to suddenly revert to the habit was concerning.

"Oh, you like thumbs better than spinach?" She let out a noise that could have been a laugh. Ted rocked her in his arms and continued to talk.

"I bet you're still hungry, aren't you?" She nodded again. "What if I found us some ice cream? Would you like some ice cream?" She raised her head and nodded, looking at him through eyes that were slightly brighter.

"Yeah, I could go for some ice cream too," Ted said loud enough to be heard by the men on the other side of the door.

Carl got the message and looked to Dr. Ziegler, who pointed in the direction of the cafeteria. He took off down the hall like an Olympic runner.

"I saw all the toys in your room. You sure have a lot. Did you know my favorite color is pink? What's your favorite color?"

"Pink," she said, her voice a little more than a whisper.

"No kidding, we both like pink. What else do you like?"

"Drowsy," the girl said with her thumb still in her mouth.

"Drowsy, are you tired, honey?"

"No, silly." She removed her thumb. "Drowsy is my doll. She can talk."

"Oh, I see. What does Drowsy say?"

"She says, 'Kiss me goodnight,' and 'I want a drink of water.'" Dawn perked up with the discussion of the doll.

"Were you in your room playing with Drowsy last night?" Ted steered the conversation.

"No."

"No? You weren't in your room last night?"

"I wasn't playing with Drowsy. I was playing with my stick-ums."

He didn't know exactly what she was talking about but thought he might have an idea.

"Oh, you mean like color forms, peel and stick?"

"No, stick-ums are magnets. You put them on the stick-um board and move them around. There's teddy bear stick-ums and flowers and one that looks like Baxter. I have a lot."

Ted remembered seeing the board she had been clutching and the collection of magnets scattered around her when Deputy Kovach upended the bed.

"Oh, so you were playing stick-ums in your room last night." He paused, unsure about how to lead into what he wanted to say next. "Did you hear anything while you were playing stick-ums?"

She nodded her head and stared up at him.

"Can you tell me what you heard?"

She clutched him tighter. "Animals in the house ... monkeys, maybe. Then Mommy and Daddy yelling."

"What were they yelling, honey?" Carl had returned and listened outside the door with Dr. Ziegler.

"They yelled 'Tommy, no; Tommy, stop!'" Tears fell down the young girl's cheeks.

"That sounds scary. What did you do?" He held on to the poor thing as she dug her fingers into his collar.

"I hid with my stick-ums."

And she had probably stayed there all night, up until the time they found her, starving, soiled, and frightened out of her wits. She had hidden with her toys scattered all around her and the stick-ums board clutched tight to her chest. Ted felt he had pushed the child more than enough and didn't want to cause her any further suffering.

Carl took the silence as his cue and entered the room with the doctor behind him. "Who wants some ice cream?" Carl held up two Styrofoam cups. "I have chocolate, and I have strawberry."

Dawn looked up at the mention of the treat. "Strawberry." She held out her hand.

Ted placed her on the cushion of the examination table as the sheriff handed her the cup and gave the other one to him. "Here you go, Deputy. You deserve it." Carl watched as Ted and the young girl dug into the ice cream, and smiled.

Ted had handled the situation well, and Dawn revealed exactly what Carl suspected. That her brother, Tommy, had attacked and killed their parents. Somehow, the boy had overlooked the fact that his sister was still in the house.

Carl attempted to work out the exponential factors of the problem in his head. It was now evident that Felix Castillo had infected at least two others prior to his untimely introduction to the front bumper of the delivery truck. Tommy Negal and Jeff Campbell had gone missing for several hours Sunday afternoon, and it was becoming clear what had happened.

That chance meeting appeared to have resulted in the transmission of the contagion to not only the Campbell and Negal families but most likely to the Barnes family as well. In addition, the Tobin boys were missing along with a dozen other of the town's citizens. That brought the possible infection count close to thirty. Carl needed an immediate course of action and had no idea what he would say to the state police when he called them for backup. *Christ, I might need to call the National Guard.* "Deputy Lutchen, could you stay here with Dawn while the doctor and I go for a walk?"

Ted agreed through a mouthful of chocolate ice cream. It was hard to tell who was enjoying the snack more, the deputy or the five-year-old girl.

Ziegler led Carl down the hall and started to fill him in. "Christ, it isn't good, not good at all. I called Oswego. Not only did Dr. Malcolm never show up, but he never called and never scheduled the transfer of the children. I contacted every facility that deals with toxicology and infectious disease, and struck out on all of them. It's as if Dr. Malcolm and the children just vanished."

Carl removed his hat and rubbed at the bridge of his nose. It was just as he feared. Dr. Malcolm had been compromised. He wrestled with how this changed the exponential factor of the situation. *If Dr. Malcolm has been infected, then so are the children's parents. Dear God!* That was three children, Dr. Malcolm, and four more adults. With the exponential probability of transmission, there was no telling how many people in town had already been compromised.

"You think maybe you should have called me a bit sooner?" Carl rubbed at the dull ache in his temples.

"As you can see, we've been inundated with a rash of absenteeism and an increase in emergency room activity. Without Dr. Malcolm, it's all I can do to keep up with the cases as they come through the door, and I still have patients to attend to on the wings."

"I get it. We're all stretched thin. But we've got a real mess here. Have you thought about what may have happened last night in the MRI?"

"I have, but I don't have any real answers yet."

"Well, keep working on it. By my count, this may have already spread to thirty or forty so far. And every minute that passes sinks us that much deeper into shit's creek, and we're already up to our necks. I need answers, and I think that MRI machine has something to do with it."

"I'm doing the best I can, Sheriff." Ziegler had walked Carl to the Lab where Burt was working. They entered the room as the coroner looked up from a pile of reports.

"So, this is where you've been hiding." Carl nodded. "Don't get up. I'm in big trouble, old man, and I need all the help I can get. You probably heard the sirens this morning."

"I did." Burt furrowed his brow, preparing himself for the bad news.

"You know about the house fire last night. Well, it wasn't any old fire. Someone left the dinner burning on the stove, and there weren't any bodies discovered in the place. The upstairs bedroom window was busted out from the inside as if something jumped through it. I found blood outside the back door and seriously doubt if anyone was in the house when it caught. I believe they were infected by their neighbors, the Campbells."

"Isn't that one of the kids that was lost in the foothills?" Burt asked.

"Bingo. He and his friend Tommy were the ones who left their bikes in the woods. I think our guy Felix got to them sometime after he left your lab. The kids and both their families are missing. We found a hell of a lot of blood over at the Campbell place ... and again, no bodies."

"Jesus Christ!" Burt gasped.

"I'm afraid it gets worse," Ziegler added. "Dr. Malcolm and the children never made it to Oswego. At this point, we have to assume they're all infected and possibly still in Garrett Grove."

"Jesus Christ!" Burt repeated. "You saw what one of those things did. Can you imagine what twenty or more are capable of?"

"Unfortunately, I can," Carl said. "And that's why I'm counting on both of you to figure out what it was about that MRI machine that put the damn thing down."

"I didn't know we moved past trying to save people." Ziegler raised his voice. "For crying out loud, we're talking about children here. We're talking about our neighbors. I'm a doctor. I took an oath to do no harm. These are your people, Sheriff. Don't you care about that?"

Carl felt the pressure rise within him. He'd been trying to keep it together as best he could, but the situation was about to go critical; he could feel it. *Who the fuck does this guy think he is, anyway?* Carl grabbed the doctor by his lab coat and lifted him off his feet. "You don't think I know that?" he screamed into Ziegler's face. "I grew up in this town, for fuck's sake. I don't need you to tell me who these people are. If you can figure out a way to save them, then I'm all ears. But you need to pull your head out of your ass, Dr. Ziegler, because I don't think there's any coming back from this. It's your job to prove me wrong."

Burt put his hands on Carl's shoulders and pulled him off the doctor. "Whoa, easy, Carl. That's not helping."

Burt's presence seemed to snap Carl out of it.

He released Ziegler and took several deep breaths. "You're right ... I'm sorry, Doctor." He took his hat off and rubbed at his temples again. "I don't know what came over me."

"No, I'm the one who should apologize. I was out of line. Truce?" Ziegler held out his hand, and Carl took it and gave it a firm shake.

"I could leave if you guys want some alone time." Burt laughed. "I could get you a bottle of wine, maybe a Barry White album."

Carl replaced his hat and looked out the window of the lab to make sure no one was in earshot. "Here's what I'm looking at. We have no idea what we're dealing with. If there is a way of fixing it, we need to figure that out ... fast. We're beyond the whole 'that's not possible, dead people don't get back up' thing, so there's no point in wasting time on that conversation. Right now, I'm thinking triage, I'm thinking containment, and I am thinking about saving the rest of them. Because if we don't get a handle on this, we're gonna lose this town. Consider yourselves officially deputized."

"What about your other deputies?" Burt asked. "What are you going to tell them? They need to know what they're up against."

It was something Carl had been considering. He was already down one officer with no idea what might have happened to Gary Forsyth. At this point, it was safe to assume he had been infected as well. That left Ted, Kovach, Rainey, and the dispatchers. Rainey was up to speed, and Carl was confident that Ted, the department's youngest officer, savior to animals and small children, would fall in line without losing his mind. It was Deputy Kovach he was worried about.

Kovach was a real by-the-book, logical officer and would probably have the most difficult time accepting the impossible.

"I didn't want to say anything until I was one hundred percent sure it was as bad as I suspected. But I guess it's time. I'm worried about Deputy Kovach; I don't see him dealing with it all that well. He doesn't have a very good imagination, and this isn't exactly your everyday situation."

"You're not the most imaginative guy on the planet either, but it's hard to argue when it's staring you in the face," Burt said. "If it walks like a duck and it talks like a duck, you know what they say."

"Okay, that doesn't even make sense, but thanks for trying. I'll take care of bringing my deputies up to speed. Do you still have what I gave you?"

The coroner pulled the .25 cal. from his jacket pocket and showed him.

"Good, although I might want you to have something with a little more stopping power, and I'd like you to carry as well, Dr. Ziegler."

"I'm not a cop; I'm a doctor. I wouldn't even know what to do with a gun." Ziegler held up his hand in a show of submission.

"Well, I saw what you did to my deputy at the morgue. If it wasn't for that arm of yours, I'd be dead right now. I'm not asking you to go shooting up the place; I just want you to be able to protect yourself if you need to. The one thing we do know is that a bullet to the head turns them off like a switch."

"Come on, Carl," Burt reasoned. "That might be easy for a guy who goes to the range twice a week, but I haven't shot a gun in a long time, and I was never a good shot anyway. Dr. Ziegler here probably doesn't have any hands-on experience." Ziegler shrugged his shoulders and shook his head. "You're talking about a headshot to a moving target. This isn't the movies. That's not easy for guys who aren't familiar with guns."

It was a valid point, but there wasn't much of a choice. "I'm just saying, it's better to have a gun and not need it than to need one and not have it."

"Fine, so let's say you give me a gun and you make me a deputy; I'm still a doctor, and I have a responsibility to my patients."

"Exactly, and if something horrible were to happen and you had to hit someone over the head with a stainless steel basin or, worst-case scenario, shoot something to protect one of your patients, then as a deputized member of the Sheriff's Department, I can protect you from any legal backlash that might come your way when the dust settles."

Ziegler nodded his head in agreement. "Okay, fair enough."

"You don't need to ask," Burt added. "I made a promise to your father before you were even born. Whatever you need from me, consider it done."

Carl put his hand on his friend's shoulder. "Thank you. Thank you both. I need to figure out how to brief my deputies, and even then, we may still need a few more hands on deck. Doctor, what's the prognosis on the girl?"

"Well, there isn't any sign of the infection; that much is certain. But I would recommend she spend the night for observation. Is there any next of kin?"

"We're working on that. My deputy will stick around for a little while. She seems to have taken to him. She'll be safe with him, at least until we find a family member to come get her."

"I hate to be talking about my own needs with all that's going on, but I need to get some lunch before I pass out. Anybody hungry?" Burt stood up and straightened his jacket, trying to adjust the weight of the gun in the pocket.

"I need to get back to the emergency room. I'll meet up with you in a little bit," Ziegler told them and turned for the door.

"Can't; I have to check back in with Ted before I leave. I'll try to return sometime this afternoon. We'll reconvene at that point. In the meantime, put some thought into that MRI machine. What happened, and why?"

"I'm on it."

The three men left the lab and headed in different directions. Carl repositioned his hat and prepared himself for the daunting task ahead of him.

Chapter 41

Father Kieran mulled around the emergency room, waiting for any news on the young man he had found on his doorstep. The center was busier than he'd ever seen in the past, and Kieran didn't think it was any coincidence. The staff appeared on edge and stretched too thin to handle the patient load, and the lack of available employees didn't strike him as coincidental either.

He walked in a slow circle past the nurses' station, through the emergency room, and then near the boy's bed, where the doctor was examining him. Most people were not allowed in the ER, but when you were dressed like a Catholic priest, you pretty much got to go wherever you wanted. Kieran made another pass and found himself in front of the boy's bed once again.

"Father," a faint voice called to him.

He looked at the bed next to the boy to see a young girl who belonged to the parish. He wasn't positive but thought her name might be Susan. She had a large bandage wrapped around her head that also covered one eye. Fresh stitches ribboned throughout a laceration that extended the entire length of her cheek. Kieran offered his kindest smile and approached her bedside.

"Yes, child." He hesitated to call her by name.

"It's Susan, Father. Susan Smith. I know I haven't been to Mass lately, but do you have a minute?" The girl looked like she had lost a fight with a woodchipper and might be feeling the effects of a sedative, as her exposed eye drooped and hung heavy.

"Of course. How can I help, Susan?"

"We were in an accident. Me and Debbie Horne were on Route 3 early this morning. I was driving, and a mountain lion ran across the road." The girl closed her eye and looked as if she might fall asleep at any moment.

"You're going to be all right. Has anyone called your parents yet?" He pulled a chair beside her bed and sat down.

"Yes, they're on the way. I didn't see it till the last minute ... the mountain lion. I-I swerved and crossed into oncoming traffic. I drove right into the other c-car. Is Debbie okay? Can you see her, Father?" Kieran looked over to where Susan pointed and saw the girl a few beds down. A flurry of nurses and doctors were at work; a basin was passed to one of the women, filled with scarlet-soaked bandages. Kieran had to stop his breath short to prevent himself from reacting in front of Susan.

"She looks as if she's resting, and that's what you should be doing as well." Kieran knew that Susan's friend would soon be with the Lord, but he wasn't about to tell Susan that. *Sometimes, an omission of truth is the merciful path.*

"Would you bless me, Father?"

"Of course." He made the sign of the cross and bowed his head. "In the name of the Father, and of the Son, and of the Holy Spirit, Amen. Through this Holy anointing may the Lord in His love and mercy help you with the grace of the Holy Spirit. May the Lord who frees you from sin save you and raise you up. Amen."

"Amen," Susan said and allowed her one exposed eye to close once again, then she looked up at him and smiled. "Thank you, Father."

"You're welcome, my child." He took her hand and comforted her. She had seen the animals coming off the mountain as well. He hadn't even imagined the problem it might create, having all those displaced animals running around town. Something had moved into their home, and the wildlife no longer felt comfortable there. The girl turned to look at the bed next to them and saw the doctor working on the boy.

"What's Billy doing here?" she asked.

Father Kieran gasped. "You know him?" He hadn't considered that the girl might recognize the mysterious boy that had shown up on his doorstep, though they both looked to be about high school age.

"That's Billy Tobin, Debbie's boyfriend. Is he okay?"

"Yes, he's going to be fine. Now get some rest, child. God bless you."

Father Kieran let go of the girl's hand and left her to sleep. Then, he walked to the nurses' station and spoke to the woman behind the desk. "I believe the boy's name is Billy Tobin."

⚫⚫⚫

Lois had been at Alice's house for about an hour before the phone rang. Will answered and ran into the living room, where the women sat on the sofa.

"They found Billy; he's in the emergency room."

"What about Eric? Is Eric with him?" Alice cried.

"They didn't say anything about Eric. They just said Billy was there, and he's unconscious."

Lois helped Alice to her feet and out the door. She followed them to the medical center in her Impala.

⚫⚫⚫

Father Kieran felt better after placing an identity on the mysterious boy. The child was under the care of physicians, which was far better than any he could offer himself. Feeling confident enough to leave the child's bedside for a moment, he followed the directory arrows down a long corridor and arrived at the cafeteria. The smell of coffee and fried food greeted him the second he stepped inside; his stomach reacted with a loud rumble. He hadn't had a moment to even think about food and couldn't recall when he had last eaten.

A friendly face looked up from a table in the back and waved him over. He approached the man and took a seat across from him.

"Father Kieran, what brings you here today?" Burt Lively took the priest's hand and shook it.

"Hello, Burt, it's a long story, really. How are you? I didn't see you at Mass on Sunday."

Burt made the sign of the cross on his forehead. "I know, Father, I was called to work. We had a bit of a problem, and I found myself at the lab most of the day."

Burt worked at the cheeseburger and large mug of coffee in front of him, which looked delicious. And when the waitress came to the table, Kieran told her he would have the same thing his friend was having. A few minutes later, she sat a mug in front of him and said his order would be out in a few minutes. He took a sip of the coffee, and his stomach made another lurching growl.

"I guess you're hungry, Father?"

"I seem to have neglected to eat breakfast this morning." He took another sip of coffee, and Burt raised his own mug as well.

"I'll drink to that," Burt said.

Kieran noticed the distinct aroma of blackberry brandy. He smiled and lowered his voice.

"My coffee is strong, but I'm afraid it isn't quite strong enough." He lifted his eyebrows and held out his mug. Burt looked around the cafeteria, reached into the breast pocket of his jacket, and removed a small flask. He unscrewed the cap and poured a generous helping of the liquor into Kieran's mug. "Bless you, my child." Kieran took a long sip and sighed.

The men sat in silence for a few minutes, sipping at their spiked coffees, until Kieran's order arrived. He tore into the burger without bothering to add any ketchup or mustard. It wasn't an uncomfortable silence, thanks to the brandy, but it was enough to allow Kieran a minute to consider what was going on in the woods behind the rectory. So much had happened in only a few days. He cleaned his plate and tipped back the rest of his mug before Burt was halfway done with his own. "Thank you, Lord. I certainly needed that."

"How are things over at the rectory, Father? Are they keeping you busy up there?" Burt asked.

Kieran looked back at the man and wondered if Burt had read it on his face. "I suppose," he said. "Burt, you've been a member of the parish since long before I came to Garrett Grove."

"Yeah, been here all my life."

"You know the area of the woods behind the church, the place they call the foothills?"

Burt straightened up in his chair and stared back at him. "Have you seen something, Father?"

Kieran glanced into his empty mug. "You've seen them as well?"

"I have, and too close for my liking. Look, if you need to talk to someone, I think you might have come to the right table."

"Are you asking me if I'd like to make a confession?" Kieran allowed an uneasy smile to cross his face.

"I'll tell you what. Why don't I start, and you can jump in anytime you want."

Kieran listen as Burt told him everything, explaining how the body of Felix Castillo had been found early Sunday morning, less than a mile from the steps of the rectory, and how the corpse had been depleted of nearly all its fluids. He told him how the body had disappeared from the morgue and then shown up at the far end of town the following morning. Burt paused only for a moment when the waitress approached the table to fill their mugs. After she left, he told Kieran about the three children who had been admitted to the medical center Saturday night and then signed out by Dr. Malcolm. And what he believed the situation implied: that Dr. Malcolm had been compromised and a percent of the population were now infected.

Father Kieran allowed Burt to top off his mug and sat for a moment without saying a word. He hadn't even considered that the aberrations he saw in the woods were members of his own parish. He'd been thinking in terms of demons and not demonic possession, certainly not on such a grand scale. "I've seen terrible things in the past few days, my son. I can confirm that your fears are accurate. There are a great many of these beasts. They have been traveling through the foothills by night. I've seen their shadows in the woods, but they don't look like people anymore. And despite how many you think there are, you should reconsider that number. There are far more than that."

"Sweet Jesus!" Burt gasped.

Father Kieran took another long sip from his coffee. "Amen." He shared his own story about how the boy had shown up at his doorstep, half-dead and in shock. And how he hadn't even known the child's identity until only a moment ago. "From what you told me about these creatures, how Abe was infected and how the deputy was possessed, it's a miracle the boy survived."

"There's something else, Father. When we put Abe into the MRI, it did something to him. Something came out of him. It looked like a cloud of smoke. I don't know ... it looked evil."

It was exactly what Kieran had seen that first day in the woods, and he knew Burt was right. *It is evil ... it is the fallen Angel.* "The Lord works in mysterious ways. But Satan's works are far more mysterious. There is a presence in Garrett Grove, and that presence is pure evil."

"How do you stop evil, Father?"

"The only way to fight the darkness is with the light of the Holy Spirit, the power of Jesus Christ." The men continued to talk and drink their spiked coffee. The brandy helped to loosen their tongues and allowed for an even exchange that might have otherwise been hindered by insecurities and customary expectations. And rather than meeting as priest and parishioner, the two men met as equals over a meal and a cup of coffee. "I'm glad I ran into you, Mr. Lively," Kieran said.

"So am I, Father. It's always good to have a man of God on the team."

Chapter 42

Billy Tobin remained unresponsive. He was in shock and suffering from acute blood loss as well as dehydration. His temperature was high, but he didn't appear to have sustained any head trauma. Dr. Freedman explained to the boy's family how Father Kieran had brought him in and that one of the girls involved in the auto accident identified him. Unfortunately, there was still no information to the whereabouts of his brother, Eric; Alice and Will were near hysterics.

Lois tried to console them but was distracted herself by the flurry of activity going on around them. Chilton was too busy for a Tuesday afternoon. Not only did the facility appear understaffed but there was an increase in emergency room cases. She looked toward the nurses' station just in time to see Carl approaching from the connecting hallway. "I'll be right back," she told her sister and brother-in-law, then marched up to Carl and intercepted him at the desk. She caught him off guard and ripped into him with guns blazing.

"Where the hell have you been, and why didn't you start looking for my nephews sooner? Eric is still out there, and Billy's unconscious! Just what the hell are your officers even doing, for Christ's sake?"

Carl backed up a step, clearly caught off guard by her assault. "Lois, slow down. My men are doing all they can to find your nephews. You know I can't report anyone missing until forty-eight ho—Wait, did you say Billy is here?"

"No thanks to you! Father Kieran brought him in less than an hour ago. He's in bad shape, and Eric is still missing."

"Where's Father Kieran now?"

"How the hell would I know? I can't believe you. My nephews are missing, and you make my sister wait. That's not the Carl I thought I knew. Not the man I—" She stopped talking for fear of what she might say next, feeling the steam rise within her like a kettle about to boil over.

"Look, Lois," he said, lowering his voice. "I'm doing everything I can, not just for your family but the whole goddamn town. There's a lot going on that you have no idea about. So, if you would please give me a break and let me do my job. And please stop yelling at me."

She hadn't planned on ambushing the guy but was out of her mind after what Ziegler told her last night. Not to mention, she had driven all over God's creation looking for Carl in an attempt to get to the bottom of it. At this point, she didn't know what to think.

"How could you treat my sister like that?"

"Walk with me." Carl took her by the arm and led her out the emergency room door. The fresh air did little to change the mood, and Lois felt the heat continue to simmer within her. "Goddammit, Lois. I'm trying to protect your family. You have no idea what's going on."

She folded her arms and pressed her lips together, considering whether her next attack should be a frontal assault or one a bit more tactical; she opted for the tactical approach. "Well, I talked to Dr. Ziegler last night, so why don't you try me. You might be surprised just what I have an idea about." *Bullseye.* Lois watched his jaw drop like she had hit him with a right cross. Still, Carl wasn't as easy to manipulate as most men and was far more intuitive. He stepped back and took a defensive pose.

"What exactly did he tell you?"

Lois balked and attempted to recover, but the man had called her bluff.

"He told me the children might be suffering from something a bit more serious than the flu." She scanned his poker face and could tell he was waiting to see what else she knew.

"Okay, what else?"

"Well, he suggested we take a family vacation. So why don't you tell me just what the hell is going on here. What happened to Rob and the Richards kids that has Dr. Ziegler so freaked out? And what's got your department so busy you can't find the time to look for my nephews? Eric's still out there somewhere."

Carl removed his hat and scanned the parking lot to the left and the right. Then he stepped in, just inches from her, and lowered his voice once again.

"Maybe you *should* consider leaving Garrett Grove for a week or two. Pick Troy up after school and take him upstate, just for a little while."

His words settled over her like a glacier as an icy frost took Lois's breath. Now she was the one who had been caught off guard. It was one thing to hear it from Dr. Ziegler, but Carl wasn't the type to jump to conclusions. If he was telling her to get out of town, it was a warning to be taken seriously. Lois covered her mouth with both hands, allowing a gasp to slip through her fingers.

"My God, Carl! What is it? Is it that contagious?" Tears pooled in the corners of her eyes.

He rested his hands on her shoulders and looked directly into her. "It's worse than I could even explain. I don't want to see anything happen to you or your family. I'm sorry about your nephews, but I'm really doing all I can. People are dying, more than a few. So please take your family and get the hell out of town."

Her tears swelled and overflowed their banks as Lois struggled to process the words. Then Carl pulled her to him and wrapped his arms around her; she hugged him back and cried into his chest. She tried to speak but found it difficult to accept the fleeting moment of comfort. It felt more than familiar to be wrapped in his arms with her head resting against his chest. It was a feeling she had never forgotten, even after all these years. Warm, safe, complete. *God, he still smells the same... he still feels the same.* It was hard to describe, but if she had to, Lois would have said it felt a lot like coming home.

The trio of children cut through the ballpark, passed the outfield and the firehouse, crossed over the railroad tracks, and entered the Village where Janis lived. The pup's tail started wagging the moment she saw her master approaching. "How's my good girl?" Peanuts ran from one child to the next, unable to make up her mind whose face she wanted to lick first.

Janis's aunt met them at the door. "I don't think we have any cookies left, but there might be some Ring Dings. Are you guys hungry?" Which had been a silly question since the answer was obvious. Lynn went to the kitchen to rustle up a snack while the children scrambled up the stairs. They maneuvered around a stack of boxes and entered the room with Peanuts underfoot every step of the way.

Wendy sat on the bed and cut right to the chase. "If these things have been around for so long, how come we're just finding out about them now?"

"That's what my grandfather was working on. My mom doesn't tell me, but I know she knows more about it than she says. Wait right here." Janis walked into the hallway and proceeded to rummage through the stack of boxes until she located what she was looking for. "Here it is," she said, returning to the bedroom.

She held what looked like a photo album, put it on the bed, and opened it. The first page showed some very old black and white pictures of people wearing dated and funny-looking clothes. The next page showed a hole in the earth so deep the people were using ladders to climb into it.

Janis flipped to another page that contained the photos she was looking for. Various pictures of the small teeth were revealed, exactly like the ones she had in her case. There were labels above each of the photographs. One said Cahokia and showed several shots of the teeth and the jawbone they had come from.

"If you had to guess, do you think those things had a mouth like this?" Janis asked.

It was hard to tell what kind of an animal the jawbone belonged to. It looked canine, only much more dangerous. Troy hadn't gotten a good look at what chased him and could only imagine. "I guess so; I don't know, really. I was running so fast I didn't see. It's kind of hard to tell from looking at a picture."

"Yeah," Wendy said. "But do you think it's possible?"

"I guess it's possible."

"Good. So, maybe they're like bears and need to hibernate, only they hibernate for a *really* long time," Wendy continued. "Maybe it's like your mom said. I know she was just playing and trying to scare us, but maybe there's something true in her story that she didn't even know. Maybe there isn't anything called an Ojanox, but maybe there's something that only comes out after it's hibernated for a long time. Like the Ojanox coming out at Halloween. Maybe that's why no one knows about it. By time it comes back, everyone that was around is long gone."

Troy stared at the girl who had grabbed him in the haunted house, kissed him, and declared herself his girlfriend. *That makes a lot of sense.* At the moment, he felt like the maturity difference was a whole lot more than two years between him and Wendy. She was smart, everything she said made sense, and it just rolled off the top of her head. Troy sat there with his jaw open, searching for some intelligent remark to contribute ... He had nothing.

"That's got to be it," Janis said. "The Ojanox, or whatever you want to call it, shows up after a long sleep, goes into a town like Cahokia, or Garrett Grove, and kills everybody. Then goes back to sleep. After a hundred years or so, it just becomes one big mystery, and everyone is like, I wonder what happened to Garrett Grove."

Now they were both moving too fast for him to follow, almost as if they had rehearsed it. Troy suddenly felt like the stupid kid in the room and wanted more than anything to add to the conversation. "So, how do you kill them? It doesn't sound like anyone has ever been very good at that."

Both girls nodded as he spoke, making him feel somewhat relevant. Janis flipped to the next set of pictures, one that showed a few arrowheads and a spearhead. The others depicted a large dagger surrounded by several round objects worn into perfect globes. The tiny balls resembled bullets or musket balls. *That's it.* Troy focused on the picture of the weapons that looked to be made up of the same material and knew exactly what it was.

"Oh my God, that's lodestone!" Troy shouted as Janis's aunt entered the room carrying a tray of snacks.

Janis slammed the book shut, and all three of the children looked up at once.

"What's going on in here?" Lynn smiled and surveyed the room.

"Nothing, Aunt Lynn. You just scared us." Janis set the book on the floor behind her.

"Y-yeah ... scared us." Troy attempted to act like he hadn't been caught red-handed.

"Mmm-hmm, if you say so." Lynn set the tray of Ring Dings and juice on Janis's dresser, inciting Peanuts to lift her head up at the smell of food.

"Thank you," the children said nearly in unison, and Lynn left them to whatever it was that they had been doing.

Once she was gone, Wendy leaned in and punched Troy in the arm. "You almost blew it, dork."

He rubbed where she had hit him, trying not to show how much it had actually hurt. They each grabbed a cake, and the dog inhaled every crumb that fell to the floor.

"Now, what was this you were saying, lodestone?" Wendy asked as Janis opened the book to the page they had been looking at.

"Those little balls. My dad said the cave that he and your mom are working in is full of these things. They're all made of lodestone. It's magnetic and hard to work with, so they took a long time to make. That means that they must have really needed them."

"Do you think these are the same thing ... lodestones?" Wendy asked.

"I don't know for sure, but if I had to guess. What are the odds your mom studies these things and has pictures of the teeth and weapons? I'd say if your mom's job took her to that cave, then those weapons are *all* made from lodestones."

The girls nodded and appeared to agree with his line of reasoning, Wendy especially.

"Do you think it's like garlic for a vampire or kryptonite to Superman?" Janis asked.

"I guess the people from Cahokia and the Lenape thought so. I don't know, really." Troy had given up his wealth of information and needed the girls to take over again. Then it occurred to him. It had been at the tip of his mind, just waiting to come out. "My dad said the whole cave is made out of lodestone. He also called it magnetite, and if all of those bones up there are from the Ojanox ..." He shook his head. *Jeez, even I'm calling it Ojanox.* It was a stupid name his mother had come up with, and now they were all using it, which was more than just a little embarrassing.

Wendy nearly spit the cupcake out of her mouth. "That's it! Only maybe they weren't hibernating; maybe they were trapped in the cave. Maybe they couldn't escape because of the magnetite."

It sounded as right as anything else they had come up with so far. At least it didn't sound wrong to Troy. Still, he wondered about the bones. *If there's bones up there, then they died in the cave.* It didn't all make sense yet but felt like it was coming together.

"So, if you kill it with lodestone and you can trap it in a cave, how do we get some of that stuff? Because I'm not going out on Halloween without some protection," Janis said.

THE OJANOX

"That's a good question." Wendy squinted as she concentrated. "We have to get your dad to bring some home for us, or—" She looked at Janis. "Or you got to ask your mom to get some."

Both Troy and Janis looked doubtful at the possibilities of either idea being very successful. Then Wendy presented an alternate option. "Or ... we need to visit that cave and get some of it ourselves."

● ● ●

With the small opening to the unknown area blocked off and everyone made aware of the potential danger, Don, Stephanie, and the rest of the team moved on to the secondary chamber of the cavern. The murals in this section of the cave were even more elaborate than the ones they had photographed yesterday. There appeared to be exactly twelve individual scenes with a distinct chronology to them. Don still couldn't recall where he had seen it all before.

The first mural depicted a near entirely black landscape with a singular object set in the center that looked like a massive brown cloud. Shades of yellow sulfur and the most volatile green had been added to the shape, giving it the appearance of smog or swamp gas. The peculiar choice of color looked as if the artist had merely been experimenting with hue and technique and hadn't perfected either. At least Don thought so. But Stephanie and Gail focused a great deal of time and attention on this one mural alone. Stephanie pointed to the top right corner of the mural, where the only piece of vivid color entered the scene. It was white with accents of gold and crimson and looked like a secondary cloud sitting in the far distance. A polar opposite of the dark-colored haze that resembled pollution.

There was nothing ambiguous about the next mural. The scene was a fiery explosion of reds, yellows, and oranges. The scarlet was so red and the yellow so warmingly powerful, Donald could almost imagine the heat and force of the blast. He held his breath, staring at the dynamic piece of art. The flash from Gail's bulb accentuated the scene, bringing the mural to life and adding to the illusion that the explosion was currently happening.

"How were they able to capture such a vivid image?" he asked.

"It's beautiful, isn't it?" Stephanie said. He jumped, not realizing she was standing next to him. He'd been so enrapt by the mural he didn't notice she was practically on top of him. "They were quite advanced in culture and art. We could have learned much from them."

The murals continued to line the walls on the left side of the tunnel, which was now being referred to as "the secondary chamber." The flash of the camera splayed across the mural's surface, nearly triggering the memory within Don. And for a second, he could almost recall what it all reminded him of, but the moment passed without him latching on to it. He dismissed it, figuring it would eventually come to him.

The third painting was a picture of the earth sitting amongst the heavens. Donald stared in disbelief at the rendition of the blue planet sitting in its correct position in the cosmos, carefully nestled between the violet gasses of Venus and the red sands of Mars. *That's impossible.* There was no way the Lenape could have knowledge of the solar system like this. Sure, they would have known about the sun and the moon, but how could they have learned the positioning of all the other celestial objects? Orion was fixed in the furthest corner of the cave wall. Even the nebula located within the three stars of the constellation's belt were visible. And not only that, Cassiopeia, Ursa Major, and Minor were all located very close to where they would be, had they been gazing at this scene in a planetarium.

"How is this even possible?" Gail asked with her flashbulb clicking away at a feverish pace. "It's so vivid, and the accuracy is amazing."

"I get it," Don said. "This is a depiction of their creation story. It's the Big Bang, right? But how would they have known about that? This is incredible."

"Well." Stephanie cleared her throat. "Carl Jung had a theory called collective unconscious. The belief that the information we come to know as truth is not entirely organic. That all we know is derived from inherent knowledge, like code written into our DNA."

"You're saying that we know about the Big Bang because our ancestors knew about it and it was transferred in our genetic makeup?" Don tried to keep a straight face.

"It isn't the craziest theory if you think about it," Stephanie explained.

Somehow, the Lenape tribe had attained the knowledge. Was it possible they knew about the Big Bang because their ancestors knew about it, and the knowledge had become a part of their genes? Don doubted the possibility, but it was something to think about. No one could explain how infants made the connection when it came to developing the skills to put sentences together. In every culture, it was a phenomenon that baffled psychologists and physicians. One day, a baby struggled with the basics like mama and dada. Then almost overnight, they developed the ability to string words together and form coherent sentences. Oftentimes, they used words they had never been exposed to with complete cognitive understanding. Don had witnessed that himself with Troy. *Fill 'er up, Pop.* He remembered his toddling son standing in his crib.

That could be a form of what she was talking about, a collective unconsciousness lying dormant within our cells, just waiting to be triggered at the right time. For infants, the language trigger came somewhere between the ages of one and two. For the Lenape and most civilizations prior, maybe the need to understand their own creation was the springboard that ignited the creation story. Every culture had one, and it was crazy how they were all so similar.

"That's a pretty far-out theory. I don't know if I buy it, but it's definitely an icebreaker at the cocktail party." Don looked at the mural of the earth set in its proper quadrant of the solar system. It was uncanny. "Still, I can't explain how the Lenape could have gotten these details on their own. It's pretty damn amazing."

Stephanie pointed to the wall where the rendition of the universe had been painted centuries ago. "Is this lodestone as well?"

"Yeah. Crazy, isn't it? It's got to be one of the largest deposits ever recorded. This is definitely a cave for anomalies. I've never seen so much beauty in one place." He suddenly realized he was no longer looking at the mural; he had been staring at Stephanie. He offered a smile and watched her face flush crimson a second before she turned away.

"Yeah, you sure do know how to talk to women, Mr. Fischer," she said, and walked on to the next group of murals.

● ● ●

Lois pulled away from Carl and looked up at him through a haze of bloodshot tears. A million thoughts raced through her head, but not one of them made any damn sense. There was one that felt right, but she wasn't about to act on it. For a fleeting moment as Carl attempted to comfort her, she had thought about taking his face in her hands and kissing him right there in front of the emergency room entrance. Instead, she stepped back, wiped her eyes, and struggled to control herself enough to talk. "What's going on that's so bad?" He had confirmed everything that Ziegler said. "Who has died, Carl?"

He scanned the parking lot and hesitated as a man and woman exited from the doors behind them and headed to their car. "This really isn't the place. I promise I'll tell you everything, but you're not going to believe it. Christ, I don't believe it myself. I need to talk to Billy as soon as he wakes up, and I need to apologize to Alice and Will. Not to mention, I still have one missing deputy and a bitch of a headache. I will tell you, but I need to handle a few things first. Where can we talk?"

Lois thought about it for a second; it wasn't like he could just stop by and discuss it over dinner. She didn't want Troy to hear any of this ... or Don, for that matter. "Troy is at a friend's house." She checked her watch and noticed the time. She wanted to stay a little longer with Alice and Will, but she would have to call Troy and tell him that she was running a little late. *I could ask Janis's aunt if he could stay a bit longer.* That would give her enough time to hear everything Carl had to say. "Can you meet me at the house at five?"

He raised his eyebrows and offered a cautious look.

"Donald won't be home until seven, and Troy is at a friend's. It's not a public place, so there's no chance of anyone overhearing us."

"Fine, I'll be there around five. But first, I need to see if Billy is awake."

They walked back inside, through the emergency room, to the bed where Billy Tobin lay. He was still unconscious and looked pretty messed up. And he wasn't the only one. It had been a grueling day in the emergency room; at least one of the patients involved in the car accident had passed away, two others were critical.

Carl apologized to Alice and Will for not being more responsive. He explained how they had found the body on Sunday morning and were still following leads on Monday. Alice asked the obvious question: was there a connection between the murder and their son's disappearance? Carl told her no and that he wanted to be alerted as soon as Billy regained consciousness. The boy would be able to tell them where he and Eric had been, and that would be the best lead to help them find him.

"Deputy Lutchen will be here for the next few hours if you need him. He can reach me on the radio," he said before he left. Then Carl checked in on Ted. He entered the room to find Dawn fast asleep, sucking her thumb, on the examination table.

"I want you to stay here until we locate a next of kin."

"Sure, Sheriff. Um-I was wondering."

"What's that?"

"Well, the girl's dog is still in the pen and is probably hungry and thirsty again. I think someone should go take care of it?"

"Can't we just call the pound?" He had enough on his plate without having to worry about a dog.

"That's cruel, Sheriff. I'll take care of it. Besides, he seemed to like me anyway. Um, what if no one shows up for Dawn?"

Carl studied the rookie's face. Ted was practically a kid himself and looked as if he had just started shaving over the past year.

"We'll figure something out, Deputy." Carl put his hat on and started out the door.

"Sure thing, Sheriff."

Carl left the medical center with a great deal on his mind and even more on his plate. First, he needed to stop back at the station and go over things with dispatch and the rest of the officers. Then he intended to pay a visit to the armory and make a withdrawal. He promised both Burt and Dr. Ziegler something with a little more stopping power and had just the thing in mind. He checked his watch and ran to the cruiser—time was slipping away, and sunset was right around the corner. *Christ, I hope we're ready for this.* He had started to formulate a plan but had no idea if they'd be able to pull it together in time.

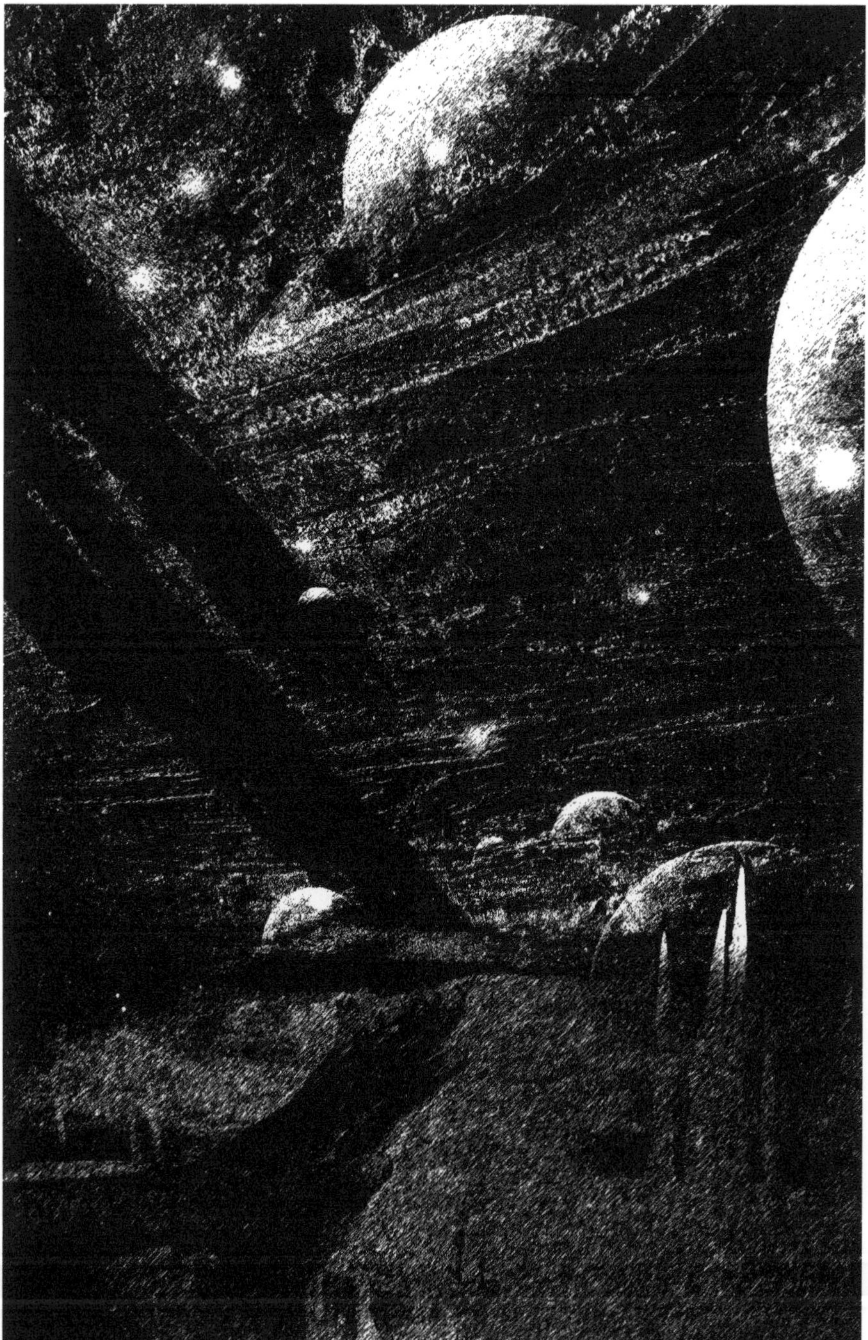

Chapter 43

Dawn Negal had eaten her ice cream and then fallen asleep while Ted remained at her bedside feeling helpless. His mind kept fixating on the child's dog, still left outside in its pen. They had fed the Shepherd enough food to nearly last it the rest of the week, but it was the water bowl that Ted was worried about. More than likely, Baxter had tipped it over again. He agonized over it, feeling responsible for the animal, and started thinking. Dawn was out like a light, and Ted figured she would sleep straight through. There was little chance she had slept the night before, curled up terrified beneath her bed.

He got up from his chair and looked out into the hallway to find two nurses passing by. "Excuse me," he said.

The girls, who couldn't be any older than Ted himself, turned on their rubber soles and stared at him. One flashed a wide Cheshire smile, and the other nurse bit her lower lip. "Yes, Officer, how can I help you?" the lip-biter asked.

"I was wondering if either of you ladies could do me a favor?" They looked at each other and giggled. "I have to step out for a moment and need someone to watch over my friend." The nurse that had spoken leaned her head into the room and saw the sleeping child.

"Oh my, she's adorable. I'm on break, so I can sit with her for a little while. How long do you think you will be?" She looked up at Ted and batted her eyes.

"Less than a half-hour; you're sure you don't mind? I really appreciate it."

"It would be my pleasure." She held out her hand and bounced on her toes once, then twice. "I'm Carole ... Carole Reiner." Ted shook her hand. "I'll be here when you get back."

Ted thanked her and sped off down the hall towards the exit. Becky Ramos, the nurse who hadn't thrown herself at the deputy, looked at her friend and slapped her arm. "Very subtle, Carole. I'm surprised you didn't just hike your skirt and ask him, 'do these panties make my ass look fat?'"

Carole laughed and watched Ted as he double stepped down the hall. She bit her lip and replied, "I think I'll try that when he comes back."

"Carole Reiner, you're terrible!"

⚫⚫⚫

Lynn worked in the kitchen, trying to get everything put away and the place in working order. She had gotten used to relocating and now considered herself a professional when it came to packing and unpacking. Since she moved in with Stephanie and Janis, they had changed houses, as well as states, three times in under two years.

Being born only eighteen months apart, Lynn and her sister had always been very close. Which helped when Stephanie separated from her husband, Brian. He had been a decent enough father but a terrible husband who respected only two things: his money and his libido.

Brian had been looking for a trophy wife and sat on the board of executives at the museum. Stephanie had studied ballet for years and still held her dancer's physique when she came to work for the MNH and, to put it mildly, was a knockout. Brian noticed her immediately and went after her like a shark. He swept Stephanie off her feet, married her in a whirlwind, and they were expecting Janis long before the honeymoon was over. At the time, he seemed like the perfect man. But it didn't take long for Brian Thompson to show his true colors.

He was neither violent nor an evil man; he just couldn't keep his dick in his pants. Brian messed around constantly and was horrible at keeping it a secret. He slept with half the interns at the museum, and the ones he wasn't sleeping with, he was working hard to do so. He had even propositioned Lynn once at a family event. Lynn had slapped him across the face and told her sister immediately. Which hadn't come as a surprise. Stephanie had seen the signs but tried to maintain the façade of a happy marriage for Janis's sake. But Brian had crossed the line by going after her own sister. Stephanie could no longer ignore his transgressions and confronted him.

The louse didn't even have the decency to deny it or try to hide the fact he was fucking every piece of ass that walked through the doors of his office. He threw the importance of his position on the board in her face, reminding her that the funding for her father's research had to go through him first. And Stephanie told him he could do the same with his funding as he did with the rest of his whores—he could *Fuck It!* The next day she contacted her lawyer and not only slapped Brian with divorce papers but filed a class-action suit against him and the museum for threatening her position as well as her funding. Most of the interns that Brian had been using as his own personal harem took the stand as witnesses to his professional misconduct. Girls he had manipulated into believing a position with the museum required they submit to a few positions of his own had been more than willing to testify. And the museum was just as willing to settle out of court. Brian was terminated, and Stephanie was offered the job of curator after her father retired. Brian was forced to pay a staggering wad in the divorce settlement along with pain and suffering compensation to not only Stephanie but every girl that had joined in the class action suit.

It hurt Brian's bottom line, but the guy had been born into money, so it didn't break him. He continued to treat Janis as if he could buy her love. But she was her mother's child, and the endless endowment of gifts didn't affect her. She was a pure soul.

Stephanie and Lynn's father passed away shortly after the divorce, and Stephanie had taken up his research. Lynn moved in to help raise Janis, which she considered a pleasure. She had never been married herself, and although she was only in her early thirties, she believed that ship had sailed. It certainly looked as if she would never have children of her own, and becoming Janis's surrogate while Stephanie was at work was the next best thing.

Lynn had tried to find her own direction and taken more than a few misguided steps along the way. She went to college for business, but after graduation, she realized she didn't have even a remote interest in it. Instead, she found work as a waitress and bartender, then spent some time on the road following the Grateful

Dead. She'd always been a free spirit. And in the music and the lifestyle, she believed she had found the secret meaning to life. For a good year and a half, she'd been under the misconception that if you dropped enough acid and listened to enough Scarlet Begonias, you could attain enlightenment. Unfortunately, despite all the laughs and amazing sex she had while she was tripping, Lynn never became enlightened. Much like her heroes, she arrived at the realization that the great prophets of the late '60s and early '70s had been misinformed. Timothy Leary had been dead wrong. Jerry Garcia, Grace Slick, and Abby Hoffman had all been ill-advised. The only thing to be attained by ingesting handfuls of LSD was a brain full of mashed potatoes.

Lynn was thankful she made it through her Deadhead days with most of her brains intact. But she had wasted far too many years chasing an illusion. She had some great memories and a few foggy recollections. One that she would never forget was the trip she made to see Jerry and the boys at Woodstock. She and her friends had been stuck on the New York State Thruway in bumper-to-bumper traffic and thought it'd be fun to show their tits to all the vehicles traveling the opposite way. One of the cars they had given an eyeful to had been driven by a priest; the guy even flashed them the peace sign. It had been a crazy time, and for the most part, her wild days were behind her. However, even now, as she unpacked the last of the dishes and placed them in the cupboard, she thought it might be nice to have a few hallucinogenic mushrooms to help with the rest of the work.

The phone rang and broke her from her daydream. Lynn picked up on the second ring. "Hello."

"Hello, this is Lois Fischer, Troy's mom."

"Hi, Mrs. Fischer, this is Lynn, Janis's aunt. How are you today? Do you want to talk to Troy?"

"Um, no. I was just calling because I'm running a little late. My nephew's in the emergency room, and I'm here with my sister. Is there any way Troy could stay a little longer? I should be able to pick him up by seven."

"No problem, Mrs. Fischer. Is your nephew going to be all right?"

"Well, it's too soon to say, but the doctor seems to think so. He's still unconscious and needs his rest."

"I'm so sorry to hear that. Troy can stay here as long as you need. Is it okay if I feed him dinner? I'm baking a chicken."

"Don't go to any trouble. I'm sorry to impose."

"Nonsense, I look forward to meeting you later. Stephanie might be home by then, and I know she's looking forward to meeting you as well. I'll see you when you get here."

"That would be great, thank you. Goodbye."

"You're quite welcome, bye." Lynn checked in on the children and told Troy his mother was running late and he would be staying for dinner. She said nothing about his cousin, thinking it best for Mrs. Fischer to tell him herself.

Baxter paced back and forth, waiting for anyone to show up and remember he was still in his pen. On most days, he'd have already gone for several walks and been allowed back in the house, but it had been a very strange day and an even stranger night. He lay on the concrete with his muzzle resting between his front paws, allowing an occasional exaggerated sigh to speak for his frustration with the entire situation.

Then the man opened the gate and appeared on the side of the house. It was the same man from before, the one with the hose. Excited, he jumped at the fence, unable to contain himself.

"Hey, buddy, I didn't forget you." Ted grabbed the leash hanging on the pen. "Do you want to go for a walk?" Baxter started to yelp and dance as if he had been offered a hot roast beef sandwich. The answer was obvious.

Ted opened the pen, and Baxter pounced, landing his front paws against the deputy's chest. Ted fastened the leash, grabbed the empty bowls and the bag of food, then led the dog out the gate. He took Baxter for an extended walk to do his business, then opened the back door of the cruiser. The dog looked up at him as if unsure. "Get in," Ted said, which was all the assurance needed. Baxter hopped into the backseat, and together, they headed back to Chilton. Ted knew there was only one problem with his plan; he hadn't yet figured out what he would say when he got caught sneaking a German Shepherd into the medical center. He hoped something would come to him.

Carl pulled into the back lot of the sheriff's department, near the door that led to the holding cells and the hallway connected to the armory. He let himself in, proceeded to the secured area, and unlocked the steel door where the weapons were stored. He scanned the stockpile and decided on two .40 cal. semi-automatics and a .357 Smith and Wesson revolver. Placing the guns into a duffle bag, he added several extra magazines and two boxes of .40 cal. bullets. He continued to fill the bag with boxes of .38 ammunition for his own weapon, three boxes of 12 gauge shotgun shells, and two boxes of 30-30 Winchester rounds. With the bag slung over his shoulder, he grabbed two shotguns from the rack and the 30-30 lever-action Marlin 336, which had always been one of his favorites. He left the armory, locked the door behind him, and deposited the cache into the trunk of his cruiser next to the helmets and riot gear they had used at the morgue.

Feeling as confident as he could under the circumstances, Carl slammed the trunk and climbed the stairs to the main floor of the station. Andrea Geary had just arrived to relieve Tara Jefferies, who was ready to walk out the door. Carl barged in, surprising both women with his brisk entrance, and began to dictate the procedures he needed executed.

"I haven't much time, so please don't make me repeat myself. I want all hands on deck tonight. I will brief the entire department at seven p.m. sharp. Tara, I know you just pulled a full shift, but I need you here. I want Deputy Kovach and Rainey here as well. Don't worry about Ted; he's still at Chilton and will probably be there most of the night." The women watched as he continued without stopping to take a breath. "Also, I need Chief Jones from the fire department and two of his men; I would prefer Koloski and Gomes. We can't count on Deputy Forsyth returning to work anytime soon, so I want you to call in Beau Jenkins and Tim Colbert." Carl finally stopped to take off his hat.

"Sheriff, you want Jenkins and Colbert; aren't they both retired from the department?" Tara wrote everything down and tried her best to keep up.

"They're about to be reinstated. Also, I want you to get in touch with the first aid squad and have a couple of paramedics here. Did you get all that?"

Both women stared at him with the same look, a cross between disbelief and concern. It had been a rough twenty-four hours for the whole department. Garrett Grove had seen more activity in one day than it usually saw in six months.

"What's going on, Sheriff?" Andrea asked.

"I'll fill you in at seven. Until then, I want you both to carry your sidearms." His words fell with the gravity of an avalanche.

Chapter 44

Lois hugged Alice and Will, told them she had to leave to pick up Troy and that she would return in a little while. She felt terrible lying to her sister, but telling her she was planning to meet Carl was out of the question.

She arrived home at ten to five and waited; Carl didn't pull up to the house until a quarter after. By then, Lois believed he wasn't going to show. She opened the front door before he even exited the cruiser, her eyes red with dark circles spreading beneath them. He walked straight into the house, took off his hat, and sat down in the kitchen. Lois immediately noticed how tired he looked and examined the crow's feet at the corners of his eyes and the grey in his hair that appeared to have doubled overnight.

Lois wrung her hands, waiting for him to begin.

"This is going to take a while," he said. "I could really use a cup of coffee and a few aspirins. Would that be possible?"

Making coffee gave Lois something to do with her hands that felt better than just fidgeting. She handed Carl a bottle of Bayer and a glass of water, and he proceeded to swallow three of the white pills and gulped down nearly half the glass. Soon the smell of coffee filled the kitchen and provided a small sense of familiarity to the uncomfortable weight of the moment. Lois pulled a pack of cigarettes out of her purse and lit one.

Carl waited while she stared at him through a grey cloud of smoke. "This is going to sound crazy. Christ, it feels crazy to even think it. First of all, whatever those three kids have, it's a lot more contagious than anyone believed. And no one knows what the hell it is. Maybe a parasite, maybe a bacterium." Lois opened her mouth to either speak or gasp but was unable to do either. She continued to stare instead. "You can't catch it like the flu, so don't worry about that. It's a bloodborne pathogen; that's the only way you can catch it ... as far as we know. A man was murdered sometime late Saturday night or Sunday morning. We found the body at the end of Foothills Drive."

"By Robert's house?"

"Right in front, to be exact. The man appeared to have died from acute blood loss, only there wasn't any found at the scene. There was a small wound on his neck. His name was Felix Castillo; he worked for Con Ed and was transported to the morgue for examination." Carl took a deep breath and paused. "Around three o'clock on Sunday, Mr. Castillo's body disappeared. At the time, we believed some kids had broken in and stolen it. Do you think that coffee is ready?"

Lois got up and walked to the counter. As she prepared the cups, she watched Carl lean across the table, grab her pack of cigarettes, and light one. She couldn't recall the last time she had seen him smoke and suddenly knew he hadn't even told her the worst of it yet. She returned to the table with the coffee and set a mug in front of him.

"Early Monday morning, a man was hit by a truck on Sunset Road. The guy's body was thrown into a drainage ditch. You know how those gullies fill up with water and muck. Well, he was dead, covered in mud, head to toe, and hadn't been carrying any identification. We didn't get a good look at him until we got him back to the morgue and washed him off. So, Burt gets him in the tub and starts hosing him down, then we see the wound on the neck. The guy in the tub—the guy who got hit by the truck ... It was Felix Castillo."

● ● ●

Wendy needed to be home shortly after five and informed Troy it was customary for him to walk her to the corner. He happily obliged and even offered to carry her books, but Wendy was having no part of it. He couldn't figure out why she wanted him to walk with her in the first place since she refused to talk and only replied with single-syllable grunts. They reached the corner where he knew they would part ways, and Troy prepared for the anticipated kiss that would follow. He leaned his head in to accept her affectionate peck on the side of his mouth and closed his eyes. After what felt like an eternity, he opened them to see Wendy already halfway down the block. There had been no kiss, no peck on the cheek, not even a *see ya later*—she just kept walking. Troy knew he had done something wrong—again—and figured he would find out what that was sooner than later. At the moment, he didn't have a clue and felt okay about it. He imagined his acceptance of the situation would also lead to further backlash. *This is impossible.* Wendy made his head spin, but somehow, he found it well worth it. He headed back to Janis's house, doing his best to forget about the whole thing.

Janis met him at the door; the smell of baked chicken filled the living room and caused Troy's stomach to growl. He followed the girl back up to her room with Peanuts trailing underfoot.

They sat on the floor once again with the photo binder spread out in front of them. Troy studied the pictures of the various weapons, trying to imagine how the Lenape had crafted them.

"You know, I was thinking," Janis said. "Maybe we don't need to go to the cave after all."

"What do you mean?"

"Well, you said it's called magnite."

"Magnetite," he corrected her.

"Right." She blushed and pushed a curl behind her ear. "Well, isn't it just a magnet?"

"Yeah, I guess so." He saw what she was getting at.

"Well, if magnetite can kill them, then maybe we could just get regular magnets and make weapons out of them. It's a lot easier to go to the toy store than the cave. Don't you think?" She offered a toothy grin that lit up her face.

"That's smart. We could buy those big magnets and make as many weapons as we need. If we make them sharp enough, they'll work better than little balls. We could get a few wrist rockets. I bet if you hit one of those things with a magnet from a wrist rocket, it would knock 'em right out."

"You're smart too, Troy. Wendy is lucky," she said, shifting her eyes down at the carpet.

"Yeah? Well, tell her that. I'm not doing very good at being a boyfriend. I make a lot of mistakes."

"No, you're doing fine. Girls are complicated. It's not you at all."

"You think so?"

Janis nodded and smiled again. "Can I ask you a question?"

"Sure, what is it?"

"Um ... what was it like when you and Wendy kissed?"

He noticed she wasn't looking at the carpet anymore; now she was looking right at him. Staring at him with eyes too blue to be real. His heart started pounding and felt like it was inside his throat, a big wet lump catching his breath. He hadn't seen the conversation taking this turn. Where the heck was all this coming from, anyway? *Dear God, they're working together. There is no way I can win if they keep changing the rules.* He gulped hard, forcing the lump down, and made a strange noise that sounded like a wheeze.

"Don't get all freaked out, man. I just want to know what it was like. I never kissed a boy before."

"Um ... good ... I guess," he said. He was sure he would pass out any minute. And even prayed that he would. Which might be the only way to get out of the awkward situation he was in. He thought about pretending to faint but knew he couldn't pull it off.

"What do you mean?" She sat cross-legged, rocking in place. "Tell me."

"I don't know ... It was kinda nice. Soft and, I don't know ... nice." He didn't know how to describe it any better than that. Wendy had caught him by surprise with the first kiss, and he hadn't really felt anything from that one. Then the second one happened, and he was a bit more ready for it. His stomach had felt funny, and he got a bit tingly all over. It was kind of like the way you felt when you stuck a paper clip in the electric outlet, only everywhere. Still, he was too nervous to put any of it into words. "Um ... it was nice."

"I want you to kiss me, Troy," Janis said, and he nearly threw up on her.

What? He couldn't breathe. *Dear God, get me out of here.* He prayed he might dissolve into the carpet.

"Just as friends, I won't tell anyone."

"I-um ... I-c—" There was nowhere to run; he could feel his legs cramping.

"If you don't kiss me, I'm gonna tell Wendy you said she was stupid." Janis folded her arms and glared at him. Troy felt like he had been kicked in the teeth.

This one was even more evil than the other. *Where do these girls learn this stuff? Is it written in a book?* He figured their mothers must teach them witchcraft; it was the only explanation. Troy knew he had fallen for the worst type of treachery imaginable. Wendy had tricked him with bologna and surprise kisses, and Janis used Ring Dings and ultimatums.

"Hey, you can't do that." He squirmed as if it would help.

"I can, and I will," she said. "So don't be a big baby. Just close your eyes and stop making such a fuss."

He searched but couldn't see any way out of this mess. What made it even worse, Troy thought it might be kind of nice to kiss her. There was something exciting about being threatened by the little demon with the blonde hair. "Fine!" he shouted and closed his eyes. "Just don't say anything."

Troy leaned in, waiting for Janis to kiss him. He puckered his lips and clenched his eyes. His heart raced like a lunatic locomotive with the anticipated feel of her lips against his. He felt her draw closer to him and realized he was smiling. Troy suddenly knew he had wanted to kiss her since she walked into class on Monday. He felt her breath close to his, sensed her lips just inches away, and then it happened.

A hot, wet tongue lapped him directly on the mouth and continued to work on his nose, his cheeks, and the entire rest of his face. He jumped at the feel of the strange sensation and opened his eyes. He looked up to find himself face-to-face with the snout of the beagle. Janis sat before him with Peanuts's muzzle zeroed in on him. The pooch continued to lap at him as if his cheeks were made of cheeseburgers.

"Gross!" he shouted.

Janis laughed and let go of the dog. "Oh my God. You should have seen your face. What a dork, ha-ha-ha." Tears streamed down her cheeks in a full deluge. She continued to bellow and point at him like it was the single funniest event of her young life.

Troy couldn't move, let alone think. He stared at her in delightful disbelief. *How could she? What the—?* That had been the greatest prank he had ever been a part of, even if he was on the receiving end. Troy knew he was dealing with a level of genius that was far superior. *Are all girls this evil? Are they all so twisted? Are they all so wonderful?*

Carl stubbed out his smoke and continued to tell Lois everything that had transpired over the past three days. "It was Felix Castillo in that tub, no doubt about it. He had died on Sunday, then got up and walked out the back door of the morgue. He'd been infected by the same thing that infected the children. Whatever it is, it changed him ... Christ." He downed the rest of his mug and walked to the counter to pour another, then returned to his seat. "Everything about him, his bones, his organs. God, his mouth—it was filled with all these damn teeth."

"He used this tongue thing to grab Abe Gorman, Burt's assistant. Tossed him across the room like a scrap of paper and killed him. I shot it three times in the chest, didn't even slow him down. Then I shot him in the head. That did it. But Christ, Lois, he had gotten up twice already. We had no idea if he was really dead. So, I secured it to the table with a roll of duct tape, and Burt cut it open." Carl let out an uncomfortable laugh that fell across the table and sat between them for a moment.

Lois held her breath, unable to recall a time when she had ever seen him so unraveled.

"We taped Abe down just to be safe, and Burt took blood samples from both men. He says it looks like a parasite with a bacterial signature. I don't understand it myself, so I called Chilton. Dr. Malcolm wasn't there; I spoke to Dr. Ziegler. Well ... he confirmed it; it's the same infection that they found in the children." He slugged back the rest of his coffee, checked his watch, and finished by telling her how the thing inside Abe had somehow controlled Deputy Rainey and what had happened when they tried to examine Abe in the MRI machine.

Lois felt the color draining from her face.

"Dr. Malcolm never made it to Oswego, he never called there, and the children were never transported. I have no reason to believe that any of them ever left town. The phones have been ringing off the hook with reports of missing persons, and I know of at least three families that were ... Well, let's just say they're gone."

"Billy and Eric were missing, and Billy has a temperature. You don't think—?" Lois clutched her pack of Parliaments in a white-knuckled death grip.

"I'll call Burt and Ziegler and have them keep an eye on him."

"Th-this isn't possible." Her hand trembled as she tried to light another smoke. She studied Carl's face and stared into his eyes, hoping to find the lie hiding somewhere beneath the surface. There was none to be found, not that she had ever known him to even bend the truth. "W-what should I do?"

"I told you. Pick up Troy and leave town as soon as possible. If tonight is anything like last night ..." He didn't finish.

"But Alice and Will are at the center with Billy, and Eric is still missing." Lois felt the room start to spin and found it impossible to think straight.

"If I can arrange to have Billy transported, will you go?" He dug into the pocket of his jacket. "Will you take your family and get the hell out of Garrett Grove? Will you please do this for me, Lois?"

"I doubt if Donald will leave the job site." She regretted saying it as soon as the words left her lips. Carl's eyes suggested he really didn't care what happened to Donald.

"Yes," she replied. "If I can't make it happen tonight, I will go first thing tomorrow. I promise."

Carl removed the object from his jacket and placed it on the table. The gun was a big nickel-plated revolver. "Take this. It's got some stopping power, and the kick isn't too bad. Remember, it's got to be the head; body shots won't do a thing."

"Tell me this isn't happening." She stared at him through a salty blur, but the look in his eyes suggested it was even worse than what he had told her. It was the first time she had ever seen him scared, and that terrified the life out of her.

Carl stood up, grabbed the gun from the table, and walked around to where she was sitting. He placed the cold steel in her hand, then set a box of .38 special ammunition in front of her.

"It's a .357, but if you use the .38s, you'll have better accuracy. Better chance at making headshots."

She knew he had put his career on the line by confiding in her and giving her one of the department's weapons. After all these years, he was still watching out for her. And how had she repaid him? By cheating on him and breaking his heart. All he ever wanted was to love her, and she had thrown it back in his face. And still, here he was ... standing in her kitchen.

Lois set the gun on the table, stood up, and threw her arms around him. She pulled him in tight and let the flood gates open. She buried her head against his chest and bawled like a child. The triggering scent of his Irish Spring wrapped around her like a warm blanket.

For a fleeting moment, time stood still. But it was already getting dark, and if Carl was right, trouble was coming. She didn't allow herself to think twice, knowing if she did, she would lose her nerve and probably never get another chance. She looked up into Carl's eyes and kissed him. Soft and slow at first, then bittersweet and intense, with a sense of urgency. She felt the blood rush to her face and throughout her arms and legs as their mouths moved in perfect synchronicity as if there weren't a mile of years between them. Before it could go any further, she took a step back, looked up at him, and smiled.

"I suggest you leave town tonight. If for some reason you can't, which would be a mistake, stay in the house and don't let anyone inside. I don't care if you know them or not. Your neighbors might not be who you think they are." He grabbed his hat and headed to the door.

"Carl," she said as he was halfway down the stairs. "I should have said no."

He looked back and tilted his head. "Huh?"

"All those years ago. You asked me if I was in love with him. I should have said no; I should have told you that I wasn't. But I knew what you would have done. And I couldn't let you take care of me and raise a child that wasn't yours."

He stared back for a moment as the silence and the magnetic pull between them intensified. "Yeah," he said. "You probably should have." Carl opened the door and stepped onto the porch, leaving Lois standing at the top of the stairs, alone with her laments.

CHAPTER 45

Deputy Ted Lutchen walked through the side entrance of the medical center with the large German Shepherd padding along beside him like they owned the place. Baxter looked up at him as they passed the waiting area and headed for the hall that led to the girl's room. Ted carried a box of Dawn's favorite toys with a doll under his arm and almost made it to the hallway before Nurse TenHove shouted at him.

"Pardon me, Deputy. You can't bring that dog in here."

He turned to her and offered the most serious face he could muster. "It's okay, ma'am, K-9 unit. Official business, Sheriff's orders." He continued on his way before she could say otherwise.

Ted escorted Baxter through the hallway and opened the door to Dawn's room. Nurse Carole jumped out of her chair as Baxter ran to her and started licking her hand. "Sorry I'm late, Nurse."

"Call me Carole," she said. "It was my pleasure; she slept the whole time." Baxter nuzzled up against her, and she obliged by rubbing his ears. "Wow, a cop who likes kids and dogs. Can I buy you a cup of coffee, Captain America?"

"That would be nice, but I don't want to leave Dawn."

"Have a seat and I'll be right back. Milk and sugar?" He nodded. "Try not to miss me while I'm gone." Carole winked as she opened the door.

Ted knew he was probably blushing, but Nurse Carole appeared happy to see his reaction, as her smiled bloomed and she winked a second time before stepping into the hallway.

● ● ●

Carl Primrose climbed the steps of the sheriff's department and stopped for a moment to survey the parking lot. Judging by the excessive number of vehicles, Tara and Andrea had followed his instructions to the letter. He entered the building and was met by the throng of people clustered around the dispatch area. They stopped what they were doing and looked up; an unnerving hush fell upon the crowd.

Carl removed his hat and nodded. "Meet me in the briefing room in five minutes!" he shouted, then skirted past them toward his office and closed the door behind him. The large group stared at him as he passed without saying a word. Carl imagined they were all thinking the same exact thing: *What the hell is this all about?*

He sat at his father's old desk and picked up the phone. Nurse TenHove answered on the second ring. "Are you still there, Doris?"

"Is that you, Sheriff? What's the big idea bringing a dog in here?"

"Excuse me."

"Your deputy just came in here with a dog. Walked through the waiting room like he owned the place. Said it was police business."

"I see." Carl knew exactly what Ted had done. "Well, it kind of is. Look, I'll take care of it when I get there. The dog belongs to the little girl we brought in earlier. We thought it would help her since she just lost her family." Carl figured he would throw the deputy some bail; Ted had really proven his worth today.

"Oh, well in that case." Doris's tone appeared to soften.

He asked if he could talk with either Burt or Dr. Ziegler, and a moment later, the phone started ringing and a familiar voice answered.

"Yeah, I mean, hello, Lab."

"Hey, Burt, it's me. Looks like I'm gonna be a little late. I want you and Ziegler to sit tight and don't go anywhere. I mean it. Don't go anywhere!"

"Is that your gut talking, Carl?"

"Right now, it's singing like Donna Summer. If you see Deputy Lutchen, tell him the same thing and that I'll see him when I get there."

"You got it. Where are you now?"

"I'm at the station recruiting a little extra help. Be careful, old man."

"Don't I always?"

Carl shook his head and hung up, thinking it best to not say anything.

Its children had rested throughout the day, and now that the sun had once again begun to set, they were ready. It summoned the brood from their sleep cycle and instructed them. They began to stir and rose to their feet, the ones that still possessed them. While some of the creatures retained a glimmer of their human resemblance, most had already evolved beyond such. It dispatched them from the mountain and sent them into the town. Soon, it would possess all that stood in its way. The first objective was to destroy the machine and the men who had used it. Then it would propagate and feast like never before.

Carl walked into the briefing room to find nearly every seat filled. Scanning the crowd, he noticed that everyone he asked for had shown up. He approached the front desk and took a seat. "Thank you all for coming."

There was a stirring and an overall look of confusion on the faces staring back at him. None of them had any idea why they were there or what he was about to say, except Deputy Rainey, of course.

"You're wondering why I asked you here, so let me cut to the chase. As some of you know, we found a body Sunday morning on Foothills Drive. Since then, there has been a house fire." He looked at Bob Jones, the fire chief, who nodded in agreement. "What you don't know is that since Sunday, there has been a spree of violent activity." The room erupted with a rash of questions and comments. Carl raised his hands to regain control and continued. "We have reason to consider the residences of both Fifteen and Sixteen Poplar to be crime scenes. We also suspect a violent crime to have taken place sometime yesterday on Stanhope Road."

A dark-haired man in the front row stood up; it was Nick Gomes, one of Bob's firemen. "Excuse me, Sheriff. You said, 'consider to be a crime scene.' Are you not sure?"

"We found bloodstains and evidence of foul play. But we didn't find any bodies. Also, we've had increased reports of missing persons." He scanned the room once again and focused on Deputy Rainey, who looked a bit green around the gills. *Stay cool, kid, and keep your mouth shut.* The last thing he needed was Rainey explaining what happened at the morgue and starting a full-blown panic in the process.

"I called you here tonight because I need your help. We're a bit low on manpower, and I plan to deputize those of you who are not already members of law enforcement. For those who are retired, consider yourselves reinstated." There was another stir of murmurs and questioning stares, but Carl sensed that a swell of camaraderie had begun to spread throughout the room as well. *This just might work.*

"Currently, Deputy Lutchen is at Chilton and will remain stationed there. Bob, thank you for coming; I see you brought two of your best men."

Bob Jones gestured to the men sitting on either side of him. "I believe you know Nick Gomes and Ed Koloski. I'd trust these men with my life."

"That's good enough for me." Carl offered a confident smile and prayed it passed for sincere. "This is what I am looking to do. I'm beefing up the force tonight as a preemptive move. More than likely, nothing will happen. But I want to be prepared for anything. Mr. Koloski, you'll partner with Deputy Kovach. You will, of course, follow his lead by the numbers." Both men nodded their heads in acknowledgment.

"Deputy Rainey, Mr. Gomes is with you. Bob, you're with me. Tim and Beau, I know it's been a while since either of you wore the uniform, but I need you both here to help secure the station with Tara and Andrea. There will be a squad car out back if we need to call for backup. Are you feeling up to it?" Carl was most concerned about retired deputies Beau Jenkins and Tim Colbert, who were damn near seventy and not as spry as they used to be. But once a cop, always a cop. He smiled when they stood up and saluted. "Great, thank you all for your help. I'm issuing sidearms. I've seen you all at the range and taught most of you myself. Mr. Gomes and Mr. Koloski, if you're ordered to holster or surrender your weapons, you are to do so on the spot. Comprende?"

"Yes, sir," the men replied in unison.

Carl waved to paramedics Michelle Marks and Joseph Santos sitting in the back row. "I'm glad you're both here. I hope we won't require your services, but I want you to be ready." They nodded in agreement.

Carl prayed he was doing the right thing and the effort would be enough. His only other option was to admit defeat and call either the state police or the Feds. At the moment, he had no idea how to do that without sounding like a raving lunatic. Best-case scenario, they would laugh and hang up the phone. But more than likely, he would be relieved of duty and placed under psychiatric observation.

"One last thing. I know it's going to sound strange, but I want you all dressed in riot gear tonight, helmets and all." This raised even more questions and concerns from the crowd, but time was running out. Carl didn't think explaining it further would help them understand any better. "Trust me on this. You are to exercise extreme caution, and I want you to wear your helmets. If anyone attempts to accost you in any way, you are authorized to use whatever means necessary to subdue them. I repeat, any means necessary. I know you have questions, but I don't have any answers now. Just be careful out there and don't take chances. Check in with dispatch regularly."

There were still questions, and Carl attempted to answer those he could. But the sun had already set and there was no time left to waste. The riot gear and weapons were distributed, and Carl instructed Tara and Andrea about what they should do in a worst-case scenario. He prayed it wouldn't come to that. Then he sent his deputies out with their new partners and climbed into his own cruiser with Bob Jones riding shotgun. Beau Jenkins and Tim Colbert stayed back with the dispatchers, locked the doors, and fastened the deadbolts once the last of the patrol cars left the parking lot.

Carl served in Vietnam, which had been an unconventional war. In a conventional war, there was a clear line between armies, as there had been in both World Wars. Army A on one side and Army B on the other, with a stretch of No-Man's-Land between them. Vietnam hadn't been anything like that. The Viet Cong created an elaborate tunnel system to ambush their enemies and used civilian decoys as weapons. They employed unconventional methods against their enemies, which had given them a tactical advantage. The American soldiers entered the jungles of Vietnam expecting a conventional war, and it had ended in a bloodbath.

Carl remembered; he had seen it firsthand. They had lost in Vietnam because they underestimated the enemy. It was a mistake his platoon had made that day on the Mekong Delta, and it was a mistake he repeated almost a decade later in Garrett Grove.

● ● ●

Lois walked up the front steps of Twenty-Two Village Road and rang the doorbell. A few moments later, an adorable little blonde girl opened the door with Troy standing behind her.

"You must be Janis," Lois said. "I'm Mrs. Fischer."

"Nice to meet you, Mrs. Fischer. We were just finishing dinner. Are you hungry?"

Not only was the girl striking but polite as well. Lois smiled, giving the child the once-over, and had to stop herself from gasping as her eyes focused on the front of the young girl's shirt. She couldn't believe what she was seeing; Janis had already begun to develop. Lois averted her eyes to stop from staring and was sure that her mouth had dropped to the floor. *How is that possible?* Lois herself hadn't started to develop until sixth grade. And if she had noticed Janis's breasts within the first few seconds of meeting her, it was a sure bet that Troy and the rest of the boys in the class had noticed as well. Lois was willing to bet that Janis's dance card would be quite full for the rest of her life; the girl was gorgeous.

Lois nearly forgot what she had been asked. "No, thank you," she replied.

"Nonsense." A woman entered from the hallway. "Hi, I'm Lynn, Janis's aunt. Come in and have something to eat. I insist." Lois stepped inside and maneuvered around several stacks of boxes. It was obvious the family was still in the process of moving in. A second later, a small beagle jumped out from behind one of the large boxes and greeted her. Lois reached down to pet the pooch, who eagerly accepted.

"Don't jump, Peanuts," Janis said, pulling the pup away by its collar.

Lois took one look at Troy and was overcome. All that had happened and all that Carl had told her hit her at once. She grabbed her son and hugged him tightly, then she kissed him on the forehead and messed his hair. Troy made a face and pulled away, obviously embarrassed by the motherly display of affection in front of his new friend.

Although the place was still cluttered with boxes, there was already a sense of warmth and home about it. Lois thought it probably had more to do with the family that lived here rather than the place itself. Janis and her aunt were clearly related, both blonde-haired and bright-eyed and awfully polite. Then it hit her. The aroma of baked chicken and buttery potatoes waltzed in from the kitchen, making Lois's mouth water. She had a vague recollection of heating up a bowl of clam chowder for lunch but wasn't sure if she had eaten any of it. So much had happened. And although she wanted to get home and not appear rude, she was famished and accepted the offer. Lois followed everyone into the kitchen, joined them at the table, and helped herself. Her taste buds reacted as if it were the first time they had ever tried food.

"Oh my, this is amazing. How on Earth do you get it to taste like this?" Lois was overwhelmed by the explosive flavor of the bird.

Lynn smiled with appreciation. "Thank you so much. The secret is beer. You take a can and shove it right up there." She motioned with her hand. "There's something about the yeast and the hops that brings out the flavor."

"I'm impressed. What brand?" Lois asked.

"Yuengling," Lynn answered. "It's a Pennsylvania brew; oldest brewery in the country."

"I went to Penn State. I can't tell you how much Yuengling I drank my first year in college. Probably had a lot to do with my freshman fifteen." Lois took another bite and swallowed. "How do you like school, Janis?"

"It's great! Troy and Wendy made me feel welcome. We eat lunch together every day." She put a spoonful of mashed potatoes in her mouth. Then, when she thought the adults weren't looking, she stuck her tongue out at Troy, showing him a wad of half-eaten spuds. He returned the compliment and displayed a mouthful of chicken. Lois had seen the entire exchange.

"Troy, that's not polite," she told him.

He apologized, then leaned over and whispered to Janis. "Why did you trade your sandwich if you don't like egg salad?"

Janis looked at the food on her plate and swirled the potatoes around with her fork for a minute. "I don't know. I could tell you didn't want to eat it, and I felt bad. Wendy took your peanut butter, and you looked sad. It made me happy to give you mine."

"Wow, that was really nice. You're so cool." He grinned and continued to eat his food.

Lois overheard every word of the conversation and bit her tongue. *Be careful, Troy, you are so close to the deep end, and you don't even know it.* She could see that Janis had a crush on her son and doubted if he even had a clue. Troy was growing up fast, but he was still quite innocent; it was clear that all this girl stuff was new to him. Lois was thankful that Troy and his two new friends were still just ten years old and she didn't have to worry too much, at least for a couple years. But how long would it be before Troy found himself torn between two women? How long before he broke one of their hearts? Would he marry the right one, or would he make a mistake he would regret the rest of his life? Lois realized she was projecting a bit.

"Can we, Mom?" Troy's voice startled her back from the place her mind had wandered.

"I'm sorry, honey. What was that?"

"Jeez, I asked if I could show Janis and Wendy Scream in the Dark, maybe tomorrow?"

She and Don had promised they would think about it, but that was before she had spoken to Dr. Ziegler. After that, the world had spun off its axis. Lois didn't plan on being anywhere near Garrett Grove this time tomorrow. But Troy's question made her think about the reality of that. Sharing dinner with Janis and her aunt made her question the possibility. How could they just leave town and say absolutely nothing? How could she just abandon everyone, the girls who were swooning over her son, their families? How could she just leave and not tell her friends or the boy who bagged her groceries at the A&P? But if she did open her mouth, people were likely to think she had gone crazy. Lois prayed it could be as simple as that. Surely, any minute, she would wake up in her kitchen with a cold bowl of clam chowder sitting in front of her, her conversation with Carl never to have taken place, and Dr. Ziegler had just been overexaggerating. Lois looked down at Troy, who was still waiting for a reply. "Sure, honey, that would be fine."

THE OJANOX

● ● ●

Charlie Silva and Darren Webb were pulling extra shifts in the wake of a rash of absenteeism due to a nasty flu bug going around. Charlie worked as a lineman for Con Edison, and Darren was a subcontractor for the phone company. With winter on the way, there were a lot of preparations that needed to be made. Garrett Grove and Parker Plains wouldn't stay up and running on their own. Tonight, the men worked together, checking the tensile strength of the mains at the substation on Route 3. All the electric and telephone lines for the Grove passed through the station, where they were relayed to the four sectors of town.

Last year's winter storms had cut power to the town for the better part of a week. Most people had fireplaces, but not everyone. And many had found themselves in the basement of the high school, which was a bomb shelter built at the start of the Cold War in case Russia decided to drop "The Big One".

Charlie and Darren started outside running diagnostics on the structural integrity of the housing units on the main high-voltage relays. Once that was completed, Charlie needed to check the transformers while Darren inspected the telecommunication relay.

The sun had gone down over an hour ago, and it was chillier now than it had been the past couple nights. Charlie zipped up his coat and rubbed his hands together as Darren exited the truck with a thermos and two Styrofoam cups. He poured one for Charlie and one for himself. "Feels like it's gonna be one cold winter."

Charlie took the offering and drank. "Hopefully, the power doesn't go down like last year. That was a fuckin' mess. It's one thing to lose a few lines, but if the station goes, this town is in deep shit."

"Good thing we're here." Darren puffed out his chest. "Should have a good month before the snow starts falling. We'll be right as rain by then."

"Hope so. They'll be a helluva lot of overtime for us." Charlie aimed his flashlight at one of the relays. "This fucker's in rough shape. Probably ain't been serviced since before last winter."

"Shit, they can give me as much overtime as they want. My kids are eating me out of house and home. Oldest one's growing so fast he needs new shoes every other month."

"How are the kids?" Charlie asked.

"Better than me. Doug's got a girlfriend. Probably getting laid right now."

"Speaking of getting laid, how's the wife? I imagine she's been missing me." Charlie laughed at himself, and Darren joined.

The sound of pebbles being scattered cut their laughter short. The entire area of the substation was covered with small stones rather than dirt or grass, which prevented weeds from growing around the transformers and relays. The men stopped laughing and looked in the direction the noise had originated.

"Probably just a raccoon or possum," Charlie said. They relaxed and focused their attention on the relay and the rest of their coffee.

The noise came again. Pebbles, not just being walked on but being scattered as if someone were throwing them by the handful.

"What the fuck?" Darren said. "Hey, who's out there?"

Another handful of stones was scattered. The noise came from the darkest part of the lot. Staring into the shadows, Darren froze as a handful of the tiny pebbles landed at his feet.

He pulled a screwdriver out of his tool belt and brandished the weapon.

"What the hell is it, Dar?" Charlie shrank back toward the truck.

"Some wise-ass kids, no doubt." Darren took a step forward. "You don't want to try me, asshole. I'm in no mood." He waved the tool to prove he meant business.

The noise came again, but no pebbles were thrown. Instead, it sounded as if someone had scooped up a handful.

"I'm getting tired of this bull—"

A golf ball-sized stone rocketed out of the shadows and struck Darren in the chest, knocking the wind out of him and nearly setting him off balance. Charlie watched it happen and recoiled as if he had been hit himself.

"Motherfucker!" Darren screamed and clutched his chest. "I'm gonna kick the shit out of you fucks." The second rock hit Darren square in the face. It had been thrown fast and hard and with incredible accuracy.

His nose erupted in a cascade of blood. It flowed from his nostrils and the newly formed gash running down the entire length of his schnozzola. He screamed through a blinding cloud of searing pain.

Charlie ran toward his friend and almost made it before the first figure darted out of the shadows. Luckily, Darren had been temporarily blinded and didn't see what was coming at them ... or how fast they were. Charlie, on the other hand, saw everything and had just enough time to realize they were in deep shit.

The creatures were small, but they weren't children, at least not human ones. The figure in front resembled something that could have been fished out of the river. Its face was bloated and dark purple in color. Large slits ran down the side of the thing's neck and looked an awful lot like gills. In a heartbeat, the strange slits flared open, exposing the muscles and veins lying underneath, making the creature appear as if its neck had been flayed open.

The second abomination was equally horrific. Its head listed to the right as if its neck had been broken. It took several lumbering steps forward, then charged the men at full speed. A blood-boiling shriek exploded from a mouth so massive and threatening, it couldn't possibly be real. At least two individual rows of jagged teeth snarled at the men as the beast descended on them.

The third creature resembled some type of primate, only far more hideous. It was covered in coarse, dark hair and wore what looked like a pair of children's pajamas. It approached on all fours, dragging its knuckles.

Torn between helping Darren and running in the other direction, Charlie froze, unable to move his feet. His bladder was a bit more decisive and let loose. He stood there, pissing himself, with just enough time to grasp what was happening. The beasts closed the distance and descended on Darren like a school of piranhas; they tore into him, ripping at his flesh and feasting on the extracted pieces. A second later, they focused their attack on Charlie. The last thing he saw was a cloud of black rushing toward him, smothering him, and forcing its way inside. A voice spoke from somewhere inside of him, but before he could make out the words ... Charlie Silva was gone.

Chapter 46

Dr. Ziegler and Nurse TenHove exhausted every possible resource trying to locate any of Dawn Negal's relatives in the area. With limited available options, Ziegler checked the child into a room on the second floor, where she could stay for the time being. He even made accommodations for her dog and the deputy. Ted Lutchen parked himself in a chair beside her bed and caught up on some much-needed rest himself.

The emergency room had finally quieted down, allowing Ziegler a little time to think. He made his final rounds, and on the way back to his office, he passed the lab where Burt was still hard at work. Next to the coroner sat the same priest who'd been mulling around the emergency room earlier. It made sense. Burt had been wearing the crucifix. Of course he was a Catholic. The man was probably having a good old heart-to-heart with the preacher. After everything they had been through, it wasn't surprising at all. *Good for you, Burt.*

Ethan Ziegler had never been very religious himself. His parents, on the other hand, were practically orthodox and tried to raise their son in the customs of the old country. It wasn't that young Ethan didn't follow the faith; he just wasn't as devout as his parents wanted him to be. He had gone to temple and become a man at his Bar Mitzvah, but as he got older, he drifted away from the practice like many young men did with every other religion. He discovered women, and that had been a significant diversion. And although his mother wanted him to marry a nice Jewish girl, they just didn't do it for him. Ethan had a thing for the Gentiles; they were a lot less frigid. It was his one weakness, which had gotten even more acute when he entered med school.

Deep down, Ziegler knew he wasn't a bad guy; he just loved women. More accurately, he loved having sex with them. He wasn't looking to settle down for any longer than a night or two, and the girls he was with didn't seem to mind. He was always honest and attentive to their needs, and he had even convinced himself that he was happy. It hadn't occurred to him until very recently that all the womanizing left him just a tad bit lonely. He watched the parents who brought their children in to be treated for strep throat, bronchitis, and chickenpox. And sometimes he thought ... it might be nice. Not to have chickenpox, but maybe, one day, it would be nice to have a kid of his own.

He wasn't getting any younger, and although it was different for men, he didn't want to look like a grandfather when he finally got around to settling down. *What the hell am I thinking?* he asked himself, not sure where all this was coming from. Possibly, it had been the sight of the priest talking to Burt, which had brought back memories of his mother and of his own faith—probably. Ziegler knew he had let his mom down with all his selfishness and skirt-chasing. She always said how proud she was of her son, the doctor, but deep down, he knew he had disappointed her.

Ziegler continued past the lab toward his office. Upon entering the room, he checked the time and decided it wasn't too late. He picked up the phone and dialed. A familiar woman's voice greeted him.

"Hi, Mom," he said.

"Ethan, is that you?"

"It's me. I wanted to see how you were. Is it hot in Florida today? How's Dad?"

"It was ninety degrees today. And your fathah's out of his mind. He thinks he's Arnald Palmah. He was out golfin' in the sun all day." The sound of her New York accent always made him smile.

"He was? Tell him he's got to take it easy. That Florida sun is no joke."

"How is my good-lookin' son, the doctah?"

"Good, Mom ... I'm terrific." Ethan doubted if he had been all that good, and now that he thought about it, he figured he'd been fooling himself for a long time.

He had believed he was happy, but listening to his mother talk about his "out of his mind fathah," he knew he had been sad, possibly for a long time.

"I miss you, Mom. I just wanted to call and tell you that."

"I miss you too, creampuff. Why don't you come down and visit your mothah? You should see Ellen Schumann's daughtah, Kim. What a knockout. She's been asking about you, Ethan. Why don't you come down here and make an honest woman out of her."

"You know, I might just take you up on that." He let out a deep sigh.

"Who is this?" she asked. "What have you done with my son? Are you feeling all right? Usually, you want to give me a hard time. What's going on up there, Doctah Zieglah?"

"Nothing, Mom, really. I just thought it might be time for a vacation. I tell you what; I got a few patients I need to watch over for the next week or so, but I'm going to book a ticket and come visit you and Dad. How does November twelfth sound?"

"Be still my heart. You're gonna make your mothah cry."

"Aww, don't cry, Mom. It's been too long. I'm looking forward to seeing you and helping Dad with his golf swing."

"He'll be glad to have it. I wish he was here. He's across the street at Hank's house."

"That's all right. Tell him I called, okay?"

"Sure thing."

"I love you, Mom."

"Aww, you made my night, creampuff. I love you too."

"Okay, goodnight."

"Goodnight."

Ethan listened as his mother hung up. It'd been too long since he last saw his folks. It would be good to visit them and take some time off. And who knew, maybe he would even ask Kim Schumann out to dinner. He hung up the phone and ran his fingers through his hair. It was getting a little shaggy, and he would have to get it cut before leaving for Florida.

He leaned back in his chair and looked up at the bulletin board hanging on the wall. The red ladybugs sat there holding the papers in place. The big black dots on their backs looked like the eyes that had stared up at him from the gurney—Abe's eyes. Lost in thought, Ethan Ziegler stared into the big black dots on the backs of the red bugs, allowing what he had already been thinking to resonate and then register. *That's it!* He jumped up from behind his desk, nearly knocking his chair over in the process.

He scrambled to the bulletin board, pulled one of the bug magnets off, and held it an inch from the surface. Then he let it go and watched as it shot back and held in place. Doing it again, he imagined the invisible force that attracted the magnet to the board's surface like a bullet. The MRI machine was essentially a giant magnet that reacted to the electrons in the body. You couldn't enter the machine if you had any metal inside you or had tattoos with metal filings. The force of the machine would literally extract the alloys from your tissue. It all made perfect sense, and he cursed himself for not realizing it sooner. He shoved the magnet into his pocket, opened the door, and stepped into the hallway.

Ziegler almost ran right into the girl as she passed, pushing her cart. He stopped just in time to avoid colliding at full speed. She jumped with a start, then saw who it was and smiled.

"Dr. Ziegler, you scared me," the young candy striper said, making eye contact.

"I'm sorry." He scanned her name tag just to be sure. *Cyndi with an i.* "Cyndi ... I didn't mean to scare you like that. I was in a bit of a hurry, I guess."

"That's okay," she said. "I don't mind."

"Well, I'll be more careful in the future."

"I was hoping you wouldn't," she said, pressing up against him. "I kinda like it rough."

Ziegler felt the blood rush to nearly every part of his body, some areas more than others. He gasped as Cyndi lowered her hand and grabbed at the bulge that had started to grow in his pants. It felt good. Ziegler envisioned bending her over and taking the girl right there in the hallway.

Cyndi moved her lips close to his and squeezed once again. "Oh, Doctor, I think you need to take my temperature with this big thermometer."

He wanted her ... as much as he had ever wanted any woman. It would be easy to find an empty room and have his way with the girl; he had done it dozens of times in the past with Jackie Gilmartin, with others as well. *Like taking candy from a candy striper.* The thought resonated in his head and turned sour. It grew like a tumor, forcing all other thoughts to the side. Ziegler struggled to contain himself but was losing the battle as Cyndi backed him against the wall and squeezed. He latched on to the object in his pocket and forced himself to focus on anything else, anything more important than getting laid.

A clear image entered Ethan Ziegler's mind; he pictured himself getting on a plane and heading south. He could see the runway in Tampa, Florida, and could feel the warmth of the sun on his face. The warm spray of the salty Gulf was so vivid he could smell it. It fused with the scent of coconut oil and afternoon thunderstorms and tugged at him like a lasso. Ziegler thought about helping his father with his golf swing and the many ways he had let his mother down. Then he side-stepped away from Cyndi-with-an-i and smiled.

"I'm sorry, Cyndi. You're a beautiful girl, and I am very flattered. But I don't think it would be a good idea to do this. I don't want to use you, and I don't think I would respect either of us very much if I did. I'm sorry."

The girl's jaw dropped as if she was expecting to receive communion. Ziegler doubted she had ever been turned down in her life. Why would any guy in his right mind? For that matter, why was *he* turning her down, and what the *hell* was he thinking?

"I'm sorry, Cyndi. But I have to take care of something." He started off down the hallway when she called to him.

"Hey, Dr. Ziegler."

"Yes." He braced himself.

"Thank you. You're a real class act."

He nodded and smiled. "Thank you, Cyndi. So are you." Ziegler double-timed it down the hall. He finally knew what had happened to Abe and knew just how to prove it.

In a blinding whirl of sight and sound ... the world erupted. The explosion shook the building with the force of an atomic bomb, nearly knocking Ziegler off his feet. His ears popped and started ringing, and the overhead fluorescents flickered on and off like strobes. He reached up and clutched the sides of his head, certain he had ruptured his ear drums. The lights flickered a second time and then went out completely. A moment later, the emergency generator kicked in, bathing the hallway in a dull amber glow. *Dear God, no!* Ziegler knew exactly where the explosion had originated. He ran down the hallway toward the back of the building, to the wing where the imaging department was located.

He tasted the smoke the second he entered the radiology wing, noxious and dark like burning plastic. Then he saw the carnage and debris. Ceiling tiles had been knocked loose and broken apart. Several light fixtures hung from the grid, suspended by their wires. Others had pulled free and smashed against the floor. The smoke grew thicker the further he progressed and nearly obscured the figure of the woman running towards him. She clutched her head like an over-inflated basketball, and the blood was everywhere. It ran down the sides of her face and through her fingers. She fixed Ziegler with a crazed stare as he approached, but the woman continued running, pausing only to snarl at him when he reached for her.

Shouts of pain and cries for help cut through the gonging inside his head; people were hurt, many were screaming, and the smoke was caustic. Ziegler did his best to navigate a path through the oppressive cloud, but his eyes burned and had started to tear. In a flash of understanding, he realized the ringing in his own ears wasn't just the residual effects from the explosion. It was the sound of an alarm ... The building was on fire.

Ziegler pressed forward, focused on helping the injured, but it was nearly impossible to see through the thick haze. It assaulted him like a stroke, causing him to choke and almost double over. He looked up to see the shadow emerge from the darkness; it stepped in front of him and stood there. There was something familiar about the figure. Ziegler squinted against the sting of smoke as the man approached him.

"You there!" he yelled. "Who is that?" By the time he saw the lab coat, it was too late.

Ziegler opened his mouth to scream, but the thing that had once been John Malcolm seized him by the throat and silenced him. It latched on to his neck with the strength of a tank and stared into his eyes. The former chief of medicine resembled little of his former self. He had lost most of his hair, though a few thin strands still clung to his scalp in random places. And his face was distorted, almost unrecognizable, and no longer looked human. Still, there was no mistaking the man beneath the monster.

Ziegler scratched at the claws wrapped around his throat as Malcolm lifted him off his feet. The air in his lungs sizzled and burned as he gasped to take a single breath. But the beast's hold on him was too powerful; its grip was inescapable. Ziegler flailed his legs and twisted his body while panic washed over him in a flood. The jet-black eyes of the monster stared into his own. Darker than midnight oil and larger than the spots on the backs of the ladybugs.

THE OJANOX

The ladybugs!

Ziegler suddenly remembered and plunged his hand into his coat pocket, grabbing for the tiny magnet within. He pulled it out just as Malcolm tightened his grip and twisted. Ethan Ziegler felt a momentary snap as his throat and spinal column were crushed.

A moment later, he felt nothing.

His feet stopped kicking, and his arms fell slack to the side; the item he had pulled from his pocket fell to the floor. The creature shook Ziegler one last time, then discarded the man like a wet dishrag, tossing his body against the wall, where it crumpled to the floor, limp, ruined, and lifeless.

In a fleeting moment, just before his world went dark, Ziegler's final thoughts had been of someone other than himself. Ethan Ziegler had been thinking about his mother.

Chapter 47

Before Donald Fischer left for the night, he instructed his men to secure the cave by roping it off and placing a barricade to impede trespassers. He also made plans with Mark Gold to have a few engineers accompany him tomorrow, the third chamber being the focal point of his concern. Don intended to take every possible precaution before he or anyone else stepped one foot in there. If it turned out to be a chasm, as he suspected, the entrance to the chamber would be permanently sealed off. And even though it was a remote possibility, the idea of someone slipping past his barricades and falling to their death sat in his belly like a handful of staples.

Stephanie was the last member of her team to leave for the night. She crossed the parking lot and approached Don where he sat in the front seat of his truck. "Hey, cowboy. So, about that invitation."

Don tilted his head and drew a blank. He had no idea what invitation she was referring to. "Huh?"

"Your son asked Janis to come over ... to see the haunted house."

"Oh! That's right. I completely forgot with all the talk of Big Bang and Collective Unconscious."

"Well, I just wanted to make sure that 'come over and look at my haunted house' wasn't code for 'I'll show you mine if you show me yours.'" They laughed for a quick second, but it was short-lived.

"They're only in fourth grade. I don't think we have to worry about that." Don hadn't had "the talk" with Troy and figured it could wait a couple years. He was pretty sure his son hadn't figured out the birds and bees on his own and was hoping Troy was just as clueless as he had been at ten years old.

"Well, maybe your son isn't there yet, but girls do mature a bit quicker; you know?"

She made a good point. Don had always felt about three or four years behind the girls his own age and spent most of his life trying to catch up.

"Why don't you come and help chaperone? The more adult eyes, the less hanky-panky."

They both laughed again and realized they were probably concerned over nothing; there was little chance that any of the kids would end up pregnant or with an STD. Neither of them had any idea they were being watched from the cliffside.

Strange dark eyes stalked the man and woman as they entered their vehicles and left the lot. Like a ravenous pack of jackals, they descended the rockface and bolted out of the darkness. They clamored over the fences, reaching the small building within seconds. Bold red letters were stenciled on the steel door and outside walls of the shed: DANGER EXPLOSIVES.

Burt and Father Kieran were sitting in the lab when the explosion shook the ground beneath them. The glass windows overlooking the hallway shattered, and the lights flickered and then went out. The roar of the concussion was deafening. Burt was thrust back into the memory of war as the very air in his lungs was stolen by the force of the blast.

Both men scrambled for cover underneath the lab table until the emergency lights turned on a moment later. Father Kieran was the first to rise to his feet, then helped steady Burt.

"Dear God. What was that?" Kieran shouted over the blare of the fire alarms. The first wisp of smoke made its way to the lab as a voice broke over the intercom system; it was impossible to understand a word being said. Staring back in confusion, Burt shook his head and shrugged. Father Kieran grabbed him by the shoulders and shouted, "I'm going to see if I can help. You stay here."

The priest opened the door and exited the lab. Burt didn't like the idea of staying behind and followed, only to find the smoke was considerably thicker in the hallway. Somewhere in the building, something was on fire. The suffocating fumes of burning plastic and toxic materials assaulted the men. Father Kieran removed his jacket and wrapped it around his face to shield him from the smoke, then instructed Burt to do the same.

Burt followed his lead, noticing the heavy object in his coat pocket. He felt around and found the gun Carl had given him. He removed it, shoved it into the waistband of his pants, then headed off behind Father Kieran, and they made their way down the hall. They hadn't gone more than a dozen steps before visibility was reduced to mere feet by the oppressive smoke.

A woman rushed at them from the haze, almost knocking Burt over as she plowed into them. Her head was bleeding, and she was in shock. With firm but compassionate hands, Father Kieran took the woman by the shoulders and stared into her eyes. She tensed up for a moment and then relaxed at the holy man's touch, allowing him to check her injuries and examine her. Burt watched as the priest removed his jacket and ripped off one of the sleeves. He carefully wrapped it around the woman's wounds and then made the sign of the cross above her forehead.

Other employees arrived to aid in the rescue effort. Father Kieran guided the woman and placed her hand in that of a large orderly, who led her away toward the ER. In a flash, Kieran was on the move and urging Burt to follow.

They pushed through the smoke, shielding their eyes as best they could from the bite of the fumes. Florescent lights that had been jarred loose hung by their wires from the ceiling. The floor was littered with broken glass and debris. Burt could tell they were close to where the blast had originated.

The temperature grew warmer as they approached the back of the building where the imaging wing was located. An orange glow at the end of the hallway was visible, and Burt could hear voices coming from the direction of the blaze.

He followed Father Kieran through the smoke and around a corner that opened into a large hallway.

The dim silhouette of two figures appeared before them in the haze. The outlines of the shadows remained motionless, and even through the oppressive smoke, Burt could tell there was something wrong.

The two figures slowly came into focus, revealing the lab coats that both men wore. Burt recognized the one with his back to them as Dr. Ziegler. The coroner called out, but his voice was baffled by the drone of the fire alarms and the jacket wrapped around his mouth. Without warning, Dr. Ziegler was lifted off his feet by the other man, who had him by the throat.

Dear God, it's one of those things. It has Ziegler!

Time stood still. Burt was unable to react and could only watch the scene unfold. The doctor fought to free himself; a second later, his arms went slack and he stopped moving. The creature tossed Ziegler's body against the far wall, where it slumped in a most sickening way. Burt's stomach turned as he watched the man flop to the floor in a broken heap.

"No!" Burt screamed. He reached to remove the gun from his waistband and advanced on the creature. However, his feet were in motion long before he had control of the weapon. The beast drew a fix on him; an insectile grin flashed across its face.

Burt managed to free the weapon from his pants and raised it eye level. But the creature was faster and darted to the right, seizing Burt by the throat with one of its powerful arms. The gun flew from his hand as the creature tightened its grip around the coroner's neck.

Burt knew he had reacted without thinking; it was a mistake that would cost him his life. The creature tightened its grip, stopping the blood from reaching his brain. The jacket wrapped around his neck was the only reason he was still alive. Burt tried to draw a breath and looked up at the monster's face. *Dr. Malcolm!* Ice water ran through Burt's veins. There was no mistaking the man he had known and worked with for years, although his features had been altered considerably. The old doctor's face looked warped and distorted. His brow had grown thicker and protruded like a Neanderthal's. His nose had flattened into a defined look of brutality. And somehow, the man had grown nearly nine inches. *This isn't an infection,* Burt realized as he was lifted off his feet.

He clawed at the hand around his throat, but it was massive and so fucking strong. Burt's world grew dim as the Malcolm-beast clenched down on his throat, its hands encompassing the circumference of his entire neck. He wondered what would break first, his spine or his windpipe, then the world went black.

The thunder of an explosion roused him from the land of darkness. It was close and felt as if it had happened on top of him. It was followed by another loud concussion and then a third. The beast finally released him, and Burt fell to the floor, gasping for air. He looked up, half-dazed, as the muzzle flashed once more, hammering another explosion into the hallway. He struggled to focus on the face and looked into the eyes of the man holding the weapon.

Father Kieran stood firm with a steady hand and Burt's gun trained on the creature. The first bullet had hit the thing in the jaw and stunned it. The priest's second round hit the creature in the temple, causing it to release its grip.

Then Father Kieran stepped forward, took aim, and fired several more rounds into the monster's skull. It ceased to move, bleeding a thick black tar that spread out across the floor. Kieran raised the pistol and made the sign of the cross in the air before him. "I will fear no evil," he said. "For thy rod and thy staff comfort me."

Chris Wyatt was the only attendant working at Frank's Texaco on Route 3. The night shift typically wasn't busy, and tonight was no different, except for the occasional truck driver leaving from Wilson's diner down the street. The temperature had dropped considerably since sunset, and Chris had gotten tired of sitting in the little booth out by the pumps. He now watched the road from the comfort of the main office connected to the garage, where he could see approaching vehicles from either direction. The radio was set to a rock station, and the King Biscuit Flower Hour had just come on. Chris turned up the small volume knob, giving Alice Cooper a bit more headroom as "Welcome to My Nightmare" crackled through the tiny speakers. A thick haze of cigarette smoke hung like a net from the Marlboro Reds Chris chained smoked. The fog permeated the air all the way into the connecting bays of the garage.

Chris was a senior and had been working at Frank's for the past four months. He didn't have any real aspirations for after graduation, but at least he would graduate. Which almost didn't happen due to his heightened infatuation for Diane Nathan, who had recently moved to town from Warren.

Diane was part German, part Polish, and exactly Chris's type. It wasn't so much the blonde hair and blue eyes that defined Chris's type as Diane's willingness to let him into her pants. He and Diane hit it off instantly, and it had been amazing. Chris had been with only one girl before meeting Diane, and it had been awkward at best. That girl was Abby Hamilton, the fire inspector's niece, who was nice enough to allow Chris to be her first. Chris didn't know what to expect, being his first time as well. But it had hurt like a bitch; it felt like Abby had clamped down on his pecker with a sandpaper vise. He didn't think it was supposed to hurt like that and had walked away with some serious road rash. Turned out, it had been even more uncomfortable for Abby, who bit her lip so hard she nearly lobbed it off.

They tried it again, but neither enjoyed it much, nor did they share any real connection. Chris liked that he was finally having sex but couldn't understand why everyone hyped it up so much. It wasn't all that great. After a month of failed attempts, Chris and Abby stopped seeing each other. Neither had taken it all that hard.

Then Diane moved to town, and Chris was knocked off his feet by her big blue eyes and long blonde hair. It was clear she was interested as well and let him steal third base the very first night. Chris noticed the difference right away and knew if Diane felt half as good on his dong as she did on his finger, his life was about to take a wonderful turn.

A week later, they were going at it like drunken rabbits. Chris had been right; Diane felt amazing and fit him like a glove. It had been a mind-numbing experience for both of them, and they proceeded to do it every chance they could. They'd run to his house after school and screw until his parents came home. Sometimes he'd sneak out in the middle of the night and climb the trellis outside her window. Then, with her parents sleeping in the room across the hall, they would attempt to stifle their sighs of desire as they humped each other's brains out. They did it in his car, in her parents' car, at the movies in the balcony, under the bleachers at the school, even in the graveyard.

It got to the point where neither of them thought it made any sense to stay at school during the day, not when they could be fucking. So, they cut class and spent their time in the park, naked and connected at the groin.

The only reason they showed up to school at all was so that they could meet at the front entrance and then walk out the back. It had come as a complete shock to Chris's mom when the principal called, telling her the boy had missed twenty-three days of school, and it was only October. His mother couldn't understand what was going on in her son's head, but his father sure did. He had met Diane and thought if Chris's mother looked like that back in high school, he never would have graduated either.

The principal agreed to give the kid another chance, and Chris promised he would buckle down and graduate. For some reason, Diane had been spared, and the principal hadn't noticed she'd skipped just as many days. It was a bullet she was glad to have missed; however, Diane had missed something else which was far more serious—her period. Diane was pregnant, and neither she nor Chris had fully wrapped their heads around the magnitude of it yet. They were still behaving as if nothing had changed, going at it like minks. Chris noticed once Diane got pregnant, she became hornier than before, which was hard to imagine. And if that was what it was like to have a pregnant girlfriend, then he was all for it. Chris Wyatt was just another guy who let the little head make all the big decisions. He wasn't the first, and he damn sure wouldn't be the last.

He lit another smoke and watched the car pull into the station from the north side of Route 3. Setting his Marlboro on the counter with the ash hanging off the edge, he stepped into the chilly October air and zipped his jacket up to his chin.

"Fill 'er up, regular," the guy said in a huff.

Chris turned on the pump, began filling, and walked back to the window to make small talk.

"Cold out tonight." Weather seemed to be the ultimate icebreaker when you had absolutely nothing to say.

The guy in the cab nodded and looked into the rearview to check the progress of the pump. "Yep, sure is."

"There was a line here during the day. Gas shortage has everyone freaking out. You picked a good time to come."

A horrible shriek pierced the night like an arrow. Chris instinctively turned in the direction from which it had come. The man in the car rolled up his window, almost as if he had been expecting it. Another cry ripped through the darkness and assaulted Chris's ears. He spun around again, completely freaked out by the inhuman noise.

There was movement on the far side of the highway; Chris froze as something broke from the shadows. The man in the car had seen it as well and started his engine. Chris tried to stop him, but it was too late.

"Wait, the pump is still running."

The guy put his foot to the floor and sped out of the station, ripping the hose from the pump. Gas poured freely from the broken nozzle and spread across the pavement in a flood.

There was movement again, this time from behind—something was coming. Chris started to run toward the office and nearly made it two complete steps before it hit him like a tank, spinning him around. Chris fell to the pavement in a lake of gasoline. He tried to get up, but before he could move, it jumped onto his chest and pinned him to the ground. He stared up at the monstrosity; it was straight out of a nightmare.

The face that loomed over him was grotesque and gargantuan, with huge cancer boils covering every inch of its skin. The massive cysts oozed yellow pus that reeked of decay and sickness. The odor invaded Chris's sinus cavity, causing him to gag and retch. One of the great boils erupted, spraying him in the face with a caustic solution that burned his skin like battery acid. Chris screamed through the pain, then the beast opened its mouth. The transfer was quick; it entered him, and the pain was gone. It was quite comfortable—in fact, it fit him like a glove.

● ● ●

Deputy Kovach had been partnered with Ed Koloski, one of the volunteer firemen. Ed was just as surprised as everyone else when the sheriff deputized him, and from what he could tell, the man had overreacted. There hadn't been a single disturbance, and it didn't look like there was going to be. The streets were quiet, which was odd. Usually, there would be at least a few teenagers walking around. After all, it was only a couple days before Halloween; surely, some kids were bound to see how far they could push the limits of mischief. But so far, the night had been uneventful.

The men stopped at Wilson's for a quick cup of coffee. They took them to go and stood in the parking lot talking.

"I grew up in Rochester, and we always called it Mischief Night," Koloski said.

"What?" Deputy Kovach cinched his face into a grimace.

"The night before Halloween. We call it Mischief Night. But in different parts of the country, they call it other names."

"Oh, you mean Goosey Night," Kovach said.

"Exactly, like Goosey Night. I never heard it called that until I moved to Garrett Grove. That's a pretty odd name, don'tcha think? What the hell is a Goosey Night?"

"What the hell is a Mischief Night? That sounds a little soft. Like a buncha fruitcakes running around grabbin' each other's asses."

Koloski laughed. "What do you think Goosey Night sounds like? I've heard it called Devil's Night too. Now that sounds a bit more ominous."

"Mischief Night," Kovach repeated. "That's gotta be the dumbest thing I ever heard. Everyone knows it's Goosey Night."

Both men jumped as the initial sound of the explosion *Ka-Boomed* in the distance and then echoed off the brick wall of the diner behind them. A towering fireball vomited into the air across the highway from where they stood.

"Jesus Christ, that's Frank's Texaco!" Kovach shouted.

"Holy Fuck!" Koloski gasped.

"Get in!" Kovach jumped into the cruiser and grabbed the mic. "This is Deputy Kovach. There's been an explosion at Frank's Texaco on Route 3. I need backup, fire equipment, and paramedics. I repeat, Frank's Texaco on Route 3. The whole place just went up like a torch, over."

"Roger that, Deputy, responders are on the way."

Kovach put the cruiser in drive and raced toward the ball of fire. The flames stretched over a hundred feet into the air, billowing and churning in on themselves as if a bomb had been dropped on Garrett Grove.

The ash on Chris Wyatt's cigarette had gotten so long and heavy, it toppled from the counter, dragging the smoldering butt with it. By then, the endless rush of gasoline streaming from the broken pump found its way into the building and pooled on the office floor. For a second, it looked as if the gas had snuffed the smoldering butt, extinguishing it completely. Then suddenly, the smallest spark came to life, igniting a flame that erupted with a whoosh, sending a river of fire racing back toward the pump. The steady flow of fuel, combined with the massive lake that had already pooled on the pavement, propelled the initial blast several stories into the air. One moment, the October sky was dark and cold; the next, it blazed like the face of the sun and burned like the very bowels of hell.

Chapter 48

Lois thanked Lynn and Janis for dinner and for allowing Troy to stay late. She threw her coat on and was about to leave when the front door opened. The new arrival stepped inside, and Lois found herself face-to-face with one of the most beautiful women she had ever seen. She attempted to speak, but the words stagnated in her throat. Janis and Peanuts rushed forward and greeted the woman, saving Lois the embarrassment of looking like a fool.

"Hi, Mom." Janis hugged her as the dog whined and licked her hand. "This is my friend, Troy, and his mom, Mrs. Fischer."

Lois followed the woman's eyes as they looked her up and down. "I'm Stephanie. It's a pleasure to meet you."

"Call me Lois. It's nice to finally meet you too." Lois shook her hand and sized her up as well. Stephanie Thompson was gorgeous; she was petite and blonde and had the perfect little figure. *No wonder why he's been working late.* Looking at the woman, Lois was surprised Don bothered to come home at all and couldn't blame him. She was beautiful.

"And you must be Troy." Stephanie shook his hand.

"Hello, Dr. Thompson. My dad said you work for the museum."

"I do," she said. "I hear you're quite the explorer yourself. Did Janis show you her arrowheads?"

"Yes, she did." Troy nodded to Janis, then turned back. "What does it look like in the cave? I bet it's cool."

"It's very cool. I've never seen Lenape artifacts in such perfect condition. And we've only just begun to uncover their secrets."

An unbridled look of wonder spread across Troy's face, as if Luke Skywalker himself had just walked through the front door. "Really? What did you find so far?"

"Troy, that's not polite," Lois leaned over and whispered.

"That's all right. I love to talk about my work." Stephanie shrugged her shoulders, and Lynn chimed in.

"It's true, she does. But I warn you, once she gets started, it'll be difficult to get her to stop." Lynn tousled Janis's golden curls. "Like mother, like daughter, right honey?" Janis nodded in agreement.

Stephanie placed her bag down on a stack of boxes that hadn't been unpacked. "Why don't I make a pot of coffee? Then I can tell you anything you want to know about the Lenape tribe and what we found in the cave."

Troy hit Lois with a look she was all too familiar with; unfortunately, he wasn't going to get his way this time.

"We should probably be going, honey. Tomorrow is a school day." Lois had no intention of sending Troy to school tomorrow. All she could think about was getting him home safely and watching over him like a Doberman Pinscher. And the longer she stood there, trying to be polite, the more she was overcome by an urgency to leave the Thompsons' house.

Stephanie seemed to sense her apprehension and stiffened up as if suddenly put on the defensive. Lois prayed no one else could pick up on the tension between them and was now certain that Stephanie was just as uncomfortable as she was.

"Maybe some other time then." Stephanie offered a smile that could have been genuine.

"That would be nice," Lois lied.

"Yeah, like tomorrow night at our house," Troy blurted. "When the girls come over to see the haunted house." Lois wished he had kept his mouth shut, but that wasn't a skill Troy had fully mastered yet. "Remember, Mom, you said we could tomorrow."

She did say that, but Lois had no idea what tomorrow held. Carl had painted a vivid end-of-the-world scenario, and she was prepared to jump ship. But when it came down to the logistics of executing that plan, she found it to be more complicated. There were a million things she needed to take care of before she could just up and leave. And the more she thought about it, the more obstacles got in her way. *Maybe this is what happened to the people of Pompeii.* Lois couldn't help but wonder if the citizens who had seen the smoke lifting from the mountain and felt the earth tremble beneath them had also found a million reasons not to leave.

Not only did she have to think about Troy and herself but she had Alice, Will, and her nephews to worry about as well. And what about her friends? How could she leave them behind without saying anything? How could she run away thinking only of herself and her own family? *That's probably what happened to the people of Pompeii. The ones that were turned into human statues had probably been thinking the same exact thing.* Lois prayed the fear wasn't visible on her face.

"Yes, of course," she told Troy. "Tomorrow will be fine." She was thinking about the eruption of Mount Vesuvius and couldn't imagine what those poor people had been thinking when the top of the mountain exploded.

That's when it happened.

The darkness outside the Thompsons' picture window dissolved into a fiery orange blaze that heated into a burning red a second later. It was followed by a concussive blast that rattled the windowpanes and shook the house. The group watched in horror as a giant fireball rose in the distance. *Vesuvius.* It was all Lois could think of. She waited for the lava to rush in and turn them all into statues. She wondered if archeologists would find them one day and ask, "*Why didn't these people just leave town?*"

● ● ●

Ted sat in a chair next to Dawn's bed while she slept and had just started to nod off when Baxter began to whine and pace the floor. Not wanting to wake the child, he tried to calm the dog by scratching him behind the ears. But Baxter continued to carry on. "What's the matter, boy?" He had taken him out to do his business less than a half-hour ago and doubted if he needed to go so soon.

Still, Baxter continued to whine and began to pant like when Ted first found him in his pen, unattended and thirsty.

He reached for the dog, and Baxter reacted by running under the bed. A second later, the room shook as if a truck had crashed into the wall on the other side of the door. The chair he sat in lifted off the floor, and then he heard it ... an explosion, much louder than a gunshot.

Baxter howled from his position beneath the bed, waking the child, who immediately started crying. She scanned the room, not sure where she was until her eyes fixed on Ted. She stretched her arms out toward him and latched on to him as he picked her up and held her tight against his chest.

Ted poked his head out the door as the lights flickered and went dark. The emergency lighting kicked on a second later, revealing several employees scrambling about like yellow jackets swarming the nest, all of them trying to figure out what the hell had happened. Ted knew that the explosion hadn't occurred on the floor they were on and imagined it had taken place on one of the lower levels.

He could already smell smoke, and a moment later, an authoritative voice barked over the intercom system. *Code Redman, Code Redman, report to the imaging wing.* Ted knew Redman was the code for a fire.

Then the radio on his belt crackled, and a familiar voice shouted through the static. "This is Deputy Kovach. There's been an explosion at Frank's Texaco on Route 3."

What? That doesn't make any sense. Frank's was on the other side of town, and there was no way he could have felt the explosion at the medical center. Listening to the rest of Kovach's transmission, Ted realized there had been a second incident that had happened simultaneously. *That isn't any coincidence.*

He picked up his radio. "This is Deputy Lutchen. There is a fire at the medical center. I repeat, we have a fire at the medical center." His transmission was followed by a long period of silence. Then Andrea's voice broke up as she attempted to verify his call. Apparently, she couldn't believe the coincidence either.

Ted confirmed the information and requested backup as well as the fire department.

Carl and Bob Jones arrived at Chilton just as Deputy Kovach's call came in, immediately followed by Deputy Lutchen's. They looked up just in time to see the dark cloud erupt from the back of the building.

"Jesus Christ," Carl said. "We're too late."

Deputy Kovach and Ed Koloski arrived at the Texaco station to find the place engulfed in flames. The intense heat made it impossible to get anywhere near the front of the station itself, forcing Kovach to run to the back lot and hit one of the shut-off valves. The pumps had already discharged an incredible amount of gasoline onto the property, but the underground tanks had not gone up, and there was no way they could once they were shut off.

As Kovach ran for the switch, Koloski radioed the fire station and informed them what equipment was needed to fight the blaze. The chief was at the medical center, where there had been another incident, which left Koloski in charge at the gas station.

The blaze diminished considerably once the fuel supply was cut off, and the only thing left to do was wait for the trucks to show up and foam the place down. Kovach returned to the cruiser, popped the trunk, and removed two chemical extinguishers. He handed one to Koloski and took one for himself. They did what they could to soak the area near the road, as some of the gas had started to spill over onto Route 3. In the distance, the sound of sirens grew louder as the Garrett Grove Fire Department responded to the call.

Father Kieran lowered the weapon and tucked it into his pocket just as the sprinkler system kicked on. He extended a hand to Burt, who stared back in disbelief. Somehow, he was still alive. The creature had had him by the throat, and Burt had been unable to breathe; the lack of blood to his brain had nearly turned off his light—permanently.

He'd been foolish to mistake his reflexes for that of a younger man. He had pulled the gun and dropped it without firing a single shot. It was Father Kieran who picked it up and ended the damn thing like he was Dirty Harry. The priest had saved Burt's life and killed the creature in a very badass fashion. Burt looked into the man's eyes as Father Kieran helped him to his feet. "I've never seen a priest do anything like that before," he said.

"I'm not your average priest." Kieran smiled.

The creature that had once been Dr. Malcolm lay dead on the floor. Bullet wounds now pierced its skull, allowing a thick, dark trail to seep from them. The black liquid mixed with the water from the sprinklers and ran through the halls like a river of ink. Father Kieran removed what was left of his jacket and threw it over the creature's face.

Burt rushed to where Dr. Ziegler had been thrown. The man's body lay twisted and broken against the wall. His neck had been crushed, and his head hung to the side at a most unnatural angle. Burt bent down and grabbed the man's hand and started to cry. "Jesus Christ," was all he could manage.

"Yes," Father Kieran said. "Jesus Christ, accept this child into your Kingdom. Forgive him of his sins and grant him everlasting life." Then he made the sign of the cross over the body.

"I think he was Jewish, Father," Burt said.

"I don't think he'll mind." Kieran offered the sign of the cross a second time.

Burt let go of Ziegler's hand and blessed himself. "No, I suppose not." He glanced down and noticed the small object that lay beside the doctor's body. He picked it up and studied the black and red ladybug magnet, turning it over in his hand, then grasped it tightly.

There was a commotion of voices from down the hall as two men rushed toward them. Burt looked up to see Carl and the fire chief.

"Burt," Carl yelled. "Oh, thank God. I thought that maybe you ..." Carl looked down at the doctor's body. "Oh God, not Ziegler."

"It got him, Carl. It was Dr. Malcolm; he came back." It was difficult to tell with the sprinklers raining down on them, but Burt was pretty sure that Carl had started to cry as well. Which was something he had never seen his friend do before.

Bob Jones approached the body of Dr. Malcolm and lifted the jacket, exposing the creature's face. "What the fuck is that?" he gasped.

"That's Satan's imp. An abomination of all things Holy," Father Kieran answered as Bob replaced the jacket and stepped backward.

"What happened to it?"

"I put it down. It killed the doctor and almost killed Burt."

Carl grabbed Burt and hugged him. "I'm sorry. I told you I would be right back. Are you all right?"

"Yeah, I guess so, but I wouldn't be if it weren't for Father Kieran here. He saved my life. We weren't in time to save Ziegler. It had him before we got here, dammit!" Burt and Carl stared at each other with the weight of a thousand suns between them. All their fears had been confirmed.

"Gentlemen." Bob stepped in. "I think it would be best if the father and Mr. Lively headed back to the emergency room. Carl, there's probably a lot of injuries, and we should keep moving." Years with the department had given the man a clear head under pressure. Even after seeing the impossible, he could pull it together and focus on the job.

Father Kieran assisted Burt to the emergency room while Carl and Bob headed toward the back of the building. They left the twisted body of Dr. Ethan Ziegler where it had landed, half propped against the wall with the sprinklers raining tears upon it. Burt had been right all along; there really was no dignity in death.

● ● ●

The medical center's fire suppression system extinguished the blaze quickly. And even without the inspector to verify, it was easy to conclude that the explosion occurred in the imaging wing. Several oxygen tanks had been placed in the same room as the MRI machine. Someone had then turned the instrument on and left. Once the machine began its cycle, the magnetic pull of the instrument became so great, it shot the tanks around the room like a couple of pinballs. It probably sucked them right into the chamber. The force would have been significant enough to shatter one or more of the valves, causing the gas to ignite. That was just Bob's theory, which seemed solid.

Carl figured Dr. Malcolm had let himself in through the back door, moved the oxygen tanks into the MRI room, and then started the machine.

There had only been three deaths and none of them caused by the explosion, at least not directly. Debbie Horne, who had made her first trip to the Mountainside Asylum just a few days ago and liked to think she looked like Crystal Gayle, passed away due to injuries she sustained from the car accident. Dr. Malcolm was the second fatality, although he had in fact died a long time ago. Dr. Ethan Ziegler was the third person to perish at Chilton Medical Center on Tuesday, October 27th. The man had saved Carl's life only yesterday, and he had been their best chance of figuring out how to save the town.

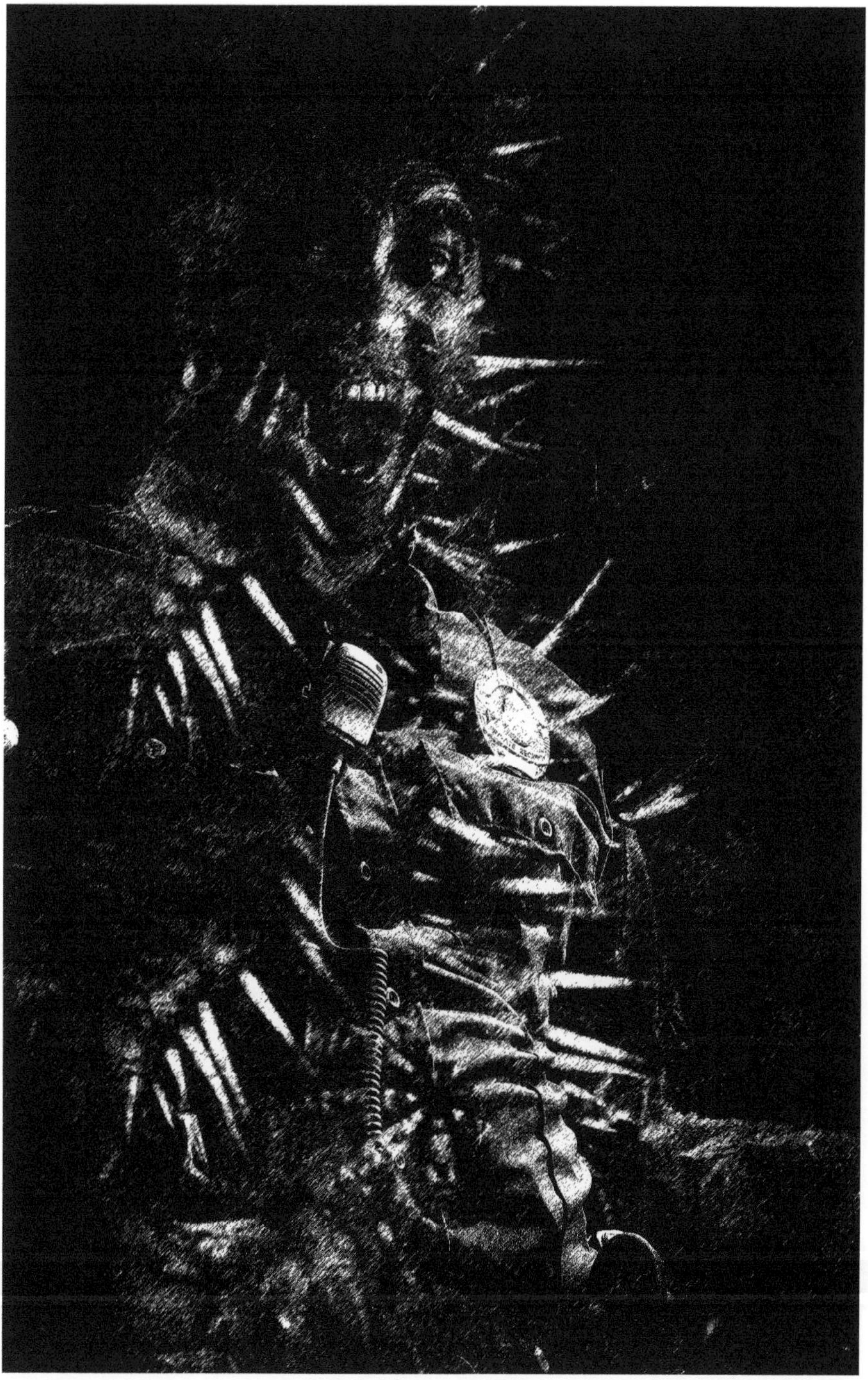

Chapter 49

Don Fischer was on his way home when the Texaco station went up like a Roman candle. He assumed the worst, thinking that a methane pocket had erupted at the quarry. They had run into several of them in the past and managed to avoid catastrophe every time. Still, the threat was always looming. He took his foot off the gas pedal, studied the blaze, and realized the explosion had originated on the south end of town and not at the quarry. He was more than relieved and continued on his way.

He nosed the old Ford into the driveway, noticing Lois's car was missing and the house was dark. Unable to imagine where they might be, he started to worry. It was unheard of for her and Troy to be out past eight o'clock on a school night. *What the hell?* He turned off the ignition, gathered his prints, and stepped out of the truck, expecting to find a note waiting for him on the kitchen table.

A quick rustling of leaves and the snapping of several branches caused Don to start. He spun on his heels toward the shadowed patch of woods along the far side of the driveway. The movement had been furtive and deliberate. He tensed up, holding his breath, half expecting someone to charge from out of the darkness. With his heart blasting cannon fire in his chest and his oiled palms growing slicker by the second, he waited, listening to the stillness of the night. Realizing it had probably been nothing more than a squirrel or a raccoon, he relaxed and exhaled a breath he had held too long. A second later, he found himself bathed in the yellow glow of headlights. Lois's Impala screamed into the driveway, almost hitting him in the process.

Troy bounced out from the backseat. "Hey, Dad, I just met Dr. Thompson. She's really cool."

"You did? That's nice, kiddo." Don struggled to relax, still tense from the sudden scare and nearly being hit by his wife's car. "Why are you guys home so late?" he asked as Lois jumped out of the vehicle and slammed the door.

She double-timed it across the lawn and made a beeline for the porch. "I'll tell you inside. Come on, Troy, get in the house."

"Did you see that?" Don stood for a moment, staring in the direction of the fire. "It looked like something blew up. I wouldn't be surprised if it was the gas station on Route 3."

"We saw it," she said. "Come on, Troy, in the house." She hurried him along.

"What the hell is going on?" He craned his head to the side, confused by her actions. "Are you all right, Lois?"

The snapping of a twig followed by the stirring of leaves caught their attention. Lois focused on the dark patch of woods near the driveway; her face faded to white as if it had been drained.

"Goddammit, Don! I said I would tell you inside. Now both of you get the *fuck* in the house!"

Neither of the Fischer men had ever heard that word come out of Lois's mouth and were bowled over by her outburst. Something had her rattled, and Don sure as hell didn't want to make it any worse. Troy appeared to get the message as well and ran straight across the lawn and into the house. Don followed his son's lead and kept his mouth shut.

● ● ●

Engine One and the ladder truck had been sent to battle the gas fire on Route 3 and were joined by retired Deputies Jenkins and Colbert. The blaze was snuffed out with a blanket of foam, revealing the broken pump as the source of the spillage. The fire had damaged part of the garage but not too severely. Fortunately,

Deputy Kovach hit the shut-off valve in time to save the structure; otherwise, it would have been much worse.

Frank Palumbo, the station's owner, showed up ranting and raving and damn near hysterical. "That damn kid!" he screamed. "When I get my hands on him, I'm gonna kill him."

"I don't think you're going to have to do that, Frank," Kovach said. The deputy stood near the remains of at least two bodies lying on the concrete, covered in foam.

Frank approached the officer, joined by Koloski and several other men. It was difficult to tell what they were looking at until one of the firemen produced a water-dispensing extinguisher and proceeded to wash away the foam.

The cadavers were charred, the remains twisted and warped, but it was obvious there was something else wrong with one of the bodies. The burnt figure had curled into the fetal position, which was horrible enough. But what shocked the men were the features of the corpse's face. Its mouth was stretched to nearly three times the size of an average human's, as if it were made of plastic and had melted. An overcrowded row of jagged teeth resembling the maw of a shark snarled up at the men. And although the fire had rendered the body a cinder, it had not affected the lethal set of choppers in the least; they hadn't even turned black.

"What the fuck is that?" Kovach took a step back.

"Jesus Christ!" Koloski and the rest of the firemen moved in for a closer look.

It was impossible to be certain, but it was a good bet that one of the bodies belonged to Chris Wyatt, the boy who had been working at the time of the fire. No one could identify what the other one might be. It looked almost human—but not enough. The arms were too short to belong to a man, and the legs looked almost canine—back-jointed and powerful. Then there was the mouth and all those horrible teeth. The sheriff had tried to prepare them for what they might encounter tonight but hadn't mentioned anything even remotely like this. They all would have said he was nuts. But for the men who witnessed the discovery at the Texaco station, seeing was believing.

The fire was visible from the second-floor office of the Garrett Gazette, where editor-in-chief Milford Whitley watched the activities from the small window that overlooked Route 3. He'd been working late, as usual, when the pumps exploded less than a block away. Before he could gather his notepad and camera, he was alerted to the sound of someone entering the building through the back door on the basement level. Figuring it was either Ginny Gunderson, the paper's only full-time reporter, or Harry Veal, the staff photographer, Milford wasn't concerned at first. It wasn't every day the Texaco station caught fire, and he imagined both employees would want a piece of the story.

Moments later, the violent sound of destruction rose from the first floor. File cabinets were being turned over; desks were tossed about. From where Milford stood, it sounded as if someone was tearing the place apart. Then he heard it, the grunting snarls of wild animals. Aggressive like dogs, but far more vicious in a deep, guttural tone. Milford grabbed the closest thing he could find to protect himself, his Wilson putter, which he often used to practice when there was little to report. Brandishing it high above his head in his best defensive posture, Milford stood at the top of the staircase, listening to the chaos ensue below. Not wishing to commit himself to confronting the creatures, he remained as still as possible.

He nearly called out but thought better of it. Milford didn't have long to think before the raging destruction drew closer to the foot of the stairs and the creatures revealed themselves. There were two of them, dressed in the tattered clothes they had all but ripped out of. Ginny's dress, the same one she had worn before leaving work yesterday, hung in shreds from her mostly scaled and deformed torso. Large reptilian eyes stared up at Milford, frozen at the top of the stairs. When Ginny screamed, revealing a mouthful of razor-sharp incisors and hooked fangs, Milford soiled himself. A moment later, the second beast howled. Harry's camera still hung around his almost prehistoric-looking neck. It pendulumed to the left and right as he bolted up the stairs at his boss. Ginny joined in the hunt, and the two ripped into Milford, who never got to use his putter again.

No one from the Gazette ever made it to the fire at the Texaco station, and no one covered the explosion at the medical center. In fact, the small-town paper never released another issue.

● ● ●

Although there were only a few deaths at the medical center, there had been a mountain of injuries. Nurse TenHove, who'd been on the floor for over twelve hours, ran from bed to bed triaging patients and shouting orders to the rest of the staff. She was built for this. Some nurses learned how to deal with the pressure over time, others struggled and never got the hang of it, but Doris TenHove was a natural. That was the thing about her generation; they had been bred to survive and were born leaders. Doris was a born leader.

Father Kieran and Burt arrived in the ER soaking wet like most who had come from the back of the building. Doris rushed to Burt and began to examine his neck. "Who tried to choke you, old man?" She turned his head from side to side.

"It's a long story," he said.

She scowled and shook her head. "Well, you'll live, so get to work. You're officially a nurse. Go scrub up and make yourself useful."

"Yes, ma'am," he said with a grin as big as Texas spreading across his face, and headed to the sink to scrub up.

"How can I help?" Father Kieran offered.

"Give these people a friendly face to look at and help anyone who asks. Help the orderlies, help the nurses, whoever needs it." Although she was concentrating on a million things at once, Doris focused in on the job with microscopic precision. "Have you seen Dr. Ziegler?" she asked.

"I'm afraid the doctor didn't make it." Father Kieran lowered his eyes and blessed himself.

Doris pressed her lips and furrowed her brow, but with no time to grieve, the sentiment was quickly pushed aside. "That is a damn shame," she said. "He was a good man."

"Yes. Yes, he was," Kieran agreed.

Carl asked Bob Jones to help him deal with the bodies of Dr. Ziegler and Dr. Malcolm. He offered the chief a condensed version of the events that had transpired since Sunday morning. And although the man raised his eyebrows more than a few times during the sheriff's rundown, he took the news surprisingly well and maintained his composure.

They transferred the bodies into two impersonal-looking black bags, loaded them onto gurneys, and transferred them to the lab's cold storage freezer. After witnessing the resurrection of Abe Gorman, Carl was unsure what to expect from the body of Dr. Ziegler. Using similar leather bindings, he proceeded to tether both men to the gurneys and fastened steel basins over their faces.

The same agonizing thought repeated in Carl's head over and over. If he had arrived only ten minutes sooner, he could have saved Ziegler. At least he would have delivered the gun he had promised the man, which might have made all the difference.

The maintenance department had gone straight to shutting down the damaged parts of the building and resetting the rest of the breakers. A moment later, the main power kicked back on, illuminating the overhead lights that hadn't been damaged in the explosion.

As Carl and Bob stepped out of the freezer, they were met by Deputy Lutchen, who gave them a look of concern. "Is everything all right, Sheriff?" he asked.

"Not exactly, Ted." Carl knew he needed all his men on the same page and that he had made a terrible mistake tonight by holding back information. "I need to show you something."

He led Ted and Bob back into the freezer where the two body bags lay secured to their gurneys. Carl approached the body of Dr. Malcolm, removed the basin, then unzipped the bag, revealing its contents. Ted's reaction was nothing like the chief's. The deputy gasped and backed away from the grotesque deformity. It was obvious his brain couldn't interpret what his eyes were seeing, and it took him almost three full minutes before he could form a sentence. The figure that lay before them looked as if it had been transported from the Stone Age.

"I-I don't—Sheriff. What is that?" he finally asked.

"That's Dr. Malcolm. At least, it used to be. He's been infected by what we think is a bacterial parasite. It turns you into that or something worse."

The men stared at the thing on the table. Even with the bullet holes in the creature's skull and the dark fluid that had flowed from the wounds, it was easy to see the deformities and mutations caused by the infection. The doctor looked as if he had devolved.

"We can't be sure how many people have been infected already, but it's highly contagious, and as far as we know, there's no cure," Carl explained. "If you see anything like this, you need to stay the hell away from it. Shoot it in the head, and then shoot it again."

"Is this what killed the Negal family?" Ted asked.

"Something exactly like this."

Bob Jones had stayed quiet up till now. "Carl?" he finally asked. "How many of these things do you think are out there?"

"If I had to guess, over thirty."

"Sweet Jesus," Bob hissed.

"I'm sure you both have more questions than I have answers. I'm coordinating another meeting. People need to know what's going on. Tomorrow morning at the courthouse. Spread the word. In the meantime, you both need to try and get some rest. I got a feeling we're *all* gonna need it."

Don followed Lois and Troy into the house and closed the door. "You mind telling me what's going on?" he asked.

"Troy, it's late. Go wash up." Lois fixed him with a look to convey it was not a request and that she was in no mood.

Troy lowered his head and proceeded straight to the bathroom.

"What's going on?" Don asked again, entering the kitchen.

"Billy is in the emergency room, and Eric is missing." She stood with her hands on her hips.

"What? What happened?"

"They've been missing since Sunday night. Billy found his way to the rectory, where he collapsed. Father Kieran brought him to Chilton but had no idea who he was. They finally identified him this afternoon." Lois shook as she delivered the news. "Eric is still missing. I was at Alice's when they called."

"Dear God." Don reached out and hugged her. Lois allowed the gesture but refused to reciprocate. "Is Billy all right? Do they have any idea where Eric might be?"

"They think he'll be okay." She struggled to control the tears welling within her. "But he has a fever and is in shock. There's still no word about Eric." She wanted to tell him everything Carl said earlier but held her tongue. Don was practical and analytical; he understood science and facts and didn't possess an ounce of imagination. Especially not about things that sounded like they came out of a *Twilight Zone* episode. "I was picking up Troy from his friend's house and saw the explosion."

"I think it was the Texaco on Route 3. I'll bet one of the pumps caught fire." He rubbed her back. "Honey, I'm sure Eric will turn up, and Billy's a tough kid. They're both going to be fine."

"I hope you're right." She had been thinking about Pompeii when the fire started and was sure it was a sign. She pulled away and looked him in the eyes. "I think we should leave town for a couple weeks." She regretted saying the words as soon as they left her lips.

"What? What are you talking about? We can't leave. I have work, and the school year just started."

"I have a bad feeling. Carl said they still don't know what's wrong with Rob and the other kids. It might be bacterial. Billy's got a fever and has been unconscious since they found him. I just think it might be a good idea." It was as close as she could come to telling him.

"I thought the sheriff said we didn't have to worry about contagion. He said Dr. Malcolm had everything under control. If you want to keep Troy home for a day or two, fine. By then, this flu or whatever it is should be over."

She knew Don wasn't about to listen to anything she had to say, and she wasn't about to waste her breath trying to convince him. *Maybe I'll just keep Troy home from school tomorrow. And maybe while you're at work, I'll pack a couple suitcases and take Troy for a little drive upstate.* But first, she would call Alice. "You're right," she said. "The explosion just has me a little freaked out."

Don stared back at her with his mouth half open. "I get it." He smiled. "It looked like one hell of a fire. Probably looked a lot worse than it really was."

"I need to call Alice." She turned to the phone. "See if she's heard anything."

Lois picked up the receiver, depressed the button several times, and listened. There was no dial tone. She tried it again, but still there was nothing.

"What is it? What's wrong?" Don asked.

"It's dead." The receiver hung slack in her hand.

"Let me see that." He took the phone from her and tried himself. He pressed the button several times, then hung up. "The fire must have knocked out the lines. I'm sure they'll be up and running by morning."

I'm not so sure about that. Now she had no way to call Alice, or anyone else for that matter. *Dear God, I can't even get in touch with Carl.*

After the sun had set and its growing army had rested, it sent them out. The one called Malcolm was instructed to destroy the machine and had taken care of the one called Ziegler. Although Malcolm had been silenced in the process, the old doctor's consciousness continued to speak, revealing the secrets of the town and the people who lived there. Soon, it would have the numbers to terminate those who had hurt it. The one called sheriff, the one called Burt, and the clever one called priest. But first, there was work to do. It released its army and commanded them to hunt.

They crept through the shadows and found their way into the simple ones' homes. They entered through open windows and unlocked doors, making their way into the bedrooms of sleeping children and unsuspecting parents, where they consumed and multiplied. Then it dispatched the ones called Webb and Silva and set them loose on the substation.

After the dust had settled, there were eighteen staff members who sustained injuries due to the explosion in the imaging wing. Burt Lively suffered an acute whiplash, which was nothing compared to what Doris wanted to do to him. Nine people were treated for smoke inhalation, five suffered head injuries, seven received damage to their eardrums, some of whom had suffered multiple injuries. Then there had been Dr. Malcolm and Dr. Ziegler.

By the time the last of the patients were treated, it was late. Burt, who had been given a brace, sat in a chair drinking a ginger ale. Not only was his neck bothering him, but he had inhaled an awful lot of smoke, which made it difficult to swallow.

"What the hell happened back there, old man?" Doris asked, taking a seat next to him.

"You wouldn't believe me if I told ya." He took a hard sip from the can and grimaced.

"Why don't you try. I just might surprise you."

"I'm sure of that." He offered a sheepish grin. "The sheriff's called a meeting tomorrow. Why don't I pick you up in the morning? You can accompany me and hear for yourself."

"I tell you what, Mr. Lively." Doris met his stare. "Why don't *you* accompany *me* tonight. I can make you something to eat and take care of that neck of yours. Who knows ... maybe I can take care of a few other things as well?"

"Nurse TenHove," he gushed. "You do surprise me."

"Wipe that stupid grin off your face before I change my mind. Now grab your coat, old man, and let's go."

Burt listened and followed her orders to the letter.

The head nurse and medical examiner left for the night and headed to her house on Fenwick Avenue. It had been years since Burt had been with a woman, and he was concerned that he might not rise to the occasion. But things worked out just fine, and he had been able to follow one of the golden rules that men his age lived by ... and he didn't waste it.

● ● ●

Alice and Will Tobin sat beside Billy's bed on the second floor, where he had been moved less than an hour before the explosion rocked the building. The lights had gone out for a little while, but the power was quickly restored, and the commotion appeared to subside. Rumors amongst the staff quickly circulated that an oxygen tank had exploded somewhere in the building. But one of the nurses assured them that it sounded worse than it had been, which didn't help ease their minds.

Alice tried to call Lois, but the lines had apparently been damaged in the explosion. That's when the nurse returned to the room carrying two coffees and asked if either of them would like something to eat. Alice was about to tell the girl she wasn't hungry when Billy started to moan. His fever was high, and he had been sweating profusely in his sleep.

She patted her son's face while the nurse checked his pulse. It was steady, but he was still burning up. Billy's eyes shot open and intently focused on them. Then he sat bolt upright and seized his mother by the arm.

"Oh, my God!" the nurse screamed.

The sheriff's station was busier than a fire ant mound. Patrol cars raced in and out of the parking lot, with the entire department pushed to the edge of exhaustion. Most men didn't return till after midnight, when they were informed about the meeting at the courthouse in the morning. There had been two separate instances, both explosions. The sheriff had been expecting some type of trouble, and he had been right.

The extra deputies made all the difference. There was far less damage to property and loss of life than if they'd been understaffed and unprepared. Deputy Rainey and Nick Gomes were the first to return to the station. They were told about the meeting, and both went home to get some well-deserved sleep. Tara, who had been on since early that morning, was relieved by Andrea, who resumed her regular position on the night shift. Kovach and Koloski stayed on duty and took turns napping in the basement, while the retired officers were thanked and sent home.

Carl was hesitant to dismiss them but believed they'd seen the worst of it. Tomorrow was another day, and he needed his deputies well-rested. Even though he already decided it was time to call in the state police. He still wasn't sure what he would tell them but knew he was in over his head and planned to make the call first thing in the morning.

He stepped out the back door of the station and opened the trunk of his cruiser. The bag of weapons containing the gun he intended to deliver to Dr. Ziegler stared up at him from the shadows. He removed the .40 cal. and tucked it into the back of his belt. Looking out across the empty parking lot, a strange sensation overtook him. The night was still and oddly quiet—too quiet. Carl knew he was being watched and scanned the darkness. He listened closely, but there was no movement—nothing at all. Slowly, he walked back into the station and ascended the stairs to his father's old office. He needed to channel the old man and quiet the screaming voice in his gut.

● ● ●

Tara Jefferies felt like she was running on fumes; she had been on duty since six a.m. and was dead on her feet. She pulled into her driveway and sat for a moment behind the wheel, collecting her thoughts. It had been one royally screwed-up day. The phone started ringing the moment she walked in the station, and it hadn't stopped. First, there'd been a report of a disturbance at the Campbell house on Poplar, then one at the Negal residence. Then, on top of that, the Tobin boys had gone missing. Thankfully, Billy had turned up, but poor Eric was still out there somewhere.

There were numerous other reports as well. Finally, the sheriff called the emergency briefing and put everyone on high alert. Good thing he did too, otherwise the fires at the medical center and the gas station would have been a whole lot worse.

Right now, the only thing Tara wanted was a hot bath and to forget this horrible day ever happened. It was more likely she would just pass out the minute she entered her apartment.

She walked to the front door, let herself in, and turned on the light. *God, it feels good to be home.* She climbed the stairs and entered the kitchen. Tara reached for the light switch. Then ... it grabbed her. Cold pressure seized her and dragged her into the kitchen with the force of a wrecking ball. She felt the pop in her teeth as her hand dislocated at the wrist. Blinding pain seared up the entire length of her arm, making it impossible to scream.

Sharp nails sunk into the flesh of her forearm as it yanked her towards him. There was just enough moonlight in the darkened kitchen to make out the distorted features of her assailant. It was Deputy Forsyth ... almost. At least the beast that lumbered before her was wearing his uniform, or what was left of it.

Thorns protruded from the man's chest and torso. The face that sat atop the distorted mass of barbs had changed drastically. More of the sharpened spines appeared to have grown from the deputy's cheeks and forehead. Dark pus ran from his eyes and down his chin as he snarled and opened his mouth. Several rows of pointed teeth erupted from his gums like tombstones from the earth.

"No, Gary!" Tara cried as he pulled her against him. The thorns jutting from his body pierced her like a gourd, impaling her upon him as her breath stopped short. She stared up into his dark, black, horrible eyes.

The thing inside of Gary Forsyth screamed as it took the woman. A thick, oily vapor seeped out of the deputy and forced itself inside her. She felt the presence enter through her mouth and then through her eyes. She resisted it at first but was so tired, and ultimately, she welcomed it. Tara Jefferies closed her eyes, joined the collective, and was gone.

●●●

Father Kieran walked towards the room where he had been directed. The head nurse, who had been nice enough to offer Burt a ride home, told him where he could find Billy Tobin. Kieran made his way to the second floor, toward room 217. He approached the door and heard the woman scream from inside. "Oh my God!"

He immediately reacted and burst through the door. He still carried the coroner's pistol tucked beneath his shirt and believed there might be one bullet left.

The boy held his mother by the arm and pulled her towards him. *He's become one of those things.* Kieran reached for the gun. He wrapped his fingers around the cold steel and prepared himself.

"Look, Father, Billy's awake. It's a miracle." The woman looked up to him and smiled.

Billy slowly turned his head toward him, looking as if he had been run over by a lawnmower. "Hello, Father," his voice barely a whisper. "Thank you for helping me." He pulled his mother close and hugged her.

Kieran eased the weapon back into his waistband. Taking a slow breath, he relaxed and offered a friendly smile. It had been a long day and an even longer night. "It is truly a miracle. You're very welcome, Billy. I'm so glad to see that you're feeling better." Although the gun was empty and wouldn't have helped any, Kieran had been prepared to do whatever he needed and knew that, soon, he would need to again. There were more of those things out there and work to be done—God's work. He had been invited to attend the meeting at the courthouse in the morning and intended to be there.

Billy raised his hand and offered it to him. Kieran shook it. Despite his compromised state, the boy's grip was firm and strong. The child had been close to death yet still possessed the strength of Samson. Kieran knew the child was sent to his door for a reason. He was a soldier, a warrior. He had been sent to do God's work as well.

"Billy, where's Eric, honey? Do you know where your brother is?" Alice's voice wavered close to tears.

"We got separated. Something was wrong with Mick; he started fighting with Eric. I don't know—I can't remember."

"He needs his rest," the nurse said. "Give him a little time. He's been through an awful lot."

Billy laid his head against the pillow, struggling to keep his eyes open.

"I'm sorry, Mom. I can't remember ... Snakes," he said. "I remember snakes," Billy whispered and then passed out.

I bet you do remember snakes. Kieran looked down at him. *The serpent is in the garden, my son.*

"Thank you for all of your help, Father Kieran." Alice grabbed the man and hugged him. "Thank you so much."

"Of course. God bless you and your family," he told them and excused himself. He didn't know if it was safe to go back to the rectory or not, but he felt the presence of the Lord, and that was enough. He drove home, let himself in, and washed the soot from his body. Nothing tried to accost him as he exited his car and entered the rectory. And Father Kieran slept better than he had in the past two nights; he slept as if he had been given a coat of armor. *For thy rod and thy staff comfort me.*

Others had not been as fortunate as Father Kieran. Far more of the Grove's citizens met fates similar to that of Tara Jefferies. They had been ambushed in their homes as the creatures invaded like rapists and murderers, spreading its germ, allowing its consciousness to fester and propagate. It entered like an intravenous drip, filling their mouths and veins, consuming their thoughts, devouring their fears. When the sun rose on Garrett Grove the following morning, there were far fewer human eyes to witness it. Its autumn rays showed through broken windows into empty kitchens, bedrooms, and nursery floors, where dark crimson stains had dried brown throughout the night.

Part Three

Chapter 50

Wednesday

Sheriff Carl Primrose pulled his cruiser into the front lot of the courthouse and did a double take, finding almost every parking spot was filled. News of the meeting had spread faster than even he anticipated. His heart quickened, and he prayed for strength; the bomb he was about to drop would be a difficult pill for most to swallow. However, he had some backup. His deputies and close to a dozen men from the fire department had all witnessed something last night, something that couldn't be explained. Carl was sure the men's stories had already spread like wildfire and was hoping their testimonies would help with what he prepared to do. He figured Burt to be a wild card who might sway the crowd either way depending on how the old man represented himself. Which was fine because this morning, Carl was counting on Father Kieran and figured the validation from the respected priest would carry the most weight. He was hoping so, at least, and drove around to the back of the building and eased the cruiser into his reserved spot.

Yesterday had been the longest day of his life, eclipsing anything that had transpired in Vietnam. Carl had struggled to settle down as he lay in bed reliving the nightmare over and over. But exhaustion proved to be too much, and sleep came regardless. He woke up feeling only slightly better than had he not slept at all. The hot shower and strong coffee helped more than anything else.

Before leaving the house, he tried calling Burt, only to find that the phones were out, which most likely had something to do with the fire at the Texaco station. Severe winters and heavy storms made it a common occurrence in this part of the state, and the Grove's residents had gotten used to losing service several times a year. Carl had dismissed it, figuring he would send one of his men to the relay station once the meeting was over.

Carl sat in his cruiser waiting for either his confidence or his gut to tell him it was time to go inside. He hoped he might make it past the front doors before being bombarded by the deluge of questions but thought it unlikely. Turning off the ignition, he watched as a familiar sedan pulled into the lot and parked a few spots over. Carl couldn't help but stare when Burt Lively exited the vehicle, walked to the passenger side, and opened the door for Doris TenHove. The old man kissed the nurse square on the lips, then proceeded to squeeze her ass with both hands. Doris returned the gesture and pinched Burt's for good measure.

You old son of a bitch! Carl watched the couple with his mouth hung open. He didn't have to be a seasoned lawman to solve this mystery; Burt had finally gotten laid. *Good for you, old man. Good for you.* He waited for Burt and Doris to enter the building, then took a deep breath, collected himself, and followed them inside.

Carl was met by a throng of people, most of whom he knew on a first-name basis. But instead of an ambush incited by an angry mob, he was greeted with smiles and shouts of "Good morning, Sheriff." Word of his quick thinking and rapid deployment of additional recruits had spread, winning him the popular vote. He wondered how long their approval would last once they heard what he was about to say. *Let's see how much you like me in another hour. I'll be lucky if you don't try to hang me.*

He approached Burt, who stood close enough to Nurse TenHove to be standing on her shoes. "Sleep well, Burt?" He exchanged a smirk with his friend, then turned to Doris. "Good morning, Nurse TenHove. You're looking exceptionally chipper today."

Doris blushed and pretended to fix her hair. "Oh, Sheriff. You have no idea." She winked.

THE OJANOX

Carl took Burt's arm and pulled him to the side, noticing the purple bruise on his friend's throat. "How's the neck?"

"Looks worse than it feels." Burt lowered his voice. "Whatever happens, I got your back. If you need my help, just give a nod and I will bail you out."

Carl pictured Burt standing up and telling the crowd how Felix Castillo's body had walked out of the morgue on its own. And that's just how he would break the ice; after that, he would throw in a bunch of medical terminology like, "really weird crap" and "smelled like a turd." Carl figured he could do without the assistance.

"Thanks, Burt. I'll let you know if I find myself in over my head."

There were far more people in attendance than Carl anticipated. From his vantage point at the front of the room, he felt exposed and on display. His hands slicked with sweat and his throat tightened as he called to the spirit of Allen Primrose for guidance. Although his old man never dealt with anything like this, Carl was sure he would have known exactly what to do if he had. He wished he was half the man his father had been. *Shit, at the moment, I would settle for one quarter.*

He stood at the podium, flanked by Deputies Kovach and Rainey on his right, and Andrea Geary and Bob Jones to his left. Burt and Father Kieran sat in the front row next to Nurse TenHove, Ed Koloski, and Nick Gomes. The rest of the attendees consisted of firemen, medical workers, and retired deputies. Scanning the crowd, Carl searched for Tara and Ted but didn't see their faces anywhere. He was about to begin when Jessica Marceau entered the room and took one of the empty seats. From what he could tell, Jessica was the only member from the town council who had shown up. Not even Mayor Gilbert had made it, which was more than unfortunate. This was going to be hard enough, and Carl didn't want to have to do it more than once.

The sound of growing whispers and concerns started to escalate as the crowd grew restless. Carl rapped his knuckles against the solid oak of the podium, casting the room into an immediate hush. He cleared his throat and began to speak; even he was surprised how easily it all came out.

"Good morning and thank you for coming." He started by retelling the story of Felix Castillo and watched as every face in the crowd turned white. However, they continued to listen, and they didn't say a word. There were looks of disbelief, but the crowd appeared to be digesting everything he told them as if they already sensed something terrible was happening in Garrett Grove and had been waiting for someone to confirm it.

Carl explained what Drs. Malcolm and Ziegler discovered when the three children were brought to the medical center and shared the news of their tragic deaths to cries of shock and surprise.

Bob Jones and a dozen other firemen were able to confirm they had also seen the strange creatures, and Deputy Rainey offered his own account of what had happened the night at the morgue. Most everyone in town knew the Campbell, Negal, and Barnes families and were shocked to hear the horrific news. Then Carl spoke about the two explosions and explained how Dr. Malcolm was responsible for the one at the medical center. He told them how the man had been controlled by the same thing that attacked his deputy.

"I intended to contact the state police and alert them of our situation, but as you know, the phones are down. Our police band radios won't reach past the mountain, so I'm sending a deputy into Warren to notify them. We'll check out the lines at the relay station and see if we can get them up and running." Carl looked to Jessica Marceau. "I was hoping the mayor would be here. Have you seen him?"

"I stopped at Mayor Gilbert's house this morning, but there was no answer. He was expecting me. I am a bit concerned."

"Okay." Carl let out a heavy sigh. "We'll check that out as well. I know you all have a lot of questions and are probably thinking I've lost my mind. But I want you to know we are doing everything we can to keep you safe."

"Sheriff." Tim Colbert stood up. "You said Mr. Lively believes there may be a correlation between the children's infections and the foothill's woods. Did you ever complete the search of the area?"

Carl shot a quick glance at Burt in the front row. They hadn't gotten back to investigate the paths at the base of the mountain, but Burt had been certain if they were going to find anything, it would be in those woods. Then all hell broke loose. "We've been spread a bit thin over the past couple of days. But we plan on getting out there today."

"I've seen these creatures near the rectory," Father Kieran said. "I believe they are gathered somewhere on the mountain. Yesterday morning, I witnessed something peculiar. Packs of animals running from the woods, all clearly frightened. Not just the smaller ones but bear and mountain lions as well. Animals that don't typically scare easily were running for their lives." This was met by an eruption of concerned voices.

"I'm sorry, but do you hear yourselves?" Fireman Nick Gomes said. "This is insane, Sheriff. How do you expect us to believe any of it? There were two fires last night, and that was a bad day for Garrett Grove. But that's all it was, just a bad day. I haven't seen any monsters or strange creatures—because there's no such thing!" He sat down after saying his piece, which was enough to spread disbelief and agitate the crowd. The sound of voices struggling to be overheard quickly escalated into an uproar.

Bob Jones watched the crowd unravel thanks to the young fireman. The sheriff had dumped a lot on their plates, which was hard enough to digest. Bob stood up, shot Nick an evil eye, and raised his hands. "Ladies and gentlemen."

The crowd ignored him, their voices growing louder by the second. Bob was usually a soft-spoken man; however, he was big with a deep booming voice and could make sure he was heard when he wanted to be.

"Ladies and gentlemen," he said again, then raised his voice and bellowed at the top of his lungs: "SHUT THE FUCK UP!"

The crowd fell silent and stared at the giant at the front of the room.

"I saw what happened to Dr. Malcolm, and I've been trying to make sense out of it all night. Something changed the doc. It was awful. His entire body was altered. Whatever this infection is, you can best believe it's real and it's no fucking joke. Dr. Malcolm looked like some type of monster, there is no other way to describe it. Now you can sit there and argue that there is no such thing, but if you saw what I did, you wouldn't waste your time. Half of my men saw something just as horrible at the gas station. I don't like it, but I believe every word the sheriff said, and I would suggest you do as well."

The shocked faces stared back at him in silence. No one said a word, except for Nick Gomes, who stood up again.

"All right, that's fine. I didn't sign on for this, but I'll play along. I'd like to volunteer to take the trip to Warren. I can alert the state police, but I want a handwritten letter from you, Sheriff. Because they're not gonna believe one word of this."

"Good idea. Thank you." Carl looked down the line at his deputies. "Does anyone know where Tara is?"

They turned to each other and shook their heads.

"All right, folks. I don't have to emphasize the need to exercise caution. Most of the activity has occurred at night, but that doesn't mean taking unnecessary risks. I will brief my deputies after the meeting, and since Mr. Gomes has agreed to make the trip to Warren, the state police should be here in a few hours—until then, please stay indoors." He met the eyes of the crowd and prayed that his words sank in. It was insane he was even having this conversation, but sanity had taken a backseat when Felix Castillo got off the slab and walked out of the morgue Sunday morning.

"I'll take Koloski and head out to the relay station," Bob Jones said. "We'll see what's going on, whether the problem is up there or if something else got burnt from the fire. In the meantime, we can use the police band and the fire radios to stay in touch. They'll only reach so far but should make do till the phones are up and running."

"Great." Carl was glad Bob had been there. "I guess that's all for now, people. Thank you and stay safe." There was a dizzying number of individual questions, and Carl did his best to answer them all. Then the crowd started to thin, and he was allowed to exit the building. The sun was bright, and from his vantage point, it looked like just another autumn day.

●●●

It had become a ritual for Don Fischer and Dr. Stephanie Thompson to meet at the trailer and enjoy a couple mugs of coffee before the sunrise.

"I don't think your wife likes me very much," Stephanie said.

Don couldn't help but laugh. "Well, I'd say, join the club. But that wouldn't be very nice of me, now would it?" He took a long sip from a mug that said *World's Greatest Geologist*.

Stephanie gave him a look of disapproval. "Oh, come on now, if it were that bad, you wouldn't be married. She seems nice. Maybe a little possessive, that's all. Troy's a real sweetheart. I think Janis may have a bit of a crush on him."

"Really? Did she say so?"

"Not in so many words. But a mother knows these things. I can tell by the way she looks at him and the way they joke around with each other. Seemed obvious to me."

"It's got to be tough moving around so much. What's going to happen when you're finished here?"

"Well, they'll send me where I'm needed. Possibly back to D.C. or who knows where."

Don hadn't noticed her aversion to the question and continued to probe.

"That's got to be hard on Janis. How does she adapt to changing schools so frequently? Has it ever become problematic?"

Stephanie stared into her coffee mug for a minute before answering him. "It's been difficult, of course. As soon as she makes friends, we end up having to move. She's taken it well so far, but I'm worried. Don't get me wrong, she's a resilient kid. Still, it kills me to put her through it. Up until now, I haven't had to worry about the whole boy thing, but she's started to notice them, and I'm pretty sure they've noticed her as well." She wasn't about to tell Don that her ten-year-old daughter had already started to develop breasts. He would figure that out when he met her. Troy had invited the girls to the house, and Don said he would be there to help chaperone.

"It sounds complicated." Don smiled.

"Everything about women is complicated. I don't know if you've noticed."

"Believe me, I've noticed. You seem to forget that I'm married. It's funny, actually. Troy has already come to some conclusions that have taken me years to figure out."

"Oh, and what conclusions might those be?" She tilted her head and met his stare.

"That trying to not look like a complete fool in front of women can be a full-time job. However, he seems to be doing a much better job than his old man."

"You don't come across foolish to me, and I'm a woman. At least I was the last time I checked. Don't be so hard on yourself; you're a brilliant geologist. How did you develop such a complex anyway? So, you didn't end up where you thought you would in life. Who does? I sure as hell didn't. But you got a beautiful son, and your wife is a real cutie too, even if she doesn't like me all that much."

"I don't think it has as much to do with you as it does with me. She's frustrated with the way things turned out and feels disappointed. I'm married to the job and am rarely at home. And when I am there, she's mad at me. She won't say it, but she only married me because I got her pregnant. She was in love with someone else. So, her life didn't turn out the way she was hoping either." He paused for a moment. "Why the hell am I telling you all this? I just met you, for crying out loud."

Stephanie wiped her eyes and swallowed back the giant lump in her throat. "That's some pretty honest shit right there. It's refreshing to hear a man talk like that. I hope Troy grows up to be just like his father. My ex screwed everything under the sun. I never heard an honest word out of the guy's mouth. Maybe your wife didn't get the man she thought she wanted, but she's lucky she got the one she did. You're a good man, Donald Fischer. Don't ever tell yourself otherwise."

For a moment, they stared at each other from across the trailer, allowing nothing but silence to resonate between them. It wasn't an uncomfortable silence. In fact, neither could remember the last time they had felt such a comfortable one.

"What's going on here?" he asked.

"Nothing," she said. "Nothing is going on here at all."

Neither spoke. They sipped coffee and sat in the quiet, enjoying each other's company. Gail was the first to knock on the trailer door and interrupt the moment. It was time to start another day, but they had had the chance to bond and enjoy a small reprieve, however fleeting it might have been.

Lois told Troy she was keeping him home from school, and he went ballistic, pouting that it wasn't fair and throwing in her face how she promised that his friends could come over. "I just want you home today, Troy. There's a lot going on right now, and I would feel better if you were here with me."

"But I have plans with Janis and Wendy, and you already said they could come over. You said so." She *had* said so. What made it worse was she had made that promise in front of Janis's mother and aunt. Lois was still trying to digest what Carl said. She hadn't left town as instructed, and there had been a huge fire. She tried to talk to Don last night, which was also a mistake, and she decided she would leave without him if that's what she had to do. The only thing that mattered was Troy's safety; Don could fend for himself like he always did. But committing herself to leaving proved to be more difficult than she imagined.

There was Alice and her family to think about. Billy was at Chilton, and Eric was still missing. She needed to talk to her sister, but the phones had been out since last night. And if they really were leaving, she still had to pack. It only made sense to keep Troy home from school. She wrestled with the same battle last night, comparing their situation to the citizens of Pompeii. Then the sky ignited. If that wasn't the biggest omen, she didn't know what was.

"I can't believe you're really gonna keep me home from school. This is so unfair." Troy started to cry.

Dammit, Troy, don't do this to me. She looked out the front window to see nothing out of the ordinary in any way. The sun was shining, and the world looked at peace. Then she thought about everything she needed to accomplish. Could she really get it all done with Troy underfoot? She hadn't told him about Billy and Eric and didn't plan to, at least not yet. She couldn't bring him to the medical center, and she still had to speak with Alice. Also, she wanted to talk to Carl and couldn't do that in front of him either. It was a no-win situation, and with a bright morning sun rising in what appeared to be an average autumn sky, Lois Fischer's world looked no different than it had on any other day. Concerns about the gas station fire and Carl's warnings of imminent danger didn't hold the same gravity they had just last night. Lois looked out the window one last time and reached for her purse.

"Fine, Troy! Get your books and let's go before you're late." She prayed it wasn't a decision she would live to regret.

●●●

After leaving the courthouse, Father Kieran returned to the rectory. The woods bordering the property were quiet. He listened to the wind rattle the fallen leaves and the branches of the indifferent oaks and maples. The lonesome howl it created didn't sound any different than it had before the creatures showed up. Almost as if they were no longer there, but Kieran knew better.

At one time in his life, Kieran believed his true calling was to serve beside his brothers in Vietnam. He hadn't been a fighter in the typical sense, but neither was David, and the bible was full of stories of unlikely heroes who prevailed over insurmountable obstacles and adversaries. However, Father Michael had had other plans and sent him to Garrett Grove to lead the parish at Our Lady of the Mountain. Which had been a true gift from the Lord. And now, Father Kieran was finally the priest and the man he knew he could be.

He'd been called upon last night to come to the aid of a member of the flock. Burt Lively had been attacked by one of the creatures from the woods. The coroner dropped his gun when the beast grabbed him by the throat. Kieran didn't have time to think. He saw the gun on the floor, picked it up, and fired.

It was a feeling he hadn't been prepared for. Kieran had never fired a gun in his life, certainly had never killed another living being. But the thing that grabbed Mr. Lively was not one of God's creatures; it was one of Satan's imps. Kieran had silenced its existence.

And it felt good.

Instead of being sent to war, he was chosen to lead the parishioners of Garrett Grove; however, war had found him regardless. He was never meant to serve in battle; his true calling was to lead his parish in the war against evil. He had simply misinterpreted the Lord's original message.

He opened the front doors of the church, dipped his hand into the holy water, and blessed himself. The first Mass of the week was today, Wednesday, at one o'clock, which was typically light in attendance. But with All Saints Day approaching and given the current situation in Garrett Grove, Father Kieran imagined there might be a slightly larger turnout. And he had a special sermon in mind for those who showed up.

After the meeting, Carl addressed his deputies and those newly appointed in the briefing room. Burt and Nurse TenHove were invited to stick around along with Jessica Marceau.

"Okay, this is how it will probably go down. Mr. Gomes is on his way to Warren, and it shouldn't take him much longer than an hour to reach the state police barracks. Backup should be here no later than noon. I imagine they will assume the operation of the department. You will be taking orders directly from them. I am still your sheriff, but it's unlikely I will be in command. I'll be too busy answering questions and caught up in so much red tape and paperwork you probably won't see me till next Christmas. They're gonna have a hard time digesting what's going on here, but the evidence speaks for itself. Once they see what we have to show them, they won't have any choice but to believe." He rubbed his temples, cleared his throat, and continued.

"I want someone to go check on Tara, and I need someone to head over to the mayor's place. I don't think I need to emphasize 'extreme caution' but I'm going to anyway. Burt, I'm hoping you can figure something out at the lab. Now that Dr. Ziegler's gone, you are our best hope. Arrange to have the bodies transported to the morgue as soon as you can."

Then he turned to the others. "Nurse TenHove, I know you're understaffed. Miss Marks and Mr. Santos will accompany you. Also, I want everyone to take a radio before you leave. Check in with dispatch every hour. No exceptions; every hour. I'm going to take Tim and check out the woods behind the Boyle place. I don't know what we're looking for, but I'm pretty sure we'll know it when we see it. Any questions?"

There were a few but nothing Carl couldn't answer. He instructed Andrea to distribute the radios and gave them their assignments. "Remember, once the staties get here, they are in charge. Until then, be careful."

Carl figured that one o'clock was the latest he would be handing over command of the department. Never in his life did he imagine he would be happy to step down.

Chapter 51

Before leaving Garrett Grove, Nick Gomes stopped at Wilson's Diner to grab a quick cup of coffee for the long trek into Warren. He parked next to a green Maverick, the only other vehicle in the empty lot, and made his way to the front entrance. Nick took one step inside the establishment and froze, half in and half out of the doorway. He surveyed the empty diner, not sure what to make of it. The place was deserted; not a soul occupied a single seat. Dick Wilson stood behind the counter, instead of at his usual station at the grill, and offered Nick a defeated roll of the eyes.

"Morning, Dick. Kind of slow, huh?" It was more than just slow; the place looked like a morgue.

"You can say that again; only had a few customers all morning. Mandy and Roger didn't show up for work. I'm guessing folks got freaked out by the fire at the Texaco and are trying to steer clear from this side of town."

Nick doubted if the fire had anything to do with it and thought it more likely that word had already spread about the bullshit Sheriff Primrose was selling. The man had laid it on thick this morning, but Nick still wasn't buying any of it. However, he'd been outnumbered. The sheriff had somehow convinced the entire crowd that the sky was falling. Nick figured it was best to let them chase ghosts while he did something that would actually help. He volunteered to make the trip to the state police barracks in Warren for two reasons. The first was to deliver the letter Sheriff Primrose had given him, and the second was to file a report with a detailed account of what transpired at the morning meeting and the near panic the sheriff had incited. One thing was sure to happen when the staties showed up in Garrett Grove; Sheriff Carl Primrose would promptly be removed from office, and that would be the end of the madman's witch hunt.

"The phones are out," Dick said. "Must have gotten damaged in the fire. Maybe that has something to do with why it's so slow."

"Yeah, probably. Say, could I get a large light and sweet and a bacon, egg, and cheese on a roll?" Nick felt bad after seeing how empty the place was and decided on the sandwich as an afterthought.

"Coming right up." Dick headed to the grill and went to work.

No one entered as Nick waited for his order, and there wasn't much traffic on the road either, which was also bizarre. When his order was up, Nick paid and left Dick a decent tip, then got back on the road.

He sipped the coffee as he pulled onto Route 3 and headed out of town. His stomach grumbled at the aroma of the freshly cooked sandwich. He hadn't had time to eat before the meeting and underestimated how hungry he was. Resting the coffee between his legs, he rummaged through the bag to get at his breakfast, then peeled away the tin foil and tore into it. His tastebuds reacted to the savory bacon that he barely chewed, and Nick swallowed two bites with the diner still visible in his rearview.

With the Gables Bridge fast approaching, Nick set the sandwich down on the passenger's seat and readjusted the cup of coffee between his thighs to better focus on his driving. The two-lane bridge had been built long before Nick's parents were even born, and a simple patch job wasn't going to do the trick; it should have been torn down and replaced years ago. There wasn't a square inch of steel that wasn't covered in rust, and the concrete was in such a state of disrepair it needed repaving every other month. If one were to push their vehicle over twenty-five while traversing the bridge, they would regret it. The blanket of ruts and numerous potholes were known to throw out the alignment of most cars and had snapped more than its share of tie rods.

Nick eased his foot off the accelerator and put both hands on the wheel. He hated driving over the damn bridge, even in the daytime. There were always accidents, since it hadn't been designed for full two-lane passage; neither lane was standard size, which forced vehicles dangerously close to the guardrails and each other as they passed.

Noticing there weren't any vehicles approaching from the other side, he tapped the brakes as the front tires of his Oldsmobile touched the bridge. Nick held his breath; a superstitious ritual he did every time he crossed the river. Sweat slicked his brow, and his pulse quickened; he chanted off the possible sudden approach of an oversized straight job, a nightmare scenario that no one wanted to experience while crossing the Gables Bridge. Fortunately, no vehicles tried to cross as Nick neared the halfway point.

The sensation of scalding heat between his legs caused Nick to jump in his seat and scream. He'd been so focused and tense that he had squeezed the Styrofoam cup, spilling the coffee onto his crotch. Then he dumped even more of it by reacting. The coffee was boiling hot and felt like someone had turned a blowtorch on his nutsack.

"Jesus!" he shouted, grabbing the cup with one hand and the steering wheel in the other. He transferred the coffee to the dashboard and managed to recover. Nick looked up just in time to watch the section of the bridge in front of him disappear.

Concrete and steel erupted in a massive concussion that shook the bridge and his vehicle with it. A thirty-foot section of the structure vaporized before him; the debris rocketed into the air and assaulted his car like machine gun fire. A chasm appeared where the Gables Bridge had once been.

Nick had enough time to hit the brakes, but it wouldn't have mattered if he didn't. The car skidded for almost three seconds, then the front tires went over the edge and were followed by the back ones. The Oldsmobile flipped once in mid-air and crashed into the Lenape River upside down.

He managed to remain conscious, thanks to his fastened seat belt—which was most unfortunate. The frigid water rushed in through the open driver's side window and hit him like a cinder block. He choked on a mouthful of river as the car was swept away with the current. The cab flooded at a rapid pace; still Nick struggled to free himself. But it was too disorienting; he was upside down and the water was arctic cold.

Working at the seatbelt with numb fingers and panic surging through his nervous system, Nick fought to hold his breath. It grew darker as the car sank deeper beneath the surface. His lungs screamed for a single breath of air, just enough to buy him a few more seconds to loosen his harness. Then the world began to blur. He clawed at the seatbelt latch, tearing off several fingernails in his last-ditch scramble for life. Nick screamed again, and a rush of dark water filled his lungs. A second later, the world went black, and everything that Nick Gomes knew ceased to exist.

● ● ●

Bill "Buzzy" Delaney worked for DuCain as the company oiler. It was his job to maintain all the heavy equipment. From the backhoes to the front-end loaders, it was Buzzy's job to ensure that all the machinery remained functional. There were grease joints that needed to be lubed every morning, batteries to be charged, and fluids topped off. Hydraulics were most important and needed to be inspected daily; a broken or dry-rotted hydraulic line could ruin your day, especially if you were the son of a bitch standing under a load when it went. So Buzzy was there every morning, shortly after Don, inspecting and maintaining DuCain's bread and butter.

Don had just finished setting a load of safety gear near the cavern entrance when he heard Buzzy scream. He looked up to see the man running full tilt, ranting like a lunatic.

"Don, Don! They're fucked—they're all fucked!" Buzzy was out of breath by the time he reached him.

"What the hell is going on? What's fucked?" Don asked.

"Someone got into the pen last night and took an axe or something to the hydraulic lines." The pen was the gated-off area where all the heavy equipment was stored overnight. Sometimes kids got into the quarry and thought it a good idea to climb up into the loaders and backhoes. The pen prevented most vandals and usually deterred trespassers.

"What? What the hell are you talking about?" It sounded like he said someone had messed with a machine.

"Someone got into the pen last night. They cut the hydraulic lines, just sliced them to ribbons."

"Christ, what machine did they get? Don't tell me they got the CAT. It's brand new, for Christ's sake." Don felt his stomach lurch as he envisioned a rather heated conversation between him and old man DuCain. *How the hell am I going to explain this?*

"All of them! Every goddamn machine we got; they cut the hydraulic lines on every damn one. And it looks like they fucked with the electrical system on the big dogs."

Don heard a loud pop originate from somewhere deep inside his head, then all he saw was red. He tore off in the direction of the pen with Buzzy trailing behind him. His blood boiled, and he could feel his pulse throb in his temples like his heart had jumped into his throat. He arrived at the pen to find the chain used to lock the gate had been shattered and lay broken on the sand. The carnage was everywhere; hoses and wires littered the ground in a tangled mess of mechanical macaroni. It reminded Don of an episode of the *Twilight Zone* where a gremlin had sat on the wing of an airplane, ripping the guts of the engine apart and tearing the plane to shreds.

Don fought the overpowering urge to vomit. *Jesus Christ, there's no way a couple of kids could have done all of this.* He kicked a massive length of hydraulic line that had been extracted from the front-end loader. The hose hadn't just been cut—it had been ripped apart.

"Oh, for fuck's sake!" Don yelled, inspecting the engine block of the CAT. The oil pan was cracked down the center, allowing a dozen gallons of oil to cover the quarry floor. He ran from the CAT to the dozer to the Komatsu—all their oil pans had been smashed. It was a total loss, and none of the equipment would be operating for a long time. Don felt dizzy and was sure he was about to pass out. He bent over and grabbed his knees, taking in slow, deep breaths.

That's when he heard the explosion. Both he and Buzzy jumped; Don was sure the mountain would rain down on him at any moment.

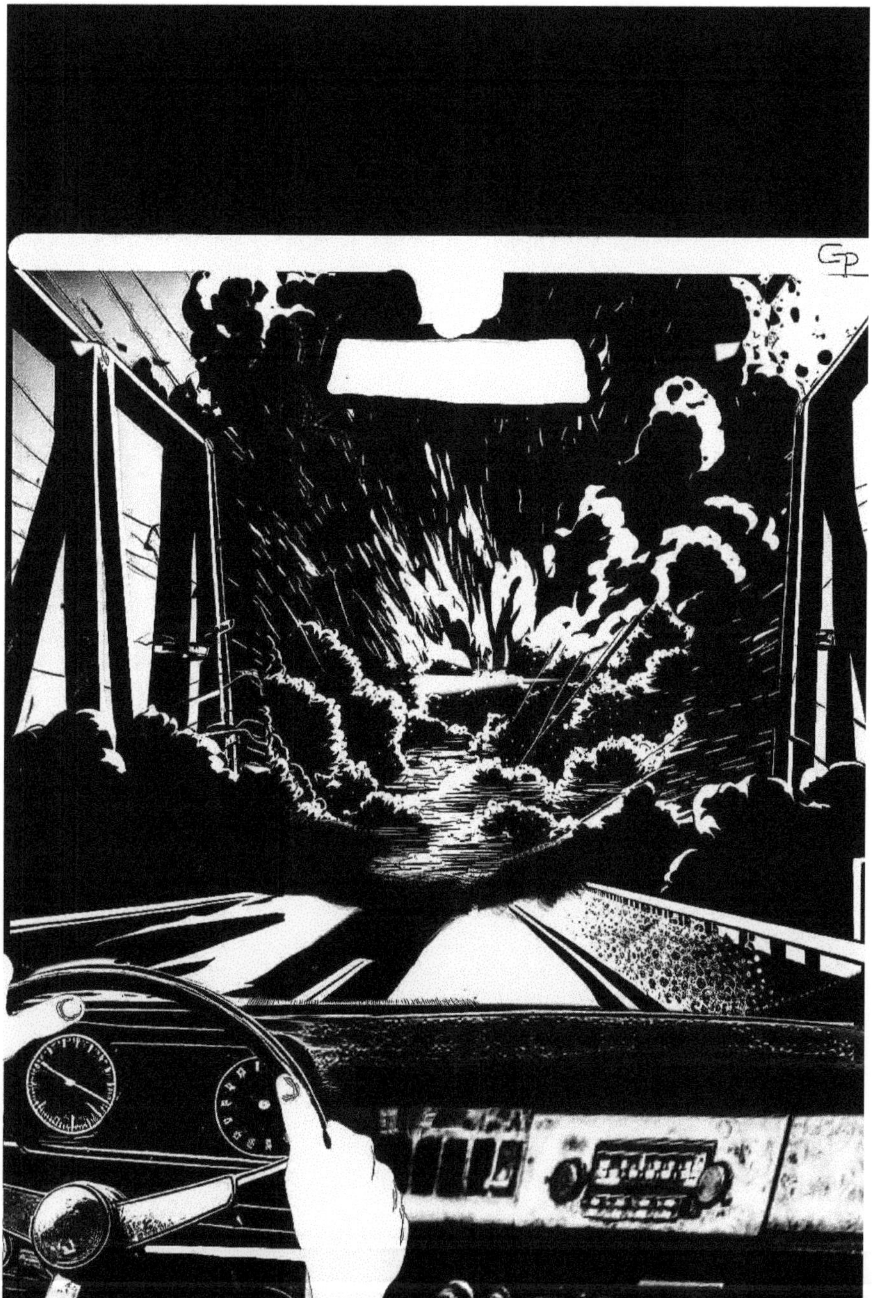

Chapter 52

After having been involved in what he believed to be a vehicular homicide, Jared Neibolt resigned himself to an extended leave of absence from his delivery position for the Fink Bakery. Rick Edwards was given half of Jared's route, and the other half went to Fred Rafer. And although the number of deliveries had been divided equally, their locations had not. Rick had drawn the short straw and been assigned the stops in Garrett Grove, the most remote of the locations. The trek over Garrett Mountain was a treacherous ride to make for only two deliveries. Sunset Road was narrow, with blind corners and a steep incline that corkscrewed like a drunken sailor along the side of the mountain. This inconvenient addition to Rick's route added an extra two hours to his day, which was a royal pain in the ass.

Rick carefully navigated the difficult two-lane road as he approached the peak, the most dangerous part of the Pass over the mountain. The slow bend and the massive outcropping of rock on the left were only half of the problem. The real danger lay on the right, where the shoulder ceased to exist just a foot past the guard rail. From there, it was a three-hundred-foot drop straight down. If any unfortunate soul were to go over the edge, it was unlikely the body would ever be recovered.

The outcropping on the left constantly rained loose granite onto the road. It was bad in October, but during the winter, it was a death trap, and the road was often closed. Rick passed two signs as he navigated the dead man's curve. One said Welcome to Garrett Grove, the other said Danger Falling Rock. "Fuck Garrett Grove," he said as he crossed the town line.

One second, he was chugging along with a white-knuckled grip on the wheel, the next, it felt like the truck had been hit by a train. A thunderous roar came from somewhere above. Rick jumped in his seat as his ears popped from what he was sure had been a detonation. With his nerves screaming and his heart on fire, he struggled to keep both hands on the wheel, knowing the hell he would find if he lost control for even one second. Dust and smoke rained down on him, and the truck was pelted with small rocks and debris. Rick checked his side mirror and watched as thousands of pounds of rock and dirt fell from the mountain and buried the road.

His hands went slick against the wheel, and his stomach cramped. There was nowhere to pull over. Not sure what he should do, Rick continued to make his way into Garrett Grove until he saw a vehicle approaching from the opposite direction. He lowered his window and flagged the car down.

"Hey!" The driver was an old man who looked at Rick as if he were on drugs. "You don't want to go that way. There's been an avalanche or something; it looks like half the mountain came down. The road is blocked."

The man snarled at Rick, then drove off toward the disaster ahead of him.

"Well, fuck you too," Rick said, figuring the old bastard would find out soon enough. He pressed his foot to the gas, leaving the avalanche and the old man behind him, and made his way into town. He would stop at the sheriff's station and tell them what happened. Then he would make the rest of his deliveries and get the hell out of Dodge. *Now I got to drive over the damn Gables Bridge.* Rick hated that bridge almost as much as he hated Sunset Road, but not nearly as much as he hated Garrett Grove.

"Fuck Garrett Grove!" he repeated.

THE OJANOX

● ● ●

Lois and Troy were leaving the house when the first explosion echoed in the distance. They stood on the front steps looking at each other for a moment, then the second blast occurred. It was a bit early to start detonating at the quarry, and Lois was sure she hadn't even heard the warning signal. Usually, there were three short blasts from a whistle that was almost as loud as the explosions themselves. Also, Don had mentioned the discovery of the cave had halted quarry production; she assumed that meant blasting as well.

The other thing that seemed odd was the first detonation sounded as if it came from the opposite side of town. But noise tended to bounce around in the valley, and it was often difficult to pinpoint the exact location of the origin. The second blast, however, definitely sounded like it came from somewhere on the mountain.

"I didn't know Dad was blasting today." Troy looked up at his mother and smiled. He loved hearing the detonations in the distance and was more than a little enamored with the idea that his father blew things up for a living.

"He doesn't tell me anything either, kiddo," Lois said and immediately wished she'd responded differently. The last thing she wanted was to put Troy in the middle of her and Donald's problems. She looked down at him and rubbed his head. "He must have forgotten to mention it. Let's get going before we're late."

"Mom, can I call Rob after school? Maybe he's feeling better and can come over too." The way he looked at her made Lois want to cry right there. How was she ever going to tell him about his friend? She didn't even know where Rob was, and Carl had told her things about the boy and his family that were impossible to digest. Again, she prayed everything would be all right.

"Come on," she said. "Let's go, kiddo."

● ● ●

The communications relay looked as if it had been torn apart by a very intentional saboteur. The wires had been ripped from their terminals, and the housings were smashed. Bob Jones and Ed Koloski gawked at the mess in disbelief. Nothing about the damage could be mistaken for accidental, which clarified a grave implication. They both saw something last night and heard what the sheriff said at the meeting this morning. The damage to the relay station proved that whatever they were dealing with was intelligent.

Bob wondered if Carl understood just how cunning this thing was. If it had wanted to prevent them from being able to call for help, it had certainly done so. The phones would be out of service for a very long time. Bob thanked God that Nick Gomes was on his way to Warren to contact the state police. He had a feeling they were going to need all the help they could get.

"Is this thing intelligent?" Koloski asked.

"It looks that way."

"What the hell are we dealing with, Chief?"

"I haven't got a clue." Bob jumped and covered his head as a massive concussion shook the ground beneath their feet. "What in the name of God?"

Both men pivoted toward the tree line to see the debris cloud rise into the air. From their vantage point just off Route 3, it looked like they were less than a mile from the explosion. Neither knew for certain, but the Gables Bridge was the only structure in that direction. Bob felt ice water run through his veins and settle in his guts. Then it occurred to him: if what they were dealing with was intelligent enough to take out the phone, then wouldn't it also attempt to destroy their only escape routes? Bob ran to the truck with Koloski hot on his heels. He peeled out of the relay station parking lot, spitting up tiny pebbles as he turned onto Route 3. He sped off towards the Gables Bridge.

Lois dropped Troy off in front of the elementary school. He opened the car door, leaned over, and gave her a kiss like he did every morning. But today she hugged him and didn't let go for quite a long time.

"Mom," he whined. "Everyone's gonna see. Stop it."

"Everyone can see me hug my son." She eased her grip and looked him in the eye. "I want you to be careful, okay?"

"Yeah, Mom. Don't worry. I'll see you after school." He pulled away and exited the car.

"Troy," she yelled after him. "I love you."

"I love you too, Mom." He slammed the door, ran up the sidewalk, and entered the building.

Troy walked down the same hallway he had walked with his mother on his first day of school. He looked at the door to the kindergarten classroom. It had appeared gigantic and terrifying, but he had been so small back then. Now he was in fourth grade and there was nothing scary about it at all. He even had a girlfriend.

He approached the door to the kindergarten class, feeling older and important, and peered through the window. There was no one inside yet.

Even the classroom looked smaller. That had been a strange first day. The children had gone insane when their moms left. Troy thought he probably would have gone nuts too if it hadn't been for Rob Boyle. The boy had remained calm and mature while the rest of the children lost it.

Troy knew his mom was hiding something about Rob. Every time he mentioned his friend's name, she acted strange. *Maybe Rob is still sick and won't be able to come out on Halloween. Maybe that's why she's acting so strange.*

"What are you looking at?"

Troy jumped at the sound of Wendy's voice; he'd been staring into the window of the kindergarten classroom, lost in his daydream.

"Oh, I was just thinking about my first day of school." He checked the hallway to see if anyone was coming, then leaned in and kissed her on the lips. Wendy's eyes flew open wide in reaction to his sudden burst of confidence, but she didn't resist.

"Wow, what's got into you?"

He felt a little embarrassed but not enough. "I don't know. I thought I was supposed to kiss my girlfriend hello."

Wendy blushed; a sheepish grin spread across her face. "Oh, okay."

They walked down the hall and turned the corner to enter the fourth-grade classroom. Troy opened the door for her, and they both stopped short.

Almost half of the class was missing. Troy scanned the rows, taking note of who was there and who was not. Despite nearly every other chair being empty, Troy was happy to see Janis had made it to school. The girl's face beamed the moment he and Wendy entered the class, and she immediately waved them over to her desk.

"I brought some money so we could stop at the toy store on the way home." She pulled out a ten-dollar bill. Troy had never even held one before and had no idea his new friend was so rich.

"Where did you get all of that money?" He stared as she held the bill up for them to see.

"Do you think it's enough to get some magnets and wrist rockets?" she asked.

"Are you kidding?" Wendy said. "You could buy half the store with all that money. Put that back in your pocket before you lose it."

Janis crammed the bill into her jeans as if it were nothing more than a bubble gum wrapper.

"It's only ten bucks," she told them. "My dad sends me money all the time. Do you think we can get what we need on the way to Troy's house? Is there a toy store close by?"

"Yeah, Marco's Playmart is on the way. We can stop there and get what we need, then you can see the haunted house." Troy heard the door to the classroom open behind him. He turned around to see Miss Boriello, his old kindergarten teacher.

"Miss Boriello, what are you doing here?" he asked.

"It's nice to see you too, Troy." She smiled, then spoke up so the entire class could hear. "Miss Walsh won't be in today, so I am going to be your teacher. I hope that's all right with everyone." They had all had Miss Boriello for kindergarten and loved her. The only students who didn't know her were Janis, Wendy, and Yvonne Munoz, who had all moved to town later.

"Do you know how to teach fourth grade, Miss Boriello?" Troy asked, and Wendy punched him in the arm.

Miss Boriello smiled. "Well, if I have any problems, maybe you could help me out, okay?"

Troy liked the idea of that. It made him feel important, mature in yet another way. "Sure, no problem."

The children took their seats and waited for Miss Boriello to begin. Troy looked around again, alarmed by just how many of his classmates were absent. There were twenty-five students in the class, but today, only twelve had shown up. Troy didn't know how to figure out percentages, but he knew it wasn't good. He raised his eyes to Wendy, who had to be thinking the same thing. That this was a lot worse than a simple case of the flu.

Miss Boriello began taking attendance. She called out name after name and waited for a reply of "here" or "present," but most of her calls went unanswered. The teacher furrowed her brow as she scanned the class. It was obvious to Troy she was concerned by the number of absentees as well; still, she smiled and continued.

Janis poked him in the back and leaned close to whisper. "Where is everyone?" she asked. "You don't think we're too late, do you?"

Troy thought maybe. He had seen those things in the graveyard, and so far, the only people who believed him were Wendy and Janis. The deputy didn't listen to him and neither did his mother or father. That was the problem with being a kid; nobody listened, even when you were right. *This is bad.* Not only was half the class out sick but so was Miss Walsh. Troy wondered just how many people in town were home sick today. More so, he wondered how many people in Garrett Grove weren't even home at all.

●●●

Deputy Rainey was about to pull out of the municipal building parking lot when the Fink Bakery truck came to a screeching halt next to his cruiser. He'd heard the explosions and thought it odd that there'd been no warning signal from the quarry. He was about to take a trip up there to see who forgot to sound the alarm when the driver of the truck rolled down his window and yelled:

"Oh, Jesus Christ. It's a real fucking mess. You got to get up there before someone gets killed."

"Easy!" Deputy Rainey yelled back. "What the hell are you talking about?"

"There's been an avalanche on Sunset Road. I swear to God it looks like half the damn mountain came down."

"What? When was this?"

"About fifteen minutes ago. It happened right behind me. If I'd been just a few minutes later, I'd be dead right now. God, it's a mess."

Rainey turned on the cherries and picked up the radio. "This is Deputy Rainey en route to Sunset Road. There's been a report of an avalanche at the top of the Pass." He took off in the direction of the high school; from there, it was two miles up Sunset Road to the top of the Pass.

"This is Primrose. I'm on my way. ETA ten minutes."

"Roger that, Sheriff," the deputy said as he pulled out onto the turnpike and sped off.

"Sheriff, this is Andrea, do you want more backup? I could get Deputy Kovach to meet you both up there."

"Negative. I'll be in contact as soon as we have a look."

"10-4, Sheriff." Andrea's voice broke up as she signed off.

Chapter 53

Deputy Kovach had just pulled up to Tara's house and was about to report to Rainey's call when he heard the sheriff's transmission. *What the hell is that all about? An avalanche? That has to be a phony report.* Sure, Sunset Road was dangerous, and some loose rock fell from time to time, but there'd never been anything like an avalanche. He exited the cruiser, walked up the stone path to Tara's front porch, and stopped. The door had been left open. He unholstered his weapon and grabbed his handheld radio.

"This is Deputy Kovach. I'm at Tara's place. Someone left the door open, and she may need assistance."

"Kovach, this is the sheriff; I'm dispatching Deputy Colbert to your position. Do not enter the house until backup arrives. I repeat, do not enter the house until backup arrives."

"Copy, Sheriff." Kovach had no intention of disobeying the man and stood outside Tara's door, looking into the house. He peered in through the cracked open door and noticed there were footprints; something that resembled tar had been tracked throughout the house. The footprints led out the front door and continued along the walkway. *Whoever made these has already left.*

Kovach could hear the sirens in the distance and knew Colbert was on his way, but a gnawing sensation continued to eat at him. *Something's wrong; I can feel it.*

As much as he didn't want to break protocol, Tara was a fellow deputy, not to mention a friend. Despite every rule he knew about waiting for backup and years of always doing the job exactly by the book, Deputy Kovach pushed the front door inward and entered the house.

"Deputy Jeffries!" he shouted. "Tara, it's Joel. Are you all right?" His call was answered with silence; the house was still.

Joel Kovach climbed the steps, following the dark footprints with his gun drawn. "Tara, are you there?" There was dead quiet. He turned the corner at the top of the stairs and entered the kitchen to find the floor covered in the same black fluid. Someone had walked through the mess, then left out the front door. It resembled tar or possibly oil. Then Kovach noticed a second set of prints, the owner of which had walked around the kitchen in circles, then exited to somewhere in the back of the house.

He followed the tracks down a hallway to where they ended at a closed door. The prints staining the carpet were smaller than the other set, and Kovach was almost positive they belonged to Tara. *Sweet Jesus*. He was certain something had happened to her. Kovach could hear the fast-approaching sirens and decided to proceed—he had already broken protocol. If Tara was injured and needed medical assistance, there wasn't any time to spare. He held his breath, turned the knob, and let the door swing inward—the room was empty. Black footprints led across the carpet to the bed sitting in the center of the room. There, they scuffed and smeared and disappeared; it looked as if Tara had walked into the room and crept underneath the bed.

"Tara, are you in here?" The only sound Kovach heard was the beating of his own heart, fast and loud inside his temples. He forced himself to suppress his jangled nerves and proceeded toward the bed. It reminded him of the scene at the Negal house, where he had lifted the mattress and found the little girl hiding underneath. A sense of déjà-vu washed over him.

Tara's bed was much bigger than Dawn Negal's, and there was no way he could overturn it. He knelt on one knee, removed the mag-light from his belt, and clicked it on. With his gun in one hand and the light in the other, he lifted the duvet and cast the beam into the darkness.

There was a flurry of motion, then white-hot pain. He screamed as it ripped into his soft flesh. It felt like he had stuck his arm inside a furnace; the sensation of a million fire ants tearing into his skin simultaneously set every nerve in his body screaming. Kovach buckled under the gargantuan pain. *Jesus Christ!* The single thought raced through his mind as he struggled to free himself. Finally, it released him. The deputy fell back and crashed into the dresser with his arm spouting a river of red. He looked down at the massive bite that had been taken out of him; his skin and muscle had been extracted. A heavy flow of arterial fluid pulsed in time to the beat of his frantic heart. Kovach's vision blurred, and pain flooded his entire world.

There was a deep gurgling sound as something emerged from under the bed. It clawed its way from out of the shadows and lifted its head. Insanity tipped Kovach over the edge. A maniacal laugh escaped his lips. The creature that lumbered before him was Tara Jeffries—only it wasn't Tara anymore. She still wore her uniform and still possessed distinct facial features, but that's where the similarities ended. Her body had grown; her muscles had doubled in size and ripped through the fabric of her clothing. She had been waiting for him, hiding under the bed.

Kovach tried to focus on a single rational thought but could only focus on the blinding pain. The room heaved and spun off its axis, making it impossible to see straight. He tried to raise his gun, attempted to aim his weapon, but was too dizzy and there was so much blood. It covered the floor and shot onto the bedspread in arcing spasms.

Tara crawled through the carnage and grabbed Kovach by the leg. Her skin was mottled and grey like a cadaver left in the hot sun. Puncture wounds covered her face and body, and dark tar ran from every wound; it oozed from her eyes and mouth as well.

The Tara-creature hissed as Kovach raised his gun and pulled the trigger. The bullet entered her shoulder. With the speed and accuracy of a jaguar, she lunged at him and tore into his belly with her bare hands. Tara buried her face into the deputy's guts and started to feed on him. Kovach tried to scream but only managed a weak gargle. He choked on his own blood and bile as the woman ripped him apart. He had disobeyed the sheriff and broken protocol; it was the last mistake he ever made.

●●●

Bob Jones and Ed Koloski stood on the Grove side of the Lenape River; neither had words to describe what lay before them. The Gables Bridge had been destroyed. Twisted metal dangled over the edge on either side, half submerged by the raging current. The structure had been old, the steel and concrete both brittle from age and decomposition, and the bridge had disintegrated as if it had been made of sand.

Both men had spent years working for the fire department and were familiar with the sound of an explosion. Even though the bridge was old, there had been plenty of life left in it. It hadn't collapsed on its own, it had been destroyed, but the question was by who, or more accurately … by what?

Koloski turned to the chief. "This is bad; someone did this on purpose."

Bob didn't know how to respond. It was worse than bad; Garrett Grove was in deep shit. He prayed that Nick Gomes had made it out of town before the bridge had been destroyed. What worried Bob even more was that while he and Koloski were en route to the bridge, he could have sworn he had heard a second explosion. He hoped he was mistaken.

●●●

It looked as if half of the mountain had come down. Carl got out of his cruiser and stared at the debris. Giant boulders had fallen from the cliff face and destroyed the road. They not only blocked the passage but had hit the pavement with such force, the blacktop had buckled from the impact. Carl imagined it would take at least a week to clear the mess, even with a bucket loader on each side.

He looked up at the area where the rocks had come dislodged. *This was no accident. No way.* Someone had set off a charge. By the sound of it, there had been two separate detonations used to take down the cliff wall. One thing was certain; no one was getting out of town this way.

Carl knew he was in over his head. Whatever they were dealing with was smart enough to send Dr. Malcolm to destroy the MRI machine and now showed a tactical initiative by cutting off one of the town's only means of escape. *Damn!*

THE OJANOX

The bridge? The realization resonated in his head like a bassoon. They had all heard two blasts; there had been a second detonation that hadn't come from the direction of the mountain. *Jesus Christ, not the bridge!*

Carl ran to the cruiser and opened the door; the radio crackled with static.

"Sheriff, come in, Sheriff."

"Go ahead." His gut churned sour.

"Sheriff, it's Bob Jones." Carl braced himself but knew it was futile. "Sheriff, the Gables Bridge has been destroyed. It looks like someone may have set charges underneath it. There's nothing left." Carl stared at the pile of dump-truck size boulders blocking Sunset Road. There was no way out of town.

Deputy Rainey pulled up behind the sheriff's cruiser with his lights flashing. Carl was sure the young officer had been listening to the transmission and waved him over just as Bob started speaking again.

"Someone sabotaged the communications relay as well. The phones won't be working any time soon."

Carl depressed the button and spoke into the mic. "Did Nick Gomes make it out of town before the bridge was destroyed?" He waited for a reply.

"I think so." Carl let out a sigh of relief. If Nick had made it out of town, then the state police would find their way into Garrett Grove one way or another. "Sheriff, I could have sworn I heard a second detonation. Any idea what that was?"

Carl had already kept information from his people, and Dr. Ziegler had paid the price because of it; he wasn't about to do it again. They had a right to know just how bad things were. "Someone set charges to the rock face above Sunset Road. The Pass is blocked; there's no way in or out of Garrett Grove." Carl could only imagine what was going through the minds of every deputy and dispatcher listening to the transmission. He had expected the state police to be stepping in and taking control of the situation sometime this morning; it looked like it was going to take much longer than that.

"Bob, are your men armed?"

"No, we turned in our weapons last night."

"I want you to return to the station and get them." He cleared his throat and nodded to Rainey. "This is Sheriff Primrose. I want *all* deputies and dispatchers to carry loaded sidearms at all times. I also want every member of the fire department issued a weapon. Andrea, coordinate with Chief Jones the distribution of guns to his men. Do you copy?"

"Copy that, Sheriff." Andrea's voice sounded shaken. Carl knew she had monitored the entire transmission and understood the gravity of the situation. The people of Garrett Grove were on their own until help arrived ... if it ever did.

After attending the morning meeting, Burt Lively drove Doris TenHove to the medical center, where she had left her car the night before. He pulled into the employee's parking area and hit the brakes. The emptiness of the lot was glaring, with less than half the number of vehicles occupying their usual spots.

"Oh dear. Not again," Doris gasped. Yesterday, the place had been plagued with a rash of absenteeism, and if the state of the parking lot was any indication of what today held, they were in big trouble.

"This isn't good," Burt said. "I can't even stick around and help."

"It's okay," she said, grabbing her purse from the front seat. "I'll figure something out; I always do. But once Michelle and Joe finish dropping the bodies off, please send them back. I'm going to need them."

"I will, and if I get done early, I'll come right over." Burt put his hand on Doris's thigh and slid it up her skirt to within an inch of the goods. She placed her hand on top of his and stopped him, but not before allowing him to graze his target.

"Mind yourself, old man. I think we both know what this means," she said, referring to the empty parking lot. "Be careful, and don't do anything stupid ... Nothing more than usual, that is." She leaned over, kissed him firm on the lips, then slapped him across the face.

"I'll try to swing by around noon, if I can."

Doris exited the vehicle and walked to the employees' entrance. Burt focused on her backside the entire time.

The emergency room was empty except for Dr. Freedman, Nurse Burnes, and one candy striper—Doris wasn't sure but thought the girl's name might be Cindy.

None of the beds were occupied, as last night's patients had all been discharged or admitted to the second floor. There had been no new emergency room patients, which was also strange; Doris figured there should have been at least one.

"Oh my. Where is everyone?" She had a feeling she didn't want to know the answer.

Doris walked to the front desk and picked up the phone. The internal lines were working, but there was still no way to call outside. *Doesn't hurt to try.* Only twelve hours ago, the center had looked like a MASH unit. There had been a heavy influx of injuries from the explosion in the imaging wing, and they'd been terribly short-staffed. Firemen, deputies, and paramedics had flooded the emergency room and bailed them out of what could have been a far greater disaster. Doris doubted the center could handle anything even remotely serious happening right now. She scanned the empty waiting area. *God help us.*

Dr. Freedman approached the desk with a cup of coffee in his hand.

"Nurse TenHove. Do you have any idea what's going on?" The man looked lost, as if he were waiting for someone to tell him what to do. He had no clue what was happening, and Doris thought it was probably better that way. She doubted if he would be able to handle it.

"I really couldn't say, Doctor," she replied. "I hear there's a flu bug going around."

●●●

Carl and Deputy Rainey set up barricades and Road Closed signs at the base of Sunset Road, two miles below the rockslide. There wasn't much more they could do. The detour sat at almost the exact spot where Felix Castillo had been hit by the bread truck. Carl looked over to the ditch where the man's body had landed, wishing he could go back to Sunday morning and do things over. Not that it would have made much difference.

The disappearance of the children and Dr. Malcolm was nothing he could have predicted or done anything about. But the Felix Castillo fiasco weighed heavy on his shoulders; it hadn't been all Burt's fault. They had the chance to nip it in the bud Sunday night, but Carl decided to bury the evidence and hide the fact they had lost the body. He and Burt had gone back to the morgue and gotten drunk when they should have continued searching the foothills. It could have made all the difference ... and that was on him.

Things were bad—really bad. The bridge was out, and so was the Sunset Pass. The phone lines had been destroyed, and the radios only reached so far. The damn mountain interfered with the signals, making sure no communications left the Grove. The Lenape called it Lonesome Mountain, and Carl thought they had nailed it with that one.

How many people have already been compromised? Which led him to the next question: *How many of those things are out there?* It was something he didn't want to think about, but he *had* to.

He needed answers fast, and with Dr. Ziegler gone, he was counting on Burt to figure something out. If there were as many of those things as he thought, they were going to need a plan.

Maybe there's a chance we could clear the road. If the guys at the quarry can get a bulldozer up here, they might be able to move some of the larger stones out of the way. Carl figured if he could still get people out of town, that would solve most of his problems.

He picked up his radio. "Sheriff Primrose to Deputy Kovach; come in, Deputy Kovach." He was met with silence. "Sheriff Primrose to Deputy Colbert." Tim didn't answer either. Carl's head started to throb again. "Andrea, this is Carl. Has Kovach or Colbert returned to base or contacted you yet?"

"Negative, Sheriff. I haven't heard from either one. They're still checking in on Tara."

"Deputy Rainy and I are en route to Tara's house. I want you to send Deputy Jenkins to the quarry. See if they can spare a front-end loader or a bulldozer and get it up to this mess on Sunset. Tell them Sheriff's orders."

"10-4, Sheriff." Andrea signed off.

Chapter 54

Deputy Colbert arrived at Tara's house to backup Deputy Kovach but was too late to do the man any good. He found the front door open, and when he called into the house, there was no answer. He followed the dark footprints up the stairs and into the kitchen, just as Kovach had. The same dark substance had been tracked all over the linoleum floor. It looked like motor oil that hadn't been changed in far too long. The goop had dried but not before someone had walked through it in circles, as if in a drunken stupor. The smaller of the two sets of prints led into the hallway and then to one of the bedrooms.

Colbert heard a faint noise coming from the room at the end of the hall. It almost sounded like something sloshing around, something wet. He unholstered his weapon and made his way in the direction of the strange noise. The closer he got to the bedroom, the louder it grew and the more pronounced it became—now he was sure it was a slurping sound. *What the hell is that?* He slowly approached the room.

The retired deputy poked his head through the doorway and froze, his mind unable to comprehend the scene spread out before him. The ocean of crimson and the haphazard arrangement of discarded organs sent Colbert's defenses into overdrive. Tara Jefferies had her face buried in Deputy Kovach's guts. She dug into the man's belly like one of those dead things in the movies. *She's fucking eating him like a zombie.* The woman was so intent on her meal that she hadn't noticed him standing in the doorway. She reached deep into Kovach's belly and pulled out a long strand of the man's intestines.

Kovach was dead—his face was stark white, and his uniform was saturated in blood. He still held his gun in one hand and flashlight in the other, and lay with his back against the dresser while the thing that had once been his coworker feasted on his insides.

Dear God, Sheriff Primrose was right. Colbert had listened to the man but hadn't quite believed him. Some of it—but not the part about the dead guy walking around killing people. But now ... *Jesus Christ! Carl was right.*

Colbert had retired over three years ago, but he still went to the range twice a week. "Hey!" he shouted into the room. The thing that had once been Tara Jefferies lifted her head and hissed at him. Colbert watched a piece of Kovach's intestine fall from the woman's mouth like a yo-yo bobbing at the end of a string. It stretched from its own weight and swung for a moment before coming loose and splatting onto the floor.

Tara opened her mouth and screamed; the noise penetrated Colbert's skull like a bullet. He didn't have time to think as the creature sprang to its feet and came at him. But having been trained by Allen Primrose, he didn't need to think and just reacted. He raised his weapon and fired. The bullet hit Tara in the front of her skull, peeling back the top inch of her hair and the bone beneath it. She looked at the deputy as if in shock, with eyes the color of midnight. He fired a second round, which hit its mark one inch below the first. Tara stopped moving and fell face first onto the floor. The same dark fluid oozed from her wounds like an overturned bottle of soy sauce. Deputy Colbert swallowed hard and thought he might be able to control the urge, then every muscle in his body contracted, and he vomited onto Tara's bedroom carpet. Wiping his chin, he ran out the front door, glad to be in the open air.

Jesus Christ, Carl. You were right.

●●●

Four corpses lay strapped to the freezer shelves in the morgue, all of which had stainless steel pans covering their faces. Burt hated to treat the body of Dr. Ziegler in such a way but believed the man would have understood. He wasn't about to take chances either way. *If it bothers you, Zig, you can let me know next time I see ya.* The way things were looking, Burt thought that might be sooner than later.

From his initial examination of the bodies, it looked as if two had been infected with the toxin and two had not. It was obvious in the case of Dr. Malcolm and the thing found at the Texaco fire. But Dr. Ziegler and the body of the gas station attendant appeared to be fine. If the attendant had been exposed, Burt was guessing the extreme heat from the blast had fried the man's brains to a cinder, incinerating the infection in the process.

To play it safe, Burt took tissue samples from all the cadavers and examined them under the microscope. The two from the fire had been seriously damaged, and he needed to cut deep into the flesh to extract the samples. And as suspected, he found signs of the infection in both Dr. Malcolm and the creature from the fire, but it was also present in the attendant as well. The only body that was clean was Dr. Ziegler's.

Burt removed the stainless steel basin from Ziegler's head. The man's throat and spinal cord had been crushed. His injuries were extensive and indicative of an aggressive attack. Which struck Burt as counterproductive. Infections didn't get stronger by killing their hosts. But this had been different; this had been a premeditated attack and carried out in a fit of rage.

"Looks like you pissed it off, Doc," Burt whispered. Ziegler had stopped Rainey from killing the sheriff and been operating the MRI machine that killed Abe Gorman.

Before Abe died, something had been extracted from his body. It appeared to be some type of gas or vapor and looked an awful lot like smoke. *Was that the physical presence of the infection itself?* It wasn't the most unbelievable thing he had seen this week.

Burt continued to examine the samples from the other bodies, comparing them to the ones taken from Castillo and Abe. In all cases, the infection appeared to have died along with the hosts.

His mind wandered to thoughts of Doris and their night together. Doris had been a very receptive lover; a childish grin found its way onto Burt's face as he relived the evening. He had taken a shower, and Doris had given him a fresh set of clothes belonging to her late husband. After being saturated in smoke, the hot water and new set of duds made Burt feel like a new man. And Doris had done a bit more afterwards to make him feel even better. At some point in the evening, he had transferred his belongings from his old coat into the new one and tossed it in the trash without realizing he no longer had Carl's gun.

Burt refocused the microscope, examining the tissue sample taken from Dr. Malcolm. Something about the cellular structure of the bacterium had struck him as familiar when he first inspected it the other night. But after scouring his old medical journals, he'd been unable to identify it. He wasn't any closer to figuring it out now and knew that Carl was counting on him. With a slick sweat breaking on his brow, Burt could feel the stress getting to him. He removed his jacket and placed it on the table.

He took his glasses from his shirt pocket, put them on, and looked into the lens once again. The red blood cells were compromised; the proteins had been denatured. And although the cellular damage indicated a bacterial toxin, there was something about it that wasn't exactly organic. Then, something happened. It was slow at first, hardly detectable at all. But ... there was movement on the slide.

Burt squinted and rubbed his eyes, then he adjusted the magnification and looked again. It was gradual, but sure enough, there was cellular movement within the sample. Only these cells were dead. "What the hell?" he gasped.

He refocused the aperture again and watched the red blood cells migrate to the right side of the slide. *Why in that direction?* He removed the slide, turned it around, and replaced it under the lens to see if the cells would continue moving, only this time to the left. He looked into the lens and held his breath. The cells stopped moving for a moment, then resumed their previous course of direction, gravitating to the right once again.

What's going on?

Burt repeated the action, removing the slide and rotating it, and the exact same thing happened. The red blood cells stopped moving for a second, then reversed direction and began to migrate to the right. "It's like they're being pulled by something," he whispered.

There'd been no movement on the slide only a moment ago. *So, what changed?* Then he noticed it. He had taken off his jacket and set it on the table near the microscope—on the right side. But that didn't make sense. Burt picked up the jacket, moved it to the other side of the microscope, and looked through the lens.

The red blood cells stopped for a quick second, then slowly began to migrate to the left.

"Son of a bitch!" he shouted. He had no idea what it meant, but he knew it had something to do with the jacket, or maybe ...

Burt grabbed the jacket and started to remove the items from the pockets. He pulled out a handful of change, the small bottle of the teeth he had taken from the ashes, and his car keys. He thought that was it, then felt one last smaller item in the very bottom of the left pocket. He reached in and pulled out the tiny ladybug. He stared at the bright red design with the little black dots on its back and flipped it over. A round magnet sat in the center of the bug's body. "Jesus Christ," he gasped. "The MRI is one big fucking magnet!"

He held the magnet against the right side of the slide and looked into the lens. He watched as the cells gravitated to the right. He repeated the experiment, switching the magnet to the left side of the lens ... The cells immediately changed direction and raced in that direction as well. The cells were being drawn by the magnet. *How is that possible?* Burt knew magnets worked on metal and polarized ores, that opposite poles attracted and like poles repelled, but he had never seen anything like this.

He jumped up from his seat and walked around the room to stretch his legs. "Okay," he said out loud. "It's a blood infection affected by magnetization. It attacks the red cells like a poison and has a bacterial signature." He paced the lab several times, then walked down the hall to the office. The book he had been looking at the other night still lay on his desk. He sat down and thumbed through the pages.

The desk and the chair he sat in shook for a quick second, causing Burt to pause; a half second later, he heard the explosion. It echoed in the distance, sounding as if it had happened somewhere on the south side of town. It was followed by a second detonation, louder and closer than the first, possibly originating from somewhere on the mountain. Then there were sirens. Burt swallowed back a sour pit that had formed in his throat. *What in the hell was that?*

It hit him in the leg, a quick pressure that was easily dismissed, then it happened again. Deputy Ted Lutchen slept in the chair next to the bed and woke when the strange sensation touched his leg a second time. He opened his eyes to see the eager face of the German Shepherd staring up at him. The dog whined, then slapped his paw onto the deputy's knee.

"I'll bet I know what that means."

Baxter cocked his head to the left and whined again. The girl in the bed rolled over and opened her eyes. She offered the deputy a confused look as she rubbed the sleep crumbs away. Then she saw her dog and smiled. Baxter looked at her and whined a third time.

"He needs to pee," Dawn said.

Ted yawned, stretched his back, then got up and grabbed the dog's leash. "Well, I guess we should take him out then."

Dawn jumped off the bed and helped him with the leash. Then Ted opened the door and the three stepped into the hallway. He checked to the left and right but didn't see anyone in either direction. There were no nurses working at the front desk and not so much as a janitor sweeping the floor. Ted held his breath and offered the child his most confident smile. They looked up at the sound of a squeaking door hinge to see a lone orderly emerge from one of the rooms. The man started when he saw the trio, as if he hadn't expected to see anyone himself, but Ted figured it had more to do with the presence of the dog.

"Good morning," Ted said. "Where is everyone?"

"I have no idea." The man appeared shaken and out of breath. "I've been wondering the same thing since I got here."

The orderly approached them, pushing a cartful of breakfast trays.

"Are you here by yourself?" Ted asked.

"No one showed up for work today. I mean some did, but more than half of the staff is out. And there's no way to get in touch with them, not with the phones out." The man's voice trembled as if he were on the verge of tears.

"You're taking care of the patients alone?"

"Elisabeth is here somewhere, but other than that, it's just me. And someone had to feed them."

"Okay, we'll help you. I'm Deputy Lutchen, and this is Dawn, and this guy who has to go potty is Baxter."

The man shook Ted's hand. "I'm Greg. Nice to meet you."

"Same here, Greg. We're going to take Baxter out, then we'll come back and give you a hand."

The sheriff's words echoed in Ted's head like a gong, and a picture of the men laid out in the freezer flashed before him. The events of yesterday felt like an impossible nightmare, but Ted knew it wouldn't help anyone to dwell on it. There were people who needed him, patients who had been left behind by a staff that hadn't shown up for work—or had been unable to. Ted didn't know which group to feel sorry for.

He and Dawn headed to the first floor and then outside to allow Baxter to relieve himself, only to find the rest of the facility was equally deserted. Although some staff had made it in, the absence of the ones who hadn't was more than noticeable.

While the pup chowed down, the trio ate at the nurses' station.

"How many patients are on this floor?" Ted asked.

"Eighteen to twenty."

"And on the other floors. Would you say about the same?"

"Yeah, sure. I mean give or take. Probably about the same." Greg gave Ted a puzzled look.

"So, about sixty patients. Is that what you think?" Ted watched Dawn as she ate from a single-serving-size bowl of Fruit Loops.

"Sounds about right."

"Are most of the patients mobile, or are they bedridden?" Ted continued. "I mean, do you think they could be moved if they had to be?"

"Why do you ask? What's going on?" Greg's voice wavered.

"I'm just wondering what you think. How many could be moved if you had to?"

"I don't know. I guess about three-quarters if we absolutely had to. But I don't know why you would, unless you know something I don't. Do you? Deputy, do you know something that I don't?"

Ted thought about what the man had said. About three quarters of the patients could be moved if they had to, approximately forty-five of them. Leaving roughly fifteen that were either bedridden or couldn't be moved for other reasons. That wasn't a very good ratio.

"No, I don't know anything that you don't. I was just wondering in case there was a problem like we had last night. Let's just hope that doesn't happen." Ted tried to look confident but was unsure if he pulled it off.

"Yeah," Greg said. "Let's hope not."

Chapter 55

Deputy Beau Jenkins pulled into the quarry and was intercepted by Don Fischer, who charged the cruiser waving his arms in the air with his face as red as salmon. Jenkins put the cruiser in park and rolled down the window a few inches.

"What seems to be the problem?" Beau asked, leaning back from the open window.

"Someone broke in here last night and destroyed all the machinery! Everything—the Komatsu, the Deere, even the CAT. We're talking hundreds of thousands of dollars in damage. You got to arrest these little bastards!" Don screamed at the older man who had just pulled up.

"Whoa, just slow down a second and start over. What are you talking about?"

Donald tried to regain his composure and took several deep breaths. Not wanting to look like a mental patient, he started over. "We keep all our equipment locked up in the pen. Look, it would be easier to just show you."

Jenkins exited the cruiser and allowed Don to lead him to the equipment pen. The damage was obvious as soon as they entered the storage area.

"Someone got into here last night. See the chain?" Don pointed to the broken links scattered around the gate. Jenkins examined them, then moved on to the equipment as Don continued. "They ripped the hydraulic lines out of the fittings.

Do you have any idea how difficult that is? Those are under high pressure. And look at this; they cracked all the oil pans."

The deputy walked around the heavy machinery, examining the damage. The hydraulic lines had indeed been yanked from their fittings. They hadn't been cut or sliced. He bent down to look at the oil pan on one of the big machines. It hadn't just cracked; it had been smashed by something heavy and powerful.

"This wasn't a couple of kids messing around, Mr. Fischer. This is a whole lot more deliberate than something kids would do. This was someone trying to make a point. Someone wanted to hit you where it hurts—the wallet."

"What are you talking about?"

"Do you have any enemies, Mr. Fischer? More importantly, does your boss have any enemies? Is there someone who might have something to gain by seeing the quarry shut down?"

"What? Of course I don't have any enemies. I'm a geologist, not Jimmy Hoffa, for Christ's sake."

"What about your boss, Mr. DuCain?"

"I have no idea. He's never here, stays at the corporate office in Virginia. Who would want to do something like this?" Some of the workers had gathered around to watch him lose his mind. Stephanie and Gail stood near the entrance of the cavern looking at him as well. He couldn't see their faces but imagined they were surprised to see this side of him.

"Did you and your men walk through the area this morning?" Jenkins asked.

Don looked at the sand around the equipment and realized what he had done. Both he and Buzzy had walked around the machines nearly a dozen times assessing the damage. "Oh Christ."

"Hmm-mmm." Jenkins studied the tracks, stepping around them to examine a bit closer. "I see three distinct sets of tracks. Judging by those boots you're wearing, I can see a lot of them belong to you. The other set of boot prints, I'm guessing belong to your man over there." He pointed to Buzzy, who stood just outside the pen. "Then there's another set; unfortunately, you men stepped on most of them."

Don knew he had done most of that himself.

"The guy who made those tracks was one big son of a bitch. That's at least a size thirteen boot, probably bigger, I'm guessing." The deputy pointed to one of the oversized tracks.

"So, it wasn't kids?"

"I don't think so, Mr. Fischer. I'd say the owner of these prints was definitely not a kid."

Don wondered if they had an enemy that he didn't know about, someone who wanted DuCain out of business. It didn't sound right; the quarry had been there for years and no other company had any vested interest in the mountain. None of it made any sense. "How did you even know to come here this morning, Deputy?" Don finally asked the obvious. "No one called; the phones are out."

"You heard the explosions a little while ago?"

Donald nodded.

"Well, there've been a couple situations in town. The Gables Bridge was destroyed and the other being a rockslide on Sunset Road; both look like they were done intentionally. I'm here because the sheriff wanted to get one of those machines up to the Pass to start clearing the road."

Don felt the blood drain from his face. Things were about to get worse. He could feel it.

"After seeing this, Mr. Fischer, I'm wondering if all your explosives are accounted for. Do you mind if we have a look?"

Don's lungs cramped like he had been kicked in the chest. *This isn't happening.* He wanted to scream and tear his hair out, but all he could do was look at the deputy and say, "Follow me."

He led Jenkins to the explosives shed, a miniature bunker set far away from the trailers behind two chain-link fences. The shed itself was constructed out of double cinderblock, reinforced by a steel interior. The doors were solid steel as well, with three padlocks, each one thicker than a man's finger.

All the locks had been broken and not cut as if done by a saw or pair of bolt cutters. They had been shattered, like they had been flash-frozen and then smashed. Don opened the door, expecting the shed to be empty. He was surprised to see it wasn't, but there was a hell of a lot of shit missing.

He grabbed the inventory sheet off the door and looked through it but could already see what was gone; it was his job to keep track of all of it. In total, six blasting caps along with fifteen sticks of dynamite, three rolls of primer cord, and two detonators had been removed from the shed. He went over the list with the deputy.

"Do you still think this was done by kids, Mr. Fischer?" The deputy studied the inventory sheet.

"What the hell should I do?" A serrated blade of tension stabbed Don in the center of his forehead as he struggled to form a cohesive thought.

"I would suggest you find a safer place to store the explosives that *haven't* been stolen from your job site. This shed isn't as safe as you think. I need to report this to the sheriff. I imagine he'll want to question you. I'm sure you understand."

The throbbing in his skull escalated. Don had never even spent a night in the drunk tank and couldn't imagine the trouble he might be facing. Someone had stolen explosives from his job and used them to blow up part of the mountain. *I am so fucked.*

"Why would someone do this, and why would they want to block the road?"

"I think I'll let the sheriff answer that, Mr. Fischer." The deputy walked to the cruiser and called the sheriff on the radio.

Sheriff Primrose and Deputy Rainey arrived at Tara's house moments before Beau Jenkins tried to contact him. Carl exited the vehicle, leaving the call unanswered, and raced across the front lawn to where Deputy Colbert stood on the walkway vomiting into the bushes. Both men approached him as he bent over and heaved one last time.

Colbert's face had gone grey; a thin layer of sweat slicked his brow. The man looked like he had aged ten years in the past hour.

"What the hell is it, Tim? What happened?" Carl watched his old partner attempt to regain control of his stomach. Tim dry-heaved, then straightened himself upright.

The men were alerted by the sound of shuffled footsteps coming from the foyer, just on the other side of the open door. Carl looked up in time to see Deputy Kovach emerge from the house. A scream rose in his throat but never left his lips.

Kovach's innards hung from a gaping wound in his abdomen. Carl moved to help the man, then recoiled in shock as the deputy's lips pulled back in a snarl. A thick oil-like substance coated the deputy's teeth and gums and had consumed his eyes as well. Kovach took an awkward step forward, and a splash of organs dumped out of him onto the front steps. His legs tangled in a coil of large intestines, the pink bands tightening around his ankles as he approached.

Tim Colbert attempted to retreat but tripped over a planter set along the walkway. He fell backward, landing hard on his ass, and looked up at Kovach. The beast glared at him through a lifeless black abyss and opened his mouth.

Carl froze, expecting a serpentine tongue like the one used by Felix Castillo to rocket from the deputy's mouth. But the only thing that came out was a tendril of dark smoke. It lifted from Kovach's open jaws and swirled before his face like a churning cloud. Then it shot like a viper at Colbert, who lay on the ground trying to right himself.

The smoke disappeared into Colbert's open mouth. The man recoiled, grabbing his throat, and rolled onto his back, gagging.

Carl and Rainey each took a step backward as Kovach turned toward them and opened his mouth even wider. Carl finally reacted and raised his gun. But before he could pull the trigger, the front of the man's face disappeared in a crimson wash. Deputy Rainey fired a second round into Kovach's chest, and the abomination toppled to the ground in a lifeless heap.

Colbert convulsed on the ground with dark threads rising from his nostrils in tiny wisps. The man opened his mouth, allowing even more of the strange substance to disperse into the air around him. Carl jumped as Deputy Rainey fired a round into the top of Colbert's head. The man fell back against the pavement and stopped moving; the cloud was carried away on the wind.

The concussion from Rainey's bullets ripped through Carl like a cardiac arrest. He'd jumped at the sound of the first one, his muscles clenching in his throat and shoulders. Then his stomach twisted as the smell of gunpowder fused with Kovach's innards in a putrefying waft. By the time the deputy fired a second time, Carl had been frozen with fear. The urge to vomit rose in his esophagus, forcing him to bite back and swallow hard. It had happened so fast and so sudden, that he just stood there. He had ordered his men not to hesitate, and Deputy Rainey followed his directions to the tee. He watched as the young officer reloaded his weapon.

"Are you all right, Sheriff?" Rainey asked.

"Yeah," he said, knowing that he wasn't ... not even a little.

Lois stared across the empty floor of the medical center to the reception area where Doris TenHove stood. A mutual understanding exchanged between them in a flash—something terrible was happening, yet they were both still here. Lois imagined a similar look had been shared by the passengers on the *Titanic* after the last lifeboat had been lowered into the water. Some had missed the opportunity to abandon ship, while others had not taken the threat seriously. They all died the same in the end, regardless to which group they belonged.

Which group do you belong to, Nurse TenHove? Lois thought the woman was probably wondering the same thing about her. Lois knew she fit into both. She had heard the warning from Carl and even taken heed, at least for a moment. Then she let reason and rationale stop her from reacting. Lois looked at the nurse behind the desk and realized the woman probably didn't belong to either category. Nurse TenHove was here because she chose to be. She was here out of a sense of duty and commitment to the people entrusted in her care. She wasn't about to leave her patients behind, even if that meant going down with the ship.

Lois held her head up and approached the reception desk.

"Good morning, Mrs. Fischer," Doris said.

"I'm not so sure that it is, Nurse TenHove. Could we speak candidly? You know, one woman to another." Lois placed her purse on the counter and met Doris's stare.

"What would you like to talk about?" Doris laid her clipboard next to Lois's purse. "Would it have something to do with the meeting at the courthouse this morning?"

"I didn't know there was a meeting, but I spoke with the sheriff yesterday about some things that I'm having a difficult time accepting. You look like you might know what I'm talking about. Can you help me understand what's going on?"

"I take it you haven't seen anything to convince you?" Doris lowered her voice. "Dr. Malcolm came back last night."

Lois's spirit picked up for a brief second but was shattered just as quickly.

"Only it wasn't Dr. Malcolm anymore. Something had happened to him; he had changed. His face looked more like an ape's or something prehistoric. And he killed Dr. Ziegler."

Tears welled up in the corners of Lois's eyes as the concussion of her own heartbeat echoed in her head like a bass drum. The stark white light of the waiting area assaulted her, and the suffocating smell of alcohol and disinfectant suddenly made her sick. She gasped and tried to wrap her head around what the nurse had said. She had just seen Dr. Ziegler yesterday. *No, that can't be.*

"I'm sorry, Mrs. Fischer. Dr. Ziegler died trying to stop Dr. Malcolm. Don't worry, your family is upstairs and they're safe. Billy was moved to the second floor before the explosion happened."

"Explosion! What explosion?" Lois raised her voice in a dramatic contrast to the silence of the waiting area. "What are you talking about?"

Doris reached across the counter and took Lois's hands. "Dr. Malcolm set off an explosion in the imaging wing. There was an awful lot of damage, and there was a fire. We had quite a few injuries, but your family is safe." The nurse held Lois's hands tight and looked her in the eyes. "The sheriff had a meeting at the courthouse this morning for all deputies and emergency care workers. It's an infection ... It's changing people, turning them into something awful. And it's highly contagious. Those who become infected can pass it on. There doesn't appear to be any cure, but Burt Lively is trying to find one." Doris TenHove leaned in closer and lowered her voice even more. "Mrs. Fischer, the infection appears to be intelligent. It made Dr. Malcolm set off the explosion."

Carl had already told her a great deal about the infection, which she had struggled to accept. He told her to take Troy and get out of town, and before that, Dr. Ziegler had suggested she do the same. Each time, Lois had convinced herself that neither man knew what they were talking about. She wondered how long she would accept what Nurse TenHove was saying before she found a way to talk herself out of it a third time.

"Carl, I mean the sheriff, told me all of this yesterday, but I just couldn't believe it."

"It's difficult to believe, Mrs. Fischer. Why weren't you at the meeting this morning? I mean, if the sheriff took his time to tell you all this, I would think he would want you there as well."

Lois had never felt more foolish in her life. It was obvious why she hadn't been told about the meeting: Carl hadn't expected her to still be in Garrett Grove.

"I don't suppose the sheriff made any preparations to have Billy transferred, did he?"

"No, I imagine with everything that happened yesterday, it was overlooked. I know this all sounds crazy, like something out of comic book, but you need to do everything you can to keep you family safe, Mrs. Fischer, trust me." The woman's words fell heavy and hit Lois like a brick.

She had let Troy go to school today. *How could I have been so stupid?* "What about you, Nurse TenHove; what are you going to do?"

The woman smiled, and it showed in her eyes; it was a genuine smile if Lois had ever seen one. "I am going to take care of my patients. That's what I am going to do. I was just considering how I would accomplish that, as short-staffed as we are. But I need to start doing something because I have a feeling we may be in for some trouble like we have never seen."

Lois could feel the seconds ticking away and sensed the lifeboats being lowered around them while she and Nurse TenHove spoke about the things they should be doing instead of actually doing any of it.

● ● ●

When Kovach emerged from the house, disemboweled and infected, all Carl could do was stare as the man lumbered toward them, dragging his organs like a toy wagon. He had been expecting the assault to come in the form of a serpentine tongue, like the one Castillo had developed, but that hadn't been the case. The real threat was the dark cloud that surfaced from the creature's mouth; it was the same stuff that had been extracted from Abe. *That's how this thing spreads.*

It had been lightning quick, and then the creature turned its sights on them. Rainey had already been ambushed once by this presence; he had raised his weapon and put Deputy Kovach down, then he fired on Colbert before the man had time to get up. All the while Carl watched, unable to move.

"Come in, Sheriff. This is Deputy Jenkins at the quarry." Beau had been trying to reach him for the past half hour.

Carl picked up his handheld. "Copy that. How are we looking?"

"Bad, Sheriff." Carl winced. "Someone broke in here last night or early this morning. Whoever it was made off with an awful lot of dynamite, some blasting caps, and a few other items. I'm guessing that's what was used on the bridge and the mountain."

Carl figured the explosives had come from the quarry; it was the only place in town with a readily available supply. "Beau, what's the chance of getting one of those machines up to Sunset Road? You told them what happened?"

"Unfortunately, whoever stole the explosives also sabotaged the machines. They ripped them apart, Sheriff. They're not going anywhere." Beau finished the transmission and was met with an extremely long interval of silence.

"Roger that." Carl turned to Deputy Rainey, removed his hat, and rubbed the bridge of his nose, just between his eyes. His headache had come back and begun to throb like a pulse. "David, let's get these bodies in the house before anyone sees them. They'll have to stay here till someone can come pick them up."

It was a horrible way to treat his own people, but Carl didn't have much of a choice. They were taxed to the limit. Burt didn't have the extra manpower, and now neither did he. The department had lost three deputies, and Carl was guessing that once they stepped inside the house, they would find the body of Tara Jefferies as well. That would bring the count to four, including Deputy Forsyth, who had to be considered compromised as well.

"Sheriff," Rainey said, scanning the neighborhood. "Where is everyone? With all the gunshots, someone should have gotten curious."

Carl looked toward the other houses on the block. The deputy was right; not a single neighbor had gotten curious and checked to see what was going on. If there was one thing people always did, it was put themselves in harm's way. Gunshots, car accident, fires—their natural reaction was to open their doors and see what the hell was going on. But not a single neighbor had so much as cracked a curtain. Carl had a bad feeling that if anyone was home behind those closed doors, they had a lot more to worry about than a few gunshots.

"Come on, David," he said. "Let's move these bodies."

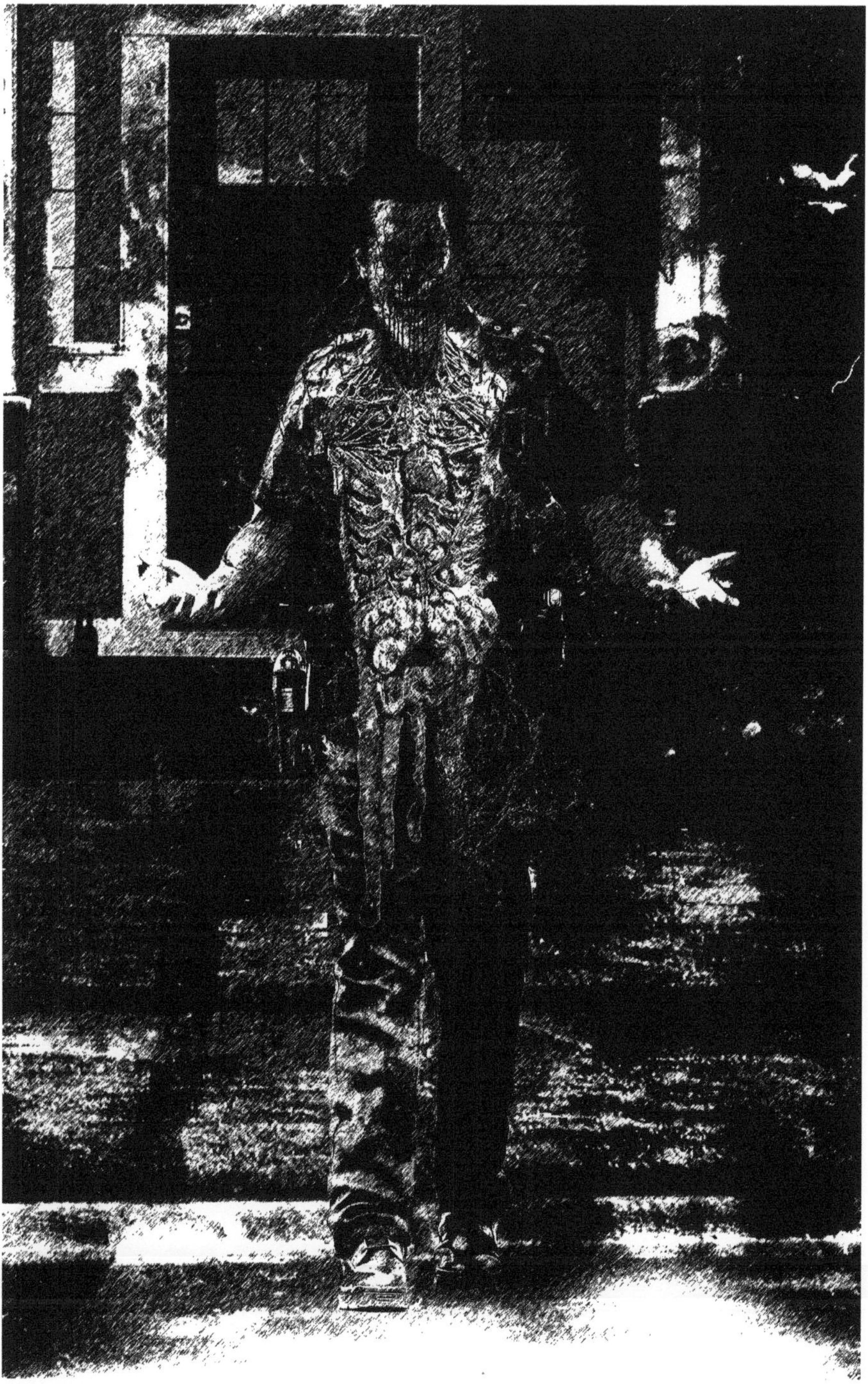

Chapter 56

The original owners and staff of the Garrett Mountain Sanatorium had abandoned the facility decades ago, but the place didn't remain empty for long. Its new occupants, the multitude of woodland creatures who found their way in through the broken windows and breaches in the foundation, enjoyed the relative escape from the elements that the structure offered. But now, they, too, had vacated the premises. It was no longer hospitable for any living creature.

A necrotic puissance had invaded their home, festering like a cancer or a mold into every crevice of the old hospital. The animals could smell it. Unnatural and intrusive, a combination of ammonia and hot metal and something far worse—the odor of poison. Most animals recognized the smells of things that could kill them. The thing that had taken over the sanatorium smelled exactly like that, like something that would kill you.

But it wasn't just the stench that sent the tiny critters running for their lives, it was the malevolent awareness that tainted every square inch of the place. It occupied the complex like a hermit crab taking a new shell, the structure not only acting as its home but a living extension of the presence itself.

Garrett Mountain had been a place of suffering for decades, and the infestation that now gestated in the basement sensed that. Like a memory hanging in the air, an echo reverberating off the walls, repeating itself over and over, it had acted like a homing beacon and attracted the Entity like a moth to a flame.

The place was dark and cold and reminded the creature of the emptiness of its origin. The emptiness to which it would again return—after it destroyed every living creature on this rock.

Now the basement of the sanatorium resembled a mass grave. The bodies of the infected lay on the cold floor, side by side and on top of one another. The process had begun. Soon, its children would wake, and they would be ravenous.

Miss Boriello called an early recess since half the class was missing and the children who were present hadn't been paying attention to her lesson anyway. The kids were too preoccupied by the emptiness of the classroom. The trio of new friends retreated to their usual spot on the playground and began calculating how to spend Janis's ten dollars. To Wendy and Troy, the sight of the crisp bill was equivalent to being handed the keys to Fort Knox. But Janis was unfazed; cash was just another thing her father threw at her to compensate for his absence, like toys, jewelry, or *Star Wars* figures.

Wendy was also a child of divorced parents. She lived with her mother, who worked an excessive number of hours. But she was a happy child, for the most part, although she did get aggravated with Troy from time to time. And although Troy thought it was his fault, that wasn't the case. Wendy's parents had gone through a messy divorce—was there any other kind? She hadn't seen much of her dad since he remarried, and he already had children with his new wife.

Her mother felt scorned by the man who left her for a much younger woman. But rather than keeping the marital problems to herself, she used her daughter as her personal counselor. Wendy was fed an endless diet of gripes focused on the shortcomings of her father and the entire male population. Men were immature and women were forced to tolerate their foolish antics—"so you better get used to it, Wendy." It was a miracle she turned out as adjusted as she had.

Wendy was a survivor and possibly the smartest kid in the class. It was easy for her to discern her mother's rantings for the slander that it was. However, it had tainted her opinion of boys ... just a little. Wendy knew women were superior to their male counterparts and it was only a matter of time before they took their rightful place in the hierarchy. She was a natural-born feminist—Gloria Steinem, eat your heart out. For the most part, she'd been disgusted by the foolishness of the boys at her previous school before moving to Garrett Grove. Then September came and she met Troy, who was different. And just like that, all the things her mother said didn't apply anymore. She'd found an exception to the rule, and that changed everything she thought she knew about boys. Her mother had been very wrong; boys weren't bad at all. In fact, Wendy thought she kind of liked them.

"Well, if nobody's gonna say anything, I guess I will," Wendy spoke up. "Half the class is missing. Every day, there's less and less. At this rate, how long will it be before one of *us* doesn't show up?"

The trio scanned the ever-shrinking population of students gathered on the playground. It wasn't only fourth graders who were missing, it was nearly half the students from every class. It was noticeable to all of them, especially Janis, who had watched the numbers decrease since arriving three days ago.

"Why aren't the adults doing anything?" Janis asked. "We can't be the only ones who notice."

Troy wondered if the grownups even knew something was going on. Adults were concerned about other things, like work and paying bills, and were so caught up in their day-to-day activities they probably hadn't even noticed.

"What does your mom think, Janis?" Troy figured if there was anyone in town who might know something, it would be Dr. Thompson. "I mean, she studies this stuff."

"She didn't say anything. She's been working a lot lately."

Troy nodded; his father had been doing the same thing.

"I don't think she knows anything's going on. It's not like she's friends with a lot of people in town." Janis blew a long blonde curl out of her eyes.

"Well, no one's going to listen to *us*," Wendy said. "I mean, we're saying that whatever chased Troy through the graveyard is responsible for all the missing kids. That's what we're saying, right?" Janis and Troy nodded in agreement. "Do you think they're all dead?"

Troy allowed her words to resonate. He had been thinking an awful lot about it. "I think that if one of those things gets you, then you become one yourself." A wave of guilt washed over him; his entire body stiffened, and he braced himself for what he was about to say. "I don't think Rob had the flu. I think he ran into one of those things last week. When I found him in my garage after the party, he wasn't himself. H-he came after me like he wanted to bite me."

"What?" Wendy gasped. "Why didn't you say something before?"

"I dunno. I guess I was trying to forget. I was hoping it really was the flu. I told the sheriff; I think he believed me. Maybe he knows something's wrong."

"You should have said something about this right away," Wendy scolded, then her stern look softened into a smile. "It's okay. It must have been scary."

"Yeah," Janis said.

"So, what's the plan? Because if there are that many"—Troy looked around, trying to calculate how many children were missing—"how are we going to stop them?"

"Well, we don't know that *everyone* turned into those things. Maybe it just kills you and you don't change," Janis said, trying to be optimistic.

And although it was a horrible attempt, Troy thought she made a good point. They didn't really know anything, not for sure. Rob had acted strangely, and Troy had been chased by something he couldn't explain.

"I don't know," Wendy said. "To be safe, we should assume everybody did. That's what always happens in the movies. You know, werewolves, zombies, vampires."

"Yeah, but those things aren't real," Troy said.

"Well, up until a couple days ago, there was no such thing as an Ojanox either, but I'd say we have a big Ojanox problem."

Troy cringed every time Wendy said the name and wished his mom had come up with something that didn't sound so ridiculous.

"If there's that many, we won't be able to stop them, but at least we can protect ourselves when the time comes," Janis said. "We have to try to make some adults believe us. What about your mother, Troy? She made up that story and seemed nice."

"I don't know; she didn't even believe me when I told her something chased me."

"What about the sheriff?" Wendy asked.

Troy figured if there was anyone in town who had an idea what was going on and could help them, it was Sheriff Primrose.

"So where do we start, and how do we convince people?" Janis asked.

Troy shifted where he sat in the grass just beneath the tire swings and scanned the playground once again. Which gave him an idea. They weren't going to get a larger crowd than the one they had right now, and he thought with the girls beside him, the other children might just take him seriously.

He looked from Wendy to Janis and then back. A strange sensation swelled in his chest. It felt a bit like butterflies, making his stomach shaky and his nerves all aflutter, but there was something exhilarating about it as well. A surge of confidence rose within him, and a strange warmness spread across his face and rushed to the top of his head. Then before he could talk himself out of it, he climbed onto the large truck tire at the base of the monkey bars and shouted loud enough for all the children to hear.

"Hey, everyone!"

The kids turned and looked at him as if he were nuts, then quickly refocused on what they had been doing.

"Everyone, I got something important to say. I'm serious!" he yelled. "Don't you even care that all our friends are missing?" Which seemed to grab the attention of a few of them. Caroline Smith and Kelly Rainey approached him where he stood atop the large tire. They were joined by Scott Cole and Steve Lambert. Then slowly, other children began to take notice and gravitate toward him.

"Okay, dork. What the heck are you talking about?" one of the fifth-grade boys barked out.

"My name is Troy," he said. "And I saw something the other day in the graveyard." Wendy's jaw dropped as she watched him, and Janis wore a smile a mile wide. "I was chased by something Monday after school. There was more than one of them, and they were really fast. I didn't get a good look because I was running, but they weren't friendly."

Looks of doubt and disbelief suggested that most of the children thought he was playing with them. But Troy saw another look on more than just a few of the faces in the crowd. It was a look of understanding. Some of the kids had seen something too. "Maybe some of you have seen these things yourself. I don't think I am the only one. What I saw almost looked like giant dogs, but they were super-fast and moved kinda funny."

"I thought I was the only one," Caroline Smith said. "I heard something in the backyard last night and looked out my bedroom window. It looked like a monster; I thought I was dreaming."

There was a stirring as many of the children nodded their heads in agreement.

"My friend Rob got sick last week, and then he showed up in my garage in the middle of the night. He walked to my house in his bare feet. At first, I thought he was sleepwalking, but then he tried to grab me. I think he wanted to bite me."

"You mean like a vampire?" Ralph Walsh, one of the third graders, asked.

"Yeah, I think exactly like a vampire. And I think that's why our friends aren't in school. I think if you get bit by one of those things, then you turn into one." Troy raised his hands not even aware of what he was doing.

Janis leaned over and whispered in Wendy's ear. "He's a natural. Where did all of this come from?"

"I have no idea," Wendy answered without taking her eyes off Troy.

"Look around." Troy spread his hands out to emphasize the number of missing classmates. "Where is everyone? There's no way they're *all* sick. In fact, I don't think *anyone* is. I think they all ran into one of those things. That's what I think."

"My brother never came home last night," a young girl said.

"My mom said that my cousin is missing and the sheriff can't do anything about it yet," another boy shouted.

"Oh, give me a break!" Jerry Santos, one of the popular fifth-grade students, pushed through the crowd. "You all sound like a bunch of babies. Everyone has the flu, that's all."

"You're wrong, Jerry. I saw one too!" The cry came from one of Jerry's fifth-grade classmates. "Something happened to my neighbors—the whole family. They all disappeared, just like that."

"I'm not saying this because I want to scare you!" Troy raised his voice. "I'm telling you because I want you to be ready. I want you to convince your parents that something's wrong. If we all do that, then there's a chance we can stop these things."

"What can we do?" someone yelled.

"The first thing is to protect yourself. We aren't sure, but we think that magnets might hurt them. Especially if you were to use a sling shot and the magnet was sharp."

"How do you know all of this, huh?"

"Yeah, how do you know, Troy?"

The children were skeptical but at least they were still listening, which was a good thing.

"Yeah, big mouth, how do you know?" Jerry continued to heckle.

"Because his father is the geologist at the quarry, and Mr. Fischer discovered a cave made out of lodestone." Wendy jumped onto the tire and joined him. "It's really old and filled with weapons the Lenni Lenape used to fight these things centuries ago."

Troy stared in shock to see her standing by his side on top of the tire. He had never said those exact words, but she had decided to run with it anyway. "My dad said that the whole cave is made from lodestone and that's what the weapons are made from."

"Oh yeah, what the heck is a lodestone, dumbass?" Jerry asked.

"It's a natural magnet found in nature."

"Oh, come on. That's stupid!"

"It's true! My mother is an archeologist in charge of the cave." Janis grabbed onto the top of the tire and pulled herself up. They were quickly running out of room, but having the girls on either side filled Troy with even more confidence, and it appeared to help the other children take them seriously. "She works for the Museum of Natural History, and she's been studying these things for a long time. Everything that Troy and Wendy said is the truth."

"If you don't believe them, then you should look at these," Janis said, pulling something from her pocket. She held out a handful of teeth and began to show them to the children standing closest to the front.

Cries of excitement and awe spread as Janis stepped off the tire and maneuvered through the crowd with her strange collection of sharply pointed teeth.

"Oh my God, it's true," one of the younger girls cried, and was met with a flurry of agreement.

"They're so sharp!"

"You need to tell your parents that something bad is about to happen," Troy said. "Then you need to find whatever magnets you can and a slingshot or a wrist rocket. It won't be easy to hit them, they're really fast, but it's better than nothing. And don't go outside at night. They chased me just as it was getting dark, so they probably come out more at night. That's why we haven't seen too many of them."

Troy watched the faces in the crowd change from doubt to acceptance. They had done it; they had convinced them. Maybe not Jerry and a few of the other fifth graders, but if the rest of the kids told their parents, then maybe that was enough to get the grownups to see what was going on. His eyes followed Janis as she made her way back to the tire, and spotted Miss Boriello standing there. She stared back at him with her hands on her hips and looked upset.

"Troy Fischer, Wendy Sirocka, and Janis Thompson, come with me to the principal's office ... now!" Miss Boriello stormed off towards the school.

Troy knew they were in trouble, but they had done it. They had begun to spread the word. It was a small group, just a bunch of kids in elementary school, but every movement had to start somewhere.

Chapter 57

Deputy Rainey and the sheriff arrived at the mayor's house to find two cars in the driveway and received no answer after knocking on the front door for nearly five minutes.

"Thanks for covering my ass today," Carl told his deputy.

"It's my honor, Sheriff. Besides, it's the least I could do for almost killing you the other night."

"I'm trying to forget you did that." Carl jiggled the knob to find it locked. Then after pressing his shoulder against the door, he backed up and slammed his weight hard against the wood. The door flew inward. Deputy Rainey had his revolver drawn and at the ready.

"Mayor, it's Sheriff Primrose. If you're home, say something."

The men entered the hallway and spotted the blood trail. It painted the floor in large splatters and had dried dark brown, always dark brown. It traversed the staircase of the bi-level, leading both up and down, making it impossible to tell which direction the victim had traveled. If Carl had to guess, he would have said down.

The men navigated the staircase with their guns drawn, trying hard not to step in the gore-soaked treads. They entered onto the first floor to find a large family room. The blood was everywhere. It had poured out of its owner at an alarming rate, coating the tile and soaking into the carpets like a flood. It trailed to a back door smeared with bloody handprints.

Carl removed a handkerchief from his pocket and opened the back door. The trail that led outside into the backyard consisted entirely of the strange dark fluid. Carl imagined that whoever left the house had undergone a change similar to the one experienced by Felix Castillo.

"Sheriff, I don't think we're going to find the mayor."

Deputy Rainey had been right; neither Mayor Gilbert nor his wife were anywhere to be found. The blood trail began in the master bedroom, where an apparent struggle had taken place. Two separate blood stains on the bed indicated more than one victim, which confirmed what Carl imagined to be true, that the couple had been ambushed in the bedroom while they slept.

Only one of the neighbors had bothered to poke their head out to see what was going on. And when Carl and David knocked on the doors of the other seven houses on the block, no one answered. It was obvious to Carl that last night had been an unimaginable loss. While they had been busy fighting fires, more than half the town had slipped through their fingers. They had lost a major battle last night, the outcome of which tipped the scales drastically against them.

If there was any way to save the ones who were left, Carl knew he needed to get to them first. He had to keep them safe, and the only way to do that was to round up every last soul and get them some place secure. He was down men, and the plan he was considering would take an army. Still, Carl knew it was the only way.

What's the safest place in town? He needed something fortified and easy to protect, a place with only one or two entrances that could be guarded with an arsenal. Something like a vault or a bunker. *Son of a bitch!* It came to him in a flash; Carl knew exactly what he needed to do. They needed to get everyone into a bomb shelter, and he knew just the place. The high school basement was a shelter ... It was a goddamn fortress too!

The high school was built on solid bedrock, which had been blasted out to form the fallout shelter. The solid concrete and steel structure was stocked with K-rations and potable water and was originally designed for a percent of the town's population to ride out a nuclear winter if the commies decided to drop the big one. The fire department ran routine inspections and oversaw the job of keeping the place stocked. Most of the goods were old, but they didn't go bad; they were made for survival, not flavor.

Carl didn't want to estimate just how many of the town's citizens were missing and prayed there was enough room in the shelter. The real problem would be rounding everyone up and convincing them of the danger. Both he and Deputy Rainey needed to get back to the station and arm the rest of the fire department and anyone comfortable with a weapon. Then he needed to send out a message to every neighborhood in the Grove and get every living soul in that shelter before sundown. He knew if he failed, none of them would live to see another.

● ● ●

Burt didn't know what he was looking for. Something he had once come across in a medical text reminded him of what the children initially appeared to be suffering from. It wasn't a flu bug but a toxin with a biological signature that destroyed the cell proteins. There were clear characteristics of poisoning, but no toxin was capable of mutating the human body and taking over the host's mind. This sounded more like possession than poisoning.

And something in the blood was causing the cells to gravitate towards the magnet.

"I guess you've got too much iron in your blood, Dr. Malcolm," Burt mumbled to himself as he sat in his office thumbing through the medical journal. He laughed at his own joke, although there hadn't been anything all that funny or original about it. "Too much iron," he repeated.

He leaned back in his chair, took off his glasses, and rubbed the bridge of his nose, attempting to collect his thoughts. He wondered if maybe there was a bit more to that after all. The MRI had extracted something from Abe's body, and Burt had every reason to believe it was the infection itself. Also, the blood sample taken from Dr. Malcolm was attracted to the ladybug magnet. *What if the blood has been poisoned by something metallic?*

Then it clicked. Burt knew what he had been looking for in the medical text.

He flipped to the section where he believed he would find what he was looking for. He had already pored through the section on toxicity but had somehow missed it. Then, there it was, staring at him in black and white. *Mercury poisoning.*

In severe cases, there was listed an array of symptoms almost identical to what the children had initially exhibited. High fever, bleeding of the gums, and the possibility of severe brain damage. Denaturalization of the cellular protein was also common in extreme cases. Of course, nothing as extreme as what happened to Felix Castillo, but Burt thought he was getting somewhere.

Heavy metals like mercury present in the blood would explain the magnetic attraction. In cases of mercury poisoning caused by ingesting seafood, it wasn't exactly the fish that ate the poison, it was a bacterial cycle. First the localized bacteria fed on the mercury contaminant, and then the fish fed on the bacteria. This went up the food chain until a human was infected from eating a bad piece of fish. Technically, a bacterium could absorb just about any substance and then infect a host. It was ubiquitous and resilient as hell. There were strains capable of surviving in arsenic, molten magma inside active volcanoes, and at the greatest depths of the oceans.

Burt had no idea where this bacterium had originated, but it was here now, and it was infecting the people of Garrett Grove. Science had always considered it to be a simple life-form, but what if it wasn't as simple as everyone thought? What if it was intelligent? This one was intelligent enough to control a human brain and make it do things against its will. Burt thought that sounded more than just intelligent, it sounded superior.

He got up from the desk and walked back to the lab with the book in his hand. "I just need to know how to stop you," he said out loud. "If the MRI killed you, then it's all in the strength of the magnet."

He returned to the microscope and looked through the lens again. He took the magnet from his pocket and placed it on the table next to the slide. The cells began to move once again.

"Maybe it just isn't strong enough," he said. "Maybe it has to be concentrated." Burt took the magnet and placed it directly against the slide. He looked through the lens to see if the proximity of the magnet altered the speed of movement.

Something did happen on the slide, only not what Burt expected. The red blood cells looked as if they were vibrating. They weren't traveling in one singular direction; they appeared torn between moving in many.

"Son of a bitch."

Then several of the cells started to separate. A cleavage line formed down the center, dividing them into two individual but very different cells on either side.

Dear God. Burt watched as the magnet separated the infection from the human cell. The bacterial cell was like nothing he had ever seen before; it had attached itself to the blood cell and transformed it. The direct contact of the magnet removed the bacterium, leaving the red blood cell unfazed.

The strange regression occurred in one cell after another. The infected cell would begin to vibrate as if bombarded by sound waves, then the cleavage line would form, resulting in the separation of the parasite from the host.

"I got you, you bastard!" Burt shouted into the empty lab. He had successfully extracted the infection from the sample, just as the MRI had done to Abe Gorman. It had killed the man, and Burt was fairly certain the process would do the same to anyone else; he didn't put much hope in the possibility of anyone ever coming back from this. But he had found a way to stop it. That was if they could figure out how to subject the infected to a great enough magnetic force.

It wasn't Burt's field of study, but he had come up with a working theory. "Jesus Christ, Doc. You knew!" Burt realized Dr. Ziegler had been on to something. The man had dropped the ladybug magnet when the creature grabbed him. That had to be why he was holding it in the first place. "You knew, Doc, and the bastard killed you." Burt made the sign of the cross on himself and went back to work. Now more than ever, he wished the phones were working; he couldn't wait to tell Carl the news.

Bob Jones relayed the sheriff's orders to the rest of his men and was the first to arrive at the station with Ed Koloski. The requisition orders had been waiting for them along with a small arsenal of semi-automatic handguns, which Andrea had procured from the armory. Most of Bob's men were seasoned hunters and familiar with the operation of weapons. Bob doubted it would have mattered if they weren't; it sounded as if the sheriff was looking to outfit an army regardless. The men started to show up and were each met by both Bob and Andrea, who gave them the rundown as they were sworn in as official deputies of Garrett Grove.

Ed Koloski watched as the chief conducted a brief heart-to-heart with each of his fellow firefighters and did his best to convince himself this was really happening. Ed was a practical man, for the most part, who relied on logic and reason. At the moment, his best logic told him that seeing was believing. Still, some things were beyond understanding. Most of the men had witnessed something unexplainable last night, and now they were cut off from the rest of the world by something clearly intelligent.

The world held many mysteries about things that had yet to be explained. Natural occurrences like lightning and tornadoes had remained unexplainable for ages until someone finally identified their cause. Koloski believed what they were dealing with was just something humanity had yet to identify. He had a few theories and was leaning toward one that didn't sit well. Ed was under the impression that whatever had been found in the Texaco fire wasn't terrestrial. Or if it was, it was a life-form that hadn't been recorded in any of the science books. Logic told him it was something new, something far more advanced than any of them could comprehend.

"This is Sheriff Primrose to base." The sheriff's voice crackled over the dispatch speakers.

"Come in, Sheriff," Andrea answered.

"Did you equip the men from the fire department yet?"

"Almost done, Sheriff, just waiting for a few more guys to show up."

Koloski offered the chief a dubious glance. Five of their men were still unaccounted for. They had not responded when Bob sent out the call, and none of them had shown up to the meeting at the courthouse. Koloski was beginning to doubt if they would show up at all.

"Andrea, I want Bob Jones and Ed Koloski to meet me at the high school in half an hour."

She looked to the chief, who offered her a thumbs-up. "He said he will see you there."

"Also, I need Bob to leave two men at the station, then I want you to call Deputy Jenkins back to base. There are two cruisers with the keys in them at 12 Gray Street. Have Jenkins drive the men there to pick them up and bring them back to base; we are going to need them."

"That's Tara's address, Sheriff. What happened?" She held her breath and waited for his reply.

"I'm sorry, Andrea. Tara didn't make it." A pause as fatal as a stroke caused Andrea's heart to somersault in her chest. She froze at the microphone, waiting for the sheriff to continue. "We lost Deputies Kovach and Colbert as well ... I'm sorry."

"No—" She croaked, unable to move. *Not Joel.* The words echoed in her head. Andrea let out a noise that sounded like a feral animal caught in a trap, then she screamed at the top of her lungs. "No!"

Bob rushed behind the desk and scooped her into his giant arms as the dispatcher wailed like a lost child at the mall. Koloski watched and knew without a doubt that the five missing firemen were not going to make it to the station—ever.

Chapter 58

The stained glass windows at Our Lady of the Mountain depicted the Stations of the Cross. The large, ornate renditions of Christ's Passion sat on either side of the main room, refracting the morning sun in a polychromatic waltz of light. Father Kieran prepared for the noon Mass, stopping to pray at each station as he did. He blessed himself in front of the rendition of the Savior being comforted by Mary Magdalene.

Typically, the weekday Masses were light and reserved for the older members of the parish. Father Kieran didn't know who or how many might attend, since there was nothing typical about today. He finished his prayer, blessed himself, and approached the next station when he was startled by the sound of someone clearing their throat.

"Excuse me, Father?" the voice of a young woman echoed off the tall ceiling.

He turned to find a girl he had not seen in quite some time. Her parents were active members of the church, and she still attended Mass on the usual Catholic holidays. However, it surprised Kieran to see her standing there, two hours before Mass.

"I didn't mean to interrupt you, Father. It's Allison, Allison Aigans." Dark circles hung beneath her deep bloodshot eyes; she had been crying.

"Of course, Allison. What's wrong, child?" Father Kieran blessed himself and walked to where she stood.

"I know I haven't been around much lately." She attempted to control her sobbing. "I'm scared, Father. My boyfriend is missing, and I know something terrible has happened to him." Allison looked around to the small cubicles on the back wall. "I was wondering if you had time for a confession?"

"Of course, right this way." Father Kieran led the girl to the confessionals and entered the one on the left-hand side. Allison stood outside, allowing the father a few moments before entering herself. She walked in and knelt at the tiny window.

"Bless me, Father, for I have sinned. It's been over a year since my last confession."

Father Kieran offered the sign of the cross. "In the name of the Father, and of the Son, and of the Holy Spirit, Amen."

Allison managed to control her tears and continued. "Father, I have taken the Lord's name in vain. I've disrespected my mother and father, and I have lied." She hesitated and took in a deep breath. "Father, I have fornicated with my boyfriend and have lusted in my heart. I've not been a very good Catholic and have been cruel to my sister."

"I see," he said. "Is there anything else you wish to confess?"

"Yes, Father." She took another deep breath and wiped her eyes with a tissue. "I think my boyfriend is dead."

Father Kieran straightened up in the confessional. "Oh. And why do you think that?"

"He's missing, Father. His parents went away and left him home alone. We were going to spend the week together."

"I see."

"Mick has been missing since Sunday. I went to his house, and he wasn't there. Also, his friends are missing as well. I think they went back up the mountain."

Father Kieran cleared his throat and listened intently as the girl continued.

"Saturday night, we all went to the old sanatorium. Do you know of it, Father?"

"Yes, I've heard stories. I believe it's quite dangerous up there."

"It is, Father, especially now. There's something up there, and I think it's evil. I think Mick went back there and he ran into it. Only this time, I don't think he was able to outrun it."

"You said it's evil. Did you see something, Allison?"

"We went there with Billy, and he had a flashlight."

Kieran nodded at the mention of the boy's name. He was beginning to get a clearer picture of what might have happened.

"We were about to go inside the building." Her voice tightened against the words. "Something ran across the front steps, only it didn't look like anything, really. It almost looked like smoke, or a cloud. It was very fast. Then it was behind us, chasing us, and we started to run. It flew over our heads like a bird or something. If it hadn't been for Mick, I think it would have killed us. You probably think I am crazy, but it's true, and I think it killed Mick and his friends."

"Bless you, my child." Kieran now knew how the mysterious boy had shown up on his doorstep. Billy Tobin was a warrior, much like King David. "I don't think you are crazy at all. I believe you."

"You do? I thought you might have me committed. I didn't know who to talk to, and there was no way I could tell my parents."

"Trust in the Lord, my child. You did the right thing. I have seen something similar, and you are correct, Allison; it is evil." He heard the girl's corduroy slacks swooshing as she moved in the confessional.

"What have you seen, Father?"

"I saw the same presence myself. It is evil, and it has begun to spread. I don't know what happened to your boyfriend, Mick, but the boy you spoke of, the one named Billy."

"Yes, Father." Allison raised her voice.

"Billy Tobin, I believe his name is. He showed up on my doorstep in bad shape." He listened as the girl gasped, and continued. "I tended to Billy and brought him to the medical center. He woke last night and is going to be fine. He is a fighter."

"Yes. He is, Father."

"So are you, my child," he told her.

"No, not me."

"Yes, you, Allison. You are the first to speak out against the evil that has come to the parish. You should be proud of yourself."

"I didn't know what to do, Father."

"I'd say you knew exactly what to do. You turned to the Lord. I believe James said it best: *If any of you lacks wisdom, let him ask God, who gives generously to all without reproach, and it will be given to him.*"

"Thank you, Father." Allison blessed herself.

"You are quite welcome, my child. Heavenly Father, Lord Jesus Christ, forgive this woman of her sins and give her the strength to stand against the evil that walks by night. Allison, I want you to say three Hail Marys and four Our Fathers, and I would like you to attend Mass at noon."

"Of course, Father."

"Allison, if the Lord called upon you to stand against evil, would you? Would you fight for the ones you love; would you fight for Mick?"

"Father." She had stopped crying. "I would do anything for the ones I love."

That was all Father Kieran had wanted to hear. Allison was the first. He prayed that more would follow in her footsteps. Simon Peter had been the first as well.

"You are absolved of your sins," he said. "Go forth, my child, and do the Lord's bidding. Stand against evil and spread the word of our savior Jesus Christ. In the name of the Father, and of the Son, and of the Holy Spirit, Amen."

"Amen. Thank you, Father." Allison left the confessional and walked up the aisle to a pew at the front of the church. She knelt and began her penance.

Father Kieran sat in the silence of the confessional for a moment, giving thanks to the Lord. He prayed for the protection of Allison and the rest of his flock and asked for guidance. *If it is your will, then surely you will deliver a sign; I trust in you, Heavenly Father.*

He left the confessional and stopped in his tracks. A line of people had formed at the back of the church. Father Kieran allowed a gasp to escape his lips. There were nearly twenty people gathered in the aisle. They had all shown up to receive confession. The Lord had delivered.

He looked at the faces of his parishioners; some he recognized and others he had never seen before. They all wore the same look. It told Kieran they had all seen something, something they couldn't explain. Something that could only be interpreted through the scriptures.

●●●

Stephanie watched the sheriff's cruiser leave the quarry from her vantage point at the entrance of the cave. She checked her watch to see it was nearly ten thirty. She couldn't imagine what was holding up Barry and Joe; they were always punctual, arriving at the dig site no later than seven a.m. every morning. She had heard the explosions earlier and hoped that nothing happened to them or anyone else. Last night, there had been that huge fire, and now this. Neither of the explosions sounded all that far away, and Stephanie figured they originated somewhere in town.

They had just started to work in the cave when Don was alerted to a problem on the job site. From what she overheard, it sounded like vandalism or something. Don had freaked out and sprinted to where the heavy machinery was kept. Stephanie watched with growing concern. Until now, she'd never seen him act like that. Then the sheriff's cruiser showed up, which looked like even more bad news. Don and the deputy walked around the machines for a few minutes and disappeared to the far end of the quarry. Whatever had happened, it wasn't good.

Then the deputy returned to his vehicle and left out the front entrance. She watched as Don stormed across the dust lot of the quarry, bounded up the steps of his trailer, and slammed the door behind him. It was obvious he was in distress, and she wanted to help.

"Gail, I'll be back in a few minutes. I got to check on something. Okay?" Stephanie made her way to the trailer.

She didn't bother to knock and walked into the supervisor's trailer to find Don standing in the middle of the room with his back to her. "Hey," she called. "Are you okay? What the heck was that all about?"

He stood there breathing heavy. The guy was pissed off; that much was obvious.

"It's nothing!" he barked.

Stephanie jumped back, shocked and caught off guard by his aggression. "Whoa, easy, cowboy. I just came to see if you were okay." Unsure how to respond, she walked up behind him and put her hand on his shoulder. "What's going on, Don?"

He spun around like a rattlesnake, reacting to the touch of her hand. His face was dark red, his fists were clenched, and his chest puffed out. The penetrating glare in his eyes frightened her, causing Stephanie to gasp. What happened next surprised her even more.

She felt the heat rise in her own face as it flushed like a fever; her breath hitched and became ragged. Donald stared at her, his features wild like some crazed animal. The moment seemed to stagnate as Stephanie watched his eyes glaring into her own for what felt like years. Then they lowered, focusing on her chest and proceeding to scan the rest of her in a most magnetic way. She had no idea she was doing the same until she caught herself watching his chest heave up and down like a prize fighter, then her eyes dropped even further. She felt herself go weak and reached for him.

Donald seized her by the shoulders and pulled her against him. Their mouths met and locked in a kiss that burned like the sun, their tongues intertwined and wrapped around one another's in a heated pulse. Then Donald lifted her off her feet. The next thing she knew, she was being carried across the room and lowered onto his desk.

Stephanie shoved his papers to the floor and pulled at his belt as he yanked her head back and kissed her deeper. Donald ran his hands down the sides of her body and grabbed at her breasts, squeezing them and pinching her nipples through her shirt. Stephanie moaned as he lifted the garment over her head and threw it to the floor.

She unbuckled his belt, unzipped his pants, and plunged her hand inside. It was hot against her flesh; it felt as if he were on fire. Burning, longing, and hard. She squeezed him. A gasp of pleasure escaped his mouth and echoed in the back of her throat as he kissed her deeper and stronger.

Donald dug his thumbs into the sides of her shorts and ripped them off in one motion. They caught on her boots but only for a second, then she was pulling him closer. She grabbed him and guided him into her. She tensed and offered a brief moment of resistance as he pushed himself into the warmth between her legs. Then she welcomed it, and he easily slid deep inside of her. Within seconds, they were in perfect synchronicity, working as one. Donald pushed and Stephanie arched her hips, counter to counter, movement to movement.

She cried out as he increased the pace and pulled her by the hair. Breathing into one another, their hearts beating in time. Their sighs and moans heightened, becoming louder and more urgent. Donald groaned, and Stephanie screamed, and just when the passion felt as if it were too much to bear, it happened. She clawed her fingers into his chest and felt the waves of his orgasm pulsate against that of her own.

Stephanie fell onto her back panting as Donald lowered himself and rested against her. He kissed her neck as their breaths slowed and steadied and their nerves recovered from the overload. She ran her fingers through his hair and pulled him closer. His warmth inside her was like nothing she had ever felt. She wrapped her legs around him, drawing him in even further, and started to cry. She didn't know if they were tears of joy or of sorrow. *What have I done?* She could barely ask herself. She pushed the thought out of her mind, refusing to go there. *Not yet.* For now, all she wanted was to feel his heart beating against her chest and to lay connected as one. Even if it was for just a minute more, she would take it. It was a perfect moment. She figured there would be plenty of time later to hate herself for what she had done.

● ● ●

Bob Jones and Ed Koloski met the sheriff and his deputy at the back entrance of the high school gym. The first thing the chief noticed when he stepped out and shook Carl's hand was how empty the parking lot was for a school day. Usually, there wasn't an available spot to be found, but now, as he turned three-sixty, scanning the area, it wasn't half full. The designated parking spaces of several of the staff sat vacant as well: Vice Principal Anderson was absent along with more than a few other teachers, including Mr. Gunderson, Miss Shane, and Mr. Rizlo.

The starkness of the grounds was unsettling, making the football field and track area look more like a deserted ghost town than a place where gym classes were usually held throughout the day.

"Christ, Carl. It's worse than we thought," Bob said.

"I got a feeling we don't know the half of it," Carl replied. "And we need to make sure it doesn't get any worse. When's the last time you and your men were down in the shelter?"

Bob knew what he was getting at and immediately loved the idea. "Me personally, about six months. But I send an inspection crew down four times a year to give it a once over, change batteries, and restock the water supply."

"I'd like to take a look. Can't remember the last time I was down there, probably during the flood."

Bob tried the large steel door facing the lot, half expecting it to be locked up tight, but it opened easily, allowing the men access to the gym. The place was emptier than the parking lot. The sound of their shoes echoed off the high ceiling as they squeaked across the polished wood floor. It was sinister how empty the place was. *Someone should be here.* Even if it was just a random student or a solitary gym teacher.

The men crossed the basketball courts to the far corner of the gym, where three doors stood. The ones on either side were vented on the bottom and labeled boys and girls locker room. The smell of perspiration and teen angst wafted from the slotted opening in the doors like discarded dreams. The door in the middle was of a different design, solid and sturdy and labeled Fire Dept Only. Bob retrieved a set of keys from his coat pocket, thumbed through them until he found the one he was looking for, and slid it into the lock. The thundering click of a bank vault being breached bounced off the back walls of the gym.

The door creaked on its hinges as Bob swung it open. It was heavy and thick and hadn't been oiled in some time. A mixture of mold, mildew, and dust rushed at them from the darkness. Bob reached for the wall and turned on the light, revealing a long concrete staircase that descended deep into the basement.

The chief led the rest of the men downward. The twenty or so stairs stretched out as if they went on forever, until finally, they arrived at the bottom, where Bob used the same key to open a second door.

The room was almost the size of the gym, just a bit smaller. The ceiling was high, and the main area was long and wide, with several doors situated on the side wall that led to the storage area, kitchen, bathrooms, and the air handler. Carl surveyed the room, estimating how many people could fit inside. He exhaled and cursed under his breath.

"What's the occupancy, Bob?"

"Well, it's designed to hold about a thousand, but I think if you crammed them in, you could bump that up to about twelve or thirteen hundred."

"That's it?" Carl asked.

Bob knew exactly what he was thinking, that there were a hell of a lot more people in town than that. Even if they already lost as many as he feared. That would leave a lot of people left out in the cold.

"What other shelters are there?" Carl continued to scan the room.

"Well, a few people have their own, but I wouldn't count on many opening their doors to the public. Folks can get a little funny when it comes to survival. It's kinda like asking them to give up their guns; you just don't do it. Know what I mean?"

"I do," Carl said.

Garrett Grove was a mountain community, and damn near everyone hunted. Owning a gun was like owning a set of snow tires—it was just smart.

"The basement at the medical center could do in a pinch. That could house a couple hundred more, I suppose," Bob said.

"Can you think of anyplace else?"

"Honestly, that's about it. There are a few other places that have basements, but nothing solid like a bunker or a shelter. If you're planning what I think you are, then you're looking for something strong. Not somewhere with more weaknesses than strengths."

"Exactly." Carl walked into the center of the large structure, taking in its defenses and features. Two-foot-thick columns sat staggered throughout the main area; the entire place had been fabricated out of poured concrete and reinforced structural steel. There were only two passages in or out. The first was the way the men had come in, through the gym entrance and down the stairs. The other was a back exit located in one of the smaller rooms. The air handler and filtration system area had an access hatch with a twenty-foot ladder leading to a janitorial closet located near the gym.

"I'm sure your men have checked the supplies recently, but I'd feel a whole lot better if you rechecked everything. Then we have a lot of work to do. I want everyone we can fit in either the center's basement or down here by five o'clock tonight. We're going to split our men between the two, and we're going to ride this thing out. I'm not willing to bet the lives of everyone in town that Mr. Gomes made it out before the bridge went down. At this point, we have to consider the possibility that the state police never got our message and they're not coming." Carl took his hat off and ran his hand through his hair. "It's a hell of a job to make sure that everyone gets the message. Some won't be easily convinced. But we need to make sure they understand just how serious this is. If they choose not to listen, they need to know they are on their own and we won't to be able to help them later."

The other men listened, a mixture of shock and awe on each of their faces as Carl laid out the particulars of his plan. It was a daunting task he was proposing, and they were already undermanned. Most of the heavy lifting would fall on the fire department, and Bob had a few ideas on how to get the most bang for the buck. He shared the information with the sheriff as Rainey and Koloski inspected the shelter's supplies and the integrity of the escape routes.

Carl needed to get back to the station, but first he had to stop at Chilton and check out the basement. There were a lot of patients who needed to be evacuated to the lower level, and that was going to take time and manpower. Two commodities they had little of.

Chapter 59

The three children stood in front of Principal Grace's desk, nervous and fidgeting like the James gang waiting to be sentenced. The two girls and the boy stared at the floor in a vain attempt to divert attention from their accusers. Miss Boriello glared at the little instigators with her arms folded and a scowl on her face. Both she and the principal scanned the children for any sign of weakness, but they had so far held their ground. The girls kept their emotions concealed with an innocent look that would have fooled even a hanging judge. Troy, however, allowed his eyes to dart from the left to the right as if he were trying to locate the nearest escape route. Principal Grace zeroed in on him; she had found the weak link. "Troy Fischer," she asserted. "Would you mind telling me just what you thought you were doing out there?"

Troy jumped and was sure his eyes doubled in size when she called on him. He had tried his best not to be noticed and prayed she would seek her answers from either Janis or Wendy. Sweat rolled down the back of his neck as he struggled to swallow, only to find his mouth too dry to perform the task. He had no idea what to say as he stood between his comrades, and looked to them for guidance. Wendy shot him a quick glance that resembled nothing like support. If he had to guess what she was thinking, it was close to, *"Say something, you idiot!"*

"I um," he said, looking to his cohorts one last time. It was no use, even Janis turned away when he peered in her direction. Troy knew he was on his own; the women had sold him out. His father had warned him this would happen one day, only he hadn't thought it would be so soon. There was only one thing left to do, and he figured that maybe this was the opportunity he'd been looking for. However, with the older women staring at him and the younger ones acting like they couldn't remember his name, he felt less than optimistic about the outcome.

"I was trying to explain to the rest of the school why so many students are out sick," he said.

"Is that so, Mr. Fischer? And what exactly did you tell everyone?" Principal Grace squinted down at him over her glasses, making him feel even smaller than he already did.

"I-um-told them-um." His ears began to ring, causing him to feel even more light-headed. *Why is it so hot in here? I think I'm gonna pass out.* "I told them what happened to Rob. He was really sick and showed up at my house Saturday night in his pajamas and bare feet."

Principal Grace's eyes opened a bit wider as she leaned back in her chair. Miss Boriello, who had her arms crossed up until that point, appeared to relax a little, and her face softened some.

"He didn't recognize me," Troy continued. "It was like he was sleepwalking. Then he came after me like he wanted to bite me."

"Bite you! Troy Fischer, your friend didn't try to bite you." The principal continued to stare at him with the eyes of a skeptic, but the look on Miss Boriello's face was different. And despite the principal's initial reaction, she was still listening; they both were.

"Then he woke up and recognized me. He didn't know where he was, and he started shaking and fell down. My mom took him to Chilton, and then later she said he was getting better. But the other day I tried to call Rob's house, and nobody answered. I don't think he ever got better ... not at all." Troy struggled to control himself and fought the tears. He didn't want to appear weak in front of all the women, but it was a battle he couldn't win. The more he thought about Rob, the worse he felt. The lump grew thicker in his throat, making it impossible to swallow, and a slow tremor started to crawl up his legs. He felt the first tear well up and overflow; it ran down his cheek and fell to the floor.

Wendy saw what was happening and so did Janis. The girls offered their support, each in their own way. Wendy took Troy's hand and squeezed it, while Janis put hers on his back and comforted him.

The grown-ups watched the emotional event unfold. The sight of the girls offering their compassionate support was moving and caused Miss Boriello to wipe the tears that had begun to mist over her own eyes. Principal Grace contained herself a bit better but appeared affected by the display as well.

"I'm sorry to hear about Robert. I know you have been friends for a long time. Troy, if you ever need to talk to anyone, that's what I am here for. You can always come see me."

He managed to stop the rest of the tears from falling, which was difficult with Wendy and Janis touching him. Their attention made him feel like crying even more. "Yes, ma'am, I know." He wanted to tell her everything he told the kids on the playground but couldn't push the words out of his mouth.

"Okay then." Principal Grace leaned over her desk. "The next time the three of you wish to address the student body, I want to hear about it first. It looked like you were inciting a riot out there." The three nodded their heads in agreement, although none of them knew what she was talking about. Whatever it was didn't sound good. "Mr. Fischer, might I suggest you consider running for class president. We are going to have an election in November, and I think with these two young ladies as your campaign managers, you would probably win by a landslide."

The principal smiled, and the children knew they had been spared. Troy had been certain they were in deep. He wasn't sure what had happened, but it felt like it went well.

"You three better go back to class," she said, and they walked out of her office, leaving the two women behind. The adults waited until the children entered the classroom before they started speaking.

"Jill," the principal said, "I didn't want to push him; he was clearly upset. What else did Troy have to say out there on the playground?"

Miss Boriello poked her head out the door to be sure the children weren't in earshot. "He was speaking about all the absenteeism and said he didn't believe there was a flu going around. He said something chased him through the graveyard the other day and they needed to be careful because there was something in Garrett Grove. He wanted the other children to warn their parents." Jill Boriello told her boss everything she had overheard before making her presence known on the playground. She explained how Troy delivered his message like George Patton preparing his men for battle. Initially, she had been upset with the boy, but after seeing his reaction in the office, she realized there was more to it. It hadn't been a joke, and he wasn't trying to scare the other children; Troy was scared himself. He believed every word he said, which was why he had been so effective.

Grace Austin looked up at the woman and took off her glasses. "What do you think about what's going on here, Jill? I've never known Sharon Walsh to not show up to work. There's no way for her to call with the phones out, but it's still so unlike her. Also, Karen Doremus didn't come in either. I had to combine two classes into one because I didn't have a substitute to fill her place. Where is everyone? Nearly half of the students are missing today. It just doesn't make any sense. Do you have any idea what's going on?"

"I don't know any more than you, but something strange is happening in Garrett Grove. I help my next-door neighbor, she's older and has a hard time with certain things. I bring in her papers and help with the groceries since she doesn't have any children of her own. Well, I picked up her newspaper this morning and let myself in through the front door. I called out, but there was no answer, which I thought was strange because she has no way of leaving the house on her own. She wasn't in the kitchen or her bedroom; she wasn't anywhere in the house. She was gone, Grace, and it looked like there had been a struggle. Her refrigerator door was left open; the milk had been spilt on the floor and left there." She started to choke on the words, finding it difficult to hold her composure. "There was something else on the floor. It looked like tar or ink. It was black, and it smelled horrible."

"Dear Lord, what did you do?"

"That's where it gets even stranger. I stopped by the sheriff's office to tell them about Mrs. Martin, and there was a big meeting going on in the courthouse. I didn't feel comfortable walking in there, so I stopped one of the deputies on his way in. I think his name is Kovach, and he said they would check into it. But he was in an awful rush, and I could tell by the way he was acting that whatever was going on in that courthouse was important."

"Do you think I should consider closing the school? It's not like we could get in touch with the sheriff if something were to happen. I thought the phones would be back on by now. It's beginning to feel a bit tense. These children are my responsibility, and their parents count on us to keep them safe. Is there more going on than either of us know about?"

THE OJANOX

"I don't know, Grace. I just don't know."

Chapter 60

Lois took the stairs instead of using the elevator. After considering the recent fire that had taken place in the medical center, she wasn't about to risk getting stuck with the million things she needed to accomplish before picking up Troy at two forty-five. She had to convey the magnitude of the situation to her sister and brother-in-law, and prayed she wouldn't sound like a lunatic when she did. With her mind focused a bit more on what needed to be done rather than on where she was going, she rounded the landing and almost ran into the massive German Shepherd. The dog looked at her for a tense moment, then started to pant and wag its tail. Lois was startled by the sudden appearance of the animal and froze in her tracks. It was more the presence of the animal in such a place that struck her rather than the formidable size of the pup. She smiled, unsure how the dog would respond, and searched for a proper greeting. "Who's a good dog?" she believed would work.

And it had, as the dog sat down and raised his paw for Lois to shake. She took it and scratched the pup between the ears. "You are a good boy, aren't you?" Now that the dog was sitting, she could see he was in fact a boy, a big boy by the looks of it. "What are you doing here?"

"Baxter, come back here," the voice of a young girl called from one flight up. It was followed by the sound of fast approaching footsteps, then a sheriff's officer and a small child appeared.

"There you are," the girl said. "Bad dog, don't run away like that."

"I'm sorry about that. Oh-hello, Mrs. Fischer." Deputy Lutchen stood before her with a leash in his hand.

"Lois is fine," she said. "Nice to see you, Deputy Lutchen. And who is this?" Lois smiled at the girl.

"Dawn," she said, rocking back and forth and hiding behind the deputy's leg. The girl wore a pair of pajamas with fuzzy slippers. Her hair was wet as if she had just washed it, and she was carrying a doll that looked like it had also doubled as the dog's chew toy at one time.

"It's nice to meet you, Dawn." She turned to Ted. "What brings you here, Deputy?"

"Well, um, Lois. It's a long story, but we came here yesterday for the doc to check out my friend. Then we got stuck here last night. I'm sure you heard what happened." Dawn pressed against his leg and wrapped her arms around it.

"Nurse TenHove told me." Lois didn't want to say too much in front of the child and could tell the deputy was thinking the same thing. "My nephew was admitted yesterday, and I'm on my way to see him. My sister and brother-in-law are here with him."

"I think I saw them; the Tobins, right?"

"Yeah, that's them. I was hoping Billy would be released. I'd like to take a little trip with the family, you know, sooner than later." Lois watched the deputy's facial features deflate and knew he was about to say something she didn't want to hear.

"Mrs. Fischer." Lois held her breath and waited for him to drop the bomb. "There's been a situation—actually, a couple." He leaned closer so he could whisper without Dawn hearing. "The Gables Bridge is out of service as well as Sunset Road. We can't leave town."

Lois scanned his eyes to see if he was exaggerating. "What are you talking about?" Then she remembered the explosions she had heard early this morning. One of the blasts sounded like it came from the south side of town by Route 3, and the other one sounded as if it had originated from the mountain. *Dear God!* She suddenly knew why there had never been a warning siren. The explosions hadn't happened at the quarry—DuCain always sounded the horn before they blasted; it was the law. Visions of Pompeii and of lifeboats flooded into her head.

How could I have been so stupid? She had not only ignored the warning signs but she had also missed the lifeboats; she was a member of both groups. And now she had jeopardized Troy's safety as well.

"Mrs. Fischer, I didn't believe your son the other day. I should have."

Sirens sounded in her ears as the urgency to cry out welled up within her throat. Her hands shook, and her bottom lip had begun to tremble. "I need to see my sister," Lois said as she pushed past the dog, the deputy, and the little girl. "Excuse me, please." She covered her face and bounded up the stairs, trying to hide her hysterics.

"Nice to meet you, Mrs. Fischer," the child said as the woman ran past them.

Lois heard the innocent voice and burst into tears as she ascended the next flight and exploded onto the second floor. The door slammed shut, depositing her in an empty hallway. Lois doubled over and clutched her knees as the tears tore through her like an avalanche. She struggled to control her breath and fight it. Finally, she succumbed to emotion and wailed. *How could I have been so stupid? How could I have been so stupid?*

Ted had heard the frantic transmissions concerning the bridge and the Sunset Pass on his walkie-talkie. Things were unraveling at an alarming rate. An hour later, he heard the reports about Tara, Kovach, and Deputy Colbert. He could only stare at the radio as the sheriff broke the news to Andrea. He and Joel Kovach were working together when they found young Dawn hiding underneath her bed. And now the man was dead? That just couldn't be. Tara and Colbert? It wasn't possible. A thousand thoughts flooded his brain as he sat in silence, radio in hand and the world gone insane. He needed to be out there helping his fellow officers, but Dawn needed him too. With everything that was happening, there was no way she could survive on her own, although she had done a better job of it than most already. Still, she was Ted's responsibility, and he damn sure wasn't about to let her out of his sight.

Shortly after Ted heard the grim news, the sheriff asked him to check out the basement and said he would be arriving soon as well. So after Dawn had washed up and gotten a fresh pair of clothes, they headed down the stairs with Baxter leading the way and Drowsy, Dawn's favorite doll, tucked underneath her arm.

They opened the door to the basement, and Baxter was the first to enter. Ted and Dawn followed the pooch into the dark, musty chamber.

"It smells funny down here." Dawn wrinkled her nose at the damp odor.

Ted surveyed the room, which was big but not enormous by any means. He had been expecting the basement's footprint to be reflective of how large the medical center was. Which it wasn't; in fact, compared to the rest of the building, the basement was rather small. The foundation had been dug out only large enough to allow for the boilers, furnaces, and mechanical equipment. A network of pipes ran across the ceiling in every direction, along with the venting and filtration ducts. The pipes were painted an array of colors, and many of them were labeled for their various usage. There were hot-and-cold-water lines along with oxygen and nitrous lines as well. Several were labeled caustic, but Ted couldn't imagine what was inside them. Still, with all the equipment in the basement, there was room for quite a few people, which was what he had been thinking when he spoke to Greg the orderly this morning. Then the sheriff called and asked him to take a look. *Great minds.*

"I don't like it down here, Ted." Dawn nuzzled up against his leg and scanned the room. "It smells funny."

"Of course it smells funny." Ted looked down at her and smiled. "That's what leprechauns smell like. I bet there's a couple of 'em down here."

Dawn's stare doubled in size as she scoped out the room. "I don't see any leprechauns."

"That's because they're hiding. If you saw them, they would have to give you some of their gold." He struggled to keep a straight face.

Dawn let go of his leg and took a few steps into the room. A moment later, she was exploring with Baxter at her side.

"Not too far." He was happy to see a bit of her confidence return as she looked back and offered a quick nod, her head already filled with thoughts of leprechaun's gold.

There was a loud thud from the door behind them being thrown open. Baxter barked twice when Carl and Nurse TenHove entered the basement.

"How's our patient doing this morning?" Carl asked.

"Much better. I was worried with all the commotion going on last night. But I think she's more resilient than any of us. I can't even imagine after everything." Ted spoke low enough so that Dawn couldn't hear, even though she and the dog had already moved off to the middle of the basement floor.

Nurse TenHove shook her head with a scowl fixed to her face. "I see that dog is still here, Deputy." She peered at him over her glasses, then cracked a smile. "But I suppose it's okay, as long as you keep an eye on him."

Carl took several steps into the large area and removed his hat, surveying the room as he spun around on his bootheels. "Nurse TenHove." He turned to her. "How many patients do you have, and what will it take to get all of them down here before this evening?"

She stared at him with her mouth open as if he had asked her to construct an ark out of toothpicks, then the look of gobsmacked frustration was replaced as she began to ponder the question.

"Sixty-three, to be exact," she said. "But there are a few problems with that, Sheriff. First, nearly half of my staff didn't show up today. If I had enough orderlies and nurses, we could move the portable cots and supplies, which is the hardest part. The service elevator runs all the way down; the bay is in the back of the room." Doris took an exasperated breath and pointed to its location. "Transporting the patients is easy enough, except for the ones on the third floor. Many can't be moved. Some are on life support, and others are in critical condition or recovering from surgery. Without trained personnel, I wouldn't risk it. Then there's the elderly, and some are in traction. I'd say I have about twenty patients that I wouldn't try to move."

"Would you still make that recommendation if their lives depended on it?" Carl stood before Doris and stared into her eyes, allowing the gravity of the situation to register.

"I understand what you're asking, Sheriff. And yes, from a triage aspect, there are at least fifteen patients that I wouldn't even try to move." Doris bit down and wiped her eyes. She understood full well what this meant. "Some might not even survive the trip in the elevator and will have to be left on the third floor. I will remain with them."

"We'll cross that bridge when we get there. Right now, you need to show me where you keep those extra cots, and I want you to start taking inventory of any medications and first aid equipment you'll need down here as well. Also, we're going to need medical supplies for the high school. There's going to be about twelve hundred there, and I want to be prepared for anything."

"I don't have the manpower to do half of this," she emphasized.

"I'll take care of that." Carl replaced his hat and nodded to his deputy. "Ted and Dawn will assist you with the medication, and I'll get you some help. I take it there's still some staff available; we're going to need all hands on deck to pull this off. I'm hoping there are a few doctors here as well?"

"I know Dr. Freedman and Dr. Halasz are around. The intercom system is working, so I can make an announcement if you need me to."

"I'm going to need a doctor at the high school along with first aid supplies ... just in case."

"How long do you plan to keep everyone down here, Sheriff?" Ted asked.

Carl inspected the area once again, noticing the girl and her dog, who had ventured to the far end of the basement. "As long as it takes or until help arrives. We can't be certain the outside world is aware of our situation. I doubt our messenger made it to Warren. By my estimate, and I pray to God I'm wrong, I believe we've lost somewhere between a third to one half of the town overnight. If we don't have everyone locked away safely in either this basement or the shelter, I don't think any of us will see the morning. For the most part, these things have been attacking at night, but that changed today. The ones we saw went down quick and didn't appear as strong as the ones we ran into the other night. I'm only guessing, but I'm inclined to believe they are stronger at night. We've got just about six hours before sunset, then the shit is really going to hit the fan."

Ted and Doris understood the gravity of the situation and nodded in agreement. There was little time left to accomplish an impossible amount of work. If they managed to execute what the sheriff asked and they got most of the people into the shelters, there would still be losses. But when it came to triage, a calculated percent of casualties was acceptable, provided you could save the majority.

Andrea Geary sat at the dispatch station unable to wrap her head around the moment. What the sheriff had said just wasn't possible; she refused to believe it.

Joel had gone to Tara's house to check on her whereabouts. She had told him goodbye just an hour ago and could still smell his Old Spice on her clothes. The clock that hung above her station thundered with every passing punctuation of the second hand. It hammered inside her, threatening to rip her from her delicate hold on reality. *You can't be dead.* Somehow, the sheriff had gotten it wrong.

She and Joel Kovach had been seeing each other for three months now and had done a good job of keeping a lid on it. They'd worked together for five years without Andrea ever suspecting he had feelings for her in that regard. Joel was as straight and by the book as they came, certainly not the type to date a coworker. But they had been talking a bit more lately, and then, out of the clear blue, he asked her to the movies.

Andrea couldn't have been more shocked and had probably insulted the poor guy by how surprised she acted. But she agreed, and they had a nice night out together. Joel Kovach was a gentleman who opened the car door for her and was always ready with a match for her cigarette. They'd gone out a few times after that, and Andrea believed she had feelings for him. But it had been over two months and she was still waiting for him to make a move. *Maybe he doesn't like me that much?* Joel had never gone any further than touching her breast through her shirt when they kissed. And Andrea had started to think that nothing would ever come of it.

That was until about two weeks ago, when Joel shocked the shit out of her. They had gotten together at her place, and Andrea made his favorite, roast beef with green beans and mashed potatoes. They shared a few glasses of red wine with dinner and had gotten a little drunk in the process.

Apparently, alcohol was the universal primer and all the confidence Joel needed. Before they could make it to the bedroom, Joel had Andrea half naked on the kitchen table with her legs in the air. From there, they proceeded to the couch, and then onto the floor. They finally made it to the bedroom with Andrea's clothes littered throughout the house like a trail of breadcrumbs. Joel had gone at her with an urgency to make up for lost time. They finished several hours later, bathed in sweat, exhausted, sore, and punch-drunk. Joel had literally fucked her brains out.

They had gone out again last Friday for an encore performance. Andrea had never experienced anything like that with another man and was beginning to think she might be falling for him. Joel gave her the eye at work when no one was looking, asked her to sneak off to the back room for a little foreplay and dirty talk. She even offered to give him a good tongue-lashing in the literal sense one day, but Joel was far too "by the book" to try such a thing at work. But Andrea figured he might *come* around.

This coming Friday was the night before Halloween, and neither were scheduled to work. They'd been looking forward to devouring each other like a couple of teenagers. Andrea couldn't believe any of it was real; she was damn near forty years old and having the best fucking sex of her life. She had never been so happy.

As far as Andrea knew, Sheriff Primrose didn't have a clue they were seeing each other. Which wasn't an excuse for how he treated her; the bastard had been so cold. He had delivered the news of their coworkers' deaths as if it were just another traffic accident. The room suddenly felt much smaller, and the ringing in Andrea's ears and the booming of the clock on the wall had become deafening. *You can't be dead; you just can't be.* She hadn't even kissed him goodbye.

Andrea struggled to pull herself together, but images of Joel's face appeared on every surface she stared at. Then Deputy Rainey entered the station and approached her. He wrapped his arms around her and said something that was lost in the din. Andrea stood up to accept his comfort and again allowed the tears to overflow their banks.

"I know," Rainey said. "I loved him too."

"Y-you know?" she asked between sobs. "Was it obvious?"

"Not at all." He held her a bit tighter. "I just saw the way he looked at you. He really loved you."

"Do you think so?"

"I know so. I'm a cop; it's my job to know these things."

"We were trying to be so careful." Andrea let out a strangled cry.

"No one has any idea. I'm sure of it." Rainey lowered his voice. "Are you gonna be okay, Andrea? Things are going to get crazy, and I think we're in for a fight. If you can't do it, just say so; we can get Jenkins to cover for you."

Andrea stepped back and wiped at her eyes. She took a heavy breath to steady herself, then straightened her shirt and walked back to the dispatch station. "Thank you, David, but I will be fine. I am a sheriff's deputy, and I am trained to work under pressure. Now, what needs to be handled first, and what exactly are we looking at?"

Rainey smiled and nodded his head. "Bob Jones is getting the fire department together. Half the men are going to the medical center and the other half to the high school. As soon as Jenkins and the other guys get back, we're going to start canvassing the neighborhoods. We need to let everyone in town know exactly what they have to do. It's going to be a big clusterfuck if we don't execute it to the letter. I hope your driving skills are up to snuff; as soon as we're ready, we'll be leaving the station."

"All right," Andrea said. "Let's do this."

⬤ ⬤ ⬤

Chris Fredricks was the first of Bob's men to arrive at the high school. The chief watched the boy, who had just turned nineteen and still lived with his parents, pull into the back parking lot in his Ford pickup. He was followed by another man in a similar-style vehicle, then another and yet another. Bob smiled as he watched the parade. If there was one thing you could count on, it was a fireman. Garrett Grove was a volunteer unit. These guys didn't do it for a paycheck, they ran into burning houses because they wanted to help people, and Bob trusted every last one of them. He counted at least ten heads so far, and the chatter on the radio told him that the other team had started to arrive at the medical center as well. He still hadn't heard from Deputy Rainey but wasn't worried a bit about the men assigned to his detail. *With any luck, we just might pull this off.*

⬤ ⬤ ⬤

Stephanie lay with her legs wrapped tightly around Don's waist and her fingers in his hair. She prayed that the moment wouldn't pass, that reality could wait just a bit longer to resume. Their breaths worked in tandem, and their pulses had synched. Stephanie could feel his heartbeat inside her and refused to let go. She couldn't remember ever feeling so completely fulfilled.

Don eased back and looked into her eyes. He pressed his lips against hers and kissed her; it was long, and slow, and bittersweet. Then she relaxed her grip and let him go.

He helped her off the desk and hugged her. "I had no idea it could be like that," he whispered in her ear.

Stephanie backed away and picked her clothes up off the floor. She offered a thin smile but didn't reply. She barely knew what she was thinking, let alone what to say, which even she found ironic.

"I've never—" he started.

"I know." She shrugged her shoulders and fumbled with her shirt. "You don't have to say anything. I was there too."

A smile as wide as the Ganges spread across his face. "What the hell was that?"

She approached him and kissed his cheek. "Amazing, that's what."

"Yeah, and then some. I sure as hell don't remember it being—"

She pressed her finger against his lips. "You talk too much. We don't need to fill the silence with words that won't change anything. It was perfect ... Let's just leave it at that. It can't go anywhere." *Christ! I just fucked a married man!* She buttoned her shorts and kicked on her boots as the tears started to fall, then she rushed past him toward the door. Donald grabbed her by the arm and spun her around before she could leave.

"There's nothing left of my marriage ... not that there ever was. We only got married to raise Troy. You said it yourself; life doesn't always turn out the way you expect it. Well, I sure as hell didn't expect this, but it happened, and I'm not letting you walk out that door."

She stood with her mouth open and her brain spinning a mile a minute. *What the hell is happening? I'm not stealing another woman's husband!* After what Brian had done to her, how could she entertain it ... even for a minute? But no man had ever made her feel like that before. It had been raw and animalistic, and so impossibly perfect. *Christ, what a horrible bitch I must be. Who does this?*

Donald took a step closer, and Stephanie's heart screamed; she put her hands against his chest and pushed him away. "We both need to calm down and think clearly. We have a lot of work to do, and if I stay in this trailer a minute longer, we both know what will happen. So, I'm walking out this door and going back to work. Meet me and Gail in the cave when you've got yourself together. We'll talk about this later."

Donald put his hand under her chin and lifted her head. She allowed him to kiss her, and then she walked out of the trailer and closed the door behind her.

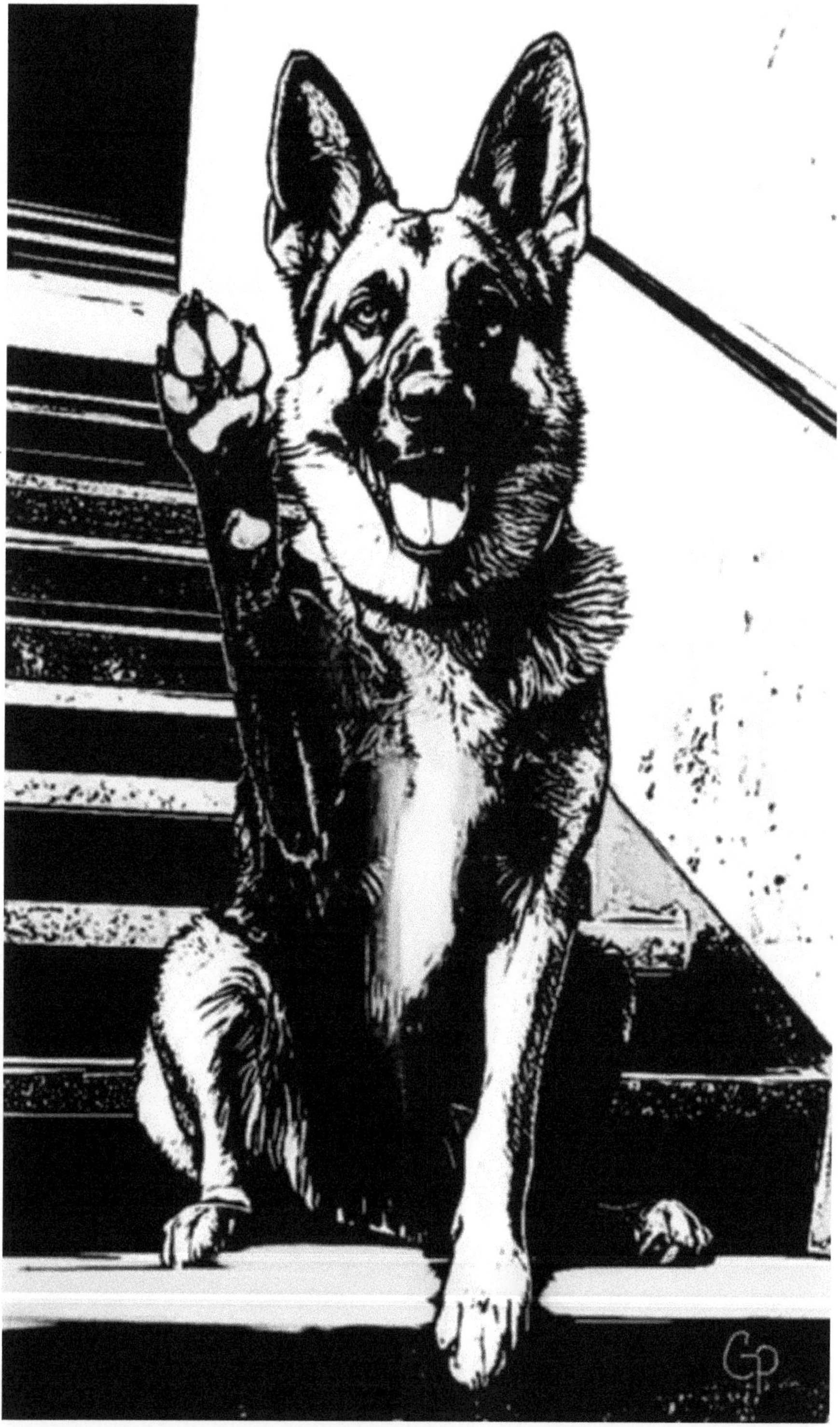
GP

Chapter 61

Lois struggled to control her sobs, her breath raking in her chest, heavy and fast like a diesel engine. Her hands trembled, and the hair on her arms bristled as if in tune to the static emptiness of the medical center. The acrid tang of disinfectant fused with the underlying stench of bedpans. Lois winced and forced herself to focus. She couldn't afford to lose it now; there were others who needed her. But as she emerged into the stark fluorescent light of the second-floor hallway, her grip on sanity slipped even more.

She searched to the left and right, expecting to find a doctor or even an orderly making their rounds. But there was no one. The long span of polished tile stretched out before her like a deserted runway. The drone of a nearby vending machine was the only sound, a jarring contrast that Lois could feel resonating in her teeth. Hunched over with her hands still on her knees, she focused on the small square of flooring and exhaled. The sudden squeaking of rubber soles on tile startled her. Lois looked up to see a young nurse exit one of the rooms. The girl plodded toward the reception area with her eyes glued in front of her and hadn't seen Lois doubled over in the hallway. The nurse moved fast, as if she had too many tasks to accomplish and no idea where to begin. Lois could see the girl was struggling as well, but somehow, she had managed to pull herself together and focus on the job. A wave of guilt washed over Lois as she watched the young girl. With all the strength she could muster, she straightened her back, wiped her cheeks, and approached the desk where the nurse stood, separating medications into tiny plastic cups.

"Excuse me."

The girl jumped, spilling several of the pills onto the counter.

"Oh." Her hands shook as she scrambled to gather them. "I'm sorry. I didn't see you there."

"I didn't mean to startle you. I was looking for my nephew; his name is Billy Tobin." Lois watched the girl fumble with the medication and could tell from the glazed look in the nurse's eyes that she was on the verge of tears. Pushing her own fear and anxiety to the side, Lois reached over the desk and took her hand.

"Here," she said. "Let me help you with that." Lois walked around the counter.

"I'm sorry," the nurse said in a voice as frail as a shiver. Then the tears started; the girl broke down and threw her arms around her.

Lois felt the child's sobs convulsing and radiating throughout their embrace. She hugged her back and forced herself to stay strong. "I thought I was going to be the only one who cried today."

The nurse chuckled between a series of tears, then stepped back and attempted to regain a fraction of her composure. "I'm sorry. That's so unprofessional of me."

Lois noticed the girl's name tag: Carole. "I don't think so." Lois pulled a tissue from her purse and handed to her.

"Hardly anyone came to work today." She struggled to control her breathing as she spoke. "At first, I thought—well, to tell you the truth, I don't know what I thought. But people have been talking, and some of the stories are starting to make sense after everything that's happened in the past twenty-four hours."

Lois searched for some words of reassurance, though she'd been struggling herself.

"Carole, right?" The girl nodded. "My name's Lois. I know exactly how you feel. I can't even count how many times I've cried today. You should have seen me a few minutes ago." Lois brushed a piece of hair from the girl's eyes. "But you know what? You came to work, and you stuck around because you know people are counting on you." Carole nodded in understanding. "I know your patients are glad you're here. And I also know we're going to get through this."

"Thank you." Carole wiped her cheek and picked up the medicine bottle. "Do you think you could stay and help me for a few minutes, just until I get the morning meds out? I never had to do it by myself before." Her giant eyes pleaded as she fought to hold it together.

"Of course. I'd be happy to. And when we're done, I want to introduce you to my nephew Billy."

A shadow crossed the girl's face. "I was a senior when Billy was a sophomore. I don't know if you've heard about Billy's girlfriend, Debbie—Debbie Horne?" Lois shook her head; she had never met the girl. "Debbie was in a car accident yesterday ... She didn't make it. I don't think Billy knows yet." Carole's voice trembled as she delivered the news.

Dear God. How much more? A black cloud had settled over Garrett Grove. The extent of grief that plagued the town in such a short period of time was impossible to comprehend. Lois tried to recall when it all started. Saturday night, just five days ago? It had all started when Rob showed up in her garage dressed in only his pajamas.

"We're not going to say anything about that to Billy. He's been through enough already, and I don't want to upset him any more."

Carole nodded and looked up when a woman's voice broke over the intercom system. *"Attention all staff. There is a mandatory meeting in the cafeteria in fifteen minutes. Please be advised, in fifteen minutes, there will be a mandatory meeting for all staff. Thank you."*

"That can't be good," Carole said. "Lois, will you come with me, please?"

Lois checked her watch and smiled. "Of course." There was still time before she had to pick Troy up at school. Together, the women finished filling the tiny plastic cups and distributed the medication to the patients on the second floor. Then they checked in on Billy to find him sitting up eating his breakfast, which was the best news Lois had received all day. She hugged Alice and Will and promised she would be back soon.

She had been mistaken.

● ● ●

It took longer to distribute the medication than either woman anticipated, and Carole and Lois arrived several minutes late to the meeting. They entered through the double doors of the cafeteria and were bowled over by the crowd. The place was packed and not just with medical staff but a good number of the town's volunteer firemen. Head Nurse TenHove stood at the front of the room, flanked by Deputy Lutchen, the little girl named Dawn, and her dog. Lois scanned the room, overwhelmed by the sea of faces, most of whom she knew. It was a stark contrast to how empty the rest of the building was.

Lois and Carole started to push their way through the crowd when the doors burst open behind them. Lois spun around to find herself face-to-face with Carl.

She could read it in the expression on his face: *God Dammit, Lois. What the hell are you still doing here?*

He shook his head, then pushed his way to the front of the room. "I need to talk to you," he whispered to her.

Lois felt as if she had betrayed the man yet again and by doing so had also put her family in harm's way. She studied how weary he looked. Fresh crops of grey hair were visible at his temples, and his face was ashen and hard, as if he had aged years since yesterday.

He stood in front of the room and removed his hat. "We are officially under a state of emergency," he addressed the crowd and was bombarded by a flurry of comments and questions. He raised his hands and continued. "As you can see, a lot of people are missing. And if we don't work together, things will get a whole lot worse."

"What's going on, Sheriff? Where is everybody?" Dr. Freedman shouted.

"There's been an outbreak, Doctor. It started over the weekend and has continued to spread. We don't fully understand it, and that's why we need to get everyone to safety. This infection killed Dr. Malcolm and Dr. Ziegler. It appears to manifest in the body and control the host. A lot of people have already been infected, and we need to protect ourselves. This thing has killed four of my deputies already."

"How are we going to protect ourselves if it's killing cops?" a young man shouted.

"We're moving everyone into the shelters, and that's why I need you. The patients can't fend for themselves, so with the help of the fire department, we plan to move everyone into the basement. We're going to ride this out till help arrives."

"Why isn't help here already?"

He held his hands up again. "I'm afraid we're on our own. Both the Gables Bridge and the Sunset Pass have been destroyed."

"What?"

"What do mean destroyed?" Dr. Freedman shouted.

"Someone broke into the quarry and stole some explosives. They sabotaged the bridge and the Pass."

The room erupted in a flurry of voices louder than before. Most of which were cries of concern rather than screams of unacceptance. They had all seen something, had all heard the strange shrieks or witnessed their neighbors disappearing one by one over the past few days.

"No one may be coming for a little while. So I need to get everyone into the shelters, and I need your help. But time is of the essence, we have until about five o'clock. We need to be locked up tight before it gets dark. So listen to the firemen and work with them. Nurse TenHove is in charge; if you can't find either her or myself, speak to Deputy Lutchen." Carl pointed to Ted, who had given his hat to the little girl holding his hand.

Lois scanned the faces in the crowd, noticing how the combined looks of loss and despair were replaced by a sense of urgency. Carl had given them something to do and, with it, instilled a sense of purpose. Lois smiled as the crowd began to rush to their assigned tasks.

● ● ●

Nurse TenHove coordinated the allocation of work with the help of Deputy Lutchen and Derek Fisk from the fire department. For the most part, everyone had taken the sheriff's message seriously. However, there were two men who did not agree with Carl's all-for-one mentality and took it upon themselves to leave after the meeting ended.

Both Mark Walsh and Theo Spellman worked in the janitorial department. They had witnessed what happened in the imaging wing last night and figured they were better off on their own. Mark left out the back door, hopped into his van, and headed home to ride out the storm with his elderly mother. Theo simply walked out the front and never punched his timecard. He drove home to be with his pregnant wife, Nancy, and loaded his shotgun. He had his own family to care for and wasn't about to play hero for four bucks an hour. He damn sure wasn't about to die in some dusty basement. Neither man ever returned to work, or anywhere else for that matter.

●●●

Carl took Lois by the arm and led her down the hall until he found an empty room, then urged her inside.

"Goddammit, Lois. I told you to leave. What are you still doing here?"

"It isn't that easy. The phones were out, and I couldn't get in touch with Alice. Billy is upstairs, and Eric is still missing. Then Troy gave me a hard time about missing school. I swear I must be the only mother whose child wants to go to school." Her voice trembled as she told him. "I can't explain, but the more I knew, the more reasons I found to talk myself out of it. It was all just so impossible I didn't know what to think."

He started to pace the floor. "Did you think I was making it up? Have I ever given you a reason not to take me seriously?" He rubbed his temples and squinted as if in pain.

"No."

"Then why now, of all times, would you choose not to listen? Christ, you should be miles away from here. I can't guarantee I can keep you safe."

"That's not what you told everyone in there."

"No, but if I said they might die tonight, I'd have a damn panic on my hands."

"You don't think you can protect them? Don't you think the shelters will work?"

"Honestly ... I don't know. I hope so, but we have no idea what the hell we're dealing with. It's nothing anyone has ever seen, and it's superior in every way. Why didn't you leave, Lois?" Carl took his radio off his hip and handed it to her. "Do you still have the gun I gave you?"

She nodded and pulled it out of her purse, then she took the radio from his hand.

"Hold on to this in case we get separated. Just press the button and talk right here." He pointed to the microphone. "I have another, and I'll hear you."

"Thank you." She watched it tremble in her unsteady hands.

THE OJANOX

Carl checked his watch. "We still have time. You said Troy is at school. At two thirty, I'll take you there myself, we'll pick up Troy, and then I want you both in the shelter at the high school, no questions."

"Why not here with my sister and her family?"

Carl opened his mouth to speak, then stopped and looked away. Lois knew he was hiding something but didn't press further. "We'll figure it all out later," he said. "In the meantime, I need your help. There are a lot of patients that need to be relocated to the basement, and there's more work than people to do it. Maybe you could talk Alice and Will into pitching in too."

She studied his eyes, which looked even older than they had a minute ago. Deep crow's feet crawled from the corners as if he hadn't slept in weeks. Lois deposited the radio in her purse and took out her cigarettes. She lit one, then offered the pack to Carl, who accepted.

"I'm sorry I didn't listen—again. How are you going to get everyone into the shelters?"

He took a long drag and exhaled. "I don't think I will. Some—but not everyone. A good number will think they'd be better off on their own, and I can't force them. But I have an idea that should convince most."

Lois studied the lines in his face, allowing her heart to tear apart more than she thought it possibly could. She had put him through so much, and he was still going out of his way to help. Her marrying Donald had destroyed him, and then he had gone off to fight, which affected him even more. The war had changed Carl. It wasn't something everyone could pick up on, but she had and was sure that Burt had as well. He carried something back with him after leaving Vietnam, a burden he shared with no one. It was written on his face like the deep lines he now wore.

"Are you okay?" He had been talking to her.

"What?"

"There's a lot to do. I asked you if you were up to this."

"Yeah, I'm all right," she lied.

Carl held the door open for her, and they left the room empty once again. The smoke from their cigarettes was the only proof that they had ever been there at all.

When Lois walked into the room, Alice seized her into a bear hug and refused to let go. Billy, who had been sitting in a chair earlier, was now on his feet attempting to stretch his legs.

"Aunt Lois, how are you?"

"Never mind me, what about you? Are you sure you should be standing?"

"It's okay," he said. "I'm torn up a bit, but it's good to walk some. My head bothers me more than my legs. I still don't remember too much."

"Well, don't overdo it just yet," she said as Nurse Carole entered the room, causing Billy's disposition to brighten.

"I'm here to check on my patient."

Lois had asked the girl to show up and occupy Billy so she could speak to Will and Alice.

"If you wouldn't mind excusing us for a few minutes." Carole smiled while the rest of the family retreated to the hallway.

Lois told them about Carl's plans to get everyone into the shelters. Alice and Will had been through so much with the boys in the past few days, and the news didn't strike them nearly as absurd as Lois thought it might. There was some doubt, and Will jokingly asked if she'd been drinking, but they were rather easy to convince. The empty halls of the center and the fire the night before had primed them for just about anything. Also, they'd been served breakfast by a Sheriff's Deputy, a little girl in her pajamas, and a German Shepherd. They already knew something serious was going on.

Will and Alice agreed to help in any way they could. They always liked Carl and knew he cared about the people in town, even Billy, who had been one royal pain in his ass.

Stephanie and Gail were standing before one of the murals when Don entered the secondary chamber of the cave. He nodded and looked around for the other men. "Where are Barry and Joe? Don't tell me they're still not here?"

THE OJANOX

"Never showed up," Gail replied and snapped several photos in quick succession.

Stephanie caught his eye as he approached, and smiled. He offered one in return, then they both looked away.

The mural they examined the previous day was the most intriguing piece of work Don had witnessed so far. It was an accurate depiction of Earth's position in the solar system. The fact that it had been painted over five hundred years ago was mind-boggling.

The painting they now focused on was also of the planet, only in this one, the strange cloud had encompassed the earth, making the sphere look as if it were enveloped in fog. It was dirty and dark and looked toxic. The previous murals showed the cloud in the cosmos as a massive singularity, but this depicted it as part of Earth's atmosphere. Don had no idea what any of it meant but still found them fascinating. After all, it'd been a very long time since human eyes had gazed upon any of this.

Gail snapped away, with the flash of her camera making the place look more like a disco or one of the rooms in Troy's haunted house.

Stephanie moved on to the next mural and brushed against Don when she passed. "Oh, excuse me," she whispered, and continued.

The fourth mural wasn't a view of the planet, or even from space—it was a depiction of life on Earth. Reptiles and other lizard-like creatures had been drawn on the walls and colored with vibrant inks. The creatures appeared prehistoric, or at least some of them did. One looked similar to a small dinosaur that Don had seen in *National Geographic Magazine*. The paintings also held a striking similarity to the ones at the entrance of the cavern. The dark smoke, present in the picture of the woman and the holy man, was also visible in these and covered the reptiles in a most intrusive way. It surrounded their heads and invaded the beasts through their eyes and nostrils.

"Is that the same stuff surrounding the earth in this mural?" Don compared the two.

"It looks that way, doesn't it?" Stephanie nodded. "What do you make of it?"

"Well." Don thought about it for a moment. "Here it looks like a cloud or some type of pollution. It isn't painted in a flattering way. The Lenape didn't like it. But they didn't have pollution back then, did they? And here the animals are breathing it in, just like the murals in the front of the cave." Don stepped closer to the wall to get a better look. "Look at this. The snake and the lizard have those same black eyes, just like the man and woman in the other murals—just like it!" Don felt he could almost remember what it all reminded him of; it was on the tip of his memory.

"Pretty good, Mr. Fischer." Stephanie nodded in agreement. "Very perceptive, I'm impressed."

Don realized Stephanie knew exactly what she was looking at and had long before she arrived on his job site. She was hiding something. He hadn't been certain of it before, but their dynamic had changed, and now, he was positive.

Chapter 62

Bob Jones walked through the hallway of the high school, feeling like a giant as he passed the lockers and classrooms. He had gone to Garrett High, but the place felt a whole lot bigger back then. Of course, he had been smaller himself, but there was more to it than that. It wasn't just a matter of comparative perception; everything appeared larger to children. Bob figured it had more to do with the larger worldview shared by adults that made the places of one's childhood appear smaller. It happened after you went out on your own and had taken in all the experiences that eluded childhood. The good as well as the bad.

The world had happened to Bob after graduating from Garrett High. Prior to his senior year, the furthest he had ever been outside of town was his cousin's house in Pennsylvania. He had had one girlfriend, Sally Simpson, who he believed he would marry one day. And back then, he had even wanted to be an architect.

The country hadn't gotten involved in Vietnam yet, and although some of his friends had tried to convince him to join the Army, that hadn't interested Bob. He planned to attend college after high school; however, life had other plans. Bob's father suffered a stroke and become unable to work. And that had been the end of Bob's college plans, along with any dream of ever becoming an architect. He got a job in a print shop to help with the bills and found himself working an average of sixty hours a week.

He and Sally broke up the same year his father had the stroke, never to be married, not that Bob would have had much time for it. Which was no consolation, and it had hurt like a bitch. A few months later, Sally met a man named Earl Hillman and married the guy in a flash. Earl lived in Warren on a large piece of land his grandfather had left him. It was set far enough back into the woods and away from the neighbors so none of them could hear Sally scream on the nights when Earl came home drunk and proceeded to beat the tar out of her. The beatings went on for a few months, with each consecutive injury worse than the previous. Sally was treated for a concussion one week; the next, she was getting her arm set in a cast. And even though the couple lived in Warren, news traveled fast. Sally still came into town to visit her parents, who became increasingly concerned for her safety.

Bob had heard the stories about Sally and ran into her at the store one day. She wore a large pair of sunglasses, but the bruises under her eyes were visible. He offered to intervene, and Sally told him to mind his own business. And there was nothing more Bob could offer to do; it wasn't like she was his girlfriend anymore, despite how he still felt about her.

The following week, Sally showed up to see Dr. Malcolm with three broken ribs and a fractured pelvis. She was in rough shape, and Malcolm wanted to admit her on the spot, but Sally had refused, settling for a compression wrap and a prescription of codeine.

Bob decided he would approach Sally one more time and try to talk some sense into her. But she stopped showing up in Garrett Grove altogether. As the weeks passed without a word from Sally, her parents became more and more alarmed. Then Earl stopped answering their phone calls and had become even more elusive than usual.

Sally's folks finally notified the state police in Warren, who sent a patrol out to Earl's place to talk to the couple. The man was drunk when the officers arrived, and Sally was nowhere to be found. Earl became defensive, took a swing at one of the cops, was handcuffed and tossed into the back of the car. It was obvious to

THE OJANOX

the troopers that the man was hiding something. They decided to take a tour of the property and found a freshly turned piece of soil the size of a grave.

Earl had killed Sally with a hunting knife and then buried her face down under nine inches of dirt. He hadn't even taken the time to properly hide her body. He had shown her no more respect in death than he had while she was alive. The troopers then removed Earl from the vehicle and stomped the living shit out of him. They broke his jaw, collarbone, and his left arm, which was proceeded by his court-appointed lawyer accomplishing the impossible. The case was overturned because the defendant's rights had been violated by the two officers. The charges were dropped by the state, and Earl Hillman had been free to go.

Life didn't change all that much for Earl. He still frequented the bars most days and began to boast about how he beat the case and showed those bastard cops just who they were messing with. The only thing that was different: he no longer had a live-in punching bag to come home to.

That was around the time Bob Jones took up drinking. He had suddenly found a reason to visit the bars himself, at least the ones that Earl Hillman preferred. He had been frequenting a dive called Sneaky Pete's, just enough to not look out of place but not often enough to be noticed.

"I'll take a Bud, and give my friend here another," Bob told the bartender one Saturday afternoon.

Earl looked up and raised his glass. "Thank you, friend."

The bartender poured Earl another shot of Wild Turkey and set a Bud long neck in front of Bob, who took a long sip and lit up a smoke.

"Want one?" He offered a cigarette to Earl, who accepted. "I see you 'round here some. Name's Brady, Cal Brady." Bob held out his hand.

"Earl. Nice to meet ya. From town?" he slurred.

"Na," Bob said. "Parker Plains, out by the rubber mill, been working there for the past two years. You know how hard it is to get the smell of burnt rubber out of your clothes?"

"Can't say that I do." Earl lifted his shot and sucked it back. "Woo, that'll put hair on yer nutsack. Know whatta mean, Cal?"

Bob laughed and took another sip of his beer. "Sure do. Bartender, another one for my friend here."

The bartender poured the drink and gave Bob a look that suggested, *Be careful of the company you keep*. Bob returned an understanding nod.

"Thanks, man." Earl turned from his refill. "Excuse me, gotta drain the old lizard," he said as he got up and made the drunken shuffle to the men's room.

Bob smiled and waited until the door closed behind the man, then took a calculated look around the bar to make sure he wasn't being watched. He removed a small piece of tinfoil from his cigarette pack, unfolded it, and emptied the powdery contents into Earl's whiskey. Giving the drink a quick stir with his finger, he crumpled the foil into a ball and waited. It hadn't been easy to find what he was looking for, but his longtime friend Peter Gillick had just gotten a job at Chilton Medical. Peter had been a good friend of Sally's as well and didn't want to know the details. "This will do the trick, trust me," Pete assured him when he handed Bob the packet of pills.

Earl returned to his place at the bar, downed his shot and several more after, and thirty minutes later was slurring his words with his head bobbing up and down like a yo-yo. The bartender, now pissed, came over to evict the man, who apparently made it a habit to get shit-faced and obnoxious. Bob laid a fifty on the counter and leaned toward the barkeep. "Please excuse my friend. I think he's had a little too much to drink."

The man took the crisp bill, slid it into his front pocket, and gave Bob another look that suggested, *I didn't see a fucking thing.*

Bob scooped up Earl, walked him outside, and deposited him into the front seat of his pickup.

The man didn't wake up once during the two hours it took to drive to the Queensland Pine Barrens. He finally started to stir when Bob pulled off the road and turned onto the wooded path.

The Pine Barrens were an expansive stretch of acreage that served as a game preserve and national forest. It was easy to get lost in such a massive piece of wilderness, but Bob knew where he was going and had mapped out the trails weeks prior. They were less than a mile from the spot he had picked out when Earl raised his head and opened his eyes.

"Wha the faah?" Earl slurred, then noticed the duct tape that bound his hands and feet. He struggled to move, but Bob had wrapped the seatbelt around him to secure him in place. Earl scowled at the man driving the truck, and a shock of recognition smacked his face.

"You, wha? Why ya do this?" He was still drunk and sedated from the Rohypnol.

THE OJANOX

"You like that, Earl? Keep struggling; won't do you a damn bit of good," Bob said.

"Lemme go, ya fuck!"

"Ha-ha," Bob laughed and punched Earl in the mouth. The guy's head snapped hard to the right; his lips split open and began to bleed. Bob thought he had possibly killed him right there and felt a surge of disappointment when Earl's head dropped to his chest and stopped moving. A second later, the guy started to snore, and a huge smile spread out across Bob's face.

Earl Hillman woke up an hour after Bob had parked the truck and carried him into the woods. He found himself seated on the forest floor, propped against a large pine with his arms drawn and duct-taped behind his back. Struggling to lift his head, he looked up to find Bob standing over him. After several moments of futile struggling, he stopped resisting and faced his captor.

"Why?" he asked. "What I do to you?"

Bob punched him in the face again, knocking out two teeth in the process. "It's not what you did to me," Bob hissed and knelt in front of the man. "It's what you did to Sally."

A look of disgust slicked Earl's features. He spit a bloody clot onto the ground and snarled. "Fuck that bitch and fuck you too!"

Bob nodded and reached into the knapsack set between his feet. He pulled out several large Tupperware containers filled with a dark liquid.

"What the hell is that? Lemme go, prick!" Earl screamed. "Help ... help me!"

"Yes," Bob agreed. "Help—help us!" He yelled even louder than Earl. "Scream all you want, asshole. You're five miles deep in the woods, and no one can hear you. But don't worry, you're gonna get plenty of practice. In fact, I think before this is over, you'll be damn tired of screaming." Bob opened one of the containers and threw the contents onto Earl. The dark liquid splashed him in the face and coated his clothes.

"Hey, what the hell is that?"

"That, my friend, is chicken blood." Bob took another container and stepped back to one of the many dens that littered the woods around them. Bob emptied half the container's contents onto one of the mounds of grasses and fallen limbs. Then he poured out a trail leading to the pine where Earl was tied. A muffled grunt broke the silence and was answered by another from nearby. "Oh-no. Do you hear that, Earl?" Bob fished out a third container and splashed the contents onto Earl's clothes and the ground where he sat.

"What the fuck is that?" Earl screamed.

"That, my friend, is a mama boar, and she sounds vewy hungwy, wabbit." Bob removed a hunting knife from its sheath and approached Earl.

"Get away from me!"

"Shut the fuck up, scumbag!" Bob barked, bringing the knife down into Earl's thigh. The man bellowed as Bob twisted the blade. He ripped it out of the man's flesh, leaving a wound six inches long and two inches deep. A scarlet river flowed from the gash and mixed with chicken blood on the ground. "With any luck, you'll bleed to death before they tear you apart. But honestly, you don't look that lucky to me."

The grunts grew louder as the scent of blood was detected by the local residents. The excitement of their rooting was picked up like a telegraph signal from the neighboring burrows. Bob had checked out the area a week earlier and found no less than forty individual dens in a fifty-yard radius. And if there was one thing wild boar couldn't resist, it was the scent of blood. That shit drove them nuts.

He removed the last plastic container from the knapsack and stood in front of Earl. He held it over the man's head and poured it slowly on top of him. It soaked his hair, covered his face, and dripped down the front of his clothes. "This is for Sally," he said as he turned, picked up his bag, and headed back to the truck.

Earl screamed until his vocal cords crackled like a paper fire. Bob continued walking, never turning back once to look at the man. Before he made it halfway to the truck, the timbre and velocity of Earl's cries amped into a tantric frenzy. The shrill that now pierced the night was the hysterical bleats of a man in agony. It should have been difficult to listen to—one would think—but Bob wanted to remember every minute of it. It took less time than Bob anticipated for the boar to take care of old Earl. All in all, the man had been consumed in just under fifty minutes.

Bob sat in the truck and waited, allowing several hours to pass so the animals could finish off the last of the scraps and head back home to sleep off their dinner. He returned later to see what was left of the man who had murdered his high school sweetheart—there wasn't enough to fill a waste basket. Bob scattered the remains near the various burrows and cleaned up what he could. He hadn't been able to save Sally, but one thing was for certain: Earl Hillman would never hurt another soul.

Bob Senior passed away later that year and was buried in the graveyard behind the Lutheran church, just a short distance from the plot where Carl's father would find his ultimate rest. Many of Bob's friends were sent to war only to return to the same piece of earth soon after. Bob had missed the draft, but the weight he carried after that day in the barrens was as heavy as any burden he would have taken home from Vietnam.

Bob had listened to the man die as a testament to Sally; it was the least he could do for her. And the moment had seared into his brain like a branding iron. The sound of Earl's gut-wrenching cries had begun to haunt him. At first in his dreams. Bob could hear Earl Hillman scream for mercy. He could see the man bound to the tree, covered in chicken blood. The bastard had deserved to die, and Bob believed he could carry the weight. But it would be years before Bob Jones could sleep through the night, and he would never erase the soundtrack that played on an endless loop when he closed his eyes. He told himself he had done the right thing and Earl had received far more mercy than he deserved. The bastard didn't get any less than he had given Sally.

●●●

Much had changed in the world since Bob last walked the halls of the high school, but nothing quite as much as Bob himself. He'd lived through things he never could have fathomed as a boy. He had grown, and he had gained the perspective of a man who carried a tremendous weight—and to carry that weight, one needed large shoulders. As Bob Jones navigated the narrow hallways, he was aware of the size of his shoulders and the tremendous weight they supported. Years ago, when he went to school here, Bob hadn't carried any of it. But that was a long time ago, and he was a different man now.

He turned down the main hall and entered the administration office, where a grey-haired woman stood behind the counter.

"Bob Jones, what brings you here? We aren't scheduled for another fire drill till next month." The woman looked at him through a pair of thick glasses.

"Miss Tailor, you're looking as attractive as ever," he told the woman, who was old enough to be his mother.

"Oh, you fresh thing. What can I do ya for, Bob?"

"I was wondering if Mr. Garish was in. I'd like to speak to him if I could."

"He's here, but he's in one of those moods. We had a number of staff absentees, and with the phones out, I had no way of finding substitutes. Oddly enough, even more students didn't show up as well. Is there something going on that I should know about?" She leaned over the counter and waited for the juicy gossip.

"There is, and we're asking the entire town to meet at the gym by five o'clock tonight. We need everyone in the shelter before sundown. I don't have time to give you all the details now because I really need to speak to Mr. Garish and then get the shelter ready. But believe me, ma'am, you want to take this seriously—as if your life depended on it."

"Oh, my dear," she said. "What should I do about classes?"

"I'm going to talk to the principal about that. I'm sure we'll have an answer for you in a few minutes. Just promise me, no matter what happens, that you will be in that shelter tonight. Okay?"

"Who am I to argue with the fire chief?" She forced a nervous smile and nodded to the principal's office.

Bob felt he had conveyed the urgency and was almost certain Miss Tailor would be in the shelter before the sun went down. He prayed they would be as successful with the rest of the town's citizens.

He walked around the counter and knocked on the solid oak door. There was brief commotion as if something had fallen or been moved in a hurry, followed by the startled voice of the principal saying, "Come in."

"Hello, Mr. Garish."

The principal looked disheveled and worn, as if he had been up all night. His shirt was opened at the collar, his tie was undone, and dark circles spread out around his eyes. He jumped up and shook Bob's hand.

"Mr. Jones, what brings you here this morning?" The man popped two Alka-Seltzer into a glass of water and watched the tablets fizzle.

"I'm sure you've noticed the number of students and faculty that didn't show up today."

The principal tilted back the glass of fizz and drank it down. "Ha, yes, I've noticed, believe me I've noticed. My secretary, Julie, never made it in. I um, well,

THE OJANOX

I hope she's okay. We had plans for lunch, and she never misses lunch. I hope her husband didn't—what I mean is, I hope she's all right." The man began to root through a stack of papers, unable to find what he was looking for.

"Mr. Garish, the sheriff has given me orders to take control of your gym and the shelter as well. I'm going to need you to make an announcement at one o'clock for all students and their families to report to the gym between four and five o'clock." Bob spoke with just enough authority to make his point.

"Oh my, that sounds serious. I knew something happened when I heard the explosions this morning. Was it methane? Is it poisonous gas?" The man continued to move the papers around his desk in an erratic fashion.

"No, sir, there's been an outbreak. The explosions you heard were detonations set off at the Gables Bridge and on Sunset Road. I'm afraid there's no way in or out of town. It's very important that you notify the entire staff as well as the students."

"Oh yes. Do you think Julie is all right? Maybe she's on her way here?"

"I don't know, sir. But you and everyone else in this school need to be in that shelter by five at the latest. It might be a good idea for you to dismiss the students early so they have time to go home and talk to their parents." Bob studied the frantic movements of the principal as he searched his desk. The guy was already out of his mind, and the shit hadn't fully hit the fan.

"Yes, yes, that's a good idea. I should probably stop by Julie's house and make sure she's all right. Oh—I don't know—maybe that's not such a good idea. Perhaps you could? She lives on Woodland Place."

"I'll see what I can do." Bob was struck with a horrible premonition and hoped to God that the rest of the town hadn't already lost it like Mr. Garish. "I'll coordinate the closing of the school with Miss Tailor. She'll know what to tell the students and faculty."

"Oh, that would be perfect. Thank you, Mr. Jones." Principal Melvin Garish continued to look for God-knows-what.

Bob turned and left his office without saying another word. It was obvious the guy was banging his secretary and had his priorities jacked up. He probably hadn't been wrapped too tight to begin with and possessed zero coping skills. Bob doubted the guy would even make it till sundown at the rate he was going. More than likely, he would end up getting shot by Julie's husband.

Bob proceeded to convey the gravity of the situation to Miss Tailor, and the woman handled it much better than her boss. He gave her explicit instructions about what to say when she made her announcement. It was all he could do since he didn't have the time to visit each classroom himself. Bob hoped the younger people in town were dealing with the situation better than the principal. Lord knew they couldn't be doing any worse.

Chapter 63

Don coordinated with Mark Gold to have the remaining explosives relocated to a secondary safe site. A surprising number of DuCain employees had not shown up for some reason, and for the first time that morning, Don had a moment to evaluate his situation.

It was the worst case of vandalism he had ever seen, and it had happened on his watch. He couldn't imagine the trouble he was looking at with the company's explosives being stolen and then used in an act of terrorism. He was sure that charges would be brought up. *Can I go to jail for this?* At the very least, old man DuCain would see him swing from the tallest tree.

Then he thought about what had happened in the trailer with Stephanie, but the vision was replaced by an image of Lois and Troy. *Christ!* He had fucked up on so many levels and in such a short period of time. It had been amazing with Stephanie, like nothing he had ever experienced. *But was it worth fucking up your life?* The truth was he didn't know. Which was probably the wrong head doing the talking. He forced himself to get a grip and made his way toward the secondary chamber, where Stephanie and Gail stopped to examine something they had found near one of the murals.

Propped against the far wall were what appeared to be several cylinders carved out of either wood or cane. Stephanie inspected the tubular objects with her flashlight, being careful not to disturb them. They were approximately three feet long, no more than an inch and a half wide, with a small hole bored into each one near its base. The women were intently focused on the objects and neglected to see the mural that adorned the wall above them. But Don saw it and started to fit the pieces together.

"What do you think these were used for?" Gail asked.

"They almost look like water vessels or some type of storage unit," Stephanie said as she examined them.

"No, that's not what they are," Don said.

Stephanie looked up at him. "What makes you say that?"

He turned his flashlight onto the mural above them. The beam revealed exactly what the tubes had been used for, which had nothing to do with transporting water. The cylinders were weapons, and by the look of it, effective ones at that.

The scene on the cavern wall depicted a battle where many of the black-eyed creatures assembled against the Lenape. Some of the tribe members had been pinned down and consumed by the smoke-like substance, while others battled their attackers. Several of the beasts possessed clear human features, others looked like animals, and there were some that appeared to be a cross between the two, with both human and distinct reptilian features, all with the same horrific black eyes.

The tribe members that fought the beasts carried the same cane cylinders the women had found, and were using them like slings to hurl projectiles at their enemies. It was obvious to Don what the small hole in the side of the tubes was for. That was where the musket balls were inserted. From what the mural suggested, the weapons appeared effective, as many of the creatures had dropped and others were crying out in pain.

Stephanie looked from the mural to the tubes with a smirk of satisfaction on her face.

"This is the proof we've been looking for. You have no idea how important a find this is." She wiped at her cheek. "I wish my father was here to see this."

"This is just mythology we're looking at, right?" Donald asked; he studied the faces of the women who stood before him, not sure he wanted an answer.

"I don't think so," Stephanie said, examining the mural. "I think this is their story. This was how the Lenape disappeared. And this was how they fought them off." She motioned toward the cylinders.

"What exactly do you mean, fought them off? Who was them?"

"There has been a lot of stories and many different names for these creatures. The Lenape called it the Dark One—Matantu. The Mayans referred to it as Ah Puch. There are countless names for this Entity; it's been called everything from Apopis to Tezcatlipoca."

Don was pretty sure he had just had sex with the crazy girl from the museum and wondered how long it would be until she started making stuffed animals from locks of his hair. "Come on. Are you seriously saying the Lenape tribe went to war against the Devil?"

"Not in the biblical sense, of course not. And don't look at me like you think I'm nuts. My father spent his life studying the disappearances of countless civilizations, and nearly all of them recorded depictions of creatures like this. You said it yourself; it had to take the Lenape a long time to turn lodestone into perfect-sized musket balls. And they must have done it for a good reason."

"So, you're implying that these creatures are responsible for the disappearance of countless civilizations from different countries—hell different continents—and from different periods in Earth's history … seriously?" Don looked around the floor of the cave, noticing just how many of the spherical stones littered the place.

"It makes for a compelling reason to believe in a force like a Devil, doesn't it?"

"You said Entity, but all I see are a bunch of animals and humans fighting against each other. Maybe the Lenape painted their enemies as beasts because of the ferocity of their attackers? It's impossible that the same creatures could have been in all those countless places at different times in history."

"It is possible. My father believed that the Entity called Matantu, also called Apopis, and even Satan, is an ancient life-form that has been here since the beginning. Look at this," she said, returning to the murals they had examined yesterday. "This shows two possible Entities." She pointed out the two different-colored clouds in the painting. "Now just hear me out because I can see you want to argue with me."

Don remained quiet and listened.

"In too many cultures for it to be considered coincidental, the story of creation is similar to this. Two opposing forces in the universe before there was anything else. One represented by the depiction of light, while the other 'Entity' a juxtaposition of dark."

"You're talking about matter and anti-matter." Don preferred to speak scientifically.

"Perhaps," Stephanie agreed, "or creation and destruction. Or maybe simply good and evil, who knows?" She shrugged. "It's been speculated by countless civilizations that when the two came together, the universe was created. Look here." She pointed to the mural that Don believed was the Big Bang.

"And the collective unconscious is how different civilizations were able to come to similar creation stories," Gail added.

"Thank you, Gail." Stephanie glowed as if her own child had just won the spelling bee. "And you can see in the next mural the way the darkness enveloped the earth. It looks as if it may have gotten trapped, possibly in our atmosphere." She moved further down the row of paintings. "If you look at the next three murals as a linear succession, you can see a timeline. I've seen similar depictions in Mayan cave drawings as well as on vessel pottery from the Indus River Valley."

Don stepped back so he could see all three paintings at once. The first one showed the ether-like substance entering the reptilian creatures, which could have been a scene from the Jurassic or Cretaceous era. The second scene could easily have taken place millions of years after the previous. The dark substance had moved on to primitive primates that Don thought resembled Australopithecus. He knew little about the evolution of the human race but was familiar with the discovery of the fossils in Ethiopia in '74, suspected to be early humans. The ape-like creatures depicted in this mural looked an awful lot like the primates that dated back about four million years ago. They certainly didn't look as evolved as the Homo erectus, which hadn't come along for another three million years after that.

"Is that an Australopithecus?" he finally asked.

"Don't you just love this guy?" Stephanie said to Gail, who only smiled, pointed her camera at Don, and took his picture.

The flash of the bulb caught him by surprise and temporarily blinded him. "Please don't do that," he said.

"Sorry." Gail turned around and snapped a few more shots of the mural.

"I think that's exactly what it's supposed to represent, or at least some early descendant of ours."

"How would the Lenape have knowledge of any of this? These are all fairly new discoveries we're talking about." Don looked at the women, who both wore

I-told-you-so smirks on their faces. "You're gonna say collective unconscious, I guess." Both women nodded.

The next mural showed the substance affecting what was clearly Homo sapiens. The humans were members of the Lenape tribe.

"It's obvious this is a depiction of the progression of time, from prehistoric creatures to early humans, all the way to the time of the Lenape."

Don couldn't argue; it appeared that way to him as well. He was nearly positive that the one drawing was the very same primates that had been discovered in Ethiopia.

Stephanie used her flashlight to illuminate the next mural, since the floodlights were casting too many shadows into the furthest reaches of the cave. Don trained his light on the wall as well and was taken aback by what he saw. A momentary hush fell over the group as the mural was revealed in full light. Stephanie broke the silence and gasped at the scene painted before them.

The Lenape had immortalized several of their children on the cavern wall, all of whom possessed the same characteristic pitch-black eyes and mouthful of the horrible, pointed teeth.

"That might explain the small skeletons near the entrance," Don whispered.

Stephanie nodded in agreement and lowered her head. "The depiction of children is another commonality that's been recorded in other cultures. There is something about them that plays a significant role of importance to this Entity."

The totality of Stephanie's words hit Don like a bread truck. "You keep saying Entity, and I think you're implying consciousness. But are these murals suggesting that whatever the Lenape and these other cultures encountered turned them into creatures, like zombies or vampires or something?"

"All myths originate from some factual experience. The legend of the zombie originated in the Caribbean and speaks of people returning from the grave and walking the earth. It looks as if our holy man here did just that. At least that's what the mural implies. The legend of Dracula is based on the very real, Vladimir the Impaler, the Prince of Romania who was known to drink the blood of his enemies. Bram Stoker took a bit of the myth and threw his own spin on the story with other legends he had heard of. But the question is did Stoker come up with the story as an original idea, or was it derived from a greater place, collective unconscious?" Stephanie beamed as she hit her stride and continued. "Stoker assigned some very real qualities to the creature we all came to know as the vampire. For one, he gave his creature sharp fangs that were used to puncture the flesh of its victims. Also, the creature was limited to darkness. I don't know if you noticed what all these murals have in common, but take a closer look."

It didn't take long for Don to figure out what she was talking about; he was surprised he hadn't noticed it sooner. Not one of the murals was set during the day; the absence of sunlight was apparent. In fact, in most of the paintings, either the moon or stars were depicted in the background. "They all take place at night. None of them during the day."

"Don't get me wrong. I'm not saying that whatever attacked the Lenape tribe, or the inhabitants of Cahokia was a zombie or a vampire, but there is a good possibility it was the Entity that inspired the myth. In fact, my father believed that this Entity was responsible for our myths about most modern monsters. What if this presence is responsible for the belief in Satan and evil itself?"

"And the Lenape killed Satan by throwing rocks at him?" Don said.

"A vampire can be killed with a wooden stake through the heart and by sunlight," Gail added.

"Don't forget the silver bullet," Don ribbed.

"That's a werewolf, not a vampire," Gail corrected him.

Don nodded as if he should have known that. He reexamined the mural of the battle scene where the Lenape fought the creatures. "So, lodestones are like wooden stakes to these things; that's what you're getting at, right?"

"Well, it looks as if that's what the Lenape used to fight them. And some of those stones are embedded into the remains we found at the front of the cave. I'm no physician, but if I had to guess a cause of death."

"So, a peaceful people come across something they've never seen before and figure out how to defeat it with magnetite?" Don shook his head.

"I never said they defeated it. If anything, it was the other way around. The Lenape in this area vanished," Stephanie said. "None of the cultures that recorded these creatures survived. This is only the latest of a string of singularities that correlate the presence of a terrestrial anomaly that science has yet to categorize."

"That is up until now." Gail smiled at her boss. "With all this, you're looking at a Nobel Prize, Doc."

"That's nice, but you know they don't issue a Nobel Prize for archeology." Stephanie grimaced.

"Well, maybe they'll make an exception this time. After all, we're talking about the discovery of the century. At the very least, they'll name it after you. How does The Thompson-Habilis sound?" Gail laughed.

"Actually, it's not my discovery," Stephanie said. "It's yours, Don. How would you like a new life-form named after you ... 'The Fischer'?" She gave him a wink and flashed a quick smile.

"I don't know if I like the idea of a creature that resembles Count Dracula running around with my name." Don averted his eyes from her gaze for fear of Gail catching him. "If the Lenape got wiped out, then who created all these murals? I mean if they were all dead, someone had to be left to paint them."

"That's a good question." Stephanie picked up one of the lodestone balls and held it in her open palm. "Since the cave was sealed when you found it, I'm guessing whoever painted them never made it out. I wouldn't be surprised if some of these bones belong to our artist."

It was a morbid thought, but Don was inclined to agree. The cave had been buried under a ton of bedrock and concealed from his equipment by the massive deposit of magnetite. He hadn't even known it was there. "So, what happened to the original creature? I mean, you're saying that smokey substance was the original creature and it's been wiping out civilizations for damn near all of history. So, what happens? Does it hibernate, or does it go away for a few hundred years? What's your take on that?"

Stephanie shrugged her shoulders. "That's the million-dollar question. If I knew that, I'd be on the cover of *National Geographic*, not sandwiched between articles about the rainforest and the Gypsy Moth caterpillar."

"Well, maybe the Lenape killed it after all. You know, kind of the way Rocky Balboa and Apollo Creed knocked each other out at the end." It was an analogy Don could wrap his head around and helped add a little levity to all the doom and gloom of the moment.

"It's possible, except the Lenape weren't the first to use the lodestone. We found similar weapons at Cahokia and quite a few sites in Asia."

"So, you think this is really the same Entity in all those places. Why not individual entities instead of the same one?"

"Well, it's been my father's hypothesis, and I agree for several reasons. I guess the major one being that every original depiction of the Entity, where it existed in space, shows it as a singularity. Like a single-celled organism, an amoeba, only a lot more dangerous." Stephanie took a rubber band and pulled her hair back into a ponytail. A thin sweat broke across her forehead. She continued. "The museum has a skull they keep tucked away from the public. It isn't clear what species the skull belongs to. While it has clear primate features, there are reptilian qualities as well. But we're almost positive it started out as human. The mouth is filled with these horrible teeth, for the most part. But the back jaw contains human molars."

"How do you know they're human?" he asked.

"Because some of them have fillings. Some early dentist drilled out the cavities and filled the molars with gold. I don't know what type of creature it ended up as, but it started out life as a human; that much we are sure of."

"And you're positive it isn't a hoax?"

"Pretty elaborate hoax to make an entire civilization disappear."

The three of them sat in the silence of the cave for a moment as the gravity of what Stephanie said echoed off the walls like a cry for help. Finally, it was Gail who broke the silence. "I'm glad that whatever did this is long gone."

Stephanie looked at her assistant for a long moment, then nodded her head in agreement. "Yeah, me too," she replied.

Chapter 64

At 11:05 a.m. on Wednesday, October 28, Jessica Marceau became the mayor of Garrett Grove. Deputy David Rainey swore her in under the authority of Sheriff Carl Primrose. Jessica won the election without even submitting her bid for candidacy. She sat at the desk of former Mayor Gilbert staring at the papers in front of her. Not only had Mayor Gilbert gone missing but so had the Deputy Mayor and three members of the town council.

"I can't believe I am doing this. I've been the mayor for seven minutes, and I'm already Joseph Stalin." She proceeded to sign the orders.

"You're no Stalin. You're going to save this town," Rainey said.

"I don't like this one bit. What the sheriff is proposing is nothing short of what Russia did to the Ukraine in '32."

"We're doing this so we can take care of the people. Things are going to get crazy, and the sheriff is trying to gather as many resources as he can. He knows what he's doing."

"Well, that makes one of us because I'm flying blind here." She signed the last paper and put the pen down. "Tell me again that I'm doing the right thing, Deputy."

"You did the right thing, Mayor Marceau," Deputy Rainey told her as he picked up the papers and walked to the door. "And if you don't mind my saying, Joseph Stalin could never pull off that dress."

She laughed despite how horrible she felt. "Deputy Rainey," she called to him as he prepared to leave. "If we're both still here next week, you can take me out to dinner. I like Italian. That's an executive order, by the way." She forced herself to smile.

The Deputy stopped and gave her a look of surprise. "Yes, ma'am," he said, and walked out of the office.

Twenty minutes after Deputy Rainey left the mayor's office, he entered the A&P food store on Route 3, flanked by seven burley firemen. Usually, such a sight would raise an eyebrow or two; however, there weren't enough customers to notice, or employees. But Günter Bentley, the store manager, noticed the men and greeted them at the door.

"Ist der sumsing I can help you vit today, Deputy?" Günter had been born in West Berlin before the wall was built. Fortunately, he lived on the prosperous side and had been spared the communist presence that many of his cousins endured in the east. Raised under the watchful eye of his Uncle Sam, Günter had always dreamt of visiting America. He loved all things American, from cheeseburgers to baseball to Mickey Mouse. But what Günter loved most about America had nothing to do with the food or the pastimes. It was something every man his age could agree on no matter what country they were born in. The single greatest thing about America was Marilyn Monroe. Günter Bentley moved to the states in 1967 and married a girl who looked nothing like Norma Jean Baker. And although Hazel was no movie star, she was attractive, knew how to cook a mean cheeseburger, and was one hundred percent red-blooded all-American girl, which Günter found incredibly sexy. They had three children, and Günter became the manager of the supermarket. It wasn't exactly a Cinderella story, but for Günter, it was the American dream, and he was happy. He tried to lose the German accent, but old habits died hard. And even though he looked German and sounded German, his heart was as Yankee Doodle as they came.

THE OJANOX

Deputy Rainey smiled and greeted the man when he approached. "Hi, Günter. How are you today?"

"I am goot, zank you. And yourself?" Günter studied the men.

"Not so good, I'm afraid. I have a court order signed by the mayor." He handed him the paper. "I'm going to be requisitioning quite a bit of food. But I assure you, you will be reimbursed every dime." The firemen carried lists and orders of their own and hustled past the deputy and the manager.

"Vait! Dis must be sum mistake. I must clear dis vit my boss." Günter checked the paperwork.

"Whatever you got to do, Günter. We're not going to clean you out, but we are going to take a lot of the non-perishables. I'm sorry, but this is an emergency. There's nothing I can do about it." Deputy Rainey took Günter by the arm and led him far enough away so that the girls at the registers couldn't hear him. "Günter, I want you and your family at the high school by five o'clock. Close the store early and be there—no matter what. This is serious, I mean it. If you love your family, and I know that you do, make sure you are at the school by five. Only bring what you can carry and any medicine the children might need."

Günter's face went slack. He grew up a mile from communist Germany and took warnings seriously. "Mein Gott!" His native tongue resurfaced. "Vas ist das?"

"Life and death, Herr Bentley, life and death."

Deputy Rainey's words resonated like a detonation. Günter Bentley stepped to the side and allowed the men to collect everything they intended. He did his best to inventory the items, assisted by Claire Rizvi, one of the few cashiers that showed up to work that morning. The deputy and the men didn't clean the place out entirely, but they had come damn close. A half hour later, the firemen loaded the bags into their trucks and left. Günter watched as they pulled away, wondering if what he was feeling was anything compared to how his countrymen felt at the end of the war when the Russians arrived to liberate Berlin.

● ● ●

Harrison's Army and Navy had been around since 1955, serving Garrett Grove's avid hunters and fishermen for all their seasonal necessities. One could renew their game license, pick up a dozen night crawlers, and purchase a new pair of wranglers in one convenient trip. Tyler Harrison inherited the family business in '75 after his father Herman passed away at the ripe old age of fifty-seven. Herman Harrison had been a hunting enthusiast who not only held the record for the largest small mouth to ever come out of King Lake, at a whopping six pounds seven ounces, but was the only hunter to come off the mountain with a full 14-pointer. Both the rack and the bass were displayed proudly on the wall behind the register at the store on Route 3. There wasn't a gun Herman wasn't comfortable with, and he knew more knots than any fisherman in town. He'd been hunting since he was old enough to carry a shotgun and claimed to have never had a misfire in all his years in the woods. Strangely enough, Herman had never been stung by a wasp in all his years as a hunter either, that was until the fall of '75.

Herman set out in the early morning hours at the very start of buck season with the intention of beating his own 14-point record. The south face of Garrett Mountain had experienced a bout of Indian summer, and there were still a lot of chiggers and no-see-ums, and the little bastards had started to feast on Herman in the early morning sun. He never liked to use bug spray because the deer could smell the chemical from over a mile away. And any time he did, he always came home empty-handed.

Still, if he had squirted just a dab or two that Saturday, he might not have been so preoccupied when the buggers started swarming around his head. The black flies were especially bad that year and descended on Herman like sailors on a prostitute. They first attacked the back of his neck and then went to work on his face. Herman swatted at them, then set his shotgun down in a fit of rage. He was more than a little pissed off but not nearly as much as the hive of wood wasps he turned up with the butt of his gun. They were far more aggressive than the black flies and stung Herman repeatedly. He tore off running as soon as the first one hit him in the neck, and it took nearly a quarter of a mile at a full sprint to ditch the last of the wasps. It was then that Herman found it difficult to breathe and could feel his throat swelling up. He had no idea he was allergic to wasp stings, wood wasps especially. Having been lucky, or unlucky, to make it to fifty-seven without ever being stung, how could he?

He was found by a couple of hikers later that afternoon. By the time Herman was brought back into town, he was a dark shade of purple and his entire body had swelled so much it took Burt Lively an hour and a half to cut the man's boots off.

His son, Tyler, didn't inherit the outdoor gene from his old man and had no interest in killing Bambi's mother, or father for that matter. He reluctantly took over the family business at his mother's insistence but felt no love for the vocation. Tyler hated the outdoors almost as much as he hated mornings. He preferred going to sleep at five a.m. as opposed to waking up at that time. He'd been a fan of the disco era, and although the movement was coming to an end, that didn't mean the party was over.

The seventies had been a coke-fueled blur for Tyler and his friends, who spent their weekends at the clubs in Millville, the nearest city within a hundred-mile radius of the Grove. And although it wasn't mandatory to do cocaine while disco dancing, the two went hand in hand. It helped some men to be more outgoing, and for others, it acted as an aphrodisiac. For Tyler, it had done both and allowed him to feel less self-conscious. It also helped him to feel comfortable around other men who were interested in the same things he was—which was other men. Garrett Grove wasn't exactly the place where Tyler could openly display his sexuality. It would be decades before this little redneck burb would be ready for that.

Millville, on the other hand, was a bit less judgmental. Tyler had always had feelings for boys but kept them hidden for fear of what Herman would have done to him. As far as Tyler knew, there weren't any other men in town who shared the same tastes as he—although he would have been surprised to learn how many truly did. So Tyler kept his feelings concealed from his bigoted father throughout the week, but on Friday and Saturday nights, he was the dancing queen at the disco inferno.

Lately, he'd been seeing a guy from Millville named Carmine, who was far more comfortable in his own sexuality. Carmine had been interested in showing Tyler the ropes and promised to be gentle with him the first time. There had been nothing gentle about it—which was just fine for Tyler because, as it turned out, that was just how he liked it. The cocaine heightened the experience, fueling the men's appetites as well as the duration of the act. It had been a rollercoaster ride for several months when Tyler realized he might have real feelings for Carmine. He'd recently been thinking of expressing the idea of an exclusive relationship to his friend. Monogamy was uncommon within their circle, and Tyler didn't know if Carmine was ready for such a suggestion. Part of the magic of the lifestyle was the mystery of not knowing who you might end up with at the end of the night.

It had been weighing on his mind lately and was what he'd been thinking about when Deputy Beau Jenkins walked into the store with several firemen at his side. Tyler recognized one of them, Richard Marek, a guy he had gone to school with. Richard was a volunteer fireman and was in great shape. Tyler stared at Richard as he entered the store and received a surprising gaze in return. He had given him *the look*. Tyler wondered if maybe he wasn't quite as ready for a monogamous relationship as he thought.

"Hello, gentlemen, how can I help you?" Tyler asked as Beau approached the counter.

"Good morning, Mr. Harrison. How's business today?" Beau smiled, removed a manila envelope from under his arm, opened it, and pulled out several sheets of paper.

"Ughh," Tyler grunted. "How does it look? The only thing I've sold all morning is a dozen night crawlers."

"Well, I have some good news for you then." Beau handed him the papers, and Tyler began to read them. "The mayor has given me orders to requisition a few items from your establishment. You are to send the bill to the town treasurer, and you will be reimbursed for everything. Of course, the mayor is hoping for our usual discount."

Tyler finished reading the documents and looked past Beau towards Richard. "Well, I suppose I could let you take a few things. Lord knows I could sure use the sales to boost business. What are you men looking for?" He couldn't help smiling at Richard as he asked the question. The months with Carmine had helped build his confidence.

"Well, today's your lucky day, my friend," Beau replied with the smoothness of a used car salesman. "We need all the weapons and ammunition, and a large amount of the camping supplies."

Tyler's jaw dropped. "You're shitting me, right?"

"'Fraid not, sir. It's all here in black and white. I assure you, you will be paid in full as soon as checks are cut next quarter."

Herman would have fought the deputy tooth and nail and never allowed that much inventory to walk out the store at a discounted price, even if he had to sit on it for a year to get full retail. But Tyler wasn't his old man, and to him, it sounded too good to be true. Business had been slow lately, and today there had only been

THE OJANOX

one customer before the men arrived. Tyler's lips parted, and a huge smile spread across his face.

"Help yourselves to whatever you need, Deputy. I'll unlock the cases for you."

The firemen fanned out and began to collect the items. Richard approached the counter and leaned over to speak to Tyler.

"You're going to want to be at either the medical center or the high school by five tonight. Something major is happening in town, and if you value your safety, you will be there." Tyler watched the young fireman's eyes check him up and down. "I'll be at the high school; I sure hope I see you there." Richard nodded and joined the other men at the back of the store.

Tyler watched as he walked away, thinking that today had certainly been a day for surprises. "I wouldn't miss it for the world," he said to himself.

There were other businesses that received visits from Garrett Grove's newly appointed deputies that afternoon. Ed Koloski headed a crew of men who proceeded to liberate every walkie-talkie and battery from the Radio Shack on Route 3. Frederick Nathan, the acting manager and only employee who had shown up for work, was unconvinced the signature on the paperwork was legitimate and asked the men to kindly leave the store.

When firemen Eric Collins and Kevin Grish began to remove items from the shelves, Frederick intervened and attempted to stop the men. He grabbed the radios from Kevin's hands and tried to prevent the man from taking any more. Kevin, who had been up half the night fighting the fire at the Texaco, was not in the mood. He dropped the rest of what he was holding and hit Frederick with a right cross that sent the manager toppling into a display of Atari game systems.

The cases flew in every direction as the man crashed into them, landing hard on his backside. The firemen continued to rifle through the store, collecting the items they had been tasked to collect.

Koloski extended his hand to help the man from the floor, but Frederick ignored the gesture. "You'll be hearing from my lawyer," he barked at the fireman.

"If we're lucky," Koloski replied. "I hope we'll be around that long."

A similar confrontation took place between fireman Kurt Hamilton and Howard Bell, the owner of Bell's Hardware. It hadn't been as physical as the incident at the Radio Shack, but it still sat like a bad oyster in Koloski's gut. His men were fatigued, on edge, and some had displayed a sense of entitlement. The mayor had given them permission to be bullies, and Koloski didn't like the talk he was hearing. Things were beginning to fall apart, and it wouldn't take much to push the men over the edge. They were volunteers, not seasoned vets, and they damn sure weren't law enforcement. But now they held documents that said they didn't have to be polite, and some of the guys were a bit rough around the edges to begin with. Koloski wondered what it would take to turn some of them into an angry mob. He didn't think it would take a whole hell of a lot.

●●●

The operation at the medical center went smoother than most of the supply runs, due to the presence of Sheriff Primrose and Deputy Lutchen. Cots were moved six at a time on the freight elevator, from the second floor to the basement, while Nurse TenHove worked with Lois, Will, and Alice in the pharmacy, separating medications and supplies into two equal stockpiles. There was still the matter of transporting patients, but at the rate they were going, Carl figured the task would be completed no later than three o'clock. At that point, Dr. Freedman and several of the staff would be sent to the high school

It was nearly twelve, and soon the entire town's population would receive their own call to action. Carl prayed they would follow directions. His men were already spread thin, and there was no way to round up people individually. *At least things are going smooth here,* he said to himself as he made his way to the pharmacy. A sudden shout of profanities erupted from somewhere down the hall.

Carl rounded a corner and arrived at the first-floor freight elevator to find a nurse and two firemen yelling at someone inside.

"What's going on?" Carl shouted.

Fireman Grady Martin turned to him with a look of exasperation "It's stuck between floors. I've got two men in there."

"Is it a breaker or something we can reset?" he asked.

THE OJANOX

"Dee Riker went to check it out." Grady and the other fireman worked at the doors and managed to pry them open, but the elevator was stuck below the first floor, closer to the basement.

"Can you go through the top to get them out? Isn't there a hatch?" the nurse asked.

"Yeah, in the movies, there's always a hatch; in real life, there isn't," Grady said.

The nurse looked at him as if she had just been told there was no such thing as Santa Claus. Then another fireman bounded around corner, sweating and out of breath.

"It's fried," he panted. "The circuit board is completely fried. It must have been damaged last night during the fire."

"Are you serious?" Grady shouted.

"Yeah, man, that was the last trip," Dee answered.

Carl felt his stomach turn and could swear he smelled the sizzling circuits even though they were on another floor. It had been going too well. He quickly reassessed the situation and didn't like their chances. There was no way that they could get all the patients and equipment into the basement by way of the stairs, not by five o'clock. *Christ, this is bad.*

"How many cots have been moved already?" Carl asked.

"I think about thirty," Grady answered.

"It will have to do." Carl wiped his brow. "Everything else is taking the stairs. We're going to have to start moving patients sooner than expected. Anyone who is bedridden or can't make the trip will have to ride it out on the floors."

The nurse glared at him with a mixture of hatred and disbelief in her eyes. "You can't just leave the patients unprotected."

"I didn't say they'd be unprotected; I said they'd be riding it out on the floors. My men and I will stay and protect them."

"I'll help you, Sheriff," Grady said.

"Thank you. Now let's get these men out of the elevator and get to work. Our job just got a hell of a lot harder."

Carl checked his watch; it was just twelve, and they still hadn't started to move patients yet. He prayed that the sensation in his gut was the stale donut he had eaten but knew better. Trouble was coming, and they weren't ready for it. *God, I hope they're doing better at the high school.*

Chapter 65

Father Kieran listened to more confessions that Wednesday morning than he had the entire month of October. He'd asked the Lord for a sign, and his prayers were answered. The men, women, and children arrived to confess their sins and ask for forgiveness, and Father Kieran offered them absolution. Then he presented each with a similar penance.

"Would you stand against the powers of evil and fight in the name of the Lord?"

Their replies had all been the same. "Yes, Father. I will."

Kieran then suggested they go back to their homes, collect their firearms, and return in time for Mass. Many of the congregation had already experienced a loss, whether it was a family member or a neighbor. Garrett Grove had undergone a change in the past few days, and everyone noticed it. It had been rapid and impossible to dismiss, like waking up one morning to find your nose missing. Now the congregation was ready to take action.

A young girl named Diane Nathan had recently discovered she was pregnant. She had lost her boyfriend in the fire at the Texaco station and was struggling with something horrible she saw on her street this morning. Two sheriff's officers had fired on their fellow deputies as Diane watched from her bedroom window, and one of the men had already been on the ground. The other had suffered a terrible stomach wound before being shot in the head. The officers moved the bodies into the house and then left. None of it made sense; the world had gone insane. First, she had heard the news about Chris and felt as if she could die herself; now men were being gunned down right outside her front door.

"The Lord works in mysterious ways, but I am afraid that Satan's works are even more mysterious. What you saw today was the work of a fallen angel. I'm terribly sorry about your friend Chris. He is with Jesus and is watching over you. He brought you here today."

"Yes, Father. I know," she said.

"The child that you carry is a blessing from the Lord, and that child needs his mother's protection. Will you do what's necessary to protect the child?"

"I will, Father." She looked to the man for direction.

"Then there is work that must be done. You may have to fight, but be not afraid; I will stand beside you. Trust in the Lord and your sins shall be forgiven. Go now and prepare for the Mass." Father Kieran listened to their confessions and delivered the same message to each of them. Then he told the ever-growing line at the back of the church that he would be more than happy to listen to the rest of their confessions after Mass. He retreated to the sacristy and prepared as the congregation took their seats. The usual organist had not shown up for the Mass, which weighed heavy on Kieran as he dressed in his chambers. Then as if on a breeze, the opening notes of "Blessed Assurance" lifted upon the air and greeted him behind the door. Kieran poked his head out to find Allison Aigans seated at the organ with the sheet music in front of her.

"Praise God." He made the sign of the cross on his forehead.

●●●

Troy sat beneath the monkey bars with Janis on one side and Wendy on the other. What happened in the principal's office had gotten him thinking about Rob and the possibility that he might never see him again. He had the perfect opportunity to tell Principal Grace and Miss Boriello what he told the kids on the playground. Instead, he told them about Rob and started to cry. Troy felt he had messed up big-time.

The wind picked up, sending a gusting chill across the playground. Troy turned to Wendy, who opened her lunch box, pulled out a bag of Chips Ahoy, and handed them to him.

"Here," she said. "I know how much you like them."

Then Janis placed a salami sandwich in front of him. "You can have my sandwich, if you want."

"I'm sorry about Rob," Wendy told him.

"It might just be the flu," Janis added. "We should stop by his house after school."

"I don't think he's home. I really don't." Troy struggled not to cry again but wasn't sure he would be successful. He zipped his coat as the wind picked up, sending an even icier chill in their direction.

A growing shadow inched its way across the playground, and the change in light was noticeable. Janis looked up at the darkening clouds as they began to block the sun. "Looks like it's gonna rain," she said, and Troy stiffened. "What's wrong?" she asked.

Troy watched the dark clouds stretch across the sky. The first one passed before the sun and moved on, but in the distance, there were more that followed. Also, the wind had increased, a clear sign it was going to rain.

He had been staring at the sky, not saying a word, when Janis finally raised her voice. "Hey, Troy, what's going on?"

"No," he hissed. "The other day when those things chased me, it had just started to rain. The sky got dark, and then when the storm came, so did they."

The girls now wore the same look as he. "What should we do?" Wendy asked.

"We're not ready yet."

They looked at him as if he might hold the answers. Troy froze between the gazes of his friends as his mind went blank. He tried to think quickly, not his strong suit. It was all he could do to concentrate as the sky grew darker and the clouds drew near. If he was right, that was all the camouflage the creatures needed.

The bell rang, calling the children back into the building, and woke Troy from his unproductive trance. Racking his brain hadn't done him any good, but the sound of that annoying bell had. His eyes flew open wide, and suddenly, Troy knew exactly what to do.

He pulled both girls close and spoke low so not to be overheard. They nodded in agreement as he explained his plan. Then they closed their lunch boxes and waited while the other children assembled at the back doors. They followed the crowd at a snail's pace, making sure they were at the very back of the line. As the three friends stepped into the building, Troy turned to them and mouthed the word—*Now!*

● ● ●

The supply parties arrived at the back lot of the high school, where Bob and his men busied themselves separating the goods into two stockpiles. The mission had been a success, with Deputy Jenkins and his men delivering enough weapons and ammunitions to lay siege on a third-world nation. An array of handguns, shotguns, and rifles were laid out in the beds of two full-size pickups. Deputy Rainey's men appeared to have cleaned out the A&P, and Koloski's group had done equally as well at the hardware store and Radio Shack. The men were all issued a weapon as well as extra ammunition and a radio.

Bob wanted to make sure the supplies were stowed away in both locations before they initiated phase two of the sheriff's plan. He spoke into the radio: "Come in, Sheriff. This is Bob over at the high school."

Carl heard the chief's voice break over the radio and left his position in the stairwell to get better reception near the front entrance.

"Yeah, Bob. How are you making out over there?" Carl stepped out the front door, feeling the sweat on his skin chill to the cool air.

"We're just about set over here. Shopping went as expected, with only a few incidents. I'm about to send over your share of the goods."

"Any chance you can spare a couple more men, Bob? The freight elevator shit the bed, and we're carrying everything down the stairs." Carl winced at the pain between his eyes. A dull thud of pressure caused them to water. Startled, he spun about as a discarded newspaper, kicked up by a sudden wind, rattled across the blacktop.

"Oh Christ, that's not good!" Bob exclaimed. "I'll send who I can, but I'm about to call my man at the station and give him the go ahead. We're running out of time, Carl."

"I know. Don't take anyone off the roundup crew. We need all those men out in the field." A dark shadow crept across the parking lot, covering the area where

THE OJANOX

Carl stood. He looked up as the first heavy cloud passed in front of the sun. The throbbing in his head beat like a broken finger in response to the sudden change in air pressure.

"Disregard that request. I want all available men to begin the round up as soon as possible. I'll make do with who I have here. I think we got less time than we thought."

"What are you talking about? It's still early enough."

"Have you noticed the sky? I think we're in for some weather. I don't like how dark those clouds look in the distance."

From where Bob Jones stood, the skies were as clear as a bell, but he was facing the east, and typically, most storm fronts hit Garrett Grove from the west. He walked out to the middle of the parking lot, where he could get a better look over the top of the school. As soon he got a few feet away from the building, he felt the temperature drop as the breeze hit him. He peered toward the west and saw what the sheriff was talking about. Thick, dark clouds had begun to gather in the western sky and were rapidly approaching Garrett Mountain.

"I think you're right, Carl. I'll make the call. Ed Koloski and Chris Fredricks are on their way now, and you can put them to work if you need them. Stay in touch and keep me posted on your progress."

"10-4." Carl replaced the radio to his hip and made his way back to the building. The newspaper that had been blown across the parking lot cartwheeled through the air and snagged in the bushes next to the front door. He noticed the headlines on the page: REAGAN LEADS IN THE POLLS. He read the line as he entered the building. "Jesus Christ, it really is the end of the world," he said as the door closed behind him.

● ● ●

Allison played the intro to "How Great Thou Art," and the congregation rose on cue. Father Kieran made his slow progression up the aisle with two parishioners acting as altar boys since none of the usual ones had shown up. Diane Nathan and Josh Wilson were each assigned to read one of the scriptures before the Gospel. Father Kieran knelt at the altar, blessed himself, then opened the good book to the first page marker.

"In the name of the Father, and of the Son, and of the Holy Spirit, Amen."

The entire room answered him with a thunderous "Amen" that even surprised Father Kieran.

He continued, "Lord, have mercy. Christ, have mercy. Lord, have mercy." The congregation repeated every line. Father Kieran delivered the Homily and recited the Apostle's Creed, then instructed the parish to be seated. "Let us pray." He bowed his head, and they all followed. "Heavenly Father, for the sick and the suffering, Lord, hear our prayer. For our dearly departed brothers and sisters, Lord, hear our prayer. For Pope Paul, Francis our Bishop, and all of the Angels and Saints, Lord, hear our prayer."

He gazed upon the congregation and smiled. "Brothers and sisters, we find ourselves in a crisis. I look out among you today, and I see the children of the Lord. Some of you I have known for many years, and some I have just met. And I say, Praise be to God, for His flock is great. When I was a younger priest, I faced a crisis of my own. I questioned my place in this world, as the war in Vietnam had begun. I sought counsel from a senior member of the church, my mentor, Father Michael. And I prayed to the Lord for an answer to the problems that plagued me. The Lord worked through Father Michael, and I was sent here to Garrett Grove to lead the congregation. I trusted in God, and He showed me the way. Today, you have come with a crisis of your own. For some, it is a crisis of grief; for others, a crisis of guidance, possibly even a crisis of faith. Well, I say God Bless you all. Your crisis is a sign of your commitment. For those who have no faith have no crisis. Everyone sitting before you today sought solace in the House of the Lord, and that is a sign of strength. Blessed are the meek, for they shall inherit the Earth. And blessed are those who stand against the powers of evil and come in the name of the Lord."

Father Kieran blessed himself and took a seat behind the altar. The congregation began to take notice of one another and looked around the church to see the faces of the brothers and sisters who had also heard the call. Dick Wilson had closed the diner early and sat next to Frank Palumbo, the owner of the Texaco station. Both men were struggling to make sense out of a world that had changed overnight. Dick had watched his employees and customers disappear one by one, and Frank had literally witnessed his livelihood go up in flames. A man by the name of Rick Edwards, who drove for the Fink Bakery, decided to stop by the church after finding himself unable to leave town. He'd nearly been killed this morning by an avalanche on Sunset Road, which got him wondering about the last time he'd been to church; he figured a confession was in order. Bill Hamilton, the fire inspector, sat next to Amy Sterling, who worked part-time at Wilson's when Mandy wasn't there.

Julie and Luke Evans held hands as they listened to the sermon from the third row. They had been going through a difficult time in their marriage, and today, Luke convinced his wife to play hooky from her job at the high school. They woke last night to the sound of someone screaming in the street outside their home. It had been a terrifying animal-like scream, and after turning on the porch light and finding no one outside, they got to talking. The couple stayed up all night and made love in the early morning light. Julie cooked breakfast, and they had even taken a shower together, which was something they hadn't done in years. Julie didn't tell Luke she'd been sleeping with Principal Garish and decided that she would go to confession to help her cope with the burden. Father Kieran offered her a penance for her sins.

In the back row sat a man whose face was terribly scarred. Jim Reilly had simply been in the wrong place at the wrong time and had the unfortunate experience of ending up on the radar of the class bully. The thug had thrown a cherry bomb into the boys' room toilet moments before Jim entered the stall. The shrapnel from the explosion left him disfigured for life. He received a settlement from the school, but it couldn't buy him a new face. Jim found himself in a crisis of faith in the months and years that followed the accident but had finally found the Lord and been a loyal member of the church ever since; he never missed a Wednesday afternoon Mass. He believed he had a great deal to be thankful for; at least he hadn't been sitting on the toilet when it exploded.

Jim, who used to be called Jimmy, watched as the young girl approached the podium, just to the left of the altar. Diane Nathan stood before the congregation with trembling hands, cleared her throat, and began to speak.

"Today's reading is a Letter from Paul to the Corinthians. *And when I came to you brothers, I did not come proclaiming the testimony of God with lofty speech or wisdom. For I decided to know nothing among you except Jesus Christ and Him crucified. And I was with you in weakness and in fear and in much trembling, and my speech and my message were not in plausible words of wisdom, but in demonstration of the Spirit, and of the power, so that your faith might not rest in the wisdom of men, but in the power of God. This is the word of the Lord.*"

"Thanks be to God," the congregation responded as Diane blessed herself and returned to her seat. Father Kieran offered the girl a look of approval.

Josh Wilson read from the Book of Revelation for the second reading and did an equally impressive job. Father Kieran waited for the boy to be seated before he approached the altar to deliver the Gospel. He listened to the sound of the wind as it picked up outside the church and paused for a moment before continuing. The rustle of leaves being blown against the front doors broke the silence. It echoed throughout the large church, off the vaulted ceiling, and against the stained glass windows.

"Before we continue, I believe the Lord has given us a sign. If there is anything in your vehicles you would like to bring inside, whether it be food, clothing, or weapons, I believe that now is the time to collect those items. We will continue with the Mass when everyone has returned."

Almost every man in the church stood up and walked out the front door to their vehicles. Many of the women joined them as well. They had all come with the same goal in mind. They were looking for guidance, and there wasn't a soul in the place that hadn't lost something along the way. Whether it had been within the past couple days or years ago in a high school bathroom, they had all lost something, and they were prepared to fight for what they still had left.

The parishioners returned to the church carrying duffle bags filled with food and clothing. Some brought sleeping bags, portable lanterns, and flashlights. Father Kieran watched as the shotgun cases began to stack up against the back wall of the church near the confessionals. His heart swelled as he witnessed the flock parade into the church; they had come prepared to go to war. He always knew he had been chosen to lead during a time of conflict. And even though he had been spared from serving in Vietnam, he had been chosen after all. He returned to the altar after the last man took his seat. Looking out at the congregation, a sense of elation consumed him. It was warm, and overpowering, and spread out to his arms and legs. Kieran wiped his eyes and held out his hands.

"Thanks be to God," he said.

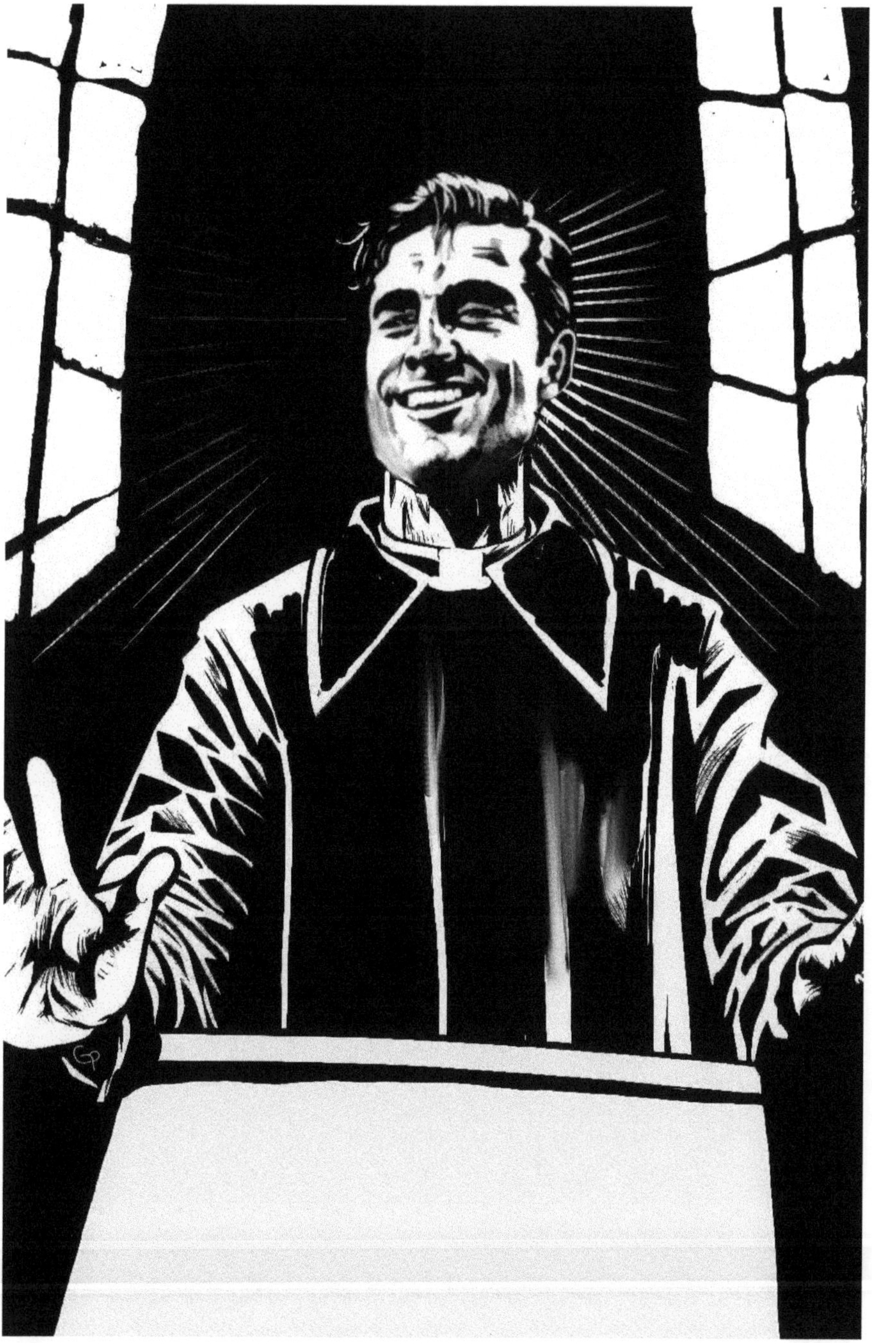

Chapter 66

They followed the crowd at a snail's pace, making sure they were at the very back of the line. As the three friends stepped into the building, Troy turned to them and mouthed the word—*Now!*

Janis held the door from closing as Troy reached for the fire alarm, grabbed the handle, and pulled. At first, nothing happened. His heart floundered in his chest. It was the only plan he could think of, and he was sure it'd been a good one. He looked at Wendy, who shrugged her shoulders; neither knew what to do next. Then the thunderous sound of a dozen bells bleating at once filled the air.

Wendy's eyes lit up, and a huge smile crossed her face. She and Troy spun around, exited the building, and descended the stairs as Janis allowed the heavy door to slam behind them. Inside, the pandemonium had already begun. None of the staff had been prepared for the unscheduled fire drill. On top of that, the children never knew what to do or where to go, even when there were adults who knew what was happening.

The three children ran across the playground to the back part of the lot that bordered the ball field. Wendy was the first to hit the small four-foot fence and scaled it like a gazelle. Janis followed with an equal amount of grace. Troy was so excited he almost tripped before he even made it there but managed to right himself and bound over the small obstacle, although not quite as gracefully as the girls had.

They tore across the pitcher's mound and into the outfield before anyone emerged from the school. Janis proved to be the fastest and made it to the railroad tracks ten steps before the others. Troy and Wendy caught up to her and burst onto the dusty tracks laughing and ecstatic. It had worked like a charm, and it had been Troy's idea.

"Let's go before anyone knows we're missing." Wendy urged them down the tracks in the direction of Marco's Playmart.

"Oh my God, that was amazing," Janis cried. "I thought my heart was gonna explode." She punched Troy in the arm and gave him a look of approval.

Wendy leaned next to him and kissed him on the cheek. "That was pretty smart."

Troy beamed and felt as if he had finally done something right after being uncertain for so long. It was a feeling he thought he could get used to.

They ran down the tracks, congratulating each other on the amazing job they had done, when a strong gust of wind kicked up some loose dust, blowing the fine particles into the air. Troy looked toward the threatening sky; the clouds appeared to gain speed as they passed across the sun like horses on a carousel. He shivered and zipped his jacket even more, noticing it had gotten much colder since they'd left school. *Rain's almost here.* They needed to hurry if they were going to pull this off. Troy prayed that Mrs. Marco wouldn't question him about why he and the girls weren't in school. If he was lucky, someone else would be working at the register instead of her.

It was only two blocks from the school to the toy store, and they arrived at the back of the store in no time, out of breath and elated from their victory. They stopped for a few seconds and attempted to collect themselves in preparation for the second phase of the mission.

Troy had the hardest time settling down and found it impossible to wipe the smile from his face. Wendy looked at him and shook her head.

"You're gonna get us busted looking like that," she said.

He stared back at her as if he'd been injured. "Looking like what?"

"Come on, Troy," Janis said. "You look like you just pulled the fire alarm at the school. You can't go in there like that; we'll definitely get caught."

"She's right." Wendy nodded. "You're staying here. Me and Janis will go in and get what we need while you keep a lookout. And try not to get noticed by anyone."

Before he could argue, both girls had flung their lunch boxes at him and disappeared around the side of the building.

He felt a bit foolish standing there holding three lunch boxes, but that still didn't prevent him from grinning like an idiot. He looked around the building and tried to play it cool, doubting he was doing a very good job of it. Hopefully, no one would come along and see him standing there, acting as guilty as a dog with its head in the toilet.

He stood next to a dumpster filled with cardboard. He and Rob had liberated a stockpile of the stuff from the trash bin to build the Scream in the Dark haunted house in his dad's garage. Which felt like a very long time ago. Troy tried to remember the day he and Rob had gone over the details of the maze.

●●●

The whole plan had come quickly to the two boys as they sat on the playground during lunch recess. It had been late September when they first got to designing what would be the highlight of the party. Troy was going to lead the kids through the maze to where Rob would be hiding in the coffin.

"I bet Tommy throws up this year," Rob said as he sat on the grass with his notebook opened to a rough sketch of the maze drawn onto one of the pages.

"Yeah, he almost did last year, and that wasn't even scary. This is going to be so much better." Troy leaned over to look at what his friend had drawn.

"Everybody is going to walk in here." Rob pointed to the entrance. "What should we do first?"

"We need to start off with a big scare. That's what always happens in the movies."

"You mean like someone jumps out or chases them?"

"It should be pitch-black so they can't see anything. And they should be trapped. And then BAMM!" Troy screamed at Rob and startled him, causing the boy to scribble across the page with his pencil.

"Quit it, jerk!" he yelled. "That's not funny."

Rob tried not to smile but couldn't help himself, and then both boys burst out laughing. It had been pretty funny, after all.

"I want to do something in the first room that will make them scream," Troy said, trying to regain himself.

Rob put his pencil under his chin and started to think about what Troy had just said. "That's it!" Rob shouted.

"What, what's it?"

"We can call the haunted house Scream in the Dark."

"Oh my God! That's awesome. Scream in the Dark," he repeated, loving the way it sounded. "Now we just have to *make* them scream in the dark."

"We will. Don't look now, but I think someone's staring at you." He nodded to the girl on the swings across the playground.

Troy looked up and saw her sitting by herself. "You mean Wendy? I don't think she's staring at me. I don't think she even knows who I am."

"Are you kidding me? She's been staring at you the whole time. Tell you the truth, I think she's been looking at you since she moved here last month." Rob went back to doodling on his pad.

"Don't be stupid; she's just a girl. What would she be looking at us for?"

"My dad says that one day I'm gonna wake up and I'm gonna want to be friends with girls. I don't know why, but maybe Wendy wants to be friends with boys. My mom says that girls are more mature." Rob had been blessed with a wealth of knowledge for a fourth-grade boy and was always sharing his pearls of wisdom.

"I don't believe that, and the only people who say that are girls," Troy said.

"Well, my dad agreed with my mom when she said it."

"Yeah, my dad agrees with my mom a lot too, but I know he doesn't really feel that way. I think he does it just so she won't yell at him." Troy looked over at Wendy and caught her staring at them. *Oh my God! She is staring at us.*

"I think you should ask her." Rob elbowed him.

"Ask her what?"

"Duh." Rob made a face. "Ask her to come to the party, you dork."

Wendy averted her eyes when Troy looked up again. He had never said all that much to her. She was nice enough and all, but she was still a girl, and they didn't have that much in common. "Oh, come on, I'd feel stupid. Besides, I don't think she would want to come anyway."

"You'll never know if you don't ask. But I bet she says yes." Rob gave Troy a look of confidence that said, *go for it*. "Unless, you're chicken ... Is that what it is?"

Troy felt heat rise within him. Now he *had* to ask. It was a no-win situation either way. If he did ask, she would say no, and he would feel like a total jerk. But if he didn't, then he would be a chicken, and that was even worse. He looked at his friend and considered pulling his hair out.

"That's okay if you're chicken," Rob said. "I'm sure there are a lot of chickens in the fourth grade. I mean ... I don't know any, but I'm sure there are a whole bunch."

"Fine!" Troy shouted, then grabbed Rob's pencil and broke it in two pieces. He stood up and threw the pencil back to his friend. "Here's your stupid pencil, jerk face."

Troy walked across the playground to where the girl sat on the swings with her feet dangling a few inches from the ground. She looked down as he approached and started to rock back and forth. He stopped in front of her, lost his nerve, and stared at the top of her head for a moment. Her hair was dark and shiny, and Troy thought it looked incredibly soft. He had no idea why a thought like that had popped into his head, but for some reason, it had.

Then Wendy looked up at him, and for the first time, Troy noticed just how big her eyes were. They reminded him of Bambi's eyes in the Disney movie. He had never noticed, but she had long eyelashes too. He suddenly felt self-conscious and forgot why he had come over in the first place.

"What?" she snapped.

"What?" he repeated and realized he had been staring.

"What are you looking at?" she asked.

This was getting more awkward by the second. "I'm sorry. I wanted to see if you might ... um. Well, I mean if you don't want to ... that's ... um." He looked back at Rob and wanted to kill him. This was his fault, and now he was stuck looking like an idiot. Rob nodded to him and smiled, which helped him regain a little of his composure.

"I don't understand, Troy," she said.

Hearing Wendy say his name struck him like a hammer. That had been the first time she had ever said it, and he suddenly felt much better.

"I was wondering if you would like to come to my Halloween party. It's a costume party, and I'm building a haunted house." Troy let out a sigh of relief. At least he didn't have to worry about being called a chicken.

"Oh." Wendy acted surprised by the question. Then she looked back at the ground and began to rock again. "I have to ask my mom."

"Sure." Troy knew what that meant. He bowed his head and turned around to walk away.

"Hey, Troy," she called him back. "I'm sure she'll say yes. Is it okay if I dress as Princess Leia?"

He looked back with his mouth hung open. Had she actually said what he thought? "Yeah, that would be awesome. I love *Star Wars*. It's, like, the greatest movie of all time."

"Well, you're really going to like my costume then. I can't wait to see the haunted house. I hope it's scary."

"Oh, you can count on that. It's gonna be awesome."

"Thanks for asking me."

"Okay," he said. A warm rush spread across Troy's face as he turned back, almost breaking into a sprint to return to his friend's side. He sat down and didn't say a word.

"Told you," Rob said.

"Shut up." Troy wiped the sweat from his forehead.

"You owe me a new pencil, you big dork." Rob threw the broken pieces at him, causing a fresh fit of laughter.

Troy had no idea how Rob had known, but he had. There was something about Wendy that was different than the other girls in class. She was cool, and she even liked *Star Wars*; that was unbelievable.

"Now all we need to do is figure out the haunted house and we're all set. If this isn't scary, we're both gonna look stupid." Rob was right. They couldn't call it Scream in the Dark if it wasn't scary. That would be a big letdown for everyone.

Troy picked up the broken pencil pieces and played with them for a moment, trying to think what might scare everyone. He held them up in front of his eyes and looked at his friend, giving Rob the appearance as if he were behind bars, like in a jail cell. He thought about that for a second. *A jail cell! What if… that's it!*

"I got it!" he shouted. Troy leaned over and explained his idea for the first room and how scary it would be if they could pull it off. Rob snatched the sharpened

THE OJANOX

half of the pencil from his friend and began to sketch out the bars of a cage. Troy showed him where it should be hidden in the wall so the kids couldn't see it until the strobe light went on ... when the monsters were inches from their faces. It was brilliant. Their friends really were going to scream in the dark.

⬤ ⬤ ⬤

"Hey dork!" Wendy shouted.

Troy looked up to see the girls had returned.

"I thought I told you not to look guilty. Jeez, you're still grinning like a weirdo. Let's go before someone sees you like that."

It didn't bother Troy that Wendy thought he looked like a fool. He had forgotten all about that day on the playground and how he and Rob had planned out the haunted house room by room. That was the day he asked Wendy to go to the party, and he thought it was the day that he realized he liked her.

Janis held up a bag full of items.

"Did you get everything?" Troy asked.

Janis shook the bag and grinned. "We sure did, and then some. I didn't know you could buy so much with ten dollars."

Wendy started walking towards the train tracks and called back, "Come on, we can talk on the way. Look at the sky."

Troy noticed that the storm was nearly on top of them. He hurried to join her, juggling the lunch boxes as he ran, and Janis followed.

The sky had grown even darker. Heavy clouds with deep purple bellies loomed overhead and appeared ready to dump. The wind had also picked up, causing the temperature to drop. The children hustled to get to Troy's house, which was only a few blocks away, when the first flash of lightning cracked across the sky. About ten seconds later, it was followed by a slow rumble that reminded Troy of the bowling alley. The storm was coming, and they had little time left to get to his house.

"We need to hurry; let's go." Wendy started to run, and Troy and Janis took off after her.

Another bolt lit up the sky like a light saber. Troy was reminded of the day in the graveyard and the creatures that chased him. He kept his eyes focused on the path in front of him, not wanting to look to the left or right for fear of seeing the horrible beasts. He told himself, *As long as I don't look, they won't be there.* He prayed that was true.

Chapter 67

Deputy Jenkins and fireman Drew Halberg waited in the office of the fire station, staring at the radio. Soon they would get the go ahead to start the second phase of the operation. In all his years on the force, Beau had never experienced anything close to the nightmare the past twenty-four hours had been. First the Texaco station had gone up like a Roman candle, then the explosion at the medical center, and now his friends were dying. Tara was dead, Kovach was dead, even Tim Colbert, who had been Beau's partner for more years than he could remember.

Beau, Tim, and Allen Primrose had been the lifeblood of the department back in the day, long before Vietnam and the kids had started smoking grass. In his day, teenagers were content to swipe a little booze from their parents' liquor cabinets. That was all you needed to have a good time or get into a girl's pants; everyone knew liquor was quicker. He missed the days when all it took was a couple shots to put lead in the old pencil and grease the wheels. It had been longer than Beau could remember since his one-eyed trouser trout had even moved. It was a sick joke what happened to men his age, when the mind was still willing but the body was no longer able.

Years ago, it had been difficult to keep the damn thing from popping out of his pants every time a pretty skirt walked by. The sucker used to stand at attention and watch him shave every morning; now all it did was hang there and watch him tie his shoes. And it didn't appear interested in that either.

If anyone ever wants to make a million bucks, all they have to do is invent a pill that gives old guys boners.

"Chief Jones to base. Come in, Drew." The radio crackled to life.

Both men stared at it for a moment, then the young fireman leaned in. "Go ahead, Chief."

"Hit it, son. That's a go for Operation Air Raid."

"Roger that, Chief." Drew turned to Beau, who sat at the control desk.

"Well, here goes nothing," Beau said as he hit the control panel.

The siren screamed to life, erupting from the speakers attached to the exterior of the building and the ones positioned throughout the town. The growing timbre of the wail increased in volume and ceased to rest. It had been set to run continuously, which was a much different signal than the three short blasts for a brush or house fire. There was no mistaking what this signal meant as it grew louder without pause; it was the air raid warning, alerting everyone to report to the shelter.

Beau doubted if many would take it seriously, since it was '79 not '59. Most would just think the siren was broken. But they had been instructed to keep it running no matter what, which was sure to get folks' attention.

Then the bay doors opened, and Gabriel Ford pulled out of the station in the ladder truck, laying on the air horn as he did. He drove past the municipal building and headed onto the turnpike, followed by Tank Ferguson in the pump truck, also laying on the horn.

Three sheriff's cruisers took off from behind the station with their cherries flashing and sirens screaming. David Rainey was followed by Glenn Gillick and Mike Turino; the men had been given their own individual routes and neighborhoods to canvass. The first part of the job was to get the sirens going; the second was to canvass the neighborhoods and deliver the message.

Beau examined the exasperated look on Drew's face. The poor kid couldn't be any older than twenty-one and still had years to go before his pecker gave out on him. But sure enough, one day it would. Beau swore to himself that if he survived this nightmare, he would get right to work on that boner pill. Now that was a million-dollar idea.

THE OJANOX

Carl worked transporting medical equipment into the basement. The supplies had arrived, and the weapons were in the process of being distributed. He ascended the landing into the lobby and heard the initial scream of the fire whistle. It wouldn't be long before one of his men showed up at the elementary school, which meant he and Lois needed to get moving. He wanted her and Troy in that high school shelter long before the storm hit. She had questioned why he didn't want her staying at the medical center with Alice and Will, and he had avoided answering. The truth was he didn't hold much faith in the center's ability to weather an attack; the high school was the only structure he felt somewhat confident about.

He froze as a flash of bright blue lit up the front entrance of the building. It was followed by a slow rumble of thunder that set his hackles standing. The storm had moved much quicker than he anticipated. Men ran both in and out of the building, carrying boxes and weapons in a desperate attempt to beat the rain. Nurse TenHove worked with Alice and Lois, transporting medications to the basement, when the lightning struck.

Lois and Carl looked at each other and exchanged an understood message; it was time. She set the box down and turned to her sister. "I have to go get Troy. Will you be okay till I get back?"

"I'll be fine," Alice said and hugged her. "Will is here and so is Billy, but hurry back."

"I will." Lois kissed Alice on the cheek and released her as a loud clap of thunder rocked the building like an avalanche.

"Nurse TenHove, it's time to get the patients into the basement. I'll be back as soon as I can," Carl instructed her as Deputy Lutchen and the little girl emerged into the lobby with the Shepherd at their heels. "Ted, keep them safe till I get back. The storm is about to hit, and we don't have much time." He had to shout to be heard over the siren.

He and Lois exited the main entrance and were bombarded by the blare of a fire whistle screaming as if it were in pain. A sharp crack of lightning spread across the sky like the crooked fingers of an arthritic man. It was followed by a concussion of thunder that felt as if it were on top of them. They entered the cruiser, and Carl turned over the ignition as the first fat drops of rain smacked against the windshield, loud as popcorn.

"Don't worry." He hit the gas and sped out of the parking lot. "One of my men is at the school making sure everything goes as planned."

Lois nodded, but a look of dread washed across her face. Another set of fat raindrops hit the windshield, and the sky grew even darker. It was going to be one hell of a storm.

Burt needed to share his discovery with Carl and had told Nurse TenHove he would do his best to be there by noon. It was already past twelve, and his stomach had started to do the Hokey Pokey. He now knew the bacterium carried a metallic signature, but it was still unclear what exact type of metal had caused the poisoning. If he had to guess, he was leaning toward a combination of several, with iron and mercury being the likely suspects. Still, there was something about the cellular composition that was entirely foreign, and he was willing to bet that if a chemist had a good look with a photon microscope, they would find at least one unidentifiable metal. It was only a hunch, but Burt was usually good when it came to his hunches.

The infection was vulnerable to magnetization, which meant if a powerful enough magnet were focused on any of the creatures, then it should be sufficient to kill it. Unfortunately, it would also kill the host; and from what they had seen so far, it appeared impossible to survive the infection. The fact that Malcolm had been sent to destroy the MRI machine proved he was on the right track. But there wasn't a powerful enough magnetic current that could be used on command or was transportable. Whatever they were dealing with was one clever son of a bitch.

He snatched his coat from the table, shut off the lights, and opened the back door of the lab. A blast of cold air slapped him across the face as soon as he stepped outside. Burt made his way to his sedan, feeling good about the progress he had made. Carl would be pleased, and he hoped to run into him soon. He fumbled with his keys for a moment as the first bolt of lightning lit up the sky. The wind picked up slightly, and the temperature felt as if it had dropped in a matter of seconds. It was going to rain; with any luck, he would be at Chilton before it started. It wasn't far, and it looked like they were in for a real boomer.

At first, it sounded like someone had crept up behind him and screamed. Then he recognized the familiar blare of the fire whistle. It grew louder and bolder, and Burt anticipated the ebb and flow of the siren's typical rhythm. But there was no pause of the steady horn as it reached full timbre, cutting through the air like a jet engine.

"Jesus H. Christ. What the hell is going on?" He turned toward the direction of the whistle. The siren continued, uninterrupted and steady. Burt had been around during the Cuban Missile Crisis and knew exactly what a steady siren meant. It was the universal signal for an air raid. *But that's not possible.* He wondered if the switchboard at the station had fried. Then he heard the horns from the trucks in the distance. Something was going on, and it sure as hell didn't sound good.

A hard drop of rain fell from the sky and landed against his face. It was followed by another that hit the ground in front of him. The droplets were so big and fat he heard them as they smacked against the pavement. Burt looked up and saw how dark and threatening the sky had become. The storm was moving fast, and the sudden cloud cover held the potential for disaster. If these things were predisposed to darkness, the storm was going to put the people of Garrett Grove at a huge disadvantage.

The din of police sirens mixed with the wail of the fire whistle, but Burt heard something else in the background. It was the sound of voices shouting over bullhorns; it was impossible for Burt to decipher a damn thing they were saying.

He jumped into his sedan and sped out of the parking lot toward the medical center. Even with the windows rolled up, it was impossible to hear himself think. Burt dug his hand into his jacket pocket, looking to find the gun Carl had given him. Which was no longer there, not that it had done him a damn bit of good. He hoped it would be useful to Father Kieran; at least *he* had figured out what to do with it.

"Brothers and Sisters, A demon-oppressed man who was blind and mute was brought to Jesus, and he healed him so that the man spoke and saw. And all of the people were amazed and said, "Can this be the son of David?" But the Pharisees heard it and said, "It is only by Beelzebub, the prince of darkness, that this man casts out demons. Knowing their thoughts, Jesus said unto them, "No city or house divided against itself will stand. If Satan casts out Satan, he is divided against himself. How will his kingdom stand? If I cast out demons by Beelzebub, by whom do your sons cast them out? But if it is by the Spirit of God that I cast out demons, then the Kingdom of God has come upon you. How can someone enter a strong man's house and plunder his goods, unless he first binds the strong man. Whoever is not with me is against me, and whoever does not gather with me scatters."

"This is the word of the Lord."

A loud clap of thunder echoed in the distance as Father Kieran finished delivering the Gospel. The congregation took notice of the dramatic accent and interpreted it as a sign. Father Kieran was sure it was and welcomed it. "Brothers and Sisters, the time has come for you to gather with me. For we are a house undivided, and we are strong in the Holy Spirit. It is not by chance you all chose to be in the house of the Lord on today of all days. I feel the time for action is near, and I would like to bless everyone as you receive the Sacrament of the Eucharist. But we must hurry." Another concussion of thunder rattled the stained glass windows in their frames. "Forgive me if I rush this a bit, but I don't think we have much time. Please line up."

Father Kieran took the vessel containing the Eucharist from the altar and held it up. "On the night he was betrayed, he took bread, gave it to his disciples, and said, 'Take this, all of you, and eat from it; this is my body. Do this in remembrance of me.'"

The line quickly gathered, and Father Kieran blessed every man, woman, and child that approached the altar. He administered the Sacrament and was almost finished when the fire whistle began to sound. The siren increased in volume, ceasing to stop.

THE OJANOX

Father Kieran stood before them and spoke loud enough so they all could hear. "Brothers and Sisters, the time has come to stand. Stand in the name of the Lord." He reached beneath his robe into his waistband and removed the handgun. "I could use some twenty-five caliber bullets if anyone has a few they could spare."

The congregation erupted with an inspired roar of approval as the sirens were joined by the sounds of fire trucks in the distance. Another flash of lightning illuminated the images depicted in the stained glass windows and was followed by a loud rumble. No less than seven men approached Father Kieran and offered him ammunition for his weapon. He thanked them all with the same reply: "God bless you."

※ ※ ※

The fire alarm came as a shock to the staff at the elementary school. No one had scheduled a fire drill, and they were having a difficult time getting the children lined up on the playground. It would have been an impossible task for those who had made it to work if attendance hadn't been so light. Miss Davis, Miss Boriello, and Principal Grace worked like sheepdogs to round up the kids; it was looking like one of the little pranksters had pulled the alarm near the back entrance.

It was hard to get an accurate head count, but it looked like everyone was present. Principal Grace gave the go ahead for the children to return to their classrooms. With the sky growing darker by the second and the threat of rain looming in the distance, they all knew they'd be lucky to get everyone back inside before the storm hit.

Then the fire whistle started to howl. The children turned toward the station, which was less than two blocks away.

"What now?" Miss Boriello shouted as two fire trucks sped past the school blaring their horns.

The children, excited by the sight of the trucks, began to stray from their neatly formed lines and made their way closer to the street to get a better look. The siren grew louder and louder and refused to stop. It was something Jill Boriello never imagined she would hear in her lifetime: the single continuous blast of the air raid siren. *That's not possible. Maybe it's broken.* She watched as three police cruisers screamed past the school with their sirens blaring and their lights flashing.

One of the cruisers pulled up to the front of the school and that set the rest of the children in motion. They broke into two groups, with half of them heading toward the sheriff's vehicle and the other half meandering toward the back fence to get a better look at the fire house.

Jill Boriello screamed to be heard over the blare of the sirens and horns but was unable to raise the children's attention. She looked across the playground to Principal Grace, who had also lost control. Jill cupped her hands on the sides of her mouth and shouted once again, then felt something strain in the back of her throat. It was no use; things were falling apart, and she knew she needed to act.

From where she stood on the steps, Jill could see things unraveling fast. She turned back toward the door and looked inside, hoping to find anything that might help. The area was empty except for a few extra desks and the bin where the phys. ed. equipment was kept. It wasn't much, just a few balls and a large parachute. Then she saw it. Jill spun on her heels and ran into the school.

A second later, she stormed out the back door with a bright orange flag and something in her mouth. She started to wave the flag as if it were the last lap of the Daytona 500, then Jill bit down on the object between her lips and blew into it as hard as she could. The professional referee's whistle cut through the roar of the sirens like a scalpel, demanding the attention of every student on the playground. They turned on cue, as if they had all been caught cheating on a math test. Then she took the whistle out of her mouth and screamed. "Get inside NOW!" She waved the flag towards the open door, and every single child made their way back into the building with their tails tucked between their legs. Not one remained behind to watch the policeman get out of his car and enter the building.

Principal Grace watched the kindergarten teacher take matters into her own hands. "I have got to get that woman a raise," she said to herself.

After the last child entered the building, the rain started, followed by a violent bolt of lightning that sizzled out of the west. They had gotten the children back into the building ... just in time. Principal Grace followed the last student inside and met the deputy in the hallway. They walked to her office and closed the door behind them.

Chapter 68

Troy and the girls arrived at his house before the rain started, with the thunder and lightning following them the entire way. He led his friends around the back to a flowerpot beside the door. He bent down and retrieved a key from underneath, then let them inside as a loud clap of thunder exploded overhead, causing all of them to jump.

They entered the first-floor rec room where Donald Fisher kept a large drawing board, an array of blueprints, and a couple small toolboxes. Janis poured the contents of her shopping bag onto the drawing board to show Troy what she and Wendy had bought.

Troy noticed the three wrist rockets were not the cheap, flimsy kind. These were the ones the big kids used to break bottles. He picked one up and examined it.

"Radical," he said, checking out the feel of it in his hand.

There were also several boxes of magnets that Wendy and Janis began to open and dump out onto the table. They were heavy and thick and looked like they would do the job—provided they could fashion the magnets into sharp enough projectiles.

Troy opened one of his dad's toolboxes, rooted around until he found what he was looking for, and produced a large pair of tin snips. "This should do it," he said and grabbed one of the large magnets. He positioned it between the blades of the snips and pressed down on the handles as hard as he could. Nothing happened. He tried again using all his strength and pushed even harder this time.

"Jeez, that's tougher than I thought." A bead of sweat fell from his forehead to the floor as he struggled to work the tool.

"Maybe you're doing it wrong," Wendy said.

"Ughhh." He bore down harder onto the magnet, feeling he might get it this time. The snips scratched into the magnet's surface, but the object remained intact.

Wendy dug into the toolbox and stood up with a hammer and chisel in her hand and a great smile on her face. She handed the tools to Troy. "Here, maybe these'll work."

Troy figured they couldn't do any worse than the tin snips. He took the tools and examined them, thinking maybe she was right. Troy laid the magnet on the hard tile floor, then rested the chisel against it. He raised the hammer, struck the top of the chisel. The magnet shattered into two pieces that shot like a couple of pinballs across the floor.

"Whoa!" he shouted as the pieces scattered.

"Yeah!" Janis and Wendy screamed in unison, then proceeded to collect the fragments.

Using the hammer and chisel, Troy cracked magnet after magnet, and the girls ran around collecting the sharp pieces. Together, they manufactured a stockpile of shrapnel and nearly depleted their supply of intact magnets.

"Let's try a couple out to make sure they work," Troy said to the girls, who nodded in agreement. Each child grabbed a wrist rocket and pocketed a handful of the shards.

He led them into the backyard where two large chestnut trees stood. Spiny cones littered the ground, and a family of squirrels were busy cracking them open and extracting the nuts. The animals looked up for a moment when the children exited the house, then went right back to work. Thunder continued to rumble in the distance, and the sky had gotten darker since they'd gone inside to manufacture their weapons.

"We better hurry up," Troy said, looking up at the sky.

"Okay, just a couple practice shots and we'll go." Janis placed a magnet into the pouch of the wrist rocket and pulled back on the rubber tubing. She aimed at the trunk of the closest chestnut tree and let go of the pouch.

The magnet whistled through the air and connected with the tree, making a wet *Thwack* as it buried itself into the bark.

"No way!" Troy shouted. "That works even better than I thought it would."

Thwack

Wendy sent a magnet flying into the tree, landing a few inches above the one Janis had let loose.

"So cool," Troy said and loaded his own projectile into the pouch of his wrist rocket. He pulled back on the tubing, surprised to find just how difficult it was, and grimaced. *Darn, how the heck did a couple girls do it?*

He finally managed to pull the bands back as far as he could and aimed the magnet at the trunk of the tree. He let go of the pouch, and the bands released. The magnet flew up and over his head and the rubber tubing snapped hard against his fingers.

"Ouch!" he yelled and shook his hand to knock the sting out of it.

Both girls smiled at his ineffective attempt to work the wrist rocket, and Wendy even let out a small chuckle. Troy felt the heat rise in his face. Embarrassed by his inadequacy but still determined, he loaded another magnet into the pouch, pulled back even harder, and aimed at the trunk of the chestnut tree. He wasn't sure what he had done wrong the first time but thought it might have been the way he released the magnet. He hadn't been that sure of himself and fumbled at the last minute. *That's why.*

He focused on the target and took a deep breath. Then he released the pouch, and the projectile sizzled away from him like a bottle rocket.

The magnet buried itself into the trunk of the tree with a hearty *Thwack*, landing even closer to where Janis's magnet had hit. Troy pumped his fists in a victory celebration.

"Hooray!" Wendy gave him the thumbs-up, and Janis showed him a toothy grin as a sign of approval. The squirrels weren't pleased with what they were up to and had taken to the trees to escape from the commotion.

A low rumble of thunder cascaded over the mountain, lasting for almost a full five seconds. As it faded, it was replaced by another sound that was very different and much higher pitched. The children looked at each other when the fire whistle started to blow and grew in intensity.

At first Troy thought it had something to do with the alarm he had pulled at the school. He stood there frozen with the siren screaming. But there was something different about the whistle, the way it continued to bellow out in one long, monotonous drone. It sounded as if it were broken or something.

Troy eyed the girls as a sharp flash of blue lit his face like the strobe of a camera. Lightning zigzagged across the sky, followed by a tremendous single clap of thunder that made all of them jump.

Other sirens joined in, accompanied by the deep bass blast of the horns from the fire trucks. Seconds later, there were voices barking out announcements over loudspeakers.

Oh no, they're coming. He turned to find both Janis and Wendy wore the same look of terror on their faces. He prayed the girls were ready but in truth was more worried how he would react.

It sounded like the world was coming to an end with all the sirens and horns blasting out in competition with one another. He tried to listen to what the voices were saying, but it was impossible to make out over the noise.

Troy didn't know what horror was headed their way, even though he had already encountered the strange creatures. He prayed he was wrong about the whole thing and the three of them would be able to laugh about it tomorrow. But as the noise continued to assault their ears and the sky turned black, he doubted they would.

As if the universe were listening to what was going on in his head, the rain started to fall. Just a drop or two at first, then a second later, the heavens opened and a torrent fell in a ceaseless downpour. It only took a moment to soak the children thoroughly. And although they weren't far from the back door, it was impossible to see the house from where they stood.

Troy ran to the girls, who huddled together, shielding themselves from the wind and rain. He grabbed his friends and urged them in the direction of the house but was halted when a shriek cut through the storm like a heart attack. The children tensed in horror as the color drained from their faces. There was a second shriek, more mournful than the first and sounding much closer.

Troy took both girls by the hand and forced himself to act, sloshing through the wet grass towards the back door. The heavy rain made it difficult to see as it hammered against his face and stung his skin. Janis and Wendy cried out, disoriented from the sudden downpour, but Troy continued to push onward. It was like being stuck in a dream; no matter how hard he tried to gain ground, it was impossible to move forward. Troy felt as if he were walking on a peanut butter sandwich as his feet sank into the over-saturated ground. Biting down, he leaned into the rain and pulled the girls along.

He saw it. Running along the right side of the house. It was one of those things, not exactly what he had seen in the graveyard but close enough. This one was bigger and didn't appear as quick, but it was difficult to tell with the rain in his eyes. The creature screeched like a wild cat caught in a trap as it skirted the fence on the side of his property. Then it spotted them and took off with a determination and speed that Troy remembered all too well.

"Run!" Troy yelled with his heart exploding in his chest. He watched the beast's accelerated approach and knew they would never reach the back door in time.

Chapter 69

The ladder truck navigated its way through the Village with its lights flashing and sirens wailing. The residents who were still alive to hear the commotion looked out to see the big red spectacle with its newly mounted equipment fixed to the roof and the ladder itself. Gabriel Ford, who sat behind the wheel, grabbed the microphone and delivered the message. His booming voice exploded through the dozen external speakers attached to the truck.

"Citizens of Garrett Grove, this is an emergency. I repeat, this is an emergency. Report to the air raid shelter at the high school immediately. This is not a drill. Bring only what you can carry on your person and any medication you require. All citizens, report to the high school immediately." Gabriel continued to repeat the message as he maneuvered the vehicle at a snail's pace through the community.

The town's siren had been howling for a good fifteen minutes, and now it was up to the fire department to deliver the message and get people moving. But as Gabriel was leaving the Village and turning onto Winding Way, the skies erupted, complicating matters. The rain came down in a torrent of heavy droplets, making it almost impossible to see out the windshield, even with the wipers set on high. He white-knuckled the steering wheel with one hand as he gripped the microphone with the other.

"I repeat, this is an emergency. If you have children at the elementary or junior high school, you do *not* need to pick them up. They are already being transported to the high school. All citizens of Garrett Grove, this is not a drill."

Lynn Donovan poked her head out the front door as the fire truck rolled past and delivered its message. *Dear God, what's going on?* She looked down at the frightened beagle hiding behind a stack of boxes. "That doesn't sound very good at all, Peanuts. I think we better do what they say. If Janis is already there, she'll be looking for us."

Lynn ran to the kitchen to grab her car keys and the leash; she fixed it to Peanut's collar and urged the pooch along. "Come on, sweetie. Let's go." But the dog wasn't having it and parked itself in the hallway. Lynn pulled and begged the beagle to move. Finally, she got so frustrated, she scooped the dog in her arms and carried it outside into the rain. They were both soaked by the time they reached the car. Lynn plopped Peanuts into the passenger seat, pulled out of the drive, and made her way to the high school.

● ● ●

Deputy David Rainey arrived at the school moments before the rain started. He ushered Principal Grace into her office, closed the door behind them, and delivered the sheriff's message. The look of dumbfounded bewilderment on her face suggested she had either not heard him the first time or found the news impossible to digest.

"What—?" she asked. "Taking the children—I don't understand."

Rainey raised his voice and spoke in a deliberate, authoritative tone. "Miss Austin, in fifteen minutes, you and your entire staff, along with every child in the building, are going to line up and walk out the front door. You'll be transported to the high school, where you will remain in the shelter until the threat has passed. I don't have time to explain this a third time, so I need you to work with me and help get the children to safety."

Grace's hands began to tremble; the deputy's message appeared to register and hit home. However, she remained seated like a deer frozen in the headlights.

"We need to move—now, Miss Austin!"

Which got her on her feet and moving. She followed the deputy into the hallway and looked out the main entrance. Three school buses sat at the front curb idling, and a second police cruiser had pulled up behind them. Two people exited the vehicle and ran toward the building.

"We need to do this now!" Rainey urged as she led him into the third-grade class. They delivered their announcement to the stunned children and an even more surprised Miss Davis, and then made their way to the next room. They entered the fourth-grade class, but before Principal Grace could speak, she was ambushed by a frantic Miss Boriello. The woman was on the verge of tears.

"I can't find them anywhere. They must have snuck off during the fire drill."

"Wait a second," Grace said, trying to calm her. "Who are you talking about? Who can't you find?"

"Troy Fischer, Wendy Sirocka, and Janis Thompson. I looked everywhere."

Principal Grace suppressed a squeal and bit her lip. It was the same children who had made a scene on the playground, the ones who had warned the other students that something was wrong. "Jesus Christ," she said. "The little shits were right."

The door behind them was thrown open as Sheriff Primrose and Lois Fischer burst into the room. Lois scanned the class and started shouting. "Where is he? Where is Troy?" Her voice trembled as she spoke.

Principal Grace ushered Lois and Carl into the hallway. "Mrs. Fischer, someone pulled the fire alarm; we believe that Troy and the girls snuck out during the commotion."

"You don't know where my son is!?" Lois screamed. "Just what kind of a place are you running here?"

"We think he left with Wendy Sirocka and Janis Thompson. They couldn't be gone any more than a half hour at most."

Lois balled her fists and cursed under her breath. "He's been hanging out with girls for less than a week and he's already lost his damn mind!"

"We'll find them," Carl said, attempting to pacify the situation. "There's only a few places they could be." He took Lois by the arm and urged her down the hallway. "Get them moving, David," he called to Deputy Rainey as he hurried Lois out the front door and into the rain.

Minutes later, Principal Grace and the rest of the staff led a parade of children out the front doors of Garrett elementary and onto the buses sitting at the curb.

She counted heads as they took their seats, allowing the number of those who were missing to sink in. Nearly half were absent. She couldn't bear to imagine where they might be or what had kept them home ... if that's even where they were.

● ● ●

Burt entered through the emergency room doors of the medical center and did a double take. When he left the place earlier, it had looked like a ghost town, but now it held all the intention of a termite mound. Firemen and orderlies ran to the left and right carrying boxes of supplies, while nurses escorted patients followed by candy stripers holding IV bags. Doris wasn't behind the desk and was nowhere to be seen. Burt followed the conga line of activity all the way to the main entrance, only to find the area even more congested. Finally, he spotted Doris directing patients down a stairwell. Her eyes fixed on him, standing there with his jaw open, and she rushed to his side.

"You're a sight, old man." She kissed him.

"What the hell is going on here?" he asked as men passed them on either side.

Doris wiped her eyes and swallowed. "Where have you been, under a rock? The Gables Bridge and Sunset Pass were destroyed this morning. The sheriff doesn't think help is coming and has ordered everyone into the shelters both here and at the high school. There isn't much time, and I need your help—again." She leaned in and whispered in his ear: "Do this for me and I'll do something that will really curl your toes."

Burt was about to offer a witty reply when Ed Koloski burst through the lobby's double doors pushing a cart loaded to the hilt with heavy fire power and ammunition. Burt eyed the stockpile, and his hand once again searched his empty pocket for Carl's gun, which still wasn't there. "If you would excuse me a second, dear. This won't take but a minute." He intercepted Koloski and approached the array of weaponry with a grin on his face.

"See anything you like, Mr. Lively?" Koloski said.

"As a matter of fact, I do." Burt picked up a nickel-plated 9 mm Beretta from the cart and tested the feel of the weapon in his hand. The brown leather grip was comfortable, and it had a good balance to it. "I think this will do nicely, thank you."

"Excellent choice." He handed Burt a box of cartridges and then reached for a second. "Just in case you don't hit anything with the first fifty rounds."

Burt smiled. He liked the guy—a snarky bastard, much like himself.

"Um, excuse me, boys." Nurse TenHove joined the men at the cart.

"I don't suppose you have anything for my lady friend?" Burt asked.

Ed reacted as if he'd been insulted and then cracked another wide grin. "I have just the thing." He rifled through the selection and came up with a snub-nosed .25.

Doris soured her face and then pointed to a chrome .357 magnum with an eight-inch barrel that looked a lot like the gun Dirty Harry carried. "What about that one?"

"The customer is always right," Ed said and handed her the weapon. "And might I say, it matches your eyes perfectly." He handed her a box of ammunition, then pulled out a small duffle bag for her and Burt to stow their gear. "Thanks for shopping," he replied, then proceeded to push the cart to the entrance of the stairwell. His progress was halted when Deputy Lutchen stepped in front of him.

●●●

Andrea Geary peered into the rearview mirror of the bus, scanning the faces of the children as she pulled into the parking lot of the high school. It had been a short ten-minute drive, and thanks to Miss Davis, the kids remained well behaved for the most part, though it was obvious they were shaken up. The second and third bus pulled in directly behind them; the operation had gone off without a hitch. A cluster of concerned parents waited for their children near the back of the building, where Bob Jones and several of his men stood, directing everyone into the shelter. Andrea opened the door, and Bob stepped in out of the rain.

"Okay, everyone. We're going to have a little campout, so if your parents aren't here yet, don't worry, they will be soon. No pushing, nice and easy, right this way." He spoke loud enough to be heard over the sirens and with just enough authority.

None of the children made a peep as the large fireman instructed them, not even Jerry Santos, known heckler and class clown. The boy walked toward the front of the bus with his head lowered and exited in an orderly fashion.

"Jerry, Jerry!" His mother ran up and hugged her son hard enough to strangle him.

The boy and his mom were ushered through the back doors and shown into the shelter. Other parents were there to meet the buses as well and ran to their children as if they had been separated for years. However, there was a large number who hadn't arrived yet.

Andrea watched the children as they stepped off the bus and scanned the crowd. One little girl stood in the rain with her bottom lip quivering and the worst case of puppy dog eyes Andrea had ever seen. The child's mommy and daddy didn't run up to greet her, and Andrea had a feeling they weren't going to. It was all happening so fast.

She leapt from her seat behind the wheel and charged out of the bus into the rain. Andrea rushed to the little girl's side and knelt before her.

"Hi, sweetie. My name's Andrea. I am going to take care of you until your parents get here. Is that okay?"

The child looked up, unable to speak. Tears ran from the corners of her eyes and disappeared in the rain. She nodded her head and allowed Andrea to take her by the hand. Several other children who also hadn't found their parents saw what Andrea had done and flocked to her side like a raft of ducklings. Miss Davis joined the group with a waddling of her own, and together, the women led the children into the shelter.

● ● ●

Fireman Anthony Leone drove the second bus, accompanied by Principal Grace and most of the youngest students, who had been crying the entire trip. By the time he entered the lot, Anthony had had his fill of children. He thought that rather than spend the night locked in a basement with a hundred screaming kids, he just might be better off on his own. He saw first-hand the thing that had burned up in the Texaco fire, and it was scary as hell. But the idea of stepping into that shelter with all those kids sounded a whole lot scarier. He had a .38 tucked in his waistband and was thinking of a quiet place where he could ride this thing out alone.

The little ones exited the bus kicking and screaming, and there wasn't a thing Principal Grace or Bob Jones could do to pacify them. Some of their parents had shown up, but the majority had not. And it was going to be a real clusterfuck if they didn't get there soon. Anthony hoped the chief knew how to handle that but doubted if he did.

●●●

The last bus pulled up to the school with a mixture of third and fourth graders and Miss Boriello holding the reins. Brandon Canfield, who was only a few years out of high school himself, sat behind the wheel. He stopped at the back of the gym and opened the door to the elements. The rain hammered sideways in torrential sheets and forced its way into the bus.

"Okay, everyone. We're going to get a little wet, but if we move quickly, it won't be too bad," Miss Boriello announced, then began to lead the children off. She turned back to Brandon and offered a quick smile.

Cars continued to pull into the lot, directed by firemen dressed in bright yellow slickers. The skies grew darker by the second, and the storm strengthened. Bob Jones looked up as another flash of lightning lit up the sky. He shouted something to one of his men, but his words were stifled by the storm.

●●●

Ted scanned the rifle selection, picked up a bolt action 30-06, and examined the scope. He slung it over his shoulder and removed a Mossberg 12-gauge as well. Then, without saying a word, he grabbed one of the duffel bags and proceeded to fill it with several boxes of shotgun shells, three boxes of 30-06 cartridges, one hundred .40 cal. bullets, and a semi-automatic handgun. Dawn crept up next to him, taking her usual spot at his side. She tilted the oversized deputy hat back on her head to get a better look at what he was doing.

Ted grabbed a walkie-talkie off the cart and handed it to her. "Here, this is for you."

Dawn smiled and accepted the gift, then stepped back to be with her dog.

The front doors burst open, allowing the blare of sirens and horns to flood the lobby; Chris Fredericks entered pushing another cart of weapons.

"How are we looking with the patients, Nurse TenHove?" Ted shouted to be heard over the weather and alarms.

"There are only a few more that can be moved. The rest have to stay on the third floor."

"Okay then." Ted turned to the firemen. "Ed, you're with Nurse TenHove and myself on the third floor, and Chris, you're in the basement." The young firemen nodded in agreement, then Ted turned to Burt, who wrapped his arm around Doris's waist.

"Wherever she goes, I go," the coroner said, pulling Doris close.

That makes four. Ted knew he still had one small problem. He looked down at Dawn and exhaled. *What am I going to do with you?* He needed to get her tucked away safely in the basement but figured the only way she'd leave his side was kicking and screaming. He opened his mouth to speak, not sure what he would say, when a familiar face came into view.

Ted reached out and took Nurse Carole by the arm; the girl's eyes lit up when she saw him.

"Carole, I really need your help." Ted bent down to look Dawn in the eyes. "Honey, I want you to stay in the basement with Carole. She'll watch over you, and help you look for leprechaun gold. Okay?"

Dawn shook her head and bit her bottom lip. Her eyes grew wide and watered over, then she reached out and latched onto Ted, burying her head in the crook of his shoulder like a tick in the carpet. *This isn't going to work.* A dozen worst-case scenarios raced through his head at the thought of forcing Dawn to stay in the basement; none of them ended well.

"Okay, she's with us," he said, looking up at Nurse TenHove, who scowled for a moment, then let her own face soften.

"I'll come too," Carole said, straightening the hat on Dawn's head.

"Well, Deputy. That's about the last of them," Doris called over the dizzying commotion as several straggling patients were directed into the basement.

"All right, get these guns downstairs and distributed!" Ted yelled to Chris Fredericks, then he turned to Ed. "Koloski, find yourself a weapon and grab as much ammo as you can carry. We're headed to the third floor—now."

THE OJANOX

A bucket brigade of men formed on the staircase, making quick work of transporting the remainder of supplies and weapons into the basement. Koloski filled several bags, handing one to Carole and slinging another over his shoulder. Then ...

The sky exploded.

Lightning lit up the entire front of the building, causing the lights to flicker for a moment. Outside, the rain fell in monsoon proportions, and the sky was so dark it looked like night had already descended.

A sudden scream ripped through the air, loud enough to have come from inside the building. It overpowered the shrill of the sirens and echoed off the stark walls of the medical center. Ted stopped moving and looked at the members of his party. *Dear God, this is it.*

"Lock it up!" Ted shouted. He had hoped Sheriff Primrose would make it back before they needed to seal the doors, but there was no time. The sheriff was on his own. The patients that could be moved were in the basement, and a handful of residents had arrived seeking shelter. Not many, though; Ted prayed they had gone to the high school instead.

A pair of firemen ran to the front doors, wrapped a thick chain around the handles, and padlocked them shut. The other exits had been secured as well, and that was all they could do. The real protection relied on their firepower and the strength of the shelter door.

The third floor was a different story. It wasn't safe, and there was no way to fortify it. Ted figured it was up to luck and God—hopefully, one of them was on their side. He urged his group into the stairway, with Nurse TenHove and Burt in the lead, and Dawn, Carole, and Baxter following behind. Ted hurried them along with Koloski bringing up the rear, leaving the rest of the firemen finishing their transport in the lobby.

"Don't take too long with that!" he called back and made his way up the stairs. Ted's heart pounded like a greyhound with a case of pre-race jitters. Blood and adrenaline rushed to his head, making him feel almost intoxicated. He tried to steady his breathing as he took the stairs two at a time, but it was no use.

A second shriek ripped through the building, followed by the deafening roar of destruction. There was a violent crash, the electric shatter of breaking glass, and, a half second later, the sound of the building being ripped apart from the ground up.

"Faster!" Ted screamed and forced his party up the stairs. They reached the landing and rounded the turn when the door to the second floor burst open. A blur of movement flew out at them. It was on Burt and Doris in flash. Ted didn't have time to raise his gun and could only watch the ambush unfold in front of him.

●●●

Firemen Glenn Gillick and Mike Turino had volunteered to drive the police cruisers and were each given a specific neighborhood to canvass. The vehicles were outfitted with external bullhorns that Deputy Rainey and Andrea had removed from the storage locker. The men set out just before the rain started, delivering the same message as those in the trucks. Glenn steered the cruiser with one hand and operated the microphone with the other.

"Attention citizens of Garrett Grove, this is not a drill. Report to the shelter at the high school immediately, bring whatever medications you require. The children from the elementary and junior high schools are already en route. You are ordered by the sheriff's department to report to the high school immediately."

Glenn couldn't tell if the message was making a difference. There were few cars on the road and even fewer people had opened their front doors to see what was going on. As far as he could tell, Operation Round Up was a wash out. Still, he had a job to do and would continue until told otherwise. He headed toward the north end of town, making a left turn on Foothills Drive. It was near impossible to see through the windshield, even with the wipers set to high, and Glenn didn't notice the man until the last second. He slammed on the brakes as the figure darted in front of the vehicle. The back tires locked up, and the cruiser skidded, then fishtailed to the left.

The cruiser came to an abrupt halt, throwing Glenn hard against the steering wheel. He looked out the window, then checked the rearview, ready to give the prick a piece of his mind. But the road was empty, the guy had disappeared. "What the f—" he hissed into the cab, scanning the street again for the lunatic who had jumped in front of him. Still, there was no one. Glen shook his head and took his foot off the brake. "Fucking jerkoff."

THE OJANOX

It smashed into the driver's side with the power of a train. Glenn's head snapped hard to the right as the tires lifted from the impact. *Jesus Christ!* He checked his mirrors again, expecting to find the car that had hit him, but there was nothing. The heavy rain beat down on the deserted road.

The dark blur moved across the front of the cruiser and came at him in a flash. Glenn hit the accelerator; his foot pressed firmly to the floor as the tires screamed for traction. But he reacted a full second too late. It slammed into the car a second time and lifted the driver's side into the air. Before he could react, Glenn found himself upside down, and he hadn't been wearing his seatbelt. His head smacked against the roof of the cab, and his vision clouded. The world before him warped into a liquid wave of shadows. The windshield cracked into a million tiny spiderwebs, and the driver's side glass imploded.

There was a flurry of movement outside, both in front of and behind him. Then the howling started, carnal and urgent like a pack of wolverines had surrounded the vehicle. Glenn struggled to move, but his concussed brain wouldn't have it. They were on him in a frenzy, clawing their way into the car, grabbing his arms and legs, dragging him out into the street.

The rain fell hard into his eyes, making it impossible to see his attackers. But he felt them, a thousand individual teeth sinking into his flesh. It invaded him like a disease, filling his sinuses and ceasing his breath. Glenn was probed like a lab rat as it took everything he had been and consumed what it needed. And just like that, the pain was gone.

Darkness came early to the small town of Garrett Grove. The storm descended from the heavens, and the brood was awakened. It spoke to them in an urgent voice and commanded them to feed. Many of its children had already turned; others were well on their way. There was work to be done. A battle to be waged. An entire world waiting to be devoured.

Chapter 70

Troy diverted to the left, dragging the girls behind him. He yanked their arms so hard he was sure he would pull one from the socket. Still, he forced his legs to move like never before and led them through the backyard to the side door of the garage—the very door he and his cousins used to ambush his friends the night of the party, just a few days ago. *Is it still open?* He remembered his mom had asked him to lock it, but so much had happened since then.

The sirens continued to scream, and the deluge was unending, but above the roar was the sound of the beast that pursued them. Troy could hear it closing in as they approached the garage door. They were almost there. With just a few more steps to go, Troy felt his arm jerk and was suddenly pulled backward by the unseen force. He turned in time to see Janis's feet slip out from under her. She skated across the lawn for a moment, frozen in position, then came down hard on her backside. She splashed onto the wet grass and almost took him with her. Troy rushed to her side. Then he saw it—headed fast in their direction—almost on top of them. His throat tightened until it was almost impossible to breathe; panic rose in his chest and forced the blood to his face. He struggled to lift Janis from the ground, but his palms were slick from rain, and her hand slipped in his grasp.

It ran towards them in an almost apish way, on all fours, in bounding strides that were difficult to follow. Horns or possibly tusks protruded from the sides of the creature's face and the top of its head. It appeared hairless, but it was impossible to tell in the rain and from the speed at which it moved. The clearest feature was the beast's mouth, a massive opening filled with hundreds of those horrible pointed teeth. Troy knew it was over; there wasn't enough time to help Janis to her feet and make it to the garage. *No!* A scream entered his throat and silenced the noise. He sprang to action, and the world warped into slow-motion, as if it were playing out frame by frame.

He grabbed both her hands, planted his feet, and pulled the girl with all his strength. Janis shot into the air like a Jack-in-the-box, nearly knocking him down in the process. As he took her in his arms, he looked over her shoulder; the beast was now less than ten feet away. It lowered its head and bore down on them, preparing to make its final attack. There wasn't time to turn. Troy knew there was no chance they would make it to the garage.

Then there was movement, fast and reactive, just from the corner of his sight. The creature erupted with an oppressive scream. Then it fell to the ground, twisting and writhing like an uncoiled spring, clawing at its body as if it were on fire. Troy heard the snap of the elastic bands as Wendy released her second projectile. The magnet penetrated the ape-thing's side, causing the beast to shriek even louder. What looked like smoke began to pour from its open wounds. A steady stream of black lifted into the air and was absorbed by the rain. At least it looked like that to Troy, who was transfixed by the spectacle. The creature flopped around like a fish out of water and then stopped moving.

It worked. It actually worked! Troy turned to Wendy, who held her wrist rocket in the ready position. Her chest heaved in and out, and a wicked grin spread out like a rash across her face. But the moment of celebration was squashed when two more creatures blasted from the side of the house.

The children spun on their heels and slammed against the garage door. *Please be open, please be open,* Troy prayed as he fumbled with the knob. It slipped within his grip, and his heart stopped; his vision reduced to a series of pulsing lights. He grasped it again and twisted. The door opened, and they poured into the darkness of the garage. Slamming it hard behind them, Troy engaged the lock and pulled the girls away.

The entire building shook as the creatures slammed against the outside wall. The three children stood in the graveyard room, dripping and breathless, with a coffin set on the floor to their right and several headstones propped up behind them. Troy looked for something strong to wedge against the door, but everything had been made of cardboard. There wasn't anything sturdy that would stop the beasts for long.

"Follow me!" he shouted to the girls, who both looked close to tears. He led them through a doorway, then grabbed the piece of drywall Billy had used Saturday night. He leaned it against the wall behind them, knowing it wouldn't do much. Still, it was better than nothing, and he thought it might buy them a few extra seconds.

The garage shook again as the creatures threw themselves against the exterior like battering rams.

Troy ducked and urged the girls through a small trapdoor concealed at the base of the wall to their left. He led them into the inner workings of the haunted house, where all the secrets were kept, a place that only he knew everything about. Even Rob hadn't been around to see all the finishing touches he had made to the hidden passage. He navigated the girls down the tight corridor, past the board used to move the tangle of rat hoses and the pulleys that controlled the dayglow spiders. He moved them through the darkness until they couldn't proceed any further. They had come to the end of the passage—the dead end. Now they were trapped.

The pounding of the rain against the roof sounded like marbles being dropped from the sky. It rattled their nerves to the point of hysterics and jarred their senses. In a deafening roar, the side door crashed inward, and hell followed. A scream like a cross between a leopard and an eagle cut through the garage like a bandsaw. Troy pulled Wendy and Janis close; trying to be as quiet as possible, he spoke to them. It was so loud inside the small area he was unsure if they had heard a word he said. A second beast howled like a wolf caught in a bear trap. Troy fumbled in his pockets as the monsters ripped the graveyard room apart at the seams. There was no way to know if the creatures would follow the laid-out maze of the haunted house or just tear the place to shreds to get to them. He ran his foot along the floor, searching in the dark until it brushed against what he was looking for. There were too many things that could go wrong, especially if the girls hadn't heard him.

Something shrieked as it entered the rat room and fought with the hoses spread out across the floor. They were getting closer—much closer. Saturday night,

Wendy had taken his hand and kissed him, just on the other side of the wall where they now hid. It felt like so long ago. Now they were crammed in the tight passage, fighting for their lives. *I hope this works,* Troy pleaded as Wendy's hand brushed against his.

Chapter 71

Principal Melvin Garish was more than a little distracted when Chief Jones visited him earlier. His preoccupation with his secretary, Julie Evans, was acute. For some reason, today of all days, the girl had decided to stay home from work. Melvin had listened as the chief relayed his instructions concerning early dismissal, but with thoughts of Julie eclipsing much of the message. Fortunately, Mrs. Tailor had also listened and carried out the chief's instructions to the letter. The announcement was delivered over the school's PA system for the faculty and students to hear. Everyone was to report back to the shelter no later than five o'clock. Melvin even stayed and listened to the announcement himself, then he exited the school and drove to Julie's house to see if her husband's car was in the driveway.

For the past month and a half, Mel had been giving Julie a little extracurricular physical education on their lunch breaks while Mr. Evans was at work. Sometimes, she would let him have her in the parking lot of the school in Mel's Chevy van. The fact that Julie was married thrilled Mel to no end. She'd been his secretary for years and had approached him about a raise. Mel informed her it would be a lot easier to fit it into the budget if she allowed him to fit it into her first. Julie had taken the proposal in stride and then took him up on the offer. And it had been amazing. Julie told him she and her husband, Luke, had been having problems for a long time and he hadn't touched her in over six months. Also, Mr. Evans had never been a fan of oral—giving or receiving. "What guy doesn't love a blowjob?" she had said. Apparently, the guy she had married. Fortunately for Mel, not only was he a fan of receiving, but he was a giver as well. Which Julie seemed to appreciate—at least for a while.

Then one day out of the blue, she told him it was over, which only made Mel want her more. He enjoyed the cat and mouse games she played and knew if he pressed hard enough, she would acquiesce to his advances. It was like a drug for Mel, and Julie was his fix. She was all he could think about. But it had started to affect his performance at work and even interfered with his sleep.

Mel noticed Julie had become more aloof than usual, fending off his plays with greater success than she had in the past. When she didn't show up for work today, he had been frantic. It was Wednesday, after all, and they always snuck off to her house on Wednesday for a little hanky-panky. He had been so desperate to see her at one point he even attempted to call her at home. However, the phones were still out.

Mel pulled his van to the curb across the street from the Evans' residence. He noticed Julie's car in the driveway and was pleased to see the absence of her husband's. "You little minx," he whispered, convincing himself this was all part of the game she'd been playing and she was probably expecting him. He imagined her waiting in the living room, naked on all fours. Mel felt the excitement growing just thinking about his secretary like that and shifted in the driver's seat to adjust his tightening pants.

There was only one light on in the house and, from what he could tell, no movement at any of the windows. Figuring it was time to make his move, he opened the door and stepped into the rain. The heavy wind snatched the umbrella from his grip and sent it careening down the street. He raised his collar as a brilliant blue flash of light sizzled across the sky, but was drenched before he made it two steps.

Mel sloshed up the walkway to Julie's front door with the constant blare of the fire whistle droning like a broken record. He looked around one last time, convinced himself he was doing the right thing, and climbed the steps of the porch. He reached for the doorbell and held his breath, then pressed his finger against it. The chime was barely audible over the whistle, so Mel pressed the button three more times. He waited, craning his neck to look through the small

THE OJANOX

window. Then, a wash of movement, just out of the corner of his eye, darted across the yard and disappeared behind the house.

Mel bolted around, alerted by the motion, but saw nothing. *Probably a branch or garbage can tossed in the wind.* He turned back to ring the bell once more, and it happened. The figure smashed into him with the force of a head-on collision and knocked him into the screen door, shattering the storm windows and the frame as well.

Mel felt the wind rush out of his lungs as he fell onto his back. He looked up and was blinded by a deluge of overflowing water cascading down from the gutters. *What's happening?* He struggled to focus, squinted against the downpour, and was met by the creature's stare. *Fuuuck!* Something inside Mel's head fried like an overloaded fuse. The vision before him was impossible to comprehend.

The creature positioned itself on the center of his chest and sized him up through eight individual orbital sockets. Four eyes situated on either side of its skull stared down at him. Coarse black hairs as thick as fettuccini protruded from a face with a bulbous forehead and a beak-like nose. Antennae jutted from the top of the creature's head, probing and searching the air in front of Mel's face.

He struggled to push the beast off him, his hands grabbing at the coarse hairs covering its body. Mel screamed as all six of the monster's legs dug into him with their pointed mandibles. They punctured his flesh and pinned him to the wooden porch like a calendar tacked to a wall.

Then the creature erupted, vomiting a thick green sludge that covered his face. It flowed into his mouth and his eyes, a concoction as foul as death. Mel gagged as the vile snot landed on his tongue. It tingled and twinged, and then it started to burn. A noxious odor filled his sinuses; he howled as the feel of a hundred soldering irons pressed against his flesh. The smell of fat, hair, and vomit rendered in a deep fryer was all-consuming as the substance went to work on him like an acid. A prehistoric acidic compound, to be precise. One that had gone extinct over two million years ago.

Mel's face putrefied, congealing into something that looked an awful lot like cherry Jello. He tried to scream but was unable, his voice box melted along with his flesh. Instead, he gurgled and struggled to look up at the nightmarish creature. An agonizing second later, his eyes popped like tiny water balloons. Then the monstrosity spread its jaws and slurped up Melvin Garish's face like a spoonful of Campbell's cream of mushroom soup.

The ladder truck crawled through the neighborhood where only days before, a small girl hid beneath her bed as her brother attacked their parents. Brian Miller had called the police about the constant howling of his neighbor's dog, claiming to be concerned that something may have happened. In truth, Brian had been trying to sleep and the damn dog wouldn't shut the fuck up. He had just gotten home from a back-breaking night shift at Faber Chemical, taken a hot shower, and climbed into bed when the hound started going at it.

He had never been all that chummy with the Negal family, thought their son, Tommy, was a snot-nosed brat, and imagined, in a couple years, the little girl would be blasting her boom box and roller skating in front of his house with her friends. No doubt when Brian was trying to sleep. It hadn't occurred to him that something had really happened to the family; he simply thought they had left the dog unattended. He expected as much from Tommy; the kid didn't have his head screwed on tight.

He watched the truck pass with its lights flashing and siren blaring. The town's whistle was already loud enough to wake the dead, and now someone was screaming over a loudspeaker.

"Attention, this is not a drill. Report to the shelter at the high school immediately. This is an emergency. Bring only what you can carry and any medication you require. Children from the elementary and junior high schools are already en route. All citizens are ordered by the sheriff's department to report to the shelter at the high school. This is not a drill."

"Shut the fuck up!" Brian screamed as the truck made its way down the street. "The only emergency will be my foot in your ass if you don't quit that damn racket."

He slammed the door, attempting to shut the noise outside, but it was impossible. He walked to the kitchen, popped two Anacin into his mouth, and swallowed them dry. There was no use in fooling himself, he wouldn't be getting any sleep today. Brian rubbed his temples with the sound of a thousand clowns on a carousel bouncing against the inside of his skull like a ball bearing.

THE OJANOX

● ● ●

The thing that entered the world as Tommy Negal returned to the street where it once lived as if in answer to a call from its previous life. But the reality of it was far different. The boy had changed so much that his own mother wouldn't have recognized him—if she were still alive. Tommy had shed almost half of his body mass and morphed into something quite reptilian. The sides of the creature's neck flared into a pair of transparent leathery membranes. His lower jaw protruded, while the top appeared to have sunken in, swallowing his nose completely. The clothes he wore had fallen away, ripped to shreds from the dagger-like spines that grew from his back and torso. Webbed fingers that tapered into talons clung to the tree outside, and a pair of prehistoric eyes spotted the man in the house. With the speed of a rattler, a long black tongue shot from the creature's mouth, snatched a squirrel from its nest, and sucked it in. It crunched down on the tasty appetizer, then set its hunger on something a bit more satisfying.

● ● ●

Brian was reaching for a bottle of gin from the cabinet above the sink when the back door imploded, sending shards of glass and splinters flying inward. He spun around with the bottle in hand, prepared to fight off the intruder, but didn't have time to think as the projectile shot at him and seized his fist.

He stared as the massive tongue latched on to his hand, then his bladder let loose. The thing was no more than three feet tall and looked like it had crawled out of the Stone Age. It was mostly green with toxic red splotches and had several lethal rows of quills protruding from its body. The teeth that lined the rim of the beast's mouth looked like broken glass.

The abomination tilted its head back and allowed its great tongue to retract, taking Brian's arm with it. He was pulled only slightly off balance as the appendage was ripped from his shoulder socket. A fountain of arterial blood spouted from the ragged wound and pooled onto the floor, evacuating Brian's body fast and freely. It didn't hurt half as much as Brian imagined having his arm ripped off would. He swayed on his feet and began to lose consciousness.

The monster descended on him; its talons chewed into the porcelain tile floor as it raced toward him. There wasn't time to scream. As he fell to the floor, the massive tongue shot out again and seized him by the throat. Thankfully, it happened just as fast as the arm. The creature retracted its powerful tongue and snapped Brian's head off at the shoulders. The last vision he registered as he landed in the beast's mouth was several rows of razor-sharp teeth closing down on him. The sirens had finally ceased, and the world was quiet again, at least it was for Brian.

Lynn Donovan turned right onto Village Road with her heart racing to the drone of the sirens and adrenaline coursing through her veins like a hallucinogen. She fought the urgency to disregard the speed limit as the vehicle's windshield wipers carried out their own struggle against the never-ending rain. Both were losing the battle. Peanuts, who lay in the passenger's seat, whined and looked up at her, distraught as only a beagle in a thunderstorm could be.

"It's okay, girl. We'll be there in a minute."

Lynn approached the green light at the intersection of Jackson and brought the car to a slow crawl. A cross between instinct and zero visibility cautioned her to check both ways before inching forward onto the main drag. The blare of a horn, louder than the sirens and almost on top of them, caused her to slam on the brakes. Peanuts tumbled off the seat and onto the floor with a yelp as a station wagon sliced through the red light, missing them by less than a foot. Lynn watched the derelict vehicle scream down the road and was prepared to pull out a second time when four large animals tore through the intersection in pursuit. It was difficult to focus on them due to the heavy rain and the speed at which they moved, but Lynn thought they resembled oversized dogs. One of them jumped through the intersection dragging its arms like a gorilla.

Lynn turned in the opposite direction with a bit less respect for the speed limit, her tires spinning out on the wet surface until they finally gripped the pavement. The car fishtailed as Lynn banked onto Elm Street; she noticed the smoke right away. A house had caught fire and been consumed by the blaze. Flames erupted from every window on the first and second floors, and the roof had started to collapse. Then she saw it—stoic like a pillar on the front lawn, staring at the inferno. It had to be over seven feet tall and looked like it had been dredged out of a swamp. Although Lynn sailed past it doing fifty, she was certain she had seen gills lining the sides of the beast's neck. And she was positive she had seen scales covering its body like plates of armor. Lynn had a feeling her bladder had let go but was too terrified to check.

She blasted through the next intersection and stole a glimpse in the rearview. The enormous beast had followed her and was approaching fast. *What the fuck?* Hoping to coax just a bit more out of the screaming engine, Lynn pressed her foot to the floor. With the high school just two blocks away, she gripped the wheel with both hands and prayed. But it was almost on top of her, and she knew there was no way she would make it.

She steered to the right, and her back tires lost traction. They caught a second later as the vehicle turned onto Mandeville and approached the school. She checked the mirror again to find her pursuer just a few strides behind. Now she could see the long tentacles the thing used to propel itself and the suction cups that lined its appendages. Madness threatened to invade, but Lynn fought to maintain her wits. The front of the high school loomed into view ... Lynn's heart sank. Bright yellow creatures swarmed the lot and occupied the area. They were slimy and smooth and looked like they had been dragged from the depths themselves. There was nowhere to go.

She was about to drive past the parking lot when one of the yellow creatures began flapping its arms to get her attention. Lynn stared at the strange sight and was filled with a wash of recognition. It wasn't a creature, but it had been difficult to tell in the storm. Men in bright yellow raincoats waved her down and directed her passage. She sailed past the first man and was nearly thrown from her seat when the explosion rocked the car. It had been loud enough to pop her ears and to start Peanuts barking.

● ● ●

Firemen John Sampson and Eric Collins were stationed at the front entrance when the Pinto approached with the monstrosity nearly on top of it. Neither man could believe what they were seeing even though they'd been told to expect the unexpected. John waved the car in, then unslung the 12-gauge from his shoulder.

It came at him fast and looked like it had fallen out of some unlucky fisherman's net. He followed it in his sights and fired the first shot. The creature shrieked but didn't slow, not even a little, as pink ooze sloshed from a grapefruit-size wound in its side.

"Fuck, it has to be a head shot," John cursed under his breath. He exhaled and fired, this time taking out a chunk of the squid-beast's shoulder. A huge chunk of blubber fell, and more of the pink goo spurted out onto the wet pavement.

The monster entered the parking lot and came at him; John slammed another shell into the chamber and fired, this time missing his mark completely. He took a frantic step backward and pulled the pump. A thunderous concussion detonated from inches away. The beast's head exploded as the 30-06 slug from Eric Collin's Remington connected dead center. The repulsive heap fell to the pavement before the men's feet; it even smelled like it had been pulled out of the sea.

Lynn Donovan slammed on the brakes, bringing her Pinto to a halt at the back entrance of the gym. Bob Jones and Brandon Canfield rushed to her aid and helped her and the pup from the vehicle. "M—mmm—hel." She tried to speak but was incapable.

"Jesus Christ," Bob Jones said, arriving at the car from the side of the building. It hadn't been the first abomination the men had encountered, and far too many of the town's citizens had not been as lucky as Lynn Donovan. "Men, we can't stay out here much longer. We're going to have to chain the doors soon."

Eric Collins stepped back from the body of the creature. "What about Sheriff Primrose? He's still out there."

"I'm well aware of that," Bob said, lifting his radio from his hip. "Jones to Primrose. Dammit, Carl. Come in!"

THE OJANOX

●●●

Teresa Sirocka had been dealt a raw deal and was pissed about it. Her ex had left her for a younger chippy who was already pumping out little rug rats of their own. The deadbeat barely saw Wendy as it was, and now he had a one-year-old and another on the way. Since the divorce, Teresa hadn't had time to breathe, let alone go on dates herself. Not that she was interested. Being a single mom was demanding; she worked most days, and keeping up with Wendy was a full-time job—the girl was too damn smart. But her daughter was a good kid, far ahead of the curve, and unfortunately for Teresa, Wendy had already noticed boys.

Teresa had tried to fill her daughter's head with notions and cautionary warnings about the male members of the species—they were not to be trusted. And it appeared to sink in for a while. Then Wendy attended a Halloween party last Saturday, and when Teresa arrived to pick her up, she saw her daughter kissing a boy on the front steps … All was lost. That was how it started. First, it's sneaking kisses at a boy's Halloween party, next she'd be having sex in his basement after school. It was just a matter of time before Wendy found herself married to a cute boy who was sticking it to some chippy half his age. She'd end up a single mother with no time for herself, standing in front of the television ironing a mountain of laundry.

Days of our Lives provided the much-needed background noise while Teresa worked the iron and thought about her daughter. She knew she'd been projecting her own issues onto her, but she had every right to be concerned; Wendy was her only child, after all.

Teresa was startled by the sudden eruption of sirens and horns in the distance. The town's fire whistle blew and refused to cease, growing in both timbre and duration. Then the distorted blare of voices echoed a message from not far away. She stopped what she was doing and ran to the stairs to listen closer. The man mentioned something about reporting to the shelter and then said something about the elementary school. Teresa panicked. Wendy was there and would be frantic and lost without her. She grabbed her keys and ran to her car without listening to the rest of the message or even turning off the iron. A second later, Teresa was tearing through the Village, driving too fast to be safe, and missed her turn on Jackson Ave. She quickly hung a U-turn and headed to the elementary school to pick up Wendy.

When she left the house, the skies were only dark, but before she had driven a mile, they were pouring down rain. Teresa turned the wipers on high, but even that wasn't enough to slap away the deluge. She took a right at Bell's Hardware and brought the station wagon to a full stop. Something was going on in front of the building. It almost looked like a pack of monkeys were attempting to break into the store, jumping and clawing at the windows and front door. Then Teresa noticed they weren't exactly monkeys, at least none she had ever seen in *National Geographic*. They were far too large, and something about their movements was all wrong. She watched, breathless and frozen, as one of the creatures turned to her and screamed. The shrill voice pierced her ears, sending a rash of gooseflesh down her arms and the length of her spine. The mouth on the creature was massive, far too big to belong to anything of this world, and housed a forest of jagged teeth.

Teresa threw the car in reverse and punched it, bouncing over the curb as she misjudged the turn. Several of the creatures took notice and abandoned their attack on the hardware store, suddenly moving her way. They bounded after her, hopping like apes with murderous intent as she fled.

Teresa pressed the pedal to the floor as she approached the light on Jackson Ave. She scanned the rearview to see her pursuers were nearly upon her. Knowing they would overtake her if she stopped or even slowed, she laid on the horn and blasted through the red light without looking, almost smashing into a Pinto at the intersection. Fortunately, the other driver stopped in time as Teresa sailed past with the strange primates in pursuit.

Unable to process what was happening and preoccupied by the sight of the beasts in the mirror, Teresa struggled to maintain control of the vehicle and outrun the monsters. She came upon the turn for the elementary school but continued straight for fear of leading the creatures to her daughter. Not knowing that Wendy and the other children had already left, Teresa did what she thought was best. She beelined down the Turnpike toward the east end of town. It wasn't that far of a stretch, and at the speed she was moving, it didn't take long for her to reach the end of the line.

She crashed through the old wooden fence at the entrance of the King Lake Recreational Center just as the first beast caught up to the vehicle and seized the

THE OJANOX

bumper. It pulled itself onto the back and leered at Teresa through the large back window of the station wagon. It was primitive and evil and looked more like a gargoyle than any monkey. It was joined by another that looked similar but not identical, except for the mouth and all those horrible teeth.

Teresa pressed her foot to the floor, and the car chewed up the short distance across the dirt parking lot of the rec center. King Lake loomed before her in all its enormity. Formed by glaciers several million years ago, it was nearly as deep as it was wide, and far too big to see the opposite shoreline. The rain diminished her visibility, making it impossible to judge how far she was from the bank. She steered the car toward the massive body of water. The vehicle shook with a lurch as a third beast landed on the roof.

With the steering wheel gripped tightly in her hand, Teresa prayed that she hadn't messed her daughter up too much. She knew she had filled Wendy's head with burdens no child should have to carry. She had dumped all her baggage into her daughter's knapsack and sent her off to school with a head full of nonsense. In truth, Teresa had done the best she could with the cards she was dealt.

"I'm sorry, Wendy. I love you," she said as the wagon hit the elevated bank of King Lake and was propelled twenty feet over the water. It came down hard, like it had hit a concrete wall, scattering the beasts on impact. Teresa's head smacked against the roof of the car, knocking her unconscious. She was spared the intrusion from a creature that never should have found its way to Earth to begin with.

The frigid water filled the car and sucked it to the bottom of the lake. Teresa Sirocka was one of the lucky ones who died that day in Garrett Grove. Burt Lively had been incorrect—sometimes there *was* dignity in death.

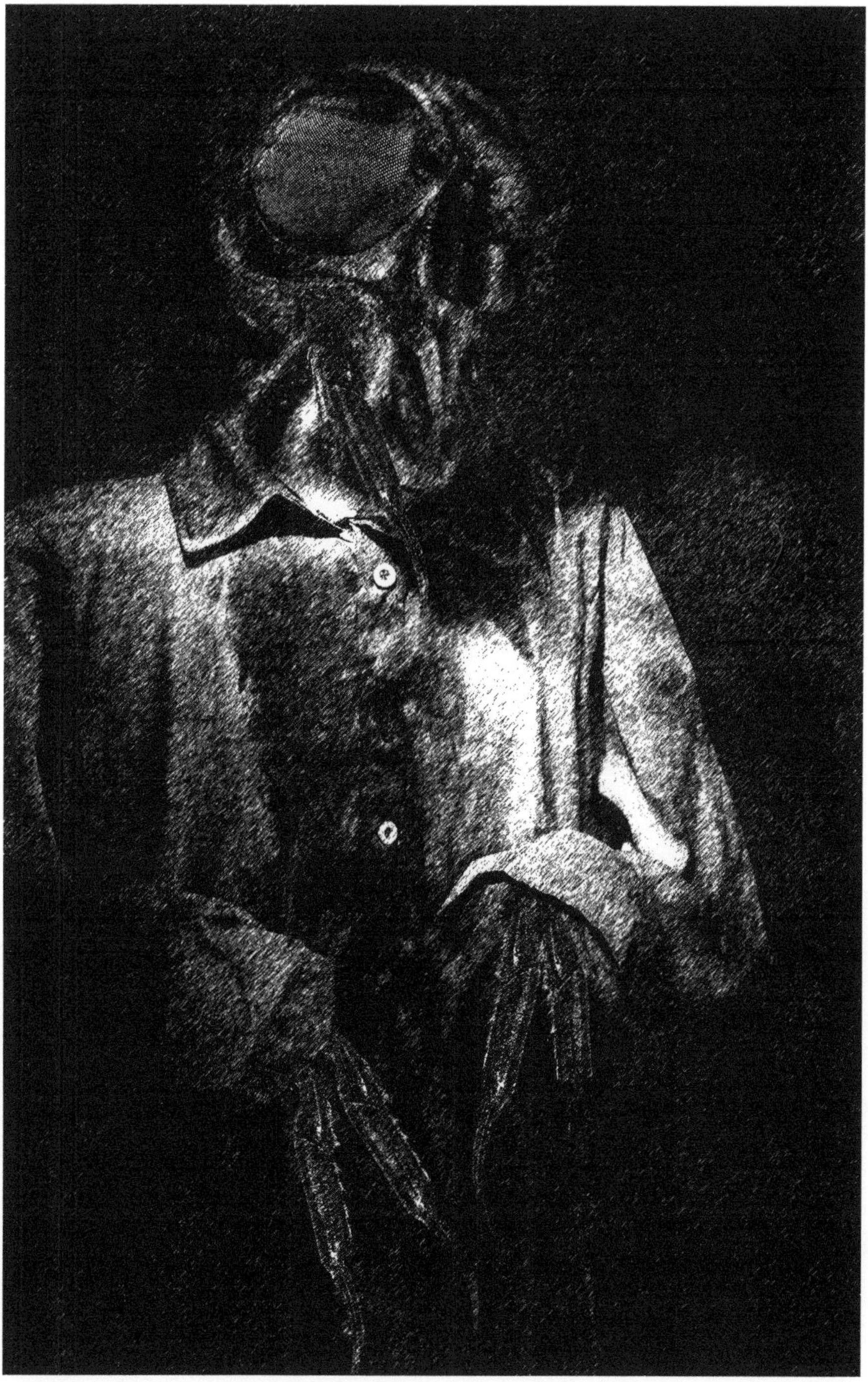

Chapter 72

The medical supplies were divided into two large stockpiles, one for the high school and another for the shelter in the medical center's basement. A third smaller allocation was stashed away at the nurses' station on the third floor, where the immobile patients remained. Dr. James Freedman and Michelle Marks loaded their share of the medication and equipment into the ambulance and sped off to join the group at the school. Michelle turned on the lights and sirens and pulled out of the parking lot. It was only a half a mile to the school, but the rain was relentless; she kept it well below the speed limit. Dr. Freedman sat in the passenger's seat, bouncing his legs up and down like he needed to use the bathroom.

"I don't see why they had to send us," he whined. "They could have sent Dr. Halasz."

"Maybe they needed someone qualified enough to deal with whatever might happen." Michelle believed the best way to deal with doctors like Freedman was to pander to their egos—even though she knew it had been a random decision on Nurse TenHove's part and qualifications had nothing to do with it.

"Yes, that's probably it," he said, then took to tapping the dashboard with his hand.

Michelle looked over at him and gritted her teeth, anxious to get to the high school before Freedman drove her batshit crazy; she pushed the gas a bit harder.

Michelle worked the day shift with Joe Santos. They were a good team; Joe knew his stuff. They had reported to the scene of the accident on Route 3 yesterday morning to find that none of the occupants of the vehicles had been wearing their seatbelts. Although the drivers and passengers of both cars had survived their initial injuries, it had been obvious to Michelle that not all of them would make it and came as no surprise when one of the high school girls and the old woman passed away late last night. It was sad, but it was part of the job and something you needed to know how to deal with or you had no business working in the field. Michelle found that almost impossible at first; she had lacked the much-needed ability to detach. She started out wide-eyed, compassionate, and looking to save the world. Joe recognized his coworker's naivety and had a heart-to-heart with her that first week.

"I get it, you became a paramedic because you want to help people. You're looking to save them all. But here's the thing." He pulled the ambulance over and looked her in the eyes. "You can try, but you never will. And if you can't accept that, you are in the wrong line of work."

Michelle smiled and thanked him but thought Joe was just another jaded prick. She believed she could handle anything and she would be the exception to the rule. She *was* going to save them—all of them. Joe was detached; he no longer cared. *How can you save anyone if you don't care?*

In the spring of '77, Michelle received her wake-up call. The King Dam had overflowed after heavy rains and an early thaw, flooding the south end of town and the low-lying communities along Route 202. She and Joe were dispatched to help the fire department rescue citizens stranded by the frigid rising waters. The biggest problem they were dealing with was hypothermia, as many had already been in the water for nearly an hour.

The fire department used boats to extract people from their homes and submerged vehicles, then began to deliver them to the paramedics on the banks. But their limited numbers were overwhelmed quickly as victims were passed along at a feverish pace. Michelle, Joe, and the other paramedics worked in a frenzy to keep up with the growing number of patients, handing out blankets, applying heat packs, and dressing wounds. But there was only so much they could do. Michelle focused on the job and went to work like a professional as she struggled

THE OJANOX

to keep up. Then she heard the hysterical screams from a woman who had just been delivered to the shoreline. Michelle was the closest and rushed to her aid. The woman howled in agony and thrust the baby into Michelle's arms.

"My baby!! Please save my baby!"

Michelle took the bundle of blankets and parted the covers to examine the child. Cold—lifeless—milky-white eyes stared back at her. The tiny thing had turned blue and shriveled up in a most awful way from the frigid water. Michelle touched the infant's skin and knew the little girl had been under for far too long. She proceeded to rub the child's chest while the frantic mother howled as if the baby had been ripped from her womb.

One of the firemen who had witnessed the scene intervened and ushered the woman into an ambulance, assuring her that her baby was in safe hands. Michelle continued to stand there, rubbing the child, staring into its milky-dead eyes, rocking the frozen bundle in her arms. Then the world stopped spinning. Michelle gazed into the pleading eyes of the baby she couldn't save. She placed her lips over the child's mouth and breathed into its frozen lungs. She was told later that Joe had to wrestle the dead infant from her grips. Michelle didn't remember any of it.

The doctors said she experienced a traumatic breakdown that afternoon. She was put on medical leave and started counseling after spending over a month in the hospital. St. Claire's specialized in psychiatry and mental illness. The treatment helped, but the daily visits from Joe helped Michelle even more. He had attempted to prepare her for the ugliness of the world, but she hadn't wanted to hear it. And the day of the flood had been a baptism by fire. They talked a lot over the following six months. And although she was never able to get the image out of her mind, she eventually managed to get a full night's sleep. Less than a year later, Michelle wanted to go back to work.

Joe wasn't the only one who doubted if that was a good idea, but Michelle was cleared by her psychiatrist and, much to everyone's surprise, appeared to have rebounded from her breakdown. She was allowed to come back, in a probationary capacity, and reassigned to work with her old partner. Joe was skeptical at first, but after a few weeks of seeing Michelle in action, even he had to admit she appeared ready. Michelle found a way to disconnect and turn off the emotion switch; she had bounced back from a place no one believed she would have returned.

Unfortunately, Michelle's ability to "turn it off" transcended into other aspects of her life. She became disconnected from her family and friends. And when it came to relationships, the most she was interested in were one-night stands. She wasn't about to get that close to anyone. Her shrink might have been concerned about such behavior, but by then, she had stopped seeing him.

She lived alone without any pets or even a house plant. She rarely spoke to her family, and if she ever felt the urge, she would stop at one of the bars on 202, pick up a random quarry worker, get her rocks off—hopefully—and kick the guy out the next morning. It was acceptable for men to do, and it suited Michelle's needs just fine. Best of all, now she could pull a dead child from a tangled car wreck and not feel a thing. *Because you can't save them all—right?*

"What the hell is that?" Dr. Freedman screamed as the massive figure dropped from the trees in front of them.

Michelle reacted quickly, slamming the brakes and causing the ambulance to skid for about fifty feet before coming to a complete stop. The doctor was lifted from his seat and smacked his head against the windshield. Michelle looked at him with her jaw hung open. *You're a doctor, for Christ's sake, and you never heard of a fucking seatbelt?* Freedman flopped back into his seat with fresh blood pouring from a gash in his forehead.

"My head. What are you doing?" He stared at her through a veil of red.

The thing in front of them rose to its feet and squared off. It was difficult to see through the cascade of rain and the slap of the wipers, but Michelle thought whatever it was looked a lot like a man. But no ordinary man, the guy was massive, with arms as big as cinder blocks. Also, the bastard was naked. His muscles and veins bulged and popped as if they might burst through his skin. Then Michelle noticed the grotesque abnormality of the guy's package swinging between his legs; it almost touched the ground.

"What the fuck?" She watched as the freak approached the vehicle. "Oh, no the fuck you don't," she said, punching the gas and turning the wheel to the right. The front tires of the ambulance bounced over the curb and skidded onto the sidewalk. Dr. Freedman was tossed like a salad as Michelle maneuvered the vehicle around the thing in the street. She had no idea what it was, but she wasn't about to let it anywhere near her, not with a dick the size of a baseball bat.

She got a better look at the creature as the ambulance lurched over the sidewalk and into the field. Although it initially looked like a man, it was clearly not. It was hairless and stared at Michelle with eyes as black as the devil's asshole. It shrieked as she drove away, revealing a mouth full of razor-sharp bad intentions. She pressed the gas harder and made a split-second decision to head for the fence bordering the high school football field.

The beast crouched low to squat, then pushed off the ground with its massive legs. It took to the air, flying over the ambulance and landing on the far side. It raised both of its hulking arms and smashed the passenger's door where Freedman sat, bringing the vehicle to a complete stop. It proceeded to shake and tear apart the sheet metal as if it were nothing more than the front page of the *Sunday Times*.

"You have to save me; I'm a doctor! I'm important!" Freedman turned to Michelle and pleaded.

She grimaced at him as the gorgon smashed the window and seized the self-righteous bastard by the throat. Freedman latched on to her arm as the beast attempted to extract him from the ambulance. She was yanked toward him and struggled to free herself from his clutches, but the doctor held on for dear life. Michelle braced her feet against the floor, reached into her jacket pocket with her free hand, and removed the .38 she had been issued the previous night. She aimed the pistol at the doctor and pulled the trigger. The bullet hit Freedman just below the cheek, which was enough to do the trick.

The man's eyes bulged outward, and then his jaw went slack. Blood leaked from the small wound, and he released his hold on her. The monster ripped him from his seat like a child plucking a dandelion from the front lawn. His feet flailed and kicked off one of his shoes, which landed on the seat next to Michelle, who punched the gas and took off through the field. She checked the rearview mirror to find the beast had discontinued its pursuit for the moment and gone to work on the very important doctor. She wondered what the creature intended to do with the giant shaft between its legs. *Better him than me.* Michelle picked up Dr. Freedman's discarded shoe and tossed it out the broken window, then pointed the ambulance toward the school and floored it. The paramedic replaced the gun in her jacket pocket and smashed through the fence.

The men in the yellow rainslickers stationed in the back parking lot saw the vehicle approaching. Michelle slammed on the brakes and turned the wheel, bringing the ambulance to a screeching spin-out, stopping at the gym door. Bob Jones and Brandon Canfield rushed to her aid and immediately noticed the damage to the vehicle.

"Jesus, what happened?" Bob yelled.

"Something got Dr. Freedman. I tried to save him, but there was nothing I could do." Michelle did her best to look distraught and even managed to shed a few tears, but she wasn't sure if the act had been convincing enough. She had turned that switch off a long time ago. "The medicine and supplies are in the back," she told the firemen as she pretended to give a flying fuck about the man she had just shot in the face.

Deputy David Rainey oversaw the operation at the elementary school, making sure all the children were loaded safely onto the buses and the building was clear. He assisted his kid sister, Kelly, and her best friend, Caroline, and assured them everything would be all right, that he would meet them at the high school. The evacuation had been a success, except for the three missing children who left the school during the unplanned fire drill. Sheriff Primrose and Lois Fischer set out after them, but the kids couldn't have picked a worse time to play hooky. With any luck, they would survive long enough to get their fannies tanned by their parents. The streets of Garrett Grove weren't safe for anyone, especially three children.

David did a final sweep of the school to make sure no other students had slipped through the cracks. He checked the classrooms and principal's office on the first floor; all were clear, which left only the basement. David took the stairs and proceeded to check the boys' bathroom. "Hello," he called into the empty lavatory, receiving no reply. He made his way back into the hallway and was greeted by the sound laughter. "Hello," he called again.

There were footsteps, soft and furtive, coming from the girls' room. It was followed by another burst of laughter. *Dear God. We missed one.*

He entered the bathroom expecting to find the child standing there ... but stopped short. The place was empty; there wasn't anyone inside.

"He-he." The voice floated from the back of the room.

"Hello," he called. "We need to get you out of here." David took a step forward, then froze when the strange voice answered him.

Hello ...

THE OJANOX

It wasn't the voice of a little girl; it was hoarse, distorted, as if the owner had spoken through a mouthful of dirt. Then it spoke again.

Hello, David ... did you miss me?

Searing pain erupted behind the deputy's temples and in the center of his head. It was the same voice from the other night. The one he had heard at the morgue.

Don't move, David.

He tried to run, but his muscles wouldn't respond. His legs felt cemented in place, his arms frozen at his sides, and his head screamed like it had been placed in a vise with the torque bar being tightened. Tears streamed from his eyes as he fought to pull himself from the overwhelming compulsion to remain right where he was. Then the door to the back stall swung open, followed by the sound of wetness slapping against the floor. A hand reached out and revealed itself. Dark, moldy skin hung from the twisted bones; deep red sores ate into the flesh like an acid.

Slosh ... Slosh ... Slosh

The thing that emerged from the stall looked like it had been underwater for a very long time and something had been taking bites out of its hide for even longer. Most of its skin had turned black, making it difficult to see the leeches that crawled across the creature's face and eyes. Still, David saw them.

He no longer felt his legs and had no idea he had stopped resisting the pervasive invasion within his head. The deputy stared slack-jawed at the abomination, rocking back and forth on his heels as the beast penetrated his brain and ransacked the shelves. It felt like being raped, a violation of his memories and emotions. The presence ravaged his psyche, and David's stomach tightened, then he vomited on the floor.

Oh, David ... this will do nicely.

The voice originated from deep within his skull, and then ... it released him.

Deputy Rainey woke to find himself in the girls' bathroom, standing over a puddle of vomit. He was alone; the creature that had been there only a moment ago was gone. *But how?* He didn't wait for a reply and spun on his heels out of the bathroom, up the stairs, and toward the front doors. He ran straight to his cruiser and jumped in. Somehow, he had been spared ... a second time. He damn sure wasn't going to wait around and offer it a third.

His ears rang, and his stomach lurched from the acrid taste in his mouth. David could still hear the awful presence tearing through his brain; he had never felt so

693

violated. Putting the cruiser in drive and pressing his foot on the gas, he sped off toward the high school. He was overcome by an urgency to see his kid sister, a compulsion he was unable to describe and one he couldn't resist.

Chapter 73

Beau Jenkins rolled his eyes at Drew Halberg, shrugged his shoulders, and raised his hand, indicating the number five. The siren had rung nonstop for the past twenty minutes, which had to be long enough. They would give it another five and then head to the high school. Neither man wanted to miss their chance to get inside; Chief Jones would soon be locking the doors for the night. Drew set the timer to five minutes, its longest duration, and slid in behind the wheel of the remaining pump truck. Beau Jenkins joined him, hopping into the passenger's seat.

By the time they reached the Turnpike, the sky was as dark as a solar eclipse. The storm was a full-on barn burner, and Beau was hit with the realization that he and the kid had waited too long. The main drag of Garrett Grove looked like a war zone. From their position, Beau could see at least two houses engulfed in flames and a tangle of burning vehicles littering the road. Drew swerved wide around an overturned Volkswagen Beetle and slowed to look at a truck that had crashed into the front window of the Plains Pharmacy. The vehicle was smoldering, and it looked like people were still stuck inside.

"Sweet Jesus," Beau said as Drew pulled the truck to the side of the road. The retired officer leaned his head out the window to get a better look, then motioned to the boy.

"Don't stop the truck, kid!" he shouted.

"But—there's people," Drew cried.

Beau watched in horror, feeling his own blood turn to ice in his veins. He suppressed the urge to scream and could only stare in silence as the creatures rushed toward the disabled truck. There were five of them, each one more hideous than the next. Their malicious intent was evident from the violent flailing of their bodies as they descended upon the vehicle's occupants. With ape-like strength, they smashed the windows of the truck and extracted the man with ease. He fought to get away, kicking and throwing his fists at his attackers, but there were too many of them. The beasts seized him; as if engaged in some barbaric game of tug-of-war, they tried to tear the man in multiple directions. His right arm separated at the shoulder; the attacker took off with his prize in hand, tearing into the torn flesh like a short rib. Beau could see the man was screaming but couldn't hear him over the rain and sirens. The other assailants swarmed him and wrestled the man to the ground, then they turned on the woman in the passenger's seat and began to tear into her as well.

"I said don't stop the fucking truck, kid!" Beau screamed, sure he was about to vomit or pass out.

Drew didn't need to be told twice and pressed his foot on the gas.

Beau didn't know he had drawn his revolver and sat there with it trembling in his hand.

"What was that?" Drew asked. "We should have helped those people."

Beau focused on the road in front of them. "It was too late, kid." He rolled down his window the rest of the way as they approached another car stopped in the middle of the street. There was something on top of the vehicle, slamming its mitts against the roof, clawing and scratching to get inside. Beau looked closer at the scene and noticed there were still people in this car as well. The faces of three children stared back at him from their position in the backseat.

"You can slow down now," Beau said, leaning out the window. He aimed his .38 and fired. The round hit the creature in the chest, which only seemed to piss it off. The thing on the roof of the car looked like every picture Beau had seen of Bigfoot, only smaller. It was covered in long, matted hair that hung from its limbs in tangled clumps. He fired a second round and hit the beast in the jaw, drawing its full attention. The mini-Bigfoot shrieked, jumped off the roof of the car, and ran toward the truck at top speed.

THE OJANOX

Beau fired off two quick rounds, missing the beast completely. It was too fast, and it was almost on them. The creature took a giant stride in their direction; Beau focused his sights on the area in front of it and squeezed the trigger. The round penetrated the thing's skull just above its left eye. The Yeti's legs gave out, and it fell to the pavement less than three feet from the truck. Beau jumped out and fired another round into the back of the creature's head, just to be safe. He reloaded as fast as his fingers would move and ran to the disabled vehicle.

"Oh, sank Gott, Herr Jenkins! You saved us!" Günter Bentley exited the car with his wife, Hazel, and his three children.

Drew opened the back door and motioned for the family to pile in. Günter's three little girls looked to their father to make sure it was safe to enter the stranger's vehicle. He assured them it was. "Ja, children, move along. Deez are mine friendz." He shooed the girls and his wife, Hazel, into the backseat.

"You're in the front with us, Günter," Beau told him and waited for the man to climb in. Günter jumped up and checked the backseat to make sure his family was safe and sound.

"All set den, sehr gut, ya sehr gut."

Beau grabbed the door handle and lifted his foot into the cab. Before he could pull himself into the vehicle, he felt it wrap around his leg. He clutched at the handle and seat as it grabbed him from behind and yanked him off balance. Looking up at Drew, he opened his mouth to scream but was ripped into the street. He came down hard on the pavement and nearly blacked out from the impact. The wind rushed from his lungs in one crushing blow as the unseen force clamped down even tighter.

"Get them out of here!" he called back to Drew as the beast dragged him away and he disappeared in the rain.

Drew stared in disbelief; it had happened so fast.

Günter reached over and slammed the door shut. "I sink ve better do as he saiz, ya."

The young fireman hit the gas and took off down the Turnpike at breakneck speed. The truck handled well in the rain but still fishtailed at first.

Günter turned to his family again. "Ya, I sink ve vill be vearing are seatbelts den, quickly, children."

The Bentley brood listened to their father, and all fastened their seatbelts, including Hazel. Drew looked in the rearview mirror for any movement in the street but didn't see a thing. He had no idea what happened to Deputy Jenkins, but the man had gone out a hero. He had saved Günter's family, and that was a noble way to spend the last day of your retirement—also a rather dignified way to die.

⬤⬤⬤

Cars, trucks, and vans continued to arrive at the high school as the people of town realized the urgency of the situation. One of the vehicles had been chased by something that looked like it belonged on a platter at Red Lobster. Then Michelle Marks tore across the football field and smashed through the back fence. After coming to a screeching halt at the gym doors, something gigantic, naked, and clearly male chased after her, dragging the body of Dr. Freedman in its grip—the creature had resumed its pursuit. Bob's men were ready and dispatched the abnormality before it ever breached the parking lot. The freakishly endowed creature and Dr. Freedman now lay somewhere near the visitors' thirty-yard line.

The steady flow of vehicles trickled down to almost none, but Bob still held out hope. He wanted to give the citizens and his men every opportunity to get back before he locked the place up tight. Drew Halberg and Deputy Jenkins were working the siren at the station, others were canvassing the town in the trucks, and Carl, along with several of his deputies, hadn't returned either.

He looked up as a Plymouth Skylark took the turn into the parking lot way too fast and almost collided with a light pole before swerving and making its way to the back doors. The car came to a skidding halt, and a woman wearing a bright pink slicker stepped out into the rain. Bob rushed to assist her and offered his hand.

"Right this way, miss," he said.

"Who're you calling miss, sailor?" Tyler Harrison looked out from under the brim of his Day-Glo rain slicker. He smiled at the chief, then batted his eyes.

Bob released his hand and stared with his jaw slack.

"Why don'tcha take a picture; it'll last longer," Tyler said, then hurried into the warmth of the gym, where he was directed to the basement.

Bob shook his head, looked at Brandon Canfield, and shrugged his shoulders. He grabbed his radio again, praying this time he would get an answer.

THE OJANOX

"Jones to Primrose. Answer your radio, Carl."
But there was still no reply.

● ● ●

Howard Bell didn't listen to the warning he received from Ed Koloski. *Who the hell does that guy think he is anyway? Coming in with his gang of hoodlums, looting the place, waving around fake documents.* The bastards had ransacked the hardware store like a bunch of mobsters. As far as Howard Bell was concerned, the only emergency in town was the fire department had appointed themselves the secret police. No way in hell he was about to close his business at the recommendation of a couple thugs. He didn't care what the document said, even if it did state he would be reimbursed.

It didn't help that Howard wasn't in the best frame of mind when the men showed up this morning. Lately, he and his wife, Kim, had been fighting even more than usual, and he had a good idea she was screwing around behind his back. He didn't know with who and had no idea how to deal with it. They got married right after high school, much to Howard's surprise. Kim was a fox, way out of his league. Still, she had chosen him, with all his faults and insecurities, of which he had a boxcar full—insecure about his appearance, his weight, the size of his dick, you name it. In truth, the only thing different about Howard Bell was his debilitating insecurity issue. Kim hadn't been cheating, but she was sick and tired of being accused of it.

Monday morning, after Howard left for work, Kim had packed a suitcase full of clothes, loaded their two-year old son in the car, and headed to her parents' place in Nashua, New Hampshire. Howard came home to a note, an empty house, and proceeded to lose his shit. Figuring he'd been right all along, he drank himself sick and then started hitting the valium. When Kim didn't return home on Tuesday, Howard considered taking the whole bottle of the little yellow tablets. After getting no answer at her parents' house, he knew she wasn't coming back. And the phones had stopped working. Then Ed Koloski and the sheriff's gestapo showed up and damn near cleaned the place out.

Now he was expected to close shop and spend the night in the basement of the high school. What if Kim changed her mind and came home? What if the phones started working? There were too many variables. But the real reason why Howard Bell didn't want to go was because he had been ordered. Howard didn't like being ordered around—not one bit.

Soon after the men left, the fire whistle blew. Apparently, they were serious about getting everyone in the shelter. Then the rain started, which didn't help Howard's disposition. Rainy days always got him down, and when Howard got down, he got dark ... and not just a little. A psychiatrist might have diagnosed his manic depression and prescribed a medication that helped, rather than the valium, which only made things worse.

Howard watched the rain hammer the parking lot from his storefront window. The sky was as grey as his mood, and it occurred to him in a moment of clarity, he had driven Kim away. But thoughts of such were pushed to the side when the first beast appeared. It ran in front of the store, chasing a Volkswagen Beetle up Jackson Ave. The thing looked primitive and wore a mechanic's uniform. Howard tried to tell himself he imagined the strange sight but was unable to when a second one showed up in the lot. This creature could almost have passed for human if it weren't for the face, which looked warped and deformed, as if it had melted.

He stared at the nightmare, unable to pretend it wasn't real. Then several more abominations found their way into the lot. They maneuvered on all fours and were fast as hell. Howard locked the deadbolt, drawing the attention of the primates in the process, causing them to descend upon the building like a plague. They tore at the windows and doors in a frenzied heat to get at the man inside. He retreated to the back of the store and then into the basement. The place was built well, but it wasn't a fortress, not by a long shot. The atrocities quickly found their way inside and proceeded to rip the store apart. Howard shrank to the furthest reaches of the cellar as chaos ensued overhead.

He told himself it was all his fault; he had driven Kim away with his constant accusations and this was what he deserved. He listened as the sound of destruction drew nearer and knew the freaks had found the door to the basement. It was the end of the world; he was sure of that. And with Kim gone, there was no sense in going on anyway. Howard knew that as he searched through his stock of supplies on the back shelf. He removed the bottle of Quaker State anti-freeze and cracked it open. The deafening smash as the beasts tore the basement door from its hinges almost caused him to drop the container. He raised the bottle to his lips and swallowed as much of the vile contents that his body would allow. Howard Bell died before the first creature made it off the staircase. They say suicide is the coward's way out, but whoever said that had no idea how much courage it took him to swallow that quart of anti-freeze. Some might even say that it took a hell of a lot of guts.

● ● ●

Howard Bell wasn't the only resident of Garrett Grove who decided to end their own life that day. Marcie and Gottfried Eichmann heard the alarm and took the warning seriously. Baby Lavern was still nursing, and Marcie had just run a warm bath for both her and the child. Then the whistle went off. Gottfried immediately took to gathering everything he thought they might need for the baby, throwing diapers and ointments into bags, and cans of formula in case Marcie went through a dry spell. Then he proceeded to load everything into the car.

Marcie stood at the front door watching her husband load the trunk when the storm hit. It came down fast and sudden, soaking Gottfried in seconds. It was then that Marcie noticed the woman lumbering up the sidewalk as if she were drunk, with her arms hung slack at her sides. Something was very wrong with the woman, her mindless shuffle, the intoxicated sway of her body, not to mention she appeared unfazed by the storm.

Gottfried spotted her and approached to see if she was all right. But it was apparent she was not. He walked toward her with his arms held out as she turned and entered the driveway. The woman lunged at him with the speed and accuracy of a viper. Her mouth clamped down on the side of Gottfried's neck, and in a hot flash, a kiwi-size section of his flesh was torn away. He tried to scream, but the shock gripped him before he could react. A rivulet of crimson pulsed outward from where his carotid artery had been breached, soaking both he and the woman, running down the driveway and into the street. He fell to the pavement and bled out while Marcie watched from the front door, clutching baby Lavern to her breast.

Marcie screamed as Gottfried's leg twitched for the last time, then the attacker turned toward her and the baby. A section of the woman's face was missing; thick white worms crawled within the gaping wound. Marcie froze at the front door, staring at Gottfried's body where it lay in the driveway and the impossible features of the monster that had killed him. Her world heaved and spun out of control, and something inside her popped like an overloaded circuit breaker. Before she could move from her position, three more figures appeared on the far side of the property.

Marcie slammed the door and attempted to lock it but was unable to execute the action with Lavern stuck to her breast. *Dear God, they're going to eat my baby!* The thought resonated in her head and tipped Marcie the rest of the way over the edge. She had seen the movies about the living dead and wasn't about to let that happen to her or her baby. She ran up the stairs, into the bathroom, and locked the door behind her. The floor shook beneath her as the first intruder entered the house. Marcie stared at the tubful of bathwater, nice and warm, soothing, and relaxing. She had just drawn it for her and Lavern and couldn't think of a nicer place. She lowered the baby into the tub, pushed her under the water, and started to sing.

"Hush little baby, don't say a word."

It took less than a minute for the child to stop struggling; by then, there was little that remained of Marcie. She threw open the top drawer of the vanity and removed Gottfried's straight razor. She slid the cold steel across her throat with enough force to not only sever the vein but her windpipe as well. It was unsure whether Marcie bled to death or suffocated. At least she hadn't been eaten ... not until the beasts found her lifeless body on the bathroom floor.

● ● ●

Sven Peterson watched the creatures tear at the cedar panels on the side of his house. His wife and two boys retreated to the back bedroom as the place was dismantled board by board. He first saw the creatures enter his neighbor's yard and attack several children playing with slingshots. Sven couldn't be sure if the kids had gotten away, as they ran to the far side of the property. By then, there were more of the strange attackers. Sven got a good look at them, thinking they almost resembled gargoyles as they ripped the plywood from his house. Soon they would be inside, and it would be all over for the Peterson clan. Sven had always been a practical man, didn't believe in ghosts, UFOs, or even Bigfoot, and had no way of knowing exactly how he might react in a situation like that. If Sven had been asked on Tuesday if he was the type of guy who would use a shotgun on his entire family and then turn it on himself, he would have said *Absolutely not!* But on Tuesday, he never imagined he would be around to witness the end of the world.

●●●

Angelo and Donna Franco heard the warning signal and took the message seriously. After the week they had had on Poplar Ave. with the house fire and the disappearance of several of their neighbors, they weren't about to take chances. The whistle sounded, and then a fire truck drove by, delivering its message. So, Angelo and Donna did what any self-respecting Italian couple would do … they got their asses to church! Which appeared to be a popular decision. They arrived at Our Lady of the Mountain to find the parking lot more than half full, which was unheard of for a Wednesday afternoon. The couple exited the car and hurried through the rain toward the entrance just as the front doors burst open. Two men carrying hunting rifles greeted them with hearty smiles.

"Welcome, friends," one man said. "Glad you could make it."

"Hurry on now. Don't want to stand there too long," the other man told them, then shouted over his shoulder. "Look alive! We got company!" He dropped to his knee and raised the rifle level with his eye. Angelo and Donna were rushed into the church by the first man, who then turned and pumped a round into his shotgun.

Donna jumped into her husband's arms when the first shot was fired. It was followed by a second and then a third as the men took action. The couple stood in the center of the aisle clutching each other in shock. They had come to the church to find solace in faith during a time of crisis; what they found was something different. Suddenly, a man they knew very well charged toward them. Father Kieran had performed the ceremony at their wedding eighteen months ago. The Francos knew him to be a compassionate, understanding man who was old-fashioned like every other Catholic priest. They liked him, felt comfortable in his church, and had made it their church as well.

Father Kieran barreled toward them with the small caliber pistol raised above his head. "Stand back. The evil ones are upon us," he shouted as he passed the couple and ran out the front door. Several parishioners followed him. The sound of gunfire stifled the blare of the sirens and pouring rain. Donna and Angelo stared at each other, unsure if they should give thanks or run for their lives.

●●●

Carl maneuvered the cruiser through the Village. He'd been concerned the cloud cover of the storm would provide enough darkness for the creatures to wage an attack but never imagined the destruction that could take place in such a short time. Lois stared out the window in silence, tears streaming down her cheeks as she directed him to Janis's house. They arrived a moment later, and Carl brought the cruiser to a screeching halt in the driveway.

The place looked dark and empty, but it was impossible to tell in the storm. "Stay here!" He grabbed her purse, removed the handgun, and thrust it into her hand. "For Christ's sake, hold on to this. You're going to need it!"

Lois stared at him through a river of tears. Carl wasn't even sure she had heard him, but there was no time to repeat himself. He had waited too long to start the evacuation and the relocation of patients into the center's basement. Every move he had made had only been reactionary, ineffective, and counterproductive. How many deaths was he responsible for? How many men had he lost by making the wrong call? He was in over his head and had no idea how to bail himself out. He had even missed the chance to send for help.

Lightning flashed blue overhead as he ran to the house. Thunder immediately followed, causing Carl to jump as he climbed the steps. *Please don't let the power go out.* He tried the handle, only to find it locked, then backed away and kicked without knocking. The door flew inward, and Carl rushed into the house with his firearm raised. A moment later, he exited and jumped in the cruiser.

"That's a good sign." He nodded to Lois. "If they were here, they're probably already at the high school." He threw the car in reverse and backed out of the driveway just as the windows of the house across the street exploded outward. The concussion shook the cruiser, and a wall of flames billowed across the lawn and rushed toward them. Carl grabbed Lois, forced her down, and lay on top of her. She screamed as shards of glass and pieces of debris landed on the hood of the vehicle.

For Christ's sake. I'm going to lose the entire town.

"Where does the other girl live?" he shouted and drove away from the destruction.

Lois pointed forward; her hand shook with a spastic tremble.

"We're gonna find them," he said. "But we need to stay focused. I know you're scared, just stay with me, Lois."

Lois stared down at the gun in her lap, then looked back at him. "Wendy lives two blocks up on Winding Way." She continued to point ahead as they left the carnage behind them.

"You there, Bob?" Carl shouted into the mic. He took the turn onto Winding Way and was jolted by the blare of a horn. The pickup truck screamed toward them, taking up both lanes of the road. Carl dropped the mic and pulled the wheel hard to the left. Every muscle in his body tensed, anticipating the impact. The cruiser's tires bit into the pavement and squealed, sending the vehicle and its passengers over the curb and through a hedgerow. Carl regained control and steered back onto the roadway as the pickup continued without stopping. *Jesus Christ!* It had been too close. He looked over at Lois, who gripped the dashboard with both hands. All the color had drained from her face. *Too fucking close!* He gripped the wheel and hyper-focused on the road in front of them.

"Carl, thank God. Where are you?" Bob's voice boomed through the speaker.

"We're still trying to locate the kids. Are they there yet? They might be with the girl's aunt, Lynn Donovan."

There was a pause that felt like it lasted a year before Bob answered. "The Donovan woman showed up about fifteen minutes ago looking for her niece. But no sign of the kids yet."

"Roger that," Carl replied. "I'll be in touch as soon as we find them." He knew exactly what Bob was thinking: they couldn't keep the school open much longer. Soon, they would have to bolt and chain the doors shut. But neither man spoke a word about what was on their minds.

"Copy that, Carl. We'll leave the lights on for ya."

Chapter 74

Don and Stephanie sat with Gail at the entrance of the cave eating a late lunch and watching the dark clouds gather in the west. There were periods of awkward silence and moments where they caught themselves staring at each other. They had crossed a major line without giving it a second thought. Don couldn't believe he had acted so impulsively and was sure Stephanie felt the same. Still, despite the guilt, he didn't regret what had happened. It had been incredible, erotic, and confusing as hell. After lunch was finished, they acted like nothing happened and went back to work.

The back of the second chamber was where the final three cave paintings were located. Don and the women rearranged the work lights to illuminate the far-right corner, revealing the image that had been painted over four hundred years ago. It was a depiction of a ritual involving several Lenape children. They were adorned in elaborate clothes and jewelry, and the elders of the tribe looked as if they were praying to them. There was nothing dark or ominous about this painting, no black eyes or jagged teeth like there were in the others. This mural was a juxtaposition of the ones they had previously examined.

"Did they worship their kids?" Don asked.

"No more than we do ours," Stephanie answered. "There were certain rituals intended only for children, but their interactions weren't that different."

Don turned his flashlight on and examined the children. Each wore an elaborate medallion around their necks, a large emblem of an ornate sunburst nearly as big as their chests. Don had a good idea what the necklaces were made of—magnetite—the same as the weapons and the cave itself.

Gail clicked off a series of shots, running another roll of film dry. She reached into her bag to replace it and rummaged around for a few seconds. "I have to head to my Jeep and grab some more film. I'll be right back." She made her way toward the front of the cave, and Don and Stephanie found themselves alone once again.

They stared at each other for a full minute without talking. Finally, Don broke the silence. "You're probably thinking I'm an asshole."

Stephanie burst out laughing. "And you must think I'm the biggest slut going. You're married, for Christ's sake, and I just dropped my pants like some love-sick teenager on prom night." She turned away, shaking her head.

"Don't be so hard on yourself." He smiled. "I'm kinda irresistible."

"Well, Mr. Irresistible, let's try to move on from this. It doesn't take a collective unconscious to know this doesn't end well. Either way, someone gets hurt. I don't want to be responsible for that, and I don't need to go through it myself. Not again."

Don stared off into the farthest reaches of the cave, where the small opening disappeared into nothingness. "I understand," he said.

An uncomfortable silence fell over them, accompanied by an icy chill racing in from the cavern's entrance. The moment was shattered by a loud clap of thunder that resonated off the lodestone walls. They jumped at the sudden sound, then moved to the front of the cave to check the coming storm.

"I hope Gail hurries back, or she's gonna get drenched," Don said and poked his head outside. The town's whistle sounded a moment later, growing in volume as it echoed throughout the quarry. Don waited for the rise and fall of its pitch, but the whistle continued to belch out an endless cry. "That can't be right," he said. "That's the air raid signal."

"You mean the duck and cover kind?" Stephanie raised her brows in question.

"Yeah, that kind. The siren must be broken."

Outside, the rain started to fall against the dusty hardpan. Don looked toward the parking lot to watch Gail retrieve her bag and start running up the slope of the hill toward the cave. There was another quick flash of lightning, then the skies exploded, dumping rain in a fat torrential downpour. They backed away from the entrance as a cascade of water sheeted off the cliff in front of them. A horrible shriek sliced through the din of the storm, high-pitched and ear-shattering like the wail of a great cat caught in a trap. Stephanie turned to Don, wide-eyed and terrified. The cry was followed by another, even more mournful than the first.

"Probably a mountain lion!" he shouted to be heard.

Then he saw it.

At first, he thought the rain had loosened the rock on the western ridge, but as he looked closer, he realized it wasn't rock or mud or anything like that. Something was making its way down the rockface on the opposite side of the quarry. It was an animal of some type, clinging to the cliff. But it was moving too fast. Then he noticed the second one and then a third descending the rock. Soon, there were a dozen of the things rushing toward the canyon floor.

The air in his lungs sizzled like molten metal as he finally exhaled, unaware he had been holding his breath. Don gripped the wall next to him as the tremble started in his legs and worked its way throughout his body. It happened so fast. Terror spiked with uncertainty running through his veins as he watched the impossible scene unfold. *What in the name of God?*

From where Don stood, they looked like spiders—huge fucking spiders! The damn things were almost the size of a grown man. Even at a distance with the rain, he could see the creatures had nearly as many legs as spiders and were covered with dark brown hair, everywhere but on their heads, which was reddish orange.

"What the fuck?" Stephanie cried and hid behind Don.

The creatures had made their way to the ground and took off in several directions, scampering across the hardpack to where Buzzy and Mark had set off to relocate the explosives.

At first, Don thought the red part of the strange arachnid's body was the head, but now he could see them clearer. It was a stinger, and they weren't exactly spiders. The monstrosities that descended the quarry walls looked more like scorpions with deadly red stingers at the end of their tails. "Jesus Christ!" Don hissed as he watched the beasts make their way toward the trailers. His men had no idea what was headed their way.

Then something else emerged on the canyon floor that wasn't a spider or a scorpion. It was a man, and something was terribly wrong with him. His head hung limp and lolled from side to side as he shuffled through the wet dirt on a left foot that appeared to be broken at the ankle. The injury didn't impede the man's speed in the slightest; he ran straight toward the trailers with his foot flopping behind him.

Gail, who had been preoccupied with her equipment and the rain, ascended the rise and finally spotted the creatures. She screamed, dropped her bag, and bolted toward Don, who stood at the entrance, waiting to assist her. He hung out of the cave as much as he dared but took a step backward when another cry echoed from the direction of the trailers. It was high-pitched, intense, and agonizing, sounding like someone was being burned alive.

"Help me!" Gail screamed. She ran the last few steps to the entrance, reached out, and latched on to Don's hand.

He grabbed her and started to pull her inside, then froze when the front of her shirt exploded, basting him in a wash of crimson. The giant pincer drove itself into her back and penetrated the photographer's torso. A look of disbelief stole across her face as the red ball pushed its way through her skin, skewering her like a beef kebob. She grabbed at the impaling object as the creature lifted her with its monstrous tail and held her up for Don and Stephanie to see.

At only a few feet away, Don was able to get his first good look at the creature. There were characteristics that were scorpion, like the tail and the pincer, but there were some spider-like qualities to it as well. Thick black hair covered the creature's entire body, which had to be over five feet long. It had at least eight legs, as far as Don could tell, but that was where the arachnid similarities ended. Don stared at the impossible with a heart-stopping scream stuck in his throat.

Where the monster's head should have been sat the face of a human woman ... and there was something familiar about it. Don wasn't sure who had been the owner of the face, but he recognized the look in its eyes immediately. They were horrible, and piercing, and pitch-black.

Blood poured from Gail's mouth and cascaded from the massive opening in her chest; still, she continued to fight against the beast, kicking and flailing and beating against its giant pincer. The monster backed away from the entrance with the woman suspended from its deadly mandible and howled. The repulsive sound of its voice churned Don's stomach. He wanted to run, but his entire body had gone numb. He stood transfixed, staring at a dozen rows of God-awful razor-sharp teeth. The very same as the ones depicted in the murals.

He moved to the side to shield Stephanie from the creature, only to find she wasn't there. She had retreated to the back of the cave; he thought he should probably do the same. But he could only stand there, watching. Gail stopped fighting a few seconds later; her body went slack as the life dripped out of her. The scorpion-creature shook her one last time, then tossed her body away like a scrap of paper.

The great freak opened its human mouth and howled again, allowing a tendril of dark smoke to lift from its maw. Black eyes stared down at Don and began to smolder as if something inside them was burning. The thick cloud poured forth and accumulated around the creature's hideous head in a swirling mass. Don stood there, hypnotized by the concentric motion of the cloud, until a thunderous crash from the direction of the trailers broke his trance. He backed away, but the beast held its ground, with the growing cloud picking up momentum and churning before him.

Don felt the air disrupted near his head as something whistled past him. The beast bellowed with a thunderous squeal that penetrated deep into the cave. It reared up on its hind legs and came down hard, twisting and writhing like an ant under a magnifying glass. The whistle of a second object sailed past his head a moment later, and the creature screamed as if it were about to erupt. It curled up like a giant pill bug and rolled down the slope of the hill, where it came to rest and stopped moving.

Don spun on his heels to see Stephanie standing behind him. She held one of the wooden tubes in her right hand and several lodestone musket balls in the other. Her breath was ragged and exaggerated; tears coursed down her cheeks.

"Get your ass out of the way before you get yourself killed!" she screamed and loaded another musket ball into the tube.

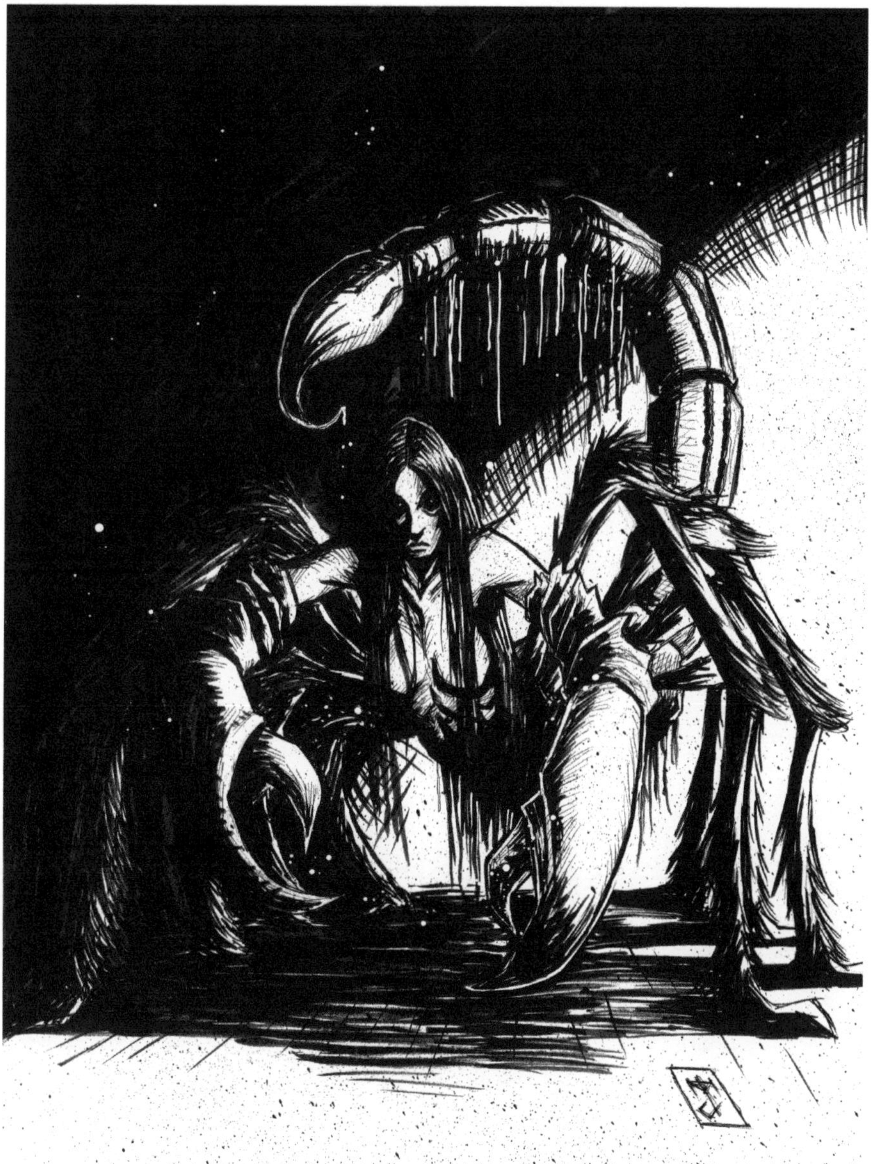

Chapter 75

Troy and the girls huddled together in the tight confines of the makeshift cage. To flee their pursuers, he had led them through the concealed opening that originated in the graveyard room to the narrow hallway where the inner workings and mechanisms that controlled Scream in the Dark ran through the center of the garage. With nowhere left to run, they had made their way in the dark, past the rat room and the spider palace, only to come to a dead end in the confines of the cage. Troy prayed it was hidden enough but knew the only thing between them and the creatures was a thin layer of cardboard.

He pulled the girls close and explained his plan but couldn't be sure they had even heard him over the sirens and the pouring rain. Sliding his foot forward, he found what he was looking for and prayed the cord was still plugged in. He rested the tip of his sneaker on the plastic switch, dug into his coat pocket, and removed the item. The ghouls were closer now. Their grunts and barks bounced against the walls of the maze, making it impossible to pinpoint their exact location. Troy was almost certain they were now in the rat room, following the path of least resistance, which he had been counting on.

The wheel that controlled the Day-Glo spiders began to spin at a feverish pace as the fiends ripped the hanging arachnids from the ceiling. The diversion of fishing line and plastic decorations lasted about two seconds, and the creatures pounced into the space in front of them. The rancid stench of sour milk and wet dog filled the confining area, causing Troy to gag. He held his breath and fought the urge to vomit. But they were so close, inches away on the other side of the makeshift cage, standing in the exact spot where Wendy had kissed him. The overpowering stink of the beasts was oppressive and awoke Troy to a horrible possibility. If he could smell them, then could they smell him and the girls as well?

An ear-splitting shriek erupted in front of them, and Troy knew their hiding place had been discovered. It was now or never. He pressed his foot down on the small plastic button taped to the floor. The strobe light came to life, filling the room with a white-hot pulse, illuminating the creatures before them. The boom box exploded, blaring its soundtrack of prerecorded screams, adding to the confusion of the moment. Troy, Wendy, and Janis found themselves face-to-face with the repulsive creatures just as the Tobin boys had ambushed the children Saturday night. The searing light had the exact effect Troy had hoped for. The demons screamed and shielded their eyes, howling and writhing as the pulse hammered at them like a branding iron.

Troy released the magnet he held in the pouch of his wrist rocket, sending the projectile point-blank into the first creature's chest. The monster hissed and jumped back in the confines of the small area. Troy loaded another round into the pouch as Wendy and Janis released their weapons of destruction. It was impossible to miss from the short distance, and the sound that came out of the creatures when the projectiles made contact was ghastly. The children loaded their weapons and released their arsenal on the beasts, who twisted and screamed and fell to the floor tweaking like a couple of trout.

Troy urged the girls back the way they had come through the tight passage, leaving the creatures behind. They exited into the storm to find the fire whistle no longer ringing and no creatures in sight.

"Quick!" he yelled. "Back into the house!"

Both girls wore similar expressions; half-crazed and wild-eyed, they stared back at him. He wondered if he looked the same as he led them across the backyard, into the house, and slammed the door behind them.

"That was amazing!" Wendy shouted, grabbing him and kissing him on the cheek.

"You saved us," Janis cried and planted one on his other.

THE OJANOX

The celebration was short-lived when something hard and heavy slammed against the back door. The children jumped and looked up to see the horrendous face. The creature that stood before them was repulsive. It stared through the eye-level window set into the door and began to sway to the left and right as if moving to a tune only it could hear. It looked slow and deformed, as if something had gone wrong in the mutation process. Troy watched the distorted head bob about like it belonged to a drunk or a toddler; he assessed that the threat was minimal.

Then the freak reared back and opened its mouth, revealing a lethal set of fangs. It screamed at the children as both sides of its neck flared like a cobra ready to strike. Horrible black eyes pierced Troy like an arrow, now making the creature look as dangerous as a switchblade.

It butted its head against the glass, sending shards flying in every direction. It took out a sizable section of wood with its single blow and nearly gained access. Wendy scooped up a handful of magnets from the drawing table and deposited them into her pockets. She turned to join Troy and Janis, who were already headed for the stairs, when the back door exploded inward. The cobra-looking horror stepped into the rec room, dripping puddles onto the tile floor.

It was on them before anyone had a chance to load their weapons. Swift and accurate, it approached the children where they stood frozen in place. It took an exaggerated step and lunged at Wendy. The beast's foot slipped in one of the large puddles of rainwater, and suddenly it was airborne, losing its balance and coming down hard on its back. The creature's massive head slapped against the tile floor with a resonating thud.

Troy didn't hesitate and forced Wendy and Janis up the stairs toward the front door. He was about to tell them to head outside when they rounded the landing and headed to the second floor. His heart stopped. There were no exits on that level of the house; they would be trapped. The magnets weren't exactly a super weapon; they took too long to reload and too many shots to take down the creatures. They would soon find themselves outnumbered and out of magnets.

The beast that had fallen let out another mournful shriek and regained its footing. Troy noticed movement out of the corner of his eye but didn't dare look back. Panic flooded his brain, making it impossible to focus on any constructive thought. He ascended the stairs in pursuit of the girls and was nearing the first landing when the front door flew open as if it had been hit with a battering ram. Splinters of the jamb sailed past his head, and the door almost smashed into him.

Sheriff Primrose rushed into the house with a rifle pointed in front of him. There was just enough time for Troy to duck before the sheriff started firing. The concussion of the weapon was deafening as each shot ripped through the stairwell like a wrecking ball. Troy was sure he had been hit. He closed his eyes and hugged the carpet as the sheriff fired round after round.

● ● ●

Carl and Lois turned onto Pine Street and saw the children run from the garage to the back door. A small pack of the strange brutes spotted the kids as well and took off after them.

"Oh, Carl, hurry!" Lois screamed.

After finding both girls' houses empty, they'd sped to the Fischer residence with the urgency of a four-alarm fire. Carl slammed the brakes and leapt out of the vehicle before it came to a complete stop. He ascended the front steps and took a running jump at the door, kicking it in mid-air. The flimsy wooden structure flew inward, and Carl found himself facing Troy with several of the crazed beasts hot on the boy's tail. The child ducked just as Carl aimed the Marlin and fired at the first attacker.

The seven-round, reloadable 30-30 was deadly accurate and Carl's weapon of choice. But the thing was close enough behind the child to be on top of him. It stretched out a hulking arm and lunged for Troy; its mangled fingers reached for the boy as the gun thundered. The bullet connected with its mark, taking out a massive portion of the monster's head; it fell backward into the rec room, where it ceased to move. But more followed and rushed through the back door. Carl fired on the horde, making the most with each shot, taking the time to aim for the heads. But their breach was too fast; they flooded into the house in a swarm and zeroed in on them.

"Everyone, outside now!" he screamed to the girls at the top of the stairs, and lifted Troy off the floor. They followed him and met Lois on the front lawn. Carl turned, fired off his last round, and reloaded. His fingers flew in a dizzying blur as the group tore across the lawn toward the squad car. Lois urged them into the backseat, then entered the vehicle herself. A second later, Carl pounced behind the wheel, threw the car in reverse, and screamed out of the driveway. He took a hard right, and the Fischer residence faded from view. The vile ghouls poured out the front door like a plague. More of the beasts gathered on the front lawn like a demonic band of trick-or-treaters.

Lois turned to the three children in the backseat and opened her mouth to speak. She reached out and took Troy by the hand as the tears flooded onto her cheeks.

Chapter 76

Chris Fredericks took the lead position of the bucket brigade at the top of the stairs. He handed weapons and supplies to Phil Reardon, who passed them along to Derek Fisk, who in turn delivered the cache to Dee Riker at the bottom of the stairs. A severe flash of lightning lit up the entire lobby of the medical center as if someone had thrown a flash bang through the front window. Chris thrust the weapons into Phil's hands at a faster pace but froze when a shriek sliced the air like a machete. It was followed by a second that sounded closer than the first.

"Don't take too long with that!" Deputy Lutchen called from the stairwell.

A second later, Chris heard the sound of chains being threaded through the front doors.

Chris watched the front lobby with growing concern. Shadows reflected off the glass, growing darker by the second. Underneath the sound of the rain and sirens, he was sure he heard something else, the guttural grunting of wild animals. Moments later, the front windows of the lobby exploded inward; a horde of bodies poured through the opening like a flood. Chris lowered his hand to his side and gripped the .38 he'd been issued, but the weapon never left the waistband of his jeans. He was knocked into the cart and blinded by the throng of bodies that fell on him. Some went right to biting and clawing, but a far worse sensation overtook Chris. It entered him like an electric current and tasted like a tin of copper pennies, ravaging what was useful and tossing the rest to the side like a piece of leftover meatloaf.

● ● ●

Derek Fisk was standing at the bottom of the stairwell when the creatures breached the building. He watched as they descended on Chris Fredericks, then attacked Phil Reardon. Derek spun about, colliding into Dee Riker, and shoved the boy backward into the basement. None of them had considered for a minute they'd be ambushed before they were safely locked inside the shelter. Steel cleats had been secured to the wall on either side of the door with four-inch lag bolts. The half-inch reinforced steel plates they were designed to support were tempered and strong enough to prevent even King Kong from getting inside. Provided they were set in place first.

Derek turned back to see Phil Reardon overcome by the swarm of creatures. Growing tendrils of dark smoke lifted into the air and swirled before the man's face. Phil's eyes rolled into the back of his skull and glossed to a black onyx, then he screamed. "Lock the door, now!"

The sight of the smoke disappearing into Phil's mouth was enough to break Derek from the spell. He slammed the door shut, leaving his friend behind on the stairs. He engaged the dead bolt and turned to Dee, who was there to help and slid the first plate into the steel cleats. The men moved fast and inserted the rest as the horde of demons made their way down the stairs. Several other firemen joined them at the door, stacking sandbags against it, and then stepped back.

They retreated to a barricade of filing cabinets set approximately thirty feet from the door. Weapons and boxes of ammunition were strategically placed at various vantage points on the makeshift stronghold. The gauntlet was where they would make their final stand should the monsters breach the fortification of the shelter door. If that happened, Derek didn't think it mattered how many weapons they had. *God help us if they do.*

They had a ton of firepower, but there were also a lot of patients and staff that would be useless once the fighting started. The firemen would perform well, but as Derek surveyed his forces, he realized there were less of them than he initially thought. Dee Riker dropped to one knee and held a shotgun trained at the basement door. The kid didn't so much as tremble. To Derek's left stood Greg, a large orderly who had fed breakfast to the patients on the second floor almost single-handedly. Greg adjusted the sight of his weapon, and it looked to Derek as if the guy knew what he was doing. Further down the line of defense were Fred Ramos, Kevin Grish, and Kurt Harrington, the fire inspector's nephew. All the men were avid hunters and comfortable handling firearms.

Behind them stood a second firing line of medical staff who had taken up arms, using several overturned carts for cover. Lee Chen, the lab tech, crouched next to Joe Santos from the first aid squad, but the most surprising of the volunteers was the center's own Dr. Halasz. Derek didn't know what to expect from any of them but was thankful for the extra guns pointed at the door.

Derek scanned the room, taking in the terrified looks on the faces staring back at him. The patients in their cots, the nurses attending to them, and the citizens who arrived seeking shelter—they had all heard the attack in the stairwell. Derek focused on a young girl with a bandage wrapped around her head; she had been involved in a traffic accident yesterday. An older man sat holding her hand, most likely the girl's father. Derek jumped and spun about as the first beast threw itself at the basement door. He watched the door with a laser focus; it appeared as if it was going to hold. The second concussion rattled it in its jamb, and Derek could have sworn the cleats had moved.

He turned to Dee and the rest of his men. "Remember, it has to be the head. Don't fire unless you can make the shot!"

He was met with a shared look of acknowledgement and held his breath as the third blow hammered against the door. Derek felt his legs go numb and almost ran from his position; he was certain the upper cleat on the right side had started to come loose from its anchor.

● ● ●

Garth Redman had been admitted on Monday night after experiencing severe chest pain. Dr. Halasz examined him, put him on blood thinners, and was happy to report that Garth had not had a heart attack. At the ripe old age of forty-seven and weighing in at a hefty two sixty, Garth was elated to hear the news. Now, as he lay in the back of the basement, about as far as anyone could get from the stairwell, he began to feel lightheaded. The pounding at the basement door sent a tremor racing through him with every thunderous beat. Garth started to hyperventilate, and sweat dripped from his brow. It ripped through him suddenly and with the strength of bazooka. Garth bit his tongue as his chest locked up tighter than the tin man's ass. He clutched the left side of his body and struggled to scream, but it was already too late. He fell back onto the cot, clamping down on his tongue hard enough to almost bite it in half.

The assault against the basement door ceased, and the room was still. A young nurse rushed to the aid of Garth Redman and checked for a pulse, but there was nothing. Nurse Burns looked about the room for Dr. Halasz and located him near the front door holding a pistol. She placed her hands to either side of her mouth and prepared to call out. The straining sound of metal twisting and breaking caused her to jump. She spun and faced the back of the room, where the noise had originated. It was followed by a buckling crash and several loud thuds as something massive fell against the concrete. Nurse Burns watched as the doors of the freight elevator started to spread apart. There was something in the shaft.

They parted only an inch at first, just the slightest movement. Then, the elevator doors spread a half inch more. Nurse Burns crouched behind the body of Garth Redman. She gripped the sheets of the bed with trembling hands and a hitch in her breath and watched. It happened too fast to even follow; the elevator doors mushroomed outward as the creature blasted from the shaft like a projectile. The putrid stench that followed was oppressive. It filled her sinuses like a plague.

Nurse Barnes gagged as the vile thing entered the basement, its skin looking like a cross between runny egg whites and cottage cheese. Pieces of the beast's flesh sloughed from its body and fell to the floor, discarded and forgotten. It wore what could have been a pair of jeans and flannel shirt, but it was impossible to tell since its runny epidermis had fused with its clothing. Before she could catch her breath, it was on top of her, wrapping its soupy hands around her head and lifting her off her feet. The putrefying flesh wrapped around her like a wet, rancid blanket, blinding her vision and stopping her air. She flailed in the behemoth's grip until it finally dropped her to the floor. It tilted its head back and released an enraged cry. A massive cloud of black spewed forth and descended upon the paralyzed nurse in a rush. It spilled into her and went to work, consuming her consciousness and devouring her fear.

THE OJANOX

● ● ●

Derek was alerted by the sound of twisting metal and the crash of the freight elevator when the cables snapped. Earlier, the car had gotten stuck between the basement and the first floor, the circuit board blackened like a tin of Jiffy Pop. The men trapped inside were rescued, but there was no repairing it. Derek and the rest of the firemen figured the stalled elevator car would act as an impenetrable barrier and didn't give the shaft a second thought. The oversight was catastrophic.

The men stationed at the barricade could only watch as the horror unfolded. The elevator doors disappeared in a blur; a second later, the vile mutation bolted from the ravaged opening like a discharged bullet. The stench that followed was oppressive. Then it took her, grabbing and tossing the young nurse like a fitted sheet. As she lay on her back with the terror towering above her, the even more impossible happened. A plume of fog, almost black in color, poured out of the thing's mouth. It swirled for a moment, gathering and building in mass, then pounced on the girl. It surrounded her, entered her, then moved on to the others. The strange cloud attacked those in the neighboring beds, hopping from cot to cot in a storm. The rest of the patients and staff screamed and fought to get away from the dense mass, but it was everywhere.

A second flurry of movement thrust itself from the nonexistent elevator doors. Derek struggled to focus through the hysterical mass of fleeing bodies, expecting to find more of the dark substance. But what he saw looked nothing like the descending cloud. Hundreds, possibly thousands of birds, or what had once been birds, poured forth like the eighth deadly plague. Their bulbous bodies were larger than hawks and featherless with pink oily skin like newborn mice. The wings that propelled them upward were leathery and transparent, like bats with beaks tapering into sharp, defined points. Hideous chuffing, barking noises filled the basement, making them sound more like a pack of wild dogs than any murder of crows. The demon-flock circled overhead for a moment, then dive-bombed the unprotected patients in their cots.

Whatever was affecting the people of Garrett Grove had also affected the wildlife. The ravens—or possibly hawks—had been infected by the same thing that got Dr. Malcolm. The pterodactyl-like beasts dive-bombed the defenseless victims with pinpoint accuracy, tearing and impaling them with their talons and beaks, causing an ocean of red to flow throughout the entire basement.

The pandemonium and sensory overload were hypnotizing. Derek's head spun and his vision blurred as the swirling clouds of smoke and flying bodies increased in speed and momentum. He struggled to refocus, raised his shotgun, and fired at one of the demons as it banked toward him. It fell to the floor, twisting and convulsing; he stepped closer and pumped a second slug into it.

The onslaught from the open shaft was endless. Creatures resembling primates breached the shelter; others that looked reptilian joined the winged horde and ripped into the crowd like an army of chainsaws.

●●●

The firemen guarding the front entrance turned their attention to the back of the room and onto the flying militia. They fired into the dizzying flock, their bullets felling many of the creatures but missing even more. Behind them, the basement door imploded with the force of a detonation. The steel slab, the plates, the cleats, and even the sandbags rocketed into the barricade of carts and cabinets, scattering the men like a handful of marbles. A degradation of atrocities stormed through the entrance and joined the slaughter.

The first beasts to push through the doorway were dropped by the firemen's defenses, but the magnitude of the attack was too great for so few guns. Kevin Grish landed on his back when the door collided with the barricade. A creature that looked like a cross between a tarantula and a Labrador raced toward him and pounced on his chest. The transfer was instantaneous—the freak ravaged Kevin like a chew toy.

Fred Ramos faired a little better than Kevin did, rising to his feet and firing several rounds into the mass of deformities. But he was silenced just as fast when one of the winged beasts swooped down on him from behind. Fred dropped his weapon as the ice water chill of spinal fluid leeched from his body. The strange bird had clipped the back of his neck with the front edge of its wing, slicing through the meat, the bone, and cartilage like a brisket. The man's head separated from his already crumpling torso and fell to the floor. Fred's lips continued to move, trying to deliver one final message, but his vocal cords were two feet away.

THE OJANOX

Kurt Harrington watched his friend's head roll across the floor, hypnotized from the shock. He never raised his gun to defend himself and slipped into a full catatonic state in two seconds. The swirling mass of black rushed in, took hold of the reins, and got the operation up and running again. Of course, Kurt was no longer able to participate.

Dr. Halasz and Joe Santos fired into the crowd of attackers at a frenzied pace. The doctor, who'd never shot a gun in his life, missed almost every target. Lee Chen also found it difficult to reload fast enough to keep up with the masses and was the first member of their group to be compromised. Joe was the next man to fall when he stepped up to fire at the thing that latched on to Lee. He emptied his revolver into the creature and proceeded to reload. However, none of his rounds had been head shots, and the beast was on him like a horny teenager. The doctor turned tail and ran, tossing his weapon in the process.

● ● ●

Susan Smith lay on a cot in the center of the basement, clinging to her father for dear life. She and her friends had encountered something the other night at the old sanitorium. Although none of them had seen it, one thing had been obvious: it was dangerous. If it hadn't been for Mick Petrie, she doubted if any of them would have made it off the mountain alive. Which might have been better in the long run. She buried her face into her father's chest and tried to block out the surrounding terror. Her head pounded from the concussion she'd received in yesterday's accident, and the madness around them made it worse. Her father pulled her closer as the man in the next cot choked on a vapor of suffocating smoke. A splattering of blood sprayed across the sheets, freckling his face with crimson. He wiped it away and attempted to shield his daughter. A young girl, no more than five or six, approached them with her arms outstretched. Susan didn't notice the child's eyes until it was too late. The girl latched on and bit into Susan's neck like a barracuda attacking a piece of squid. Susan screamed and beat at the monster to free herself but was unable. Her father stood up and latched on to the child's back with both hands but was thrown off balance by an unseen force. It picked him up and carried him away. Mr. Smith was gone before he hit the floor.

● ● ●

"Fall back!" Derek screamed as a primitive ghoul staggered toward his position. He blasted the beast in the face and navigated a retreat toward the center of the room. Dee and Greg rallied around him, leveling a path through the flying horde, making their way to the far wall. There were fewer screams to be heard, and the sound of gunfire was now minimal. The barking of the soaring pterodactyls and shrieking of the beasts was all that was left. Derek and his men reached the wall, slammed their backs against it, and sidestepped toward a set of steel doors.

Looking out across the scarlet river, surveying the total loss, Derek spotted two faces. The young nurses huddled together beneath one of the cots, their terrified eyes pleading for help. He continued along the wall to the set of doors and waved to the women, but they remained under the bed clutching one another. Derek gave them another exaggerated wave and opened the door behind him, urging them to follow. Finally, the nurses rose to their feet, hesitated for a moment, and ran. One of the winged devils spotted the two girls. It changed direction, banking in midair, and swooped down on the nurses, who were unaware of the threat. Derek saw it and reacted. He fired over the girls' heads and hit his mark. The mutant bird fell to the floor spewing a trail of oozing tar, then burst into a waft of tendrils that rose into the air and fused with the dense fog.

Derek ushered everyone into the utility room and slammed the door behind him. He went for the lock only to find there wasn't one. He quickly wedged the shotgun between the knob and the floor, pressed his back against the door, and planted his feet. He looked to the rest of his party. *Five ... only five!* The nurses were out of breath and terrified, Dee was frantic, and Greg faced the back wall trying to control himself. The large orderly had taken to rocking back and forth on his heels, as if moving to a tune only he could hear. Derek stared at the man for a moment and then returned his focus to the door behind him.

● ● ●

It started as an itch, one he was unable to scratch. Deep inside his head, with a pressure that made his eyes water. Greg thought he might vomit. He reloaded his

12-gauge as the pressure grew more intense and approached the threshold of pain. Shaking his head and biting down, he tried to deny the intrusion. Then it spoke.

Now, Greg...

The penetrating voice was commanding, and Greg was powerless to resist. He spun about, raised the weapon, and pulled the trigger. The group watched as Dee took a round to the chest and fell to the floor. Derek had enough time to realize he was next and managed to latch on to the barrel of Greg's gun. The weapon exploded, leaving a three-inch hole in Derek's torso. He continued to hold on to the weapon for a moment before collapsing next to the body of his fallen comrade.

The nurses backed away from the man, crying and clutching one another. Greg approached the door, kicked Derek's shotgun from under the knob, and yanked it open. The world was eclipsed in a rush of black. The charging smoke rushed in, pinned the women to the wall, and devoured them.

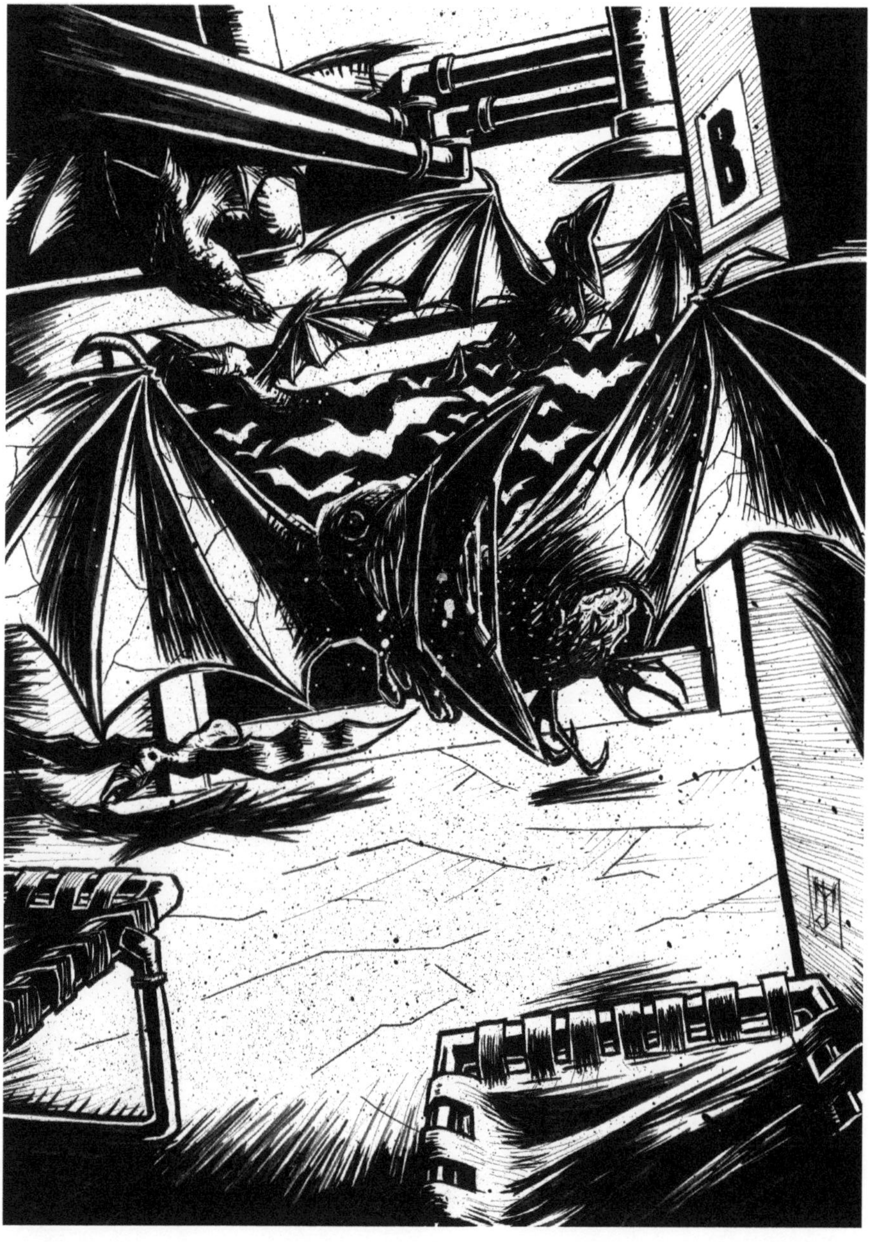
B

Chapter 77

Deputy Ted Lutchen rushed his party up the staircase just as the first ghoul crashed through the front windows. Doris and Burt led the way, with Dawn, Ted, and Baxter on their heels, and Ed Koloski and Nurse Carole bringing up the rear. The group rounded the first landing and approached the door to the second floor. Then the screaming started.

Ted didn't need to see to know the building had been breached. He could envision the throng of attackers crashing through the front window and pouring into the basement. He could also tell from the lack of gunfire the men had been taken by surprise.

"Faster!" he screamed, urging them along.

In a blur, the second-floor door flew open. The assailants lunged forward and seized Doris and Burt. Baxter reacted and pounced on the figure closest to him; he grabbed it by the arm and pulled it away from Doris.

"Get it off me!" Will Tobin screamed, trying to shake the German Shepherd, but Baxter held fast.

Ted scrambled up the stairs and grabbed the dog by the collar. "Easy, boy." Baxter was reluctant to comply but calmed at the deputy's command.

Burt had run headfirst into Billy Tobin, and although the boy was still weak, the coroner was almost knocked off his feet. Alice stood behind them; the three had been on the second floor and ran for the shelter when they heard the crash.

"We didn't make it to the basement," Will explained. "We were waiting for the n—"

"There's no time. We got to keep moving." Ted pushed the group and its new members to the third floor just as the first shot echoed in the stairwell. Seconds later, the steady concussion of gun fire bounced off the walls, sounding like the beginning of World War III.

They reached the next landing, and Doris paused at the door before opening it, as if someone might be on the other side like the Tobins had been. She held her breath, turned the knob, and hurried onto the third floor with the rest of the group behind her. Koloski was the last man to leave the stairwell and stole a glimpse over the railing before leaving. They weren't being followed, but it sounded as if a massacre were taking place in the basement. The shrill of the screaming and the concussion of gunfire rattled the plaster from the walls, and the smell of gunpowder was detectable even from where he stood.

He left the stairwell to join his party and was met by a familiar face. Fellow fireman Grady Martin stood in the hallway next to a blonde candy striper—her name tag said: Hello, my name is Cyndi. Koloski approached Grady and handed him one of the guns he had slung over his shoulder. Then he dug into the duffle bag and distributed handguns to Will, Alice, and Billy. He held one out to the Cyndi with an i, who shook her head and declined.

"There're two ways off this floor," Doris said. "This stairwell and one at the end of the hall that leads to the roof."

"What about the elevator?" Ted asked.

Doris held out a set of keys. "I turned it off and stopped the car on this floor. We can operate it if we need to, but no one can use it to come up."

"Smart." Ted scanned the hallway to the left and right. "And the patients?"

"In three rooms near the nurses' station. Far end of the hall away from this stairwell. I figured it was the safest place."

"Good job," he said. "Please lead on."

They followed Doris around the corner and down a long hallway that dead-ended near a nurses' station. Ted nodded, observing the layout. The counter itself would serve as the perfect vantage point. If the creatures found their way to the third floor, the only way they could attack was via a straight run down the hall toward them. With several shooters positioned behind the safety of the heavy counter and the rest of them hidden in the doorways, their forces were as strong as they could hope for. "This is where we make our stand," he told them. "Everybody, dig in."

The sound of gunfire was quieter now that the door to the stairwell was closed. Baxter relaxed a little bit but still clung to Dawn's side. Ted bent down eye level to the girl and lowered his voice. "I have an important job for you. Will you help watch over the patients with Carole and Cyndi?"

"Is that Drowsy?" Cyndi motioned to the doll in the child's hands, and Dawn's eyes lit up. "I had Drowsy when I was a little girl. I haven't seen her in years. Does she still talk?"

Dawn smiled and showed the girl her doll. Ted watched the exchange and let out a deep sigh. It had been hard enough to get the child to use the bathroom by herself. With Cyndi and Carole to watch over her, he could at least focus on the fight. The women brought Dawn into the room across from the station, and Baxter followed.

Ted turned to the others and surveyed the strength of the group. Burt and Doris both held large-caliber revolvers and appeared ready to use them. Doris looked a bit more prepared than the old coroner, but looks could be deceiving. Then there was Koloski and Martin; Ted had seen them both at the range on numerous occasions and didn't doubt their ability. Which left the Tobins, possibly the weak links in the chain of defense. But this was the lot he had drawn, and it would have to do. He prayed the vantage point of the nurses' station would allow them the edge they needed, but there was no way to know for sure. He listened as the sound of gunfire lessened and then stopped. Nothing ... not a scream or a single shot sounded out. A gripping chill settled in the back of his neck. Things had gone terribly wrong in the basement.

"All right, I want someone in each of the doorways and two with me behind the counter."

The nurses' station sat on the left side of the hallway across from the three rooms with the patients. The door to a janitorial closet sat next to the station on the same side of the hall. With his army of eight, Ted figured he would stagger his firepower at choke-off points in each doorway with a sniper team positioned at the counter. He was a good shot with a scope, and if he could get a decent rifleman with him behind the desk, they would have a formidable line of defense.

"Who's good with a rifle?" he asked.

He wasn't surprised when Koloski raised his hand, then Billy Tobin stepped up as well. Ted threw the kid a skeptical look, but Will spoke up.

"He is. I've seen him hit a dime from fifty feet with a 30-30."

"You up for it, kid?" Ted asked, but he could tell from the cold determination in Billy Tobin's stare that he didn't need to ask.

Chapter 78

Jessica Marceau stood at the window of her new office overlooking the Turnpike. The town she grew up in now looked alien and unrecognizable. Abandoned vehicles and wrecks littered the two-lane street in front of the municipal building. A Volkswagen Beetle lay overturned near the entrance to the parking lot. Its front window had been smashed; a dark burgundy trail stretched out across the pavement like a carpet. Several of the businesses on the main drag were burning out of control, while others appeared to have been vandalized or looted. She watched as a station wagon careened past the building doing well over fifty in the twenty-five mile per hour speed zone. Four hideous ape-like creatures pursued it like a pack of bloodhounds. One of the strange vertebrates looked as if it were wearing a mechanic's uniform. "Grease monkey," Jessica said and cackled into the empty room. The sudden outburst even startled her, as she took to rocking in place, cradling herself in her arms.

She had been ordered to report to the shelter at the high school, but that felt like abandoning ship. How could she turn tail and hide while there were still people on the streets? She was the mayor, after all—newly appointed, of course. It looked like it would be the shortest term ever served. There were other things on the streets as well ... horrible things. Some looked reptilian, others appeared to be from the primate family, and less than an hour ago, something had slithered across the front parking lot that could have crawled out of the Black Lagoon.

Jessica jumped back from the window as a shower of sparks exploded from one of the transformers across the street near the Lutheran church. "Oh my," she giggled. "That can't be good." The lights in the mayor's office didn't flicker or dim; they stopped working at once, leaving her standing in the dark. The last of the dim daylight was fading fast, and Jessica let out another burst of laughter, making her sound like she was raving mad. In truth, Jessica Marceau was well on her way.

● ● ●

Bob Jones watched from the side of the school as the brown Ford pickup banked hard into the parking lot with the massive creature hanging from the driver's side window. The operator of the vehicle had his foot pinned to the floor and missed running down John Sampson and Eric Collins by inches. Both firemen jumped out of the way at the last second as the truck and its unwelcomed passenger slammed into a light pole. A moment later, the entire shooting match went up in flames. The beast paid no attention to the fact that it was now on fire and continued to claw its way into the vehicle. Both the driver and assailant burned to death in less than a minute.

There were other vehicles that carried unwanted passengers, leading the creatures right to the high school. Bob and his men had been lucky so far and managed to put them down, but he knew their luck would eventually run out. Things were getting worse by the second, and it was looking like the round-up crew had done the best they could. However, far fewer citizens had shown up than even Bob anticipated. Either people hadn't taken the warning seriously or most of the town had already been massacred in their sleep. At least they got the kids out of the elementary and junior high schools. Bob figured whoever was still out there was taking things seriously now.

The pump truck entered the lot, driving past the still-burning pickup. It pulled up to where Bob stood, the doors opened, and Drew Halberg stepped out. Expecting to see Deputy Jenkins join him, the chief did a double take when the manager of the A&P exited the vehicle. Günter Bentley was followed by his entire family.

"Hello, Chief Jones," Günter greeted him. "Dis ist mine beautiful vife, Hazel. And deez are mine chilrun; dis ist Gretel, und dis ist Gisela, und dis ist mine little princess, Marilyn." The three toe-headed children stared up at Bob with their giant blue eyes.

The absence of Deputy Jenkins was obvious, and Bob didn't have to ask to know what had happened. He winced and shook his head. He had known the man almost as long as he had known Carl, and now he was gone. Bob could feel it in the air, pressing down against him and weighing on his shoulders. It was loss and pain, and no one was beyond its reach. Before this day was over, Bob knew that everyone in Garrett Grove would experience it on some level. He stood there and kept a watchful eye; time was running out ... for all of them.

●●●

Mike Turino enjoyed getting the chance to sit behind the wheel of the police cruiser. Although he had ridden in them before, this was his first time in the front seat. As a kid, Mike found himself in trouble a bit more often than other boys his age. Nothing serious, just some underage drinking and vandalism, and the one occasion when he got caught stealing from the Radio Shack. Which was the first time Deputy Jenkins had made him ride in the back of the cruiser.

When Mike turned eighteen, things got a bit more complicated. It started out simple enough, tossing back a few with his buddies, sharing a bottle on a Saturday afternoon at the lake, but in truth, there was nothing simple about it. A light switch had been turned on, and Mike found a sense of ease and comfort that only booze could bring. He was a likable drunk, a hit at the parties, and was even able to talk to girls without acting like a buffoon. He had suddenly found the missing ingredient of life, thanks to John Barleycorn. Simply put, Mike liked beer ... it made him a jolly good fellow.

Mike had known Brenda Pritchard since high school, but they had never talked much. That was until one night at the old sanatorium. The six-pack he downed on the walk up to the place was all the liquid bravado Mike needed to approach her. Brenda twirled her hair when he spoke, laughed at his jokes, and let him get to third base on one of the cots in the old hospital. And from there, it was game on. Mike asked Brenda to the drive-in the following Saturday, and she agreed. He packed a case of Michelob into his cooler, thinking if Brenda had a few drinks in her, it would be easier to get the rest of the way around the bases. Before the movie was half over, with only two six-packs down, she proved his theory correct. They had sloppy, drunken sex in the backseat.

Later, when they made their way back to Garrett Grove, Mike was what most people would call piss drunk. He succeeded in keeping the Buick on the road and managed to get them to the edge of town without hitting a tree. He slowed as he approached the Gables Bridge and gripped the wheel with determination. It was going well too; Mike even made it halfway across before the truck barreled at them from the other side. Then he panicked. To avoid swiping the straight job, Mike jerked the steering wheel a bit too hard to the right. The Buick collided with the guardrail, sending the passenger's side into a concrete pier. Brenda, who wasn't wearing her seatbelt but had been relaxed to sleep by the combination of alcohol and drunken sex, smacked her head against the window and rebounded like a ragdoll. Fortunate for her, the doctors said if she had been sober, she most likely would have suffered worse injuries than a few contusions and hematomas to her face. Mike walked away without a scratch.

Although Brenda's injuries were minimal, her father, Gerald Pritchard, Esq., was none too pleased. The King County prosecutor was determined to see Mike swing for jeopardizing the safety of his daughter and filed negligence charges against him. Mike went before the judge and was forced to pay five hundred dollars in restitution, Brenda's hospital bills, and was sentenced to serve thirty days.

Deputies Colbert and Jenkins drove Mike from the courthouse to the county jail. They both knew Mike from town and had witnessed how the boy's drinking escalated over the years. Still, he was a good guy, and they liked him—even though they had each thrown him in the drunk tank on various occasions. They sent him off to jail with three packs of smokes, a deck of cards, and fifty bucks. The deputies told him he was allowed to bring the cigarettes, even the cards, but he would have to hide the cash.

"How the hell am I supposed to sneak this in?" Mike asked.

"You know." Deputy Colbert tossed him a rubber glove. "In the old jail wallet." Both officers tried to stifle their laughter.

THE OJANOX

"You mean in my ass?!" Mike blurted with a look of indignation.

"Well, look at it this way," Jenkins said. "As long as you have the money, chances are nothing else will have to go up there." He razzed the guy, though people seldom got raped in county jail, that was more of a state prison thing.

"It's easy, kid," Colbert explained. "Rip one of the fingers off the glove and put the money in it. Then tie it good and tight, spit on it, and you know—up the ole pooper." The deputy struggled to keep a straight face while he explained the process. The officers had an even harder time when Mike went to work concealing the cash. By the look on the kid's face, it was more than a little uncomfortable. Even funnier was when they brought Mike into the jail to get processed.

"What do you have to declare as property?" the guard asked.

"Three packs of smokes and a deck of cards," Mike answered.

The guard scribbled onto his paperwork. "Any money?" he asked.

Mike froze as he felt the fold of bills quiver inside him.

"Money ... what do you mean?" He started to panic and thought for sure he was busted.

The guard threw him a dirty look. "Do you have any money, kid? You're allowed to have up to fifty dollars."

Colbert and Jenkins erupted into a gale of laughter. Mike tightened his face and scowled at the deputies who had been fucking with him all along and had probably pulled this one countless times before.

The guard cracked a smile and laughed himself. "It's in your ass, isn't it? Yeah. It's in your ass." Apparently, the joke was an oldie but a goodie. Mike was just happy the deputies hadn't given him the fifty bucks in quarters.

Mike did his time in county, and Brenda even came to visit. She said she felt bad for what her father had done. She gave Mike an old-fashioned hand job in the visiting booth. In fact, her father's actions backfired terribly, and Mike's jailbird status affected the prosecutor's daughter better than a dozen oysters and a bottle of Black Fly.

● ● ●

Once the town fire whistle stopped ringing, Mike delivered his message for the last time and headed for the high school. That's when he saw the girl waving from the alley between the diner and the beauty parlor. He turned into the parking lot, and the girl ran to the cruiser.

"Thank God." She was drenched. "My asshole boyfriend was supposed to pick me up an hour ago."

"I know you." Mike recognized the girl from the A&P. "You're Claire, right?"

"What the f—" Claire looked as if she might jump out of the car. "You're no cop. You're that guy Mike." She grabbed the handle, then thought better about it.

"Easy, I'm helping the sheriff. You could have been killed out there."

"I hid in the alley for the past hour. What the fuck is going on? Man, you wouldn't believe the shit I've seen." Claire pulled a pack of waterlogged smokes from her coat. "I don't suppose you got a butt, dude?"

Mike handed her his pack, then turned on the heat and focused the vents on her.

"My hero," she said and lit up. "So ... this is cool. First time I ever rode in the front." Claire looked into the backseat, and Mike knew they had at least one thing in common.

"Want to feel something even cooler?" he asked with an evil grin on his face.

"Dude, if you whip out your dick, I swear to God—" She tensed up and slid further away from him.

"Relax, that's not what I mean." Mike turned on the cherries, hit the siren, and punched his foot to the floor. The cruiser took off like a pulsar as they made their way back into town. Claire cracked a wicked grin of her own as she braced herself in the passenger's seat. She was glad the guy hadn't whipped his dick out.

● ● ●

Father Kieran took a sentry position at the front entrance of the church, flanked by Dick Wilson, and the terribly scarred, Jim Reilly. The priest now brandished a S&W .357, gifted to him by a member of the flock. With the coroner's .25 safely tucked in the waistband of his slacks, he kept a watchful eye on the parking lot and surrounding area. Stationed at the entrance to the sacristy was Dick's nephew, Josh, Frank Palumbo (the owner of the Texaco station), and Fire Inspector, Bill Harrington. The only other entrance was an emergency exit near the organ, where

THE OJANOX

Luke Evans, Julie's husband, a truck driver named Rick Edwards; and Angelo Franco, who had just arrived with his wife, Donna, stood watch. All of the parties were backed up by larger groups of men and women who had been assigned the tasks of reloading and weapon replacement.

The overhang at the front entrance prevented the heavy rains from assaulting the men and offered an excellent vantage point. So far, only a few of the demons had been brave enough to leave the darkness of the woods and venture near the church. Kieran and his men made quick work of them. The priest's presence fueled the morale of the men and women of the flock, inspiring a determination and sense of courage most never knew they possessed. Kieran turned to the man with the scars on his face. Jimmy stood fast with his rifle raised and at the ready, filling the priest with an overwhelming sense of pride.

"You are a warrior, James," Kieran told him. "A fitting name for such." He patted the man on the back.

"Don't worry, Father. Nothing is getting past me."

"God bless you, my son." Father Kieran then turned to the man on his left. "Brother Richard, the Lord is with you."

Dick Wilson returned a smile and focused his attention on the tree line at the edge of the lot, but the downpour made it nearly impossible to see. A sudden ripple of movement caught his attention as something emerged from the woods. "I think we have company, Father."

Kieran raised a set of binoculars and peered across the parking lot; two creatures lumbered out from between the trees and made their way into the open. They were slow and there was only a couple, but that didn't mean they were alone. He raised his hand to Dick. "Hold steady. Don't fire until I give the word."

The demons that entered the lot were abominations. They were bald, and their skin hung slack as if it was too big for their bodies. Their ears were pointed, and Kieran thought they resembled bats or some type of rodent. He could see the onyx black of their eyes, with the help of the binoculars, and how misshapen their features were. One beast turned to the other, and there was an evident exchange, as if they were communicating the plan of their attack. There was an intelligence at work, a malevolent one. Kieran knew the imps were waiting for him to make the first move. He scanned the woods, adjusting the focus of his binoculars, and saw the rest of them. An army of repulsive creatures hid behind the cover of the tree line.

"I see you," he said under his breath. "Brother Richard, gather more men to flank our position."

Dick retreated into the church and did as the Father asked. He returned with the recruits, who took their positions on either side of the men.

"No one fires till I give the word," Kieran said. "They are trying to wait us out, trying to test our defenses. They will learn, you cannot test the Lord. Hold fast, men."

Josh Wilson held point at the entrance of the sacristy, where he and his men could see across the side lawn all the way to the rectory. A tangle of trees on either side of the house provided enough cover for something to hide within, but there hadn't been any movement yet. He scanned the area and squinted to get a better look. There was motion. Slow and concealed, but he caught it just as something moved from the far corner of the building to the wooded area.

"You sneaky bastards," he hissed. The men to either side of him gripped their weapons and stared off in the same direction. There was something out there; they all saw it now. "What the hell are they waiting for?" Josh wondered what was happening at the other entrances and called to Allison Aigans, who stood behind him in the reloading party. He sent her to check on the other groups and report back.

It felt good for Allison to have something to do after losing her mind over the past few days. It was unlike Mick to disappear like he had. When she learned the Tobin boys were missing too, it all made sense. Billy Tobin had a way of talking people into doing things. She knew the boys had gone back to the sanatorium and sensed that something terrible had happened. She wanted to talk to someone about it, but things got very strange at school after that. More people went missing, and not just a few. Almost half of Allison's homeroom class didn't show up for school yesterday, including Susan and Debbie. So, she left school early and drove to King Lake to figure out her next move. It was where she and Mick had made love the first time. She remembered how it felt to hold him close as they lay in the sand beneath the stars. Just being there reminded her of him and made her feel as if he was still with her. But Allison knew he wasn't, and she knew something had happened to him. That was when she decided to head to the church.

She approached the men at the side entrance near the organ and asked if they had any information. Similar sightings of the creatures were reported, lurking just behind the tree line, waiting for the right moment. Allison shared the group's information with Father Kieran and reported back to Josh with explicit instructions for everyone to hold their fire until they got the word.

It was a waiting game, and Kieran had a good idea what the demons were up to. They were waiting for nightfall; that was when they would strike. And it was approaching fast. The evil one thought Kieran's forces would fold once the attack began. But the priest was clever and had a counter-maneuver in mind. Once tonight's victory was in hand, they would bring the war to the Devil's doorstep and slaughter Satan in his sleep.

Chapter 79

The third floor of the medical center went dark as several of the transformers in town overloaded. It took the emergency generator almost a full minute before it kicked on. The dim red glow of the auxiliary lighting cast long, deformed shadows across the faces of those standing outside the nurses' station. Ted and the members of his group stared at each other in the wash of twilight. All was silent, save the hammering of the rain against the windows. The gunfire had ceased, the cries from the basement had been quelled, and the strange disquiet that fell upon them was unsettling. Ted waited, listening for any sound other than the rain or wind. Finally, he turned to Koloski.

"Your man in the basement, Fisk, right?"

"Yeah, Derek Fisk," Koloski answered as Ted lifted the walkie-talkie to his lips.

"This is Deputy Lutchen to Fireman Fisk, come in, Derek." A crackle of static filtered through the speaker and echoed throughout the hallway.

"Deputy Lutchen to anyone in the basement. Come in, over." Ted waited for a response, but there was nothing. He thought it possible the concrete of the shelter might be preventing the signal from getting through but had a feeling it was worse than that. The looks on the faces staring back at him suggested they thought the same. Then the radio garbled, and a voice spoke through the speaker.

"Ted, it's Carl. What's the situation at the center?"

"We were ambushed, Sheriff. I can't get through to anyone in the basement. It sounded like a damn war down there." There was a long period of silence, and Ted was about to repeat the message when the sheriff replied.

"You're on the third floor, Ted?"

Ted looked at the anxious faces of Alice and Will Tobin and knew what they were thinking. Lois had left with the sheriff to pick up Troy. "Roger that, Sheriff. I'm on the third floor with the Tobin family, Nurse TenHove, Coroner Lively, Koloski, Martin, and several others."

"Roger that." Carl sounded relieved. "I need you to hold tight till I can get some backup over there. I have no idea how soon that might be. How are your defenses?"

"I think we have a tactical advantage, sir. I can set up a gauntlet and pick them off if they attack."

Burt grabbed the radio out of Ted's hand. "Carl, I figured out why the MRI machine killed it. It's a giant magnet, and this thing is made of some type of metallic alloy."

The radio crackled, and the sound of several people talking at once distorted the speaker. "All right!" the sheriff shouted and was followed by a moment of silence. "Yeah, I was just told the same thing about ten minutes ago by a group of fourth graders. But good job, Burt. Glad you're safe, and I hope that info helps us."

"I take it you found the kids?"

"That's a big 10-4—" There was a loud garble of static and the sound of a woman screaming, *"Look Out,"* then there was silence.

Ted grabbed the radio. "Sheriff, come in. Sheriff!"

There was no response.

"What happened?" Alice pleaded with him, but Ted didn't have any answers for her.

He tried to reach the sheriff again with the same result ... static. There was a tremendous thud as the floor shook beneath their feet, then the sound of shrieking filled the hallway. The beasts had found out where they were and had begun to ascend the stairs. Terror flashed from face to face, and time stood still ... for a moment. They had all anticipated this, and although they prayed it would not come to fruition, they sprang to action and took their assigned positions.

THE OJANOX

Ted, Billy, and Koloski retreated behind the nurses' station, while Grady Martin took point in the room closest to the adjacent hallway's intersection. Alice stood in the doorway of the janitorial closet between Martin and the station, and the rest of the group made their way to the rooms on the opposite side of the hall. Will on point, Doris in the center, and Burt in the last, nearest the exit to the roof. Patients occupied the three rooms, and Dawn, Carole, and Cyndi were tucked away in the last one behind Burt.

A high-pitched shriek ruptured the air; the group leveled their weapons in the direction from which it had come. They stared down the hallway, waiting for something to charge. Every one of them jumped when something large slammed against the stairwell door. The force on the opposite side proceeded to batter the steel and the surrounding frame with relentless abandon. The group gathered their munitions, checked their weapons, and prayed it would be enough.

A clowder of fists assaulted the door until it gave way under the strain and was ripped from its hinges. The bodies swarmed the hall and flooded toward them. Ted rested the 30-30 on the counter and focused his scope on the area where the two hallways intersected. He had a good vantage point with a perfect line of sight. Anything coming their way would have to pass his firing line. He wiped a drop of sweat from his nose and watched as the first shadow bounced off the far wall. Then a darting figure rounded the corner and screamed. Ted didn't even have time to fire as three other members of his team let loose on the beast. It dropped to the floor and ceased to move.

The dark glow of the emergency lights added to the tension as they waited for the next attacker to appear. The flailing shadows grew shorter as a mass of figures bounded around the corner and advanced on their position. The sound of eight different weapons firing simultaneously in the narrow hallway was deafening and intoxicating. Smoke filled the area as the group continued to fire and the bodies of the assailants piled up at the end of the hall.

The gauntlet was effective. Grady and Will were closest to the approaching horde, and the number of enemies was endless. Ted was now certain the men and women in the basement had been slaughtered. His attention was suddenly drawn to Will Tobin, who had stopped firing his weapon.

The pile of bodies littering the floor helped slow the progress of the creatures, but it didn't stop them. Will reloaded his rifle, slamming the last cartridge into the chamber, but the monsters were closer than ever. He raised the barrel and froze when one of the beasts lumbered in front of him. *No!* Will stared at the shirt the thing wore. It was a John Deere T-shirt covered in dirt and blood ... his blood froze in his veins. The creature was bald except for a few stubborn strands of hair that clung to its scalp, and its skin was a greyish green. Its head hung slack, and its features were deformed, but there was no denying. "Oh God, no," Will cried with the rifle trembling in his hands.

The creature that started out life as Eric Tobin lunged at the man in the doorway. It still wore the clothes it had on when the boy went missing Sunday afternoon. The John Deere shirt belonged to Will, but Eric was always borrowing it. Will lowered the rifle, backed up into the room, and his youngest child followed. The Eric-creature allowed its lower jaw to descend, revealing an impossible mouthful of teeth. It leapt at the man and tackled him to the floor.

"I'm sorry, son. Please forgive me," Will said as the thing lowered its horrible mouth to his neck. Will pulled the trigger of the .38 he had removed from his belt, and the back of Eric's head sprayed against the far wall. The body of the boy slumped into his father's arms. Will Tobin sat up and pulled Eric close. "Eric," the man cried. "What have they done to my boy?" Will had thought about turning the weapon on himself. But there was no way he could allow his own son to exist as an abomination. His face was deformed; his body was twisted. No father should have to see their child like that. The man sat on the floor holding his son, rocking back and forth as he had when Eric was a baby. "I'm so sorry," he repeated.

It was a burden Will Tobin wouldn't carry for long. Several small creatures scurried into the room and surrounded him. They moved much like spiders, and one appeared to have appendages growing from its abdomen. Their strange black eyes sized him up. Will raised the weapon and pointed it at the creature closest to him, but before he could fire, the beast opened its mouth and sprayed a hazy film. The filament latched onto his fingers, sealing his grip in place, making it impossible to pull the trigger.

THE OJANOX

As Will stared into the strange arachnid eyes, a second creature shuffled toward him and spread its jaws wide. There one second, gone the next. Will's anguish and burdens disappeared in a splash of red as the ghoul pounced on his chest and went to work with its sharp, sharp, teeth.

● ● ●

Grady Martin took position in the room directly across from Will Tobin and had an unobstructed view when the creature backed the man into the room. Three smaller creeps entered shortly afterward, and Will never returned to his post. It didn't take a genius to figure out what had happened. Grady considered himself fortunate for choosing the shotgun over the hunting rifle and had also grabbed a .45 as a sidearm. Both weapons were easy to reload, and Grady had a jacket full of extra magazines and shotgun shells. He unloaded on the approaching horde. The sound of gunfire echoed off every surface, and the din of the battle was intoxicating. The ink-like blood that oozed from the attackers' bodies covered the walls and ceilings and ran like a river down the center of the floor.

The smell of gunpowder and gore made Grady delirious. Sweat dripped from his brow and landed at his feet. Smoke filled the hallway and swirled about his head as if it had a life of its own; it tasted like copper pennies. The nauseating funk had begun to tickle in the very back of his throat. Grady struggled to breathe and fought to stay focused. Then he felt it between his eyes and at the base of his skull. An itch ... impossible to scratch ... it gnawed at him like a rat chewing into his soft tissue. Then he heard it.

Grady ...

He dropped the shotgun and froze in the doorway. Gunfire continued to erupt around him as the other members of the group fired blindly at their targets, unable to see due to the smoke. Grady listened to the voice as it gnawed deeper into his brain ... such a hungry little rat. A nibble here, a morsel there, until a sizable portion of the man had been devoured like a Triscuit.

Grady stepped into the line of fire but was somehow spared from being hit. He walked along the wall to where Alice Tobin stood. The woman's attention focused on the battle before her, she hadn't seen the man as he approached. She fired her last round and proceeded to reload the weapon. Sliding the last bullet into the cylinder, Alice looked up in time to see the .45 pointed at her temple.

Grady pulled the trigger, and the pistol discharged. The slug tore through the woman's head from point-blank range. Alice Tobin was dead before her body hit the floor—she had been one of the fortunate ones.

The four patients in the room where the body of Will Tobin lay had not been as fortunate. After the three spider-like beasts picked the man clean, they helped themselves to the sleeping patients. However, they weren't exactly sleeping, just unresponsive. All were hooked up to various life-support systems to keep their vital organs functioning. Three of the four were considered brain dead and didn't feel a thing when the arachnids began to nibble on them. But the patient in the furthest bed near the window had been in a coma.

It's said when you are in a coma, you are aware, you can hear people talking, touching your hand, even a change in temperature. But no one ever mentions what happens when a giant spider decides to turn you into a late-afternoon snack. The woman in the bed near the window could have enlightened the students at Johns Hopkins; she could have told them—you can feel it—you can feel every single excruciating nibble.

Doris watched the fireman raise his weapon and fire on Alice Tobin. Even through the dense cover of smoke, she could tell he was no longer himself. She followed the man in the sights of her revolver and pulled the trigger. The hollow click of the empty chamber resonated within her. Fumbling for the shells in her pocket, Doris sped through the task of reloading as Grady stepped over the woman's body and made his way toward the nurses' station. *Dear God, he's going to kill them.* She slammed the last round into the cylinder, raised the weapon, and fired. A large chunk of plaster wall vaporized behind him. She steadied her hand and focused on the area just above Grady's left ear and pressed on the trigger. The piercing sounds of breaking glass invaded the room behind her. Doris pivoted to see the beasts throw themselves through the window. They were on the beds in a frenzy, tearing into the patients.

Four hideous monstrosities had somehow scaled the exterior of the building and located their position. They scrambled over the window ledge and attacked the patients in the beds, not all of which were unresponsive. Doris watched the river of red spread out before her. One of the creatures threw itself at the wall and clung to it in a gravity-defying exhibition. It stared at Doris, licking its maw with a tongue that was much too long. It scurried toward the nurse, and she fired on it until she depleted her ammunition. It snapped its tongue in her direction, almost making contact, and that was all Doris needed to get her ass moving. She bolted into the hallway and headed to the farthest room. She prayed Burt wouldn't shoot her by mistake.

The horde advanced on Doris's position as she fled down the hall and darted through the doorway. She plowed into Burt, who was reloading his weapon. Doris frantically scanned the room to find Carole, Cyndi, and Dawn sitting on one of the beds. There was movement behind them ... shadows against the window. Doris saw the beasts just before they crashed through the glass.

"Look out!" she screamed.

Chapter 80

Carl sped away from the Fischer residence, leaving the house and carnage behind. He scanned the faces of his three young passengers in the rearview. Troy sat in the middle, between the girls, with tears streaming down his cheeks. The dark-haired girl occupied the passenger's side, her eyes vacant and her complexion a ghostly white. It had been too close of a call; only a matter of seconds and things would have turned out horribly different. Carl continued to check his passengers and noticed the blonde who sat directly behind him. The girl stared back at him, beaming with a huge smile on her face. Carl did a quick double take as their eyes met.

"Sheriff," she said, "you can kill them with magnets."

"What?" Carl's jaw dropped. "What did you say?"

"The Ojanox, you can kill them with magnets." She held up a wrist rocket and a handful of broken magnets. "That's why we left school. We needed to get weapons before it got dark."

Lois looked at Carl and then turned to Janis at the mention of the name.

"I'm sorry—" Carl squinted.

"Janis," she said.

"I'm sorry, Janis. But how do you know this, and what the hell is an Ojanox?"

"Those things out there, you can kill them with magnets, but they got to be really sharp," Janis continued. "My mom is an archeologist, and she's studying the cave at the quarry. She's known about the Ojanox for years."

Carl could see the girl's testimony had a soothing effect on the other children, who were now ready to chime in. Troy fidgeted in his seat, busting to speak up.

"How do you know they're called Ojanox?" Carl asked.

"That's what Mom called them," Troy said. "She told us the story, then they chased me through the graveyard on Monday. Wendy said they sounded like Ojanox because how they hid and tried to get me."

"What the hell is an Ojanox?" He turned to Lois and shrugged, wondering how three fourth graders had done a better job than his entire department. They'd figured out what was happening, given it a name, and made him look about as inept as all the three stooges put together.

"I told the kids a ghost story Saturday night at the party," Lois said. "It was a combination of something I wrote in college and a little improv. I made up the name years ago, Ojanox, mostly because I liked the way it looked on paper. Troy didn't care for it much." She looked at her son in the backseat, who crinkled his nose as if he smelled something rancid. "I'm sorry I didn't believe you the other day. You said something chased you; I thought it might be a dog or you were confused. I'm so sorry, kiddo."

"It's okay, Mom," Troy said.

"Oh, I get it." Carl nodded. "But how did you figure out the magnets?"

"My mother has pictures of what they found at Cahokia. And Troy said the cave up at the quarry had weapons just like it and they were all made of lodestone."

"What!?" He turned to Lois again. "What cave? How come I'm just hearing about this? Why didn't anyone at DuCain notify me?"

Lois shrugged and raised her hands. "I figured you knew."

The radio crackled before Carl could finish. *"Deputy Lutchen to anyone in the basement. Come in, over."* Carl held his breath and waited for someone to answer Ted's call. He knew the medical center's basement wasn't that secure and had wanted to get Lois and Troy to the high school instead. Still, her sister's family was there, and if something happened, and it sounded like it already might have, Lois would never forgive herself. Silence filled the cab as they waited for a reply.

Janis looked across the backseat to her friends and offered a toothy grin, which seemed to ease their apprehension. It was amazing what one look could do, and Janis had the ability to affect the world with her bright eyes and genuine smile. It helped comfort Wendy especially, who struggled to maintain her tough exterior; the little Italian girl relaxed a bit, then returned the gesture.

Janis was just happy to finally have friends who liked her for who she was. The first day of school, when she walked into the classroom, all the boys started acting goofy, just like the boys in her old school. But not Troy, he had smiled and said hello while the other kids were snickering and whispering to each other. Troy hadn't acted like a dork just because of her changing body.

She was self-conscious about the stupid things as it was and couldn't wear half her clothes anymore. Everything was either too tight or made her look ridiculous; at least that's what Janis thought. At first, she tried to hide them, telling her mom and aunt how much she hated being a girl. They tried to console her and told Janis one day she would feel comfortable and maybe even like them. But she didn't think it likely. And the idea of the new school was terrifying. Especially after the way the boys in her old school acted. They all wanted to talk to her; they acted goofy and said the dumbest things. Now she would be walking into a new classroom with her new boobs, and everyone was going to see them. And she had been right. Miss Walsh introduced her, and all the boys snickered; even the girls gave her dirty looks. Janis had wanted to crawl into a hole and die.

Then at lunch, she noticed Troy and Wendy sitting by themselves, sharing their sandwiches, and acting like grown-ups. Janis didn't know if it was jealousy, but she thought it would be nice to have a friend like that. Someone to talk to and share her lunch with; someone who didn't act like a total dork. The girl seemed nice too, but that wasn't why she first approached them. She wanted to know the boy who was immune to the power of the boobies.

"Hi," she'd said. "Can I sit with you? Those boys are acting silly." And that was how it all started. Wendy and Troy welcomed her and treated her like one of them. It was obvious Troy was uncomfortable, but Janis thought that it was kind of cute. And he never stared at her boobs; in fact, he deliberately didn't look at them. So, she decided to mess with him and asked him why the other boys were treating her different. Wendy knew what she was up to and played along. It made Troy even more uncomfortable, and it looked like he was about to explode when he finally shouted, "It's because you have boobs!"

It was priceless. There was something about Troy that was refreshing, and he and Wendy made her feel like she was going to fit in after all. She had missed the chance to go to the Halloween party by less than a week and wished she had moved to town sooner. It probably wouldn't have made a difference, but she wondered … If she did, maybe Troy would have kissed someone else instead of Wendy … maybe.

Janis looked across the seat and smiled at her new friends. Both Wendy and Troy returned the gesture, which made her feel better than she had in a long time. They made her feel like she belonged in Garrett Grove.

● ● ●

Andrea Geary's head spun from the sensory overload coming at her from every direction. The shelter at the high school was a flurry of activity. The ocean of faces and the roar of a thousand different conversations was intoxicating, but it was a thankful respite. For the moment, thoughts of Joel and of her loss had been put to the side as she busied herself helping others. She handed out blankets, assisted children and the elderly, and answered as many questions as she possibly could—but most of which she was unable.

"Have you seen my boy?" a distraught woman asked.

"How long do we have to stay down here?" an older gentleman questioned.

"I can't find my mommy. Have you seen my mommy?" a frightened girl cried.

"Excuse me, but could you tell me where the bathroom is?" That was one question she could answer. The others were impossible to, and each one chiseled at her heart. She took it all in, all the faces, all of the pain, and all of the loss.

But every now and then, she would be offered a glimmer of hope and see an entire family lucky enough to have been reunited. Unfortunately, luck was in short supply and most of the families in Garrett Grove had not walked away intact. Andrea smiled at Günter Bentley from the A&P, who sat with his wife and three golden-haired daughters. The girls looked as if they had stepped out of a nursery rhyme as they huddled in close to their father. Principal Grace had gathered no less than fifty children and occupied their interest with a story she was telling. Another cluster of children flocked around a woman and her pet beagle. The dog was in heaven from the attention the children gave it and at serious risk of overdosing on belly rubs.

Andrea handed out the last of the blankets and turned down the small hallway toward the ladies' room. She rounded the corner and stopped short; one of the firemen had a man in a bright paisley shirt backed up against the wall and was in the process of giving him a serious mouth-to-mouth session. The men separated when they noticed Andrea. The one against the wall pressed his lips and smirked, while the fireman attempted to act as if nothing had happened, like Andrea hadn't seen him with his tongue in the other guy's throat. She excused herself and proceeded to the ladies' room.

Andrea entered the bathroom to find Jill Boriello running her hands at the sink and staring into the mirror. The woman reacted to the deputy's uniform and introduced herself. "Can you tell me anything about what's going on out there?" the teacher asked.

"I don't know much, really." Andrea forced the same smile she'd been offering for the past two hours. "Right now, this is the safest place you could be."

"I went to my neighbor's house this morning," Jill said. "She was missing, and the place had been torn apart."

Andrea's upper lip began to tremble, and then the lump in her throat she had so far managed to swallow rose and nearly choked her. A half second later, the first tear leaked from the corner of her eye. "I'm sorry," she cried. "I lost someone today."

"I'm so sorry." Jill gasped. "That was horrible of me."

"No-no." Andrea brushed it off and attempted to control herself. "We've all lost someone. I know things are insane and you're scared. I'll tell you what I know."

Jill Boriello took the deputy's hand and listened to everything she had to say about the disappearances that plagued the town, starting with the death of Felix Castillo, up to the sheriff's decision to evacuate everyone into the shelters. Her reactions were a mixture of shock and awe and even understanding. Then she told the deputy how three of her own students had addressed the entire student body earlier today. Somehow, the kids knew what was going on, while the parents and teachers were in the dark. Then the boy and the two girls vanished during the fire drill, just before the world went to hell.

"Has there been any word on the missing children from my class?" Jill asked.

"I'm sorry." Andrea frowned. "Our radios don't work in the shelter, but I know the sheriff is looking. He'll find them."

"I pray that he does. I'll never forgive myself if something happens to them." Jill let out a muted cry. "You see, I'm the kindergarten teacher, and this morning, Troy asked if I even knew how to teach fourth grade. I guess I don't. I mean ... I lost three kids on my first day."

Andrea took the teacher in her arms as she broke down and sobbed onto her shoulder. There was nothing she could say to take away her burden. There was so much sadness in the basement of the shelter you could feel it in the air. It was heavy; it had weight. Andrea herself had every right to cry and to mourn the loss of her coworkers and the man she loved. And Jill Boriello had every right to mourn the loss of her neighbor and the disappearance of her students. If you couldn't cry over missing children, then what could you cry over? The woman had every right to feel her pain, and who was Andrea to talk her out of it? She'd earned it; they all had.

The teacher jumped at the sound of someone throwing a firecracker just outside the bathroom door. Jill looked at the deputy with frantic eyes, searching for answers. But Andrea thought differently of the sound and rushed the woman into one of the bathroom stalls.

"Whatever you do." Andrea stared her in the eyes. "Stay down and don't come out." The deputy unholstered her weapon and closed the stall door, leaving the teacher inside.

Jill covered her ears as the roar of semi-automatic weapons fire cannoned from somewhere in the shelter. The woman began to cry as bullets rattled off the concrete ceiling and echoed in the old, moldy bathroom.

Chapter 81

The pump and ladder trucks pulled in behind one another. Tank Ferguson and Gabriel Ford had canvassed the town, delivered their message, and made it back safely. And they had each done one better in the process. The cabs and even the backs of the vehicles were loaded with passengers both men had picked up along the way. Nearly forty people in total clung to the ladders and side walls of the fire trucks and jumped off when they arrived at the back entrance of the school.

Bob Jones and Brandon Canfield assisted the soaking wet passengers to safety and directed them into the shelter. Then one of the yellow school buses pulled in behind the trucks. Bob thought they had all been parked in the back lot and had no idea someone had taken one out. The door opened, and a swarm of people exited and made their way to the gym. The group shuffled along at a snail's pace, using their canes and walkers to assist themselves along.

Botany Village, the senior house! Bob realized they had forgotten about the place. He cursed himself as he made his way to the bus. *How could I be so stupid?* He leaned to look inside and found a smiling Anthony Leone staring back at him.

After delivering a busload of screaming first graders, Anthony had second thoughts about spending the night in the shelter. In fact, he had more than just second thoughts and had taken the school bus with every intention of riding it out on his own. That was until he passed Botany Village and saw the frightened faces staring at him from the windows. They had forgotten about the place; no one had been sent to take care of the town's senior population. There was no way they could make it to the shelter on their own.

So, Anthony pulled into the lot, went from door to door, and loaded everyone on the bus. He had driven by thinking only of himself and was caught completely off guard when the altruistic inspiration overcame him. It was as if his own heart had grown—three sizes like the Grinch himself. The crowd from Botany were so grateful they had broken into a few verses of "For He's a Jolly Good Fellow." Who would have thought Anthony Leone a jolly good fellow? Certainly not Bob, or Anthony, for that matter.

Bob was about to say something, couldn't find the exact words, and gave Anthony a thumbs-up like he was Fonzie. The sound of screeching tires alerted him to the police cruiser as it pulled in. He half expected to see Carl; instead, Deputy Rainey exited the vehicle and proceeded straight to the trunk. The man removed several rifles and a large bag, then made his way across the pavement toward the front doors.

"Deputy Rainey, what's it looking like out there? Did you see the sheriff or any of my men in the cruisers?"

Rainey kept his head down and stared at the pavement to keep the rain from hitting him in the face. "It's not good; the town looks like a war zone. I stayed behind at the school to make sure everyone got out, then did a quick once-over down the Turnpike. No sign of the sheriff or your men. Those things are everywhere; we need to lock this place up right away." Rainey stepped into the gym and out of the rain, then proceeded to make his way to the shelter.

"Deputy," Bob called to him. "Shouldn't we wait for the sheriff? I've still got men out there!"

Rainey spun around like a water moccasin. His face was white as death, and he looked as if he had seen the devil himself. "If the sheriff isn't here in five minutes, it's because he's already dead. The same thing goes for your men." Water dripped from the deputy's clothes and the arsenal he carried with him. "If we're going to keep these people alive, we need to lock the doors before it's too late."

"Understood," Bob replied, and stepped back as the deputy turned and headed across the wooden floor toward the basement. The deputy had seen something terrible out there. Bob didn't want to imagine what might happen if even one of

THE OJANOX

those horrors found their way into the basement. Rainey was right; they couldn't wait much longer; it was getting darker by the second. Bob picked up his radio and made one last try. After that ...

● ● ●

Deputy David Rainey walked across the gym floor toward the entrance of the shelter, paying no attention to the trail of rainwater left in his wake. He toted two rifles slung over his shoulder and transferred the duffle bag from his right hand to his left. He had loaded it with as much ammo as he could fit. The M1 Carbine had been his father's in WWII. The old man had mailed the Garand back home piece by piece once the war had ended, and Uncle Sam had been none the wiser. It was a reliable weapon and a favorite among servicemen for years. David had fired it only a few times, since you couldn't just take a semi-automatic weapon up to Garrett Mountain. But the sheriff had allowed it at the range from time to time, mostly because he wanted to fire it himself. It was an impressive firearm with lethal stopping power. David had been compelled to stop by his house and transfer the gun to the trunk of his cruiser. But for some reason, he had no memory of ever doing so.

He rubbed his temples, trying to soothe the dull thud that had settled between his eyes and the sides of his head. It was an annoying ache, constant and grating, and one he couldn't shake. David approached the door to the stairwell and stepped inside. He gazed down the long set of steps, remembering he had been there just earlier today. It felt longer than that, and even longer since he had gotten any sleep. More than anything, David Rainey just wanted to close his eyes, needed to, but there was no time. There was work to be done.

David stepped onto the landing, engaged the deadbolt, and descended the steps toward the shelter. Closing the basement door behind him, David placed the duffle bag on the floor and looked out across the room. *Dear God! There's so many of them. How did they all get here? And how long before they realize I've discovered their nest?* He moved slow and deliberate, removing the weapons from his shoulder. He placed the M1 to the side and wedged the other rifle between the doorknob and the floor.

"Carl, this is Bob, come in." The radio remained silent, not even the static audible over the thundering drive of the rain. "Bob Jones to Sheriff Primrose, come in."

He waited and then tried to reach the other men. Glenn Gillick and Mike Turino were in patrol cruisers delivering the evacuation message. Neither man answered. Bob's stomach twisted as he waited for a reply from any of them. Something had happened; he was sure of it. A cross between what the deputy said and the feeling in his gut told him neither Carl nor his men were coming. There was nothing left to do but chain the doors. The lives of every person in the basement depended on it.

"Carl, I don't know if you can hear me, but I'm locking the doors. If you're out there I hope you're somewhere safe. Jesus Christ, Carl, answer me!" Bob tightened his fist against the radio and prayed.

"If anyone can hear me, God be with you." Bob waited for Brandon to enter the building and closed the doors behind him. The men laced the large chain through the handles and padlocked it shut. The gravity of the moment hung in the air like a dead man at the end of a noose. Neither said a word as they made their way to the entrance of the shelter on the opposite side of the gym.

The first gunshot sounded more like a firecracker than a bullet. The second and third happened in rapid succession, causing Bob to freeze in mid-step. *Was that a gunshot? Why on Earth would someone be shooting a weapon?* The singular bursts were followed by the sound of semi-automatic weapon fire. Bob bolted across the wood floor like a cheetah. *Dear God!* There were women and senior citizens down there, and there were so many children!

The gathered horde still hadn't noticed him, but soon they would. David worked fast, unzipping the duffle bag and loading as many extra magazines as possible into his pockets and waistband. He replaced his .38 with a .40 and added several extra magazines to his belt as well. There was no way he could take out all of them, but he had to try while he still had the element of surprise. David positioned himself in

THE OJANOX

a shallow nook beside the door, which offered a clear view of the entire basement. He raised the M1 eye level, sighted the first beast, and placed his finger on the trigger.

●●●

Peanuts lay on her back with her paws in the air as the children took turns rubbing her belly. Lynn Donovan did her best to entertain the kids from Janis's elementary school and keep their minds occupied, but Peanuts stole the show. The pup let out a noise from the back of her throat that sounded like she was moaning, and her eyes rolled back in her head.

Lynn had arrived at the high school to find Janis and her two friends had gone missing during the fire drill. She was ready to go back out and look for them but had been stopped by the fire chief, who said no one could leave the school. Lynn herself had been pursued by something monstrous on her way to the shelter. It looked part sea creature and part man but behaved like nothing she had seen in her life. She thought if this was an acid flashback, it was the worst trip ever.

"Is this your dog?" Lynn looked up at the man who spoke. He had dark hair, appeared close to her age, and wore a shirt with a FD insignia on it.

"This is Peanuts," the young girl rubbing the pup's belly replied.

Lynn got up from the floor and extended her hand. "Hi, I'm Lynn Donovan."

"Nice to meet you. Drew Halberg with the fire department. Just making my rounds, seeing if everyone is all right."

"Do all firemen carry guns?" she asked, noticing the weapon on his hip.

"Well, it's just a precautionary measure."

"I hope you don't expect to have to use it down here."

"You know what they say," he told her. "Better to have one and not need it than the other way around."

"Like a condom," Lynn laughed.

Drew's face turned red at the remark. "Yeah, something like that."

Now that Lynn was on her feet, she was better able to see and noticed just how many men in the basement were armed. Firemen with shotguns mulled around as if they were on patrol; some carried weapons on their hips. There were several other men in the crowd who had taken up arms as well.

"I feel safer already," she said, her attention drawn to the deputy who had just entered the shelter and closed the door behind him. Drew continued to talk, but Lynn focused on the young officer as he placed a bag on the floor and then wedged one of his weapons against the door. There was something off about the way the guy was acting, scanning the room with his wild eyes and then proceeding to load ammunition into his pockets. He looked as if he were terrified—as if he were preparing for something.

"I haven't seen you around. Are you new in town?" Drew asked.

Lynn hadn't heard a word he said. "I'm sorry, but do you know that guy over there?"

Drew Halberg turned to the door and began to walk toward the man who had backed up against the wall. "Deputy Rainey," Drew called. "What the heck are you doing over there?"

Lynn watched the color drain from the deputy's face when the fireman called to him. Panic and fear flooded his features, and suddenly, Lynn knew what the deputy intended to do. She opened her mouth to yell as the man stepped out from the nook and raised his weapon. But time was either moving too fast or it had stopped completely, and Lynn was unable to speak. Then the deputy fired.

Lynn jumped as something wet splashed across her face and into her open mouth. She looked down and saw the red splattered across her shirt. The fireman standing in front of her swayed for a moment and then fell to his side on the concrete. Lynn stood in shock, not sure what was happening.

"Drew," she called out.

The deputy fired again, and Lynn knew exactly what was going on. One of the men patrolling the basement screamed and fell onto his back as the deputy's bullet caught him in the chest. The sound of a third bullet echoed off the ceiling like an avalanche. Then the deputy unloaded his weapon at a feverish pace, sweeping the barrel of his gun from left to right, into the crowd. Lynn darted around and threw herself at the group of children. She pushed them to the floor, attempting to shield everyone as they wiggled and squirmed from the concussion of each explosion.

Gunfire ripped through the shelter like cherry bombs in a toilet. Another man was thrown backward as the deputy's bullets tore into him. Chips of concrete flew into the air as weapon fire ricocheted off every surface. Screams and cries of terror lifted from the trapped citizens, who scrambled to flee from the attack but had nowhere to run. Men, women, and even children were caught in the crosshairs of Deputy Rainey's weapon and slaughtered in a bath of crimson.

Lynn struggled to protect the children but was losing her grip to gather them together. "No!" screamed the girl who had been rubbing the dog's belly. She jumped to her feet and ran from the man with the gun. Lynn watched as the deputy turned his weapon on the child and drew down on her. *God no!* Lynn rose to her feet and took off after her. The girl hadn't gotten far, and Lynn snatched her up and cradled her like a bag of groceries. She shielded the child and attempted to crouch as low as she could.

The explosion from the deputy's weapon was more jarring than the bullet that entered her back. It felt no worse than getting hit with a snowball; cold at first, then her legs gave out from under her. Lynn dropped the child and fell to the floor. She tried to reach for the little girl, who simply stood there. "Get down," she managed. But she was already too late. A pinprick of red appeared on the front of the girl's dress. It grew to the size of a quarter and then to that of a grapefruit. The child fell on her back and was quiet.

Lynn was aware of movement, a great deal of it, and the fading resonance of sound. Children and adults running in every direction, bodies falling, and surfaces painted red. The rapid fire had been replaced by the methodical blast of single shots, and then there was another sound. Growling and barking followed by a horrible whimper and the echo of the gun. Lynn raised her head enough to see the small body laying at the feet of the monster. "No, Peanuts," she cried. Lynn Donovan lowered her head and stopped breathing.

●●●

Deputy Rainey discarded the spent rifle and removed the pistol from his holster. He fired into the throng of deformities, making head shots when he could and avoiding their counterattacks. The creatures had infected far more of the town's population than either he or the sheriff anticipated. Men, women, and so many children had been compromised, taken over by the virus and turned into something unimaginable. Their deformed features and hideous bodies rose up and turned on him, but David was fast and laid waste to their suffering. The roar of the fight was so consuming he never noticed the constant itch deep within his skull, and the voice inside him sounded too much like his own to be anything else.

● ● ●

A group of children from the fourth-grade class had spent the afternoon gathered around Principal Grace, playing games and listening to stories. Kelly Rainey, Caroline Smith, and Scott Cole sat together, giddy, punch-drunk, and feeling more and more apprehensive as the minutes passed. Some of the children's parents made it to the shelter, but for everyone that did show up, there were at least two who had not. Kelly saw her brother, David, when he entered through the basement door. She perked up and left the group to approach him. He didn't notice her and went straight to checking his equipment and locking the door.

Then David stepped out and started shooting. Kelly jumped at the sound of the first explosion, her breath frozen in her chest and every hair on her body stood at attention. A man in the crowd screamed and then fell to the floor. Kelly wondered what the man had done. There had to be some reason why her brother would shoot him. David turned his gun on another person. Bullets sailed past Kelly's head as he fired into the crowd, connecting with one of the third graders from her school. And then he started shooting at the mothers, and the fathers, and even more of the children. *What's happening?* It was more than Kelly's ten-year-old mind could comprehend; she stood fast, unable to move as her brother gunned down her friends and classmates.

"Get down, Kelly!" Principal Grace screamed and ran towards her.

Kelly turned in time to see the bright splatch of crimson spread out across the front of Scott Cole's shirt. The boy fell backward onto the floor, causing the other children of the group to scream and take off running. David shot them in the back, picking them off one by one. A spray of bullets danced across the arms of Mrs. Smith, who attempted to shield her daughter from the attack. Both she and Caroline fell together amongst the other bodies.

Principal Grace dove at Kelly and tackled her to the floor. Kelly struggled to breathe as the weight of the principal bore down on her. Somewhere off to her right, she could hear a dog barking. She twisted and turned under the woman's weight and managed to slide out from underneath her. Principal Grace stared at

THE OJANOX

Kelly without blinking as the bullets exploded around them. A thin line of blood trickled from a small hole in the woman's forehead. The little that was left of Kelly's resolve vanished like a wisp of smoke.

A shadow crossed her face as she sat with tears in her eyes. Kelly looked up into the barrel of the gun pointed at her head. It was her brother, only it wasn't David at all. The face she saw was contorted and twisted and unrecognizable.

David stared down at the small creature on the floor before him and pressed his finger to the trigger. Then one of the firemen rushed forward, grabbing at his weapon. The men wrestled and stumbled backward over the litter of bodies. David managed to throw the fireman aside and turned his weapon on him, firing several bullets into the man. He scanned the room for the target he had been focused on but was unable to locate it. He moved on to his next, emptied his weapon, and reloaded a fresh magazine.

Kelly had crawled back beneath the body of Principal Grace. She cried and covered her ears, struggling to block the sound of her brother's bullets. But the resonating sound of the weapon and the cries of her classmates would stay with Kelly the rest of her life.

Andrea opened the bathroom door and stepped into the roar of semi-automatic weapon fire. She crouched low as she made her way through the hall toward the shelter. The sound of women screaming and children crying was just audible over the deafening concussions. Someone was unloading the hammers of hell on the people of Garrett Grove. Andrea turned the corner with her weapon drawn and stopped in her tracks.

She watched David Rainey as he tossed an old semi-automatic rifle to the side and drew a pistol. *Christ, where did he get a weapon like that?* She scanned the tangled mass of bodies through the haze of red. David had to have fired at least five magazines on the crowd. So much blood, so many bodies, and far too many of them were children. It was impossible to tell who was living and who was dead amidst the gun smoke and crimson. She held her breath as her partner approached a woman and shot her in the head.

No!" Andrea broke cover and fired. Her first bullet went wide; she pulled the trigger again as she advanced. Rainey turned and raised his weapon in her direction, but Andrea rushed him and fired. "Drop it, David!"

The bullet hit David Rainey in the shoulder. The features of his face suddenly changed as he looked down at the wound and examined the blood with his fingers. He looked back at Andrea with a question on his lips and confusion in his eyes, but the moment of recognition vanished. David's face twisted into a snarl; he lifted his gun in Andrea's direction.

She felt the slug bite into her thigh and almost toppled over from the pain. Struggling to maintain her focus, she gritted her teeth and pulled the trigger. David fell backward as the bullet took him in the chest. He lay on the floor flailing and scrambling to get back on his feet.

Andrea closed the distance between them as fast as her injured leg would allow. She came up on the deputy and kicked his weapon to the side. Blood sprayed from his mouth; he looked up at her with fear and hatred in his eyes. Then in a flash, his features softened, and the glaze in his stare lifted.

"Andrea." He coughed. "You have to help me. They're everywhere."

She stood over him with her weapon drawn. "What are you talking about? Why, David?" The gun trembled in her hands as the tears fell from her cheeks and hit the red-stained floor.

"They're infected. I had to kill the monsters; I had to put them down. Just like I did for Kovach."

Andrea's breath stopped cold. Her eyes blurred as Rainey's words slipped between her ribs like a dagger and pierced her heart. *Just like I did for Kovach.* They continued to resonate on an endless loop. *Just like I did for Kovach.* The gun wavered in her hands; her throat tightened, and the tears flowed without resistance. The slow tremors in her arms ebbed throughout her entire body and raked deep within. The man she loved, dear sweet Joel, gunned down by one of their own. Killed by David Rainey in cold blood. Andrea forced herself to focus past the pain in her chest and allowed the throbbing in her leg to propel her anger even further. She aimed her weapon at the man who killed Joel Kovach and exhaled.

"You're the only monster I see," she hissed and pulled the trigger.

The presence had first invaded Deputy David Rainey's head Sunday night at the morgue as he stood over the reanimated body of Abe Gorman. It invaded him a second time that afternoon in the girl's bathroom at the elementary school, only this time, it left something behind. Just a suggestion, an itch the deputy felt compelled to scratch. It was impossible to ignore and too tempting to refuse. It played with David as if he were no more than an ant beneath a magnifying glass, ransacking his brain like a thief until it found exactly what it was looking for. It saw the semi-automatic weapon David owned and seized the opportunity. It was exactly what was needed to reduce the simple ones' numbers and render them defenseless. David had no recollection of stopping at the house, using his service revolver, and leaving his parents' bodies lying in the kitchen. He also didn't remember removing the weapons and blowing out the pilot light before leaving. When David entered the shelter at the high school, he believed he had finally stumbled upon the creature's nest and that he was looking at those who had already fallen to the beast. David would never remember raising his weapon on his own sister and nearly pulling the trigger.

It had ransacked his brain twice, but there would never be a third. David Rainey would never have to live with the knowledge of what he had done. He would never know the number of children he had slaughtered or parents he had gunned down in cold blood. And the last thing to invade David Rainey's brain was the .38 caliber slug fired by his coworker Andrea Geary.

Chapter 82

The men working at the quarry saw the abominations descend the cliff face, but no one was able to digest what they were seeing until it was too late. By then, the strange insect-like creatures were already upon them. Mark and Buzzy fled toward the trailers with a handful of the other rockhounds but were outmatched by the speed of the beasts. The stingers at the ends of their tails were not only sharp but dripped an ancient poison more lethal than any other known to man. It possessed the equivalent toxicity of the box jellyfish and the blue-ringed octopus combined. This particular brand of venom had disappeared when the dinosaurs went extinct—which was a good thing; otherwise, nothing else would have ever populated the blue planet.

The scorpion-human hybrids were joined by other creatures a bit more humanoid in appearance, although not entirely. The large, deformed zombies appeared to have maintained a better hold on their own DNA signature than the insects had. However, the flood of new information being transmitted to their mitochondria as well as their own DNA sent their bodies' cellular processors into overdrive. It was impossible to translate. In some cases, the rapid transfer altered the host to its original primitive state. But in most, the human body found the multiple genetic codes impossible to decipher, resulting in a transformation into myriad creatures.

It was a collector, a harvester, and had consumed information since the beginning of time. The simple ones were easily molded and made the perfect foot soldiers. They were malleable but far from impervious. They could only last so long with its seed inside them. But the young, the children were much stronger and could last a great deal longer. They were the only vessel powerful enough to contain its true essence.

It had divided into three, the original three, and had kept them safe. The one called Butchie was there to protect, but the flesh of the simple ones had grown weak. Even the original three were waning, and the time to replace them was soon.

It could have chosen any of the children from town, but after possessing the mind of Robert Boyle and tasting his friend in the graveyard, it craved the one called Troy. The child had made a game of creating fear, and that was a consciousness worth possessing. A controller of fear could possibly withstand the whole of its presence. Soon, it would have the child; it was just a matter of time.

Stephanie's father, Dr. Edgar Donovan, had studied the disappearance of civilizations for the greater part of his career. Countless depictions similar to those in the DuCain cavern had been found across the globe. From the Indus River Valley to the Olmecs, and even the Mayans, the correlation of recorded events was near identical. The die-off of biological life in each location always coincided with archeological findings that were beyond explanation. The possible causation of such led Dr. Donovan and his colleagues to dig deeper into more recent occurrences, specifically those taking place in the new world. There had been at least three between the years 1400 and 1600, the first being Cahokia, also known as America's forgotten city, located in modern-day Illinois. Cahokia was home to somewhere between 10,000 and 20,000 Native Americans who simply vanished overnight. Similar paintings and unidentifiable teeth were uncovered at the site. An animal skull had been found containing human molars that had been drilled and filled with gold. There had been the lost colony of Roanoke in 1587, where Donovan had worked the excavation himself. And then there was the disappearance of the Lenape Tribe in the eastern US, which occurred somewhere around 1600. All previous excavations showed a recorded history of each civilization's battle with an unstoppable force. One Donovan and his partners referred to as The Dark One.

Stephanie followed in her father's footsteps, studying at his side for years and then taking over the research after his death. Together, they postulated that the force responsible for countless disappearances, the Entity called The Dark One, had originated from antimatter. They also believed it to be cognizant. As a juxtaposition to matter, the Dark One was the antithesis of creation. Thinking in terms of matter as creation, the destructive force of antimatter wasn't that far of a stretch.

The battle between good and evil was recorded in every religion and in every culture. The monotheistic God didn't come about until somewhere around 5000 B.C. Evidence of this Entity had been around much longer than that. In fact, the Dark One appeared to be present since there were hands to record it. It was the original evil, the original sin. And Stephanie believed this Entity was the inspiration behind the story of the Devil himself. She also believed it was the originator of nearly every mythological creature story known to man, from the Kraken to the werewolf and even the vampire.

There were countless names for the Entity and far too much evidence to ignore. The signature teeth were found in each location, usually alongside weapons manufactured from magnetite. The only other information Stephanie Thompson was sure of was the Entity's preoccupation with children. She couldn't explain why, although she had a working theory.

●●●

A second beast stood at the entrance of the cave with blood dripping from its stinger. It approached the small opening and backed away howling as if it had been scalded. The onyx eyes surveyed the area for a breach in the defenses and found none. It reared back on its haunches, exposing a lamella-lined abdomen, and screamed; the humanish face at the end of the monster contorted as it stared at Stephanie. Again, she raised the ancient weapon in the direction of the abomination and threatened to unleash her arsenal. The display was effective, and the scorpion retreated into the quarry, then sped off toward the trailers in search of a more accessible meal.

Don stood behind her, half-concealed by a small outcropping, with his analytical mind performing calisthenics. *It's not possible.* He searched for logic and rational explanations and found none. Gail's blood was still wet on his brow. He held out his palms and stared at the exaggerated tremble of his hands. It radiated into his chest and threatened to overtake him. Everything Stephanie had said, all the insanity about lost civilizations and entities—it had all been true. But that was impossible. He opened his mouth to speak, but a dry croak was all that left his lips. Don reached out and grabbed the rock to steady himself as the world turned grey around him. Outside, the fire whistle stopped ringing, leaving only the shrieks of the creatures and the screams from the last of their victims.

Stephanie lowered the weapon and approached him. "Are you all right?" she asked.

Don shook his head. "I—I didn't—"

"Easy, you've got to breathe or you're going to pass out." She placed the musket balls and weapon on the rock in front of Don and took him by the shoulders. "Easy, in and out, like that."

He followed her lead and focused on his breathing. He was certain he would faint, and then the moment passed. After several seconds, he looked up at her and spoke. "I'm sorry I didn't believe you."

Stephanie offered a half-smile and wiped the tears from her face. She had been able to act and fend off their attacker but was struggling just as much as he was. She held up her hand and steadied herself. "It's impossible to believe. Not something I ever imagined witnessing in my own lifetime."

"You said this thing is responsible for the disappearance at Cahokia." Now the questions were flooding into Don's head at a faster pace than he could process and spit out. "Where has it been all this time? Why did it wait till now to show up?"

"I don't think it waited, exactly. I think maybe it was either trapped in here or hibernating in your cave."

Don swayed and clutched at the rock. "You're telling me I let this thing out?!"

"You wanted to make a name for yourself in the field of geology—congratulations."

It hit Don in a frenzy, the vandalism at the quarry, the missing explosives, the destruction of the bridge and the Sunset Pass. His heart beat faster as he realized the implications. "Jesus Christ! Just how intelligent is this thing? Is it capable of tactical thought?"

Stephanie pressed her lips together and tilted her head. "Well, how intelligent would something have to be to wipe out an entire civilization?"

Don knew the answer before he even asked. It was Combat 101. If you wanted to conquer your enemies, the first thing you needed to do was isolate them—destroy every escape route and leave them trapped. Then you could pick them off one by one. *For fuck's sake, Garrett Grove's cut off from the rest of the world.* And Lois and Troy were out there in the middle of it.

He had been so worried about himself, about his job, and hadn't stopped to think about his family. *What have I done?* But Don knew. He had been the same guy he had always been, only caring about Don, only focused on his own life, and the hell with everyone else. He prayed there was still time, that it wasn't already too late.

"We have to get back to town and warn everyone. They have no idea what they're up against."

"You wouldn't last five minutes out there." Stephanie walked to the tangle of bones in the center of the floor and removed the stone dagger from the remains. She tested the balance of the lodestone weapon and slid it behind her belt. "I know what you're thinking. I need to help my family too, but we're no good to them dead. And this cave is the only thing protecting us from being ripped apart. Our only chance of helping them is in the daylight. I'm sorry, but we have to wait till morning."

"We can't just sit here. We need to warn them."

Stephanie pointed to the opening, where several of the massive arachnids gathered at a distance. "I'd say from the sound of the sirens, they already know."

Don hated it but knew she was right. They would never make it even if they tried. The things outside hovered near the cave's entrance, never daring to step too close. They appeared to be more afraid of the cave itself than they were of the actual weapons, which had taken more than a few shots to be effective. He knew their only chance of survival was to wait inside the safety of the cavern, at least until morning. He prayed that daylight would offer the protection they needed to make it back to town. "So, how the hell do we stop these things?"

"Are you serious?" She turned toward him and shook her head as if he hadn't been paying attention. "This thing has been around forever. It's responsible for the disappearance of countless civilizations, hundreds of thousands of people—and that's just the ones we know about. You don't stop it; you can only get the fuck out of its way."

"Oh bullshit!" Don barked. "It's vulnerable to lodestone, to magnetism, that means it has a weakness and can be stopped. It must have a metallic signature in its makeup if magnetite affects it adversely. The Lenape figured out a way to trap it, and it would still be stuck in this cave if I hadn't come along and blown it up."

"I said maybe it was trapped. Or maybe it was just sleeping. The point is, nothing anyone has done in the past has been effective because it keeps coming back. I think it only goes away once the food source is depleted in its hunting grounds. Right now, it's found a home in Garrett Grove, and it's not going to stop until it's destroyed everything in its path." She stared at him, out of breath with tears streaming down her cheeks.

"So, what are you suggesting we do?"

"We wait till morning, then we go find our families and get out of town. I don't care if we have to walk over the mountain all the way to California."

"I thought this was the chance of a lifetime to study your father's work." Don wished he could take back the words as soon as they left his lips.

"I can't study it if I'm dead," Stephanie hissed. "I'm a scientist, not a statistic. You of all people should understand that."

Her words cut back at him like a broadsword, and he deserved that. "I'm sorry. I'm just not ready to write off the entire town. We can't even be sure how many of those things are out there. For all we know"—he pointed to the entrance—"that could be it. Somehow it got stuck in this cave, either trapped or hibernating. And if it was trapped, the Lenape figured out a way to lure it inside." The analytical gears and pistons were firing again, and he was able to think straight. "There are only a few skeletons in here, so the Lenape didn't lure an army of creatures in here; they lured the Entity itself. Whatever this thing really is, it was trapped inside this cave."

Don picked up one of the flashlights and started walking as he reasoned the impossible possibilities of the scenario. "Okay, if this thing is an Entity, like you said, then it has to have a main consciousness. A central intelligence hidden somewhere. When a country goes to war, the president doesn't join the troops on the frontline. Shit! You killed that thing with a handful of rocks. Why would it expose itself? If it were me, I would be holed up somewhere while I sent my peons out to do the dirty work." He turned on the light and directed it onto the far wall, revealing the mural of the children. He stared at it for a moment, thinking. *What about this place is so damn familiar? Where have I seen something like this before?* "In fact, if I was this thing, I would be hiding until the coast was clear before I showed my ass. I'd be worried someone might try to pull the same shit that the Lenape did."

Don made his way into the second chamber, inspecting each mural along the way. He turned to find Stephanie a step behind him, hanging on every word. "You know what I think?" he asked. "I think this thing isn't half as smart as you give it credit for. I mean, if it's as old as you say and as powerful as you tell me, then it's pretty goddamn stupid. I'll bet it's grown so cocky and sure of itself it had no idea what was happening when the Lenape pulled the rug out from under it. I bet if we get a look at the rest of these murals, we'll find out just how stupid this thing is."

Don turned the light on Stephanie. The look on her face spoke volumes; it was the broken look of someone who had accepted their fate.

"The Lenape tribe in this area were slaughtered," she said. A sizzle of lightning flashed outside the cave, illuminating half her face as she spoke. "They were exterminated like a colony of ants."

Chapter 83

Janis looked across the backseat of the cruiser at her friends. She offered a toothy smile that helped ease their apprehension. Although she was soaked from running through the rain and falling onto the wet grass, her bubbling attitude hadn't dimmed a single watt. Her warmth was infectious like a plate of fresh chocolate chip cookies and radiated outward. Troy could feel it filling the backseat as if a space heater had been focused on them. Then a voice spoke over the sheriff's radio.

"Deputy Lutchen to anyone in the basement. Come in, over."

Troy sat between the girls and pulled them in close as the sheriff started speaking. "Do you think we're gonna get in trouble for pulling the fire alarm?" he asked.

Both Janis and Wendy laughed and elbowed him in the ribs. Apparently, neither thought there was anything to worry about. Their attention was drawn again when another voice crackled through the tiny speaker.

"Carl, I figured out why the MRI machine killed it. It's a giant magnet, and this thing is made of some type of metallic alloy."

Janis sat upright at the mention of the magnets and began to smack the back of the sheriff's seat. Wendy and Troy also chimed in shouting, "I told you; you see—you see." They were so excited that they had figured it out first, none of them could contain themselves.

"All right!" the sheriff shouted and turned to the back seat. "Would you mind keeping it down back there?"

The group of children settled down and sat upright. Troy had never been yelled at by the sheriff and had no idea he could shout so loud. Janis, however, started to snicker almost right away, which in turn got Wendy giggling. A second later, both girls were unable to control themselves. Troy relaxed a bit and joined them. Even his mother and the sheriff were infected by the laughter and offered smiles of their own.

"Yeah, I was just told the same thing about ten minutes ago by a group of fourth graders." Carl laughed and looked in the rearview mirror. "But good job, Burt. Glad you're safe, and I hope that info helps us."

"I take it you found the kids?" the voice asked.

"That's a big 10-4—"

It shot at them in a blur, screaming across the Turnpike from out of the side street. Dark and fast and on top of them in an instant. Lois grabbed the dashboard and screamed, "Look out!" Then the world was eclipsed.

It hit them with the force of a charging rhino, tossing everyone in the vehicle about as if they were nothing more than a little girl's dolls. It crashed into the driver's side rear quarter panel, and the back windshield imploded. Glass rained down on the children in a violent barrage. The sound of crumpling metal and breaking glass was all that anyone could hear. Suddenly, they were spinning out of control and around like a pinwheel for what felt like an eternity.

Janis had been trying to contain her laughter when the car was struck. She was thrown hard to the left, propelled toward the back passenger door. Her head hit the glass with a sickening thud nearly as loud as the initial impact. The girl's smile disappeared, and her face went slack.

Janis's eyes rolled into the back of her head, and her body went limp. She collapsed into Troy's lap. Her blonde curls darkened as blood flowed from the wound and began to spread. It matted her hair, ran down her face, and soaked into Troy's jeans. He tried to focus on his friend, but a million impossible thoughts assaulted his senses as he struggled to comprehend what was happening.

The vehicle continued to spin out of control on the wet pavement until it finally came to a halt several seconds later. Troy looked down in horror at the sight of the indentation on the side of Janis's head. Every nerve in his body fired at the same time, and he had no idea what to do. He didn't know if he should touch her or not, if he should attempt to cover the wound to stop the bleeding or not dare try. With tears coursing down his cheeks, Troy looked up and screamed.

"MOM—HELP!"

⬤ ⬤ ⬤

Mike Turino pushed the cruiser to fifty-five miles per hour while Claire Rizvi cheered him on with cries of approval. Her cold, wet T-shirt clung to her like a second skin even though Mike had turned on the heater—and he dug the way she looked in it. The scenery flew past as they barreled down Garrett Grove's deserted streets like they had been granted a free pass.

Mike was so mesmerized by Claire's goods he didn't realize he had blown the stop sign until it was too late. He smashed into the back of the sheriff's vehicle without ever taking his foot off the gas. Mike and Claire were thrown at the windshield like a pair of crash test dummies.

Mike's chest was formally introduced to the steering wheel and caved inward. Claire's body continued travelling fifty-five miles an hour as she left the seat and hit the windshield. She was expelled from the vehicle, sailed over the sheriff's cruiser, and hit the Turnpike before coming to a rest some thirty feet away. By then, she was nothing more than a stubborn stain that would never come out. The sheriff's vehicle continued to spin for a half a minute before it finally stopped on the side of the road, ruined and inoperable. Rain pounded the wreckage, mixing with the gasoline that had begun to seep from the cracked tank of the cruiser.

⬤ ⬤ ⬤

Carl's vision swam and his head spun, but he retained enough awareness to understand they had been in an accident. He had hit his head on either the window or the steering wheel, and blood dripped from a small cut above his left eye. He turned to Lois, who had been wearing her seatbelt, but she was already on the move. A cry as piercing as a cattle bolt erupted from the backseat. Carl turned to look and was washed away by the sea of red. There was so much, and it was impossible to tell whose blood it was at first. Then he saw the little girl sprawled in Troy's lap. *Dear God!* His pulse flew off the rails as he unfastened his seatbelt and attempted to exit the vehicle. But his door refused to open as he pressed against it.

Lois had already exited the car and run into the street. Carl followed, sliding across the seat and out the passenger's side. He threw his hat on to shield himself from the rain and reached Lois as she opened the back door. Wendy stepped out of the backseat first, hysterical and convulsing; she was swept out of the way into Lois's arms. Carl rushed in next to Troy and nearly cried out. His gut twisted as he looked down at the child laying in her friend's lap. The head wound was massive and had been dented in close to an inch or more.

Troy held on to the girl, his body shaking, the tremors ripping through him in concussive waves. Blood soaked his clothes and ran between his fingers and underneath his nails. Janis lay motionless in his arms.

"I've got her, Troy," Carl said and slid his hands between the girl's head and Troy's legs. "Let me take her. Slide out of the car."

The boy didn't move, only sat there crying and in shock until Lois reached in and offered her hand. He took it, slid across the seat, and buried his face in her bosom next to Wendy, who had done the same.

Carl looked for something to cover the wound and spied the wet sweatshirt on the seat. Being as careful as possible, he wrapped it around her head, managed to get his arms around her, and eased Janis out of the vehicle. She was so light and frail and hung limp like a doll in his arms. As Carl stepped out of the car, he smelled it. There was no mistaking that smell, not for a guy who had seen as much napalm as Carl had. It was gasoline, thick and heavy and leaking from the cruiser's tank. He moved as fast as he dared, trying not to jar the child or cause her further injury.

He stepped from the cruiser into the pouring rain and surveyed the scene. The other vehicle had come to rest further down the road. Although it was impossible to tell the condition of the driver, it was obvious the passenger hadn't made it. There was no time to worry about that asshole anyway.

"Over here!" A shout came from across the street. Carl looked to find the owner of the voice standing in the parking lot near the main entrance of the municipal building.

THE OJANOX

"Follow me," he called to the others and started moving. They were out of options, and at least there were medical supplies in the building. But as Carl watched the sweatshirt turn a deep scarlet, he doubted if it would make any difference. Janis didn't so much as stir as he raced into the parking lot carrying her.

Jessica Marceau had witnessed the accident from her second-floor window. She met them at the side entrance to the sheriff's department. "The keys are in my right pocket!" Carl yelled out.

Jessica dug in and pulled them out in one quick motion. She ran up the steps, opened the door, and held it for the others. Carl rushed into the building just as the first cruiser caught fire and exploded. The gasoline had spread quickly, and a moment later, the second vehicle detonated. There was no need to check on the condition of the driver. Carl focused on the girl and made his way toward the back of the station, where several cots were set up.

He entered the room with Janis's condition looking more dire by the second and motioned for Lois to take the other children down the hall. They would only get in his way and there was nothing they could do to help. He lowered Janis onto the cot and heard the deadbolt engage as Jessica locked the door behind them. The mayor rushed in to join him with a first aid kit and a flashlight. She turned it on and searched for gauze, bandages, and whatever else she could find.

Carl removed the sweatshirt from Janis's head, revealing the injury. Jessica gasped and continued to lay out gauze for the sheriff to use. He examined the intrusive dent in the child's skull, then fumbled about to find a pulse. He searched every inch of her neck but was unable to find even the faintest sign of life. *Don't die on me, Janis,* he chanted to himself as he pressed into her flesh with his fingertips. Then—he felt it—so faint it was nothing more than a tremble. But it was something; it was still a pulse. She was still alive.

He eased the gauze over the wound. The first layer soaked through in seconds, but the next layer appeared to slow the flow of blood, at least a little. There wasn't much he could do. The child had a massive concussion and needed a doctor, but Chilton was a war zone. Jessica removed a large bandage and assisted Carl as he proceeded to wrap it around Janis's head.

He finished the wrap, which appeared to stop the flow of blood a bit more. Then Janis's eyes fluttered, and a faint moan escaped from between her lips.

"Where is your car?" he asked the mayor. The medical center was off-limits, but one of the doctors and a paramedic would be at the high school by now. If they could get Janis there, there was a chance they could save her.

"In the back lot," Jessica answered.

"Thank God." Carl rested Janis's head against the pillow, stood up, and grabbed his radio. "Bob, come in. It's Carl, come in, Bob."

There was a blast of static, and then a man spoke; his voice was unrecognizable. The strained sobs warbled through the small speaker. "H-he killed them, C-Carl. Jesus Christ, it's a bloodbath."

The sheriff and mayor stared at each other, unable to make any sense out of the chief's transmission. "What are you talking about, Bob? What's going on?"

There was a long pause before Bob returned. "Your deputy—Rainey. He went insane and killed them. It's awful—God, Carl, it's so fucking awful. He slaughtered them. Christ, Carl—the children!"

Carl hadn't known Bob Jones to register a visible emotion the entire time he had known him. He had seen the man pull bodies from house fires. The guy was a rock if there ever was one. But his words came over the radio too fast and distorted to comprehend. Carl struggled to grasp what the man was saying. "What are you talking about, Bob? You're not making sense."

"Rainey! Deputy Rainey went crazy and shot the place up. It's a massacre, Carl. Jesus Christ, he killed them."

It hit Carl like a derelict squad car. He wasn't sure how he knew, probably a feeling in his gut. But suddenly he understood what the chief was talking about. Deputy Rainey had walked into the shelter and fired on the civilians. Only it hadn't been David Rainey at all. It may have looked like him and had no doubt been wearing the deputy's skin. But whatever it was that had gone into that shelter wasn't Deputy Rainey. It was the thing that had gotten into his head. *Dear God, it never left!* It had used the deputy as a weapon against his own people. *Dear Lord, please save us.* Carl pinched the bridge of his nose and winced as he prayed to whoever might still be listening.

THE OJANOX

● ● ●

By the time Bob Jones and Brandon Canfield forced their way into the shelter, it was already too late. They were assaulted by the oppressive cloud of gun smoke and gagging stench of gore. A river of red ran from the twisted tangle of bodies strewn about the floor. The neglectful way in which their arms and torsos tangled and heaped was nothing either man was prepared to witness. Bob had seen how disfigured and unrecognizable a flame could render the human body. He also knew what a man looked like after he was eaten alive by a pack of wild boar. But what lay before him was worse than any of that. And he had sent everyone into the shelter himself.

Bob struggled to keep his head and tend to the injured, but the stench of bodily fluids was as thick as a landslide. Brandon had an even harder time keeping a grip on the contents of his stomach and ran back up the stairs to purge on the gym floor. He returned minutes later looking pale and beat down. They moved from one pile of corpses to the next, checking for pulses and trying to focus on one single body at a time. There were some moans, a few cries, and even the occasional screams, but they were scarce. A chilling hush blanketed the large room, snuffing out all other sounds. The lack of injuries was surprising; the lack of survivors was staggering.

The gravity weighed heavier with each step the men took toward the center of the room. A discarded semi-automatic rifle lay on the floor next to several spent magazines, all tossed about in a haphazard fashion. Bob averted his eyes, frantic to find a single soul he could help, but it was impossible not to focus on the carnage. Parents had used their own bodies as shields to protect their helpless children. The rifle's bullets had torn through the little ones regardless; flesh was no match for a .30 caliber fired at close range.

The chief stood beside another cluster of victims and knelt to check for pulses. He was met by the unblinking stare of a child hidden beneath a tangle of limbs. Bob rolled one of the bodies to the side, revealing the terrified little girl. He held out his hand, thankful he had found a survivor. "I've got you," he said. "It's all over."

The girl allowed the fireman to lift her from the heap and buried her face into the crook of his neck. He stepped away from the mess and carried her toward the hallway leading to the smaller rooms. Bob passed the women's bathroom and jumped back when the door flew open and the woman rushed at him.

Jill Boriello had hidden in the bathroom as instructed and didn't move. She had waited until the bullets stopped flying before even leaving the stall. "Oh, God!" she cried. "I'll take her." The teacher held out her hands and took the young girl. "I've got you, Kelly," she said, but Kelly hadn't heard a word she said.

"Stay here," Bob told her and turned to leave. "This might not be over yet."

Bob made his way back into the nightmare of the main area with a bit more clarity than he had previously. The act of helping one individual lifted him enough to keep going and inspired the idea there might be others. His hopes lifted even more when he saw the deputy in the center of the room. The woman had fallen to the floor and was struggling to get to her feet.

"Andrea," he shouted and approached her. "Are you all right?" The deputy lifted a hand, revealing the .38 in her grip. Bob stopped in his tracks and removed his own sidearm, concerned it had been Andrea who was responsible for all the death. But as she rose to her feet and holstered her weapon, the idea became less likely. The deputy limped a few steps and kicked at a body on the floor in front of her.

Bob made his way toward her but kept his weapon in hand. He reached Andrea and gasped. On the floor lay the body of Deputy Rainey. He had been shot several times in the chest and once in the forehead. An arsenal of ammunition decorated his utility belt. Bob knew—Rainey had been the shooter.

"Dear God," he hissed.

"He killed them." Andrea focused on the body with a blind intensity. It looked as if she were staring through the man.

Bob noticed the wound in her leg and offered a hand, but Andrea refused and pushed him away. The rigid steel glare in her eyes and the icy tone of her voice told Bob everything. He recalled hearing how Rainey had nearly killed Carl at the morgue, how the creature got inside his head and manipulated the deputy like a puppet. Bob knew it had happened again, or the creature had never left at all. The result was the same either way. Deputy Rainey was used as a weapon and had slaughtered almost everyone in the shelter. The look in Andrea's eyes told Bob even more. She had silenced the beast.

THE OJANOX

Several people emerged from one of the back rooms, led by Michelle Marks. The woman sent them straight to work, turning her own emotion switch off and focusing on the job at hand. She tended to the victims' wounds, helped them to their feet, and led them away from the massacre. The small group of survivors lumbered off like war prisoners still untrusting of their rescuers. Looks of shock, horror, and disbelief filled the faces of those who had been spared. Although no one had been spared at all, not really. Everyone had lost something—a child, a mother, their spouse.

There was one miracle that occurred in the basement of the high school. Günter Bentley and his entire family had managed to survive the massacre. A combination of where they had been sitting when the shooting started, the man's instructions to his family to lie as if they had already been shot, and dumb blind luck were to thank. They were the only family to survive intact. Not that many had been intact before the shooting started.

Of the ten men Bob had stationed in the basement, only two survived. Anthony Leone suffered a grazing wound to the temple, and Rich Marek had been unharmed. Both men aided in helping with the survivors alongside Bob, Brandon Canfield, and Michelle's tiny group.

Their numbers were few, and those who were left were in no shape to defend themselves. The groups were taken into one of the back rooms, where they huddled together in silence. Survivor's guilt and shock swept them up like a blanket. Bob whispered a few instructions to Michelle and then returned to the gym to check the doors and resecure their defenses. That's what he told her at least. In all honesty, he needed to step away for a moment. The thick smell of gore still ripe in the air was inescapable. He climbed the long staircase, a weight like no other imposed upon him, and he entered into the openness of the high school gym. He was relieved for a brief moment until Carl's voice flooded through the radio's speaker.

Then Bob lost it. It rushed at him at a thousand miles an hour. The face of every fallen child appeared in his mind like a Polaroid. Every pulse he had checked on, every blood-soaked body, like a snapshot on his brain. He saw the look in Andrea's eyes, the body of Deputy Rainey, the snarl on the face of Earl Hillman, and he saw Sally. Dear, sweet, perfect Sally. He saw her as she was when she had loved him years and years ago, and he saw her the day she arrived in town with her face bruised and shoulder dislocated. Then a different picture of his first love entered the chief's mind: an image of Sally face first under nine inches of loose dirt. Bob broke down and let his tears fall. He had been holding them for so long, but the dam had finally broken.

His breath hitched in his throat as he tried to tell Carl what happened. "H-he killed them, C-Carl. Jesus Christ, it's a bloodbath." Bob's tears hammered through him like the rain. A second later, the lights in the gym flickered and then went black.

The first transformer blew when a random bolt of lightning hit the pole across the street from the sheriff's department. Jessica Marceau witnessed the explosion as the overload cut power to the surrounding area and interrupted service in the Village. The unthinkable happened not long after when a Chevy truck driven by Denny Birch crashed into a second telephone pole on Mandeville. After having Dr. Freedman remove a Hula Popper from the side of his head, Denny had spent the morning nursing his pain the only way he knew how—with a fifth of Jack. By the time he realized the fire whistle wasn't broken and was on his way to the high school, Denny was sufficiently shit-faced. He hit the pole doing fifty-five miles an hour and cracked it in half like a wishbone. Denny was killed on impact—which was unfortunate. The loss of two transformers plus a mile of damaged high-tension line was devastating. The substation on Route 3 overloaded, and Garrett Grove went dark minutes before nightfall.

Chapter 84

The three small creatures watched while their numbers advanced. They remained hidden, observing the entrances of the church, assessing not only the simple ones' strength but their weakness. The shared consciousness of the one coursed through them and was then relayed to the horde. They instructed and ordered the execution of the attack. The strange bodies once belonging to Robert Boyle, Erin Richards, and Ben Richards resembled nothing human in the least. Their distorted features, reptilian and sleek, were designed for speed and evasion. They watched through collective eyes from every possible angle. They listened as the simple ones gathered under the watch of their cunning leader and discussed their defenses.

The sentinel guarded over the three. It had been called Butchie, a being consumed by random chaos. Now it was a soldier, ruled by intention. But the vessel was strained and wouldn't last forever. The three were waning as well and would soon need to be discarded, replaced by new vessels, fresh skin to contain its essence. Then, when it finished with this colony, it could move on to the next. The map of humanity spread out in detail before it. Places called Warren, Parker Plains, and Millville were in the thoughts of the consumed. The simple ones had sealed their demise, populating the sphere on top of one another. Now nothing could stop it from spreading as it had always intended. One by one, colony to colony, city to city.

The three transmitted the plan to the soldiers surrounding the church. It directed them and ordered the attack. Then they retreated further into the woods and waited.

●●●

The lights in the church winced out, and their artificial illumination was replaced with the natural glow of a hundred or more candles set in every corner and all the pews. Lanterns were lit and flashlights were aimed into the dark as a bastion of beasts cascaded across the parking lot in a wave.

"Here they come!" Father Kieran shouted over the driving rain. Weapons were drawn and extra guns were positioned at the ready. The people of the parish reacted and worked together as if they had trained for years. "Steady," he called out to every man and woman. The horde made a rapid advance past the sixth row of parked vehicles and continued to the fifth.

"Steady now, steady!"

The legion of demons breached the fourth row of vehicles and approached the third. "Fire!" Kieran screamed and leveled his revolver into the writhing crowd. The night came alive with the thunder of gunfire blasting from every entrance of the church.

The beasts fell in rapid succession. As fast as they advanced, they were silenced. Kieran observed the men who flanked him, firing their weapons with zest, defending their church like Templar Knights. His heart swelled with pride, and he knew they would walk away victorious.

●●●

The assault on the sacristy entrance was much lighter than anticipated. Josh's men found it easy to fight off the small number of beasts advancing on their position. Josh fired into the darkness, then turned back to Allison and shouted his instructions. The girl turned and ran to Father Kieran's position to relay the information.

THE OJANOX

It felt good for Allison to stay busy. She hadn't been sure about coming to the church but had nowhere else to go. After the experience at the sanatorium, she knew whatever was out there was evil. And when Mick had gone missing, Allison had found herself alone. Now that she was here, helping Father Kieran and the others, she was certain she had done the right thing. She kept her head down, made her way to the front entrance, and delivered her message to one of the men, who passed it along to the father. A moment later, he turned back and shouted over the rattle of gunfire. Allison nodded, getting most of what he told her, then ran back to deliver the instructions to Josh.

She crouched again, staying low, and slid along the side wall of the church beneath the stained glass windows. She looked up at the portrait of Jesus and Mary Magdalene; it was the very image Father Kieran had been looking at earlier. The woman stood before the Lord, risking her own life to offer him a drink while his own disciples fled. She had never left his side and had been the first to see him resurrected. But for some reason, it was always Peter who was exalted. The man had denied Jesus and hid when he was crucified. But not Mary, she had remained faithful to the Lord. Allison felt proud to belong to a sisterhood of such devotion. She made the sign of the cross on her forehead and stopped to pray.

A dark shadow darted behind the window a second before the glass imploded. A polychromatic waterfall of art and color rained over Allison and onto the carpet. She shielded her eyes from the force of the shock, then the beasts were on her, grabbing her by the arms and throat. Allison was propelled upward and forced out the window into the night. She landed hard and was dragged across the lawn in a flurry. Her body jerked and bounced off the pavement as she was yanked into the parking lot and then carried off into the woods. Finally, the monster released her.

Allison lay on her back gasping for breath. Rain fell hard into her eyes, blurring her sight and obscuring the vision before her. It drew in closer and hovered over her, and then it spread its lips. The demon's teeth were pointed; its eyes were piercing and black. The creature's grey skin hung in loose tatters no longer fitting its small child-like body. Then it sneered at her and drew in even closer. The first waft of smoke lifted from its jaws and swirled before her in hypnotic waves.

"The Lord is my Shepherd," she said as dark tendrils gathered about. "I will fear no evil."

The beast made a strange gurgling sound that could have been laughter, but it was impossible to tell over the din of the rain. It pounced and entered Allison like a tidal wave; it extracted what it needed and ransacked all that was left.

● ● ●

Julie Evans and Amy Sterling huddled in the center of the church, away from the fighting taking place at all three entrances. Neither woman thought it was nearly far enough. What did a part-time waitress and a high school secretary know about guns and combat, anyway? They had met earlier today and confided in one another. Julie about her recent infidelity with Mr. Garish, the principal, and Amy about the possibility that Father Kieran was out of his holy-rolling mind. The way the congregation had swallowed the priest's dogma, hook, line, and sinker, was more than unsettling. Amy had arrived shortly after Allison and watched Father Kieran systematically recruit his followers one by one in a cult-like fashion. Allison had swallowed the bait like a proselyte. Amy watched the transformation take place in the high school girl and knew the priest was dangerous. And although Amy knew it was no longer safe to be outside, she believed she had made a grave mistake by coming to Our Lady of the Mountain.

● ● ●

"I don't know if I will be any good with a weapon, Father," Allison had told the priest, then turned to Amy and smiled. Only a few of the parishioners had gathered when the three spoke earlier.

"You may not need to take up arms today, my child," Father Kieran had told her in a calm but deliberate tone. "But before the war is over, the time will come when you must."

"You expect an ongoing battle?" Neither Allison nor Amy had anticipated a lasting confrontation.

"Fear not," he assured them. "We will be victorious this evening. But I believe you have information that will aid in our counterattack. You know where the evil resides."

"The sanatorium," Allison gasped.

"Yes. If we are to defeat the beast, we must slay it while it sleeps. For the light is the Lord's domain, and no evil can walk by day. That is when we will strike."

That's when every red light in Amy's head fired at once. "You want to fight this thing on its home turf?"

"Worry not, young Amy." His voice was cold and calculating like a used car salesman. "The Lord is with you and no harm shall pass."

Amy wanted to mention the countless souls who had put their lives in the hands of God only to die horrible deaths. The Bible was full of such stories. She wanted to offer an alternate option, one where they defended themselves until morning and then got the fuck out of Dodge. Instead, she kept her mouth shut, knowing there was no swaying the preacher; it was too late for that.

"When the sun rises tomorrow," Kieran continued, "we will descend upon the sanatorium and vanquish the beast while it sleeps."

Allison met the priest with a huge smile, and Amy had offered one as well. However, hers was only meant to appease and buy some time until she came up with a plan of her own. One that got her out of Garrett Grove and far from the congregation of kamikaze nutjobs.

Amy told Julie what she had witnessed this afternoon, and the secretary was on board, for the most part. Unfortunately, her husband, Luke, had already bought the priest's message and taken up arms at the side entrance of the church, which was going to complicate things. The women watched Allison Aigans run from station to station delivering messages for the priest and his men like a good little minion. The girl stopped at one of the stained glass windows to pray for a moment. The depiction of Jesus and Mary Magdalene was one of twelve individual scenes, six on either side of the church in every window. The Stations of the Cross were staples in all Catholic churches. The mastery of craftsmanship in all was breathtaking.

Before either woman could react, the window where Allison was standing shattered into a thousand shards of red, blue, and gold. Then they were upon her. The beasts bounded through the opening and snatched Allison up like a door prize at a tricky tray. Amy froze as the monsters carried Allison off into the night.

The Erin-creature crawled onto the girl's chest, opened its mouth, and allowed the ether to slip out like a shadow. It swirled and grew in intensity, then penetrated the terrified child. Everything that had been Allison was consumed and categorized in a heartbeat. It knew everything the priest intended to do and how to defend against him. The information was simultaneously shared with the others, the one that had been called Ben and the one called Robert. The three communicated as one and transmitted the information to the hive. They accessed the collected memories and drew upon a vision of the one called Troy, the boy, the creator of fear. Fully understanding and able to now think in the simple ones' own language, it spoke to the soldiers. *If they want a fight, then they will get one. Let them come ... and let them scream in the dark.*

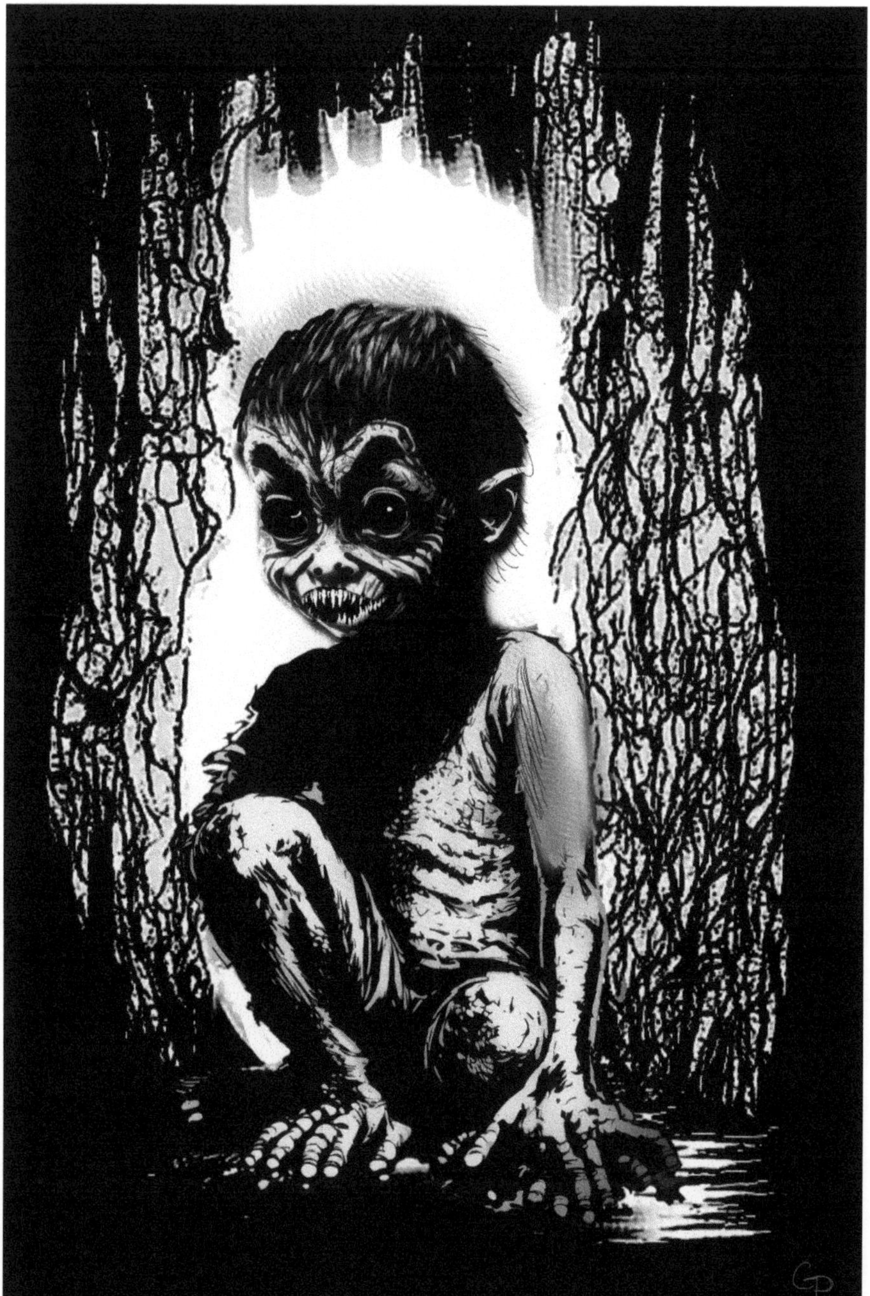

Chapter 85

Burt slid the last cartridge into his weapon and was almost knocked to the floor when Doris TenHove rounded the corner and barreled into him. Realizing her position in the hall had been compromised by the fast-approaching horde, he craned his head from the doorway to get a better look. Although much was obscured by the thick cloud of smoke and the encroaching swarm, Burt looked up in time to see Grady Martin rush the nurses' station and raise his weapon. The fireman ambushed the area where Ted, Billy, and Ed Koloski were stationed, and fired. His bullet hit Koloski in the chest and leveled the man like a bag of Portland cement. Burt pulled the hammer back on his own gun and prepared to fire when Doris screamed from behind him. The room erupted with the sound of broken glass and the cries from the other women. He spun in time to see Doris take the first shot.

At least three of the horrible devils crashed through the window on the far side of the room. Nurse Carole and Cyndi, the candy striper, stood closest to the carnage and were taken by surprise. Doris's bullet hit one of the demons in the shoulder as it seized Carole and snapped her out of the building like a rubber band. Cyndi dodged the second beast's advances and evaded its grasp by inches. The girl rushed toward Burt with Dawn and Baxter at her side, ducking as the coroner and head nurse unloaded their weapons on the mob.

But there were more of them, forcing their bodies through the broken window and pouncing on the patients in the beds. Burt fired as Doris reloaded, but there was too much happening at once; it was impossible to register. The dog barked, and the beasts advanced, and Burt didn't know whether his bullets were even hitting their marks. He felt himself pulled backward and almost tripped over his own feet. The unseen force yanked him out of the room and into the hallway. He found himself in the stairwell leading to the roof and looked up to see Doris and the rest of the group already on the move. The door slammed behind him. Scanning the group, he counted their numbers. Burt's legs stopped working as the realization gripped him; they had already lost half of their party.

• • •

The stairwell leading to the roof was narrower than the others in the building. An initial set of risers approached the first landing, turned left, and were followed by an additional set that led to the roof's entrance. Ted followed his group and called to them as he reached the halfway point. "This is where we make our stand!" he yelled and turned his weapon in the direction they had come.

Billy Tobin was dazed beyond tears and grappling with the loss of both parents. Ted sized him up and watched the boy sway on his feet as if in a trance. He doubted if Billy would be of much use in the fight, but with only four shooters left, Ted prayed for the opposite. They needed to focus two of their weapons on the third-floor door below them and two at the door to the roof. If the creatures had been able to scale the building and ambush them through the windows, it was a sure bet they had also found their way onto the roof. Their only chance was to hold up in the stairwell and pick off the attackers as they advanced. At least they stood the chance of dropping enough bodies at the entrances and creating a barricade of the dead.

Ted had had just enough time to grab the ammo bag before Grady Martin and the rest of the horde descended upon the nurses' station. He reloaded the 30-30 and checked the 12 gauge slung over his shoulder. "Okay, Burt. You're with me." He motioned for the coroner to join him and help protect the third-floor entrance. Which left Doris and Billy to cover the door to the roof. They would make a strong team, provided the boy hadn't already lost it. The group moved into position, flanking Cyndi, Dawn, and Baxter on the landing.

Here goes nothing. Ted jumped when a slender hand appeared in front of him.

"Give me a gun," Cyndi said and looked him in the eye.

Ted removed the .38 from his hip and handed it to her. He figured she couldn't possibly do any worse than Burt and was glad she stepped up. He replaced his sidearm with a Colt Python he removed from the bag, then set the remainder of the ammo on the landing. There wasn't much of it, and it would only last so long.

The first battalion reached the lower door and threw themselves at it like a meteor crashing into the Yucatan. Cyndi jumped but kept her weapon aimed at the door. Ted noticed and knew he had done the right thing by arming the young candy striper.

A low growl escaped from deep within Baxter's throat. The Shepherd focused on the door, his hackles standing on the back of his neck and every muscle in his body poised to pounce. Dawn extended her hand and stroked the animal, which appeared to relax him a bit. But his guard was raised when something crashed into the door a second time, causing the dog to snarl. Ted looked to the members of his party and nodded; this was it, the point of no return. He turned back as the first monstrosity broke through the door and entered the stairwell.

It attempted to climb the stairs, and Ted dropped it with his first shot. It landed face first in the doorway, creating the beginning of the barricade he prayed would impede the others. A second creature, smaller and faster than the first, scurried into the stairwell over the body. Ted fired again, missing the creature's head and hitting it in the back. Burt was unlucky with his shot as well and missed the vital areas. It darted up the stairs at Ted, who was unable to track it in his sights and stood closest to the open door. Then it lunged at the deputy, lifting from the risers and hurling itself into the air. The concussion as the beast's head exploded was deafening, and Ted was bathed in foul brain matter. He looked up into the barrel of Billy Tobin's shotgun; smoke lifted from the end. The boy had leaned over the railing and fired on the aberration at the last possible moment.

Ted turned and shot, dropping another body on top of the first, adding to the barrier. He reloaded while Burt focused his weapon on the face of a man who looked as if he might have been dead for well over a month. The necrotic features twisted and warped in a repulsive spatter of black, then the beast fell as well. Ted slammed the last round into the chamber and raised his weapon just as the door to the roof buckled in its frame.

Baxter stared at the door, lowered his front haunches, and bared his teeth in a snarl. The battering filled the narrow hallway with the dull echo of flesh connecting with steel. The force of the blows made quick work of their minimal defenses. The door flew inward, the hinges ripped from the jamb. The disfigured being that entered the doorway was an abomination to life itself. They all stared up at the horrible deformity that had once worked for the coroner's office. Burt gasped and stepped backward. Although the man's face and body had been altered, he was recognizable. Tony wore the same clothes he had on the last time Burt had seen him. His medical whites were now soiled a putrid black from the dark substance that oozed from his eyes and mouth. The man had been ranting about vampires before he fled from the lab Monday night, which wasn't far from the truth. What had happened to him was right out of a horror movie.

Burt was unable to move or draw his weapon as he stared at the man he had known. Doris was quicker to react and fired at the lab tech, her bullet striking Tony in the shoulder. Then like an uncoiled spring, Baxter pounced and launched himself at the beast. The Shepherd broke from the child's grip and seized the monster by the neck, knocking it backward to the floor. The creature and dog twisted and tumbled out the door, into the night. Dawn reacted and bolted past Billy and Doris up the stairs and after her dog.

"Dawn, no!" Doris screamed. She chased after the child with Billy Tobin hot on her heels. Together, they ascended the stairs, exited onto the roof, and were swallowed by the night.

Carl stood in the darkness of his father's old office with the radio in his blood-stained hands. The room tipped and swayed as he attempted to digest the news he had just received. It had never left Rainey's head, or it had found its way back inside. Either way, the result was the same. The deputy had gone ballistic and mowed down nearly every living soul in the high school basement. There were survivors, but their numbers were few. Andrea Geary had made it, along with two teachers from the elementary school, an administrator from the high school, and several others. Bob and Michelle Marks were in the process of isolating the injured and the lucky into one of the smaller rooms in the basement. The woman was the only known survivor with medical training and Janis's only hope. There wasn't much time, and Carl doubted if any of the doctors at the center were even left. He could load his party into the mayor's car and make a break for it. At least he had to try.

He steadied himself, stepped behind his father's desk, and looked out the window into the parking lot. Carl jumped back. An army of demons gathered behind the building. Their masses huddled together almost on top of one another. He attempted to count their numbers but was unable. The creatures looked ready to launch their attack, as if they were waiting for the order to strike. Carl's heart skipped as it tried to keep up with his racing mind. There was no chance they could make it to the high school, let alone ten steps out the back door. They were trapped. Then one of the figures advanced toward the building and revealed itself. Carl recognized the uniform despite the shape it was in. Deputy Gary Forsyth, or what was left of him, stepped up to lead the attack, his body ravaged and disfigured. He looked like a demonic pincushion or some type of hybrid porcupine. Spikes grew from his face and chest, piercing his skin and shredding his clothes.

Carl ran from the window and out of the office. There was only one place in the building where they might stand a chance. He charged into the room where Lois and the two children were and shouted, "We need to move ... now!"

Lois looked up, confused at first but immediately registered the urgency in his direction. She gathered Troy and Wendy at her side and rushed them out the door. Carl darted to the cot and threw his keys to the mayor. He laced his arms underneath Janis and lifted her as gently as he could. "I need someone to grab the mattress and first aid kit and follow me."

He led the group down the stairs with the child in his arms. Lois and Troy managed to grab the cot and followed with Wendy carting the medical supplies behind. Carl hurried them past two jail cells no bigger than three by nine and continued to the far end of the hallway. He stopped at a large steel door with a massive lock located in the dead center.

"It's the big square one!" he shouted to Jessica as she fumbled with the keys. She found the right one and inserted it into the hole. The clunking sound of heavy steel echoed down the hallway as Jessica opened the door. She pulled the handle, revealing the station's armory. Bare racks stood where weapons and ammunitions had been stored. The small room was empty except for a wooden bench and a few boxes of shells.

The mayor closed and locked the door behind them as the sound of breaking glass and splintering wood lifted from the station's back entrance. The beasts had found their way inside and begun their attack. A second later, the armory door shook as something threw itself at it. The noise was deafening. Carl's party backed away as if the extra foot might save them. Again, the sound of a battering ram slammed against the steel door, but this time it didn't move. The door held fast, at least for the moment. Carl prayed it would continue to do so. He looked down at Janis's limp body in his arms, wishing there was something he could do, but there was nothing. They weren't going anywhere.

With their defenses split, there was no way the remaining members could defend the stairwell. Ted fired into the growing mass of bodies, turned, and forced the others upward. Burt and Cyndi followed his lead and exited onto the roof. They stumbled out into the rain to find Baxter and the creature engaged in a deathmatch. The dog had the beast by the throat and tore into the man who had gone by the name of Tony, pulling him off his feet and dominating. The creature struggled to latch on to the dog but was no match for the brutality of the great Shepherd. Billy and Doris stood guard in front of Dawn with their weapons raised in either direction. They scanned the top of the building, searching for any sign of movement, but it was impossible to tell in the darkness. Baxter shook the beast with a violent tug, and the man's neck snapped loud enough to be heard over the rain. The dog released its hold and backed away as Billy rushed in and fired a shotgun round into Tony's brain.

Shadows darted at the edges of their vision. Then, one by one, they appeared; creatures of varying size and deformity moved in on them from every direction. They emerged from the stairwell and invaded on all sides. Ted huddled his party into a tight circle with their backs to one another. They raised their weapons at the approaching horde but knew it was senseless. Even Baxter shrank away from the ever-tightening circle of beasts. He drew in close to Dawn's side as she wrapped her arms around his leg.

All that was left of their party, Ted, Billy, Doris, Burt, and Cyndi, backed against one another with Dawn and Baxter wedged between them. They aimed their weapons outward at a throng of uncountable bodies. Over a hundred, by Ted's estimation. Not enough bullets to put down half. The creatures took another step forward, then stopped, as if taunting their prey.

Ted wondered if the others were thinking the same as he. *Is it really a sin? Surely under the circumstances...* He checked the cylinder of the Colt; four bullets left. More than enough to do the trick when pressed against the temple. He looked down at Dawn, her golden locks plastered to the side of her head from the rain, and knew he could never pull the trigger.

A fiery bolt shattered from the sky, striking somewhere in the parking lot. The blinding blue that flashed before them made it impossible to see, and it was almost a minute before their eyes were able to focus. Ted sprang to action, ready to fire on the creatures, who would no doubt capitalize on the opportunity. He pointed his pistol into the black, but there was nothing. He spun around, surveying the rooftop and the entrance to the stairwell, but all was empty. They were gone. The creatures had retreated into the storm and spared them.

He didn't hesitate and didn't need to figure it out. "Follow me!' he shouted and led his party back into the building and out of the rain.

● ● ●

Bob and Brandon checked the integrity of the gym doors, then locked and bolted the entrance to the shelter behind them. They entered the basement and stared across the ocean of wool blankets that had been laid over the corpses, each one conforming to the figure that lay beneath it. So many dead, and it had happened so fast. The men walked down the hallway and into the small room where the survivors were gathered. The eyes that stared back at them were so far gone, they were no longer able to cry. The shattered gazes of the shell shocked and despondent looked to the men for answers, but there were none to be found.

Kelly Rainey stared at the floor while Jill Boriello cradled the girl in her arms. Andrea Geary cleaned her service revolver for probably the tenth time in the past hour. Tyler Harrison and Rich Novack had come to the realization that life was too short to hide in a closet and sat together holding hands and comforting one another in hushed, deliberate tones. Günter Bentley, perhaps the luckiest man in town, kept his family close and continued to kiss his wife and daughters on their foreheads as if they might disappear any moment. Anthony Leone kept his wits intact for the most part and assisted Michelle Marks, who appeared unfazed and in her element. Bob noticed the resilience of the woman and could have sworn she had been smiling when he entered the room. The chief took a seat near the door and motioned for Brandon to do the same. The only thing left for any of them to do was wait until morning—that and pray.

●●●

The ramming against the armory door persisted, but the reinforced steel remained intact. As the night drew on and the hours passed, the creatures' attempts to gain access diminished some but never ceased. Carl stayed alert, with his weapon drawn and his back against the wall. He looked at Lois and the children, who had all passed out from exhaustion, then he turned to the mayor, who stood watch at Janis's bedside.

She whispered so not to be heard by the others. "I think we're losing her. She's lost so much blood."

Carl nodded; he had been thinking the same thing. "I can't risk moving her till morning. If just one of those things—" His voice cracked, and it took him a moment to recover. "I wish I could."

His hands were tied, and his options were nil. If they left now, they would be overcome in seconds. Their only chance was to wait it out and try to leave in the morning. He prayed Janis would make it until then.

"No, you're right." Jessica nodded and studied the deep circles etched beneath his eyes. "How long has it been since you slept?"

"I'm not sure," he said and pinched the bridge of his nose.

"Give me that," she told him and motioned to his pistol. "I'll watch the door, and you get some sleep."

THE OJANOX

"No, I'm fine," he said, struggling not to yawn. But he was so tired, and the door had held so far. Finally, he handed over the weapon and leaned back against the wall. "Thank you. Maybe just a few minutes."

Carl fought the urge for several seconds, then closed his eyes and fell asleep. Jessica guarded the door and listened to the sounds of the creatures as they tore through the basement of the sheriff's department. But the lock held, and for the moment, they were safe. Janis's eyelids fluttered at times throughout the night, and at one point, she cried out, but her words were mumbled and impossible to understand. Although Jessica could have sworn she heard one word clearly; she was sure the girl had said Chewbacca.

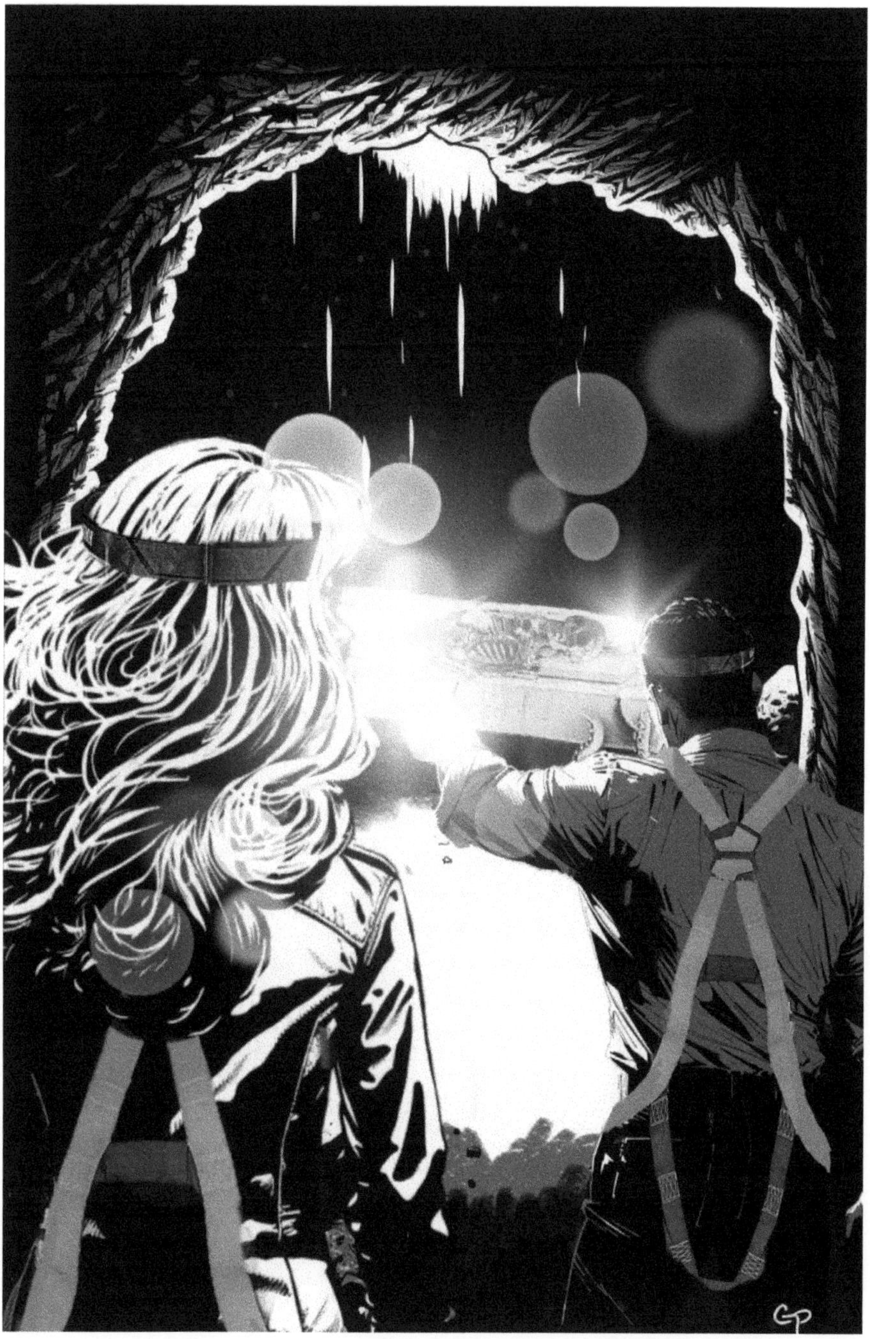

Chapter 86

Night came early to the canyon and the area once known as Lonesome Mountain. It crept in under the guise of the storm and took root like a malignancy. The generator had long since run out of fuel, and the only light to penetrate the dense murk of the cave came from the flashlights and several battery-powered lanterns. Don and Stephanie retreated to the furthest reaches of the second chamber, far from the cavern opening, and occupied themselves by studying the remainder of the murals—which was difficult with the limited illumination.

The paintings appeared to follow a linear storyline. They stood before the fifth one in sequence on the far side of the chamber. Don stepped closer and raised his light, revealing a depiction of the same children who had been in the previous painting. They were the focal point of this one, with each child laid out on what looked like three individual altars. And although Don wasn't positive where the scene had taken place, he had a good idea. The children were depicted very human, without the dark eyes or animal-like teeth. They were featured against the dark background of the lodestone; no additional colors had been added to the scenery to illustrate stars or a moon as the Lenape did in the other murals. However, at the very center of the piece, a darker color had been added. A black circular hole spread out between the children. Their altars, which Don thought looked sacrificial, were placed at equal distances around what could only be a pit or a chasm.

The children each wore an elaborate medallion around their necks. He turned the light toward Stephanie, who studied the wall with unblinking intensity, then returned his stare as well. The initial murals in the front of the cave appeared to be autonomous and almost a statement of facts. But the ones in the larger chamber were clearly a succession of a storyboard, a chronological telling of events the Lenape felt compelled to record. This one, the eleventh they had seen, adorned the right wall as the cave dipped and funneled toward the small opening in the back. With ten feet between them and the mouth of the shaft, there was enough room for one final mural. *Lucky number twelve*, Don thought as he slipped past Stephanie and moved to examine it.

He turned his light to the wall, and Stephanie joined him, both anticipating what the final mural in the series might be. Don looked closer and furrowed his brow. He scanned the small alcove with his flashlight, aiming the beam to the right and then left. The wall was stark and barren except for one swatch of color in the lower left corner. A short whiteish smear had been drug across the base of the wall and then terminated, as if the artist had been silenced while making his first brushstroke. And that was all there was of the final mural.

"That's a bit anti-climactic," he said, continuing to search the rock in a futile attempt to find a message that wasn't there.

Stephanie approached the wall, extended her hand, and touched the small swatch of paint. A wash of emotion filled her face, confusion being the dominant, but there was something else. Maybe frustration or realization, and Don was unable to tell which it might be. He himself was ticked-off to have come all this way and found a single line of paint. It would have been more gratifying had they found nothing at all. But Stephanie was still intrigued and remained silent as she studied the brushstroke as if it might still be wet.

"Well, I guess we know what happened to the artist. Got killed before they could finish."

"I guess," Stephanie replied, her thoughts elsewhere. She had turned toward the small opening that led away from the second chamber. The darkness that lay beyond called out to both of them. "You know ... Now we have to go back there."

Don shook his head. "I knew you were going to say that. And you know my answer."

THE OJANOX

"We'll never get another chance," she pleaded. "We might not survive the night. So just tell me what to do, and we'll be as careful as we can."

Don was curious himself, more than a little. But it was dangerous as hell, even if they took every precaution. He couldn't actually stop her from going back there if she was dead set. And from the look in her eye, he could tell she was. He looked toward the entrance of the cave, where the scorpion-like creatures paced about, then turned back to the small opening. To step outside was suicide; to venture into the darkness and explore what was back there would probably result in the same. Still ... he had to admit he was curious. And the only way to make sure she didn't go in there and get herself killed was if he went first. Even then, there was a good chance they would never come out. He was about to speak, then noticed the smile crease her lips and the spark that had ignited in her stare.

"Why are you smiling? I didn't say anything."

"Because you're going to. I promise I'll follow your lead, and we'll be careful every step of the way."

"I'm going to regret this."

"Thank you!" Stephanie jumped once and then grabbed his face with both hands and kissed him. It lasted only for a flash, but the exchange was electric as her lips parted and she bit him gently.

Don pulled back slowly and looked at the floor. He remembered the fight he and Lois had had in the garage the other day and wondered where she and Troy might be. It didn't feel as if they were gone, but he wasn't sure he would know if they were. He had been distant and self-absorbed for a long time. Don didn't know if there was still a chance for him to do right by either of them, but he knew he had to make it out of this cave alive. He and Stephanie had to survive the night and make it to their families.

She released her grip on his face and nodded. "Sorry," she said. "Friends?"

"Friends," he agreed. "But I'm still going to regret this."

● ● ●

After donning the necessary safety equipment and checking it for the third or fourth time, Don secured the anchor line to a fixed point in the second chamber and tethered Stephanie's harness to his own. He approached the small opening and directed his light downward. The blanketing darkness stretched out before him without depth or restraint. It felt endless, cold, and damp against his skin, yet electric as well. Don pointed his primary light down, relieved to find the rock floor. He had been most worried about an abrupt drop-off just on the other side of the opening. He exhaled, relieved somewhat but nowhere near relaxed. He cast the beam as far as it would extend and followed the floor ... flat ... solid ... and presumably safe. To the left and the right, the beam penetrated only so far before it was swallowed by the suffocating density of terminal darkness. Then he turned the beam upward. The ceiling above them formed a cylinder that extended like a chimney for what could have been miles. The great tube that towered above them looked like a funnel—a giant funnel of magnetite.

"That explains why compasses never work on Garrett Mountain," he said.

"It's amazing." She leaned in to see for herself. "The Lenape were drawn here. They believed the mountain held magical healing powers. Maybe they were right."

Don stepped from the threshold into the chamber with Stephanie following in his exact footsteps as instructed. The noticeable drop in temperature was immediate, causing their breath to condensate in plumes. Somewhere, water dripped in the distance; the resonating echoes bounced about the chamber, making it impossible to pinpoint the exact location of the source. Don wasn't sure but believed not far from where they stood was a sizable body of water. He pressed on, taking one calculated step at a time, with Stephanie in his wake.

Twelve murals. Actually, eleven murals and one brushstroke, but Don was sure there were meant to be twelve. It bugged him that the final reveal was a bust, but not as much as the certainty that he had seen it all somewhere before. It had been on the tip of his brain since they first began examining the storyboard of designs. Six on one side of the chamber and six on the other. The history of the Lenape tribe, just waiting for someone to come along and find it. From the battle against the dark-eyed beasts to the depiction of the children laid upon their stone slabs. All of it sealed tight within the mountain, behind tons and tons of rock. The thought bounced around his head for a moment. *A ton of rock. A ton of rock!*

"*That's* it!" He stopped short, raising his voice, causing Stephanie to jump.

"Jesus Christ, you scared the hell out of me. What's it?"

"A ton of rock. I don't know why I didn't think of it before; it's so damn obvious."

"Slow down, cowboy. I'm not following you."

"The murals." He bounced on his feet as he explained, excited to have finally made the connection. "They're the Stations of the Cross, just like on the windows of the Catholic church. I've been trying to figure out what the paintings reminded me of, and that's it." Don grinned as he raced to explain it all to her. "You see, Our Lady of the Mountain has twelve stained glass windows that show in succession the Passion of Jesus Christ. The story of his crucifixion and resurrection. The painting of the children helped me finally put it together. They were laid out on slabs, and their story was sealed tight in this cavern, behind a ton of rock. Just like the story of Jesus. He was placed in the tomb, and on the third day—well, you know the story."

"Yeah." She grinned back. "Of course I know. It's the basis of Christianity, the story of their salvation from sin—and, of course … death."

"Maybe this is the Lenape's same story. I mean, it's unlikely this tribe had been exposed to Christianity, but if what you say about collective unconscious holds water, it's a possibility."

"It's more than possible." Now she was beaming. "I'd say it's very likely, and now I've really got to see what's back here."

Don nodded his head in agreement, turned around, and redirected his light. He walked further into the darkness, taking one careful step at a time. His heart thrummed from the connection he had made, and the warm sense of satisfaction shielded him from the chill of the cavern. The flashlight bounced across the floor, then revealed a dark object at the end of its beam.

"What's that?" Don asked and led them closer to the shadow.

The sound of water dripping into a larger pool was louder and now closer to where they tread. He squinted to focus better and proceeded forward toward the strange dark mass. Shadows spread out to the left and right as the light danced upon the formation. Don walked up to it and shined his light down onto the structure.

"My God," he gasped.

Stephanie approached from the side and added the beam of her own light. They looked down at the ancient altar before them. It sat about four feet off the floor, supported by a pedestal at the head and the foot, all constructed from lodestone. On the dusty surface of the slab lay the skeleton of a child. The remains were no more than three feet in length, intact, and covered with jewelry. Ornate bracelets and rings adorned the child's fingers and wrists. All pieces had been fabricated from magnetite and interlaced with gold chains and links. The precious alloy reflected at them in the flashlight's beam and danced across their faces. Neither spoke as they examined the four-hundred-year-old skeleton.

The large amulet that had been placed around the child's neck now rested on the bones of the ribcage. The intricate design etched out of the lodestone was breathtaking. A sunburst originating from a concentric sphere spread out into individual rays that tapered off in waves. Gold had been incorporated into the piece as well. It looked as if it had fused with the rock at places in the center of the disc and alternating sections of the rays. In addition, the entire chain of the medallion was fabricated entirely out of gold. Stephanie reached out to touch the item, which was twice the size of her hand. She rubbed her fingers across its surface and then slid them underneath the medallion and lifted it to check the weight. She replaced it, then directed her light at the skull and leaned in. The lower jaw hung open, allowing Stephanie a clear look inside the child's mouth.

"What do you make of it?" Don asked.

"All human. No sign of anything different. This was just a normal child. No alterations to the skeletal or dental remains that I can see."

"Seriously?" Don examined the skull as well. He wasn't sure, but he felt as if his eyes had adjusted to the absolute darkness of the antechamber in the short time they'd been there. Lighter shadows danced against the dark, giving the room the appearance of artificial illumination, as if a light had been turned on and then increased in small increments. He dismissed the idea, knowing he was fooling himself; it just wasn't possible. He scanned the remainder of the cavern, checking three sixty, expecting his eyes to revert to night blind.

"Son of a bitch!" Don hissed, realizing he could see much more of the cave than he could before. He turned his light to the cavern floor in front of them; it extended for approximately ten feet and then disappeared as if it were swallowed up. Sweat beaded on his forehead despite the icy chill that gripped his heart like a glacier. Don had sensed it when he entered the cave but didn't realize how close they had come. The drop-off lay less than ten steps in front of them.

"Jesus Christ." He removed a tether of line and snaked it around the pedestal of the altar, then tied it off and fastened the other end to their safety line.

"What's going on?" she asked.

"Whatever you do, don't move. There's a drop in front of us, and I've got a feeling it's one deep son of a bitch." Don inched forward with his light aimed in front of him. He made his way to the edge of the drop, stopped two feet from the precipice, and cast the beam of light across the pit to the other side. A large circular well occupied the center of the cavern, and Don was able to make out much of the detail. It was about thirty feet across, symmetrical for the most part, and, just as he imagined, deep as hell.

A thick plume of condensation escaped his lips as he stared across the abyss in amazement. Now he was positive it was getting lighter in the cavern. He focused on the walls and shadows he hadn't been able to see before. In the distance, on the far side of the chasm, stood another mass of rock that looked exactly like an altar. He shifted his light to the right and came upon a third that was also identical. Don scanned the full circumference of the pit in search of another, but there were none. *Three altars for the three children.*

Finally, Don aimed the flashlight into the massive well. The beam was reflected at him in glints and shimmers and took him by surprise. Tiny particles of mica or possibly pyrite caught the illumination of the artificial light and flickered in the dimness like the tip of a sparkler. Don gasped and squinted, allowing his beam to dip further into the pit. He leaned over as much as he dared, curious how far down he would be able to see, and gasped.

The vison before him defied possibility. Don looked down into the well further than a five-hundred-watt bulb was even able to reveal; he stared into the pit, over a hundred feet down, by his estimation, all the way to the bottom. He saw the pool below, reflected in it the glow of his own flashlight, dancing like a million mirrors on a disco ball. The water itself was a milky white and appeared to almost absorb the light before bouncing it back, as if it were dense with a skin-like surface layer.

Then it changed. It looked like it had started to move. Ripples formed in the water below as if something were swimming within. Left to right for a moment, darting back and forth. And then—it began to swirl. Suddenly the pool stopped reflecting the light, the prismatic appearance of mirrors vanished, and the water itself began to glow like a bulb had been turned on deep below the surface. The milky-white color took on an opalesque quality and moved as if it were alive. He tried to call to Stephanie, but all that left his lips was a dry croak. He knew he should step away from the edge and retreat, but as the light grew brighter and the strange sensation of growing heat washed over him, Don was unable to move; he could only watch.

It wasn't anything like artificial light, stark and assaulting. This was warm and glowing and natural, like the sun. It continued to increase in intensity and soon filled the entire cavern, dispelling every shadow, revealing every surface of every corner in the entire cave. The walls of the pit were perfectly smooth, as if they had been eroded by rivers of time. The terrain along the perimeter was about twenty feet wide and formed a walkway that led from one altar to the next.

Now Don could see the skeletal remains on the other slabs, even from his distance forty feet away.

"What the hell is happening?" Stephanie called out from behind him. Her voice wavered and sounded on the verge of shrill.

"I—I have no idea."

"It's warm," she shouted. "And look on the other side."

Don didn't reply; his attention was drawn to the massive funnel of rock that towered above him. The scope of its dimensions was visible due to the addition of the new light source, and he had to force himself to breathe. Lost in the depth of it, Don felt smaller than he ever had, like a speck on the pistil of a flower, possibly a dust mite on the surface of the moon. It was unlike any natural formation he had ever seen or any that had been recorded. The geometric perfection that twisted above could in no way be mistaken for accidental. At the mid-point of the cavern's ceiling, an opening centered directly over the pit. It spiraled upward in an almost snail-shell pattern, but not exactly. Don thought it resembled more of a helix and was reminded of a three-dimensional image he had seen of the Milky Way. He tried to imagine the slow movement of a glacier or the steady flow of eons of water creating what lay before him but was unable to. It was too perfect, too precise, too calculated. Don thought Fibonacci would have really lost his mind had he found this.

"It's amazing," Stephanie said.

"It's more than that," he answered. "It's the geological find of the century." He turned back to her with his eyes wide and mouth agape, then smiled. He felt like a four-year-old boy on Christmas morning.

"You see that? You didn't have to go to California to make a name for yourself. It was right here, waiting for you all along."

He stared at her, noticing the sweat beading on her forehead. The cave was much warmer than when they walked in, and the light, although not overpowering in intensity and glare, revealed everything in a clarity and detail he thought he had never known. Even from where he stood, he saw the tiniest flecks of grey against the pale blue of Stephanie's eyes. He was sure he hadn't noticed them before. The pores of her skin, symmetrical and perfect, and even the faintest touch of grey in the few strands that had started to sneak into her blonde hair. He saw it all in the bath of clarity that washed up from the chasm.

Feeling more confident about their safety now that the cave was illuminated, Don motioned for Stephanie to join him near the edge. She left the side of the altar, approached him, and looked over into the pit at the strange light within.

"What do you make of it?"

"No idea." He hesitated for a moment. "Bioluminescence, possibly, but like none that we know of. Its—" The words to describe it fell short and were hard to form. "I could study this the rest of my life."

They exchanged a look but didn't speak on it, although both had been thinking the same thing. Life was a funny word to use under the circumstances. It was an uncertainty, to say the least, and not to be used lightly.

Finally, Stephanie nodded to him. "That makes two of us." Then she looked out across the pit to the other side. "I'd really like to get a look at the other altars. Do you think it would be safe for us to try?"

Don thought it was, and together, they made their way from altar to altar, examining and comparing the remains. All the skeletons had been children, and all wore identical medallions around their necks. They discovered no sign of alteration in the skeletal remains. The structure of the skulls, the jawbones, and even the teeth were all perfectly human. Which was unsettling and left questions rather than answers. Then, as if on cue, the strange illumination began to fade. It was a slow disappearance, which allowed enough time for them to navigate their way back to the small opening to the main chamber.

Outside, the rain continued to fall, the monstrous beings darted about the hardpan floor, and at some point, the electricity to the trailers and the lights in the parking lot had been cut. A mixture of excitement and awkwardness was felt by both Don and Stephanie but was spoken of only in brief intervals. They settled in with their backs against the wall of the cave in an attempt to escape the stress and confusion. Sometime during the night, despite the din of insanity that raced through both their heads, they managed to fall asleep. And although it defiantly fought to hold on, Wednesday night released its grip on Garrett Grove and acquiesced to Thursday morning. For better or worse.

● ● ●

Many of its numbers had been sacrificed. But the assault at the medical center and church had been necessary. The bodies of the simple ones were weak—its essence burned through them like an inferno. The need to replace their ravaged husks had always been the problem. But for every soldier it lost, two had been added, and the threat to its army had been neutralized. It learned of the priest's intentions with the acquisition of the one called Allison. The information she held was the key element, so it discontinued the attack and called its army back. Kieran was a clever one, and could have become a problem, but now it knew. The three, the carriers, were relocated while the others waited. It planted a vital seed of itself intended for the priest and his army, and then it, too, waited. It was good at waiting—it had waited for a long, long time.

Part Four

Chapter 87

Thursday

The Nor'easter that buffeted Garrett Grove and half the state of New York dumped a record ten inches of rain in just under five hours. The Lenape River swelled above its banks, flooding the low-lying areas of town and consuming what remained of the Gables Bridge. The damage from the heavy winds was extensive; from Route 3 to the top of Garrett Mountain, there wasn't a dwelling or business left untouched. Even the rockslide on Sunset Pass looked as if it could have been caused by the storm. On any other day, officials from Warren would have already come to check on their distant neighbors. But it wasn't any other day, and the storm had not been isolated to the Grove; Warren and the neighboring towns also experienced catastrophic damage. The power failure in Garrett Grove wasn't an anomalous occurrence either. Before the entire grid collapsed, a total of seven transformers had blown, sending an overload to the two step-down transformers at the substation, and a loss of one of the turbines. This resulted in an overload at the Con Ed Power Plant, which also effected the town of Warren, who had miles of downed lines and blown transformers of their own to deal with.

The rain had almost been enough to douse the numerous house fires that occurred throughout the town ... almost. Most were the result of extinguished pilot lights or overturned appliances as families were taken by surprise when hell smashed through their front doors and picture windows. Stoves were left on, fireplaces unattended, and candles had been knocked to the carpet. By the time the storm was over, most of the fires had burned themselves out.

An unearthly silence blanketed the streets of Garrett Grove. It spread out from the mountain like a tumor, silencing the usual chatter of wildlife in a suffocating shroud. The birds didn't call to the approaching dawn, nor did they ride the first thermal waves of the morning. Squirrels didn't scamper from branch to branch, and the chipmunks were nowhere to be seen. The larger animals were silent as well ... as if they'd never been there at all. And long before the first streaks of gold paved way for the rising sun, a deathly hush dominated a town that had once been alive.

The starkest contrast was the absence of people. Not one vehicle moved across a single stretch of pavement. The parking lot at Wilson's Diner was empty, as was the establishment itself. No coffee was prepared, no showers were turned on, and no early morning diapers were changed. Empty cribs sat in empty nurseries in empty houses on empty streets. It had been swift and impossible to stop, even for those who were aware of what was going on. The town had been infected by something far worse than anything Dr. Malcolm could have ever suspected. It had been ravaged by a plague. A plague that had silenced countless species in the past. And though it had been known by many names, they all meant the same thing ... extinction.

● ● ●

The surviving members of Ted Lutchen's group spent the night in the back room of the pharmacy at the medical center. The gauntlet they'd set up at the nurses' station had been ineffective; they were overrun and forced to retreat to the stairwell and then onto the roof, where they made their final stand. With the beasts closing in, Ted considered the unthinkable: using his weapon to spare his friends and then turning it on himself. But before he could act on the thought, it was over, the creatures ceasing their attack and disappearing into the storm.

But there had been casualties, a great number of them. Alice and Will Tobin, Ed Koloski and Grady Martin, Nurse Carole, not to mention every living soul that sought shelter in the basement. However, they found little carnage when they made their way from the roof through the third-floor hallway where the battle took place. There was a tremendous amount of blood and gore but nothing that could be identified. The creatures had assimilated or consumed what remained of the patients and fallen members of Ted's party, as well as countless numbers of their own. A fortunate Billy Tobin had been spared from finding the corpses of his entire family.

Ted kept watch throughout the night while the others rested. Even after what they had been through, they had all managed to fall asleep. Everyone except for Billy, who sat across from Ted, unblinking. The kid had lost everyone. Ted couldn't fathom how the guy was still functioning, how he hadn't broken down. The way he had chased after Dawn onto the roof without concern for his own safety surprised even Ted. The guy was a warrior. *Billy the Kid,* Ted thought as he inventoried the ammunition and weapons they had retrieved from the hallway.

Doris and Burt rested in one corner of the cramped area, while Dawn, Cyndi, and Baxter huddled together in another. All was quiet except for the occasional snores and chuffs from the coroner and the dog, then about an hour before sunrise, Ted rose to stretch his legs.

"I'll be right back," he told Billy, the only one awake.

"Are you sure it's safe?"

Ted shrugged. There was no way of knowing. The creatures had abandoned their attack when they could have easily finished the job. It was possible some had remained to scavenge the detritus of the dead, but Ted didn't think it likely. He would take a quick tour of the hallway, then make a pit stop in the men's room; his bladder had been screaming for over an hour.

He left the back room of the pharmacy with Billy locking the door behind him, then made his way through the second-floor hallway. All was quiet; the red glow of the emergency lights revealed nothing out of place. Ted kept his revolver in hand and proceeded with caution. He turned the corner, entered the men's room, and relieved himself. Standing at the sink, he stared at the unrecognizable face in the mirror. The dim light accentuated the bags under his eyes and reminded Ted of pictures he had seen of his old man. He splashed himself with cold water and was drinking down several mouthfuls when a blast of static squelched from the radio on his hip. He seized it and shouted into the mic.

"Come in. Is there someone there?"

"Thank God." The sheriff's voice was followed by another blast of static. "Good to hear your voice, Ted. What's your status?"

Ted didn't want to say too much for fear of Lois or the children overhearing. He had no idea how to share the news about those they had lost and figured delicately was the best approach.

Carl appeared to anticipate what Ted was thinking and cut in before the deputy could continue. "I'm alone. You can speak freely."

Ted took a deep breath. "Not everyone made it, Sheriff. The only ones left are Burt and Nurse TenHove, Billy Tobin, a candy striper named Cyndi, the dog, and the little girl." Ted stared at the strange face in the mirror and added, "I'm sorry."

There was a long pause before the sheriff replied. "Copy that. Tell Doris and Burt I will be there shortly after sunrise. I have a child with a massive head injury that requires immediate attention. Meet us in the emergency room and tell them to be ready. The kid's hanging on, but I don't think she's got much fight left in her."

"Roger that, Sheriff. We'll be ready when you get here." Ted ended the transmission and turned the water back on. He watched it form a funnel as it ran clockwise down the drain and tried to remember why it did that. *Why always clockwise?* His overtired mind was unable to recall what he had learned in school, how the metallic particles in the water were affected by the earth's magnetic poles. Not that it mattered. He splashed water on his face and prayed they might survive the day. Ted made his way back to his group, then led them through the abandoned medical facility to the emergency room.

They arrived on the first floor, and the group went straight to work. Doris and Burt prepared for their patient, and Ted sent Billy and Cyndi to the cafeteria to drum up something for breakfast. Dawn and Baxter remained behind, never straying from Ted's side.

"Deputy," Doris said. "I need you to contact the group at the high school. Find out if Dr. Freedman and Michelle Marks are available. Tell them their presence is required immediately."

Ted acknowledged and headed for the exit door. The sun had just begun to turn the color of the sky into a pale shade of pink.

"This is Deputy Lutchen to Bob Jones. Come in." Ted hadn't heard any of yesterday's transmissions and knew nothing of their status. He waited for a response that never came, then tried again. He knew it was impossible to transmit through the school's concrete foundation, but the dead silence led him to suspect a different explanation. He didn't know if Doris and Burt could handle what was coming their way but hoped their combined talents would be enough to save the child. A disturbing premonition gripped him, and Ted doubted if any of Garrett Grove's doctors had survived the night.

⚫⚫⚫

Carl was up before the sun and ventured out of the armory just as Ted was leaving the pharmacy. The basement of the sheriff's station revealed no sign of the menacing threat; it appeared the beasts had vacated the building sometime in the night. He cleared each room with his service revolver in hand, then made his way upstairs. Satisfied the place was secure, he contacted Ted, and although he hadn't had time to express himself, he was happy to hear his deputy's voice. But Carl was running on fumes; he couldn't remember a time he had been so thoroughly exhausted in his life, not even in Vietnam. Sure, he had been tired during the war, both physically and emotionally, but he was younger then and able to endure the sleepless nights.

Now it felt like he had been buried under a landslide, and the lack of sleep was only part of it. What affected Carl to his core was the insurmountable loss and despair that swept through his town like the angel of death. Something he said a lifetime ago came to mind: *People don't get murdered in Garrett Grove—not in my town.* He rubbed his temples, trying to force the cobwebs out of his head. He had kept Lois and Troy alive by sheer luck. If they were going to survive another day, it would take a lot more than that; he needed to stay sharp.

He tore through the supply closet, found what he was looking for, and returned to the basement. The group regarded him through bloodshot eyes when he entered the armory carrying the wooden stretcher. Wendy and Troy huddled near Janis, who had started to moan and managed a few incoherent words in her unconscious state. Carl maneuvered into the room unsure how he would break the news to Lois about Will and her sister, and knew now wasn't the time. It would be awful when he finally did, but he needed everyone as clear-headed as possible. Transporting Janis to the medical center would be difficult enough.

"The building is clear," he said. "The sun will be up in a few minutes, and I think it's safe to move Janis." Wendy and Troy met his stare. "She needs medical attention, and we'll use the stretcher to carry her." He knew the best thing he could do for the children was include them, so he assigned each of them a task and then set the stretcher beside the cot with Lois's help.

Even in the dim light of the armory, the deep purple bruise that crept across the girl's face was prominent. It flowed out from under the bandage like a stain. With the children off gathering supplies, Carl, Lois, and Jessica transferred Janis onto the stretcher, then carried her to the back of the mayor's station wagon. They grabbed everything they possibly could, knowing there was a good chance they would never return, then the group left the building.

Carl drove while Lois and Jessica did their best to secure the stretcher. Troy and Wendy sat in the backseat staring out the windows at the destruction. The spot where the two cruisers collided was the first scene of carnage they encountered. Both vehicles had burned throughout the night; all that remained were the hulking shells. When they turned left onto the Turnpike, the enormity of the devastation became apparent. A vehicle had crashed through the front window of the Plains Pharmacy; a splattering of crimson gore decorated the display shelves in a haphazard frenzy, making it look as if the owners had started to repaint the place in the dark.

The front of Bell's Hardware looked like it had been hit with a wrecking ball. Carl swerved around a Volkswagen Beetle overturned in the center of the road; a horrible dark brown stain spread out from the smashed-in windshield. Other vehicles had been left abandoned in the street as if they had run out of gas or just stopped working. The once familiar neighborhood was now a post-war scene of desolation; the absence of life was ubiquitous. Not so much as a squirrel darted from behind a single branch; the trees themselves looked as if they had witnessed something beyond unspeakable.

Houses had caught fire, many burned to their foundations. No one had been called to battle the blazes; even if they had, there had been more pressing matters than a few pieces of burning timbers.

THE OJANOX

The rain had moved on, but the wind was still strong in the wake of the storm. A cluster of papers blew across the street, and Carl knew what they were before the bills caught in the wagon's windshield wipers. The faces of Franklin and Grant stared in at the passengers as the vehicle lumbered past the Herald Bank. The front doors were destroyed; thousands of dollars now littered the parking lot and the street. Carl doubted the creatures had done that. Whoever thought the present catastrophe was a good diversion to hit the bank had either overestimated their own limitations or underestimated the nature of the catastrophe.

Carl checked the rearview to find Troy and Wendy wide-eyed with wrist rockets held at the ready.

He rounded the corner near the high school and drove straight to the entrance of the medical center. He pulled into the lot and made his way to the emergency room entrance to find Billy Tobin waiting at the door. Carl looked back at Lois, who hadn't yet seen her nephew, and prepared himself. *Son of a bitch!* He knew things were about to get even worse. He felt horrible for not having told her about Will and Alice; he had spared her a few moments of sorrow but doubted it would matter.

Ted exited the door and helped Carl with the stretcher. As they rushed into the building, Lois screamed and then started crying; her short reprieve was over. Her sobs permeated the building, echoing off every surface. A moment later, Troy's tears mixed with his mother's.

Doris directed the men where to place the stretcher. She and Burt were dressed in scrubs and had an array of equipment and supplies laid out on trays next to the bed. They transferred Janis to the bed and then began to examine her wounds. A low, almost inaudible gasp escaped from Doris's throat, but she quickly recovered and went to work. The nurse filled a needle from a bottle that said epinephrine and inserted it into the girl's arm.

"Gentlemen," she said to Carl and Ted. "I need you to remove yourselves from the area. We're working under adverse conditions and must take every precaution to prevent infection."

The men took several steps back when Burt approached and locked eyes with the sheriff. Carl nodded to his friend; the old man's voice resonated in his head as if he had spoken aloud. *This isn't going to end well, even if she does manage to survive.* Burt pulled the curtain and returned his attention to the patient.

● ● ●

Doris cut away the gauze and removed the bandages. "Oh Lord," she gasped, looking down on the wound. The child's hair was caked with dry blood, but Doris could still make out the ruinous indentation in the girl's head. The entire left side of Janis's face had bruised and swelled under the pressure of the concussion.

Together, they began to clean the wound, with Burt handing off items as Doris asked for them. The bed linens beneath the child began to turn red as the disinfectant washed the gore away. Doris had seen numerous head wounds during her time in the ER; concussions, even under the best circumstances, were difficult to predict as the brain swelled and pressed against the broken skull. Most were survivable, provided the damage wasn't too severe and the patient received prompt medical attention. But Janis had been unconscious for over twelve hours, and judging from the color of her face and the amount of blood loss, Doris believed the blood vessels in her brain had been compromised. At the very least, there had been some extent of brain damage. It was a miracle she had survived the night.

"Peanuts ..." The word escaped from Janis's lips, followed by a low moan.

Doris and Burt stared at one another, wondering how the child was still able to speak. The girl was a fighter. Burt made the sign of the cross and said a prayer. Janis moaned again and then muttered something that sounded like "you bacca," but neither were able to understand what she was trying to say. Then the corners of her mouth turned up as if she were trying to smile. She spoke again, and this time they were able to make out every word.

"Troy ... be careful."

● ● ●

Carl motioned for Ted to follow him, then led the deputy to the remains of the lobby. The entire front of the building had been smashed inward as if it were hit by a tank. Broken glass and twisted metal littered the floor, and a thick smearing of black tar trailed to the buckled basement door. Carl sensed the apprehension in his young deputy, who couldn't stop staring at the stairwell.

THE OJANOX

"I won't ask you to go down there," Carl said. "Not yet. You're sure no one survived?"

"I don't see how anyone could have," Ted replied. "I have no idea how we made it ourselves; it was the damnedest thing. They had us surrounded on the roof, we were outnumbered, then they just vanished."

"I need to get over to the high school. It went bad there too." Carl removed his hat and untucked his shirt, which was covered with Janis's blood. "That thing that got into Rainey's head ... it happened again, or it never left in the first place. He showed up at the high school last night with a fucking arsenal and killed damn near everyone. Andrea had to put him down. This thing used our own man against us. How do you protect against something that can do that?"

"Jesus, Sheriff." Ted's face went pale.

"We need to find a way to get everyone out of town before nightfall. I have no idea how we're going to do that. The pass and the bridge are out, and the river will be impossible to cross with the children and seniors." He unbuttoned his uniform and threw it to the side; the T-shirt underneath had a small smear of blood but nothing by comparison. It wouldn't comfort anyone if he showed up at the high school bathed in gore.

"I need you here, Ted. So far, they've only attacked in the dark, but stay sharp. While I'm gone, I want you to figure out an escape plan. I don't think we have another night left in us."

⬤ ⬤ ⬤

The sheriff exited out the broken front doors, and Ted returned to the emergency room to find Burt and Doris still behind the curtain, focused on their patient. There was no sign of the other members of his group. He left the area and headed to the cafeteria. Minutes later, he walked in to find everyone seated at one of the larger tables with Cyndi and the mayor busy behind a gas grill, flipping pancakes. The aroma of frying bacon and melting butter hit him like a freight train, causing his stomach to lurch in response. A stronger scent cut through the others and made his mouth water. Someone had brewed coffee, and it smelled intoxicating.

He approached the table where the small group of survivors gathered and offered his condolences. Ted Lutchen was no stranger to loss, though it had been years since he experienced it firsthand. Having spent his early years in different foster homes and then losing his adoptive parents when he was young, he knew there was little he could say that would help. He had been on his own ever since and considered himself lucky that he didn't have anyone left to lose, or so he thought.

Chapter 88

Bob Jones and the survivors at the high school spent the night huddled together in the back room, far away from the carnage in the main area. A group of just over three dozen mulled over a breakfast that had been prepared by several of the firemen; it did little to placate the grieving. Kelly Rainey clung to Jill Boriello like a baby kangaroo to its mother's pouch. Jerry Santos, Ralph Walsh, and a handful of the other children gathered around Miss Davis; none had left her side, not even to use the restroom. Tyler Harrison and Rich Marek assisted the seniors and helped feed them breakfast. The Bentley family stayed to themselves, trying their best to avoid the accusing stares from those who had not been as fortunate. It had been sheer luck that spared the Bentleys from the madman's bullets. But this morning, no one wanted to hear a damn thing about luck, so Günter and his brood sat away from the others, in the far corner eating cold cereal.

When breakfast was finished, Bob pulled Brandon to the side and led him out of the room. "You're with me. Do you have your weapon?"

Brandon showed him his sidearm, then followed the chief through the main area, past the rows of covered bodies. Bob unlocked the door to the staircase, and the men ascended. Neither had any idea what they might find in the gym or in the parking lot, but they couldn't stay in the basement; it had become a morgue.

They entered the gym to find it empty and quickly made their way to the exit doors. Bob pressed his ear to the steel and was alerted by the sound of approaching footfalls in the parking lot. He pulled back the hammer on his revolver and aimed at the center of the door.

"Hello. Is anyone there?" a familiar voice called out. "It's Sheriff Primrose."

Bob let out a sigh of relief and holstered his weapon. He motioned for Brandon to do the same, but the boy shook his head in response.

"How do we know it's really him?" Brandon asked. "It could be one of them like Rainey."

The kid had a point; they had been blindsided by an enemy that knew their weaknesses. Bob raised his weapon again and yelled through the door. "I'm here, Carl. But how do I know it's really you?"

There was a moment of silence, making Bob think the kid had been right, then Carl answered. "Good thinking. I guess there isn't much I could do to prove it without you seeing me. You probably have your guns drawn, so I'm removing my weapon and placing it on the ground. Of course, you can't see that, but when you open the door, I will keep my hands on my head. You can take my gun until you're convinced that it's me."

"Okay," he yelled. "Back away from the door."

Bob removed the chain securing the door, pushed it open, and raised his weapon; Brandon followed his lead. Carl smiled with his hands glued to the back of his head and stood there when the men emerged from the building and retrieved his weapon.

"Is it really you, Carl?" Bob squinted against the harsh morning sunlight.

"In the flesh," he said, making no sudden movement.

"Christ, it's good to see you." Bob holstered his weapon and looked at Brandon to do the same. "Put that damn thing away before you accidentally kill someone." He seized Carl in a bear hug and knocked the wind out of him.

"It's good to see you too, old friend," Carl replied, hugging him back.

Bob released him and looked down at the blood smear on the shoulder of Carl's T-shirt. "Where's your uniform?"

"We were in an accident ... One of the children." He paused. "We had to hold up in the armory until it was safe to leave. Doris and Burt are doing everything they can. Please tell me Dr. Freedman made it?"

Bob shook his head and met Carl's stare; he didn't need to answer but continued. "Michelle Marks is alive; she could assist Nurse TenHove."

Carl let out a thousand-pound sigh as they entered the gym and made their way toward the stairs. "I want you men to put your heads together," he said to both Bob and Brandon. "We have to get everyone out of town before sunset, and I need answers on how we are going to do that."

Bob shook his head and smiled.

"Tell me you have an idea."

"Not me, but I was talking to someone who does. I think it would be best to let him explain it to you, and a good idea to get everyone out of the basement." Bob's voice shook as they started down the stairwell. "It's awful down there, Carl ... It's just awful."

"I wish I had time to be a bit more sensitive to what you've all been through." Every eye zeroed in on Carl as he addressed the survivors in the back room of the shelter. "Unfortunately, time is of the essence, and right now, the important thing is getting you out of this basement and to safety. We're headed to the medical center to regroup with the others. The emergency generator is supplying minimal power, and there's hot water and plenty of beds. We're working on an evacuation plan, so as soon as you are ready—"

The promise of a hot shower got everyone on their feet and moving faster than even Carl expected. No one wanted to spend another minute trapped underground with hundreds of bodies just a stone's throw away. They gathered their limited belongings and made a mass exodus past the acre of corpses. Carl approached Andrea Geary, who was one of the last to leave the room. The glazed look in her eyes told him she was beyond shell-shocked; she had been defeated.

"He killed them, Sheriff. I didn't have a choice." Her voice lifted as if it had risen from a grave.

"I'm sorry." Carl stopped her and put his hands on her shoulders, causing Andrea to tense up. He hadn't been positive but had reason to suspect that she and Joel Kovach were romantically involved, cop intuition or maybe just his gut. "I can't imagine what you're going through. They were my men, and I loved them too; Joel was like a brother to me. And Rainey ... I swear, Andrea, we're going to get out of this; I just need you to be strong a little bit longer." Carl searched for the right thing to say, not wanting to sound cold or inappropriate. Something in his words appeared to affect Andrea, who looked up at him, a bit more clear-eyed, and forced a smile.

"Yes, Sheriff. I can do that." She left the room and headed upstairs just as Bob Jones approached with the Bentley family at his side.

"Carl," he said. "I believe Mr. Bentley has an idea you will find quite interesting."

"I'm looking forward to hearing everything you have to say, Mr. Bentley. Perhaps you could share it with me on our way to the medical center. You can all accompany me in my cruiser."

"Zat vould be goot, Herr Sheriff," Günter replied as he and his family followed the sheriff and the chief out of the basement and into the light of day.

On the way to the medical center, Günter explained his idea to Carl. It was a damn good one, and Carl couldn't believe he hadn't thought of it himself. Of course, it would have been impossible to execute yesterday due to the storm. Also, the plan couldn't accommodate a large group; however, their numbers had been greatly decreased. Carl followed the school bus to the center and listened to the supermarket manager lay out his plan in detail. And for the first time in a very long week, Carl Primrose felt hopeful. *This just might work.* It would have to; they were out of options.

Chapter 89

As the sun began to rise, Don and Stephanie stood at the mouth of the cave, staring out at the stillness of the quarry. The storm had passed, and from what they could see, there was no sign of the creatures that had descended from the mountain. They gathered all they could carry, taking several of the ancient tubes and anything that resembled a lodestone weapon, and made a break for Don's truck.

The horror of what happened to Garrett Grove was quickly revealed the moment they turned onto the Boulevard. The town was unrecognizable. Vehicles lay in tangled wrecks, abandoned, and overturned; some had been driven into storefronts, and others had been ripped apart. Numerous fires had occurred. Some of the homes and businesses were still smoldering, while others had burned to the ground. Telephone poles and trees had fallen, blocking the road with debris and downed power lines, forcing them to backtrack and find alternate routes.

A deep, guttural gasp escaped from Stephanie's throat when they turned into the Village. Don swerved at the very last second to avoid driving over the body lying in the center of the road. It was impossible to tell if it had been a man or a woman; there was little left that was identifiable. The poor soul's intestines trailed out from the remains as if they had been used for a game of jump rope; dark brown blood saturated the pavement.

Other houses had fallen in Stephanie's neighborhood. Windows were smashed in, front doors torn off their hinges, and many had caught fire. There were more corpses littering the development as well, lying on the front lawns and trapped in their vehicles; none appeared to be intact. Stephanie pointed to the Cape Cod on the left and burst into tears as Don pulled into the driveway. The house across the street was gone. A scattering of debris blanketed the front yard; the splinters that had been someone's home still smoldered.

"No!" Stephanie screamed and was out the door and running before Don came to a full stop.

There were no other cars in the driveway, and the front door had been smashed inward. Don watched Stephanie bound up the steps and disappear into the house. He quickly followed, finding pieces of the shattered jamb laying on the soaking wet carpet of the entranceway.

"Janis! Lynn!" Stephanie screamed from the back room. Don knew she was wasting her time; it was obvious the place was empty. She sprinted past him in a flurry and ascended the stairs three at a time. She called out and ran from one bedroom to the next, searching for her sister and daughter. The sound of her heavy footsteps echoed like thunder throughout the tiny house. Finally, she stopped moving as if she had found something.

"What the hell were you doing with this?" she said. A moment later, she raced down the stairs toward Don with what looked like a photo album tucked under her arm. She hurried out the front door without stopping. "They're not here. Let's go!"

●●●

They arrived at Don's house minutes later to find the place in even worse condition. Not only had the front door been smashed in a similar fashion, but the back door was broken as well. The bodies of countless creatures littered the entrance way and the first-floor rec room. A fight had taken place; by the looks of it, the creatures hadn't come out on top. All the monstrosities looked deformed, as if they were missing a few chromosomes. One of them resembled a reptile of some type, possibly a snake. Others looked more like a cross between human and primate.

Don walked through the rec room trying to piece together what might have happened. He approached the table he used for his prints and picked up the cardboard box. "Look at this," he said, turning it over so Stephanie could see.

The front of the box read *Devlin's Assorted Magnets*; the contents had been removed and the package left on the table. Don scanned the room and noticed the open toolbox in the corner, not the way he had left it. Then he saw the hammer and chisel laying amidst a litter of small black chips. He knelt, picked up the chisel, and watched as several of the chips attached themselves to the tool. He pulled off one of the magnets and showed it to Stephanie, who nodded and tilted her head to the side.

"Here," she said, taking the book from under her arm. She opened it and turned through the pages. "I think our children were looking at this. I couldn't understand what would possess Janis to go in my room and dig it out ... until now." She showed Don the page that the book had been opened to when she found it on her daughter's bed; it was titled *Cahokia* and contained several black and white photographs. The pictures were of weapons similar to the ones they had found in the cave; musket ball-sized spheres, arrowheads, daggers, and spear tips—all appeared to have been fashioned out of lodestone.

"Are you saying our kids knew what the hell was going on and figured out how to fight it?" Don looked down at the broken magnet in his hand.

"It looks that way," she said. Scanning the room, Stephanie spotted something near the back window and walked over to retrieve it. "Look!" She picked up the jagged shard of magnet and showed it to Don. The pointed angles gave the object the appearance of a sharpened projectile. The kids had used the hammer and chisel to smash the magnets into the perfect-sized weapons.

Don rifled through the empty bag left on his drawing table and fished out a receipt. "Magnets and three wrist rockets. Son of a bitch!"

"They were here." Tears brimmed heavy in the corner of Stephanie's eyes and ran onto her cheeks.

"Do you think our children did this? Is that even possible?" Don said, taking a moment to study the creatures and their wounds.

"I don't think a wrist rocket could do that kind of damage," she said. "Some look like bullet holes."

Don nodded in agreement. The damage appeared to have been caused by a large-caliber bullet. Which meant the children had held their ground until help arrived. One thing was certain, the kids had figured out what was going on long before anyone else had. And knowledge was the key ingredient to survival.

Together, he and Stephanie searched the rest of the house, but there was nothing else to be found. They were returning to the driveway when Don spotted another body in the backyard near the garage. A shiver settled into his spine, and a cramp gripped his heart in a stranglehold; something about the way it lay near the open door. He ran toward the corpse without saying a word, and Stephanie followed.

The primitive creature lay on its back with three small puncture wounds in its chest. A dark liquid oozed from the beast, matting its hair and staining the tatters of its remaining clothes. Don removed a ballpoint pen from his pocket and inserted it into one of the creature's puncture wounds.

"What are you doing?" Stephanie asked.

"I just want to see something," he said, tapping the pen into the damaged flesh until it connected with something hard. He twisted the pen and pried at the object. It popped out of the wound and landed in the grass between his feet. Don touched the back of the pen to the small black shard and watched it jump out of the grass and attach itself to the metal.

"It's a magnet." He held it up for Stephanie to see.

Her jaw fell, then she turned toward the open garage door behind them and motioned toward it. They entered the building to find two more bodies and the place torn apart. "So, this is Scream in the Dark," she said, examining what remained of the haunted house.

"What's left of it. I'd say your little girl finally saw it. They got out of here in one piece; I'm sure of it. We just need to find out where they went from here." Don remembered hearing the air raid siren but couldn't recall where any of the town's shelters were located. The only place he could think of might be the sheriff's station and figured that was as good a place as any to head to next.

He turned to exit the garage, stepping over the torn down cardboard pieces and remnants of what was left of Scream in the Dark. He approached Stephanie, who stood with her back to him, facing the same wall where a young Robert Boyle had stood just five days before. He reached out and touched her shoulder, immediately sensing the tremors ripping through her body.

"Hey, we're going to find them," he said.

THE OJANOX

Stephanie faced him, her eyes red and swollen and tears streaming down her cheeks. The tremble of her bottom lip caused her teeth to chatter. "I have a terrible feeling." She allowed Don to wrap his arms around her and draw her close.

"Don't talk like that."

"I can't help but think this is all my fault."

"You couldn't know any of this would happen. No one could."

"No." She pulled back and looked at him. "For what I did ... for what we did. I-I'm not religious, but as far as karma goes, I messed up big-time. What if this is karma. Oh, God—if something happened to any of the children, I'll never forgive myself."

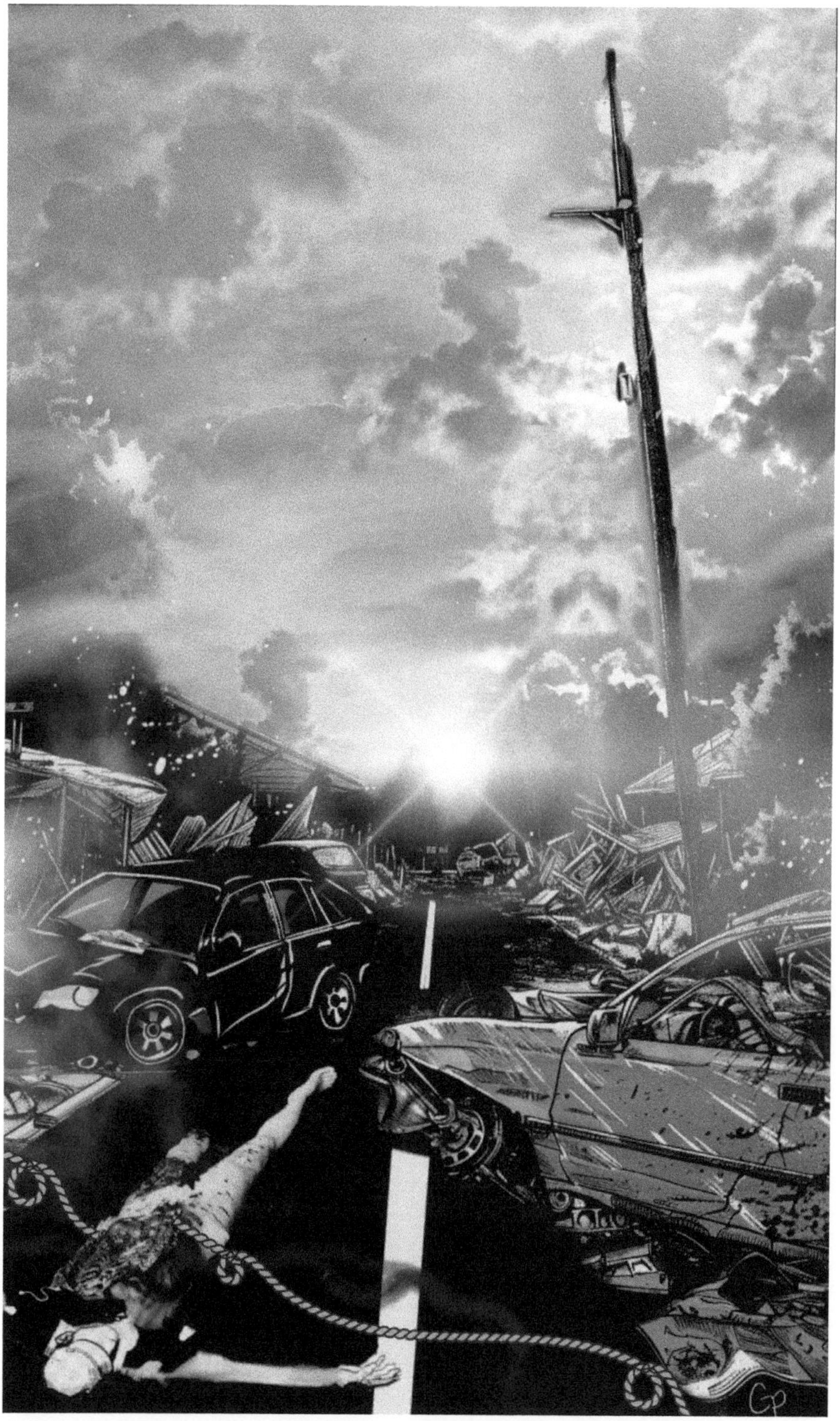

Chapter 90

The overall mood at Our Lady of the Mountain was exuberant for almost everyone except Father Kieran. Any general would consider the results of the previous night's battle a victory, but the loss of even one member of his flock was unacceptable. Allison was the first to arrive at the church, and she had been his sign from God. Her death was a significant sign as well, and her passing was devastating. More than ever, Father Kieran felt the reignited fire in his belly to bring the battle to the enemy. He wanted to hit them where it hurt, and thanks to Allison, he knew exactly where to strike. Allison had provided the strategic information and become a martyr in the process; now she was the inspirational force driving Kieran's determination to rain holy hell on the evil one.

The beasts attacked and then fled like cowards after realizing the parish was too great a force to overcome. Kieran's army kept a vigilant watch throughout the night, but the creatures never returned. When the sun rose on a new day, the newly formed militia prepared a victory meal fit for the Knights Templar. They used the rectory's gas stove to prepare the food and served breakfast in the parking lot.

Kieran knew the odds were in his favor and their best chance for a swift maneuver was to attack while the demons slept. After the meal was finished, the congregation cleaned and reloaded their weapons, packed their supplies into the vehicles, and formed a convoy leading to the top of Mountain Ave.

They filled the parking lot at Mountainside Park and left their vehicles on either side of the street. Then Father Kieran addressed his flock, offered a prayer to the Lord, and they began their arduous ascent up the abandoned Old Mountain Ave extension. The group assaulted the gate separating them from the treacherous road; rather than navigating a safe passage around it, they tore it down and trampled over it.

The old road didn't look any better in the early morning sunlight than it had the day a thousand snakes cascaded down its crumbled asphalt and attacked the Tobin brothers. It was still just as cracked and forgotten, although there were no reptiles to be found. There were no birds either, or squirrels, or chipmunks, or anything else one would expect to see in the early morning hours on Garrett Mountain. The road was silent; the only sound was the marching feet of Kieran's army.

The frenzy of the impending fight seized the crowd like a drug. It made their skin tingle with anticipation, set their nerves on fire, and filled them with a super-heightened sense of awareness, as if their morning coffee had been spiked with amphetamine.

There was one member of the flock who still wasn't buying all the gung-ho dogma the priest was selling. Amy Sterling didn't feel half as optimistic and had attempted to voice her concerns at breakfast. But she had been cut off and silenced by members of a cult that had been recruited less than twenty-four hours ago.

The loose gravel made traveling hazardous, and Amy had nearly fallen twice already. With every step that brought them closer to their destination, she became more certain she wanted no part of it. Still, she followed the others, kept her mouth shut, and waited for the right moment. She ascended the steep incline until she came to a spot where a large branch sat amidst a cluster of loose asphalt, and decided to make her move. Amy stepped onto the scattering of pebbles and allowed her foot to slip out from underneath her. She came down hard, more on her fanny than anything else, grabbed her leg, and screamed.

"Ahhh!" she cried. "My ankle." Amy grabbed her wounded foot and rocked back and forth on the loose pavement. Julie Evans rushed to her side.

"Are you all right?" Julie asked.

"I think so." Amy tried to stand but fell again when she transferred her weight.

Julie helped steady her friend while the rest of the congregation gathered around them. Father Kieran parted the crowd and knelt beside the girls. "Are you hurt badly, my child?"

"I think she sprained her ankle, Father," Julie said. Amy looked up at the priest with a tear in her eye.

"I'm afraid you won't be joining us in battle, Amy," he said. "I'm sorry."

"I can make it, Father." She tightened her face in pain.

"I'm sorry, but we can't take you." He placed his hand on her shoulder. "We will come back for you after we defeat the beasts." Kieran motioned to Dick and Josh. "Brothers, help Amy to a comfortable spot on the side of the road. Our sister has fallen." He turned and addressed the crowd. "It is here where we must part ways ... let us march!"

Dick and Josh grabbed Amy under each arm and assisted her to the side of the road. They sat her down on a patch of grass in the shade, checked to see she was comfortable, then joined Father Kieran and the rest.

Amy wiped away the tears that had come naturally, not the ones she intended to shed to sell her act. She took Julie's hand, pulled the girl close, and whispered in her ear. "Don't go up there. Please stay with me."

"I can't." Julie's eyes welled up. "Luke." Her husband had bought into what the preacher was selling, and there would be no talking him out of going. "My place is at his side ... for better or worse. I'm sorry."

"You can't." Amy tried to hold on to Julie as the girl pulled away.

"I'll come back for you." Julie turned and joined the rest of the group.

No ... no you won't. Amy wanted to scream and beg her friend to stay with her but knew there wasn't a thing she could say that would change her mind. Instead, she watched the congregation continue up the steep road until they disappeared over the crest. She removed a pack of cigarettes from her coat pocket, lit one up, and let the smoke swirl around her head on the cool October breeze. Her plan hadn't worked out quite the way she intended; she had hoped Father Kieran would have dispatched a member to stay behind with her, Julie preferably. But the priest was committed to the fight, and the thought hadn't crossed his mind. He was blinded by his own bloodlust, and Amy was the only one who had seen that. Julie knew it too but refused to leave her husband's side. *Fools.*

Amy stood up and flicked her butt into a loose patch of asphalt where another girl had fallen less than a week ago. That girl was also dead. Amy brushed the dust off her jeans and started to walk down the old, forgotten stretch of pavement, being extra careful to watch her step. The last thing she needed to do was fall and twist an ankle.

The front doors of the sanatorium had been left open, the hinges now rusted and frozen in place. Most of the windows in the building had been broken by drunken teenagers along with every mirror and interior pane of glass. Father Kieran held the large-caliber pistol in his hand and stood before the oppressive structure for the first time, the perfect sanctum for the Dark One. The grounds reeked of suffering and despondency; every pore of every brick cried out against the horrors that endured for years behind its now decaying walls. The looming monolith cast a dark shadow across the battered asphalt. Standing before the desperate structure made the priest's head swim and his eyes water. Father Kieran tried to ignore the sour pit in his stomach as it turned like a screw being threaded too tightly. He bit back against an overwhelming sense of intimidation and forced a smile, then he rallied his troops one last time before ordering them forward.

"The Lord is with us today," he said, standing tall in the shadow of the sanatorium. "Stay sharp and we will be triumphant! The beast sleeps by day; we have the element of surprise on our side. We will dispatch the demons and end their suffering. And they will be thankful that we did." Father Kieran ascended the front steps of the sanatorium and entered the building. His entire flock followed without a word of resistance.

For decades, Mountainside Sanatorium housed members of society who required isolation to prevent them from infecting the rest of the population. Now a far deadlier infection resided in the old hospital, one that made tuberculosis look like a case of the sniffles. This one possessed a consciousness, and it knew the minute Kieran and his flock entered its home. It had been waiting for them, after all ... and they were welcome. It had been a long time since the old hospital had visitors, even longer since the Entity had devoured a group so sure of themselves, so confident they had the upper hand. But the one called Allison had revealed their plans, and it was prepared. It had relocated the three that possessed its essence, separating them from the brood. Although it had little concern for the priest and his soldiers, the bodies of the little ones were weak and would soon need to be replaced with fresh hosts. There was no reason to risk unnecessary exposure when it could easily dispatch the priest's forces from where it now slept, miles away in the minds of Rob, Erin, and Ben.

Sometime between Tuesday morning and Wednesday night, Angelo and Donna Franco had come to believe in monsters, leading to a quick restoration of their faith. Although it hadn't been lacking to begin with, during times of desperation, there was always a fire sale on the product. And the young couple had bought what Father Kieran was selling ... in bulk. Even Donna, who had been paralyzed with fear only a few days ago and unable to walk across her neighbor's kitchen floor, now found herself filled with a sense of invincibility. The young couple were the last to climb the crumbling stairs and enter the foyer of the building. The overpowering funk of mold, decay, and death permeated the place like a vapor. It hit Donna in the face, causing her to gag as the putrid stench filled her mouth and sinuses. She doubled over and retched, then noticed the stains on the moldy tile floor. An army of oily black tracks covered every inch of the tile; most of them looked fresh.

Donna jumped at the jarring concussion of heavy metal slamming behind her. Although she knew she'd been the last to enter the building, she turned back toward the entrance expecting to find someone had shut the doors behind them. But no one was there ... no one had slammed the front doors ... because the doors were no longer there. The stairs, the entrance way, and the foyer she had passed through only seconds ago were all gone. A solid monochromatic ocean of dark red wavered before her. The crimson hue of the wall reminded Donna of the dried blood left on her neighbor's kitchen floor.

She spun about, reached for Angelo's hand, and came up with nothing. Her husband, who had been standing at her side, had been replaced by another wall of scarlet identical to the first.

"Angelo!" she screamed, spinning three-sixty to locate her husband and the other members of the party. Everyone had disappeared. Donna found herself surrounded by the repulsively-colored surfaces. The ceiling and floor had also been transformed into the solid shade of drying blood, making it impossible to discern where one flat surface ended and the other began. There were no visible right angles; the monotonous flow of the landscape made Donna's head swim. She swayed on her feet, overcome by a dizzying sense of vertigo. Finding it impossible to attain depth perception from the flood of sensory input, she reached out to grab on to anything that might help steady her. She took a lumbering step forward, then another. Donna's hands smacked against something wet and were sucked in up to her elbows.

She screamed and struggled to pull her arms free from the suction of the wall, but it held fast and began to pull back. Donna jerked with a violent twist and managed to yank herself free; she was slapped across the face by the warm wet liquid. It was rancid and smelled much like the stench that had hit her when she first entered the building, only far more concentrated. Examining her hands to see what had splashed her caused Donna's heart to stifle in her chest. Her arms were covered in crimson from elbows to her fingertips, dripping thick with deep red blood. Her eyes struggled to focus on the coating; it appeared to be pulsating on her skin. Then she felt it … it was moving.

Donna looked closer to find thousands of tiny red worms clinging to her flesh. They flipped and twisted along the entire length of both arms. She twitched when the first one crawled across her face and over her eyelid. Donna reacted and brushed it away but only managed to transfer more of the small creatures onto her cheek.

She screamed and began swatting at the worms, then tried to scrape them off her arms, which only aggravated them. The first one bit into the skin just above her wedding ring, followed by another that nipped her on the wrist. As if they had been waiting for a signal, the entire swarm of maggots bit into Donna's flesh on cue. Hot white light erupted behind her eyes, and every pain receptor in her brain fired as the worms burrowed into her flesh. They ate at her, digging away tiny channels into her skin and biting her face. Donna's head flailed as if in the grip of a grand mal seizure. All the while, her hands clawed to remove the worms that simply were not there.

The suggestion planted in her head had been small but effective. It took root and snowballed, her neural network doing most of the work itself.

There was an inaudible snap as the thin thread connecting Donna to reality was severed. She bucked and twisted, then hunched over and started running at top speed. Her fingernails tore deep gouges into her forearms as she attempted to scratch the worms out of her flesh. Lost in a sea of scarlet, Donna struggled to outrun insanity. But it already had control of the reins, propelling her forward with no idea she was in motion. She ran across the lobby toward the thick marble banister of the staircase with her head lowered like a battering ram. Her feet skated across a scattering of loose plaster, but somehow, she remained upright, and she continued to build up speed.

Donna's head connected with the unforgiving solid marble. The sickening crunch that her spine made when it snapped at the brainstem was audible, but it was only heard by her; she had simply mistaken it for the sound of a worm biting into the soft flesh on her neck. And Donna Franco was dead before her body hit the floor.

Not far away, a dark presence found great satisfaction in her death; it had almost been as satisfying as if it had consumed the woman itself... almost.

⬤ ⬤ ⬤

Just as Donna turned to find herself face to face with the scarlet apparition, her husband, Angelo, was thrust into a nightmare of his own. The lobby stretched out before him as if the walls, floor, and ceiling were no more tangible than the exterior of a balloon. The expanse of the room elongated, walls that had been near twenty feet in length doubled, then quadrupled in size until Angelo could no longer see where they ended. The ceiling disappeared into an infinite void. His stomach flipped, and Angelo doubled over and vomited onto the floor, but that, too, vanished as the tile beneath his feet expanded into nothingness.

He stumbled for a moment, then turned to search for his missing wife. His eyes struggled to focus on the enormity of the endless hallway but found the task impossible to accomplish. Angelo raised his gun and pointed it down the hall; he thought about firing off a round, then hesitated. The hallway grew darker, and there was movement in the far distance. He squinted at what looked like thermal waves and something suspended above the floor.

"Hello," he shouted. "Where is everyone?" Angelo began to make his way down the endless corridor. The .357 in his hand trembled, and the pulse of a bass drum beating against the back of his eyes made it impossible to see straight.

The void beneath him listed hard to the left, then pitched to the right. Angelo was thrown against one hard surface and then ricocheted into another. He managed to stay on his feet, but the gun was knocked out of his hand; he watched it tumble away down the hall. Angelo scrambled after the weapon and crouched to pick it up, but the gun was torn from his reach as if it were on a conveyer belt. With a jolt, the entire hallway heaved like the deck of a wooden ship caught in a hurricane, tossing both Angelo and the gun. He was thrown over five feet into the air, then came down hard on his side on top of the gun.

Angelo's shoulder popped out of the socket when the force of his downward momentum was halted by the unforgiving cold steel. The sensation of his extremity tearing out of the cup blinded him, and Angelo vomited once again. Searing pain like soldering irons probing his flesh brought him to the edge of unconsciousness, then pulled him back slowly. After what felt like an hour, he rose to his feet, his left arm hanging limp a good nine inches longer than the right. He winced against the pain assaulting his entire left side, picked up the weapon, and froze.

Angelo found himself in the middle of the movement he had seen in the distance. Icy breath escaped his mouth, forming long plumes of condensation in the frigid air. Huge slabs of meat, much bigger than any sides of beef Angelo had ever seen, swung back and forth, suspended from massive hooks connected to rusted chains. The encompassing stench of rot filled the air, and the only sound was that of a thousand flies as they feasted on the carcasses of spoiled flesh. The ceaseless rocking of the meat accompanied by the nauseating stench was nearly as maddening as the din of the insects as they rippled across the putrid grey flesh.

Angelo navigated a path around the slabs, being careful not to touch the meat or the flies. But the insects appeared to sense his presence, their droning song changing in pitch and timbre as he passed. All the while, the decaying carcasses swayed closer toward him as he turned sideways to clear a passage up the middle. Then he saw them ... figures coming toward him, lumbering down the hall from the opposite end.

He couldn't tell what they were but could see they were dressed in white and moved in frantic jerking motions. Sweat broke out on his forehead despite how cold it had gotten. There were two of them, much closer than they had been only a second before. They looked almost human but didn't move like any human Angelo had ever seen. Throwing their arms in the air, then bringing them down in violent sweeps, they ran at him with the intention of a freight train. Then he saw the butcher's aprons they wore and the cleavers they wielded. The fast-approaching menaces raised their weapons high into the air and then brought them down like lumberjacks against the rotting carcasses. Huge chunks of meat fell from the bones, sending swarms of flies into the air.

Angelo's lungs cramped as if they had shriveled in his chest at the ghastly sight. The creatures were featureless, devoid of any facial characteristics; they had no mouth, and no nose or eyes. But somehow their aim was deathly accurate. He froze where he stood, allowing the monsters enough time to hone in on him. Their blank canvas faces pointed in his direction, and they came at him like a tsunami. Angelo raised the gun and fired at the beast closest to him. The bullet hit it in the chest, causing the white fabric of its apron to run deep red. The second one reacted and bolted at Angelo, who turned his weapon and fired. The lunatic butcher was felled by a bullet to the forehead.

Fighting to catch his breath, Angelo regained a small amount of his composure and raced down the hall, away from the rotting meat. He stepped over the bodies he had shot. Luke Evans and Diane Nathan had both been fighting their own individual nightmares. Neither had been wearing white or carrying a clever, but Angelo's bullets had worked on them just the same.

"Angelo, where are you?" Donna's voice called to him from somewhere down the hall.

"I'm here," he shouted. "I'm coming." He passed the last slab of hanging meat as fast as his throbbing shoulder would allow. The floor continued to pitch and toss him off balance, but Donna was nowhere in sight and Angelo was rapidly approaching the end of the hall.

"Angelo!" Donna screamed. "Hurry!"

Picking up the pace, Angelo pushed through the pain with his arm stabbing at him like a molten dagger. His feet landed on black-stained tiles as he approached the ancient elevator shaft that had been pried open a decade ago by a group of drunken teenagers. Donna's voice called up from the darkness of the shaft before him. Angelo was unaware of the Entity's presence.

He stepped off of the hallway floor and onto nothing. The feeling of weightlessness never registered as his other foot followed him into the darkness. In a heartbeat, he was falling. For a fleeting moment, Angelo realized something had gone very wrong. His body cartwheeled as it fell thirty feet down the abandoned shaft toward the mangled hardware that lay rusted and corroded at the bottom.

Angelo's body smacked against the hardened steel, and just like that ... the pain in his shoulder was gone. His spine severed in three places, and his skull cracked open like a cantaloupe filled with strawberry jam.

It watched the man's body shatter against the machinery. If it had working vocal cords, it would have been laughing, but the three children had lost that faculty some time ago.

Julie Evans stepped out of reality and walked into a page straight out of Robert Boyle's notebook, which had been created and perfected in the mind of Troy Fischer. The Entity that consumed Robert was so enthralled by the idea of the ambush it couldn't resist utilizing the psychological manipulation.

Julie found herself thrust into absolute darkness, unlike the Francos, who had been consumed by visual illusion. A blanket of night closed in and suffocated her as if she was being held under water. Not even a shadow of black on black permeated the stark canvas devoid of sensory input. She reached out for anything to help navigate her way through the abyss, her fingertips tingling as they contacted nothing. A profound emptiness filled her, and fear lashed out as Julie made the quick progression from tears to sobs to hysterical panic. Her hand smacked against the wall to her right, allowing her to gain her balance, at least for a moment. When something brushed up against her left side, Julie screamed. She relaxed a second later, realizing it was the wall on the opposite side; somehow the hallway had grown impossibly narrow and closed in on her.

Julie soon found herself sandwiched between walls on either side, with just enough room to shuffle forward by turning her body sideways.

THE OJANOX

The darkness was overpowering. She sidestepped through the narrow corridor with one wall pressed snug against her back and the other tightly against her stomach and chest. She raised her arms alongside her without a thought for the firm grip on the pistol in her hand. Her ragged breath escalated; the frantic cries burnt like cinders in her chest. She forced herself to continue forward, but the hallway had grown so narrow she was unable to progress. She had come the wrong way and hadn't even realized it. Julie prepared to move in the other direction when it hit her. It blasted her in the face—hot, wet, and pungent—and Julie was acutely aware. Something stood mere inches before her and had just exhaled directly into her face.

Blinding white light erupted from every angle, searing her eyes and momentarily paralyzing her. It had happened so sudden and intensely that Julie suffered a minor heart attack on the spot. However, it wasn't enough to kill her, and the terror that followed shocked her back into the moment. The strobe flashed at a frenzied pace, revealing the cage she had pressed herself up against. The horrible beasts that occupied the space in front of her threw themselves at the bars and clawed at her. Covered in hair, their deformed faces contorted as they howled, filling the tight area with their noxious breath.

With no way to turn, she tried to sidestep in the opposite direction but found the act impossible. The walls closed in tighter around her as she struggled to move. One of the beasts smashed its grotesque face against the bars and shrieked, spraying spittle into Julie's eyes and mouth. She screamed and fought to free herself, her pulse thrumming in time to the strobe.

Julie's heart slammed against the walls of her ribcage and flooded her brain with too much blood. She stumbled over her feet and tried to force her way down the hall. She tensed up and squeezed the trigger of the weapon in her hand. Julie's arms had been raised in the confines of the hallway, and the bullet didn't have very far to travel. The hot lead slammed into her temple and bounced around inside her skull, tossing the grey matter like a Caesar salad. Her lights went out, and she fell to the floor between the bodies of her husband and Diana Nathan. Troy Fischer had been correct about the effectiveness of his idea; in the end, Julie Evans really did Scream in the Dark.

● ● ●

Jimmy Reilly flanked Father Kieran up the stairs of the old hospital and was the second man to enter the building. But the moment he cleared the threshold, he fell victim to the same mind trap as everyone else. The Dark One had left a present for the priest and his followers, one that would ensure the safety of the Entity's children while they slept in the basement.

Jimmy found himself walking through the halls of Garrett Grove High School. He knew he was late for his next class and raced down the hall to the boys' room. He passed one of the classrooms and caught a glimpse of his boyish features in the glass. His youthful face had still been intact back then, and Jimmy was beginning to forget it had ever been otherwise. The crowd of students that progressed the halls appeared to separate as he made his way forward, as if they sensed his presence and didn't wish to impede his momentum. He raced to the restroom with an overwhelming urgency to relieve himself, then turned the corner into the pungent surroundings. He entered the stall and unzipped his fly, feeling he might just piss himself. He smelled the sulfur and saw the cherry bomb sitting in the toilet a second before it exploded. The bowl shattered, throwing up tiny blades of shrapnel at him. Jimmy had enough time to close his eyes before he felt the first shard penetrate his cheek.

● ● ●

Jimmy made his way down the hallway; the memory of the past few seconds faded as he tried to figure out where he was. Late for class ... that was it. Somehow, he had gotten tied up, and he was about to miss the final bell. Worse than that, he had to piss like a goddamn racehorse. He double-timed it toward the boys' room and caught a glimpse of himself in the window of one of the classroom doors. He smiled when he saw himself; he always liked the face the Lord had blessed him with and couldn't wait for his confidence to catch up with the rest of him. He imagined he would become quite the ladies' man one day. He ran into the bathroom, barged into the first stall, and unzipped his fly. The world was eclipsed in a deafening concussion and blinding light. The pain in his face exploded like he had fallen onto a fire ant mound, the razor-sharp pieces of porcelain making quick work of his flesh.

●●●

The crowded hallway of the high school was nearly impossible for Jimmy to navigate. He was already late, and on top of that, he had to go like there was no tomorrow; if he didn't make it to the bathroom soon, he would surely piss himself, which he hadn't done since kindergarten. His bladder screamed but not as loud as the pain he felt in his face and his head. He passed one of the classrooms and turned to look in the glass as he walked by. The face that stared back at him was unrecognizable; it was horribly disfigured, as if it had been in a terrible accident years ago, and never healed correctly. Jimmy tried to force the image out of his head, thinking it had been a trick of the light or his own mind playing games with him. He rounded the corner and entered the bathroom in a frenzy with his belt undone and zipper halfway down. He ran into the stall and began to piss; he had been holding it for so long.

Before he could react, there were hands on him as someone grabbed him from behind and pushed him forward. It was Butchie Post, the school lunatic; the guy had had it out for him all year. Jimmy struggled but was unable to move while Butchie held him and pulled his pants to the floor. "Hold still, pussy!" Butchie screamed, pressing up against him.

Jimmy struggled to get away from the madman, but every move he made allowed Butchie a better hold on him. *What the hell is he trying to do?* Then he felt it press up against him as the monster forced his head into the toilet. His face submerged under the water as the lunatic pressed harder against his backside and invaded him. *Dear God, what's happening?* It was the last thing he thought before the bomb exploded and took half his head off with it.

●●●

Jimmy stumbled through the empty hallway of the high school, tripping over his own feet. Blood flowed down the front of his shirt and splattered onto the floor. His pants hung around his ankles as he shuffled off in a direction he had no idea he was heading. Bells rang in his head, making it impossible to think or even focus. He almost fell when he entered the bathroom but managed to hold on to the wall for support. Jimmy made his way to the sink, then stood before the mirror. Half of his face was missing; his left eye hung out of the socket, suspended by a mass of veins and optic nerves. His stomach somersaulted at the sight of the beast in the mirror that looked an awful lot like him. Before he could fully react, he was grabbed from behind and manhandled to the floor, unable to understand what was happening with the two percent of his brain that still worked.

"Hold still, pussy!" a familiar voice said, the owner shoving something stiff into Jimmy's ass. He lay there as the creature forced him to relive the scene over and over until Jimmy's brain was as limp as an overcooked piece of spaghetti.

Jimmy Reilly moaned on the lobby floor of the old hospital with drool running from his mouth in a steady stream; he pissed himself repeatedly.

The Entity ransacked what was let of Jimmy's frail psyche and destroyed it in less than three minutes.

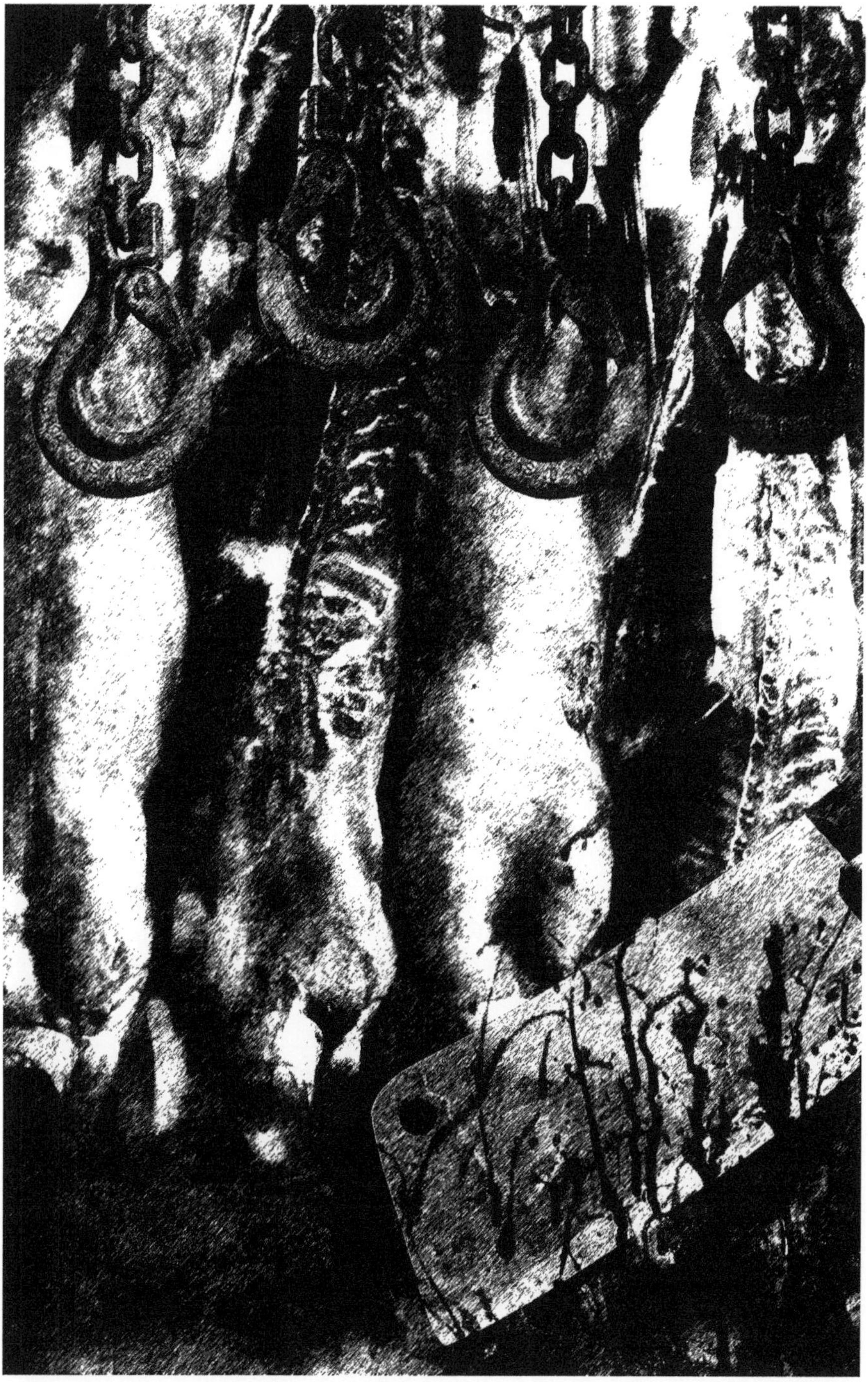

Chapter 91

Father Kieran had underestimated the enemy; even worse, he had overestimated himself. He had mistaken the creature for something as simple as a demon or a fallen angel. He was unaware of the intelligence it was capable of, nor could he fathom the measure of its hunger for domination. The priest's deceptive victory the night before had been a ruse to extract information and lull Kieran into a false sense of security; and the priest had fallen for it like a child.

The intel obtained by the portion of the Entity residing in the misshapen body of Erin Richards was all the tactical advantage needed to thwart the priest's forces at the gate. It ransacked Allison's simple mind and assimilated her into the brood. Her addition proved helpful when it came to laying the mind trap at the entrance of the nest. The enemy had simply walked into it; everything in their heads was there for the taking and easily used against them. The priest had taken down the one called Malcolm, and for that, he would suffer ... for a long time, for eternity if his mind allowed it. It had already tasted the man through the thoughts of Allison, and when the priest entered the lair, it knew all it needed to manipulate the man completely.

Sergeant Kieran McCabe ducked at the sound of artillery fire echoing in the distance. A mortar exploded a half klick from his position; the concussion was great enough to cause his ears to pop. He looked through the thicket of jungle to the other men in his platoon and motioned for them to stay down. The AK-47 he held tight to his chest was comforting yet thrilled him at the same time. He had killed more Viet Cong with the weapon than he could count and was about to add a few more to the list. He raised his hand and ordered his men to follow. He had been bred for leadership, and although he should have ranked higher than sergeant by now, he was glad he hadn't. It allowed him to fight alongside his men, as opposed to being stationed so far away from the action that the only fighting he would see was if he refused to pay one of the whores in Saigon.

He led the men through the brush and emerged first into the clearing on the other side. A cluster of commies gathered around one of the rat holes, preparing to go underground. He held up his fist, telling his men to hold tight, and removed the sidearm from his holster. The large .45 was a beauty and had one hell of a kick, also it left an exit wound the size of a grapefruit. He backed slightly into the brush and aimed at the first target. He preferred to use the .45; it was so much more personal, and he wanted to remember the kill.

Kieran fired at the man. The image froze like a Polaroid as the bullet entered the commie's forehead and exited out the back of his skull in a volcanic spew. He trained the weapon on the next man, who didn't have time to move, and fired again. Another bullseye; the man fell next to his dispatched comrade.

"This one's for Uncle Sam, you commie fuck!" Kieran hissed, squeezing off the final round at the last man as he attempted to enter the tunnel. The projectile caught him in the throat but failed to kill him; a river of crimson exited the wound in a deluge. Kieran rushed toward the man, stood over him, and pointed his .45 at the gook's head. Then ... the scenery shifted; the jungle swam into a blur of green and black, and vanished. Kieran looked down as the stained floor of the sanatorium faded into view.

THE OJANOX

He found himself standing over Dick Wilson with his weapon pointed at the diner owner's head. The man had been shot in the throat. He stared up at Kieran with terror in his eyes and scrambled to get away from the priest.

Kieran looked at the weapon in his grip; it was still smoking and hot from having been fired. *What have I done?* He scanned the floor of the old hospital and saw the bodies of the others where they had fallen. Bill Hamilton, the fire inspector, had been shot in the head and lay a few feet from the body of Frank Palumbo, the owner of the Texaco station.

Father Kieran knew it had been his bullets that took the men down ... but how? "Lord, how could you let this happen?" he demanded as Dick Wilson let out an asphyxiating gasp and collapsed on his back. The man had come to Kieran looking for salvation, hoping to find someone who might lead him in the fight against evil. The priest studied the smoking gun in his hand and started to cry. He had no recollection of drawing his weapon in the first place.

Other bodies littered the floor of the lobby; Kieran's tears fell and pooled with their spilled blood. Then he noticed the rest, the ones that were still alive, who stood there frozen in place. Josh Wilson had stopped a few feet from the main entrance; his jaw hung slack with his eyes rolled back in his skull, revealing only the whites. Others stood just as catatonic with their arms limp at their sides; many had dropped their weapons. One of the women lay before the banister; her head had been smashed in from an obscene amount of force. Kieran opened his mouth to alert the others. They had been ambushed and were being picked off one by one.

Then ...

● ● ●

Sergeant Kieran McCabe ducked at the sound of artillery fire echoing in the distance. He reloaded his side arm and waited for the exact moment to strike. He had always been destined to serve in the military and was determined to leave this war a hero, even if meant he would have to kill every last commie bastard himself. Which was exactly what he intended to do.

It played with the priest and forced the man to destroy the rest of his flock, just like a good little toy soldier. When the Entity had finally gotten bored with the man, it tossed him down the elevator shaft, where he landed next to the other creature. Neither body would go to waste and would provide some well-appreciated nourishment for its brood when they woke. The same was true for the bodies on the floor of the lobby.

It had expended a great deal of energy with the execution of the mind trap and retreated fully into the minds of the three. It rested and attempted to regain its strength. There was much that needed to be done before it moved into Warren. It needed to acquire the others, and then it needed to transfer.

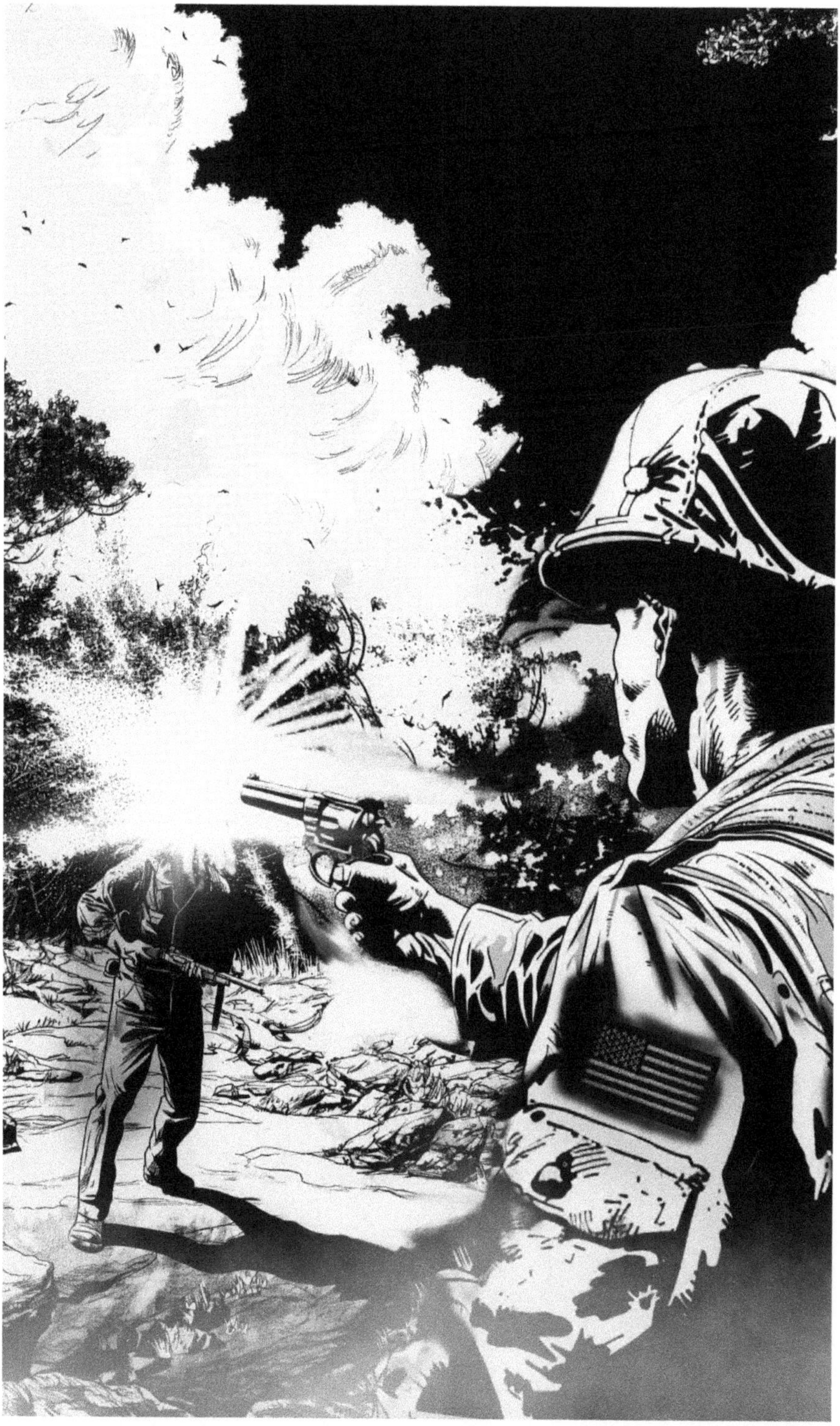

Chapter 92

The small group ate breakfast in the wake of a most somber silence. The pancakes and coffee that Cyndi and the mayor served helped to alleviate a glimmer of the sting but did nothing to placate the wounds. They were all processing the loss in their own way, and it was something they would be dealing with the rest of their lives, however long that turned out to be. So many had died—best friends, neighbors, brothers and sisters, mothers and fathers. Despair had taken residence in Garrett Grove and knocked on everyone's door.

Billy and Lois, who were reeling from the deaths of Alice, Will, and Eric, did their best to offer Wendy and Troy their bravest faces. The children were in shock after all that had transpired in the past twenty-four hours. Having been attacked by the creatures, witnessing the destruction of the town, and the accident that had left Janis fighting for her life, it was a wonder they were able to eat at all. There were others who were still missing too. Don, Stephanie, and Wendy's mother hadn't shown up to either the high school or the medical center. It was possible they had all found a safe place to hide, although with each passing moment, that possibility became more unlikely.

While the others were internalizing their pain, Billy Tobin was redirecting his and projecting. More than anything, he wanted revenge. For some reason, he had been spared while so many others had not. Thanks to Father Kieran, he had been given a second chance to make it right. Billy wondered if the man had survived the night. His memory of the past few days was still a bit foggy, but the details were coming back a little at a time. An image of the priest standing over him came to mind, followed by a vision of a thousand serpents descending the face of the old road extension. He remembered looking up at the crest of the hill and seeing Butchie Post with his arms stretched out to the heavens, like he was controlling the snakes, like they were protecting something. *Son of a bitch!* The realization smacked Billy in the face. He had known what to do a week ago but hadn't been prepared. But he was weaker now and was in no shape to lead an attack himself. He scanned the room and surveyed their limited forces; there were so few of them left. They needed more manpower; they needed an army and someone who knew their way around a battlefield. *That's what we need. We need a seasoned vet.*

The cafeteria door flew inward, and Sheriff Primrose entered, followed by Bob Jones and a small group of people. Many were seniors and children and not exactly what Billy had in mind, but there were more than a few strong men among the ranks. Billy watched the sheriff direct the crowd into the cafeteria, and it all made sense. Somehow, he had known; even years ago when he had buried the man's car keys in the snow and thought it the funniest thing, he had known.

●●●

Wendy raised her head when the doors opened and the crowd poured into the cafeteria. Her eyes grew wide with anticipation, hoping the next face she would see might be her mother's. But as the line of new arrivals thinned, it became obvious her mother was not among them. Wendy sank back in her chair and attempted to stifle her tears.

Lois was about to try to comfort the girl when Troy leaned over, put his arm around Wendy, and hugged her. Wendy leaned against his shoulder, returned the embrace, and wept into Troy's shirt. Lois got caught in mid-breath and felt the air swell in her throat. She covered her mouth with a trembling hand and tried to hide her reaction. It was the single most profound gesture she had ever seen. It was as if the children had grown up overnight. Troy and Wendy looked more like a couple who had been married for years, perfectly in tune with one another's emotions, and not a couple of ten-year-olds who had just experienced their first kiss. It also

THE OJANOX

struck Lois as far more genuine than even her own marriage. She wondered what might become of this puppy love that had blossomed under the pressure cooker of desperation. Troy kissed Wendy on the forehead, and it was too much for Lois to bear. The tears broke through her defenses and overflowed the banks. It should have made her worry about Don, but at the moment, he was the furthest thing from her mind.

● ● ●

Carl waited for the last of the new arrivals to be seated and approached the area near the front of the room, where he had addressed a much larger crowd only yesterday. He turned his hat over in his hands, searching for the appropriate words to begin.

"I'm not gonna sugarcoat it. There aren't many of us left and our options are limited." This was met with a grumble of concerns, and Carl knew he hadn't chosen the best opener. "But I've been talking with Mr. Bentley, and he has an idea that just might work. Günter is the instructor for the sailing club. He has informed me that there are three boats tucked away in the rec center at King Lake." Another murmur spread throughout the room; however, the mood had shifted some.

Most people in town knew Günter oversaw the club that met Saturday mornings to teach young boys and girls how to sail. King Lake was massive. It fed into the reservoir and supplied all the drinking water to not only the Grove but most of King County. Since it was part of the watershed, the only boats allowed on the lake were sailboats; motorboats were prohibited, as runoff from the engines polluted the drinking water. There were some fishermen in town who braved the lake in rowboats, but that was foolish since King Lake produced waves large enough to capsize the small vessels and had done so in the past. The sailing club owned three twenty-five-foot sloops, which was a bit of a luxury for the small community. They had been donated in the mid-sixties by a relatively famous mystery author who had retired to the Grove and later caught the sailing bug.

"There are three boats. To the best of my knowledge, they're the only ones in town sturdy enough to make the trip. Each boat can safely hold ten passengers." There was movement as everyone in the crowd started counting heads. Carl cut in. "You're doing the math right now. And yes, it will take two trips. It will also be dark before any of the boats return with help to pick up the rest of us. So, we're sending the women and children first; if there is any room left, we will do it the old-fashioned way." Carl held up his battered Stetson for all to see. "We'll pick names out of a hat. I've chosen pilots for the boats. Günter and Hazel Bentley will be in one, Deputy Geary and Fireman Leone will be in the second, and the third will be piloted by Fireman Marek and Mr. Harrison. With a little luck, the wind will be in our favor and the boats will return before sunset." Carl turned to Günter, who offered a questionable look, then checked his watch. "It's almost ten. Mr. Bentley and my men are going to prepare the boats, which gives everyone an hour or so to get something to eat and wash up. Anyone who would like to assist the crew, please see Mr. Bentley or Deputy Geary."

There was a stirring at one of the back tables where a group of seniors from Botany Village had gathered and were in deep discussion. "Tell him ... tell him," the others urged one of the women, who turned and raised her hand.

"Yes." Carl recognized the former town librarian who had helped him with his book reports when he was a boy. "Yes, what is it, Mrs. Harris?"

"Well, Sheriff." She lowered her arm. "My friends and I have been talking, and while we might be old, we can still do math. You don't have enough room on your boats for half the people here." Carl nodded his head and opened his mouth to speak. "Let me finish before you cut me off, young man. You can kindly keep all our names out of your hat. If there's room on the second trip, that's fine, but make sure you get everyone else out before you worry about us. We've lived our lives, raised our kids, and spent more than our fair share of seasons in Garrett Grove. And to be honest, some of us old-timers won't be around in another year anyway. That's our decision, and we won't hear anything different. Thank you."

Carl wasn't the only one taken aback by what Mrs. Harris had said. No one had been prepared for it. Conversations erupted, mixed with astonished gasps and more than a few tears. Carl swallowed back the lump in his throat, offered a smile, and averted his eyes. "Well ... I suggest the rest of you take advantage of the accommodations in the meantime."

The crowd in the cafeteria began to disperse, but Carl remained at the front of the room to go over the details with Günter and his men.

Ted excused himself from the table, leaving Cyndi and Mayor Marceau to watch over Dawn and her dog, and joined Sheriff Primrose and the others. Although he arrived in the middle of the conversation, it was easy to get the gist of what was being said.

"Dat's not possible, Sheriff," Günter said. "Dere ist no vay ve vill be back in time."

"I know." Carl nodded and lowered his voice so that no one outside the immediate circle could overhear. He motioned for Andrea, Ted, Günter, and Bob to lean in close to him. "Under no circumstances are you to come back for the rest of us. There's enough room on those boats for all the children and most of the women, and that's going to have to be good enough. When you get to Butler, notify the authorities and call the National Guard, let them deal with it. That's an order."

"Sheriff." Andrea was again on the verge of tears. "You can't be serious. You just told everyone we would come back."

"I know what I said, but I couldn't risk creating any more of a panic than we're already dealing with. If anybody starts asking questions, just play along and tell them what they need to hear."

Andrea wiped the corner of her eye and nodded in agreement. Then Günter leaned in even closer with his lips pressed tight together. "I am not very goot at lying, Sheriff."

"Then don't, Mr. Bentley. But surely you can remain silent. If a question comes up that you can't answer, then just excuse yourself and tend to the boat ... weigh anchor, trim the sails. I don't know, do whatever it is you do on a sailboat." Carl offered the man the best smile he had left, which appeared to be just enough. Then he turned to the others. "Bob, Ted, I want you to help make sure that everyone gets on the bus by eleven thirty. The boats leave at noon."

The place was buzzing with activity; some helped themselves to what the cafeteria had to offer in the way of a meal, while others headed off to freshen up. Carl looked to where Lois and the rest of her group remained seated. They had not started to move, but soon they would have no choice. Whether she liked it or not, Lois and the children were getting on one of those boats, along with Mayor Marceau and the candy striper. The dog would have to stay behind, which Carl knew would present a problem, and then there was Billy Tobin. The kid had already been through hell and was one of the few family members Lois had left. He wasn't sure how he would do it, but when it came time to pick names out of the hat, Carl was going to make sure that Billy Tobin's would be the first.

"You have your orders." Carl raised his voice to its usual timbre. "Take your team and get those boats seaworthy, Mr. Bentley. Then call us on the radio when you're ready."

Günter nodded as Andrea closed the distance between her and the sheriff and wrapped her arms around him. She pulled him close and held on tight. "Be careful, Carl." She placed a kiss on his stubbled cheek and released him.

Before he could react, she turned and left the room. It was the first time she had ever hugged him or called him by name. Bob and Ted also sped off to do as instructed, leaving Carl alone for a moment. He replaced his hat and approached the table where Lois and the others sat. They looked up at him as he stood there searching for the words to say. Before he could open his mouth, Lois cut in.

"You warned me," she said blankly.

"What?" She had caught him off guard.

"You told me to leave two days ago. But I just couldn't believe it."

"You did what you thought was right. I don't blame you; I've been second-guessing every move I make. If it's anyone's fault, it's mine."

"That's not true, Sheriff," Billy said with a voice as stiff as iron. "I knew something was wrong last week. I should have come to you, but I wanted to take care of it myself."

Troy perked his head up along with everyone else seated at the table. They listened as Billy worked through what had happened to him nearly a week ago.

"It attacked us at the old sanatorium last Saturday night. We went there after Troy's party, me, Mick, Eric, and the girls. There was something up there. It looked like smoke, or maybe a cloud ... it was hard to tell. At first, it was behind us, but then we got freaked out and started running, and the next thing we knew ... it was in front of us. Damn thing flew over our heads like a flock of birds or something. Whatever it was, it was hunting us. Mick decided to lure it into the woods so the rest of us could get away. When he got back to the car, he was bleeding, said he ran into a branch, but that's not what happened."

Carl didn't want to push but was anxious for the boy to continue. "What else, son?"

"Sunday afternoon, Eric and I decided to go back." Billy cleared his throat and wiped his eyes. "It was my idea. I forced him to go. We picked Mick up; he had this rash on his neck, worst case of poison oak I ever seen. Only it wasn't any ordinary rash. We started to walk up the old extension to the top of the mountain

… then—" He paused, trying to force the memories to the surface. "I'm not really sure what happened, but there were snakes … a lot of them, and that guy Butchie Post was there."

Carl felt his stomach churn at the mention of the name; that was one headache he didn't need to deal with at the moment.

Billy wiped his eyes again and struggled to focus. "I'm sorry, I don't remember much else."

Dawn leaned over and rested her head against Billy's arm. She was about to say something when the cafeteria doors opened once again and Burt rushed in.

The coroner approached the table still dressed in scrubs with his mask pulled below his chin. Everyone stared back, holding their breath, waiting to hear the horrible news. "You need to come with me," he said to Wendy and Troy. "Janis is awake, and she asked for you."

Chapter 93

Don and Stephanie stood outside the back entrance of the sheriff's department amidst a splattering of black stains that blanketed the lot. The security door lay buckled, torn from its hinges and shattered frame. A thick trail of the tar-like substance, left from a thousand different prints, led into the building as far as either could see.

"Hello," Don called into the seemingly quiet building. "Is anyone there?"

Stephanie followed close behind Don as he maneuvered a path around the broken door and entered the basement hallway. The couple navigated the aftermath of what could only be described as a war zone. Broken ceiling tile and light fixtures littered the floor, drywall and plaster had been ripped free from the walls, and furniture from the basement offices lay pulverized in splinters. The hallway intersected at a T; they turned right and followed until they came to a dead end. A heavy door with the word Armory written on it had been left open.

The door was intact for the most part; it had taken a beating with a rippling of dents on its surface but didn't appear to have been compromised in any way. An optimistic swell stirred within Don but was quashed when he entered the armory. He scanned the empty shelves and gunracks, then noticed the blood-soaked mattress in the far corner. Stephanie saw it only a second later and cried out. She rushed toward the cot and stood over it, staring down as time froze.

They both sensed it, heavy in the air; the children had been there, and not that long ago.

"No," Stephanie sobbed. The stain covering the pillow and mattress was bright red but had already started to turn brown where it had dried along the edges. It spread out in a circular pattern approximately the size of a dinner plate and had obviously come from a traumatic wound. She turned to Don with ribbons of tears streaming down her cheeks. "My baby!" she cried.

"Hey," he said, taking her in his arms. "That could be anyone's blood. We don't even know if they were here." But Don sensed otherwise and could tell Stephanie did as well. He also knew there was only one place left for them to look: the medical center. He took her by the hand and started to head for the door but stopped when he felt the hard object catch in the tread off his boot. Don bent down and pulled it free. He stood up holding the shard of magnet that had been left on the floor.

●●●

The ambush that took place in the medical center's basement hadn't even lasted an hour and had ended in a bloodbath with the entire group being devoured in either the literal sense or in a far more perverse fashion. Those who hadn't been fed on were invasively consumed and then added to the brood. The men who assembled to defend the basement's only entrance had overlooked the breach in the elevator shaft and were taken by surprise. Somehow, they had managed to fell many of the enemy's forces. Bodies of the creatures now littered the basement floor, lying next to the remains of the firemen, nurses, and patients. However, not everything in the basement was dead.

A piece of something had been left behind ... forgotten. The beast had been injured but still held a glimmer of the master's essence. It lifted itself on broken leathery wings and dragged itself across the floor. Running on instinct, it inched forward toward the open elevator shaft and listened. The once great creature, born for flight, projected like a radar beacon and attempted to contact the hive.

Three sets of eyes woke from their sleep and focused on the wounded creature. They scanned the basement and listened to the echoes resonating in the air. It was nearby, a presence they had been searching for. Their force spread out, dividing into three separate units, and dispersed throughout the building like a vapor. It covered the basement, where all was quiet, then traveled up the shaft to the roof, only to find more death and rot. It carried up the stairwell, entered the lobby, and detected what it was looking for. It rushed further into the building, travelled down a hallway, and found the room where the simple ones were gathered. It was here ... the boy was here.

It watched the child and listened to the thoughts of the others until it located something it could use. It zeroed in on the group's weakness and allowed its essence to return to the creature in the basement. Still strong enough to trigger the snare. Soon, it would be even stronger, with fresh vessels to carry its presence forward.

●●●

Doris and Michelle Marks stepped from behind the curtain and met Troy, Wendy, and Lois as they approached with Burt leading the way. The head nurse lowered her mask and leaned down to face the children.

"I don't know if she will be awake for long, but she wants to talk to you both." Doris turned to Lois and nodded. No one had expected Janis to survive, let alone regain consciousness. She opened the curtain and allowed the children and Lois to enter the small area while she and Michelle waited behind.

Troy approached the side of the bed and stared down at his friend. She looked small to him, thinner and weaker than he remembered, like she had wasted away overnight. A fresh bandage had been wrapped around her head, covering the entire left side of her face, including her eye. Purple bruises crawled out from under the thick gauze and stretched across her face from her nose to her cheek. When Troy touched the side of the bed, Janis's right eye fluttered, then opened, bloodshot and foggy; he wondered if she could even see through it at all. Then a faint smile creased her lips and she attempted to turn toward him, but the mountain of ice packs surrounding her head prevented her from moving.

"Y-you scared us," was all he could say, the bulge in his throat oppressively choking off the words.

Wendy slid beside him and took Janis's hand. She had already been crying, but now the flow was ceaseless.

"Why are you crying?" Janis said in a voice as frail as a teardrop. "Did I miss Halloween?"

Wendy and Troy managed to laugh.

"No, it's still a few days away," Troy said. "But I never made my costume."

Janis looked up at Wendy. "Boys," she hissed, then closed her eye and lay still.

Troy and Wendy were sure she had fallen asleep again and didn't know if they should stay, until Janis stirred and opened her eye as much as the swollen lid would allow. She looked up at them and tried to raise her head. "Watch out," she said, her voice trailing off and the words impossible to understand. "Troy." She struggled to shrug off the crashing waves of exhaustion.

There was a long pause as Janis winced; a tortured look crossed her face as if she were attempting to hush an army of jackhammers pounding inside her head. Michelle pulled back the curtain and approached the bed. "I'm sorry, but your friend needs her rest. You should probably go now."

"No!" Janis shouted and latched on to Wendy's hand. "Watch out for the bad woman! You need to watch out for the—"

"She doesn't know what she's saying," Michelle said. "She's delirious."

"Troy." Janis lowered her stare and spoke in a voice that sounded nothing like her own. "Y-you have to get all of them ... t-the Ojanox. You have to get it all ... every scrap."

Janis closed her eye and fell back against the pillow as her friends stood beside the bed, looking at her and then at one another. Troy was certain that Janis knew exactly what she was saying and hadn't been delirious. The mention of the creature's name was all the proof they needed. Still, he had no idea what she had meant about the woman. "What bad woman?" he asked, but Janis had fallen asleep.

Michelle and Doris moved to usher the children out of the emergency area and adjust the ice packs surrounding the girl's head. Troy stayed a moment longer and placed his hand on top of Wendy's and Janis's. "Don't worry," he told her. "We'll get all of them. We'll get every last scrap."

Chapter 94

The late morning sun reflected off King Lake like a million diamonds caught in a ripple of wind. From where Günter stood on the north shore, it looked like a perfect autumn day, but after surviving the past twenty-four hours, he knew it was anything but perfect. The town where he had chosen to raise his children had been erased in a heartbeat.

He opened the garage doors of the rec center and instructed his crew to back their vehicles up to the boats where they'd been stored for the winter. The three sloops had been winterized and stowed away less than a month ago, and there was little work to do to get them ready.

The first boat was backed into the water; Andrea, Richard, and Tyler busied themselves by gathering every life preserver and flotation device available. Most of them were child size, which was fortunate, since the majority of the passengers were under twelve. There were no older children among the small group of survivors, as most of the teenagers hadn't shown up to the shelters and probably hadn't taken the threat seriously. It was a shocking contrast to see an entire demographic of the population absent. Billy Tobin and Cyndi, the candy striper, were the only surviving members of their age group.

Anthony Leone released the catch on the back of the trailer, and the second boat slid gently into the water. Hazel and the Bentley girls pulled it to the dock, then tied the bow and stern lines to the cleats. Even Marylin pitched in and did her part, who was the youngest and had been around boats since the day she was born. The three girls shouted and ran around the dock like it was just another day at the lake.

Günter watched his wife and daughters, their laughter causing his heart to ache. He doubted that any of the adults in town would ever laugh like that again. No one would ever get over what had happened. With two boats already in the water and the third one close behind, Günter was anxious to get underway. As much as he had loved this town and the roots that he and his family had planted, he knew that once he reached the other side of King Lake, he would never return to Garrett Grove.

* * *

Lois stared at the empty chairs where she and Troy had sat waiting to hear news of Rob's condition. It all started just six days ago, not even a full week to the day. They had rushed Rob to this very emergency room; at the time, it appeared to be a severe case of the flu. They had sat in the waiting area trying to make sense of it all. But there wasn't any sense to be found, not in a world where an entire town could be wiped off the map in less than a week.

No one noticed the man and woman when they entered through the emergency room doors and stopped. They waited for a moment with neither one saying a word, staring at the group that had assembled near the parted curtain. Don Fischer and Stephanie Thompson looked across the empty room to see Lois, Troy, and the young dark-haired girl gathered in an embrace. Scanning the area, both of their eyes fell onto the child laying on the bed. Stephanie's gasp sliced through the air like a surgical blade.

"God. No!" Stephanie screamed and rushed past Don to where the group was gathered. She pushed her way through Doris and Michelle and latched on to her daughter's bed. "Janis!" Her cries penetrated the emergency room in a despondent echo, affecting the others as if it were happening to them, as if Janis were not just Stephanie's daughter but all of theirs. Doris followed the woman behind the curtain and attempted to explain what had happened. How Janis had been involved in a car accident and how they had done everything they could

THE OJANOX

for her. She explained how Janis had regained consciousness and spoken to her friends, which was a great sign. And although it was too soon to tell, judging from her speech and eye movements, Doris told Stephanie she was cautiously optimistic and that Janis was a very strong little girl.

Stephanie clung to her daughter's hand and lay her head next to her on the bed. Her breath burned in her lungs, and her eyes blurred from the onslaught of salty tears. Now more than ever, she was convinced that her own actions had brought this upon her daughter. *I did this to you, baby.* "Janis, I'm so sorry, baby. This is all my fault."

● ● ●

Troy looked up as Dr. Thompson ran past him, then saw his father standing near the entrance. For a moment, time stood still, then Don rushed toward his wife and son with his arms spread open. He scooped Lois, Troy, and Wendy into his arms and pulled them into a great bear hug. He kissed Lois on the forehead and squeezed them even tighter. "Oh, God. I thought I lost you."

"I knew you were all right." Troy looked up into his father's tear-soaked eyes. "I just knew it."

"I love you, kiddo," he said, reaching into his pocket and pulling out the small black magnet. He held it for them to see. "I followed your trail, from our house to the sheriff's department, and then here."

Lois searched to find the words. She held on to her family with the massive lump in her throat threatening to stop her breath. Her bottom lip trembled, and her arms shook uncontrollably; she tried to catch her breath but was unable. The world was moving at light speed, and the emotions washing over her were impossible and confusing. Loss, despair, hopelessness, and regret were compounded and juxtaposed by gratitude and an overwhelming sense of joy. Her son and husband were safe, which was a godsend, but it didn't feel real or even fair, not when so many others were gone. Alice, Will, Eric ... the entire town. Lois listened to the woman behind the curtain. Stephanie's sobs stabbed at her, and her own heart cried in harmony.

She offered Don an all-knowing look. Despite the rift that had grown between them, they were acutely in tune with one another. He nodded back to her, then looked off toward the part in the curtain. "If you kids would excuse us for a second, I think Janis's mother could use our support." He tossed Troy's hair and then turned to the dark-haired girl. "It's nice to meet you, Wendy. I'm Don."

Wendy and Troy took each other's hands as Don and Lois disappeared behind the curtain. It was hard to hear what was going on exactly, but they could see the shadows of the adults when they came together in an embrace.

● ● ●

The other members of the group watched the scene from the lobby. Jessica Marceau, Billy, Cyndi, and Carl gathered with Dawn and Baxter, watching the emotional events unfold. Jessica had begun to cry like everyone else, turned to Billy and excused herself, then made her way down the hall in search of a ladies' room. She rounded several corners and continued to walk until she found herself in an unfamiliar corridor. *This isn't the way I came.* She turned back. *And it sure isn't the way to the ladies' room.* She passed a set of double elevator doors labeled Freight and continued walking. Finally, she found it. She opened the door and entered the pitch-black darkness; Jessica froze with the door closing behind her.

Her heart raced, the overwhelming murk filling her with a sense of disorientation. She reached toward the wall beside the door and fumbled for the light switch, praying the emergency electricity was working in this part of the building. Her hand found what she was looking for and flipped the switch; one of the overhead fixtures sizzled to life, illuminating the lavatory in a dim glow.

Jessica stepped across the tile floor and entered the nearest stall. Closing the door behind her, she sat down, buried her face in her hands, and wept. She tore off a wad of tissue and used it to blot the tears from her skin. She struggled to control her breathing, knowing if she didn't get a hold of herself, she would hyperventilate. *Deep breaths in ... deep breaths out.* She focused and fought to make any sense of what was happening; there was little to be found.

The bathroom door creaked, causing Jessica to jump. She drew her hand over her lips to stifle the sound of her sobs. Holding her breath, she waited for whoever it was to enter the room. The door slammed with a loud thud, and a second later, the room went dark. Blackness wrapped around Jessica like a shroud. She sat frozen with her heart slamming against the inside of her ribcage; she could sense the person standing there in the dark. She nearly screamed when the first footstep fell against the floor. It sounded like a wet mop being thrown against the tile, sloppy and out of place. It was followed by a second, and then she smelled it, sour, foul, and oppressive. The stench of rotting fish permeated the room; the underlying tang of dank fungus smelled as if it were full of intent.

Tears fell from her cheeks onto the floor, but Jessica remained motionless, praying her presence hadn't been detected. Another wet slopping of waterlogged flesh slapped against the tile and approached the stall where she sat. The offensive stench grew stronger, turning her stomach; she knew she was about to lose what little breakfast she had eaten. It stopped at the door in front of her, followed by the sound of a steady dripping. Water rained onto the floor less than a foot away, peppered by the occasional splats of something falling that was a bit more solid. Jessica tried not to visualize the presence, but thoughts of a beast standing before her dropping pieces of its rotting flesh were impossible to sequester.

A wet thud slapped against the door, causing Jessica to jump where she sat. A second thud splattered against the steel and almost sent the door flying inward. A low hiss crept through the air and morphed into a gargle. A million scenarios raced through the mayor's mind—fighting, escape, surrender—but none that she could act on. She sat frozen as the beast pressed its rotted face against the stall door.

"*Jessica—*" it hissed, just before the door crashed inward.

●●●

Amy Sterling waited in the lot at Mountainside Park, leaning against the hood of her Corolla, smoking one Virginia Slim after the next. She hoped at least some members of the parish might return. But the distant sound of gunfire echoing off the top of the mountain hadn't lasted long, nothing like the epic battle the congregation had anticipated. Still, she held out hope that Julie had been spared and would soon return.

After two hours of silence with no sign of anyone, Amy knew the entire group had been slaughtered. There was no need to stick around any longer; no one was coming. She flicked her cigarette butt into a dry patch of brush and prayed it might catch fire and torch the entire mountain. Then she got in her car and drove down Mountain Ave for what she knew would be the last time. She never looked in the rearview at the torn down fence that once blocked the old road as it faded from view.

The drive back into town was surreal; Garrett Grove had been devastated in the short time Amy had been away. The roads were deserted, with no sign of life in any of the developments she searched. She drove by her place but was too afraid to go inside after discovering several bodies in the road outside the house. A trail of remains spread out from her driveway to the front lawn on the opposite side of the road. Amy couldn't bear to imagine what she might find inside and just kept driving. She had given up hope of locating any survivors but decided to head to the sheriff's department anyway.

When she reached the Turnpike, a reflection in the distance caught her attention; a glint of light flashed off the windshield of a Ford pickup pulling out of the municipal building's parking lot. Amy followed the vehicle from a safe distance, not wanting to alert the driver to her presence, at least not yet. She crept along while the pickup gained speed and turned onto Mandeville. It passed the high school, then veered into the medical center's parking lot, taking the turn a bit too fast and nearly colliding with a parked Jeep. Amy eased her car to the side of the road and watched the man and woman exit the truck and rush into the emergency room entrance.

Amy lit another cigarette and prepared to follow them. After her experience with Father Kieran and the church of the holy kamikazes, she was reluctant to rush in for fear of finding another group of unhinged lunatics. But the idea of remaining alone in the ghost town of Garrett Grove was even less appealing. About a half hour and several cigarettes later, she stood at the emergency room door, working up her courage to go inside. Amy pitched her last butt onto the walkway and entered the building.

● ● ●

Most who had gathered in the cafeteria to listen to the sheriff's evacuation plans made use of the amenities the center had to offer. The senior demographic found a few quiet rooms and helped themselves to the empty beds. Jill Boriello and Brandon Canfield used one of those beds for an entirely different reason; their

THE OJANOX

lovemaking served as an act of celebration for having survived the night. Although Jill had never been the type to sleep with a man she just met, today was no ordinary day, and she knew she might never get the chance to do it again.

Carl had excused himself and headed off to freshen up as well. Now sitting at a table in the back of the room, Burt, Ted, and Bob drank coffee in silence. The soothing warmth of the brandy Burt provided helped take the edge off the moment as each man prepared himself for the night they were about to face.

"I'm guessing the high school is still the safest place to holed up." Bob took a long sip from his mug.

"The boats aren't coming back, are they?" Burt asked, but already knew the answer. It would be suicide for them to even try. Ted and Bob didn't answer, but each offered the old man a look that spoke volumes. "Yeah, I figured as much. Well, I've got some more brandy back at the office; we can stop there on our way to the high school."

"I'll drink to that." Ted raised his mug. "I took a mental note of everyone in the room. We'll get most of them out with only one trip ... well, since the seniors decided to sit it out."

"I'm not very comfortable allowing them to make that decision," Burt said.

"You can't force them if they don't want to go." Bob leaned back and squinted. "What they did ensures that all the women and children will survive. You got to respect that, even if you don't agree with it."

Burt nodded, knowing the chief was right. And now that the liquor was nearly gone, a silence fell over them, with each man thinking the same thing. What chance did they have of lasting another night? There weren't enough men left to defend the shelter, not with less than ten guns against a few thousand of those things. Burt could sense Bob's apprehension at the idea of heading back into the shelter, and for good reason. The place would be ripe by now. And it was obvious that Ted wasn't about to step foot into the center's basement. The young officer had tensed up at the very mention of it. As far as Burt was concerned, he figured he would go wherever Carl and Doris did, wherever that might be. He was never the greatest soldier and certainly not the brightest by a long shot, but when it came to loyalty, Burt knew he was as faithful as a Golden Retriever.

Carl entered the cafeteria looking a good deal better than he had before he left. His hair was wet, and he now wore a fresh set of cloths he liberated from the janitorial closet—green work pants and a matching shirt with a name tag that read Theo. The men did a double take, finding it strange to see him in anything other than his uniform.

Carl approached the table, his keen power of perception kicking in when he spotted the three empty mugs. "Guess I missed the party," he said and winked.

Burt reached into his jacket and pulled out the flask. "Saved ya a pop." He offered it to his friend, giving the contents a shake. Carl's eyes widened, and he accepted the gesture, taking a seat at the table and finishing off what was left.

"Gentlemen." He checked his watch; it was just after eleven. "We should be hearing from Mr. Bentley any minute now. I want everyone we can fit on those boats." He turned to Burt. "I suppose I'd be wasting my breath if I told you I wanted you on one of them."

"You know you would," Burt said. "Besides, who would watch your back if I left?"

Car laughed. "Well, just try not to shoot me while you're busy watching my back."

"I'm not making any promises."

"If you don't want Burt to shoot you," Ted added, "just stand in front of him."

Carl and Burt turned their heads with a jerk and looked at the young deputy in disbelief; it had been more than a little out of character for Ted to say such a thing. The young deputy shifted in his seat, a flush of red spreading across his cheeks and forehead. "I-I didn't mean anything by that, M-Mr. Lively."

The sheriff and coroner exploded with a gale of genuine laughter that was contagious. Bob joined in, and even Ted relaxed, shedding a bit of his shell.

"He's got you pegged, Burt." Carl slapped Ted on the back with tears forming in the corners of his eyes.

Burt wrinkled his nose and lifted his upper lip. "He's got you pegged, Burt," he mocked. "Don't you have a toilet to scrub, Theo." He pointed to the name tag on the janitor's uniform. Which led to a fresh round of laughter that left them all

THE OJANOX

catching their breath. It lasted for a few minutes until it ebbed and then passed. The men sat at the table waiting for whatever might happen next, certain the mood was about to shift.

"I got to be honest with you." Carl lowered his voice. "We're outnumbered a thousand to one, and I don't think the doors at the high school will hold them back for long. This probably doesn't end well."

A hush fell across the table, and no one spoke for what felt like far too long. None of them noticed the boy and the young woman who had been standing there long enough to hear everything Carl had said.

"Then why don't you do something about it instead of just hiding like it's already over?" Billy Tobin stood with one of the waitresses from the diner.

The men stared back at their new arrivals. Carl's face went slack like he'd been slapped as Billy continued.

"You have the chance to act, but all you want to do is go hide again. Well, hiding doesn't work with these things. It's time to get off our asses and go after them already."

"Now look here, kid," Burt raised his voice. "We're all upset, but you can't come in here and talk to the sheriff like that."

Carl raised his hand and stopped his friend. "It's all right, Burt. He's got every right." Carl turned to Billy Tobin. "I get it. But there are thousands of those things out there, and once the sun sets, they have the upper hand. They're stronger, and faster, and strategic. I have no idea how to fight something like that."

"That's because you're thinking conventionally."

Carl straightened in his chair and stared back, slack-jawed. "What did you say?" It was as if Billy Tobin had extracted the very thought from his head.

"You can't fight these things on even ground. You can't fight them face-to-face, and you can't run and hide ... You'll lose every time."

Ted and Bob exchanged a quick look, then turned back to hear the rest of what the kid had to say.

"I take it you have a suggestion?" Carl pinched the bridge of his nose and winced.

"Yeah! Hit 'em while they're sleeping. We go in and wipe them out before the sun sets, before they have the upper hand."

"And how do you propose we do that? There's a whole lot of ground to cover on the top of that mountain, and we don't even know where to start."

Billy turned to Amy Sterling. "We know exactly where they are, Sheriff. They're hiding in the sanatorium."

It had been right in Carl's face the entire time, and deep down, he thought he had probably known it all along. *Son of a bitch ... of course!* Where else would they be hiding? The place was a fortified complex and the only structure big enough to house that many bodies. He had overlooked the obvious and never considered taking the fight to the enemy. The kid was right; Carl knew he'd been thinking conventionally and had lost every battle because of it.

"You all know Amy." Billy nodded to the girl he had walked in with. "I think you'll be interested in what she has to say."

Amy cleared her throat and began to share her story with the sheriff and the rest of the men. She told them how she showed up at the church with nowhere left to turn and been recruited by Father Kieran into going to war against the creatures. She described everything the best she could, how the priest and his followers had turn fanatical. "It felt like I had joined a cult." Amy went on to say how she faked twisting her ankle to save herself, and that Father Kieran had left her behind on the side of the road. "I walked to my car and waited for them, hoping at least someone had made it. Then I heard the gunshots." She wiped her cheeks. "It didn't last long at all, and if they did what they had gone up there to do, there would have been a lot more shooting. So, I left, and I came here."

Carl listened with a mixture of shock and disbelief plastered across his face. He couldn't believe the priest had attempted such a thing with an army that possessed little to no fighting experience. Father Kieran had gone off the deep end, but he had attempted to do what none of them had even thought to try. It was a goddamn foolish thing to do but one of the bravest ventures Carl had ever heard of. He turned to Billy and squinted. "Let me get this straight. You want to go running up there just like Father Kieran and get us all killed?" Carl lowered his head and rubbed at his temples. *Fantastic, now this damn headache is back!* Billy Tobin had been giving him one for years.

"Not at all," Billy explained. "They went barging into the place with guns blazing ... That's why it got them. You said it yourself; it's stronger, it's faster, and it's smarter. We can't go rushing in like the Magnificent Seven; we have to strike unconventionally."

"It knew we were coming," Amy said.

"Why do you think that?" Carl focused on the girl.

"Last night, they attacked the church and got Allison. They crashed through one of the windows and carried her away. After they took her, they backed off, like they had found what they came for."

"You think they wanted Allison?"

"I think it wanted something inside her ... information. Allison knew what Father Kieran intended to do. And if it can get inside your head, then maybe it read Allison's mind and decided it would be smarter to just wait for us at the sanatorium, rather than sacrificing a bunch of its soldiers trying to get into the church. We were doing a damn good job defending the place."

Jesus Christ, if that don't make a lot of fucking sense! Carl stared at Amy and Billy as the pieces clicked into place. *That's why Dr. Malcolm was sent to take out the MRI machine, and how Rainey knew to grab the heavy artillery before showing up at the high school. The goddamn thing is using our own intel against us.* "Okay. But what makes you think we'll do any better if we step inside that place?"

"You're still not looking at this right, Sheriff," Billy said. "We need to use guerilla warfare. We can't rush in there; they'll drop us before we draw our weapons. We got to torch the place from the outside ... You know, burn it to the ground."

"I have a better idea!" Don Fischer stood in the doorway with Dawn and Baxter at his side. Lois and the rest of the kids followed in a moment later. Don approached the table where the sheriff and the other men sat. "I have enough dynamite to level that place ten times over. That's how we take them out. We go up there and plant enough TNT to bring down half the mountain."

Carl opened his mouth to speak but was interrupted by a blare of static.

"Sheriff," Günter's voice crackled over the radios. "Ve are ready at the lake." Carl looked at Don and then at Billy. He smiled and nodded his head. As much as he hated to admit it, he knew the kid was right. It was an unconventional approach, and a damn good one. Not to mention, they were out of options. Carl's smile grew even wider. *This could actually work.*

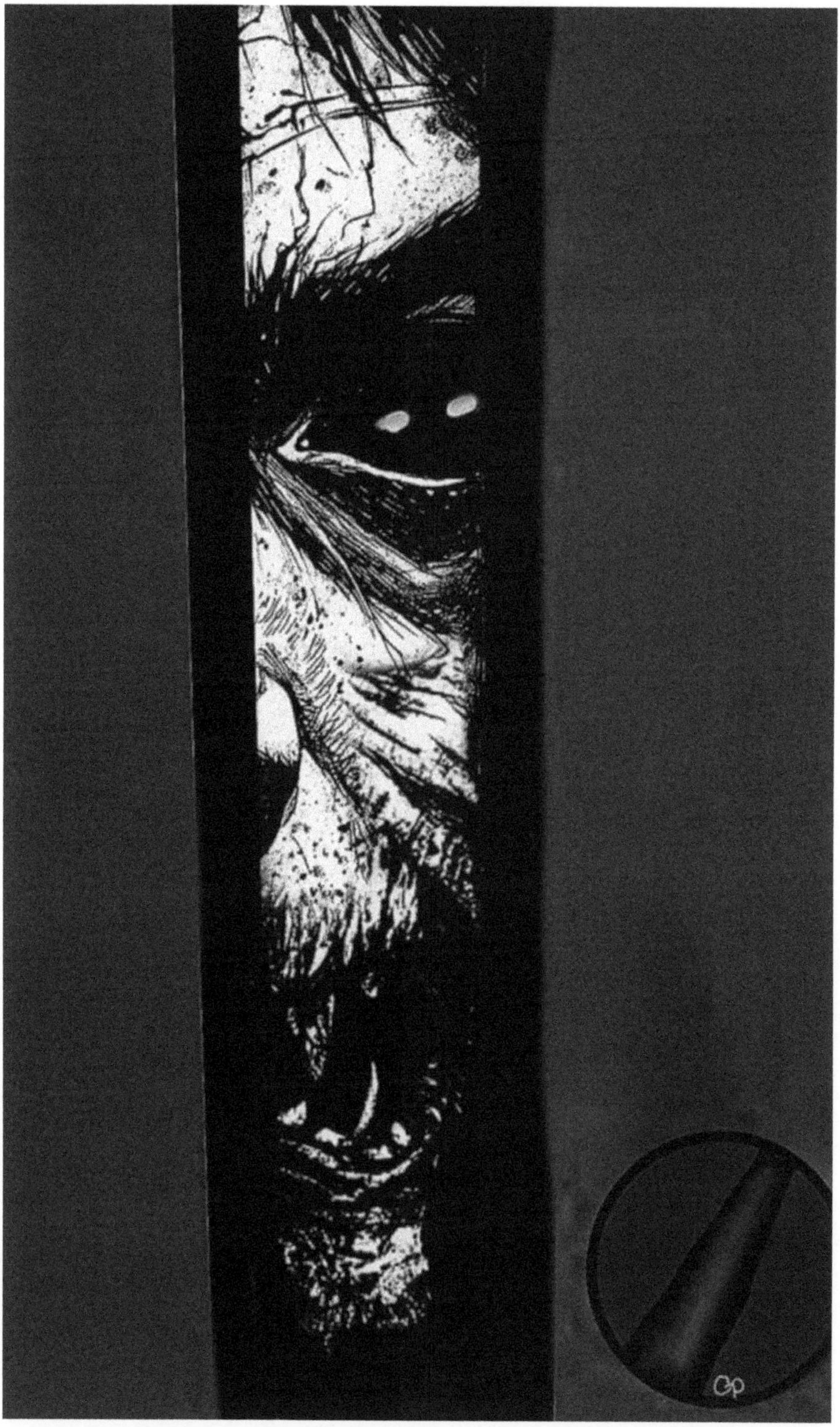

Chapter 95

Günter and his team had successfully launched all three of the vessels, inspected the safety equipment and the riggings, and deemed the boats seaworthy before placing the call to the sheriff; they were ready to sail. The wind was in their favor, which would shave a little off the estimated time of their journey, but Günter knew that could change in a flash on the open water and didn't put much stock in it. He watched the first car pull into the entrance, kicking up gravel and dust as it came to a stop in front of the rec center. Miss Davis and Jill Boriello sat in the front seat, with Kelly Rainey and two other children from the elementary school riding in the back.

"Ahh Sehr Gut," Günter said, making the sign of the cross on his forehead. He waited for the rest of the passengers to arrive, remaining as patient as he could. But the sooner they set sail, the better; Günter was more than a little anxious to put Garrett Grove several nautical miles behind him.

"She's stable at the moment," Doris explained, with Stephanie hanging on every word. "But your daughter shouldn't be moved. Even under the circumstances,

I strongly recommend she remains here. The trip could kill her." Michelle and Burt nodded in agreement; Cyndi stood by and offered her own support. "Mr. Lively and I will remain here. We'll take good care of Janis."

"You can join us," Michelle said. She and Cyndi would be acting as the medical staff for those travelling in the boats. Once again, they were splitting the teams in half, hopefully with better results than they had had the first time.

Stephanie pressed her lips together and shook her head. "Thank you, but I'm not leaving. My place is here with my daughter, and I have a feeling there are others who are going to need my help."

No one expected her to say anything otherwise. A stillness fell over the group where they stood just a few feet from Janis's bedside; there wasn't much left to say.

"Well, we should be on our way." Michelle lifted the large medical bag at her feet and turned to the candy striper.

Cyndi was unable to keep her emotions in check quite like Michelle; she had never learned how to flip that switch. She grabbed Doris and hugged the old nurse with a fierce grip, then with a quiver in her lip and tears in her eyes, she hugged the others. "Please be careful," she said before turning and following the paramedic out the side entrance.

"Thank you, Nurse TenHove, Burt," Stephanie said, holding herself together as best she could. "You saved Janis's life. I could never repay you for that." She took in an icy breath and placed her hand on her daughter's bed. "Unfortunately, I have to ask one more thing from both of you."

"You don't have to ask," Burt said and nodded his head in agreement.

"We'll take good care of her," Doris said.

Stephanie excused herself and made a beeline toward the cafeteria.

●●●

"You know I have to do this," Don explained to his family and the extended members. Wendy and Dawn occupied the seats next to Lois and Troy, with Baxter sleeping on the floor at their feet. "I'm the only one qualified to handle explosives." He tried to reassure them before they left for the boats.

THE OJANOX

"You just came back to us," Lois said with tears in her eyes. "I don't like anything about this plan."

"That's why I need to make sure these cowboys don't kill themselves. I know I'm not the hero type, but if there's one thing I'm good at, it's blowing stuff up."

"Carl knows explosives," she said, wiping her cheek. "He was a demolitions expert in the war."

Don winced and bit his lip. "I don't think you ever told me that."

"Well." Lois wrung her hands and scanned the room. "I know he doesn't like to talk about it, and it really wasn't my place to say."

"Doesn't matter." Don waved his hand and continued. "They didn't use dynamite in Vietnam, anyway. It was either C-4 or ANFO, which is the same principle, but trust me, it's not the same at all. Not to mention, that was over ten years ago. Even if he knows what he's doing, he's more than a little out of practice. I do this every week. You know I'm the most qualified."

"Dad's right, Mom." Troy lifted his head and looked up at Don. "Nobody's better at it than Dad."

Lois forced a smile and let out a long slow breath.

"I love you, guys," Don said. "Don't worry, we're going to get this thing."

"You got to get all of them." Troy's eyes widened as he spoke. "You can't miss even one; you have to get them all."

"Every scrap," Wendy added, wrapping her arm around Dawn and pulling the girl close.

"You don't have to worry about that. By the time the smoke clears, half the mountain will be gone, and every last one of those things will be dust." He leaned back in his chair and offered the group a wide smile.

Lois lowered her voice and leaned in. "And how do you plan on doing that without those things figuring out what's going on?"

He opened his mouth and then shut it just as quickly as Carl, Ted, and Billy approached the table.

"Sorry to interrupt. It's time for the rest of you to head out; the boats will be leaving shortly." Carl addressed Lois and the children, then leaned in and spoke to Don. "I'm anxious to hash out the particulars of the plan with you and the other men when you're ready. There's six of us. I'm not a big fan of that number, to be honest; I'd feel a whole lot better with a lucky seven."

Don shrugged his shoulders and nodded in reply.

"We're almost ready," Lois said, offering the children her bravest smile, then looked around the cafeteria for the missing member of their group. "Has anyone seen the mayor?"

"I just passed her in the hall," Stephanie said; no one had heard her enter the cafeteria. She approached the table and stared the sheriff in the eye. "I'm coming with you." Her words fell like mortar fire.

"I don't think—"

"Think what, Sheriff? It's a good idea? What isn't a good idea is going up there without a clue of what you're up against. Just how do you plan to get close enough without those things knowing you're there?" She stood like a tree with her hands on her hips, staring at Carl as if he were a little boy.

Carl turned to Billy and then to Don. "Well, we haven't fleshed out all the details yet. I'm guessing you have a suggestion, Dr. Thompson?"

"As a matter of fact, I do."

"She knows a whole lot more about these things than any of us, Sheriff," Don said. "I'd listen to her."

Carl pinched the bridge of his nose and scanned the members of his group. There was little time to argue. "Looks like you're our seventh man." He smiled and looked down at Don. "So, to speak." Then, checking his watch, he turned back to Lois. "You really need to get moving."

Jessica Marceau rushed into the cafeteria like a breeze. "Sorry I took so long." She rummaged through her purse. "You know, girl stuff."

Dawn stood up and grabbed Baxter by the leash. She walked him over to Ted and wrapped her arm around the deputy's leg. Ted bent down and hugged her back. "I'm gonna miss you, honey. Have fun on the boat."

Dawn allowed him to straighten the oversized deputy hat she still wore, then she took the end of Baxter's leash and placed it in his hand. "Janis is going to need someone to watch over her. Baxter can keep her company while I'm gone." The slightest tremble took hold of her bottom lip as she scratched the dog behind the ears, then kissed him on the head. "Be a good boy," she said, then allowed Ted to hug her one last time.

The deputy wiped his cheeks and stood up with the leash in hand. The three of them had been through a lifetime together in only a few short days, and the bond that had developed between them was as strong as iron.

"You really need to be leaving," Carl urged them, looking at Jessica. "Now."

"Gotcha," the mayor said, pulling a set of keys from her purse. "I'll drive."

Lois approached Billy and hugged him. "I don't like this at all, but I know there's no talking you out of it."

"Don't worry, Aunt Lois. I got nine lives."

"You're right about that," she said. "Just be careful and come back to me." Then she turned to Carl and cracked a smile. "You look like you haven't slept in a week."

"Maybe a bit longer than that," he said and raked his hands through a recently formed grey head of hair.

She threw her arm around her old high school sweetheart and kissed him on the cheek. "Take care of my family and watch your ass." She released him and turned to leave.

Troy reached into his jacket pocket and wrestled the item out. "Here you go, Dad. You might need this." He held out his wrist rocket and a handful of broken magnets. Don took them and wrapped his arms around his son.

"I love you, kiddo. I'm sorry I wasn't there to help build Scream in the Dark. I should have been there." Don knew he'd been a selfish prick and had messed up royally. He had missed every major development in his son's life and been an absent father at best. He didn't know if this was the second chance he had prayed for, but he wished that it could be.

"There's always next year," Troy said.

"Next year," he agreed, then stood up and faced his wife one last time. They shared a look that didn't require words. The weight of that one look was felt by both, as strong as an avalanche and as unstoppable as a raging river. Lois stood on her tiptoes and kissed him.

"Come back to us," she said.

The moment was broken when Wendy held up the items she'd been holding and offered them to Stephanie. The woman took the wrist rocket and handful of magnets and smiled back at the girl. "Thank you for taking care of Janis."

Carl cleared his throat loud enough for everyone to hear. He rested his hands on his utility belt and stood there dressed in his green janitor's uniform.

"Okay, we're leaving, Theo," Lois laughed, lifting the mood for a moment, then she and Jessica ushered the children along and left the cafeteria without looking back.

"If those things knew Father Kieran and his group were there, then what makes you think they won't know we're coming?" Ted asked once Lois and the others had left the room.

Stephanie looked at Don and then at Carl; she had an idea but thought she would keep it in the vault a bit longer.

"Actually ..." Billy smiled and leaned in. "We want them to know we're coming." Ted looked at him as if he were crazy. "We want them to know exactly where we are ... at least some of us."

The group hashed out the plan as best they could, but there was still a big piece of the picture that had been left out ... and for good reason. Stephanie knew it wasn't wise to share everything with everyone. Information was power when it came to this Entity, and the fewer who knew what she had in mind ... the better.

Chapter 96

Billy threw open the overhead door and entered the garage with Ted behind him. Afternoon sun flooded the two-car area reserved for tools, hunting gear, and the rest of the Tobin boys' hobbies. Will Tobin had lost the battle years ago and allowed his sons to take over the garage to store their collection of grown-up toys. Although lately the boys' interests had centered around girls, the items that Billy and Ted were looking for were something that the Tobin boys still made use of every weekend.

The two YZ 750 dirt bikes stood next to each other in the center of the garage. Billy and Eric had been riding since they were big enough for their feet to touch the ground. The trails that ran through the foothills and crossed the old extension had been the boys' stomping ground for years.

"Here." Billy pulled a large bin out from under a workbench and pried off the top. "You're gonna need these." He tossed several different sized pads and protective gear at Ted, who wasn't that much older than Billy and had spent just as much time on the trails as any boy in town. It was a mountain community, after all, and two things were guaranteed: everyone owned a gun, and damn near every boy road a dirt bike. Ted began strapping on the knee and shin pads and was nearly dressed when Billy approached with a roll of duct tape.

"What do you plan on doing with that?" he asked.

"Trust me. This is gonna save your ass." Billy yanked at the tape and started to wrap it around the bottom of Ted's legs, over his calves and ankles, and even over the shin pads.

"Can you still move your foot?"

Ted twisted his ankle to check the range of motion and to make sure he would still be able to operate the brake and gears. "Yeah, it's good."

"Perfect." Billy tossed him a helmet, then wrapped the duct tape around his own legs. He didn't know exactly what to expect from the thing hiding in the old sanatorium, but he didn't believe it would behave any different than it had in the past. It was a hunter, and all hunters were creatures of habit. They found what worked, and they usually stuck to it; they never changed tactics once they found an effective method. At least that's what he was counting on; not only was he betting his own life on it but everyone else's as well.

"This is gonna work, right?" Ted asked.

"Oh yeah. This is gonna work." Billy tilted his head and shrugged. "Probably."

⬤⬤⬤

The pump truck droned like an oil rig as Bob Jones and Brandon Canfield made their slow approach up Mountain Ave. They rounded the curve just before the entrance of the park to find a line of vehicles on either side of the street and packed into the dirt lot as well; Father Kieran's forces had never returned to retrieve them. Two men on dirt bikes blocked the road where the old extension began. Bob turned off the truck and stepped out.

"Did you do that?" he asked, looking at the remains of the downed fence.

"Not us," Ted answered, pulling off his helmet. "Must have been the others. Saves us the trouble, I guess."

"Any word from the sheriff?" Brandon joined them.

"Not yet. It'll take some time for them to get in position. We could be waiting a while."

Bob looked at the duct tape covering the bottom half of the men's legs. "Don't suppose you got any more of that stuff?"

Billy unslung his backpack and pulled out a new roll. He tossed it to Bob, who went to work wrapping his own legs, then handed the roll to Brandon, who did the same.

"Better safe than sorry." Bob cast a tentative glance up the old road, then turned his head to the sky and shielded his eyes from the glare. It was a cloudless day, and that was about the best news they would get. He removed the walkie-talkie from his belt—it was still too soon to move forward, but he was as anxious as everyone else.

"How are you looking, Carl?" He watched the radio tremble in his hand; his nerves were working overtime. Scanning the faces of the other men, Bob offered an awkward smile of encouragement that may or may not have been effective. He prayed he was the only one who could tell just how nervous he really was.

Carl stood next to Stephanie at the passenger's side of Don's truck. They both jumped when Bob's voice crackled through the small speaker as they waited in silence for Don, who had disappeared behind the demolished remains of one of the trailers to retrieve the explosives. Carl had half anticipated the blast of a detonation when the radio transmitted.

"Yeah, Bob. We're at the quarry now and should be on our way in about fifteen minutes. We'll have to take it slow, though, at least an hour or so."

"Roger that," Bob replied. "We'll get started on our end. If anything happens or you get held up, let us know. Other than that, I guess we're going silent from here."

Stephanie had suggested that once they got started, they should cease all radio transmissions. She wasn't certain but implied the Entity might be sensitive to certain frequencies as it had been to the magnetic pulse of the MRI machine. If that was the case, there was a possibility it could track them through their own radio transmissions. Of course, it was just a theory, but Don agreed and said they would be wise to follow her advice.

"I got a feeling if anything goes wrong on our end, you won't need the radio to hear about it." Don had told them he was bringing enough TNT to blow up the sanatorium three times over. If something bad did happen, they would be hearing it as far as Warren.

"Just make sure nothing goes wrong, then," Bob said.

"10-4, over and out." Carl returned the radio to his hip. He had modified his gun belt to carry the .38 on his right and a .44 on the left, with as much ammunition as he could fit jammed into every available slot and pouch. He wore it over a set of jungle-design camo fatigues they had liberated from Harrison's Army and Navy. Stephanie wore an identical set cuffed at the ankles to prevent the legs from dragging on the ground, and Don had dressed the same. The group also covered their faces in camouflage grease paint to help blend into the mountain. No one knew if the extra precautions would make a difference, but they figured it couldn't hurt.

Carl scanned the quarry and the large section of the mountain that had been removed by DuCain industries. "Where is this cave located?"

Stephanie pointed to the left, where Gail had been killed. "Just over the rise of that slope." She could see the body of the scorpion creature that had attacked them.

"You've really been studying this thing your whole life?"

"Not my whole life," she said. "My father discovered it first on the Cahokia dig. He became convinced that something was responsible for the disappearance of the civilization. It's rarely spoken of, but the native tribes weren't the only ones who vanished. There was a major die-off during that period in every species—birds, mammals, reptiles. It had to be more than coincidental."

Carl rubbed his temples and swayed on his feet for a second. Stephanie reached out to steady him. "Are you okay?" she asked. "You look a little green."

The paint he had used to cover his face was in fact mostly green. "Very funny," he replied. "It's just a headache from not enough sleep."

"Yeah, I know what you mean." She continued: "The truth is, Sheriff, there are hundreds of lost civilizations that have simply vanished from the face of the earth. And there is more than a little evidence that suggests this Entity had everything to do with them."

"Just how old is this thing?"

She shrugged. "Ageless. I don't know, as old as time itself."

"I'm guessing we're not the first to try to take it out?" He removed a canteen from his belt and took a sip.

THE OJANOX

"We'll be the first to succeed." She offered a smile and a wink.

Carl wondered if she would be as optimistic in another hour or two. He watched Don Fischer emerge from behind the work trailer with a large pack on his back and one in each hand. He'd never cared much for the man who had taken his girl. Don appeared to be a self-absorbed prick who was all wrong for Lois. But watching the guy make his way across the quarry carrying enough dynamite to change the earth's rotation, Carl thought that maybe he had misjudged him.

"Okay, I got everything," Don said with sweat streaming from his brow.

"Are those packs fireproof?" Stephanie asked.

"Wouldn't matter if they were," Don answered. "Dynamite isn't. What you really need to worry about is if I fall or drop this stuff." He set the packs down and removed the gloves he wore, a thick pair with rubber hand grips.

"What are those for?"

"For handling the dynamite. You don't want to touch it with bare hands. It will really ruin your day, probably your entire week."

"We should get going," Carl suggested.

"Hold on a second." Stephanie removed her own backpack and set it on the ground. She opened the zipper and dug deep until she located what she was looking for. She stood up and held out the three ancient medallions. The gold links woven throughout the chain and emblem caught the sunlight and reflected it back like a crystal.

"When did you grab those?" Don asked.

"Before we left this morning. I thought they might come in handy." She placed one around her neck, the large ornate medallion covering a third of her chest. Then she held one with the chain open for Don to put his head through. He did, then tucked the large piece of jewelry under his shirt.

"What are those for?" Carl asked, staring at the artifact with a skeptical look on his face.

"Let's just say, I think this might be the best camouflage we could wear today."

He raised his eyebrows, thinking she was crazy, but decided to go along with it. He leaned over, and she slipped the gaudy medallion around his neck. It was large and bulky and heavy as hell, but the woman said to wear it and he would. Carl looked at the large bags Don carried and hesitated to interject.

"Do you need me to carry some of that stuff?"

"I've got it. You two should lead, and I'll follow behind from a distance. That way if something happens, I won't bury you in an avalanche or even worse."

Both Carl and Stephanie backed up a few steps. "Okay," Carl said. "It's been a few years, but I'm sure I remember the way. Once we crest the hill, we'll find the trails. Provided they're still there and not completely overgrown."

"Lead the way," Don said.

Carl walked toward the section of quarry that DuCain had been cutting into for the past decade. Stephanie fell in at his side, while Don waited until they were far enough ahead, then followed in their footsteps.

Chapter 97

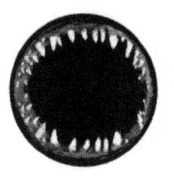

Lois sat in the passenger's seat of the mayor's station wagon as they pulled out of the parking lot and turned right. She laid her purse next to her, then turned to Troy, Wendy, and Dawn in the back, who looked up and offered their best nervous smiles. They'd been through so much but were anxious to get out of town, maybe even a little excited to travel in the boats. Jessica, who sat behind the wheel, nodded to Lois, then reached into her own purse and started rooting around. Lois hoped she might be searching for a cigarette and had been craving one herself, although she didn't think the woman was a smoker.

The mayor continued to rifle through her purse, paying more attention to what she was looking for, and missed the turnoff for the lake. Lois watched as the woman passed the side street without so much as taking her foot off the gas. "You want to take Sunset to get to the lake," she said.

Jessica smiled in agreement but continued to rifle through her purse, making no effort to turn the car around or even slow down.

The mayor pressed her foot to the gas, causing the station wagon to lurch forward with a jolt. Lois turned to her and raised her voice. "I think you need to turn around. You're going the wrong way." Troy, Wendy, and Dawn looked up from the backseat; a cross between fear and confusion washed over their faces. Something was wrong.

Jessica pushed her foot harder to the floor, and the vehicle screamed in response. Trees, signs, and houses passed in a blur as the car sped to sixty miles an hour.

Lois's heart jumped into her throat. She reached out and braced herself against the dashboard. "What are you doing?" She couldn't imagine what had gotten into the mayor for the life of her. "Jessica, slow down. You need to go the other way!" Lois realized what was happening a moment too late.

The mayor's eyes clouded. A thin black film passed before them, blocking out the whites. Their natural appearance returned a second later, accompanied by an evil grin that spread across the woman's face like a sickness. Somehow ... it had gotten to her.

Lois tore at her purse to retrieve Carl's gun. She managed to pull open the flap, but that was all. The mayor drew back her hand and lifted her fist into the air. Lois saw the flash of something metallic in her grip but couldn't focus on it. The woman struck like a viper; Jessica slammed her fist into Lois's thigh and pressed.

Lois looked down at the hypodermic as Jessica depressed the plunger. The drug entered her body in a hot rush and took effect before she could react. First, she felt it in her face, flushing her cheeks and making her jaw go slack. Then her arms and legs grew heavy and went numb. Lois struggled to open her mouth, wanting to turn and warn the children, but was unable to move a muscle. She lost feeling in her torso as her head grew too heavy to hold up. She opened her mouth to scream, and a thin line of spit fell to her chin. Her head bobbed once, then twice, then fell against her chest, and Lois Fischer faded away.

Troy beat his fists against the back of the front seat. "What did you do to my mom?" he cried.

Jessica slammed the pedal to the floor, and the wagon took off like a rocket. She looked into the rearview mirror at the children, with the dark cloud filling the retinas of her eyes.

"Troooyyy ..." an inhuman voice hissed.

The children shrunk in the backseat, shaking and clinging to one another. Troy looked at the girls, searching for an answer but unable to think. "T-th-the bad woman," he managed with tears streaming down his cheeks. He stared at his mother's lifeless body in the front and sobbed. "Mom, get up. P-p-please, get up." But it was too late.

THE OJANOX

Wendy reached into her pocket for the wrist rocket, forgetting she had given it to Dr. Thompson. She started to cry as well and latched on to Troy and Dawn.

Jessica left the syringe sticking out of Lois's thigh. After being probed in the ladies' room at the medical center, the Entity had sent her on a mission. She had washed the ink-like fluid from her face before exiting, made her way past the cafeteria, and crept down the stairs leading to the basement. The shelter was littered with bodies, but it had been easy to locate what she was looking for. The stockpile of medicine had been left in the open. With the acquisition of Dr. Malcolm and the rest of the medical staff, the creature now possessed a full working knowledge of pharmaceuticals. Jessica found the vial easily and loaded several syringes with the fluid. She deposited them into the inner compartment of her purse, retreated the way she had come, and joined the others in the cafeteria.

Lois and the children had already been expecting her to drive, which made it even easier. Soon, it would reside in the new vessels; the three young hosts were strong enough to carry its essence to the next town. Finally ... it would have the one called Troy. It had tasted the boy in the graveyard and in the memories of Robert Boyle. Its hunger was acute and nearly blinding, but soon it would possess the object of its desire.

Three withered bodies lay shaking on the floor with the shared consciousness of the one pulsing through them. There was little left of their fragile shells. The protector stood watch over them, waiting for the new vessels to arrive. In a previous life, it had gone by the name of Butchie. But the massive creature that had been chosen for its brutality looked nothing like the man it had once been. After leaving the mind trap for the priest's army and retrieving a buried memory from deep within the Butchie creature, a suitable location revealed itself. A dark place of pain and suffering, one that the protector was familiar with. It was the perfect spot for the three to rest and would serve just as well for the transfer.

Günter checked his watch and paced along the shoreline. The boats were ready to sail, but they were still five passengers short. The sheriff had given him direct orders to depart no later than one o'clock, and it was already a quarter after. He had also been told to maintain radio silence and knew the sheriff and the others would be unreachable. Still, he knew he couldn't leave without the others and wrestled with the decision until he finally broke down and picked up the walkie-talkie. "Sheriff, dis ist Günter. Ve are still vaiting for ze last passengers to arrive. Ist anyone zerr?" The radio remained silent. "Please come in, Sheriff."

Günter exhaled and checked his watch again. He continued to make his final preparations as slowly as he could. The rest of the passengers were aboard, with the children tucked below decks. The equipment was stowed, and they were ready to leave. He walked to the third boat, where Tyler and Rich sat in the back at the transom.

"I'm afraid dis ist everyone."

"What about the rest? We still have room for five more," Rich said.

"Yes, yes, I realize zat." Günter nodded, then yelled to the next boat. "Andrea, please send Jerry over here." Then he called to his wife. "Hazel, please tell Michael to join us, sank you."

The two boys exited the other boats and boarded as instructed.

"Okay zen!" Günter shouted for everyone to hear. "Follow my lead und Gott bless you." Approaching the lead boat, he untied the bowline. He made his way to the back and released the stern line from the cleat. Then he pushed the boat away from the dock and jumped in. The sailboat floated out into the open water. Hazel lowered the keel as Günter raised the main sail until it was fully extended. The others followed, and the vessels were underway. Günter tacked the sheet into the wind, and the craft was propelled forward. Moments later, the boat was gliding across the water with Hazel steering them into the openness of King Lake.

Günter checked the dock, making sure the late arrivals had not shown up. But no car had entered the parking lot and there was no one on the dock. He watched the sandy beach in front of the rec center grow smaller and smaller until it became a speck on the horizon. Then Günter set his sights in the opposite direction and never looked back. With the wind at his back and the weight of guilt pressing even harder against him, he picked up the radio one last time.

● ● ●

It became a bit easier for the group to make headway after Carl navigated a passage out of the quarry. He led them up the carved-out face of Garrett Mountain, taking longer than he thought to find the trails. It had been years since he'd been up there, but once he gained his bearings, things started to look familiar. He stumbled across the first path, a bit more overgrown than he expected, and the memories of his youth came flooding back. It was still much like he remembered.

Don lagged a couple hundred feet behind, but after seeing the amount of dynamite the guy had liberated from the quarry, Carl couldn't help but wonder if even that was far enough. He continued to look back to check on the man, but Don Fischer followed at a steady pace and hadn't lost a stride. Stephanie surprised him as well, showing more energy and endurance than himself. The woman was clearly athletic and in great shape; Carl didn't know what sport she had played but knew there had been at least one. He could feel the lack of sleep and stress affecting his own performance, but he pushed himself to keep going. *Just a little bit longer,* he chanted, wiping the sweat from his brow.

The first trail led to a steep incline with close to a forty-five-degree upgrade. The hard-packed clay had been tamped down by the feet of the Lenape tribe centuries before any of his ancestors had set foot on the continent. Then one day, the tribe that lived on Lonesome Mountain disappeared without a trace. Stephanie followed behind Carl, stepping where he did, avoiding the loose gravel at the sides of the trail.

"This Entity," Carl said, looking over his shoulder at her. "How do you suppose it found its way here in the first place? I mean, after doing what it did at … Cahokia, you say?"

"Good question," she said, matching his steps. "Best guess would be it hitched a ride on another life-form, maybe a deer that had become infected. It may have made a few stops along the way, or it could have come right here and then run into a member of the Lenape tribe. There's a painting of a holy man inside the cave; he could have been the first."

"Holy man?" Carl forced himself up the incline, his breath growing ragged in his chest.

"Yeah, and from there, it would have spread just like it did in Garrett Grove. But I'm willing to bet it never encountered a race quite like the Lenape."

"H-how do you mean?"

"Well, for one, they were in tune with nature on a spiritual level and believed in the healing powers of the mountain. Then there's the mineral deposits in the area. The Lenape had figured out a wa—" Stephanie almost ran into Carl, who had stopped short in front of her and blocked the path.

"Whoa," she said. "Are you okay?"

Carl bent over and clutched at his temple; his hands shook as he tried to catch his breath.

"Yeah, I just need a second." Carl squinted his eyes and tried to focus on the path before him, then everything went blurry. He swayed and caught hold of Stephanie. "It's my head; I've been getting these migraines for a couple days now."

Stephanie dug into her pack and removed a bottle of aspirin; she handed him three pills and her canteen.

"You're a lifesaver," he said, swallowing the tablets with a long gulp of water.

"Can never be too prepared."

"Hey, what's going on?" Don called from less than fifty feet away. He stopped and waited for them to continue moving. "Is everything all right?"

"Fine," Carl shouted. "Got a little dizzy for a second; better now. We're almost there, maybe another half an hour at most."

Don looked up the path to where Carl and Stephanie had stopped. He raised his arm and shrugged when she looked at him. *What's going on?* She shrugged herself. *I don't know.* He waited for them to continue and shifted the bags in his hands. It was bad enough that he and Buzzy had to relocate the explosives in the first place. But after the robbery, he had no choice. They had used one of the older storage areas and the temperature control wasn't half as good as it needed to be. The whole mess had been bouncing around for the past hour in the duffle bags, and it was turning into an unseasonably hot October day. Don had no idea if any of the sticks had already started to sweat and tried his best not to think about it. He watched as Carl righted himself and gave him a thumbs-up.

Come on. Let's get moving already. Don felt his heart thundering in his chest. The sooner he got this dynamite off his back wouldn't be nearly soon enough. A second later, Carl and Stephanie started moving again. He waited until they were a safe distance away, then followed in their footsteps. He felt the cold press of the lodestone medallion against his skin and wondered if it would have the effect Stephanie hoped it might. Not that he was willing to take it off and press his luck. *How much of this do you really know, and how much are you making up on the fly?* He couldn't help but second-guess Stephanie's call with the medallions. Figuring it best not to think too much about it, he told himself she knew what she was doing. *I'm only the guy carrying thirty pounds of dynamite; who am I to ask questions?*

● ● ●

Bob checked his watch and nodded to the other men; it was time to move. He took position behind the wheel, and Brandon slid into the passenger seat. Between them sat a pair of 12 gauge shotguns and a dozen boxes of shells. The men also wore sidearms and had brought almost a metric ton of ammo for both weapons. Bob gave Billy and Ted the go-ahead, then threw the truck in first and released the clutch.

Billy and Ted jumped down on the kick starts of the YZs almost simultaneously, and the bikes roared to life. Ted rechecked the shotgun hung against his back to make sure he still had easy access, then looked at Billy to do the same. Billy did, then hit the throttle and popped the clutch, causing the bike's front tire to jump twelve inches off the pavement. The YZ vomited a plume of gravel and dirt in its wake as Billy hotdogged it over the downed fence. Ted applied a bit less pressure, pulling a wheelie that only lifted about three inches. The deputy popped the bike into second, and Billy took off like a bullet ahead of him. Loose asphalt and silt, eroded from decades of weather and disrepair, was thrown into the air from their spinning tires. Ted pulled alongside Billy as the extension grew steeper and more treacherous. He motioned to the kid, shrugging his shoulders, not sure where to find what they were looking for. But the chief had gone over it with Billy, and the kid seemed to know what the man had been talking about.

The bikes ate up the incline with ease and had ascended almost half the distance to the crest when Billy veered to the left and slowed down. Ted spotted what he was headed for a second later. A small oval reflector sat on top of a fiberglass pole almost entirely obscured by the overgrowth of trees and brush. Billy led them straight to it and brought his bike to a halt; Ted did the same. The sound of the pump truck shifting into lower gears screamed as the firemen made their way up the hill behind them.

Ted followed Billy, removing a small hatchet he had fastened to the handlebars of his bike. The men walked off the road into the tangled brush and found the ancient hydrant. It was thick with vines, buried under several feet of wild thorns. "Careful, those are the bastards that got me," Billy said.

They made quick work of clearing the area, with Ted concentrating on the right side of the old plug and Billy focused on the left. They had just finished leveling the last of the vines when Bob pulled the pump truck parallel with the hydrant, blocking nearly the entire road.

Brandon jumped out of the passenger side and chocked the wheels, placing the huge wedges behind each one of the vehicle's tires as Bob leapt from the vehicle and charged at the hydrant with the largest wrench Ted had ever seen. The big man attacked the fireplug and attempted to loosen the two-and-half-inch nuts on either side. He fitted the wrench to the cap on the right and leaned in with all his weight. It didn't budge, not even a millimeter. Bob's eye bulged as he realized how seized the rusted old plug had become. The department was scheduled to service hydrants on the extension once a year … in a perfect world. But it had probably been closer to two or even three since this one had last been touched. It was also possible it had gone overlooked completely.

"Give me a fucking hand!" Bob shouted, standing up to catch his breath. Billy took the wrench in his hands and faced the chief. "Okay, one … two … three." The two men leaned into the wrench; Billy lifted himself off the ground and came down against the strain.

The sound of metal grinding against metal echoed out of the old hydrant, and the cap began to move. The wrench slammed to the ground as the nut rotated a full quarter of a turn; Bob reaffixed the wrench, and the men went back to work. This time, the cap turned easier; the ancient metal squealed, then freed itself from its lock. Bob removed it the rest of the way without Billy's help, twisting the cap off one final turn before it fell to the ground.

He moved the wrench to the other side, and he and Billy went to work again. The left cap was equally as rusted, but now the men had an idea of how much torque was required to break the seal, and they managed to remove the second cap somewhat easier.

Sweat streamed down the chief's forehead and soaked the neckline of his shirt. He moved the wrench to the top of the hydrant and gave the others a look that suggested, *Here comes the hard part.* All three men grabbed the wrench and pulled it in a counterclockwise motion. The top cap turned almost instantly, much to everyone's surprise.

"Okay, we got it from here!" Bob shouted. "Time to do this." He went to work on the top of the old plug and counted out loud. "Seven ... eight."

Billy and Ted returned to their bikes, donned their helmets, and a moment later were spitting up twin fantails of gravel and dust; they sped away from the truck and continued up the old extension road.

"Ten ... eleven." Bob continued to loosen the plug on the top of the hydrant, and after the twelfth spin, he held his breath and turned the bolt for the thirteenth time. The sound of rushing water from deep within the underground pipe grew louder and louder until finally it erupted from the open caps on either side of the plug. It flooded the ground where Bob stood, dark and murky with massive flecks of rust and sediment throughout. It took a full minute for the water to filter out the debris and take on a clear transparency. After the last of the sediment dissipated, Bob turned off the water and grabbed the first piece of equipment that Brandon had set at his feet.

The Siamese connector resembled a large Y that attached to the hydrant at the two open caps on either side. Bob made quick work of it; he torqued down on the nuts, then took the pony connection and fastened it to the LDH that Brandon ran from the truck.

The pump truck carried approximately eight hundred and fifty gallons of water in its tank. Which would last about three minutes without a steady supply being fed to it. But that could be depleted much quicker if more hoses were connected and the man operating the deck gun got too overzealous.

Bob ran from the overgrowth and leaned into the cab of the truck. He exited a moment later with as much ammo he could carry and one of the shotguns. "Okay, get up there," he yelled to Brandon, who climbed onto the back of the truck. Bob handed him the weapon and supplies, then went back to the cab to retrieve his own gun. He set his weapon and several boxes of ammunition down on the guard of the truck and concentrated on the two lengths of hose that Brandon had set on the side of the road. Both were fifty feet in length with inch and a quarter smooth water nozzles that were powerful enough to remove the yellow line from the center of a highway. Today, they would be focusing the highly concentrated water pressure on something a bit softer than blacktop.

Billy crested the hill, throttled forward, and maneuvered a wide turn through the loop in front of the old sanatorium. Ted followed close behind, getting his first good look at the place in years. It was in far worse shape than the last time he had seen it, and he was overcome by an impending sense of dread. He examined the broken windows and crumbling steps of the facility, then focused on the entrance and the pair of shoes sticking out from the open front door. Squinting to get a better look, he noticed they weren't just a pair of random shoes but were attached to a set of legs. They jutted out the open door onto the porch while the remainder of the body lay concealed within the shadows of the building. Ted considered stopping for a moment to check if the owner of the shoes was still alive, then thought better of it. He knew the only thing that would accomplish was getting himself killed and jeopardizing the entire mission. He hit the throttle and sped through the turnaround to the back of the old parking lot.

Billy had told them what happened Sunday afternoon when he, Eric, and Mick attempted their half-assed assault on the sanatorium. And Ted kept his eyes peeled for movement as he navigated the dirt bike over the treacherous cracks and divots in the ancient asphalt. They made another pass through the turnaround in front of the building, and the deputy nearly dumped his bike when the first snake darted in front of his path. It was fast and startled him when it lifted its head to strike; he managed to maintain his balance and avoid what almost looked like a timber rattler. But there was something horribly wrong with the snake. It was disproportionate and had lost nearly all its coloring. The identifying rattler markings had faded as if the reptile had been bleached, with sections of its body so swollen it looked like it had swallowed several huge meals. But that didn't appear to slow it down; the snake quickly turned and struck out at Ted a second time.

He called ahead to Billy, who was already aware they had attracted the attention of the creatures. The kid swerved his bike in a zigzag pattern, navigating a path around a gathering of snakes that appeared to emerge from thin air. Within seconds, they were everywhere, to the left and the right of the men and blocking the way back to the road. Billy gunned the throttle, lifting his front tire off the ground. He rode the wheelie through the turnaround with his back tire chewing up snakes in its path. Ted followed the kid's lead as his front tire left the pavement in a sudden jerk. He was sure he would topple over, then eased on the gas and rode it out nearly as well as the kid. He felt the bodies squish beneath the weight of the bike as he made his way back to the road.

The serpents hadn't yet made it to the street when the two men took off down the mountain toward the truck, but it wouldn't be long. Ted fought the urge to look back for fear of losing control of the bike, and trusted the snakes would continue their pursuit. *I hope you're ready.* He prayed that Bob and Brandon could handle the holy hell that was headed their way.

The sound of dirt bikes cascaded over the mountain to where the small group ascended the final steps of their climb. Don brought up the rear with the added disadvantage of the heavy cargo he carried. Making sure each foot was well-placed before moving onto the next, he plodded along a safe distance behind Carl and Stephanie. He had taken care to pack things tight and secure, but it was still dynamite and unreliable under even the best conditions. You never wanted to think you were safe. The stuff sweat nitroglycerine and had a mind of its own, no matter how careful you thought you were. Don knew it wasn't the rookies who blew themselves up; it was the seasoned vets who grew careless over the years and lost respect for the stuff. He made his way to the top of the slope and came to the crest where Carl and Stephanie had stopped to watch from the cover of the tree line. Two men on motorcycles sped past the front of the building riding wheelies, then took off down the road.

From what Don could tell, the place looked quiet, with no sign of movement in any of the windows or at the front entrance. They were still a distance away and couldn't be sure, but he thought things looked good. They hadn't been attacked by anything like they had seen at the quarry, and so far, there was no sign of snakes. He looked at Carl, who checked his watch, then held up both hands with his fingers spread; in ten minutes, they would start. Don nodded as his nerves jangled with anticipation. He didn't like the idea of just sitting around with thirty pounds of dynamite, but at least Lois and Troy were out of harm's reach. By now, they would be close to halfway across King Lake.

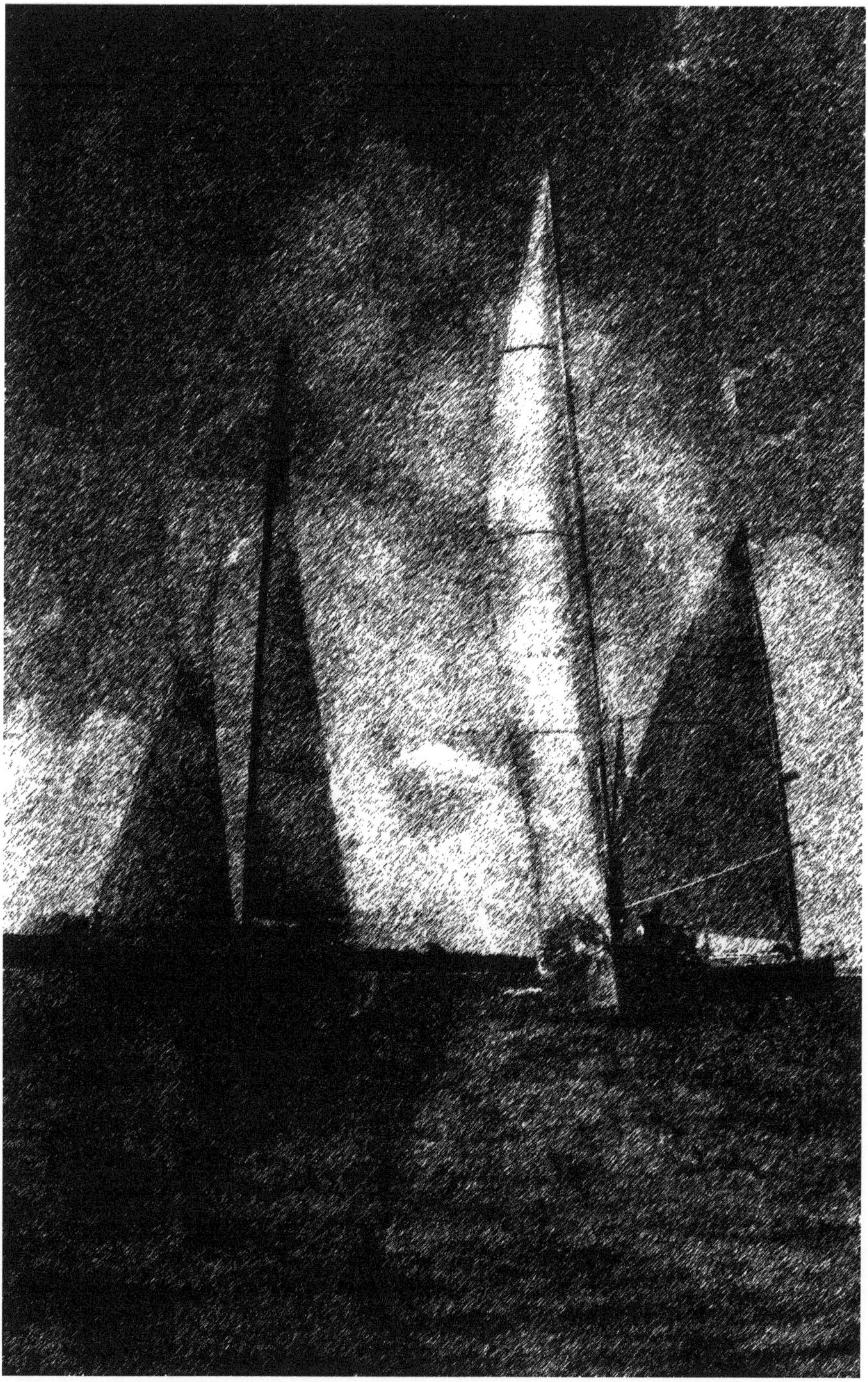

Chapter 98

Jessica Marceau pulled the station wagon into the driveway where Marion Butchie Post once lived with his mother, Margaret. No longer in control of her own actions, the mayor operated under the same power that had directed Deputy Rainey to slaughter his own people. It had taken Jessica with very little effort, projecting its essence through the freight elevator shaft to the bathroom where it found the woman alone. It hadn't been there in the physical sense and merely slipped the woman a suggestion that festered like an infection inside her. The simple ones were that easy to control; however, some were more resistant than others. Rainey had been one of the easy ones, the first time, but the one named Ziegler had severed the tie. It was a bit more difficult to regain control the second time and had been necessary to ambush the deputy when he was alone to impose the full effect of its presence.

But with Jessica, it had been a seamless insertion, as if the woman had never been in control of herself to begin with, like she'd been waiting for direction. It slipped into her consciousness and manipulated the strings the way a child might do with a toy.

The woman bounded out of the car and tore open the back door where the children sat, causing them to scream and shrink away. The one called Troy reached over the smaller child and grasped at the door handle, but it was ripped out of his hand. The great beast stood before him. The creature that had started its life called Marion towered over the station wagon, nearly a foot and a half taller and far wider than it had previously been. The clothes it wore hung in tattered shreds from the gross expansion of its muscular and skeletal design. The creature's brow protruded over its eyes as if it were made of solid brick. It howled at the children, exposing a maw that contained at least two rows of jagged teeth.

It reached into the car, seized Troy and Dawn by the collars, and yanked them out of the back seat like bags of groceries. Jessica lunged at Wendy and removed the girl from the vehicle in a similar fashion, dangling the child in the air above the driveway like a ragdoll. Wendy kicked and struggled to break free from the woman's grip, but it was useless; the mayor was too strong.

"Let me go!" Troy screamed and was carried to the side of the house. He looked back in the direction of the car to see his mother's body slumped against the passenger side window. "What did you do to my mom?" The tears cascaded down his cheeks as he was carried away into the backyard.

"I'm gonna kill you!" Troy shouted as the gargantuan monster looked down at him and howled.

In the shed behind the Post house, the one called Ben turned its head in the direction of the mountain. It listened to the sound as the men maneuvered their vehicles toward the nest. *What are they doing?* It cast its eye upon them and spotted the boy who had gotten away; the one called Billy had come back and brought others with him. It had expected the priest but hadn't given the others much concern. Still ... it was ready for them.

It called out to the serpents once again. Their bodies, still useful and not yet spent, had more than enough strength left to deal with the nuisance and protect the brood while they rested. It unleashed them on the men, knowing if any of the intruders were to find their way inside, there was still something waiting for them. Something that worked even faster than snake venom; something the priest had tasted firsthand.

The door to the shed flung open, and the three children were tossed inside onto the dirty wooden floor. Troy came down hard on his hands and knees, landing face-to-face with one of the creatures. It opened its eyes and focused on him with intent. A scream stalled in Troy's throat with the black pupils of the creature fixating on his own. Though they were much different than the last time he saw them, the eyes were still familiar. The face and the body had changed greatly as well, but there was no mistaking the thing that lay before him.

He tried to back away but couldn't move and remained on his hands and knees staring into the horribly disfigured face. The creature's eyes grew wide as if with recognition, then a single dark tear pooled in the corner of one and ran down the beast's cheek.

"Rob," Troy sobbed. "I'm sorry."

The creature that had once been a fourth grade boy who loved to look for arrowheads in the woods and build haunted houses with his best friend opened its mouth and hissed. "Troooyyy."

It had destroyed everything the child had been. His body contorted into something almost reptilian, with his arms and legs curled up underneath him like a frog. His flesh was a pallid greenish-grey and looked more like leather than skin. Folds of loose canvas, too big to cover the shrunken body, hung like flaps of stretched-out rubber. Troy fixated on the dark streak as it crawled down the creature's face. It clung as a single drop from his old friend's chin before falling onto the floor. A memory from what could have been another life flashed for a moment, then was gone. A group of children separated from their mothers for the first time, and the comforting reassurance of one boy ... Robert Boyle, and one single tear.

"Troooyyy," it hissed again, a tendril of smoke lifting out from between the creature's jaws. Unable to move, Troy watched as more of the strange substance rose from the thing's mouth and began to swirl in the air before him like a cyclone. From somewhere inside the shed, he could hear Wendy and Dawn screaming, but he was paralyzed. The swirling mass was hypnotic and made him dizzy, and he was unable to look away. It wrapped around itself, growing dark and then grey, then a mixture of the two. Troy gasped at the sight of the apparition as his eyes grew heavy.

It rushed at him like a bullet and forced itself upon him. Troy felt the icy gust fill his mouth and enter his windpipe. Before he could think, it was in his lungs and took hold of him. He sensed the satisfaction felt by the presence and watched as the monster rifled through his memories. He fought to push the invader out of his head, and it bit back. Troy collapsed against the old wooden floor as the beast stole his breath. Everything he knew, all he had ever witnessed was there for the taking; the creature sifted and ransacked and consumed what it wanted. It was eager and it was hungry. It also had no idea that Troy was still there, watching from somewhere in the darkness.

While the Rob-creature transferred its presence into Troy, a similar transfer was occurring just a few feet away. Dawn was overcome when the dark cloud left Ben Richards, and Wendy succumbed to what had resided in its twin sister, Erin. The sudden and immediate transition of the Entity's presence was fast and consuming. Neither of the girls' bodies were able to handle the onslaught of genetic information.

Wendy collapsed and started to convulse, the fever ripping through her frail body. It bore deep into her mind and attempted to take control of the child at once. But it never worked that way with the little ones; theirs was a slow burn as their malleable defenses fought off the invasion. In its lust for power and need to satiate its hunger, it had tried to consume her completely. It eased back its grip on the child. But their resistance would only last so long; it was a process they needed to go through and the reason it had first appeared as an infection—or flu, as the doctors labeled it. Its greatest disguise was how it could manifest as a sickness, which was always dismissed, until the children grew weak and its control became omnipotent.

Dawn radiated heat like an inferno and had also begun to tremble. The Entity relaxed its grip on her as well. It would have to wait to settle into its new hosts. Which wasn't anything new, it had waited many times in the past ... it was good at waiting.

It watched through the eyes of the protectors, the ones who had delivered the children. The old hosts were already losing cohesion. The one called Rob fell against the floorboards; darkness ran from its eyes and mouth, where it pooled around the body, then disappeared through the cracks. Erin and Ben ceased to move as well. The female's head smacked against the hard wood. Her dark eyes rolled back in her head and turned over white. The essence had left, and her tortured flesh had already begun to liquefy. Her brother went through a similar process as the ether spilled out of him and into Dawn. It was done much like the way a snake shed its skin; the spent bodies of Robert Boyle, Erin Richards, and her twin brother, Ben, were no longer viable. They would remain where they had been discarded, a combination of myriad creatures from multiple time periods: part human, part reptilian ... all monster.

●●●

The heavy rain from yesterday's storm eroded much of the loose gravel from the surface of the old road and gullied out many of the existing crevasses even further, leaving huge potholes and craters that made navigating the bikes difficult. Ted nearly wiped out a dozen times and was almost sent over the handlebars when his front tire caught in one of the larger cracks. Now that they were making their way down the slope and back to the truck, it was noticeable just how dangerous the old pavement had become. With the added threat of their pursuers, the need to remain upright on two wheels was paramount. Ted eased back on the throttle and applied the brake.

Billy, who wasn't nearly as daring as he had been on the way up, followed Ted's lead and descended the hill at a steady pace. By the time they reached the truck, Brandon had taken position at the deck gun, while Bob stood at the side manning the controls of the pump.

Ted pulled up to the back of the truck, threw down the kickstand, and jumped off. He headed straight to the side where Bob had set up shop and grabbed one of the hoses. It rolled out easily as Ted headed for the front of the truck and positioned himself near the right bumper. Billy followed close behind and stood at the left side with the other length of hose.

Lifting the visor of his helmet, Ted called out over the roar of the engine: "Okay, we're in position!"

Bob heard him and opened the valves, allowing the pressurized water to rush into both lengths of hose. The inch-and-three-quarter tube filled quickly and tried to jump out of Ted's hands as he reached for the nozzle. He gripped it tighter to compensate for the force of the water.

"Good to go!" Bob yelled from the side of the truck.

Ted checked to see the hose Billy held was fully loaded and the kid was ready to go as well. "We're good," he said, then stared at the crest of the hill with nervous anticipation.

He continued to watch the road for any sign of movement, then turned to Billy and shrugged his shoulders. Billy gave him the universal sign to wait a second. But there was no movement from either side, and nothing showed itself at the top of the old extension.

Ted squinted and struggled to focus on the crest of the rise, which appeared to grow hazy. At first, it was barely noticeable, and he thought he might have dust in his eyes. Then it became clearer, as if the very top of the mountain had started moving. A series of waves began to spread out, looking like the heat vapors that rose from the pavement on sweltering days. Only it wasn't summer, and Ted knew what was headed their way. The waves grew wider and stretched out to cover the entire width of the road. A pulse of movement rippled through the mass as the strange shape began to descend the mountain and make its way toward them.

Ted gripped the nozzle and planted his feet. It was an impossible scenario, but there wasn't much about the past week that wasn't. From what he could see, the kid hadn't been exaggerating at all. It looked as if every snake in the damn state was on that road. The mass of twisting bodies became more visible the closer the creatures encroached on their position. Ted felt his heart beat triple time; a cold sweat streamed down his back, slicking his shirt to his skin. "Okay, Sheriff. It's time," he said under his breath.

● ● ●

Brandon had a much better view of the approaching mass and was able to make out the individual bodies of the deformed reptiles. Something horrible had happened to them, distorting and twisting their once streamlined features. The snakes were still swift and deathly fast, but they had been disfigured. Massive boil-like growths that looked like infections distended their bellies and backs. Many of the reptiles had lost their pigment as well. The heads of the creatures had grown, and it looked like their venom sacs had tripled in size. Some resembled timber rattlers, others could have been coral or kings, but without the typical vibrant marking, it was impossible to tell for sure. Now they all looked similar, one just as lethal as the next.

The young fireman adjusted the elevation of the deck gun with the foul creatures drawing closer to the truck and the men standing in front of it. He tested

THE OJANOX

the traverse, making sure he could sweep the street quickly, and decided he was happy with the movement; he would be able to execute what he had come to do.

The truck's engine was loud, but another noise rose above it. The sound the reptiles emitted made Brandon's skin crawl. The combination of their tortured hissing and the writhing sound of their misshapen bodies slithering against the broken pavement was nauseating. He felt his stomach flip and fought to hold on to his lunch. The creatures snapped and bared their teeth and lifted their heads in the direction of the men. They had closed more than half the distance down the mountain and were now moving faster.

Brandon's hands grew slick, and his mouth went dry. With every nerve heightened, he waited for the mass of creatures to descend the last twenty feet.

"Almost ready!" he called down to Bob.

● ● ●

The chief had primed the pump and adjusted the throttle. As soon as the gun and the two hoses were fully operating, he'd need to watch the controls and adjust them accordingly. The three men would be shooting a hell of a lot of water at once, and that meant Bob would have to stay at the pump and constantly readjust it. If he allowed the RPMs to tack too high, the engine could seize, and if the PSI dipped below sixty, then the hoses wouldn't work. He needed to balance the master as well as the intake pump and the outtake. Every fireman's worst fear was the possibility of a pump becoming air locked, which happened one of two ways: from a loss of pressure or from the hydrant running dry.

Bob readied himself and took hold of the valve that fed the deck gun. As soon as Brandon gave the word, he would let it rip.

"Okay, Chief. Here we go!" Brandon called as the snakes closed the gap "One ... two ... three!"

Bob turned the valve and watched the pressure dip slightly on the main gauge. He adjusted it and listened to the sound of the engine's RPMs speeding up to feed the pump. The hoses began to fire, and Bob knew the fight had begun. He lowered his hand onto the butt of his sidearm, just to make sure it was still there. *So far, so good.* He adjusted the pressure to compensate for the high water volume coursing through the pump. Although he was curious to see what was happening, he didn't dare leave his position; he trusted the other men had it under control.

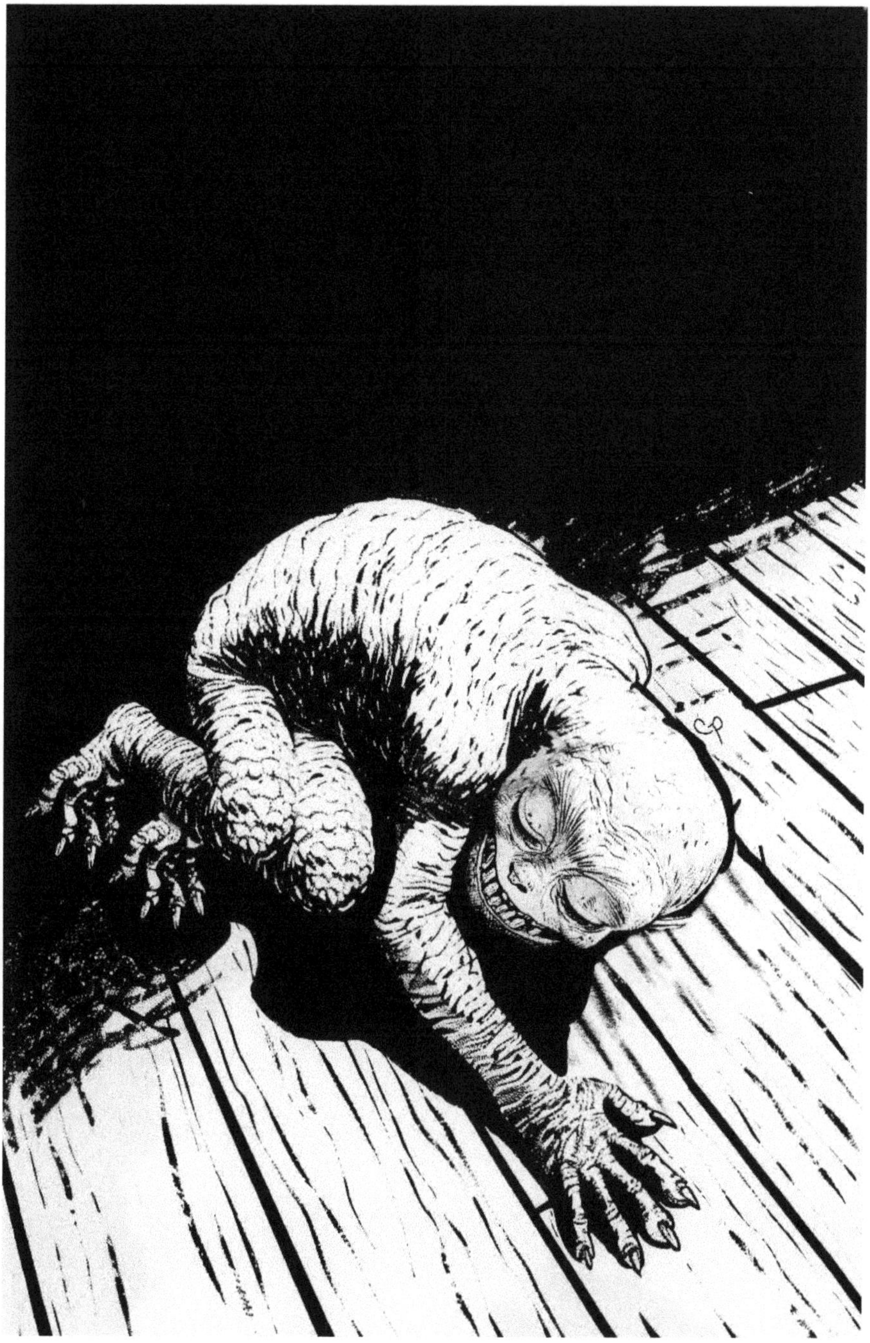
CP

Chapter 99

From where they stood at the back of the old parking lot, the asylum looked dead and forgotten; if Don had to guess, he would have said it was empty. And he would have been wrong to do so; the place was the delineation of death, but it was far from empty. Although presently inactive, the massive hive that clustered in the basement was very much there. Carl checked his watch and nodded to Stephanie and Don that it was time.

Don set the packs on the ground before him, then pulled on the thick gloves with the rubber palms and extracted a set for Carl and one for Stephanie.

"You'll need these." He handed the pair to the sheriff, who looked at them and grimaced.

"I don't think these will protect me if this stuff goes off."

"You didn't use much dynamite in the war, did you?" Don asked Carl, who shook his head and shrugged. "I didn't think so. Trust me on this. You really want to wear these when you handle dynamite."

The sheriff accepted the gloves, and both he and Stephanie pulled them on. Don unzipped the first bag, revealing an obscene amount of explosives. He had taken the time at the quarry to band the sticks into tightly wrapped bundles of ten. Two wires extended from the center of the bundles where the blasting caps had been inserted. At the other end of the wires were the timers, which were nothing more than fancy stopwatches.

Don removed the rest of the bundles from the bags, eight in total, and carefully turned back the timers to the twenty-minute mark.

"That should give us more than enough time to set them and get back here. We need to be long gone before this stuff goes off, so I'm going to give you two stacks each. Are you sure you're both ready for this?"

Stephanie offered a thumbs-up, and Carl nodded in affirmation.

Don focused on Carl, the way his hands had started to shake and the strained look in his eyes. The guy probably hadn't slept in days. "Are you sure you're up to this?" he asked again. "Because you don't look so good."

"I'm fine!" Carl snapped. "I'll be better when this is over and I can get some sleep."

Don nodded. Of course, that was it. The sheriff had been pushed to the limit since last weekend and probably hadn't eaten in over a day as well. "Okay. Whatever you do, you don't want to drop this shit; it will seriously ruin your day."

Stephanie counted the eight stacks lying before them. "If we each get two, then that leaves you with four to set. That place is huge. Are you insane?" She furrowed her brow and stared back at Don.

"I'll go around the right side, then head to the rear of the building. I'll backtrack and set the charges as I go. I want you," he told Carl, "to hit the left side and set these in the shell of the basement windows." Then turning to Stephanie: "You get the front. You see the small windows cut into the foundation on either side of the entrance?"

She nodded, examining the low-set windows.

"All you need to do is place the stack on the sill. As long as you get it close to the mark, there's enough TNT to topple this sucker like the tower of Babel."

Stephanie's face turned red. "You gave me the easy job 'cause I'm a girl!"

"Trust me," Don said. "There's nothing easy when it comes to dynamite. A million things could go wrong ... That goes for all of us."

"Okay ... you're the boss." Carl said.

Don felt the heavy medallion pressing against his chest and hoped it was enough to keep their actions concealed until they were far enough away. He set the last timer and checked his watch. "Okay, here we go." He pressed all the buttons, and the second hands began to tick down. He placed two bundles in one of the bags, two in the other, and handed them to Stephanie and Carl. Then he transferred the four bundles into his backpack and cinched it over his shoulders. "Let's do this."

Don was the first to emerge from the tree line and into the parking lot of the old hospital. Carl and Stephanie followed behind with their packages in hand.

The hulking behemoth stretched out before them, towering over the property like a monolith. The fact it had been allowed to remain at the top of the extension for so long was a mystery. Surely someone owned the property with all its counted sorrows. For whatever reason, it had been left to rot for decades. However, its time of standing sentinel at the top of Garrett Mountain was nearly at an end. Don had never stepped foot in the old sanatorium like most of the people from town; he had never partied on the grounds with his friends and had never made out with a girl at the top of Mountain Ave. But he had heard stories about the place, most of them told by his nephews, Billy and Eric. Now that he had gotten his first look at the Mountainside Sanatorium and felt the presence of the place firsthand, he was glad he had never come here. Don imagined the place had been haunted long before Stephanie's Entity had come to live here. And he didn't even believe in that stuff.

It was more than just the way the structure had been left to rot that made it look evil. Don sensed it in the very ground itself. He scanned the stonework that had crumbled and crashed to the pavement in front of the foundation. Some brave fortune seeker had climbed onto the roof and removed every copper drainpipe and gutter. A bright red heart had been spray-painted across the brick front of the building, bearing the inscription: Mark loves Lizzy. *Sorry, Mark. Looks like I'm gonna be messing up your artwork. I'm sure Lizzy will understand.*

The trio made their way across the torn-up pavement at a slow but steady pace with their hearts racing like Andretti behind the wheel. The blacktop had been overtaken by nature; large trees pushed their way up through the crumbled asphalt. Weeds and scrub brush stood nearly as tall as Stephanie and came up to Don's shoulders. They walked side-by-side and drew closer to the monstrous structure. The sound of thunder rose from the base of the road at the far left of the parking lot. There was another sound even louder than the revving of the engines and the roar of the hoses. Stephanie looked to the men; her eyes widened as the sound of a thousand snakes cried out as one.

Carl squinted; the nauseating sound penetrated his skull, and he swayed for a moment. The sensation passed; still, the chronic gasp of the serpents was an assault to the group's senses. None of them could imagine what the men on the truck were going through.

The cries continued and the roar of the truck grew louder until the trio found themselves standing at the front of the building. No one knew if the medallions Stephanie had given them were helping, but so far, nothing had come after them. They nodded to one another, preparing to set off in separate directions, when the sounds from the road suddenly changed. The high throttled thrum of the engine tacked out, and the cry of the serpents intensified as well. Their screams were now more visceral, as if they had begun to howl.

"God, something's wrong," Carl said under his breath. He turned to the others, who were already looking at him, shocked and terrified.

"We need to move now!" he shouted. "If something went wrong with the truck, we've got a lot less than twenty minutes!"

Don ran toward the right side of the building while Stephanie proceeded to the front. Carl sprang to action and headed in his assigned direction. "Christ, Bob," he cursed over the growl of the serpents. "Watch your ass!"

⬤ ⬤ ⬤

The chief opened the valve, and eighty pounds of pressurized water raced through the line. It entered the deck gun and exploded out of the nozzle in a tight, focused jet. Brandon adjusted the elevation and lowered the pitch of the spray onto the forward line of the encroaching horde. The concentrated water first pounded the pavement in front of the tangle of serpents and then centered on them. The violent power of the jet ripped into the bodies of the creatures, and the water tore them apart. Brandon cranked the traverse adjustment, sweeping the jet across the beasts; a fantail of crimson lifted into the air. Body fluids and pieces of the creatures were thrown across the pavement as if they had been hit by a cannon. Brandon swept the traverse back to the left, releasing another five-foot section of serpents from their mortal coils.

The deck gun was more than effective, making quick work of the serpents that had already closed in on the men. Ted and Billy watched the carnage as Brandon unleashed the initial defensive, then opened the nozzles of their own highly pressurized hoses and pounded the snakes from a lower angle. The combined effort of three jet streams was devastating. Heads, tails, and intestines were thrown in every direction, but mostly back the way they had come. A river of red cascaded down the hill and ran between Ted's boots; a still-rattling tail floated past him and continued down the old road.

Ted never liked snakes to begin with, had always thought they were evil, but these creatures were something far worse. They had gone through a transformation, and it looked like it didn't go quite as planned. It appeared as if there had been a design in mind, that the Entity had a clear idea of what the snakes should become. It had just been physically beyond the snakes' body structure to carry out. Ted focused his jet directly into the pile of deformities and silenced their horrible cries. The other snakes reacted to their brothers' and sisters' destruction and screamed in response; their mutated snake-like language cut through the roar of the jets like a sickle. It was horrible to listen to, deafening and tragic, and almost made Ted feel sorry for having to destroy them. Almost … he still didn't like snakes.

●●●

Billy knew the snakes would be alerted by the sound of the dirt bikes and sent to intercept them; it was the creature's first line of defense in protecting the sanatorium. He and his friends had first encountered the presence Saturday night, probably before it had assembled its army and made the old hospital its home. They may have even stumbled upon it while it was moving in. It looked like a shadow or a cloud of smoke, nothing near as threatening as the possessed creatures that attacked the medical center or the mutated vipers they now faced.

He mowed through the monsters, sweeping his jet stream from the left to right. It had been his idea to lure the creatures out with the dirt bikes, but the chief had suggested they utilize the pump truck. Directing his nozzle, Billy ripped through a tangle of serpents. He prayed the distraction would give the others enough time to breach the perimeter of the sanatorium but had no idea just how omnipotent the creature might be. Still, judging by the ear-splitting reactions of the beasts, he thought they might have a chance.

He opened the nozzle to full and blasted a manhole-sized section of snakes into hundreds of slithering pieces. Billy screamed, focusing all his hatred, until the tears finally surfaced. He had done his best to hold them back, to stifle his feelings, but the destruction of the serpents intensified his memory of what happened to his family. And the dam let go; the tears fell as if driven by their own pump and high-pressure valve. The back spray from the hose lifted into the air and rained down into the open visor of his helmet, camouflaging his tears, but it did nothing to disguise the way his hands had begun to shake and the tremors that raked through his body. However, there was too much going on for anyone to notice that Billy Tobin had lost control.

● ● ●

Bob dialed up the pressure as the demand for water from the hoses and the deck gun diminished the PSIs to the intake pump. He adjusted the setting with the RPMs racing and watched the pressure slowly climb back to eighty PSI. Snake parts and a shower of gore rained down on him where he stood at the controls. He could see the crest of the mountain, and there didn't appear to be an end to the conga line of serpents headed their way.

Then the unthinkable happened; the pressure in the pump dropped to zero and the RPMs shot through the roof. Bob watched the LDH deflate as water ceased to flow through the large-diameter hose.

"Jesus Christ, no!" he screamed, running to the hydrant. The Siamese connection had gone dry as well, and the men were gunning through the remaining water reserve at an alarming rate. Bob didn't know if the hydrant had dried up or if he was looking at an even worse scenario … a water hammer.

A second later, the pump lost its prime, becoming air locked, and they were dead in the water. Bob's only hope was that a slow stream of water would return and he would be able to reprime the pump. However, the pressurized water that rushed toward the hydrant directly behind the untimely air pocket hit the ancient plug like a two-ton hammer … a water hammer.

The old unserviced hydrant had been made of cast iron and was unable to handle the force of the hammer. The Siamese connection exploded from the impact of the pressure while Bob was standing directly over the plug. He was hit in the head by a three-inch shard of cast iron. The metal penetrated his skull, and he fell backward into a river of serpent soup. Bob Jones was dead before his head met the ground; he never saw what hit him.

●●●

The pump's reserve water supply went dry just before the hydrant erupted. At first, Ted thought the sheriff and the others had begun to set off the charges. Then he saw the huge plume of water jetting into the sky behind him. The hose in his hand went limp, and the others stopped working as well. *What the fuck happened?* But there was no time to wait for an answer; the mass of vipers regrouped and honed in on their position. He turned to Billy, who twisted and punched at the non-working nozzle in his hands. Ted watched the frantic way that Billy attacked the hose and could see the tremors raking throughout his body. He rushed to his side and yanked the hose from his hands.

"That's it. The pump is dead!" he screamed over the erupting flow of water and the shrill cry of the snakes. Ted grabbed him by the front of his jacket and shook. "We have to move, now!"

Billy looked up at him as if in a trance. "What?"

Ted seized the boy and dragged him around the side of the truck; they stopped short at the sight of the chief's body lying near the shattered hydrant. "No," Ted groaned, and approached the man who had been operating the pump. He looked down into the chief's open eyes; a portion of the man's skull was missing.

"Nooo!" Brandon screamed from the top of the truck.

"Get down," Ted called up to him. "We've got to get the hell out of here ... now!" He pulled Billy to the back of the truck where they had parked the bikes, unslung the shotgun from his back, and turned it on the horde. The snakes were almost on top of them. Ted fired at the masses, blasting a hole in their line of offense that was filled in by more creatures just as fast. He fired again and jumped when another weapon erupted to his left. Billy Tobin had regained enough of his composure to join the fight. The men continued to blast away at the snakes, with little effect other than a momentary disruption in the creatures' momentum.

"Get down here, Brandon!" Ted called, but the boy was nowhere in sight.

The serpents reached the front wheels of the pumper and made their way closer to the back tires; still, there was no sign of Brandon. Ted called to him a third time and was alerted by the sound of gunfire from the front of the vehicle. The kid had moved toward the cab and decided to battle the creatures from there.

Ted and Billy exchanged a disheartened look; there was nothing more they could do other than attempt to lead the snakes away from the truck and the sanatorium. The deputy hopped onto his bike and Billy followed. Together, they coasted away from the truck without starting the engines. It took less than twenty seconds to make it halfway down the hill, far enough to reach a safe distance. Ted popped the kickstand and dismounted the bike; he turned toward the truck to see Brandon panicked on the top of the vehicle. Brandon screamed and shot at something that had gotten too close to his feet. Ted turned away, unable to watch anymore. The next sound to leave the young fireman's lips reverberated as if the man had been set on fire; Brandon fell onto his back and screamed for another few seconds, then fell silent.

The snakes accelerated their pursuit and descended the mountain towards the men on the bikes. Billy shot into the parade of bodies, which did little to slow their attack.

"Jesus Christ." Ted scowled, then hopped back on the bike. Billy fired again at the creatures, then followed. They coasted down the hill another thirty feet and turned to shoot at the serpents once again. They repeated the process until they found themselves at the downed fence where Mountain Ave met the access road. The snakes never ceased their pursuit, but from what either men could see, the size of the horde had diminished. Ted and Billy led the rest of the monstrosities away from the sanatorium and the old extension. The diversion had worked, but it had come at a high price.

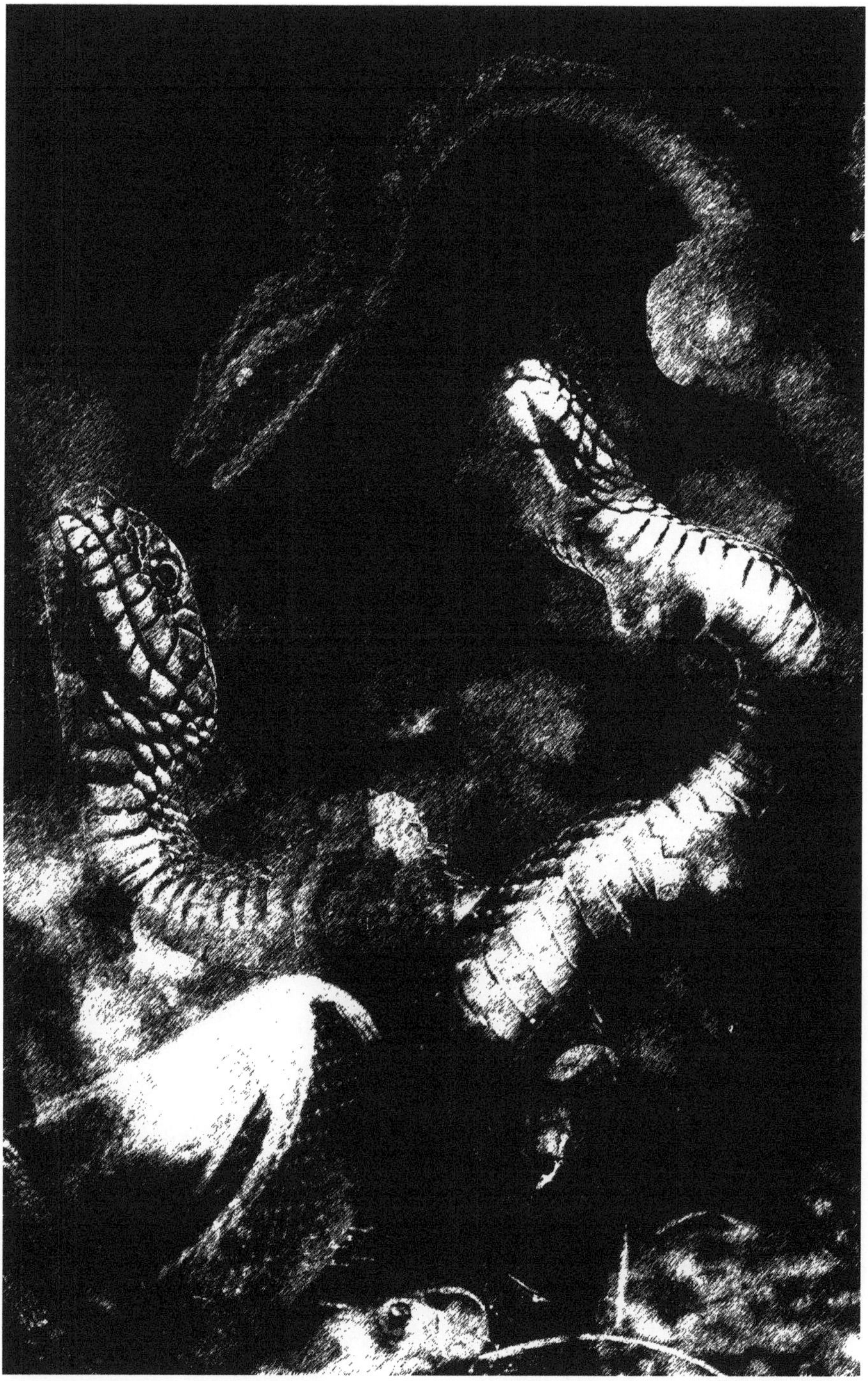

Chapter 100

Don made his way along the far side of the building and heard the horrible grinding noise of the pump when it became air locked. He didn't know what to make of it at first, thinking it was operating under normal conditions. Then the engine raced to an ear-splitting decibel, followed by the sound of an explosion. He jumped when the hydrant erupted and almost fell with the backpack of dynamite.

The landscape surrounding the sanatorium hadn't been tended to in decades, making it near impossible to wade through the chest-high tangle of weeds and scrub brush. Tightly knit vines wove throughout the property and across the face of the structure. It took Don three full minutes to navigate the right side of the building, and by the time he reached the back, nearly seven had passed. He had allowed more than enough time for Carl and Stephanie to set their charges but realized now that he would be cutting it far too close himself.

He quickened his pace as much as he dared and trudged through the overgrown weeds. Large thorns slowed his every step; Don winced as their barbs dug into his legs and tore at his jeans. Still, he forced himself to continue onward.

It took another minute to reach the furthest window in the back. He bent down to the glassless frame and was overcome by the most oppressive stench he had ever encountered. The rancid odor of death rose from the basement and smacked him in the face. Don gagged and nearly passed out. Biting back the urge to vomit, he set the first bundle of dynamite on the window ledge at the base of the foundation.

He doubled back the way he came, retracing his steps along the back of the building toward the second window. More of the deadly thorns attacked him, penetrating his skin and drawing blood. Don suffered through the pain and approached the next window.

The noxious smell was just as bad; the acrid stench of death now appeared to be everywhere. Don tasted it in his mouth and smelled it on his clothes; the odor of rotting flesh saturated the very ground. He held his breath, reached into the bag, and removed the second bundle of explosives. "Damn," he cursed, looking at the timer. Ten minutes had already passed, leaving him only another ten to set the last of the explosives and make it to safety.

Don placed the charge on the window's ledge and sped off to the right side of the building. He cursed himself for doing so, knowing full well the danger of running with explosives on his back, but the urgency to make up some time was paramount. He convinced himself he was only retracing his steps and felt somewhat confident even though he couldn't see where he was stepping. He reached the corner of the building and banked a hard right. Don picked up the pace, with the next window less than twenty feet away. Then ... his right leg went out from under him. He was thrown off balance as his foot sank into the old gopher hole, his leg disappearing into the dirt up to the knee. Don's upper body continued its forward momentum. The stomach-lurching sound his ankle made when it snapped in the forgotten burrow was consuming, and Don almost passed out.

He fell into the overgrowth with his leg held fast in the ground. Bile rose in the back of Don's throat as the pain blasted through him. He turned and vomited onto the grass, his head spinning as if he were on a carrousel. Consumed by blinding light, Don struggled to figure out what had happened. The confusion passed a heartbeat later, and Don realized with laser clarity that he still had twenty sticks of dynamite on his back with the timers set.

He pushed himself onto his hands and one good knee and attempted to lift his injured leg out of the hole. At first, it wouldn't budge; the dirt held fast against his throbbing foot. Don screamed with sweat drenching his forehead and running into his eyes. He gritted his teeth and pushed through the pain, attempting to free himself a second time. The dirt closed around him like a suction cup; then finally, it loosened and partially released its grip. Don's leg shot from the gopher hole, and he fell forward onto his face. White-hot pain blinded his vision, and the world began to go dark. He struggled to remain conscious, but it was too intense. He passed out in the grass with two full bundles of dynamite strapped to his back and less than seven minutes left.

● ● ●

Carl knelt to set the first bundle of explosives at the base of the foundation and hesitated. The changing volume of the pump engine caused him to turn toward the road. The motor's racing RPMs accelerated to a lunatic speed, then halted. Less than a full second later, the hydrant blew. Carl jumped and nearly dropped the ten sticks of dynamite through the open window into the basement below. His heart hammered in time with the rapid concussion of gunfire that followed. *Dear God ... no!* Something had gone terribly wrong, but his thoughts were drowned out when the battalion of serpents screeched as one.

The sound of weapons fire meant the men were still alive, but things hadn't gone as planned. Best-case scenario, the men could still hold off the invading army, but there were too many variables. *Shit!* Carl turned back toward the window and leaned in closer to set the package on the sill. That's when it hit him.

The foul stench rose from the basement and sucker punched him. It was the rancid smell of death with an underlying stink that Carl found far too familiar. The paralyzing funk of rotting fish filled his sinuses, causing him to freeze. It rushed at him like a predator and thrust him back in time, back to that day on the Delta. Olfactory recall kicked in as the scene replayed itself over again on the canvas of his psyche.

● ● ●

Carl found himself waist deep in the brackish waters of the Delta. Thousands of rotting fish covered the surface, putrefying in the Asian sun. He watched the chopper as it lifted into the air and then headed toward the horizon. Wiping the sweat from his brow and doing his best to keep his weapon out of the water, Carl turned and pushed forward through the gravy of dead fish and swarming haze of black flies.

The banks of the Delta lay before them, peppered with endless fields of rice paddies. Tall grasses swayed against a breeze that did nothing to diminish the oppressive heat. Carl looked back and nodded to his platoon—Hacksaw and Tank, followed by Tennessee and Tucson; the Sarge was sandwiched between Big Joe and Little Joe, leaving Goober and Ralph bringing up the rear. Carl locked eyes with Ralph, his only real friend in this God-forsaken country. The big guy had a girl waiting for him back home, and Kerri Ann was expecting their first child.

Carl froze, the sirens in his gut screaming at him. He opened his mouth to warn Ralph; it was on the tip of his lips, but his heart twisted in his chest before he could react. He knew about the landmine and that Ralph was about to step on it; still ... panic paralyzed him, and he couldn't form the words. The only thing Carl could focus on was the overpowering stench of the fish. His hands shook as the scene replayed itself in his mind's eye. *For God's sake, Ralph. Don't Move!* But he could only watch as the platoon proceeded forward, making their way closer to the shoreline. The corpses of the fish increased in density and mass and the all-consuming odor. *Dear God ... the horrible stench of fish.*

Ralph locked eyes with him and smiled. Suddenly, all other emotions were stripped away. His eyes bulged as terror rearranged his features. He knew he had stepped on it; the click echoed beneath his boot and resonated through the water to where the other men stood. Ralph opened his mouth to scream; "Loo—" was all he got out before the water erupted like a geyser.

A tidal wave of crimson washed over Carl. A baptism of pulverized fish guts marinated in Ralph's blood rained down. It entered his mouth, covered his face, and ran into his eyes. Carl felt the scream forming in his throat, but before he could release it, the scene began to fade. It was replaced by a familiar sensation in his gut. *Something's wrong ... something is very, very wrong.* He was catapulted back into the moment by the sound of someone calling his name.

"Carl!"

Every muscle in his body went rigid. Sweat poured from his brow and his hands shook as he looked around to locate the owner of the voice but found no one there. The memory of the Delta faded to a whisper, and Carl regained a sliver of his composure, realizing he had succumbed to another flashback. He stared down at the stack of dynamite in his hands. Over five minutes had passed with less than seven left until detonation. His gut twisted and spoke up once again; something was terribly wrong, much more than just what was happening with the men on the truck. He was sure someone had called his name and could almost recognize the voice as that, too, faded with the Delta.

He set the dynamite on the ledge, turned back the way he had come, and headed to the next window. Holding his breath, he placed the second bundle in the appropriate crook at the base of the foundation, then ran toward the front of the building. Carl hit the corner like a bat out of Hell to find Stephanie standing in the parking lot facing him. She lifted her arms and shrugged her shoulders. He quickly closed the distance with sweat plastering his hair to his forehead.

"What happened to you?" she asked. "You look like hell."

"It's a long story. Where's Don?" Carl looked at the far side of the building to find no sign of movement in that direction. He suddenly realized why his gut had called out so urgently. "Jesus Christ!" he cried. "Something's wrong!"

Stephanie took off after him the second he started running and followed across the busted blacktop of the parking lot. "Please, God, please, God," she chanted, with Carl leading the way.

They found Don's trail immediately and retraced his steps though the tall grass. Carl glanced at the windows lining the foundation and noticed that none of the charges had been set. *This is bad. Where the fuck are you, Don?*

The grass was taller on this side of the building and riddled with gopher holes. Carl spotted them right away and navigated a wide berth. They approached the far corner of the building when Carl noticed the mass of camouflage sprawled out in the grass. It was Don, his body laid out face first. "Christ. No!" he shouted and rushed to where the man lay.

Stephanie gasped as she approached and knelt down beside him. Don groaned and attempted to lift himself off the ground but couldn't right himself. His right ankle remained partially lodged in one of the numerous gopher holes, and it was evident what had happened.

She lifted his head and slapped him across the face. Don's eyes opened at once.

"What?" He blinked as terror flooded his features. "The dynamite!"

Carl removed the pack from Don's back and opened it; there were three minutes left on the timers. He reached in and removed the two remaining bundles, the thick rubber gloves he wore causing him to fumble for a moment. He looked down the side of the building and moved to set the last charges.

"No." Stephanie stopped him. "Give them to me. I'll never be able to lift him; you have to carry him out of here."

Carl held on to the explosives and stared back at her, knowing she was right. The woman was five foot one, two at the most, and there was no way she could move Don by herself. He would have to carry him while she set the last of the charges. It was the only way. He handed her the bundles and nodded to the side of the building.

"Set that shit and get the hell out of there!" he barked, then bent down and hefted the injured man over his shoulder in one lift. Don screamed when Carl grabbed him and started moving.

He stumbled, then Carl shifted and compensated for Don's full body weight on top of him. He started to run, slow at first, then fell into a decent stride. He continued as fast as he could, avoiding the minefield of gopher holes that now revealed themselves to be everywhere. He jumped over one and nearly landed in another, all the while wondering how Don had made it as far as he did without breaking his leg sooner.

Stephanie watched the men retreat toward the front of the building with a stack of dynamite in each of her hands. She looked down at the timers ...

She had less than two minutes left.

● ● ●

Its divided essence rested within the three new hosts. The children lay on the floor of the shed unconscious and sick. Sweat drained from their bodies as the ether pushed to accelerate the becoming process. But the harder it forced its intrusion, the worse it affected the children, their systems threatening to shut down as it sought to consume them faster than it knew possible.

It had been hyper-focused on the acquisition of the three and neglected what was happening on the mountain. It sent its eye into the vipers and watched them advance on the two remaining men. The controllable reptiles made an effective line of defense but weren't built for evolution and had almost been destroyed in the becoming process. However, their venom was more than just toxic; it was like nothing this era had ever seen.

Alarms sounded within its sensory awareness. It couldn't see what was happening but knew something was very wrong. It attempted to zero in but was unable. Rage filled its consciousness with the realization that there was an additional threat to the hive. It wasn't possible; it had left the mind trap for anything that might slip past the vipers. Nothing living could evade it, and its flawless nature had worked perfectly against the priest's group. Still, the threat was there, and it was dangerously close to the hive.

It was still too early, and it had risked much by sending the Butchie-creature out into the light. The protector's body was already showing signs of deterioration, but there was no other option. It focused its projected eye from the shed and directed it on the hive. Still, it couldn't see the threat. This had never happened before.

An echo stirred within the presence ... a memory ... this *had happened* ... once. The beings called Lenape had tricked it. Blinding rage filled its vision; it entered the hive and roused its army from their rest cycle. A glimmer stirred within it, a sense that it was risking a great deal by sending the brood into the light. But it wasn't anything close to rational thought. That was a human quality. The Entity acted on pure bestial instinct.

● ● ●

Stephanie ran along the side of the building with her heart in her throat. She sidestepped to avoid one of the massive gopher holes and proceeded to the closest window. The glass had been broken out of the frame decades ago, and as she bent to place the explosives on the sill, the penetrating funk assaulted her like an air strike. It was death ... suffocating ... rotting flesh. The creatures had amassed within the basement by the thousands; their stench was incapacitating.

She gagged and nearly vomited, then she heard the first tortured cries emanating from within. *They're awake! And now they're coming.* The clamor of the beasts as they clawed from their crypt rose in volume. Stephanie listened to the sound of their taloned hands and feet scrambling across the basement floor, and a second later, the world erupted in a chorus of shrieks. *They know I'm here.* The beasts had figured out what they were up to.

She froze for a moment too long, her legs glued to the ground. Looking down at the last remaining bundle of dynamite in her hand she watched the timer pass the one-minute mark, which finally got her moving. Stephanie raced along the side of the building at a full sprint, her muscles propelling her through the tall grass like a gazelle. It didn't matter that she was short and her legs were small; she had been a ballerina for years. Stephanie's petite dancer's legs pumped like a diesel locomotive. She reached the final window and barely stopped to set the explosive; however, it was long enough for Stephanie to focus on the minute hand as it ticked past the thirty-second mark.

The ghastly sounds erupting from the basement were deafening and frantic. The beasts had mobilized and soon would be exiting the building. Stephanie lowered her head and pushed herself to the point of collapse. It had been years since she exerted her body in such a way, but it came back as familiar practice, and she didn't miss a beat. Her heart raced quicker than the seconds on the detonators, and Stephanie knew she had less than twenty heartbeats left. One missed step, one unfortunate gopher hole, and she'd end up just another stain on the property. She made it to the corner of the building in time to see the distant figures of the men disappear behind the tree line as Carl slipped into the woods with Don on his back. They had made it. But she was still so far away and had so much distance to cover and very little time.

●●●

The basement of the old sanatorium had been gutted and left to rot. Several gurneys lay overturned in one of the back corners. Black mold from decades of rainwater seeping in through the broken windows and the no-longer-functioning drainage system coated the floor. And one of the foundation walls had caved in from the excessive rain from yesterday's storm.

Those maladies were the least of the problems that plagued the basement of the old hospital. Now it truly was a place of monsters. Many of which had already started to decompose. Their flesh, pushed beyond its capabilities, could no longer fight the infection. Blood, gore, and non-functioning organs were discarded with every movement of the horde.

At once, they were awakened by the voice. There was trouble, but the directive was obscure. They had always been sent out with clear instructions, but this was different; they had simply been roused and sent out in a general fashion. The hive reacted to the master's uncertainty and frustration; had they still possessed human emotions, it would have been labeled fear. They responded in kind with cries of rage and aggression. Scrambling to their feet, they clawed up the stairs, pushing past one another to exit the building. There wasn't a single shared concern that they were rushing into the toxic light of day.

They poured onto the first floor, trampling over what had been left of the priest's forces. The hive besieged the front door as the blinding light of day seared their eyes and burned their skin.

●●●

Stephanie sailed across the broken asphalt with her legs propelling her into the air like a gold-medal-Olympian. Carl and Don watched the woman from their position. She bolted toward them, clearing half the distance of the parking lot in a matter of seconds. Her feet looked like they never touched the ground as she took flight, pristine and streamlined.

There was movement from just inside the front entrance; something flashed out of the shadows and emerged onto the steps.

"Oh fuck!" Don said as the first beast stared out across the lot and spotted Stephanie. The creature howled, then threw a tangle of arms in front of its face to block out the sun. Behind it, a degradation of fiends followed awkwardly out the front doors.

Stephanie poured on the steam as the first ghoul stepped into the full light of day and shrieked. She spotted Don lying on the ground at the tree line and closed the distance between them. Springing off her back leg, she took to the air, sailing across the final stretch of pavement and coming down in the cool of the woods just as the horde descended the steps of the old hospital.

Seconds later, the air was sucked from their lungs as the front of the building eclipsed before them. The searing light lashed out across the parking lot, accompanied by a concussion that stripped the few remaining leaves from the trees. The detonations went off simultaneously, with the exception of the ones set in the back; those went off perhaps a second or two later, but the effect was the same. The first floor of the building disappeared as the explosion forced the concrete foundation and blockwork outward in a geyser of shrapnel. Fiery red, orange, and yellow flashed, and the exothermic chemical reaction tore the structure apart. What remained of the second and third floors caved into the massive hole created by the explosion. A titanic cloud lifted into the air and rushed across the parking lot at a couple hundred miles per hour. The group buried their heads as dust and debris rained over them and covered the ground where they lay.

The beasts that had started to make their way outside were vaporized by the two bundles that Stephanie had set at the windows on either side of the entrance. Their souls had finally been laid to rest.

It was a long time before Don, Carl, or Stephanie could raise their heads as concrete dust, pulverized building material, vaporized mold spores, and a century of pain clouded the air. It permeated every molecule. As they lay there, a strange hush fell over them and resonated in their ringing ears. Something had changed, possibly their luck. But after a tidal wave of sorrow and pain, Stephanie wasn't about to place her faith in something as impermanent as luck. She held her breath and prepared for the next tragedy to befall their dwindling group.

She didn't have to wait long.

Chapter 101

Ted and Billy led the snakes away from the sanatorium and a half mile further down Mountain Ave like a pair of Pied Pipers. The serpents followed as the men coasted their bikes down the hill, stopping every several hundred feet to allow the demonic parade to catch up, then repeating the process. It worked like a charm. Ted imagined he could lead them straight to King Lake, where they would all jump off the dock into the water like a bunch of lemmings. They balanced their bikes and waited once again in the center of the road when the top of the mountain erupted like Mt. Vesuvius.

The explosion took the two men by surprise. The concussive *Wha-Woom* popped their ears and resonated in their sinus cavities. It shook the ground beneath their bikes with such force they were nearly thrown off. A mushroom of black and brown vomited into the sky like a rocket as the sanitorium disintegrated. A growing sense of elation welled up inside Ted as he watched the dark plume spread out like a nuclear blast. He turned to Billy, who hooted and pumped his fists into the air. Then something strange happened. The snakes that had been hot on their trail stopped following, as if the explosion had jarred them from their trance. It appeared as if they had forgotten what they were doing. The serpents stopped, paused for a moment, and then dispersed into the woods in every direction.

The men looked at each other, wondering if it was really over, with neither one able to accept the possibility that it might be. Ted removed the radio from his hip and turned it back on. "Sheriff," he said. "We can see your work from here. Looks like you took out half the mountain." He watched the expanding cloud and tried again. "Sheriff, are you there?"

There was silence for a moment, then the radio blared with static and a familiar voice broke through. "Deputy Lutchen," the man shouted. "This is Burt. We have a big problem. Mayor Marceau, Lois Fischer, and the three children never made it to the boats. Günter called, he had to leave without them." The old man's voice was shaken and frantic.

"Where were they last seen?" Ted shouted into the radio.

"At the medical center when they left for the lake. They were in the mayor's station wagon!"

"Okay, Burt. We'll retrace their steps and see if we can find them. Maybe they had an accident or drove off the road."

"I already did that. I've been looking since we got the call. I checked every road between the center and the lake, and there's no sign of them."

Billy leaned in, hanging on the coroner's every word. "Where are you now, Burt?" Ted asked.

"The foothills behind the Boyle house. Carl and I thought there might be a connection back here, and it was the only other spot I could think of."

Ted remembered the morning they found Felix Castillo's body lying in the middle of Foothills Drive and thought what the coroner was saying made sense. The Boyle house bordered the woods and so did the Richards house. If there was a connection, it was very possible that it lay somewhere in the woods behind those residents. Ted let out an exaggerated breath. *This isn't over.* They all thought it would end with the destruction of the sanatorium, but they had missed something. There was still a missing piece of the puzzle somewhere staring them in the face.

"Copy that, Burt." Ted clutched the radio with a growing tremble in his hand. "As soon as I hear from the sheriff, we'll help you find them. We're coming in from the Mountain Ave side and will meet you somewhere in the middle. Have you found anything yet?"

"I came across some tracks. Three of the sets were small, but I wouldn't exactly call them human looking."

"Those could be old tracks."

"Not likely," Burt said. "The storm would have washed them away. These are fresh. There was another set too. Something big was with them ... something really big."

"Okay." Ted swallowed at the lump in his throat. "Don't take any chances, and wait for us before you do anything."

"Copy that. I'll see you when you get here." The coroner ended the transmission.

Ted was about to try the sheriff again when the radio crackled in his hand.

"Deputy Lutchen, come in, Deputy Lutchen." Ted recognized Stephanie Thompson's voice.

"This is Lutchen."

"Deputy Lutchen," her voice was ragged and out of breath. "We need your help; it's an emergency!" The radio went silent. A cold sweat broke out on Ted's forehead. He turned to Billy, who reacted and jumped down on the kickstart of his bike. A second later, the YZ roared to life with Billy Tobin gunning the throttle and the back tire smoking against the pavement as he tore back up the mountain.

● ● ●

Stephanie raised her head and squinted against the fine particles still lingering in the air. She coughed, shaking off a layer of filth as she got to her feet and attempted to regain her bearings. The breeze on top of the mountain had picked up and already begun to carry the massive dust cloud away. Its foggy billows tumbled across the parking lot and were sent toppling over the south side of Garrett Mountain in the direction of the quarry. She stared down at the two men, who were both covered in pulverized stone from head to foot.

Don spat onto the ground in front of him. "Am I dead?" He tried to get up and was instantly reminded of his injury with a sharp stabbing pain. He howled and fell back to the ground.

"Easy does it," Carl said, then helped prop him up against a large boulder. "It looks like you broke something."

Don leaned back, braced himself, and attempted to flex the ankle in question. He turned it to the right and left, then tried to wiggle his toes. "Hurts like a bitch, but I can still move it a little."

Stephanie knelt in front of him and slowly rolled up his pants. She gasped; Don's leg had already swelled to almost twice its normal width and turned a deep purple.

"Jesus. That's not good."

"I don't think it's broken," he said, moving his toes with a bit more success.

Carl shook the dust out of his hair, removed the rubber gloves from his hands, and threw them on the ground. There was a metallic *chunk* as they landed on something half buried in the silt. A glint of gold caught the sun and reflected back at them.

"What's that?" Stephanie leaned over and sifted through the mess. She lifted it by the chain; a fine layer of dust fell from the medallion. "Did you drop this?" She looked up at Carl.

"I guess so," he said, patting his chest. "Probably came off when I hit the ground." He reached for the pendant and froze with his arm outstretched. His fingers started to tremble, just slightly at first. Then his face twisted as the tremors took hold of his hand and escalated.

"Ahhh!" Carl grabbed his temples and fell to his knees. Clutching his head with his trembling hands, he continued to cry out as Stephanie rushed to his side and took him by the shoulders.

"What is it? What's wrong?" She bent over the man as he rocked back and forth on his knees. Don focused on Carl and watched with growing concern.

The fit lasted for a minute or more before it finally passed, and Carl's body relaxed. He placed his hands on the ground and raised his head. Sweat poured from his brow and coated his face.

"It's the headaches?" Don stared at him from his position against the rock.

"Y-y-yeah," Carl answered with a waver in his voice. "Christ."

"You used RTD instead of dynamite in Vietnam ... right? Came as a rubber you could mold and handle?" Don pressed.

"What?"

"I don't see what you're getting at," Stephanie said, glancing at the medallion in her hand.

"Yeah. What's with all the questions?" Carl's eyes narrowed.

THE OJANOX

"You're nitro-sick, Carl," Don stated. "It happens when you touch dynamite without gloves. The nitroglycerine seeps into your pores and gets into your bloodstream. Symptoms include a drop in blood pressure, shakes, and severe headaches." Don shifted against the rock as Carl stared at him.

"He was wearing the gloves," Stephanie said. "You saw him take them off."

"Not today," Don insisted. "The other night, when you took the explosives from my trailer and used them to blow up the Sunset Pass and the Gables Bridge." Don forced himself to his feet and limped closer to Stephanie. She took his hand, and together, they backed away from the sheriff.

"What in God's name are you talking about, Fischer?" Carl barked. "Are you out of your damn mind?"

"I thought I was. But there were two sets of prints at the shed. One belonged to a big son of a bitch, but the others looked an awful lot like those cowboy boots you're wearing."

Carl's face twisted as Don continued.

"I figured it had to be someone who knew a little about explosives. But you'd never used dynamite and didn't know you needed gloves to handle it. It got into your head, Carl ... and you never even knew it was there!"

Carl clenched his fist and gritted his teeth; he stared at the ground in front of him with his breath growing heavy in his chest. "Th-that's not p-possible!" he said as his vision blurred and the image filled his head.

●●●

Carl found himself staring down at the trunk of a car that was being loaded by a pair of busy hands. He forced himself to focus against the throbbing in his head and tune into the image more clearly. Boxes were being placed onto dark carpeting that was so familiar it jumped out at him. The trunk belonged to one of the sheriff's cruisers. The haze lifted, and the dream came back to him fully; there was writing on each of the boxes that read: Danger Explosives. Carl bit back the pain as it tore into him even deeper. When had he dreamt that? He wondered if it had been last night at the armory but knew it wasn't. Possibly the night before.

The view of the trunk faded, and Carl found himself looking at a dusty patch of ground. His eyes came to rest on the top of the old cowboy boots; they were his own. But someone else was there too, another set of boots, torn and much larger than his. They were ripped at the side stitching; the feet within them had pushed through the leather and broken the laces. His view shifted upward to examine the owner of the massive boots. The remnants of the man's clothing hung in tattered rags and barely covered his calves and thighs. Skin that had been stretched to its absolute limit ruptured from the grotesque muscles and veins bulging beneath the surface.

Carl's heart twisted as he recalled the minute details of the dream. *The man's torso was bare, covered in thick scales that resembled armor. He followed the vision upward and focused on the face that was almost too deformed to look at. The creature's forehead protruded, and its eyes were as black as coal, but there was something about it that was very familiar.* Christ! *Carl thought,* it's that psychopath Butchie Post.

The beast reached into the shed, pulled out two handfuls of the dynamite, and handed it to him. Carl watched his own bare hands accept the explosives and then place them into the trunk of the cruiser ... his cruiser. He tucked them into a box that held several timers, blasting caps, and even more dynamite.

Carl shook his head and tried to force the vision out of his mind. He clenched his fists and pressed them against his temples. *What's happening?* The pain erupted like a volcano, and Stephanie rushed to his side once again.

As Carl tried to fight off the headache, another vision crept into view and started to play out.

He watched his own hands take one of the timers, the same type he had used in Vietnam, and connect it to the two leads of the blasting cap. He then inserted the cap into a bundle of dynamite and placed it into the box with the others he had fashioned. He had made four complete stacks.

"Get away from him!" Don yelled to Stephanie.

She looked back at him through a wash of confusion.

"I said, get away from him!" Don screamed, but it was too late.

Carl's head shot back as if it were on hinges, and he zeroed in on Stephanie with a visceral intent.

THE OJANOX

●●●

It had nearly gotten into the sheriff's head the night at the morgue. Rainey had succumbed easily, and it would have taken Carl if it hadn't been for Ziegler. Still, it had tasted the man, and that was all it needed to follow his trail and wear him down. Carl had felt off for the past few days as the presence nibbled away at his defenses, attempting to get inside and control his actions. Some were easier to control than others, and Carl had been a tough nut to crack. But the man had pushed himself to the point of exhaustion, which had ultimately worked against him.

Wednesday night, after the fires at the medical center and gas station, the sheriff was close to collapsing. That's when it latched on to him and turned him into a weapon. Carl believed he had gone home and straight to sleep. Instead, he had driven to the quarry, where he met with the recently assimilated Butchie Post, Gary Forsyth, and Mandy Griggs. He had backed his cruiser up to the explosives shed that Butchie and the others had broken into.

The Entity had learned what Carl knew about explosives, but its children no longer possessed the finesse to construct such a device. Not only did it need Carl's knowledge but his fingers as well. The sheriff manufactured the weapons, then gave the stacks to Butchie, Gary, and the others. He explained where to place them underneath the bridge and in the cliff face over the pass, then he showed them how to press the button. The creatures waited until just before sunrise to initiate the countdown sequence. By then, Carl had driven home and woke up in his own bed an hour later, exhausted but under the assumption he had gotten close to a full night's sleep. But his headaches grew increasingly worse as the nitroglycerin entered his bloodstream and forced his blood pressure to bottom out.

●●●

It had sensed something wrong at the nest but been unable to see that Carl and the others were there. It woke its children prematurely from their rest and dispatched them into the light. Then ... pain ... blinding pain ... unlike any it had ever felt before. The nest had been destroyed; all its children silenced at once. Rage consumed it as it struggled to project, but still something blocked its ability to see. Sending its ether out from the shed, it sensed a familiar presence, one it had tasted before. It latched on to the man and looked through his eyes as he stood up and focused on the broken chain lying in the dirt. It scratched at the surface and nibbled away as it attempted to take control of the man once again.

● ● ●

Carl knew it was true; somehow, he had been compromised. It had found a way into his head just as it had gotten into Rainey's. *Christ! I never even suspected.* In a rush of clarity, he understood why he'd always been two steps behind the creature's every move. It had impeded his judgement and affected his decisions from the very beginning. He and Burt had been on its trail, and if they'd only gone back to the foothills, they might have been led back to the sanatorium sooner.

Then he felt it, an itch in the back of his head, impossible to scratch. It gnawed at the base of his skull, twisted like a knife, and entered his brain. The voice was far too familiar.

Carl...

Every muscle in the sheriff's body went rigid. He rose to his feet, balled his hand into a fist, and struck Stephanie under her chin. The small woman was caught off guard and lifted several inches off the ground. Her jaws slammed shut, and her head flew backwards with a violent twist. She landed hard on her back and lay there motionless.

Don lunged to grab him but stumbled on his sprained ankle and fell to the ground. Carl raised his boot and brought it down on Don's shoulder blade. He twisted his heel and drove it deep into the man's back with the full force of his body weight.

Don screamed and struggled to crawl away; he squirmed and scrambled and finally managed to roll over onto his back. Reaching up, he latched on to Carl's boot and attempted to throw him off balance. Don stopped moving when he saw the gun.

Carl pulled back the hammer of the .45 with a shaky hand. Broken blood vessels filled his eyes with crimson as he drew a bead on the man.

"This isn't you, Sheriff," Don pleaded to the man inside. "You don't want to do this." Don watched the giant barrel focus on the center of his head. There was no use ... Carl Primrose was gone; the beast had taken over.

Now, Carl ...

Carl's finger tightened on the trigger of the magnum. Like a prisoner trapped within the confines of his own mind, he could only observe as it all played out. The gun steadied in his hand as he took aim at the man on the ground.

Don closed his eyes and raised his hands. He jumped as the concussion of the explosion tore through him like a stroke; he waited for the life to flow out of him. The tremendous weight came down on him and drove the air from his lungs. He struggled to open his eyes one last time, but there was only darkness.

⬤ ⬤ ⬤

Stephanie stood over the two men, holding the softball-sized rock she had brought down on the back of the sheriff's head. She threw it to the side and scrambled to pull the man's dead weight off Don; she grabbed Carl and yanked as hard as she could. The sheriff's body flopped to the side. She knelt over Don and began to search for the bullet wound; then his eyes shot open, and he exhaled violently.

"Am I dead?" Don screamed.

"No." Stephanie continued to search with tears streaming down her cheeks. "You're still here." She grabbed his face and kissed him.

"What happened?" he asked and tried to sit up.

"I hit him over the head with a rock."

"What!?! He could have shot me!"

"I didn't have a choice ... You're welcome, by the way."

Carl groaned, rolled over onto his side, and attempted to lift his head.

"No, you don't!" Stephanie jumped to her feet, grabbed the medallion with the broken chain, and quickly tied the two ends together. She looped it over Carl's head and tucked the large pendant under his shirt against his skin.

"My head." He opened his eyes and stared up at the woman. "What happened?"

"I hit you—with a rock!" she shouted. "And I'll do it again if you try anything else. Now give me that radio." She ripped the walkie-talkie from his belt and turned it on. The sound of voices filled the tiny speaker as she bent down to retrieve the .45 lying in the dirt near Carl's side. Then she remembered his second weapon and relieved him of that as well.

"Don't get any ideas," she said, waving the large gun in his direction. "Deputy Lutchen. We need your help; it's an emergency!"

Billy and Ted returned to where they had left the truck and prepared it for evacuation. They moved the bodies of their fallen comrades as respectfully as they could and tucked them into the tall grass at the edge of the pavement. Leaving the scene of the battle behind them, they made their way up the final stretch of the mountain.

"Ugh," Carl moaned, stirring in the backseat. He woke to find his hands bound behind his back and his eyes blindfolded.

Don sat next to him and took Carl by the shoulders. "Easy, Sheriff," he said. "That thing got inside your head. It's probably been there a long time, manipulating you and clouding your judgement." He helped to steady the sheriff as the truck shuddered down the steep mountain.

"What?" Carl asked though a soupy veil of fog. But as Don said the words, the memory came back, and he remembered it all. "What have I done?" he asked, lowering his head.

"It's not your fault, Sheriff," Ted said from his position behind the wheel. "It got to you just like it got to Rainey. How do you feel now? Can you tell if it's still there?"

"Ted!" Carl called out. "Thank God you're here. I don't feel anything but a headache."

Stephanie rubbed the cut on her chin where Carl had punched her. "You're lucky that's all you got. I should have hit you harder."

THE OJANOX

"I had no idea." Carl shifted in his seat. "It called my name, and then it was like I was watching a movie or something. I heard Don talking about nitro sickness, and then I was there ... at the quarry. Jesus Christ." Carl's voice trembled on the verge of tears. "I made the damn bombs myself. I showed them how to set the timers and where to plant them. I'm responsible ... for all of this!"

"No, Sheriff." Billy Tobin sat on the other side of the man. "You had no control over this. It used you like a weapon; it's responsible for this, not you. It exploits our knowledge, and it could have taken any one of us. It chose you because of the knowledge you possessed."

"I don't feel it anymore," Carl said.

"It got into you when the medallion broke," Stephanie said, turning from the passenger's seat. "They did exactly what I thought they would; the pendants blocked it from seeing us and knowing what we were up to. Now that you're wearing it again, you should be safe ... probably."

"Which means we didn't get it after all; it's still out there," Don added.

"We have another problem." Ted looked back through the rearview. "Um ... Lois and the kids never made it to the boats."

"What!?!" Don and Carl screamed from the backseat.

"Günter Bentley said not everyone had shown up to the boats. When Burt figured out it was Lois, Jessica, and the kids, he went out looking for them but hasn't been able to find the mayor's station wagon anywhere."

"Take this goddamn blindfold off me!" Carl shouted, and Billy removed it for him. "Something went wrong. Not all of the creatures were in the sanatorium."

"He's right," Stephanie said. "And it will continue to spread unless we get all of them."

"Every last scrap," Don added under his breath.

"The Entity itself wasn't in the sanatorium. It might have been at one time, but not when we blew it up." Stephanie's eyes grew wide and welled up. "It's after the children. It can't spread without strong hosts."

"That explains the pictures in the cave." Don's face drew dark. "That's why it took Rob and the Richards twins first."

"We have to find them before it's too late," Billy said what they were all thinking. No one dared mention that since the children were already missing, it was likely they were already infected.

The truck turned onto Mountain Ave, with Ted maneuvering around the double-parked vehicles at the base of the old extension. The road twisted and turned as they continued to make their way closer to town, watching for any signs of movement or life.

"Hurry!" Don shouted from the backseat.

"Ted." Carl leaned forward. "Did Burt say anything else?"

"Yeah, he's headed into the foothills, and we're going to meet up with him. Said he was coming in from the Boyle's backyard. I told him we'd park at the Richards place. Son of a b—" Ted leaned his head forward and brought the truck to a halt.

The group stared out the window at the old house. It was in far worse shape than just disrepair and hadn't seen a paintbrush in far too long. The grass in the front lawn was knee high and contained more weeds than anything else. But the state of the place wasn't why Ted stopped the truck. Parked in the driveway was a vehicle with three of its doors wide open.

"I think we found the mayor's station wagon." Ted pulled the truck to the side of the road. "And that's Butchie fucking Post's house!"

Even from their position in the back, Don and Carl could see the tilted head of the woman in the passenger's seat and knew it was Lois. "No," Don gasped.

"God no," Carl moaned in unison.

Chapter 102

Burt walked past the two bicycles that Tommy Negal and Jeff Campbell had left in the woods nearly a week ago. There were many things left lying around by the children of Garrett Grove that were never going to get picked up. However, there weren't enough children left to worry about it. In the wake of the storm and destruction, the town had been all but washed off the map. Still, something had survived. Burt followed the strange tracks to where they entered the overgrown backyard. The tall weeds and grasses had been trampled through recently, leaving a defined path that led to an old shed set back on the property.

Something about the run-down wooden structure caused a cramp to settle in Burt's chest like a coronary. It looked evil, a place of poisonous things. Burt had no idea the shed belonged to Butchie Post and was unaware of the horrific acts that had transpired within.

Burt lifted his gun to his chest and took a step forward. The sound of a large vehicle in front of the residence broke the threatening silence. Then the radio on his hip came to life.

"Burt, it's Deputy Lutchen."

Burt grabbed the radio and whispered, "I hear your truck. I'm in back of the house and think I found something. There's an old shed—"

"Don't go in there!" Ted barked through the speaker. "We need you out front. Right now! For God's sake, hurry!"

● ● ●

Stephanie leaned into the backseat and refastened the blindfold around Carl's head.

"Wait." He struggled. "I can help."

"The only thing you can do right now is get in the way," she said, tightening the knot.

The group exited the truck and rushed to the station wagon, leaving Carl in the backseat. Don was the last one to arrive, hobbling along on his sprained ankle.

Stephanie ripped open the passenger's door of the station wagon and looked in on Lois. The woman's skin was grey, and she didn't appear to be breathing. Stephanie looked down and noticed the hypodermic needle sticking out of Lois's thigh. "Oh no," she cried.

Ted forced his way in and searched for a pulse but couldn't find one. He frantically pressed his fingers against Lois's neck as Don screamed from somewhere behind him.

The deputy removed the hypodermic and shouted into his radio. He pulled Lois out of the front seat and laid her down on the driveway. Lifting her arm, Ted searched her neck again, with the others hovering over him. After several seconds, he looked up to them. "I've got a pulse," he said. "It's weak, but she's alive." He checked her forehead for any sign of fever, then lifted her eyelids. There were no telltale indications of the infection; the woman had either been poisoned or drugged. A flurry of commotion caught his attention as something hurried toward him from the side of the house.

Burt almost knocked Ted off his feet as he pushed past him to get to the woman on the ground. He went straight to work checking Lois's vitals, listening to her breathing, finding her pulse, and then lifting her upper lip and inspecting the color of her gums.

"Is she going to be okay?" Don asked through a cascade of tears.

Ted lifted the hypodermic to his nose and sniffed. He ran back to the station wagon and focused his attention on the front seat. He spotted the two purses that had been left in the car and began to rifle through them. He shouted and emerged from the car with a vial in his hand.

"Morphine! She's been drugged." He held the vial out to Burt.

"Is she going to be all right?" Don demanded.

"Ohhh." Lois's eyes fluttered and opened to slits as she attempted to lift her head. "Wha the heyyy," she slurred.

"She should be fine, Mr. Fischer," Burt said. "But I need to get her back to the center and let Doris take a look at her."

Don knelt beside her. "Lois, where's Troy? Where are the children?"

"The mayorrr ... took them."

"In the backyard." Burt grabbed Ted. "There's something back there. Several sets of prints, by the looks of it. I think that's where you'll find them." Without another word, Billy and Ted tore off around the side of the house with Stephanie following close behind. Don attempted to get to his feet, but Burt stopped him.

"They can handle whatever's back there, I need you to help me with your wife."

Carl worked at the amateur knot used to bind his hands. He tensed his arms and twisted, slipping out of his confines, and then removed his blindfold. The pain in his head had eased slightly, and there appeared to be no sign of the presence on the edge of his periphery, at least not that he could detect.

He looked up in time to watch Stephanie disappear around the side of the house toward the backyard, then he exited the truck, causing Don to stiffen as if reacting to a predator. Carl intercepted the man before he could remove the large gun from his belt.

"Knock it off, already." He snatched the .45 from Don Fischer. A second later, Carl followed the others around the side of the house.

He caught up to Stephanie and ran past her, giving a quick nod. He raised the .45 and took position with Ted, who had already drawn his own weapon. Together, the men approached the shed door with Billy no less than five steps behind.

Carl examined the grass leading to the shed; from what he could tell, there were five sets of prints. He held his breath as he approached the door, placed his hand on the latch, and prepared to rush inside.

● ● ●

Troy waited … expecting the presence to detect him at any moment. It had slammed into his head like a nail into a two-by-four, then proceeded to ransack his memories and rifle through his consciousness. It was vile and toxic, and now it was inside him. It smelled like sulfur.

The creature was dark, never holding the same shape for long. At times, it was nothing more than a cloud, shimmering and transparent. From where he hid, Troy could see the metallic particles of the creature's makeup. They swirled and spiraled like dust, only this dust had intention. Twilight from an unknown source danced over the creature's mass and reflected into the dim. Flecks of scarlet, amber, and deep purple flashed as the formless shape lumbered across the strange landscape that Troy instinctively knew was the creature's reality.

It moved further from him, making its way across the bareness of the expanse. Then, in slow motion, the beast and the landscape began to take shape and materialize. It took on the form of a giant reptile, more dangerous looking than anything Troy had seen in his schoolbooks. The beast turned and morphed into an insect with dark hairy legs and great fangs. The spider-like creature then altered into the form of a man and then a massive ape. It continued to shift from one form to the next as it maneuvered away from Troy.

Watching from his hiding place, Troy was gripped with a sudden realization; he knew exactly where he was, impossible as it might be. His hands gripped the bars of the cage, the cold steel familiar against his flesh. It was the first room of the haunted house that he and Rob had built. Troy was standing in an exact replica of the cage in his garage—he was back inside Scream in the Dark. Then he noticed his hands on the bars in front of him; his fingers and flesh were transparent. Troy raised a palm to his face and gasped. He could see through it. A pale luster outlined his features, a stark contrast to the landscape and the makeup of the creature. His body appeared somehow illuminated, while the beast's looked dark and dirty. He moved his hand, watching the trail of incandescent light wash across the canvass before him. Troy stepped out from behind the bars of the cage and made his way into the emptiness that stretched out before him.

The creature had moved on, consumed with locating whatever it was thirsting for. The expanse was dark and vast, and there was a depth to it. The air felt heavy, and although it was alien and unfamiliar, Troy didn't feel as scared as he should. *This isn't Earth. At least, not the Earth that I know.*

There was movement; a dark shape dotting the perimeter slowly came into focus and approached. Troy froze as the featureless shape took form and he found himself standing face-to-face with the woman. It was the girl who worked at the diner; her name was Mandy. Troy remembered she had been nice to him; he had always thought she was pretty. But there was nothing pretty about Mandy anymore. Her head hung limp to the side, and her flesh was dark and murky, like the smoke from a fire. She stopped before him, staring in his direction. Except Mandy's eyes were missing. Black hollowed-out sockets fixated on Troy's position and beckoned for him to release her from the torment. Her sorrow was profound, and Troy could feel every ounce of it. The pretty waitress had been ravaged; there was nothing left of her. Mandy placed her hands against her chest and walked away into the darkness. Troy wanted to scream and to rip the hair from out of his head but found it impossible to do either. Instead, he watched Mandy disappear into the abyss ... the beast's abyss.

He turned away from the awful sight only to find Tommy Negal standing before him with his arms outstretched. His old friend stood there pleading, yearning for salvation. But there was none to be found, at least none that Troy could offer. Tommy continued his search and lurched away into the darkness.

Unable to witness any more, Troy shielded his eyes from the onslaught. But the images continued to appear. Children from his class approached and stared in his direction, all possessing the same grey eyeless features as Mandy. They were followed by others whom Troy had never met. Somehow, they sensed his presence and had come for his help. Then the landscape itself began to take shape. There was a deafening pulse, and Troy found himself standing in the foothills. A moment later, he was in the graveyard of the Lutheran church. Then Troy was on Pine Street, watching his house from the driveway. He was at the toy store, and then he was at the school, standing in the playground where he, Wendy, and Janis had eaten their lunch.

There was another pulse, and Troy found himself running. He sped through the demonic representation of his town without any idea where he was headed. Only this version wasn't his town; this was the creature's existence. By consuming every consciousness, it had constructed a dark prison where it could roam free without fear of the light. The absence of illumination was apparent in the dimness of the void. Troy felt his feet moving as the gaunt, hollowed-out faces flashed before him. Terror seized him; he realized he would never escape this hell, that he would never see the sun again. Troy ran until he found a familiar door and raced toward it. It was constructed of cardboard and wasn't much of a door at all, but it was one he recognized, one he had made himself.

Troy pushed his way through the secret passage until he came to the dead end. He stood up, wrapped his hands around the bars of the cage, and exhaled, feeling his panic subside slightly. The secret comfort of his hideaway filled him with a sense of security. He shifted his position behind the bars and slid his feet across the strange floor. His heart leapt from his chest, causing him to jump, when he knocked into the object with his sneaker. Troy positioned his foot and he waited. Troy was good at waiting.

Lois opened her eyes and looked up to see Don and Burt leaning over her. A dreamy fog glazed her stare; then her eyes widened, and it came back to her in a rush. She grabbed Don by the front of his shirt and struggled to get on her feet.

"Troy!" she screamed.

Don was almost knocked off his one good foot but managed to remain upright when she grabbed him. He and Burt helped her up the rest of the way.

"Where are they?" She wobbled a bit and frantically scanned the driveway. "Where's Troy?"

"The sheriff is searching the backyard now," Don said, trying to steady her. But the action was ineffective, and Lois slipped from his grip and bolted out of the driveway before either he or Burt could lift a hand to prevent her.

Don hobbled after her, assisted by Burt, who grabbed him under the arm, and together, they followed Lois into the backyard.

THE OJANOX

● ● ●

Carl pressed down on the latch, feeling the clasp disengage. He nodded to Ted and glanced back at Stephanie and Billy, who were only a few steps behind them. He rested his finger on the trigger of his weapon, held his breath, and eased the door inward. The old hinges strained under the stress and let out a strangled squeal. Carl pushed the door further and was bombarded when the oppressive stench rushed at him and struck him in the face. The odor of rotting meat and decay filled the small structure like the funk of a slaughterhouse. Something had died in the shed and been concealed in one of the corners or beneath the floorboards some time ago. A flashback of the Delta threatened to resurface once again, but Carl bit back and managed to fortify his resolve.

Carl noticed the dark brown stains that painted the floor. Then he saw the thick chain bolted into the wood; a steel dog collar with a padlock was attached to the other end. Carl forced himself not to imagine what it had been used for, knowing that Butchie Post had been busy long before the presence entered him. The windows had been boarded up and fortified, making it difficult to see into the back of the structure, which was still bathed in shadows. Carl shielded his mouth and nose from the assaulting odor and allowed the door to open fully inward. Sunlight fell across the floor, revealing the three small figures and the withered remains of the others.

Carl saw the children and prepared to rush in when an ear-shattering shriek erupted from the silence. A tremendous force rushed at the men from the back corner of the small building. It blasted out of the shadows and smacked into Carl and then into Ted. The deputy was thrown into the door like he had been hit by a linebacker. The wind rushed out of him, and he was knocked off his feet before he could aim his weapon. Carl didn't have time to react either as it hit him with the full force of a tornado and sent him flying backward onto the grass. The .45 was thrown from his hand and landed in a tangle of weeds somewhere behind him.

The mayor burst from the shed after crashing through the two officers. The woman's face contorted with rage; a thin cloud of the poisonous Entity had already begun to lift from her eyes. Billy and Stephanie had enough time to react and managed to raise their weapons. Billy lifted his revolver while Stephanie produced Wendy's wrist rocket. But the mayor rushed at them with the speed of a cheetah and knocked into Stephanie, who was tossed like a ragdoll. The mayor landed on Billy with her arms outstretched.

Billy felt the woman's fingernails dig into his flesh just below the shoulders as she came down on top of him. He howled and tried to fight the creature off but was unable to breathe. The woman was too strong and continued to drive her talons deeper into him. Billy started to lose consciousness. It was the speed in which the woman moved that took them by surprise; her swiftness and strength was that of a freight train and had toppled their defenses. Carl and Ted scrambled to their feet as the mayor began to tear into Billy Tobin.

A darkened mass grew around the creature's head, lifting from her eyes and mouth. It swirled and twisted in the autumn air, the metallic presence reflecting the sunlight like a thousand black diamonds. Billy found himself hypnotized within it, mindless of the pain in his chest. The mayor lifted her head and howled. A magnificent plume of darkness filled the air like an atomic blast. It gathered before her face, then concentrated its attention on Billy. A dagger-like projection focused on the boy, who had precious seconds left before he, too, was consumed. Billy remained transfixed, unable to protect himself; he forced his eyes shut and waited for the inevitable.

Billy jumped as the presence hit him with the concussion of an explosion. The sensation was unlike what he imagined, and he remained fully aware as the world around him erupted. It sounded almost like a gun being fired.

The first bullet hit Jessica Marceau in the temple. It exited the opposite side of her head, taking a lemon-sized piece of her brain with it. The second and third bullets hit her in an equally damaging fashion, but the first one had done the job. The woman fell off Billy Tobin and landed in the grass. The dark cloud dissipated the moment the bullet was introduced to her brain matter. It lifted on the breeze and quickly dispersed.

Billy waited for the end to take him as the pain in his chest returned and intensified. He opened his eyes to find himself face-to-face with the ruined body of the mayor—more than half the woman's head was missing. His vision slowly cleared, and he looked up at the smoking barrel of the gun. The weapon trembled and then wavered in and out of focus. He struggled to bring the shooter's face into view, knowing it had to be either the sheriff or Deputy Lutchen who had saved him. The weapon was lowered, and the beaming face of the coroner appeared. Burt smiled, then wiped the sweat from his brow.

"No fucking way," Billy managed. He lifted his hand and gave Burt a thumbs-up, then passed out in the grass.

⬤⬤⬤

Burt rushed to Billy's side, ripped off his own jacket, and pressed it against the boy's wounds. He had little recollection of drawing his weapon or even taking the shot and had acted on reflex alone. Now, looking down on the boy, he wondered if it had been in vain. Billy was losing blood fast, and his face had gone pale grey. Burt's jacket quickly turned scarlet as he pressed it into the boy's wounds.

"I need to get him to the center, or he's not going to make it," Burt shouted and lifted Billy off the ground. He was joined by Stephanie, who grabbed the boy by the other arm. They ran across the lawn and set him into the backseat of the mayor's station wagon before Lois or Don could react. A moment later, the car sped out of the driveway with Burt's foot pressed to the floor.

⬤⬤⬤

Ted managed to rise to his feet before Carl. He rushed into the shed and stood over the three children; they had all been infected. He knelt beside Dawn, whose eyes were open but had rolled back in her head. A cloudy dark film covered the whites and swirled within. Heat radiated from the child like an incinerator. Her body convulsed as the Entity ravaged her.

Carl positioned himself between Wendy and Troy, whose conditions were just as dire. Wendy lay bathed in sweat, convulsing with such force her head beat against the floor like a tom-tom. The swirling cloud was visible in the child's eyes as well; the Entity had attached itself completely. He lifted Troy's hand, which was limp, motionless, and blazing hot. Then he leaned over the boy and looked into his eyes.

"Troy, can you hear me?" Carl jumped as the boy latched onto his hand with the force of a snapping turtle. The dark haze in his eyes lifted, and he stopped shaking. He looked up at the sheriff with a wash of realization and opened his mouth to speak. Then, just as quickly, he was gone. The darkness returned, and Troy's eyes rolled back in his head.

"Troy!" Lois screamed as she and Don entered the shed.

They were too late; it was obvious. Troy, Wendy, and Dawn all exhibited the same symptoms Robert Boyle had shown less than a week ago. Lois rushed to her son and took him in her arms.

"Somebody do something!" The sudden shock pushed the residual effects of the morphine to the side. She turned to Don and pleaded, but he was already on the move. She watched as her husband reached into his shirt and removed something from around his neck. He leaned in and slipped the chain over Troy's head, the large medallion coming to rest on the boy's chest. The effect was immediate. Troy stopped convulsing and settled into a steady, rhythmic breathing. Then the child closed his eyes and lay there as if he were only sleeping.

Lois gasped. "How did you know?" She pulled Troy close and rocked him.

Stephanie rushed into the shed with her own medallion in hand. She knelt next to the little girl and slipped the large pendant around Dawn's neck. The second the object contacted her skin, she stopped shivering. The cloud coating her eyes vanished, and she lowered her eyelids.

Stephanie gave Carl a cautionary look as he motioned to remove his own medallion. "Not so fast," she said, lifting the leg of her pants and exposing the weapon strapped to her calf. She pulled it out and slid the magnetite dagger into Carl's belt, making sure the stone pressed against his skin. Stephanie nodded as Carl slipped the medallion off his neck, leaned over Wendy, and slowly laced the chain around the trembling child. The girl stopped shaking, closed her eyes, and settled into a restful sleep.

"We didn't get all of them." Carl let out an exaggerated sigh, his eyes focused on Stephanie.

"It got to the mayor," Stephanie said. "Something we missed. I don't know what, but now it's in the children. I think this is what it was after all along."

Don had seen the murals in the cave and knew the children were the answer as well. There was something they possessed that the creature needed, and the Lenape had used their own as bait. The skeletal remains confirmed that. The children had been left behind before the cave was sealed, and the creature had been trapped with them. Now it was inside Troy and the girls, although momentarily silenced by the medallions.

"These pendants aren't going to work forever, are they?" he asked.

"I doubt it," Stephanie replied. "It's growing inside them. I think it's only a matter of time before it takes them completely. But you said Troy's friends were sick for a while before everything went to hell, which makes me think we might still have a little time." She scanned the faces of the others. "I don't know if it will work, but I have an idea." She turned to Don, who already knew what she was about to say.

"We have to get them into the cave. You said it yourself. There's something about it that can't be explained."

"What about the cave?" Lois looked to her husband with tears in her eyes. "What's in the cave that can save Troy?"

Don shook his head, pushing aside an image of three small skeletons that had surfaced. "It's a geological anomaly," he said. "I can't say with certainty, but it's nothing science has ever recorded before. I'm not even sure it's terrestrial." He watched as Lois's eyes widened.

"I know it sounds crazy, but if there's any chance of saving them, the answer lies in that cave. And we're running out of time."

Lois pulled Troy closer to her chest. "Please," she cried to Stephanie. "Please save them."

"Quickly," Stephanie said, scooping up Dawn and heading into the sunlight. "Follow me."

The darkness of the void was suddenly illuminated. The creature that had lurked in the shadows at the perimeter of Troy's vision shrunk back and hid itself from view. Troy watched as the world in which he visited altered as well. It had been dark and transparent and inhabited by countless numbers of the creature's victims. Scores of Troy's classmates and people he knew from town wandered the desolate landscape. There were animals and beasts that had roamed the planet eons ago, along with numerous civilizations that had been assimilated over the course of Earth's brief history. Tribesmen adorned in animal skins and paint beckoned for salvation. Puritan settlers in dark garments pleaded to be released from their eternal damnation. But Troy was unable to help any of them as he hid behind the bars with their eyeless stares focusing on him.

The world was eclipsed by a blinding illumination that dispelled the dark figures and faded the landscape. White welcoming light filled his new habitat. Troy sensed a familiar presence; an unmistakable one he had known his entire life.

"Mom," he called out. There was no answer, but he knew she was close. He could smell her shampoo as if she were holding him.

The dark mass darted from place to place, panicked and desperate to escape. *You're trapped, just like me.* Troy watched from his confines.

The creature vanished into the distance and emitted the most vile, torturous sound Troy had ever heard in his life. He covered his ears and tried to block it out as each one of the beast's victims cried out together in pain.

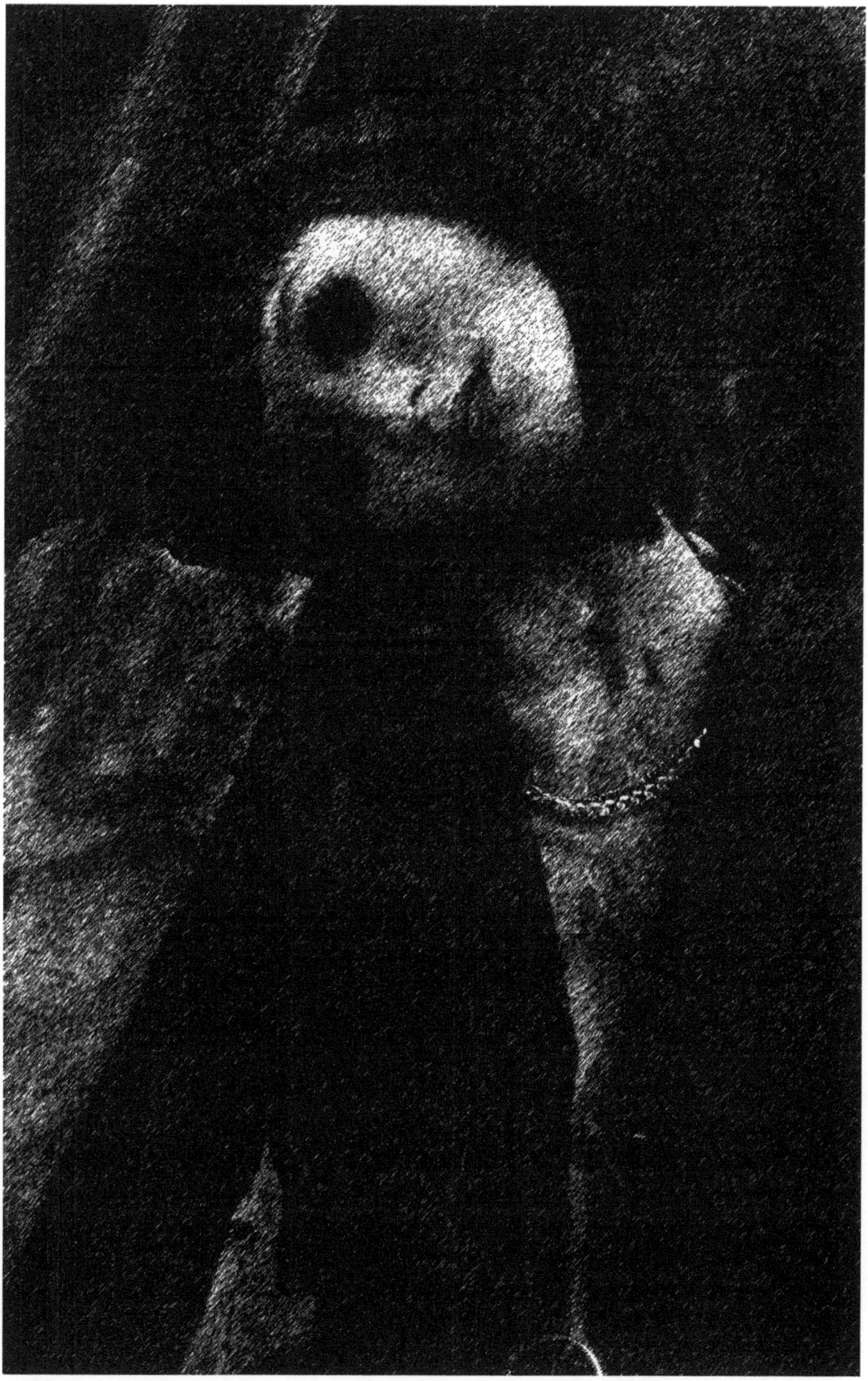

Chapter 103

Ted steered the pump truck into the main entrance of the quarry, passing several abandoned vehicles and a scattering of bodies. He stepped on the gas as Don pointed toward the ramp that led to the cavern.

Stephanie and Carl sat in the back with Dawn and Wendy cradled in their arms, while Lois and Don sat in the front holding Troy. None of the children had regained consciousness, but occasionally, Troy pulled himself closer to Lois as if he sensed her presence.

Don motioned for Ted to stop at one of the service trailers and opened the door of the truck. The pain in his leg had subsided some since he had wrapped it with the roll of duct tape that Billy had left behind. His tightly bound boot and the calf of his pants leg now acted as a makeshift cast, fastening his ankle in place. He hobbled out of the truck, retrieved a five-gallon gas can, and returned a moment later. The deputy then pulled the truck up the slope, almost to the entrance of the cave, where the generator sat.

"I need to fill the tank!" Don yelled over the roar of the truck.

"I'll take care of that." Ted said, turning off the ignition. "Get the kids inside and do whatever it is you plan on doing." He took the can from Don and headed to the generator while the others exited the truck with the children in tow. The cool air of the cavern wafted out as they made their way inside.

There was ample light in the first chamber, enough to see where they were going. They cautiously made their way into the second area when the generator roared to life, bathing the entire cavern in illumination. The massive murals painted on every wall revealed themselves to their visitors.

"This way," Don yelled before disappearing into the small opening. The darkness on the other side of the small breach was consuming as the others entered inside. Don turned on one of the flashlights, Stephanie followed his lead, then Carl did the same. "For God's sake, be careful. There's a massive drop-off in the middle of the floor. Follow exactly where I go."

No one needed to be told twice; they stayed close behind Don and Stephanie, following the beam of their lights through the darkness until they finally stopped approximately twenty feet inside the chamber.

"What is this?" Lois gasped, her voice shrill and near hysterics. She followed her husband to the stone altar. The remains of a small skeleton lay on top; the body was no larger than that of her own son's. She pulled Troy close to her chest and stepped back. "Are you out of your mind? You're not putting my son on that thing."

"You have to trust me, Lois." Don took her shoulders and stared into her eyes. "The Lenape used their children as bait. That's not what we're doing here."

Stephanie swept her arm across the altar and scattered the bones to the floor, causing the others to jump. Lois watched in horror as the woman laid Dawn onto the stone slab and positioned the medallion in the center of her chest.

Lois shook herself free from her husband's grasp and backed up several steps. Don watched in horror as she neared the ledge.

"Lois!" he screamed. "Don't move another inch. The drop-off is directly behind you."

She didn't listen and took another step, her back foot coming to rest at the very edge.

"Dear God, Lois. Don't move!"

Lois almost stepped back into the abyss but stopped two inches shy from the ledge. She looked down at Troy as his eyes fluttered. He latched on to her as if he had awakened. It was enough time for Don to reach out and pull them back. He spun her around and cast his flashlight into the massive hole in the center of the floor. Lois gaped at the chasm.

"I'm sorry, but you have to trust me," he said as Stephanie and Carl carried Wendy to the second altar. "I have no idea if this is going to work. But if we don't try, we're going to lose him." His words seemed to resonate, and Lois allowed him to lead her around the chasm to the third stone structure. She looked across the massive pit to see Stephanie rake the bones off the slab and watched Carl lay Wendy down.

She turned back as Don cleared the stone, then she placed her son on the slab. Copying what Stephanie had done, Lois fitted the large pendant in the center of Troy's chest, leaned over him, and kissed him on the cheek. He stirred for a moment, and a smile spread out across his face. "I love you, baby," Lois whispered. "Come back to me."

From where he stood, Carl could make out the far side of the chamber, which had been impossible to do when they first entered. He was taken aback by how fast his eyes had adjusted to the overwhelming darkness and watched as the Fischers placed Troy onto the altar. He had no idea what Don or Stephanie expected to take place, but so far, nothing had happened, and he was beginning to think they had come there in vain.

A shadow stepped in front of the entrance to the chamber, eclipsing the light that filtered through the passage. Carl relaxed and watched Ted as he emerged from the secondary chamber, but the deputy had stopped in the doorway and remained there. His body cast in a silhouette with the flood lights shining behind him, his features bathed in shadow and impossible to make out.

"Ted," Carl shouted. "What the hell are you doing? Come inside." He shielded his eyes to focus against the glare but couldn't make him out any clearer.

The deputy took a lumbering step into the chamber. Carl felt the hairs bristle on the back of his neck—something wasn't right. He squinted and shielded his eyes to focus better. It almost looked like Ted had carried something with him at his side, like he was trying to drag it into the chamber. Carl's jaw clenched, and his gut screamed like a siren.

The dark shadow took another step into the chamber and yanked at the baggage it was holding. There was a flurry of movement as something was tossed in their direction. Carl watched as the object cartwheeled through the air and headed directly toward Stephanie. He jumped and pushed her out of the way, knocking her to the ground as the mass landed at their feet in a tangled heap. Carl stared down at Ted's lifeless body. His head had been twisted a hundred and eighty degrees and now faced the wrong way.

"Jesus Christ!" Carl screamed and reached for his weapon, but it was too late. The massive beast slammed into him and seized him by the throat.

The creature that had once been Butchie Post now stood nearly eight feet tall. Its bulbous musculature had ruptured through its flesh. The clothes it had once worn were gone, replaced by scales and a thick layer of coarse hair covering it like an armored primate from some forgotten time.

Carl clutched at the monster's mitts as they wrapped around his neck and clamped down. The Butchie-beast released an ear-splitting shriek as if it were pleased with itself, then lifted Carl and took a step toward the center of the chamber. The sheriff's feet left the ground, and he felt himself propelled backward toward the chasm.

Stephanie regained her footing and quickly removed the wrist rocket from her coat pocket. She dug out a lodestone ball and fitted it into the weapon's pouch. Pulling back on the rubber bands, she let the projectile sail at the massive beast. The projectile missed the creature and bounced off the rock wall somewhere in the distance. She loaded another round into the pouch, drew back on the elastic, and hesitated. The beast dangled the sheriff at the edge of the drop-off; she couldn't risk it. If she hit the creature now, it would only cause it to release its grip on the sheriff. Carl would fall to his death regardless.

Across the pit, Lois and Don were helpless to do a thing when the creature entered the chamber and snatched Carl like a ragdoll. It took him by the throat in a heartbeat and, within seconds, had the man at the edge of the drop. Troy moaned and stirred behind them. Lois turned to her son, who had started to convulse once again. He shook and flailed his arms as if he were fighting the beast himself. She held on to him to prevent him from throwing himself off the narrow pedestal. Don moved to assist her as Troy thrust his arms into the air in a violent series of thrusts and jabs, the first nearly connecting with Don's chin. There was more than one battle going on in the cave, but Don suspected they were one and the same. Troy lifted his arm and clenched his fist. A second later, the beast screamed as if it had been struck.

⚫⚫⚫

Ted had just finished emptying the canister into the generator and started the engine when the huge shadow descended on him from the ridgeline above. He was eclipsed in darkness and had just enough time to look up. Then the world that Ted Lutchen knew ceased to exist.

The massive creature had watched the group exit the truck and make their way into the cavern. It didn't want to go anywhere near the rock; it had been fooled once before. But the simple ones had the children, and it could no longer see through their eyes. Something blocked its vision. Rage tore through it like a comet, infuriating every atomic particle of its makeup. It had no choice but to return to the cave and retrieve the children. Then it would ravage the others and make them pay.

It stared through the eyes that had once belonged to a boy named Marion, a boy who had never known his father, one who had experienced a lifetime's worth of abuse from the other children in just a few short years. The memories had festered inside the child and turned him sour. So much so, it had poisoned his very essence. If that hadn't been enough, the continuous rape and beatings endured during his eighteen-month sentence surely had. Butchie Post returned to Garrett Grove far worse than when he left. He had come back tainted, with a hunger for something far more debase.

The shed he kept in the backyard of the house on Mountain Ave was far enough from the road and neighbors that if any of his victims had lived long enough to scream, they would never have been heard. But they were generally at death's door by the time he fastened the dog collar to their necks and the shackles around their wrists. The people who disappeared from Warren and Parker Plains, women and men alike, had never raised the attention of the Garrett Grove Sheriff Department. Butchie had been somewhat disciplined in that regard. However, his appetite had grown stronger as he struggled to sequester his desires. It wasn't enough to incapacitate his victims, it wasn't enough to beat them within a brushstroke of death before he threw them in the trunk of his car, and it wasn't enough to strip and shackle them to the floor of his shed. Butchie's violation continued long after his victims died, and recently he had begun to take notice of the prey within his own community.

It had sensed the predator in the one called Butchie and chosen him for the role of protector; it was as if the boy had been bred for the position.

It stood in the doorway of the third chamber, watching the one called Carl. It had fought to take control of the man and had finally succeeded but was blinded to his thoughts once again. Just as it was to the children. Fury ripped through it when it spotted the little ones on the stone outcroppings. It was reminded of the pain it had felt when the tribal people had lured it inside, a burning within every particle of its essence. It pushed forward, certain that these simple creatures would never sacrifice their children. The one called Ted was now dead, and there was no one left to seal the cave.

But it had been certain before and had found itself trapped just the same. Fury had driven it to the edge, and it had ripped through the Lenape who had been left trapped within the cave. Then it had descended on the children. It tried to turn them but had been far too eager, and something had blocked its reach. With blinding rage, it had forcefully inserted its dominance, and the children had perished.

Now it felt that rage once again; it boiled within as it stood in the doorway of the chamber, watching. It lifted the body of the deputy into the air and threw it across the cavern. The man landed in a broken heap.

Chapter 104

Carl stared into the black eyes that had once belonged to Butchie Post and struggled to free himself. But his attempts were futile; the thing was massive and as strong as a bulldozer. It lifted him off his feet and dangled him at the edge of the chasm in the center of the cave. Carl kicked at the beast as it hoisted him into the air and tightened its grip on his windpipe. He felt his throat compress. The air in his lungs turned to fire and started to flame out.

Despite the increasing brightness that had crept into the cave, the perimeter of Carl's vision began to fade as his brain started to shut down. He reached blindly for his weapon only to find it wasn't there, or he was too incapacitated to locate it. He slapped at his hip with his right hand and held on to the monster's claw with his left. His arms grew heavier with each groping motion, and Carl knew it would be over soon. He thrust his hand in a final desperate motion and latched on to it, cold and hard against his belt. Carl's spirit lifted when he realized what was in his grip.

With the last ounce of strength in his reserve, Carl raised the dagger Stephanie had placed in his belt and drove it forward. The tip of the lodestone weapon connected with the creature's chest. A piercing howl erupted as if the monster had been hit with a branding iron. It released its hold on Carl's neck and dropped him to the ground. He landed at the very edge of the chasm and stumbled forward onto his knees.

The beast screamed and swatted at the searing pain in its chest. It clawed at the blade that had pierced its hide by less than an inch, knocking it to the ground, where it fell in front of Carl. The sheriff stared down at the weapon as he fought to regain his breath, unable to retrieve it.

Stephanie released the projectile and let it fly. The musket-sized rock hit the beast in the shoulder, causing an even louder concussion of torment to spew from its lungs. It threw its head backwards, stamped its feet against the floor, and turned in her direction.

She quickly reloaded another magnetic rock into the weapon's pouch and drew back on the bands. The musket ball sailed through the air at her target and missed the creature's head by less than an inch. On the other side of the chasm, Don held the wrist rocket that Troy had given him and attempted to draw a bead on the creature. Don let the projectile sail, missed his mark, and came closer to hitting Carl than connecting with the beast.

Carl struggled to fill his lungs, raking in one shallow breath after the next. The muscles in his throat screamed after almost being crushed by the oppressive strength of the monstrosity. He swayed on the precipice of consciousness, then he felt it, an itch in the base of his skull.

Carl...

Panic seized him as the horrible voice penetrated his head and spoke. He looked at the dagger laying on the floor in front of him; it had been the only thing protecting him, his only defense against the voice.

Carl...

It forced its way inside his head, knocking down the barriers he had constructed to hold back the memories of war. It ripped through the façade he had fabricated to convince himself that he was never meant to experience love. And it smashed through his rationalizations that Lois was better off without him.

Carl...

He stared down at the dusty rock floor of the cavern as his eyes glazed over and the blood vessels ruptured within.

Carl!

The presence invaded him like a virus. Carl arched his back and screamed from the very base of his core, powerful enough to tear his vocal cords down the center. He lowered his head, every muscle in his body rigid and flexed to the point of popping.

Less than twenty feet away, Stephanie watched. She spotted the ancient dagger lying on the floor, just out of the sheriff's reach. She loaded another stone into her weapon and trained her aim on her new target; she focused the bead directly at Carl's head.

⚫⚫⚫

The dimness of the void had been altered. Something had changed within, and the change had been sudden. A penetrating illumination now filtered in from the outer edges of the vast emptiness. It transformed the landscape and affected the creature, which now appeared frantic and agitated. The dark transforming mass looked as if it were searching for a way to escape.

Initially, Troy had believed that his strange new surroundings were the domain and the reality of the Ojanox, but now, he wasn't so sure. He was still very much aware and had found a familiar place to hide, but what made him even more certain was his ability to watch the creature from his vantage point without it being able to detect him. *Maybe the Ojanox created this place, but now that I'm here, it's not the only builder.* Troy thought the presence of Scream in the Dark confirmed that.

The dark shadow raced past the cage, directly in front of where Troy stood. The massive cloud of twisting particles shimmered and warped like a school of herring. Its individual atoms were in a perpetual state of motion, each one repelling the other, sending their adjacent brothers into warp speed. It looked as if the beast's body was in a constant state of flux, as if it were attempting to attain wholeness but never able to accomplish the task. *That's why it changes the people into so many different things. Too much information. It can't decide what it wants to become.*

The mass continued its frenetic movements and then rocketed away from Troy's hiding place. He skidded his foot along the floor, comforted that the object was still there. He listened to the sound of his own heart hammering inside his temples and let out an exaggerated sigh.

Troy jumped as something touched his hand. He turned to the left and watched as the outline of the girl slowly took form. Her features were unclear, transparent, and washed in the same iridescent glow as he. Then she took his hand in hers and squeezed it, and Troy knew. Wendy stood beside him within the confines of the cage; she had found her way to him. He held his breath as her outline wavered before him. A moment later, the second figure appeared.

Dawn was there as well. The child looked over at Troy, pressing herself against Wendy as close as she could get. Both girls appeared to understand what he intended to do. Wendy squeezed his hand tighter and wrapped her arm around Dawn. Their voices echoed within his head as clearly as if they had spoken out loud. Although neither had said a word, Troy understood their message. *Don't worry. I'll be ready.* He replied as Wendy released his hand. Troy pressed his foot against the object and placed his hands on the bars.

The Ojanox moved faster than it had before. It darted from place to place, frantically searching the void for a way to escape. Not sure how he had come to possess such knowledge, Troy was certain the creature was just as trapped as they were and had no idea how it had happened. It wasn't used to surprises and wasn't good at thinking on its feet. It was an instinctual creature at best.

The void itself had shrunk to a confining dimension. The Ojanox collided with some invisible barrier and ricocheted backward like an infuriated pinball. Its screams split the static air. They were impossible to bear and made Troy's stomach churn. The beast doubled back and headed toward them once again. Wendy's voice sounded inside his head, and although no words had been spoken, he knew what she said. It was the very thing he had been thinking. The beast sped toward them at a dizzying speed. Troy didn't know if it would work or if he was even strong enough. Fortunately, he didn't have time to second-guess himself as the dark mass descended on him like a storm.

Troy stepped down on the small foot switch he had taped to the floor in his own garage. There was a click, and then there was … nothing! He heard the death stomp of the switch as it engaged, and the world paused as if it were solidified in time. Hope abandoned him as he realized it had all been for nothing. He had failed, and he had been so sure his plan would work. A half a second later, the strobe light came to life, filling the void with a pulse of searing white light. The beast stopped in front of the cage and screamed. Paralyzed by the blinding light, the Ojanox froze, just inches away from the children. Troy flung his arms outward and plunged them into the distorted mass of particles. He envisioned himself seizing the beast by the throat and clamping down with all his strength.

He clenched his fists together as it squirmed. The creature writhed and bellowed and struggled to free itself. Troy sensed the monster's fear; he could taste its panic, hot and metallic like melting copper. The Ojanox threw itself against the side of the cage to get at him, but Troy held on and closed his eyes. Then ... he felt it ... The cold tightness wrapped around his own throat and clenched down.

The shock was immediate. Paralysis gripped the Entity, and it lost control of all it possessed, including Carl and the one called Butchie. The shock was fleeting, but it was just enough for Carl to regain a sense of where and who he was.

He looked up as Stephanie released her projectile and felt the air break, with the musket ball passing just inches in front of his face. The creature that towered before him appeared to stagnate, but only for a moment. Its body stiffened and tensed, then it focused its attention on the area where the Fischers stood on the other side of the chasm. The Butchie-thing shrieked and lumbered in their direction.

Carl felt the pressure build between his temples as the presence attempted to regain control. He knew once it started speaking, there would be no fighting the voice, that he had maybe a second or two at best. He sprang to his feet, stumbled on the heels of his boots, then lunged at the beast and wrapped his arms around it. He pulled it in tight and struggled to plant his feet. Carl took a step backward.

The great creature howled in shock and lashed out at the man with an exaggerated swat of its arm. It was enough to offer Carl a better hold on it. He pulled with all his strength and hooked his boot heels into the edge of the drop-off. The beast lost its own footing and was set off balance by the sheriff's momentum; it fell onto Carl as he yanked it toward him.

Carl!!!

It screamed within his head as it took him. But it was too late. Carl dug his heels into the rock and pushed backward, sending himself over the cliff. The creature was dragged along with him; they both left the rock and became airborne. Their bodies cartwheeled over one another as they plummeted toward the dark pool below.

Carl felt the presence release control of his mind. Soaring downward, he saw the faces of the men, women, and children who had died on his watch. He was responsible for all of them. He saw Gary Forsyth and David Rainey, the faces of Alice and Will Tobin, and was even offered a vision of Felix Castillo. Bob Jones appeared before him, holding out his hand. They all came to him as Carl plunged faster into the darkness with the beast clutched firmly in his grip. Dr. Malcolm looked over his glasses at him. His face was replaced by Tara Jefferies, whose face was then replaced by Mandy Griggs. Jackie Gilmartin and Abe Gorman were there. Father Kieran nodded and winked. There was another who joined him; Ethan Ziegler offered Carl a satisfied look of approval; Ziegler smiled and then disappeared.

As Carl hit the shallow water, there was only one face he saw and only one person he was left thinking about. He saw Lois, the way she looked the moment before they broke up, her eyes shining and her face unaffected by time. She looked at him and kissed him. *I was finally able to save you,* Carl thought as he hit the water. Both he and the creature were snuffed out like a flame.

Chapter 105

"No!" Lois screamed. She took a staggering step closer to the chasm, but Don stopped her. There was nothing either of them could do. She turned and buried her face into the crook of her husband's shoulder.

From across the drop-off, Stephanie watched as the sheriff and beast fell over the edge and disappeared. She could see Don and Lois clearly on the opposite side and had an idea why it had not only grown brighter within the cavern but had gotten warmer as well. There was movement from somewhere in the cave. It bounced off the walls and echoed off the ceiling, making it impossible to discern where it was coming from. Stephanie looked back at the child on the altar, then stared across the chasm to where the other girl lay. Both Wendy and Dawn appeared to be resting and didn't move a muscle. Being as careful as possible, Stephanie crept to the edge of the drop-off and peered over the side.

There was no sign of either the sheriff or the creature; both of their bodies had sunk to the bottom of the strange pool. But now Stephanie understood where the sound was coming from. The water at the bottom of the pit had begun to churn like a whirlpool or a tornado. It swirled in a counterclockwise motion and glowed with the same milky white illumination that it had the first time they saw it. She gasped as the water increased in speed and the lumens intensified. She took several steps back from the edge and the cave erupted with the deafening roar of a hurricane. It sounded as if the air itself were being ripped apart. Stephanie hurried back to the altar where Wendy lay and held on tight to the rock.

On the other side of the pit, Don and Lois jumped as the explosive sound filled the cavern. Troy flung his arms into the air once again and cried out, clawing at something only he could see. Lois tried to reach for him, but Don stopped her just before Troy lashed out at the air where her face would have been. Then the center of the pit exploded like the top of Mt. Vesuvius.

It turned on the boy and seized him. Somehow, the child had managed to hold on to a portion of himself and survive the confines of the domain. But nothing had ever managed such a thing; no creature had ever retained even a glimmer of their individuality after being consumed. It had sensed the boy was different the moment it encountered him. It had known Troy would make a valuable addition to the collective, but it had lost everything in the pursuit of this sole acquisition. It turned on the child with a rage like it had never known. It lashed out and seized Troy by the throat. Looking deeply into the strange child, it found it was still unable to penetrate him completely. It squeezed tighter and shook ... it would shake the very life out of him if need be.

Survival ... it had survived since the beginning of time itself and had only been thwarted once or twice in the past. Which had always been due to its own thirst and hubris. But it had never been stopped by a single child, and it wasn't about to let that happen now. It slammed into Troy, forcing the boy against the bars of his own hiding place. But the child held fast and tightened his own grip as well.

Troy was aware of everything as the creature stared into him and searched through his memories. He felt the beast rifle through his past and insecurities, and felt his own hatred rise within him. The sense of violation was repulsive. Troy detested the feeling and pulled the creature against the bars just as it had done to him. He stared into the dark mass and screamed within the beast's mind in a voice as loud as creation.

The two squared off against one another in an exchange of intimate knowledge. The creature had stolen countless souls over the millennia, but it had never experienced a symbiotic connection like this. It had never assimilated anything that could withstand its intrusion. And Troy, who was only ten and had just recently kissed a girl for the first time, had never imagined a connection on such a profound level.

Troy experienced the creature's entire existence, starting from the moment of its inception. He sifted through the knowledge it had gathered from the countless identities it had consumed in the past. He found himself on the playground, sitting next to his friend, talking about Scream in the Dark. He found himself behind Marco's, stealing cardboard to make their haunted house. And he found himself back in kindergarten, on his very first day of school. He sat next to the boy who would become his best friend and watched as a solitary tear ran down Robert Boyle's cheek. The visions faded, but the shadows were all still there, locked inside the beast. The resonating echoes of Rob and Erin and Ben and all the rest of his friends, waiting to be set free.

Troy screamed and pulled the monster closer. Their combined consciousness attacked itself and one another within the confines of the void, a creation manifested by them both.

Stephanie took Wendy's hand as a tower of light projected from the pit like the beacon of a lighthouse. It shot out of the mouth of the chasm, focusing its concentrated beam on the very center of the cavern's ceiling. The sound that accompanied it caused her ears to pop as it consumed the entire chamber. Her hair whipped across her face as a gale force wind emerged from nowhere. It increased in speed and tore through the cave like a cyclone, casting dust and loose fragments of rock into the air. She hovered over Wendy to protect the child from the flying debris and looked across to notice that Lois had done the same. Don hobbled toward the altar where Dawn lay to defend the child from the swirling particles as well.

The strange milky water that had begun to churn at the bottom of the pit erupted, and a waterspout jettisoned into the air. It cycloned and spiraled, following the tower of light. Together, water, air, and earth combined in a cataclysmic spectacle.

The force of the wind threatened to tear the adults from their positions, causing each of them to cling to the stone altars and onto the children to prevent them from being swept away.

The tornado of water and light lifted out of the mouth of the pit and formed a vortex. It spun counterclockwise as it lifted into the impossible lodestone formation centered in the ceiling of the cave. Now the entire cavern was as bright as a summer day and nearly as hot.

Don threw himself over Dawn to shield her from the raging cyclone and noticed that not all of the light originated from the anomaly in the center of the room. Dawn had begun to emit a light of her own. Staring down at the child, he saw where it was coming from. The medallion she wore glowed as if it had been placed in a kiln. The large stone burned a white-hot golden color; it spread out across the child's chest, filling her face with the aura. It grew brighter and brighter until Don was forced to shield his eyes from the intense glare.

He turned away and looked over at Lois and Troy. A similar brilliance had settled over his son, covering his body almost entirely. The same happened with the medallion that Wendy wore. The dark stone turned red at the center of the sunburst, then spread out to the individual fingers of its crafted sun. The glow intensified, changing from a deep red to a hot white. Then the entire stone lit up as if it were on fire.

Stephanie stared down at the spectacle for as long as she could, until she finally had to look away. She hadn't been sure what to expect when she insisted the children be brought to the cave. There was something at work that no historian or geologist or any other human would ever be able to explain. They were in the presence of something great, something powerful, something that defied explanation. The way the light spread out across the child's chest and then radiated within her face caused Stephanie to think of transformation, of creation ... They were in the presence of something holy.

●●●

Troy felt the creature struggle within his grasp but sensed his own life force slipping even faster. The beast clamped down on his throat as they faced off, staring into the other's very essence. The stream of consciousness shared between them was more than intimate; it was parasitic. Neither could survive without the other. As Troy exhaled and the monster inhaled, a steady flow of universal information passed between them.

The void came to life, burning with an even brighter light than the steady pulse that the strobe provided. The dark mass whaled itself against the bars, tightening its grip around the child's neck in a last-ditch attempt to consume him. Troy cried out with a thousand blades piercing his skull. Terror raced through the ancient enemy as the light intensified, causing the shadows to recede into the furthest reaches of the void. It panicked and focused every ounce of its energy on destroying the boy, even if that meant its own destruction.

Troy gagged and felt his body go numb. His vision blurred, and his lungs raged like a furnace. He felt his legs begin to give out from underneath him. Then the world erupted in a concentrated beam of white light. It blasted out of the center of Troy's chest and focused on the beast. He watched his hands fight to contain the swirling mass as the light consumed them. The creature bore down on his throat, and Troy slipped away. It tore free from his hands and disappeared into the blinding brilliance of the void as he lost consciousness. The last thing he heard was the wail of the creature as he, too, was silenced. Troy and the Ojanox were consumed by the light.

Lois struggled to protect Troy as he convulsed against the stone altar. With the pendant glowing as if it were on fire, the child thrashed and flailed and struck his mother in the chest. Lois stumbled and moved to return to his side but was unable. She watched as Troy arched his back and screamed like his lungs were being ripped out. A billowing plume of concentrated smoke erupted from the boy like a geyser. It rushed out of him in a flood and was swept away by the brilliant tornado of light. Dark particles shimmered as they emerged from Troy's eyes and nose, then quickly disappeared on the current of air. The flow that was expelled from the child appeared to be endless, and Lois shielded herself by turning away. Then she noticed the other children were in the grips of a similar process. The reflective particles were being ejected from all their bodies.

Seconds later, Troy collapsed against the altar with a thin tendril of smoke lifting from his lips. It was swept away and was gone. Then the swirling cyclone of light and water stopped as if it had been turned off by a switch. The chamber fell silent and began to grow dark once again. Lois looked down at Troy. His head lay tilted to the side; it was impossible to tell if he was breathing or not. She rushed to her son and took him in her arms.

She lifted him from the stone table, and his body hung limp, as if it weighed nothing at all. Then she heard the voice of the young girl, crying and frightened. Wendy coughed and called out as Stephanie took her in her arms. On the other side of the cavern, Don comforted Dawn as she, too, woke from the impossible nightmare. But Troy remained motionless. Lois pressed her cheek to his lips to check his breathing. There was nothing; he was as still as a corpse. Lois shook him and pulled him tight against her chest.

"Troy!" Lois screamed.

His skin looked blue in the fading light. Dark circles spread out beneath his eyes as if he was still wearing his vampire makeup. Lois grabbed his face and pressed her lips over his mouth. *Cold.* Troy Fischer had already started to grow cold in his mother's arms. Lois exhaled into his mouth and prayed. *Please, God, don't let him die. Don't take my son!* She breathed into him once again as the realization slipped like a knife between her ribs and pierced her heart. She had lost him.

"Troy!" she screamed at him. Lois's tears raked through her completely and penetrated her soul.

A rush of air escaped from Troy's mouth. A second later, he began to cough and fought to control his breath.

Lois's tears intensified, though for a much different reason. "Troy!" She leaned him forward and patted him on the back. "Oh, God, thank you. Th-thank you, God."

He raked in the cool air of the cavern one shallow breath at a time until, finally, the coughing fit passed. Troy opened his eyes and looked up at his mother. He tried to speak but was unable and smiled as best he could.

"I thought I lost you, kiddo." Lois continued to cry as she hugged him with all her strength. "Oh, thank God. I don't know what I would have done."

Don lifted Dawn into his arms and felt the ground lurch beneath him. He sensed what was happening and turned toward the small opening in the rock.

"Run!" he screamed. "It's about to cave in."

The entire cavern shook as if a bomb had been dropped on the mountain. Don knew the explosion at the sanatorium could be responsible for the seismic tremors but believed there was another explanation. First the ground heaved as if in the grips of a tectonic shift, and then the ceiling started to give out.

"Now!" he shouted again, but the others were already on the move. Ignoring the pain in his ankle, he carried Dawn in his arms and headed toward the exit. He gritted his teeth and met up with Lois and Troy just as the first boulder-sized stalactites started to rain down from the ceiling.

Stephanie carried Wendy and was the first to step into the second chamber. She sprinted past the ancient murals with the young girl in her arms and stepped out into the twilight of the evening a moment later.

Don and Lois followed with the floor of the cavern pitching and lurching beneath their feet. They exited into the second chamber and were halfway to the mouth of the cave when a rush of dust and debris exploded from the small opening behind them. It blanketed the cavern, making it impossible to see, but they kept moving forward through the murky cloud. They held their breath and closed their eyes. They emerged from the cave just as the roof of the second chamber collapsed. The group retreated from the billow of choking dust and made their way to the center of the quarry.

The tremors lasted for another minute or so before they finally ceased. When the dust lifted and the group was able to see clearly, the entrance to the cave lay blocked by several tons of lodestone and granite. The DuCain site was lost forever, along with everything inside.

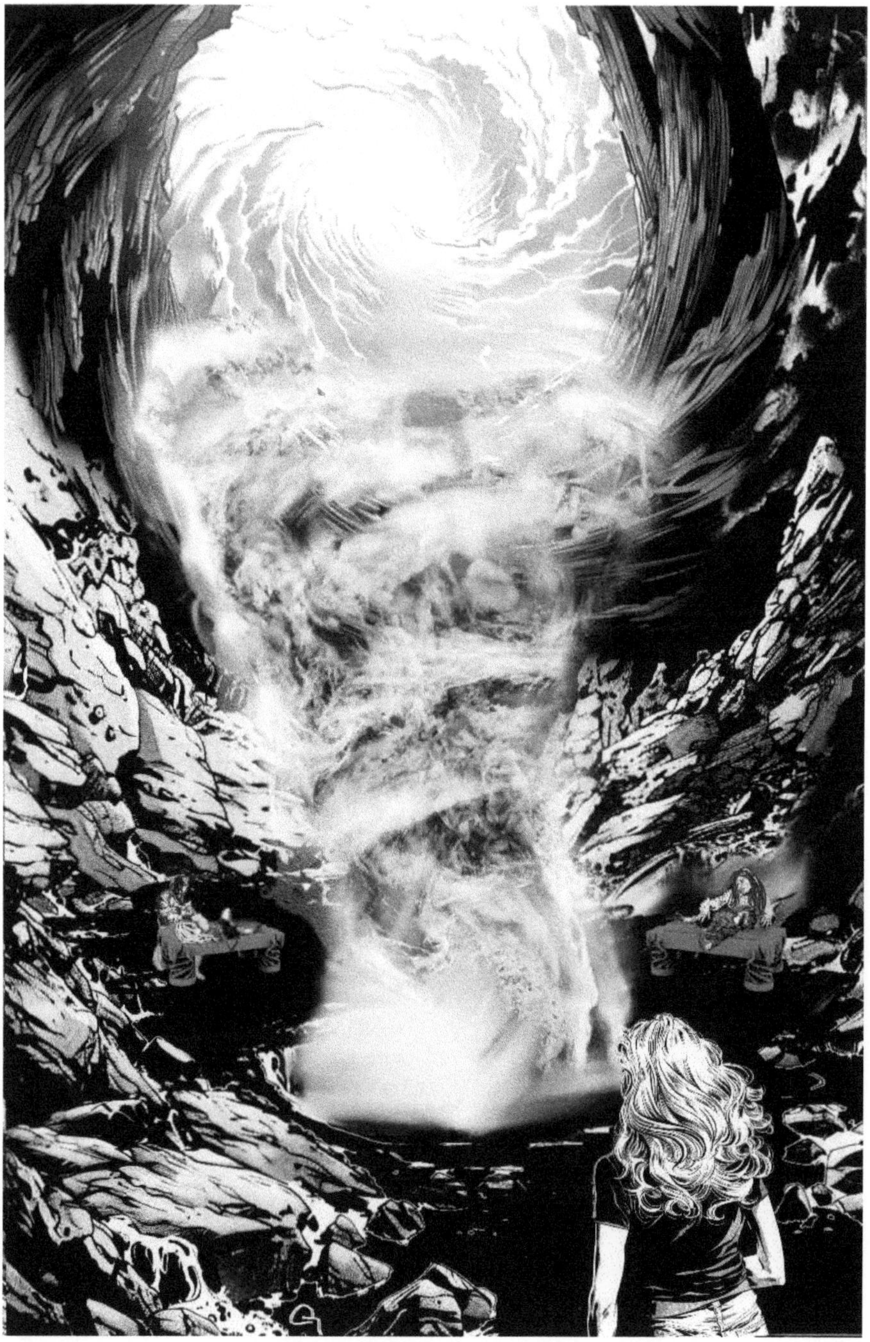

Chapter 106

A hush fell over the occupants of the truck as Don navigated a safe passage through what remained of Garrett Grove. Troy, Wendy, and Dawn stared out the windows in shell-shocked disbelief. Not a residence or business had been spared, not a soul walked the streets of the once safe neighborhoods, and not a single living creature stirred as the vehicle lumbered through town. What captured the focus of the children even more than the level of destruction was all the discarded Halloween decorations. Smashed jack-o'-lanterns littered the streets; their hollowed-out eyes stared back accusingly as they passed. Plastic skeletons had been ripped from front porches and lay strewn everywhere. The hand-painted murals on the front windows of the businesses had been broken into thousands of tiny pieces.

Doris, Burt, and several of the seniors from Botany Village watched as the first members of the group walked through the side entrance of the medical center. Baxter jumped up to greet them and began to whine the second he saw Dawn being carried in as if she'd been injured. He sniffed the entire group thoroughly, unable to find the man who had saved him, the one called Ted. Baxter let out another whine and followed them to the emergency room.

Stephanie rushed to Janis's bedside and took hold of her hand. Looking down, she noticed the slightest flush of color had returned to her daughter's cheeks. Janis lay motionless for a moment, slowly breathing in and out, then she gently turned her head and spoke. "Mom, is that you?"

"Oh, thank God!" Fresh tears streamed down Stephanie's cheeks, streaking away at the dust that covered her face. "I'm here, baby. It's over; it's finally over. Everything's going to be all right."

Burt held his breath as the rest of the group filed through the door. He waited, hoping the next face he saw would be that of his oldest friend and the man he had thought of as a son. Carl would waltz in wearing his cowboy hat, his face even more weathered from experience rather than age, and he would no doubt have a slick comment waiting on his tongue. Burt watched as Donald Fischer walked in and let the door close behind him. He locked eyes with the man and read volumes. Carl hadn't made it; his friend wasn't coming back.

"He saved us," Don said. "If it wasn't for Carl, none of us would have survived. And that thing would still be out there."

Burt wiped his eyes and nodded. Somehow, he already knew. Call it a premonition or a feeling in his gut, but Burt thought he had sensed the loss of the man right away. He sighed as a hollowness burrowed into his chest. A memory of what Carl had offered to do for him nearly a week ago crept up. He had been willing to risk his job to help Burt because that's the kind of guy Carl Primrose was. He had become Garrett Grove's sheriff because he wanted to help people. And that's exactly what he had done. *Not a bad way to go, my friend.* Burt wiped his eyes again and realized he had been wrong about one thing. As it turned out, there was quite a bit of dignity found in death after all ... quite a bit. He shook his head and gazed down at the state of the children. "Let's have a look at them, shall we?"

Troy, Wendy, and Dawn were rushed into the emergency room and placed in beds not far from where Janis lay talking to her mother. Burt and Doris examined and washed the dirt from the children's faces, checked their vital signs, and diagnosed them no worse for wear.

Troy lay back against the pillow and closed his eyes for a moment. A wave of exhaustion crashed against him like a storm. The child's eyelids appeared too heavy to fully open, even when his father called his name.

"Troy ... are you all right, kiddo?"

He cracked open his eyes and stared at his parents through the parted slits.

"Did we get them, Dad?" he asked.

"Yeah, kiddo. We got them."

Troy opened his eyes fully and looked up at his parents.

Lois gasped and lifted her hand to her mouth. She stared down at Troy in horror. His eyes had always been the same shade as hers, a deep blue the color of the sapphire. But now, something had changed. His right eye was the same as it had always been, but the left one was so dark it almost looked black. Not like the eyes of those who had been infected by the creature, completely blacked out as if by ink. Instead, Troy's iris itself had changed color and was now the shade of rich dark chocolate.

Lois turned to Don, who had noticed it as well. Neither said a word. A lifetime of unspoken resentments once threatened to tear their family apart, none of which now seemed to matter. Troy had been gone, stopped breathing for nearly a minute—they had almost lost him. Time stopped as they looked down at their son, his eyes affected by the unearthly exchange.

Don wrapped his arm around his wife as Lois took Troy's hand in her own. They had somehow survived, and somehow, they were all still together. Few had been so lucky. Troy was alive, and that in itself was a miracle. Possibly it was a sign that they, too, were worthy of a second chance.

Suddenly the curtain behind them swung open, causing them to start.

"Would you keep it down." Billy looked up from the bed. "I'm trying to sleep."

His chest was bandaged, and his face was pale, but he was still kicking; the kid really did have nine lives.

Troy turned to his cousin. "We got 'em, Billy," he said. "Every last scrap."

Billy stared back into his cousin's eyes and froze. His face turned a full shade paler as he focused on Troy's one darkened eye. "I'm not so sure about that, kiddo," Billy said. He laid his head against the pillow and stared up at the ceiling. "I'm not so sure about that at all."

AFTERWORD

Excerpt from the Warren Chronicle

After a mysterious outbreak, the town of Garrett Grove has been placed under quarantine. The unknown contaminant is responsible for numerous cases of infection and countless deaths. The National Guard was dispatched Friday to cordon off the area from neighboring communities. Dr. Devlin from the CDC stated that the contagion has been limited to the small town. The origin of the outbreak is still unknown, and the CDC has not determined whether the outbreak was viral or bacterial.

Several small boats carrying survivors arrived in Butler late Thursday. The crafts' occupants were reported to be raving and delusional with stories of monsters and strange creatures. All of the town's survivors, including those that arrived on the boats, were transported to Walter Reed Army Hospital in Washington and are under quarantine. Major David Werner reports the conditions of the survivors are grave and their survival is unlikely.

The President advises residents in the neighboring areas to stay away from the town of Garrett

Grove. The National Guard had been authorized to use extreme force to maintain the quarantine. There is no further information at this time.

Epitaph

The grounds where the old sanatorium once stood were littered with gopher holes. The inhabitants of those burrows had vacated when the dark presence moved into the old hospital. It drove them from their dens far more efficiently than any poison could have ever done. But now, something was stirring once again in one of those forgotten holes.

It pulled itself out of the ground, into the dim glow of the blue moonlight. It shook as a tremor raced throughout its body, causing even more of the animal's fur to fall from its hide. Patches where hair still clung to its flesh grew less and less with each passing minute. Its once ginger-colored coat had been reduced to a matted tangle of dark patches. Its ink-black eyes stared out across the old parking lot.

In another life, it had dined on leftover slices of turkey and hamburger that a young waitress named Mandy had been kind enough to offer. Now it feasted on consciousness and fear. The horrid-looking cat honed in on a lone mole that had lingered on the mountain for far too long. The dark presence leapt from the disfigured animal's mouth and entered the tiny rodent. It wasn't exactly satisfying, but it was a start.

The creature that had once been known as Scraps looked up at the pale moon and shivered once again. Then it darted across the parking lot and set its attention

DAEMON MANX

in another direction. Scraps headed north and followed the far side of the mountain ... directly toward the town of Warren.

April 2020 – February 2024

Thank you for reading!
Please consider leaving a rating/review on Goodreads and Amazon.

ACKNOWLEDGEMENTS

If you ever find yourself in the town of Pompton Plains, New Jersey, and drive to the very top of Mountain Avenue, you will reach Mountainside Park, but you won't find an old road extension or an abandoned sanatorium. However, the inspiration for the old hospital comes from a place called the Overbrook, which wasn't all that far away. Neither is the real Garrett Mountain, for that matter. I took great liberties when writing this book, even changing the location to upstate New York, but many of the features are similar to the town I grew up in: Chilton medical center, the graveyard behind the Lutheran Church, even the hardware store at the corner of Jackson Ave. I just changed things a little to fit the story.

It's been four years since I first started writing this book, and there are many who helped bring this monster to life. Whether their assistance was inspirational, fact-checking, information gathering, or emotional support, I couldn't have done this without them. There are topics I touched on in *The Ojanox* that required the input of professionals and tons of research. When it comes to toxicology, lab work, virology, and bacteriology, I did my best to stick to the facts. When I got it wrong—when faced with serving the story or the hard medical facts, I chose the story. So that's on me.

First, I would like to thank Wendy Nastasi and my sister, Dawn Chiossi (Danielle), for a lifetime of inspiration, support, and for listening to me talk about nothing other than this damn book for the past three years. I would also like to thank them for lending their namesakes to this story, with written consent, of course.

There are several friends who read early versions of this book whose help was instrumental. Nick Gomes and Ed Koloski helped provide feedback and were my sounding board from the very start, back in the halfway house days. Greg Gillick and Mike Turrigiano have always had my back and were there to listen to my very first attempts at horror writing. And of course, Jack Wells. Jack has been my constant go-to guy with this project for years. He read it before the first rewrite, and he still came back for more. Now that's a true friend. In truth, *The Ojanox* wouldn't be half the book it is today without Jack's knowledge, skill, and literary prowess.

My editor, Lisa Lee Tone, took every page of this manuscript and made it better with her diligent attention to detail. I'm fortunate to have Lisa in my corner to call me out when I stray from the path, and I'm thankful she was always there to rope me back in.

I'd like to thank Ben Eads for his original developmental edits on *Scream in the Dark* and for the rigorous Jedi training and instruction. (Insert Yoda voice) Because of you, a better writer, I am.

Christy Aldridge has been so much more than a cover artist, or an illustrator, or even a contributor—she has been a partner, in every sense of the word. Without Christy's hard work and dedication, this project wouldn't be half of what it is today. For the past year or more, we have been joined at the hip. She took my vision and brought it to life. Thank you, Christy, I couldn't have done this without you. Now we need to start a new project.

Thank you, Don Noble and Jeff DeSantis for contributing your amazing illustrations and talents to this project.

Many thanks to my Alpha team and proofreaders for their time, input, and suggestions: Donna Latham, Heather Ann Larson, Jae Mazer, Kerrie Roylance, Bryan Moyer, Kristen Lynch, Susan Isenberg, John O'regan, Christina Marie, and Maryanne Pacheco Chappell.

And a huge thank you to Kira (Eagle Eyes) Seamon, for tirelessly hunting through these manuscripts, making sure that all the finishing touches were properly in place. It's the little things that make the difference, and had it been up to me, far too many little things would have slipped through the cracks. Thank you, Kira for squashing all those pesky little things into oblivion.

THE OJANOX

For all my friends who follow me on social media, for all the reviewers, bloggers, influencers who support the indie horror community, thank you.

My life would have been very different if it hadn't been for my fourth-grade teacher, Mrs. Genevieve Smith, whose tutelage, undying devotion, and wealth of limitless stories molded not only myself but an entire generation. I especially would like to thank you for bringing my homework to the hospital when I broke my leg.

Thank you, Kelly Rainey, and all the fourth-grade classes of Pompton Plains school.

Anthony Lorraine helped by sharing with me his experiences in Vietnam. Without Anthony, the character of Carl Primrose would have been much different, as well as my knowledge of that moment in history. Sadly, I learned of Anthony's passing when I was still in the halfway house. He was a good friend during a dark moment in my life. I miss you, Tony.

Thank you to my family and friends who helped contribute to the inspiration of this story through a lifetime of experiences, which I in turn felt compelled to fictionalize. And finally, for my mom, who told me my first ghost story, took me trick-or-treating, and allowed me to have a Halloween party at the house when I was ten years old. And for my dad, who let me build a haunted house and still reminds me periodically that I painted his garage walls black.

And thank you to the readers and horror fans who love this genre as much as I do. Thank you for taking this journey with me and thank you for allowing me to share this story with you. I hope you enjoyed it half as much as I enjoyed writing it.

Daemon Manx

Daemon Manx Linktree

Follow me on social media